THE CAT WHO CAME IN
OFF THE ROOF

The Cat Who Came in off the Roof

Annie M.G. Schmidt

Translated from the Dutch by David Colmer

Delacorte Press

English translation copyright © 2014 by David Colmer
Jacket art and interior illustrations copyright © 2015 by Eda Kaban

All rights reserved. Published in the United States by Delacorte Press, an imprint of Random House Children's Books, a division of Penguin Random House LLC, New York. Originally published in hardcover in Dutch as *Minoes* in Amsterdam, The Netherlands, in 1970. *Minoes* copyright © 1970 by the Estate of Annie M. G. Schmidt.
This English translation was first published in paperback by Pushkin Children's Books, London, in 2014.

Delacorte Press is a registered trademark and the colophon is a trademark of Penguin Random House LLC.

Visit us on the Web! randomhousekids.com

Educators and librarians, for a variety of teaching tools, visit us at RHTeachersLibrarians.com

Library of Congress Cataloging-in-Publication Data
Schmidt, Annie M. G.
[Minoes. English]
The cat who came in off the roof / Annie M. G. Schmidt ; translated from the Dutch by David Colmer.
pages cm
Originally published in Amsterdam by De Arbeiderspers in 1970 under title: Minoes.
Summary: Minou, formerly a cat but now a woman with many cattish ways, helps Tibbs, a newspaper reporter, with information she gets from her many feline friends.
ISBN 978-0-553-53500-6 (trade hc) — ISBN 978-0-553-53503-7 (library binding) — ISBN 978-0-553-53501-3 (ebook) [1. Cats—Fiction. 2. Reporters and reporting—Fiction. 3. Shapeshifting—Fiction.] I. Colmer, David, translator. II. Title.
PZ7.S3497Cat 2016
[Fic]—dc23
2015008470

The text of this book is set in 11-point Berling.
Jacket design by Kate Gartner
Interior design by Trish Parcell

Printed in the United States of America
10 9 8 7 6 5 4 3 2 1
First American Edition

CONTENTS

— 1 —

NO NEWS ANYWHERE

"Tibble! Where's Tibble? Has anyone seen Tibble? The boss wants to talk to him. Where's he got to? *Tibble!*"

Tibble had heard them, all right. But he'd slipped down out of sight. And now he was crouched behind his desk trembling and thinking, I don't want to talk to the boss, I'm too scared. I know exactly what's going to happen. He's going to fire me.

"Ah, Tibble! There you are!"

Oh, no. They'd spotted him.

"The boss wants to see you straightaway."

He couldn't get out of it now. He had no choice but to walk down the corridor with his head hanging and stop at the door marked *Editor*.

He knocked. A voice said, "Yes."

When Tibble went in, his boss was on the phone. He pointed at an empty chair and carried on with his conversation.

Tibble sat down and waited.

This was in the building of the *Killenthorn Courier*, the newspaper Tibble worked for. Writing articles.

"So, Tibble," the editor said as he hung up the phone. "There's something important we need to discuss."

Here it comes, thought Tibble.

"These articles you write . . . They're quite good. Sometimes, even *very* good."

Tibble smiled. Maybe it wasn't going to be too bad, after all.

"But . . ."

Tibble waited patiently. Of course, there had to be a "but." Otherwise he wouldn't be sitting here.

"But . . . there's never any *news* in them. I've told you so many times. Your articles are always about cats."

Tibble was quiet for a moment. It was true. He was a real cat lover. He knew all the local cats. He even had one himself.

"But yesterday I wrote an article that didn't even mention cats," he said. "It was about spring."

"Exactly," his boss said. "It was about spring. About the little leaves appearing on the trees. Is that *news*?"

"Er . . . they were *new* leaves," Tibble said.

His boss sighed. "Listen carefully, Tibble," he said. "I like you. You're a nice guy, and you can string a story together. But we're working on a *news*paper here. And a *news*paper has to provide *news*. It has to tell people things they don't know."

"But it's already full of news," Tibble said. "Wars and stuff like that. And murders. I thought people would like to read about cats and leaves for a change."

"I'm afraid not, Tibble. Don't get me wrong, you don't need to write about murders or bank robberies. But a small town like ours is full of little news stories. You just have to find them. I've told you again and again, you're too shy. You have to approach people. You have to ask questions. But you're always too scared. Apparently you only ever associate with cats."

Again Tibble remained silent, because it was true. He *was* shy. And if you work for a newspaper, you can't afford to be shy. If you want to find out about things other people don't know about, you have to march right up to strangers. You have to be brave enough to barge in on a government minister, even if he's having a bath. And then you have to ask fearlessly, "Where were you last night?"

A good newspaperman does things like that. But not Tibble.

"Well," the editor said, "I'll give you one last chance. From now on, write articles with news in them. I want the first one on my desk tomorrow morning. And after that, I want to see two or three a week. And if you can't manage it . . ."

Tibble understood perfectly. If he didn't come up with something, he'd lose his job.

"Goodbye, Tibble."

"Goodbye, sir."

And now he was walking down the street. Light rain was falling, and everything looked gray. Tibble was taking his time. He was looking around and keeping his eyes peeled and his ears open. But there was no news anywhere. He couldn't see anything new. There was nothing he didn't already know about.

He saw cars. Parked cars and cars driving down the street. There were a few pedestrians and the occasional cat. But he wasn't allowed to write about cats anymore. In the end he was

3

so tired he sat down on a bench in Green Square, under a tree where it was still dry.

There was already somebody else sitting on the bench, and now Tibble saw who it was. It was his old teacher from school, Mr. Smith.

"Look who we have here," said Mr. Smith. "What a nice surprise, bumping into you like this. I've heard you've got a job with the *Courier*. I was always sure you'd end up at a newspaper. It's going fabulously, I suppose."

Tibble swallowed uncomfortably and said, "I'm settling in."

"You always wrote such wonderful compositions at school," Mr. Smith said. "I knew you'd go far. Yes, you're an excellent writer."

"Can't *you* tell me something I don't know?" Tibble asked.

Mr. Smith was quite insulted. "Has it gone to your head already?" he asked. "I tell you how well you write and you ask me to tell you something you don't know. . . . That's not very nice of you."

"Oh, I didn't mean it like that!" Tibble cried, blushing. He was about to explain what he *had* meant, but before he got a chance there was the sound of furious barking close by. They both looked up. A big German shepherd was racing after something, but they couldn't quite make out what that something was. It disappeared between two parked cars and the dog rushed after it. The very next instant there was a wild rustling in the tall elm tree near the cars.

"A cat," Mr. Smith said. "A cat's been treed."

"Was it a cat?" Tibble asked. "It was big. And it kind of fluttered a little. It looked more like a large bird. A stork or something like that."

"Storks don't run," Mr. Smith said.

"No, but it definitely fluttered. And cats don't flutter."

They went over to have a look.

The dog was standing under the tree and still barking furiously.

They tried to see what exactly was up there between all those branches, but the cat was completely hidden. If it *was* a cat.

"Mars! Here, boy!" Someone was calling the dog. "*Mars*, here!"

A man appeared with a leash. He clicked the leash onto the dog's collar and started pulling.

"*Grrr . . .* ," said Mars, holding his four legs stiff as the man dragged him away over the road. Tibble and Mr. Smith kept peering up for a moment. And now they saw something very high up among the new leaves.

A leg. A leg in a stylish stocking with a shiny, high-heeled shoe on the foot.

"Heavens," said Mr. Smith. "It's a lady."

"It can't be," Tibble said. "That high up? How'd she get up there so quickly?"

Now a face appeared too. A frightened face with big scared eyes and masses of red hair.

"Is it gone?" she called.

"It's gone! Come on down!" Tibble called back.

"I'm too scared," she moaned. "It's so far."

Tibble looked around. There was a van parked close by.

Cautiously, he climbed onto the roof of the van and reached out as far as he could with one hand. The woman crawled slowly to the end of her branch, then lowered herself onto another and grabbed Tibble's hand.

She turned out to be tremendously agile. In one easy leap

she was on the roof of the van, and a second hop took her down to the street.

"I dropped my case," she said. "Have you seen it anywhere round here?"

It was lying in the gutter. Mr. Smith picked it up for her.

"Here," he said. "Your clothes are all messed up too."

She brushed the dirt and leaves off her skirt and jacket and said, "It was such a big dog. . . . I can't help it, I just *have* to get up into a tree when I see a dog coming. Thanks very much for your help."

Tibble suddenly remembered his article and realized he should stop her to ask a few questions. This was definitely something unusual he could write about.

But he hesitated a little too long. He was too shy again. And off she went with that small case of hers.

"What a peculiar young woman," Mr. Smith said. "She was like a cat."

"Yes," said Tibble. "She was just like a cat."

They watched her walk off. She went round a corner.

I can still catch up with her, thought Tibble. He left Mr. Smith behind without saying goodbye and raced down the narrow street he'd seen her take. There she was. He'd ask her, "Excuse me, but I was wondering if you could tell me why you're so scared of dogs and how you're able to climb trees so fast. . . ."

But suddenly he couldn't see her anymore.

Had she gone into one of the houses? But in this part of the street there weren't any doors. Only a long stretch of fence with a garden on the other side. There wasn't a gate in the fence either; she must have slipped through the bars. Tibble peered through the fence at the garden. He could see a lawn and quite a few shrubs. But no young lady.

"She must have gone in through a door somewhere," Tibble said. "I must have just missed it. And the rain's getting heavier. I'm going home."

On the way he bought two fish and a bag of pears for his dinner. Tibble lived in an attic. It was a very nice attic with one big room he used as a living room *and* a bedroom. Plus a small kitchen, a tiny bathroom and a junk room. He had to climb a lot of stairs, but once he was up there he had a view out over lots of roofs and chimneys. His big gray cat, Fluff, was sitting there waiting for him.

"You can smell the fish, can't you?" Tibble said. "Come into the kitchen and then we'll cook them and eat them. You're getting a whole fish tonight, Fluff. And it might be the last time I can afford to buy fish at all, because tomorrow I'm going to get fired. Tomorrow I get the boot, Fluff. And then I won't earn a penny. We'll have to go out begging."

"*Mrow*," said Fluff.

"Unless I manage to write a news article tonight," Tibble said. "But it's already too late for that."

He sliced some bread and made some tea, then ate in the kitchen with Fluff. And then he went into the living room and sat down at his typewriter.

Maybe I can write something about that strange lady after all. And he started.

This afternoon, at approximately five p.m., a German shepherd chased a lady across Green Square. She

was terrified and shot up one of the tall elms, all the
way to the top. As she was too scared to climb down
again, I lent a helping hand. She then resumed her
walk before slipping through the bars of a fence and
into a garden.

Tibble read through it. It was a very *short* article. And he felt like his boss would only say, "It's about a cat *again*."

He had to do better. First a peppermint, he thought. That will clear my head.

He searched his desk for the roll of peppermints.

Huh, I was sure I had a roll of peppermints somewhere. "Do you know where I put the peppermints, Fluff?"

"*Mrow*," said Fluff.

"I didn't think so. What's the matter, do you want to go out again? Are you so keen to get back out on the roof?"

Tibble opened the kitchen window and Fluff disappeared into the darkness out on the roof.

It was still drizzling, and a gust of cold wind blew in.

Tibble went back to his typewriter, put in a clean sheet of paper, and started over again.

—2—
A STRAY CAT

While Tibble was fretting and worrying in his attic, the strange young lady was closer than he thought.

Just a couple of streets away she was sitting in a garden, tucked in behind some shrubs. Night had fallen, and it was pitch-black. A strong wind was blowing, and the garden was extremely wet.

She sat there with her little case and made a small mewing noise. First nothing happened.

She made the noise again. And now an answer came from the direction of the house.

"*Mew . . .*"

An ancient but very dignified black cat came walking toward her very slowly, then stopped suspiciously, some distance from the shrubs.

"Aunt Sooty . . . ," the young lady whispered.

The old cat spat and shrunk back.

"Now I see . . . ," she hissed. "*You!*"

"Do you still recognize me, Aunt Sooty?"

"You're Minou! My niece Minou from Victoria Avenue!"

"That's right. I heard you were living here, and here I am."

"I've already heard about it," the old cat said nervously. "About what happened to you . . . all the cats are talking about it. How could something like that happen, Minou? To you, a member of one of Killenthorn's very best cat families! What does your sister say?"

"She doesn't want to know me anymore," the young lady said. "She says it must be my own fault. She gave me the cold tail. . . ."

"*Ssss* . . . ," said Aunt Sooty. "I can't blame her. You must have done something ghastly to be punished like this. Turned into a *human*! What a horrific punishment. I wouldn't be human for all the canaries in China. Tell me, was it a magic spell?"

"I don't know," Minou said.

"But you must know *how* it happened."

"I went out as a cat and came back as a human, that's all I know."

"Incredible," Aunt Sooty said. "But it must have been your fault. You probably did something terribly *uncattish*. What was it?"

"Nothing. I didn't do anything. Not as far as I know."

"And you're wearing clothes," Aunt Sooty continued. "Did you have them on straightaway?"

"I . . . I found them somewhere," Minou said. "I couldn't roam the streets naked."

"Ugh! And you have a *case* . . . ," Aunt Sooty hissed. "What's the point of that?"

"I found it too."

"What's in it?"

"Pajamas. And a toothbrush. And a washcloth and some soap."

"So you don't wash yourself with spit anymore?"

"No."

"Then all is lost," Aunt Sooty said. "I'd still hoped that it might come good. But now I'm afraid there's no hope for you at all."

"Aunt Sooty, I'm hungry. Do you have anything I can eat?"

"I'm sorry, not a thing. I've already finished this evening's Kit-e-kat. And I have a very tidy human. She never leaves food lying around. Everything always goes straight back in the fridge."

"Is she nice?" Minou asked.

"Absolutely. Why?"

"Maybe she'd like to have me too?"

"No!" Aunt Sooty cried, horrified. "Child, the thought of it. The way you are now?"

"I'm looking for a home, Aunt Sooty. I need somewhere to stay. Can't you think of anywhere? Here in the neighborhood?"

"I'm old," Aunt Sooty said. "I almost never make it up onto the rooftops anymore. I hardly even go into other cats' gardens. But I still have a few acquaintances left. One garden up, there's Mr. Smith's cat, the teacher's. That way. Go and talk to him. He's called Simon. Cross-Eyed Simon. He's Siamese, but perfectly friendly."

"And you think maybe that teacher would . . ."

"No!" Aunt Sooty said. "You can't stay there either. But Simon knows all the cats in the whole neighborhood. And that means he knows all the humans too. He can probably point you in the right direction."

"Thank you, Aunt Sooty. Bye. I'll drop by again soon."

"If it doesn't work out, talk to the Tatter Cat. A stray. You can usually find her on the roof of the Social Security Building. Not that she has a particularly good reputation, of course. She's a scruff and a tramp. But very well informed, because of all the time she spends on the streets."

"Thanks."

"And now I'm going inside," Aunt Sooty said. "I am deeply sorry for you, Minou, but I still think you must have done something to deserve it. And one last piece of advice: Wash yourself with spit. Lick yourself. That is the beginning and end of all wisdom."

With her tail held high, Aunt Sooty strolled off through the garden and back to the house while her poor niece picked up her case and crawled through a hole in the hedge. Off in search of the cat next door.

Tibble wasn't doing well. He paced the floor of his attic and sat down every now and then at his typewriter, only to tear up everything he'd typed in a rage and rummage through the drawers in search of his peppermints. He had the idiotic idea that he couldn't think or write without a peppermint, but meanwhile it was getting later and later.

"I should actually go back out," he said. "To see if anything's happening anywhere. Something I can write about. But I don't think anyone's out on the street anymore with this weather. Strange that Fluff's staying out on the roof so long. Usually he comes back a lot sooner. I think I'll just go to bed. Tomorrow I'll go up to the boss and say, 'I'm sorry, you're right. I don't have what it takes to be a newspaperman.' And he'll say, 'Yes, I think it would be best if you started looking for something else.' And that will be that. I'll go and look for another job."

There was a quiet noise in the kitchen.

It was the bin.

"That's Fluff," Tibble said. "The scrounger! He's trying to get the fish bones out of the bin. Even though he's already had a whole fish. I'd better go have a look, otherwise he'll tip the whole bin over and I'll have to clean it all up."

Tibble got up and opened the door to the kitchen.

He was shocked by what he saw.

It wasn't Fluff. It was a woman. The young lady from the tree, who was now digging around in his rubbish bin. There was only one way she could have gotten in—through the window that opened out onto the roof.

The moment she heard him, she spun around just as she was stuffing a big fish skeleton into her mouth with her paws. No, no . . . with her *hands*, Tibble thought immediately, but she looked so much like a wet, timid stray cat that he'd almost gone, "Psssst, scat!" But he didn't say a word.

She took the bones back out of her mouth and gave him a friendly smile. Her green eyes were slightly slanted.

"I'm sorry," she said. "I was just sitting on the roof with your cat, Fluff. And it smelt so delicious. That's why I stepped in through the window for a moment. He's still out there."

She had a very respectable and ladylike way of talking. But

13

she was soaked through. Her red hair was stuck to her head in clumps, and her jacket and skirt were sopping and formless.

And suddenly he felt so sorry for her. She was just like a sad, half-drowned cat. A hungry stray!

"I'm afraid we ate all the fish," Tibble said. "But if you like . . . I could give you a sauc—" He'd almost said a saucer of milk. ". . . a glass of milk. And a sandwich, perhaps? With sardines?"

"Yes, please," she said politely, but meanwhile she was dizzy and wild-eyed with hunger.

"Perhaps you can put that back, then," Tibble said, pointing at the skeleton in her hand.

She dropped it in the bin. And there she sat, shy and wet on a kitchen chair, watching Tibble open a tin of sardines.

"May I ask your name?" Tibble said.

"Minou. *Miss* Minou."

"I'm—"

"Mr. Tibble," she said. "I know."

"Just Tibble. Everyone calls me Tibble."

"If you don't mind, I'd rather stick to *Mr.* Tibble."

"What were you doing up on the roof?" he asked.

"I, um . . . I was looking for a job."

Tibble looked at her with surprise. "On the roof?"

But she didn't answer. The sandwiches were ready. Tibble went to put the plate down on the floor, but changed his mind. She probably eats like a person, he thought. And he was right. She ate her sandwiches very daintily, with little bites and nibbles.

"You have a job at the newspaper," she said between mouthfuls. "But not for long."

"How do you know that?" Tibble cried.

14

"It's what I heard," she said. "That article didn't work out. The one about me up the tree. Too bad."

"Now, stop right there," Tibble said. "I'd like very much to know who told you that. I haven't spoken to anyone about that at all."

He waited until her mouth was empty. It was the last bite. She picked up the last crumbs with a finger and licked it clean.

Then she half closed her eyes.

She's falling asleep, Tibble thought.

But she didn't go to sleep. She sat there staring sweetly into space. And now Tibble heard a soft rumbling noise. Minou was purring.

"I asked you something," Tibble said.

"Oh, yes," she said. "Well . . . it's just something I heard."

Tibble sighed. Then he noticed that she was shivering. No wonder, with all those wet clothes.

"Don't you have anything dry to put on?"

"Yes," she said. "In my case."

Only now did Tibble notice that she still had her case with her. It was on the floor under the window.

"You should have a hot shower," he said. "And change into something dry. Otherwise you'll catch your death. The bathroom's just there."

"Thanks very much," she said. She stepped across the room to pick up her case, and when she passed him on the way back she pushed her head up against his arm for a moment, wriggling her shoulders slightly at the same time.

Tibble jumped back as if a crocodile was trying to bite him. She's rubbing up against me! he thought.

Once she'd closed the bathroom door behind her, Tibble sat down in the living room. "This is mad," he said to himself. "A strange woman comes in through the attic window. Half starved. Then purrs and rubs up against you!"

Suddenly something terrible occurred to him. Surely she doesn't . . . she won't want to stay with me, will she? She was looking for a job, she'd said. But she was obviously looking for somewhere to live. Like a cat looking for a new home.

"I don't want her here," Tibble said. "I've already got a cat. I'm way too happy living alone and doing my own thing. And anyway, I've only got one bed. I should never have let her use the shower!"

Here she was again . . . coming back into the room.

See! Tibble said to himself. Just as I thought. She was standing there in her pajamas with a dressing gown on over the top and slippers on her feet.

She gestured at the wet two-piece suit she was holding draped over one arm. "Is it all right if I dry this in front of the fire?"

"Um . . . yes, go ahead," Tibble said. "But I want to say straight away that you, um . . ."

"What?"

"Look, Miss Minou, it's fine for you to sit down for an hour or so until your clothes dry. But you can't stay here."

"No?"

"No. I'm sorry. That's absolutely out of the question."

"Oh," she said. "Not even for just one night?"

"No," Tibble said. "I don't have a bed for you."

"I don't need a bed. Back there in the junk room there's a big box. A cardboard box that used to have tinned soup in it."

16

"A box?" Tibble said. "You want to sleep in a box?"

"Absolutely. If you put some fresh newspaper in it first."

Tibble shook his head stubbornly. "I'll give you some money for a hotel," he said. "There's one just around the corner."

He reached for his wallet, but she refused point-blank. "Oh, no," she said. "There's no need. If it's really not possible, I'll just be off. I'll put my wet clothes back on and leave at once."

She stood there looking pitiful. And with such a frightened look on her face. And outside you could hear the wind and the rain. You couldn't possibly send a poor cat out onto the roof in weather like this.

"All right, fine, but just one night," Tibble said.

"Can I sleep in the box?"

"If you like. But under one condition. You have to tell me how you knew all those things about me. Who I am and where I work and what kind of article I was trying to write."

They heard a small flopping sound in the kitchen. It was Fluff, finally back from his roof walk and coming in with wet gray fur.

"He told me," Minou said, pointing at Fluff. "He told me all about you. And actually, I've spoken to lots of cats who live around here. They all said you were the nicest."

Tibble blushed. He felt strangely flattered. "You . . . you talk to cats?" he asked.

"Yes."

What nonsense, thought Tibble. The woman's quite mad.

"And, er . . . how did you come to be able to talk to cats?"

"I was one myself," she said.

Totally bonkers, thought Tibble.

Minou had sat down in front of the fire, next to Fluff. They

17

were sitting together on the rug, and Tibble could now hear two purring sounds mixed together. It sounded very peaceful. Shall I write that article about her after all? Tibble thought.

Last night I provided shelter to a purring lady who entered my apartment through the attic window and, on being asked, informed me that she had once been a cat. . . .

I'd be out on my ear the same day, thought Tibble. Now he could hear them talking to each other, the young lady and the cat. They were making little purring, meowy kinds of noises.

"What's Fluff saying now?" he asked as a joke.

"He says your peppermints are in a jam jar on the top shelf of the bookcase. You put them there yourself."

Tibble stood up to have a look. She was right.

—3—
THE TATTER CAT

"I still don't believe it," Tibble said. "You being able to talk to cats. It must be something else. Some kind of mind-reading or something."

"Maybe," Minou said dreamily. She yawned. "It's time for me to get in my box. Can I take this old paper?"

"Are you sure you don't need a blanket or a pillow or anything?"

"No, no, not at all. Fluff likes to sleep on your feet, so I've heard. Everyone has their own preference. Good night."

"Good night, Miss Minou."

At the door she turned round for a moment. "I heard a bit of news while I was out and about," she said. "On the roofs here in the neighborhood."

"News? What kind of news?"

"The Tatter Cat is due to have another litter any time now."

"Oh," said Tibble. "It's a shame, but I'm not allowed to write about cats anymore. They say it's not interesting enough."

"Too bad," said Minou.

"Did you hear anything else?"

"Just about Mr. Smith being so sad."

"Mr. Smith? Do you mean the schoolteacher? I was talking to him today. He's the one who helped me get you down out of the tree. He didn't look sad."

"He is, though."

"That doesn't sound like interesting news either," Tibble said. "Is he just down in the dumps or is it something in particular?"

"Next week it will be twenty-five years since he was made head teacher at the school," Minou said. "He was really hoping there'd be some kind of festivities. An anniversary celebration. But, no."

"Why not?"

"Nobody knows about it. Everyone's forgotten. He thought people would remember . . . but they haven't."

"Can't he remind them?"

"He refuses. He's too proud. That's what Cross-Eyed Simon says."

"Cross-Eyed Simon? That's his Siamese."

"Exactly. He's the one I spoke to. And he told me all about it. And now I'm going to get into my box."

She said a quick "*Mrow*" to Fluff. And Fluff said "*Mreeow*" in reply. That was probably "Sleep tight."

Tibble grabbed the phone book. It was much too late at night, but he still dialed Mr. Smith's number.

"I'm sorry for calling so late," Tibble blurted, "but I just heard that you'll be celebrating an anniversary soon. Twenty-five years as head teacher. Is that right?"

There was a long silence on the other end of the line. Then Mr. Smith said, "So some people have remembered."

"No, cats . . ." Tibble was about to say, but he stopped himself just in time.

"Of course they have," he said instead. "How could anyone forget something like that? You don't mind me writing an article about it, do you?"

"I'd be delighted," said Mr. Smith.

"Could I drop by to talk to you about it? It is *rather* late . . . but I would very much like to hand in the article tomorrow morning. Something about your life and about the school . . ."

"Come straight over," said Mr. Smith.

It was three in the morning by the time Tibble got back home again. He had a pad full of notes about Mr. Smith's life and work. He tiptoed through the attic and, before sitting down at the typewriter, peeked into the junk room.

Minou was curled up in the box asleep.

She saved me, thought Tibble. I've got an article. I just have to write it up.

When he finally went to bed, he told a sleepy Fluff: "I'll hand it in tomorrow. It's a good article. And it's real news."

Fluff lay down on his feet and went back to sleep.

I'll thank her in the morning . . . this strange Miss Minou, Tibble thought, and then he fell asleep too.

But when he got up the next morning she was gone.

The box was empty. There was fresh newspaper spread out over the bottom, and everything had been left neat and tidy. Her clothes were gone as well and so was her case.

"Did she say anything, Fluff, before she left?"

"*Mrow . . . ,*" said Fluff. But Tibble didn't understand.

"Well," he said. "I'm actually quite relieved. I've got my attic to myself again."

Then he saw the article lying on his desk. "It's fantastic," he cried out loud. "I'm going into the office and I've got something for the paper. They won't fire me. At least . . . not today." His happiness disappeared. He'd be trudging around town again tonight searching for another story.

There was a smell of coffee. He went into the kitchen and saw that Miss Minou had made some coffee for him. And done the dishes too. That was nice.

The window was open. She'd left the way she'd come: through the attic window.

At least the weather's better, Tibble thought. She won't have to wander around in the rain. He wondered if she was out talking to cats again? If she'd stayed here . . . he thought. If I'd let her stay . . . maybe she'd have brought some news home for me every day. He felt like shouting out through the window, over the rooftops, "Puss, puss, puss . . . Mi-nou!"

But he restrained himself. "Bah, how selfish can you get?" he said to himself. "You only want to let her stay because you think there might be something in it for you. What a nasty character trait! Forget about her and find your own news. Don't be so shy. Anyway, she's gone for good. She's probably miles away by now."

But at that moment Minou was very close by. She was sitting on the roof of the Social Security Building, the highest roof in the vicinity. She was talking to the Tatter Cat.

The Tatter Cat was called that because she was battered and tattered. She was always dirty, and she usually had muddy paws. Her tail was thin and wispy, there was a chunk out of her left ear, and her coat was drab and patchy.

"Your kittens are due soon," Minou said.

"Oh, put a cork in it," said the Tatter Cat. "Sometimes I wonder if it's ever going to stop. My whole life's one stinking litter after the other."

"How many children do you have?" Minou asked.

The Tatter Cat scratched herself at length. "How would I bleedin' know?" she said. She had a filthy mouth. But living on the street will do that to a cat. "Anyway, let's not talk about me," the Tatter Cat said. "This thing with you is much, much worse. How can something like that even exist? What did it?"

She stared at Minou with fear in her yellow eyes.

"I wish I knew. And the worst thing is, I'm not even *all* human. It's all so half and half."

"But you are all human. From head to toe."

"I mean *inside*," Minou said. "I still have almost all my cattish characteristics. I purr, I hiss, I rub up against people. I wash with a washcloth, but otherwise . . . I wonder if I still like mice. I'll have to try one."

"Do you still know the Great Yawl-Yowl Song?" the Tatter Cat asked.

"I think so."

"Sing a few bars, then."

23

Minou opened her mouth and a horrific, raucous caterwauling came out of it, a howling, shrieking, wailing sound.

The Tatter Cat joined in immediately, and together they screeched at the top of their voices. They kept going until someone opened a nearby attic window and hurled a large empty bottle at them. It hit the roof between them and smashed to pieces, driving them apart.

"All in the game!" the Tatter Cat cried cheerfully. "You know what? It's only temporary! You'll get over it. Someone who sings as well as you do *stays* cat. Feel your upper lip. You sure you don't have any whiskers?"

Minou felt her lip. "No," she said.

"And your tail? How's that?"

"Gone completely."

"Do you feel sometimes to see if it's growing back?"

"Of course. But there's no sign of it. Not even a tiny little bump."

"Have you got a house?" the Tatter Cat asked.

"I thought I did for a while . . . but I think it's off."

"With the young guy from the paper?"

"Yes," said Minou. "I'm still kind of hoping he'll call me. I left my case over there behind a chimney, in the gutter."

"You're much better off on the streets," the Tatter Cat said. "The life of a stray. Come with me. I'll introduce you to tons of my kids. Most of 'em have really made something of themselves. One of my sons is the cafeteria cat in the factory. And one of my daughters is the Council Cat. She lives in the town hall. And then there's—"

"Shhh . . . be quiet for a sec," Minou said.

They stopped talking. From across the roofs they heard a voice, "Puss, puss, puss . . . Mi-nou, Mi-nou, Mi-nou-nou-nou-nou."

"There you have it," Minou said. "He's calling me."

"Stay here," the Tatter Cat hissed. "Don't go to him. Don't give up your freedom. Next thing he'll be taking you to the vet in a basket . . . for a shot!"

Minou hesitated. "I think I'll go anyway," she said.

"You're mad," the Tatter Cat said. "Come with me. I know an old caravan at the back of a yard. . . . That'll be a roof over your head. You can take things easy while you turn back into a cat."

"Puss, puss, puss . . . Mi-nou!"

"I'm going," Minou said.

"No, stay here! Use your brain. If you have a litter, they'll drown your kittens."

"Puss, puss . . . Miss Minou!" the voice called.

"I'll come and visit," Minou said. "Here on the roof. Bye."

She jumped down to a lower level, nimbly climbed a sloping, tiled roof, and lowered herself down on the other side. Then she crawled along the gutter on all fours, grabbed her case, stood up, and stepped over in front of the kitchen window.

"Here I am," she said.

"Come in," said Tibble.

—4—

THE CAT PRESS AGENCY

"Sit down, Tibble," the editor said.

Tibble sat down. It had been exactly one week since he had last sat on this chair, blinking in the light. It had been a very unpleasant conversation, but things were different now.

"I don't know what's got into you, Tibble," his boss said. "But you've changed a lot. Last week I almost kicked you out, you know that? I was going to fire you, I'd made up my mind. I guess it was pretty clear. Then I said I'd give you one last chance. And lo and behold! In this one week you've come up with all kinds of interesting news. You were the first to know about Mr. Smith and his anniversary. And you were the first to know about the new swimming pool. That was *secret*. But you *still* found out about it. . . . I can't help but wonder, how did you find out about that?"

"Well . . . ," Tibble said. "I talked to some people here and there."

"Some people here and there" was just Minou. And Minou had heard it from the Council Cat, who always sat in on the closed council meetings at the town hall.

"And that article about the hoard they found next to the church," his boss said. "A pot full of old coins buried in the churchyard! You didn't waste any time with that one either. You were the first on the scene yet again."

Tibble smiled modestly. One of the Tatter Cat's daughters had provided that bit of news. It had been the Church Cat, Ecumenica. And she herself had found the pot of old coins while scratching in the churchyard for simple toiletry reasons. Tibble had gone straight to the sexton and told him. And then he'd written an article about it.

"Keep it up, Tibble," his boss said. "You don't seem to be shy at all anymore."

Tibble blushed. It wasn't true . . . unfortunately. He was still as shy as ever. The news all came from the cats; he only needed to write it up. Although . . . he did often need to check that the things he'd heard were actually true. But usually a single phone call was enough to take care of that. "Excuse me, Mr. Whatever, I heard that so-and-so did this or that, is that true?" Up till now it had always been true. The cats hadn't told him any fibs.

And there were so many cats in Killenthorn. Every building had at least one. Now, at this very moment, there was one sitting on the windowsill in the editor's office.

It was the Editorial Cat. He blinked at Tibble.

That cat listens to everything, Tibble thought. I hope he doesn't tell nasty stories about me.

"And so," the editor continued, "I've been thinking of increasing your salary at the end of the month."

"Thank you, sir, great," Tibble said. He snuck a glance at the Editorial Cat and felt himself blushing again. There was a hint of cold contempt in the cat's eyes. He probably thought Tibble was groveling.

A little later, out on the street, where the sun was shining, Tibble felt a tremendous urge to run and skip; he was that relieved.

And when he saw someone he knew, he shouted out "Hello" at the top of his voice.

It was Bibi, a little girl who lived nearby and sometimes visited him in his attic.

"Would you like an ice cream?" Tibble asked. "Come on, I'll buy you an extra-large one."

Bibi was in Mr. Smith's class at school and told Tibble that they were having a drawing competition. She was going to do a really big picture.

"What are you going to draw?" Tibble asked.

"A cat," Bibi said.

"Do you like cats?"

"I love all animals." She licked her big pink ice cream.

"When you've finished your drawing, come and show it to me," Tibble said, and went home.

Minou had been living in his attic for a week now, and all things considered, it wasn't too bad. What it actually came down to was that he now had two cats instead of just one.

Minou slept in the box. And she did most of her sleeping in the daytime. At night she'd go out through the kitchen window, then wander over the rooftops and through the back gardens, talking to the many cats in the surrounding area and not coming home to her box until early in the morning.

The most important thing was that she provided him with news. The first few days it had been Fluff who had busied himself searching for the latest stories. But Fluff wasn't a real news cat. He mostly came back with gossip about catfights, or boasting about a rat he'd smelt near the docks or a fish head he'd found somewhere. He wasn't really interested in human rumors.

No, the great source of news was the Tatter Cat. She knew everything.

That was mainly because she was a stray who swiped her meat scraps from all layers of society. And because she had an extensive family.

The Tatter Cat had children and grandchildren all over town.

Minou met her at night on the roof of the Social Security Building and always took a small bag of fish for her.

"Thanks," the Tatter Cat would say. "My daughter, the Council Cat, is waiting for you at the town hall. She's sitting on one of the marble lions out front and she's got some news for you. . . ."

Or "The Butcher's Cat wanted to tell you something. He's in the third garden on the left after the chestnut. . . ."

That same night Minou went down the Social Security Building fire escape, slunk over a courtyard, and slipped through a rear gate into an alley. And from there to the prearranged spot where some cat or other would be waiting.

"Soon we'll have to change our meeting spot," the Tatter Cat said. "My kids are going to be born in a few days, I can feel it, and then I'll have to stay close to the little monsters and won't be able to come up on the rooftops. But that won't matter. The message service will still work. All the cats have been informed. They know your human is waiting for news, and they're watching out for it. They're keeping their eyes peeled and their ears open. They'll pass it on."

"Where are you going to have your kittens?" Minou asked. "Have you found a good spot?"

"Not yet," the Tatter Cat said. "But I will."

"Can't you move in with us? In the attic?"

"Never!" the Tatter Cat cried. "I'll never give up my freedom! And stop nagging."

"My human's very nice," Minou said.

"I know. He's a good human, as far as that goes. . . . But I just don't like the species. They're not too bad until they grow up . . . some of them, at least. Do you know Bibi?"

"No."

"She's drawing me," the Tatter Cat said. "In detail! And she likes the way I look, even now, with this big gut. She thinks I'm beautiful! Can you believe it? Anyway, I'll let you know where I am when the time comes. Somewhere in town, close to a radio."

"Why close to a radio?"

"I like a bit of background music when I'm having kittens," the Tatter Cat said. "It makes it easier. And more cheerful. Remember that, if it ever happens to you."

When Minou came home with some news story or other and told Tibble how she'd got it, he cried, "It's all so organized! One cat passes it on to the next. . . . It's a kind of cat press agency."

"I'm not sure I like the sound of that," Minou said hesitantly. "A cat press . . . it makes me think of a garlic press. Squished cat."

"Not a *cat-press* agency," Tibble said, "a cat *press agency*."

The arrangement had saved him, and as far as he was concerned, things were going excellently.

Sometimes, when he came in, he'd find Minou in a corner of the room. She'd be crouched down on the floor, dead still and staring at a hole in the skirting board.

"Miss Minou! That's one more habit you have to break! Lying in wait at a mouse hole! That's not the kind of thing a lady does!"

She stood up and tried to get back into his good books by rubbing her head against his shoulder.

"That's not right either," Tibble sighed. "Real ladies don't rub up against people. At most they rub them up the wrong way. I wish you'd stop doing all these catty things."

"*Catty* is not the correct word," Minou said. "It's called *cattish*."

"Fine, cattish. But I feel like you're getting more and more cattish. It would be much better if you had more to do with people. Instead of just seeing cats all the time. You should go out on the rooftops less often and down on the street more—in the daytime."

"I don't dare, Mr. Tibble. I'm scared of people."

"Nonsense. People aren't scary at all!"

She looked at him for a moment with her slanting eyes, then turned away shyly.

How can I say something like that? he thought. When I'm so shy and scared myself? When I prefer the company of cats?

But he decided to stick to his guns.

"What's that I see!" he cried.

Minou was washing herself. She'd licked her wrist and was rubbing behind her ear with the wet spot.

"That takes the cake! Yuck!"

"It's—it's just . . . ," Minou stammered, "I was hoping it would make it go faster."

"Make what faster? Washing?"

"No, that's faster in the shower. I mean, turning into a cat. I still haven't given up hope that . . . I'd just prefer to be a cat again."

Tibble slumped down on the couch.

"Listen," he said. "I wish you'd stop all this nonsense. You never *were* a cat. It's all in your imagination. You dreamt it."

She didn't answer.

"Honestly," Tibble went on. "Absolute nonsense."

Minou yawned and stood up.

"What are you doing?"

"I'm going to get in my box," she said.

Fluff curled around her legs and, together with the gray

cat, she made her way over to the corner of the attic where she kept her box.

Tibble called after her in an angry voice, "If you *were* a cat . . . *whose* cat were you?"

No answer came. He heard a quiet, purring meow. A conversation in Cattish. Two cats talking behind the partition.

—5—

TIBBLE'S SECRETARY

One afternoon when Tibble was climbing the stairs to his attic, he heard a furious screeching coming from his flat; it sounded like two cats fighting.

He raced up the rest of the staircase three steps at a time and stormed into his living room.

He had a visitor. But it wasn't exactly a tea party.

Crouched on the floor was the little girl, Bibi. Minou was across from her, also on the floor. There was an empty box next to them, and they both had a hand on something. They were yelling at each other at the top of their lungs.

"What is it? What have you got there?" Tibble cried.

"Let go!" Bibi screamed.

"What's under your hands?" Tibble asked again. "*Miss Minou!* Will you please let go immediately!"

Minou looked up at him with an expression that was more cattish than ever.

There was a vicious, murderous glint in her eyes, and she refused to let go. She closed the hand with the small, sharp nails even tighter around whatever it was she was holding.

"Let go, I said!" Tibble smacked her hand, hard. She slid back and hissed furiously, but she did let go. In almost the same instant, though, she lashed out, clawing him painfully on the nose.

And now Tibble saw what it was: a white mouse. Still unharmed.

Gently Bibi picked up the mouse and put it back in its box, but she was crying from fright and indignation.

"It's *my* mouse," she sobbed. "I only got it out to show her, and then she jumped on it. I'm leaving. And I'm never coming back."

"Wait, Bibi, please," Tibble said. "Don't rush off. Listen. This is Miss Minou. She's, um . . . she's . . ." He thought for a moment. "She's my secretary and she doesn't mean any harm. Not at all. In fact, she really loves mice."

Minou was on her feet now and staring down at the closed box. You could tell she loved mice, but not the way Tibble meant.

"Isn't that right, Miss Minou?" Tibble asked. "You didn't want to hurt the poor mouse, did you?"

Minou leant over to rub her head against his shoulder, but he took a step to one side.

"What else have you got there, Bibi?" Tibble asked, pointing at a large collecting tin.

"I'm going round with the tin," Bibi said. "Collecting money.

It's for the present. The present for Mr. Smith's anniversary. And you've got blood on your nose."

Tibble wiped his nose with his hand. There was blood all over it.

"Don't worry about that," he said. "I'll put some money in your tin."

"And I've come to show you my drawing," Bibi said. She unrolled a big sheet of paper, and Tibble and Minou shouted out together, "That's the Tatter Cat! It looks just like her."

"It's for the drawing competition at school," Bibi said. "I just came by to show you."

"It's beautiful," Tibble said, and felt yet another drop of blood running down his face.

"If I go and look for a bandage in the bathroom," he said gruffly, "I hope that *you*, Miss Minou, will be able to control yourself for a moment." He put the mouse box on his desk, gave Minou a menacing look, and backed out of the room.

I've got a secretary, he thought. That sounds excellent, very posh. But she happens to be a secretary who wouldn't hesitate to gobble up a little girl's white mouse if she got a chance.

He hurried back into the living room with a crooked bandage on his nose and was surprised to discover that Minou and Bibi had become great friends in the meantime. The mouse box was still safe on his desk.

"Can I see the attic?" Bibi asked. "The whole attic?"

"Sure," Tibble said. "Look around. I've actually got two ca—I mean . . . I have a cat too. As well as a secretary. Um . . . he's called Fluff, but he's out on the roof. Miss Minou, would you show Bibi the rest of the attic? Then I'll get to work."

Sitting at his desk, he heard the two of them whispering in the junk room behind the partition. He was very glad that Minou had found a friend, and when Bibi finally left he said, "Drop in again, if you like."

"That'd be fun," Bibi said.

"Don't forget your tin. I put something in it."

"Oh, yeah," Bibi said.

"And don't forget your drawing either."

"Oh, yeah."

"And don't forget your box with the, um . . . *you-know-what* in it." He was too scared to say the word *mouse* in front of his secretary.

"Oh, yeah."

"And I hope you win first prize!" Tibble called after her.

Downstairs, in the house the attic belonged to, lived Mrs. Van Dam.

Fortunately Tibble had his own front door and his own staircase, so he didn't have to go through her house to come in or go out.

That afternoon, Mrs. Van Dam said to her husband: "Put that newspaper down for a second. I need to talk to you."

"What about?" her husband asked.

"About that upstairs neighbor of ours."

"Oh, you mean that young fellow? Tibble? What about him?"

"I don't think he's alone up there."

"What do you mean he's not alone?"

"I think he has a woman living with him."

"Oh," said Mr. Van Dam, "that must be nice for him." And he picked his newspaper up again.

"Yes, but I think it's a very *strange* young woman," his wife said.

"Either way, it's none of our business," he said.

It was quiet for a moment. Then she said, "She spends all her time up on the roof."

"Who?"

"The woman upstairs. At nighttime she goes out on the roof."

"How do you know?" Mr. Van Dam asked. "Do you go up on the roof at night to have a look?"

"No, but the lady across the road looks out of her attic window sometimes and she always sees her sitting there. With cats on both sides of her."

"You know I don't like gossip," Mr. Van Dam said irritably. He carried on reading while his wife went to the front door, because someone had rung the doorbell.

It was Bibi with her collecting tin.

"Would you like to make a donation for Mr. Smith's present?" she asked.

"I'd love to," said Mrs. Van Dam. "Come in and sit down for a moment."

Bibi sat on a chair with her legs dangling and the tin on her knee, the drawing under one arm and the mouse box next to her.

"Tell us, have you been upstairs yet? To the attic flat?" Mrs. Van Dam asked casually.

"Yes," Bibi said. "To Mr. Tibble and Miss Minou's."

"Miss Minou?" Mrs. Van Dam asked sweetly, putting a coin in the tin. "Who's that?"

"His secretary."

"Goodness."

"She sleeps in a box," said Bibi.

Now Mr. Van Dam looked up over his reading glasses. "In a box?"

"Yes, in a big cardboard box. She just fits. Curled up. And she always goes out through the window, onto the roof. And she talks to cats."

"Oh," said Mr. Van Dam.

"She can talk to all the cats," Bibi explained, "because she used to be one herself."

"Who says so?"

"She does. And now I have to go."

"Don't forget your tin," said Mrs. Van Dam. "And here, don't forget this roll of paper. And your box."

Once Bibi was gone, she said, "There. What did I tell you? Do we have a strange woman living upstairs or don't we?"

"She does sound a little odd," said Mr. Van Dam. "But I still think it's no concern of ours."

"Listen," she said. "When it comes down to it, it's *our* attic. Tibble rents the attic from *us*. And I have a right to know what's going on under *my* roof."

"What are you doing?" her husband asked.

"I'm going up there."

"Just like that? What are you going to say?"

"I don't know. I'll think of something."

Even though it was a warm spring day and she only had to take two steps out on the street, Mrs. Van Dam put on her fur coat.

She was going to ring the doorbell, but Bibi had left the front door open, so it wasn't necessary and she went straight up the stairs. It was a tall, steep staircase, and she was puffing in her thick fur coat.

"Hello, Mrs. Van Dam," said Tibble.

"Hello, Mr. Tibble. Sorry for barging in on you like this . . ."

"No problem at all, come in. Can I take your coat?"

"No, no. I'm not staying," Mrs. Van Dam said as she stepped into the living room.

There was no one there except Tibble.

"Haven't you made it lovely," she said, looking around every-where. "And what a cute little kitchen . . . and that gorgeous view out over the roofs."

"Shall I make some tea?"

"No, thank you. I was really only popping in. I just wanted to tell you that I always read your articles in the paper. Lovely articles . . . And this must be the storage space. . . . You don't mind me having a look, do you?"

"There's only junk in there," Tibble said. "Old chairs and boxes. Things like that."

But she slipped past him, chattering cheerfully.

"Oh, I always love poking around in places like this!" she said. "Old corners of old attics."

Tibble tagged along helplessly behind her. Now she'd reached the big cardboard box and was bending over it. The movement made the floor creak under her weight.

Minou woke up. She opened one eye. Then she leapt up out of the box with a shriek.

Mrs. Van Dam recoiled in fright. Furious cat eyes glared at

40

her. A hand with sharp pink nails moved toward her and the creature *hissed*.

"Sorry . . . ," Mrs. Van Dam spluttered, backing up quickly. She turned to flee, but Tibble stopped her with a friendly gesture. "May I introduce you to my secretary, Miss Minou . . . and this is my downstairs neighbor, Mrs. Van Dam."

Mrs. Van Dam turned back nervously. The strange creature was just an ordinary young woman with a polite smile.

"Pleased to meet you," said Mrs. Van Dam.

"Won't you sit down for a moment?"

"No, no. I really must be going. It was lovely of you to show me round your flat."

She peered at the bandage on Tibble's nose for a moment and then said, "Bye."

After she'd left, Tibble let out a deep sigh and said, "This attic is hers. She's my landlady."

"How horrible!" Minou said.

"No, it's all right. What's horrible about it? I just pay the rent. And otherwise we don't have anything to do with her."

"That's not what I mean," Minou said. "I mean, how horrible . . . there must have been at least twenty."

"Twenty? Twenty what?"

"Cats."

"Twenty cats? Where?"

"In that coat . . . ," Minou said with a shudder. "That fur coat. I was lying there asleep in my box and suddenly I wake up with a start and there's twenty dead cats standing in front of me."

"Oh, that's why you hissed at her. You came this close to clawing her. You have to control yourself a little better, Miss

41

Minou. Clawing the landlady just because she's wearing a coat made of cat fur. Shame on you!"

"If she comes back I really will claw her," said Minou.

"Nonsense. She bought that coat in a shop, and when she bought it those cats were long dead. It's all because you don't mix enough with people. You spend too much time up on the rooftops. You don't get down to the streets enough."

"I was on the street last night."

"You have to get out in the *daytime*. Go out and do some shopping like other people."

"All right. But I'm waiting till dark," Minou said.

"No, the shops will be shut then. You have to go now."

"I wouldn't dare."

"We need bread and biscuits," Tibble continued.

"I'm too scared."

"And we've run out of fish. You could pop by the fishmonger's. He's got a stall on the corner of Green Square."

"Oh," said Minou. "Maybe I can learn to be brave enough. Once I'm out on the street."

"I'm sure of it," Tibble said. "You'll get better and better at it. Just . . ."

"What?"

"I'd prefer it if you didn't rub up against the fishmonger."

—6—

THE NEIGHBORHOOD

Minou walked down the street with a shopping basket over one arm.

Besides that first time when the dog treed her, she'd never seen this neighborhood in the daytime. She only really knew the town from the rooftops and in the dark. And she knew the back gardens better than the streets and squares.

She felt like slinking along and hiding behind parked cars and in doorways as she went, darting from one to the other. The people and traffic made her very uneasy.

"But I don't have to sneak around," she told herself. "I'm a human going out to do some shopping. Here comes a doggy. There's no need to get frightened; it's only a little dog . . . and I mustn't hiss at it. And I definitely shouldn't stop to sniff the rubbish bins. I'm going shopping, like all the other humans out and about in this part of town."

From very far away Minou smelt the fish stall on Green Square and started walking faster and faster to get there sooner.

And when she was almost there, she circled it a couple of times at a distance until she suddenly thought, I can *buy* some fish. I've got a purse. I don't need to beg and I don't need to steal. She went up to the fishmonger. He smelt delicious, and Minou slipped in a quick rub of her head against his shoulder. He didn't notice; he was too busy gutting fish.

She bought herring and mackerel, and lots of everything, and after she'd paid she brushed her head against the fishmonger's arm once again. He looked up with surprise, but Minou just strode off on her way to the baker's.

She passed Mr. Smith's school. The windows were open; she could hear children singing, and she could see the class sitting there. Bibi was there too.

Now a cat jumped up onto the school wall. It was the School Cat. "Nosey-nosey first," he said.

Minou pushed her nose forward and felt the School Cat's cold pink nose against it. This was how the cats here in town greeted each other when they weren't fighting.

"If you give me a piece of fish," the School Cat said, "I'll tell you some news for the paper."

Minou gave him some.

"Fantastic news," the School Cat said. "The Spanish Armada has been defeated. By Sir Francis Drake. Make sure they put it in the paper."

"Thanks," said Minou.

Two houses up sat Cross-Eyed Simon, Mr. Smith's Siamese.

"Give me a piece of fish," he said, "and I'll tell you something."

Once he had the piece in his claws, he said: "You should never listen to the School Cat. He always sits in on the history lessons. He thinks it's exciting and doesn't realize it all happened ages ago."

"I got that," Minou said. "But what did *you* want to tell me?"

"That," said Simon.

"You're all just after the fish," Minou said. "I'm glad I bought a lot."

Now she passed the factory. It was the deodorant factory. This was where they made spray cans with smells in them, and it stank of disgusting violets. Nowhere near as nice as the fish stall.

Minou was about to hurry past when the factory cat came up to her. The Deodorant Cat was one of the Tatter Cat's sons. He had a very strong smell of violets about him.

"I suppose you've got some news for me if I give you some fish," Minou said.

"How'd you guess?" the cat asked.

"You can have a piece of mackerel."

"Firstly," said the Deodorant Cat, "the nicest cafeteria boy in the whole factory just got fired. He's over there now. He's called Billy. It's a terrible shame because he was really kind to me and patted me every day."

"Why'd they fire him?" Minou asked.

"He was always too late."

"Oh, that's a shame," said Minou. "But it's not news for the paper."

"No? Fine, that was 'Firstly,' then. Now comes 'Secondly.' There are plans to expand our factory. I sat in on a secret meeting today. They're going to turn this whole neighborhood into one big perfume factory."

"That's real news," said Minou. "Thanks."

"But they don't have permission yet!" The cat called after her. "The councillor still has to approve it."

Minou hadn't bumped into many people during her shopping expedition, but she had met quite a few cats, and there were a few more on her way to the baker's.

The baker's wife was standing behind the counter, and there were already a couple of women in the shop. Minou waited politely for her turn, but while she was standing there looking around, Muffin the Bakery Cat came into the shop from the house, meowing loudly.

She's after my fish, thought Minou, but then she heard what Muffin was saying.

"*Meow, meow*! Now, now!" the cat cried. "Tell her now!"

Minou hurried up to the counter and said, "Your little boy Jack has got the kerosene bottle. Upstairs, in the bathroom."

The baker's wife looked at her with shock, dropped the bread rolls on the counter, and ran out of the shop without a word.

Minou felt the stares of the other customers. It was very intimidating, and she was about to hurry off when the baker's wife came back.

"It was true," she panted. "I got upstairs and there was my three-year-old, little Jack . . . with the kerosene bottle . . . pouring it out. . . . You can't leave them alone for a second. . . . Thank you so much for warning me."

Suddenly she stopped and looked at Minou.

46

"How did you know?" she asked. "You can't see into our bathroom from down here."

Minou was about to say, "Muffin told me," but then she saw the women staring at her. She stumbled over her words. "I . . . it was just a feeling."

"Well, thank you anyway. Whose turn is it?"

"The young lady can go first," said the other customers.

Minou asked for bread and biscuits and paid.

No sooner had she left the shop than they started talking behind her back.

"That's Mr. Tibble's young lady. . . ."

"She's his secretary . . . and she sleeps in a box. . . ."

"And she sits on the roof at night. . . ."

"A very strange young lady . . ."

"Well," said the baker's wife after listening to it all, "she may be strange, but she certainly did me a tremendous favor. End of story. A small loaf of brown, you said?"

Meanwhile Tibble was waiting.

More than an hour had passed since Minou went out to do some shopping. Just bread and fish, that couldn't take this long.

He sat at his desk, nervously chewing his nails. Just when he was starting to wonder whether he should go out to look for her, the phone rang.

"Hello," said Tibble.

"Hello, Mr. Tibble, this is Mrs. Van Dam speaking. From downstairs, you know. I'm calling from a phone box. Your secretary is up a tree. And she can't get down again."

"Oh, thank you very much," Tibble said.

"You're welcome."

Too late he shouted, "Which tree?" But she'd already hung up.

"Here we go again!" Tibble cried. "What a pain!" And he ran down to the street.

Green Square first, that was where most of the trees were.

When he arrived, he saw where she was at once. There was a large group of people gathered round. It wasn't the same tree as last time; it was another one that was even taller. Bibi was there too because school had just finished for the day.

"A dog chased her," Bibi said.

"Uh-huh," sighed Tibble. He wasn't surprised. "How do we get her back down again?"

"The fishmonger's already at it," Bibi said. "He's up in the tree. He's helping her down."

Amid great interest, the fishmonger helped Minou down through the branches. First onto the roof of the greengrocer's van, then down onto the street.

"Thank you very much," she said, sniffing at his sleeve one last time. "Oh, my basket must be here somewhere."

Tibble picked it up. There were biscuits and bread in it and a little bit of fish.

"We have to do something about it," Tibble said when they were back home. "Things really can't go on like this, Miss Minou."

She was sitting in the corner looking very repentant.

"It was the same dog again," she said. "He's called Mars."

"It's not just getting stuck in trees," Tibble said. "It's all these cattish traits. . . . You have to stop acting like that."

48

"Being rescued by the fishmonger was lovely," Minou said wistfully.

That annoyed Tibble even more, but before he could say anything she blurted, "Oh, yeah, I heard some news too while I was out." She told him about the expansion of the perfume factory. It calmed him down a little; he had something new to write about.

—7—

"YOUR SISTER CAME BY"

When Minou went up on the roof that night, the Tatter Cat wasn't there. Instead there was another cat waiting for her. The School Cat.

"She says hi," he said. "She couldn't make it."

"Have the kittens arrived?"

"Seventeen or so, I think," said the School Cat.

"Where are they?"

"You know the parking lot behind the gas station? It's best to stick to the gardens until you get to the big hawthorn, then go through the hedge. There are a couple of abandoned campers there. She's moved into one of them. Temporarily."

"I'll go straight there," said Minou.

"Give me some fish before you go."

"It's not for you, it's for the Tatter Cat. I've got some milk with me too."

"I don't want any milk. If you give me a piece of fish I'll tell you some news. For the paper."

Minou gave him a tiny piece.

"Guy Fawkes tried to blow up the Houses of Parliament," the School Cat said. "Make sure it's in tomorrow's paper."

"Thanks," said Minou. He'd been sitting in on the history lesson again.

She passed through shadowy gardens to the garage where they repaired cars in the daytime. The garage was closed, but the petrol station was open; it was all lit up and they had the radio on. All night long.

It seemed the Tatter Cat had got what she wanted. Background music.

The parking lot behind the gas station was dark. And very quiet. There were a few overnight cars and right at the back there was a row of campers.

An ordinary person would have found it difficult to find their way on such a dark night, but Minou, with all her cattish traits, had excellent eyesight and easily found the Tatter Cat's home.

It was an old, run-down camper. There was a broken window with a curtain flapping in the wind and the door was half open. Inside, the Tatter Cat was lying on an old blanket on the floor. Under her, a tangle of kittens.

"Six of them!" she cried indignantly. "*Six!* Unbelievable. What did I do to deserve something like this? Can you see them? Get out from under me, you riffraff!" she said to the babies. "Look, now you can see them better. There's *one* ginger.

51

He's a dead ringer for his dad, the Pump Cat. And the rest are all tortoiseshells, like me. And now give me something to eat. I'm dying of hunger."

Minou knelt down next to her and looked at the six writhing kittens.

They had tiny little tails and blind eyes and teensy little claws. In the distance the radio was playing.

"Hear it?" the Tatter Cat asked. "Cozy, huh? It's all modern conveniences here."

"Is it safe?" Minou asked. "Whose camper is it?"

"Nobody's. It's been empty for years. Nobody ever comes here. Did you see the Pump Cat around anywhere?"

"No."

"He hasn't been here *once* to see his children," the Tatter Cat said. "Not that I want him hanging round the place, but still! And now give me that fish. You've got milk too. In a bottle. Are you expecting me to drink out of a bottle?"

"Be quiet now. I've brought a saucer."

While the mother cat lapped up the milk, Minou looked around. "I wouldn't feel at ease here," she said. "A parking lot, that means people. Lots of people in the daytime."

"We're in a quiet corner," the Tatter Cat said.

"But your children would be much safer in Mr. Tibble's attic."

The Tatter Cat made an angry gesture that sent her kittens sprawling and set off a chorus of pathetic squeaking.

"Shut your traps!" their mother roared. "They just guzzle away all day and all night. And the least little thing has 'em screaming blue murder!"

Then she shot Minou a vicious glare through the dark with

her burning yellow eyes. And she hissed, "If you take my kids away, I'll scratch your eyes out."

"Take them away? I'd take you too, of course."

"Thanks for the offer, but I'm fine right here."

"Later, when they're bigger, I could look for homes for them."

"No need. They'll make their own way. Let 'em become strays, like me. They should steer clear of humans. I always say there are two kinds of human. One kind's nasty lowlife skunks."

She was quiet for a moment and took a big bite of poached fish.

Minou waited patiently.

"And the other kind?" she asked.

"I've forgotten the other kind," the Tatter Cat said. "*Erk-erk-erk-erk* . . ." A gagging sound came up out of her throat.

Minou patted her on her skinny shoulders and the Tatter Cat spat out a fish bone.

"Just what I needed," she said. "Choking on a stupid bone. Be a bit careful next time you bring me some fish, will you? I've got enough problems as it is with this whole kitten nursery hanging off me. But you know what's so great here? I'm really close to all those posh gardens. Because just over there"—she waved one paw—"it's all big fancy houses."

"They have dogs at big fancy houses," said Minou.

"Sometimes, but if you're lucky they keep 'em chained up. And the blackbirds in those gardens are as fat as the ladies who live in the houses. And in weather like this, they always leave the garden doors open. You can sneak in and there's always something to nick. It'd actually be better if *you* came to live here with *me*. Why not? There's plenty of room. We can go hunting together! And I'm sure, very sure, that if you ate a nice fat thrush, you'd soon turn back into a respectable cat again—that's right!"

"What's the matter?"

"I'm such a moron," the Tatter Cat said. "I forgot there was something I had to tell you. . . . All this maternal love has gone to my head."

"That's OK. Tell me now."

"It's not for the paper. It's a personal message for you. Your aunt was here. Your aunt Sooty. She wanted to talk to you, but she's too old to go up on the rooftops, and that's why she left the message with me."

"What did she want?"

"She asked if you'd drop by. She's had a visit from your sister."

Minou jumped. "My . . . my sister? But she lives miles away. Right out on the other side of town. What was she doing here?"

"Take it easy," said the Tatter Cat. "That's all I know. I'm as *purrplexed* as you. Ha-ha, good joke, huh? And when you come tomorrow, make sure you get all the bones out of the fish first."

"Is it all right if I bring my human to visit? Just once?" Minou asked. "And Bibi?"

"Bibi's OK," the Tatter Cat said without hesitating. "She drew me. Have you seen it?"

"It's a beautiful likeness," said Minou.

"But I don't know about Tibble . . . I'm scared he'll start fussing," said the Tatter Cat. "He's a fusser. Even worse than you. He'll want to take my babies away . . . arrange vets and shots and looking for homes . . . all that . . ."

"I'll tell him he's not allowed to make a fuss," Minou said. "See you tomorrow."

* * *

On the way home she took a detour through Aunt Sooty's garden. She stayed in among the shrubs, but as soon as she let out a short meow, her elderly aunt came out through the cat flap.

"You haven't made much progress," Aunt Sooty said disapprovingly. "No tail, no whiskers, and you're still wearing that horrible two-piece suit."

"I heard—" Minou began.

"Yes, yes," Aunt Sooty interrupted her. "Your sister was here."

Minou trembled and her voice was a little hoarse when she asked, "My sister from Victoria Avenue?"

"Yes, of course it was the one from Victoria Avenue," Aunt Sooty said. "You don't have any other sisters, do you?"

"She chased me away," said Minou. "Out of the house and out of the garden. She was angry at me. Because I wasn't a cat anymore. I wasn't allowed to come back, ever, that's what she said. "

"Quite understandable." Aunt Sooty nodded. "But she says hello. She's not angry anymore. She feels sorry for you."

"Can I go back?" Minou asked. "Does she want me back?"

"Not like you are now!" Aunt Sooty exclaimed. "First you have to turn back into a respectable cat, obviously."

"It was such a lovely garden on Victoria Avenue," Minou said. "It was my own garden and my own house . . . and our Woman was kind to us. Do you think the Woman would want me back?"

"Of course she would, as long as you're normal again," Aunt Sooty said. "And shall I let you in on a secret? Your sister has

55

found out where it came from. This . . . condition of yours. She had the same thing."

"*What?*" Minou cried. "Is she—"

"Shhh . . . not so loud," Aunt Sooty said. "No, she isn't . . . but almost. She started getting human traits too. Her whiskers fell out. . . . Her tail began to disappear. . . . It was all because you ate out of the rubbish bin at the institute. That's what your sister says."

"Is that what caused it?" Minou asked. "That was the building next door to our house in Victoria Avenue. . . . There was always a rubbish bin outside. And sometimes I found something to eat in it."

"Exactly," said Aunt Sooty. "You ate more of it than your sister. She got over it."

"Just like that? Did it go away of its own accord?"

"No, she says she found some kind of cure . . . something that made her normal again. But if you want to know the details, you have to drop by."

"Oh," said Minou.

"And if I were you, I'd do it sooner rather than later," said Aunt Sooty. "It's gone on long enough. What are you waiting for?"

"I'm not a hundred percent sure I want to," said Minou.

"You're mad!" Aunt Sooty cried. "Your one chance, your last chance to turn back into a proper cat. And you're not sure you want to!"

"I'm umming and aahing," said Minou.

Aunt Sooty went back into the house in a huff and Minou went home, to her own roof, where she sat down to watch the moon rise over the Social Security Building. The smell of blossoms rose up from the gardens far below, and in the gutters around the roofs there were all kinds of cat smells. It was very confusing.

The next morning Tibble gave her a package.

"A present," he said. "Because I've had a pay raise."

"How beautiful, thank you," said Minou. It was a pair of gloves.

"They're for the reception," explained Tibble.

"The reception?"

"There's a reception this afternoon at the Metropole Hotel. To celebrate Mr. Smith's anniversary. And I'd like you to come with me, Miss Minou. A lot of people will be coming."

"Then I don't want to," said Minou.

"It would be very good for you," said Tibble. "And for me too. We're both shy and we both have to Learn to Dare. I think the fishmonger will be there too."

"Oh," said Minou.

"I bought the gloves," Tibble said, "because I thought, then, if you scratch someone, it won't be so bad."

—8—

MR. SMITH'S RECEPTION

"I think I'd rather go back home," Minou said. "I'm scared."

They were on Green Square in front of the Metropole Hotel, where the reception for Mr. Smith was being held. There were a lot of cars out front, and people were streaming into the hotel.

Minou was wearing her new gloves, but now that she'd seen how busy it was, she felt very nervous.

"Don't be afraid," Tibble said. "Look, there's Bibi coming out of the hotel."

Bibi skipped up to them with a beaming smile on her face.

"What have you got there?" Tibble cried. "A camera!"

"First prize," said Bibi. "I won first prize in the drawing competition."

"And rightly so!"

"It's hanging on the wall," Bibi said. "In the reception room. They've hung up all our drawings. And they let me help present the gift."

"Are you going back in again?" Minou asked.

Bibi shook her head. "This afternoon is for grown-ups," she said. "We've already had our party. At school."

She walked on and Tibble said, "Come on, Miss Minou, let's go in. And remember! No purring, no hissing and don't rub up against anyone, not even the fishmonger."

"There won't be any dogs, will there?" Minou asked anxiously.

"No. Dogs don't come to receptions."

Inside, it was extremely crowded. Mr. Smith and his wife were sitting on a raised platform with floral arrangements left and right, and the children's drawings were on the wall behind them. It was a lovely exhibition, and the picture of the Tatter Cat was hanging in pride of place with a card saying *First Prize* next to it.

"Ah, look!" cried Mr. Smith. "There's Tibble. My dear Tibble, I'm so pleased you could make it. Look at the present I got from all the people in the neighborhood. A color TV! Isn't that fantastic?"

Tibble shook Mr. Smith's hand and said, "This is my secretary, Miss Minou."

"How do you do?" said Mr. Smith. "I believe I've seen you before, haven't I? In a tree . . ."

Other people came up to shake his hand and congratulate him, and Tibble and Minou walked on. All round the room there were groups of people gathered together to talk. There was the fishmonger. He waved at Minou and she blushed. The baker's wife nodded hello as well, and Minou started to feel more and more at ease.

It's going well, thought Tibble with a sense of relief. She's not cattish at all today.

Mrs. Van Dam was there too, in her fur coat, talking to a few other ladies, who nudged each other and looked in their direction.

Minou started getting nervous again. "Just ignore them," said Tibble.

They came to a table with all kinds of delicious snacks on it. Pieces of sliced sausage on toothpicks. And blocks of cheese on toothpicks.

"Can you just help yourself?" Minou asked.

"Later," said Tibble.

Now a large man wearing glasses and a pin-striped suit came in.

The room fell silent. Everyone bowed their heads low and respectfully in greeting.

"Is that the mayor?" Minou whispered.

"No," Tibble whispered back. "It's the owner of the factory, Mr. Ellmore. He's really important. And he does a lot of good."

"What's he do that's good?" Minou asked.

"He gives money to all kinds of charities."

Minou had more questions, but people around them had started going "Shhhh."

"Mr. Ellmore's about to speak," they said. Everyone pushed forward to listen, and Minou and Tibble got separated in the crowd.

Tibble was pushed over to one side, while Minou was jostled all the way to the front, close to the small table behind which Mr. Ellmore was giving his speech.

"Mr. Smith," he began, "ladies and gentlemen . . ."

Everyone was quiet.

"I am delighted to see so many people here this afternoon. . . ."

Mr. Ellmore was holding his car key in one hand and swung it gently back and forth over the table while speaking.

He swung it gently back and forth over the table.

Tibble looked at Minou and saw to his shock that her eyes were moving from side to side like at a tennis match. She wasn't listening at all; she was just staring intently at the swinging key, like a cat that's seen something move.

She's about to cuff it, thought Tibble, and he coughed very loudly, but she didn't notice.

"Many among us were once taught by Mr. Smith . . . ," the speaker continued. "And we all—"

Whack.

Minou's gloved hand smacked the key and sent it clattering over the table.

Mr. Ellmore was dumbstruck and stared at Minou with astonishment. All the people around her glared. Now she looked like a trapped cat searching for an escape route. Tibble tried to push forward, but all of a sudden she dived down and disappeared among the skirts and legs as she headed for the big table covered with snacks. She was gone.

Fortunately Mr. Ellmore resumed his speech, and the listening people soon forgot the incident.

Tibble snuck glances left and right and tried to look under the table. Had she crept in under it?

Now the speech was over and Mr. Smith gave a few words of thanks. Then waiters came round with trays of drinks and people began eating the snacks. Tibble moped around between the drinking, mingling groups. Where was she?

Maybe she'd slipped out of the door without anyone seeing? Minou was very good at slinking around and tiptoeing and slipping away unnoticed. Maybe she was home in the attic, in her box.

Tibble sighed. It had all gone so well. She hadn't hissed at anyone and she hadn't scratched anyone . . . she hadn't even rubbed up against the fishmonger. But now she'd come up with something new. Another cattish trait.

He decided to stay a little longer.

Minou hadn't gone home. She was still in the hotel. She'd made it through a door without anyone noticing and now she was in another room. A smaller room, a kind of conference room. There was a table with chairs, a big planter box in one corner with lots of plants in it, and a goldfish bowl on a cabinet.

She was alone in the room, and she walked straight over to the fishbowl. Two fat goldfish were swimming around in slow circles with gulping mouths and bulging eyes. Completely at ease, swishing their tails now and then.

Minou bent over the fishbowl.

"This is really not allowed," she said to herself. "It's so cattish. In a moment I won't be able to control myself. Leave now, Minou. . . . Turn around."

But the fish were magnets. Two golden magnets tugging on her eyes. All by itself, her right hand with the beautiful long glove reached out to the bowl, just above it and—

Voices sounded close by and she pulled her hand back *just* in time. *Just* in time, she hid behind the planter box, because the door opened and two people came in.

One was Mr. Smith. The other was Mr. Ellmore.

Minou crouched down behind the ferns and creepers and didn't make a sound.

"I was hoping to speak to you for a moment," Mr. Smith said. "It's so busy in there, and nice and quiet here. This is what it's about: we, the local residents, would like to set up an association. The Animal Lovers' Association."

Ah, thought Minou behind the plants. News for Mr. Tibble. I'd better listen carefully.

"You know that there are an awful lot of animal lovers here in Killenthorn," Mr. Smith said. "Almost everyone has a cat. The aim of our association is to help as many animals as possible. We want to set up a home for poor stray cats, we'd like an animal hospital . . . and we hope to show films about animals. I myself," Mr. Smith continued, "am busy preparing a public reading about cats. It's going to be called 'The Cat Through the Ages: A Feline History.'"

More news, thought Minou.

"And I wanted to ask you," Mr. Smith said, "if you would be willing to be the president of our Animal Lovers' Association."

"Hm . . . ," said Mr. Ellmore. "Why *me*?"

"You're so well known," Mr. Smith said. "And you're so popular here in town. You're also a known animal lover. You have a cat yourself, I believe."

"I have a dog," said Mr. Ellmore. "Mars."

Minou started to quake so violently in her corner that the plants began shaking too. *Mars!* That was the dog that had treed her twice already.

"Hm . . . ," Mr. Ellmore said again. "Of course I'd *love* to do it, but you see . . . I'm so terribly busy. I'm already in so many associations and on so many committees. I'm already president of the Child Welfare Commission. . . ."

"It won't involve a lot of work," Mr. Smith said. "You won't need to do very much. It's more about your name. Everyone has so much faith in you."

Mr. Ellmore walked across the room and back again with his hands behind his back. He came very close to the planter box, looked at the goldfish for a moment, and then peered at the plants for what seemed like a very long time.

He can see me, thought Minou.

But he just pulled a dry leaf off a geranium and said, "Well, all right, then."

"Wonderful, wonderful!" cried Mr. Smith. "Thank you very much. We'll be in touch. Now I'd better get back to my party."

They left the room and Minou dared to breathe again.

She came out and saw an enormous black tom sitting on the ledge of the open window. It was the Hotel Cat. The Metropole Cat.

"That room's off-limits," the cat said. "I'm not allowed in there. Because of the fish. Did you see them?"

"I almost caught one," Minou said. "I have to go back to that room with all the people . . . but I'm scared."

"Your human's looking for you," the Metropole Cat said.

64

"Out front, on the terrace. If you climb out through the window you can go round the side. Then you won't need to go through the people."

With a little leap Minou was outside.

"Bye," she said, and walked around to the front, where Tibble was pacing back and forth.

"Miss Minou . . . ," he began in a strict voice.

"I've got some more news," she said.

She told him what she'd overheard and Tibble nodded gratefully.

But when they were back home in the attic, he said, "I think you really need to do something about it . . . all these cattish traits . . . this cattish behavior of yours. . . ."

"What can I do about it?"

"You have to go see a doctor."

"I don't want to," said Minou. "Doctors give you shots."

"No, I don't mean an ordinary doctor."

"What do you mean? An animal doctor?"

"No, I mean a head doctor. The kind of doctor you talk to when you have problems."

"I don't have any problems," said Minou.

"*I* do," said Tibble.

"Then *you* should go to a head doctor."

"My problems are caused by you, Miss Minou. By your strange habits. It was going so well this afternoon at the reception. You were behaving yourself perfectly . . . until you suddenly whacked that key ring with your paw—I mean, with your hand. Secretaries don't do things like that."

—9—

THE HEAD DOCTOR

And so the next day Minou found herself sitting in Dr. Gilt's office.

"Perhaps you can start by telling me your name," the doctor said, holding a pen over a card for his files.

"Minou."

MINOU, he wrote down. "Is that your first name? Or your surname?"

"It's the name they gave me."

"Ah, Minou is your given name. What's your family name?"

She was silent for a very long time, watching a fly buzz past the window. Then she said, "I don't think I have one."

"Really? What's your father's name?" the doctor asked, holding his pen ready again.

Minou thought for a moment, trying to remember, then said quietly, "He was a tom . . ."

TOM, wrote the doctor.

"At the back of a house . . ."

BACKHOUSE . . .

"Near one of the parks."

PARKES . . .

"Tom Backhouse-Parkes," said the doctor, reading what he'd noted down. "That's your name too then. Miss M. Backhouse-Parkes. Now tell me, what's bothering you?"

"Bothering me?" Minou asked. "Nothing's bothering me at all."

"But you wanted to see me. You must have had some reason."

"My human sent me."

"Your what?"

"My human, the Man I live with. He says I'm too cattish."

"Too what?"

"Too cattish. And he says I keep getting more and more cattish."

"Does he mean perhaps that you bear some resemblance to a cat?"

"Exactly," Minou said.

"Well," said the doctor. "Let's start at the beginning. Tell me a little about your parents. What did your father do?"

"He was a stray," Minou said. "I never knew him. I can't tell you anything about him."

"And your mother?"

"My mother was a tabby."

"Pardon?" The doctor looked at her over his glasses.

"She was a tabby. She's dead. They had her put to sleep."

"Mother, dead. Happened in her sleep," the doctor mumbled, and wrote it down.

"Not *happened* in her sleep, they *had her* put to sleep," Minou said.

"How terrible," the doctor said.

"Yes, there was nothing they could do. She'd been hit by a car. Blinded by the lights, but it was a long time ago."

"Well, carry on. Brothers or sisters?"

"There were five of us."

"And you were the eldest?"

"All five of us were the same age."

"Quintuplets? You don't get many of them."

"Course you do," said Minou. "Common as dirt. They gave away three of us when we were six weeks old. I was left over with my sister. The woman thought we were the cutest."

She smiled tenderly at the memory, and in the silence that followed the doctor clearly heard her purring. It sounded very peaceful. He was a great cat lover. He had one himself, Jemima, upstairs in his apartment.

"The woman?" he asked. "Was that your mother?"

"No," Minou said. "The Woman was our human. She said I had the most adorable tail."

"Aha," said the doctor. "And when did you lose it?"

"Lose what?"

"Your tail."

She gazed pensively at him, looking so much like a cat that he started to think, Oh, maybe she's still got one. Maybe it's curled up under her skirt.

"I ate something out of a rubbish bin," Minou said. "An *institute's* rubbish bin. That's what did it. But I've still got loads of cattish traits. I purr and I hiss. And I climb up into a tree when I see a dog."

"And is that a problem? Does it bother you?"

"Not me," Minou said. "But my human finds it unbecoming."

"Who's your human?"

"Mr. Tibble from the paper. I'm his secretary. It's all going very well, but I still feel one hundred percent cat."

"And is that a problem?" the doctor asked again.

"Things do get complicated," Minou said. "And sometimes it's very confusing being two creatures at the same time. Half cat and half human."

"Ah . . . ," said the doctor. "Sometimes it's very confusing being *all* human."

"Really?"

"Absolutely."

Minou had never thought of that. She found it an interesting idea. "Still, I'd rather just be one or the other," she said.

"And which would you prefer?"

"That's just it . . . I wish I knew. I can't make up my mind. Sometimes I think I'd be so glad to be a cat again. . . . Creeping under the golden chain tree with your tail up and the flowers brushing over your fur . . . and singing on the rooftops with the other cats and hunting in a garden when the young starlings have just left the nest. Sometimes I even miss the tray. Scratching in the kitty litter. But on the other hand . . . being a lady has advantages too."

"You'll just have to wait and see how it turns out," said the doctor.

"I thought . . . ," Minou said. "Maybe you can give me a mixture. Or drops. Something to . . ."

"Something to what? Turn you back into a cat?"

"No," said Minou. "I can't make up my mind."

"Well, when you have," the doctor said, "come back here. I don't have any mixtures or drops for you, but talking always helps."

There was a scratching at the door. It was the Doctor's Cat, Jemima.

"My cat wants to come in," the doctor said, "but she knows she's not allowed in here when I have a patient."

Minou listened for a moment to the meowing on the other side of the door.

"You're wanted upstairs," she said. "Your wife is grilling some chicken."

"How do you know we're having chicken?" the doctor asked.

"And she's just burnt her thumb on the grill. . . . You're needed up there right away," Minou said. "I'll be off, then, Doctor, and I'll come back when I know what I want."

The doctor ran upstairs to his apartment. His wife had a big blister on her thumb and she was furious at the grill.

"How did you know something had happened?" she asked.

"A very charming cat told me," the doctor said, and went to get some ointment.

On her way home Minou heard the horrible news about the Tatter Cat. Cross-Eyed Simon told her.

"That's terrible," Minou said. "Her leg, you say? Broken? Was it a car? And where is she now? Are her children alone?"

"Don't ask so many questions at once," said Simon. "Maybe it's not as bad as it sounds. I heard it from the Pump Cat, and he always exaggerates. Someone hit her."

"Hit her?"

"That's right, with a bottle. And she only just managed to drag herself home to the caravan and her babies."

"I'll go straight there," said Minou. "I'll just get some food and milk for her first."

She found the Tatter Cat in the caravan with her kittens, surlier and angrier than ever.

"What happened?" Minou asked, kneeling down next to the blanket. "Is it bad? Is your leg broken? Are you bleeding?"

"They've crippled me," said the stray. "With a bottle of wine. A full one. No holding back there! Have you ever heard the likes? Maybe I should feel honored to get bashed with a bottle of burgundy!"

"Let me feel if anything's broken," said Minou.

"Don't touch me!" screeched the Tatter Cat.

"I just wanted to check it."

"Well, don't! Keep your hands to yourself."

"But if you've broken a leg, surely we need to do something about it."

"I'll get over it. It's all part of the game."

"But I could take you somewhere . . . up to our attic."

"I don't want to be taken anywhere. I'd rather die. I'm fine right here."

Minou sighed and gave the Tatter Cat some milk and some meat.

"Just in time," said the cat. "I was dry as a bone. I always drink

71

from the tap in the parking lot. There's a puddle under it. But it's on the other side of the parking lot and I can hardly walk."

When she'd had enough to drink, she said, "It was my own stupid fault."

"Tell me what happened."

"I'm walking through those posh gardens," said the Tatter Cat, "when I go past that big white house with all the roses. Mostly I'm too scared to go into their garden 'cause they've got a dog. But this time they've got him shut up in the garage. He's barking like crazy, but I just ignore him because he can't get to me anyway. The french doors are open, and I smell some very tasty smells inside. And I was hungry. Because with six of these squeaky little worms you stay hungry, take it from me. Anyway, I look in. And there's nobody in the room. But there is a big table set with food and a bunch of roses. I couldn't care less about the roses, of course, but I smelt salmon. So what do you do? You seize the opportunity."

"You went in?"

"Of course I went in. I jumped up on the table and landed with my feet right there in the salmon. And then I saw how much more there was! Lobster and chicken and sliced beef. Cream and shrimps and little bowls with all kinds of sauces. And all kinds of mashes and mushes . . . *Mrwah!*" The Tatter Cat drooled all over her babies.

"And then?"

"And then! It made my head spin, it was incredible. I was dizzy from all that food. I didn't know what to start on first. Idiot that I was. If I'd just eaten some of the salmon, at least I'd have had something. But those smells went to my head.

72

And now I can't believe I let the chance go by. I didn't have a single bite. *Mreeuw!*"

"Go on, what happened?"

"What do you think? All of a sudden there they were."

"Who?"

"The humans. The man and the woman. I hadn't heard them come in. Stupid, but . . . it was like I was drunk. I dived off the table and tried to get out through the french doors, but *she* was standing there with an umbrella and took a swing at me. So I shot back in the other direction, but that's where *he* was. He'd grabbed a full bottle of wine off the table. And *that* hurt! *Mrwowow!*" the Tatter Cat whimpered.

"How did you get out of there?"

"Don't ask me. I got out, that's for sure. I think I skidded past her legs and got a whack of the umbrella too, but I'm not sure about that. I shot into the garden. At first I didn't notice anything, but when I tried to jump over the hedge . . . something was wrong. I couldn't jump anymore. I couldn't climb either."

"How'd you get over it?" Minou asked.

"The dog. They let the dog out of the garage. I heard him coming. He was getting close and there weren't any holes in the hedge. None at all. I thought, you've had it now, old Tatter Cat. Crippled and up against a dog like that . . . You haven't got a chance. But I clawed him on the nose and that made him back up for a moment. And when the horrible thing attacked again, I suddenly thought of my litter of babies here, and that got me up over the hedge. *How* I don't know, but I made it."

"And how's walking going now?" Minou asked.

"Lousy. I just drag myself around at a snail's pace. But I'll get over it. It's all part of the game. That's the life of a stray. Anyway, at least I'm glad I gave that disgusting dog a scratch he won't forget in a hurry."

"What's the dog called?" Minou asked.

"Mars."

"What?"

"Oh, you know him, do you?"

"I know him," Minou said, ". . . but then it must have been his owner who hit you?"

"Yes, of course, that's what I'm telling you. Ellmore, he's called. He's the owner of the Deodorant Factory. Where my son, the Deodorant Cat, lives."

"He's also the president of an association," said Minou. "The Animal Lovers' Association."

"And there you have it," the Tatter Cat mocked. "The same old story, no surprise there. Humans . . . they're all scum."

"That's terrible," Bibi said after hearing the story. "What a horrible man. The poor Tatter Cat."

"You should go visit her," Minou said. "You know where she is."

"Yes, I've already been there once. In the old camper. Do you think she'd mind if I took a few photos of her babies?"

Bibi took her camera with her everywhere and was constantly snapping photos. The pictures were mostly very crooked, but they were all in focus.

Bibi and Minou had become good friends. Now they were sitting together on a bench in the park.

"Did Tibble put it in the paper?" Bibi asked. "I mean, about Mr. Ellmore and the Tatter Cat?"

"No," Minou said. "He's not allowed to write about cats. That's what he said."

"But this isn't just about cats! It's about the . . . the president of . . . what was it called again?"

"The Animal Lovers' Association."

"Well, that should go straight in the paper. A man like that crippling a poor mother cat."

"Yes, I think so too," said Minou, "but Tibble doesn't want to."

She looked past Bibi at the low-hanging branch of an elm. Bibi followed her gaze. A little bird was sitting there, singing. Bibi turned back to Minou and was shocked. . . . There was a very unpleasant look in her eye . . . just like that time with the mouse. . . .

"*Minou!*" Bibi screamed.

Minou jumped.

"I didn't do anything," she said. But she had a very guilty expression on her face.

"It's absolutely not allowed, remember that," Bibi said. "Birds are just as nice as cats."

"When I used to live in Victoria Avenue . . . ," Minou said dreamily.

"When you lived where?"

"Victoria Avenue. As a cat. I used to catch birds. . . . Behind the house, next to the patio, there was a golden chain tree. . . . That's where I caught most of them, and they were so . . ."

"I'm not listening anymore," Bibi shouted, running off with her camera.

—10—

CATS AREN'T WITNESSES

"I don't understand," Minou said for the umpteenth time. "This *has* to go in the paper: *Tatter Cat Crippled by the President of the Animal Lovers' Association.*"

"No," said Tibble. "'Cats aren't news,' that's what my boss says."

"Hitting a poor old mother cat with a bottle!" said Minou. "She might never recover."

"I'm not entirely surprised," Tibble said hesitantly, "at someone losing their temper when they suddenly see a stray cat standing on their salmon. And I *can* imagine them grabbing whatever's at hand to knock it off the table."

"Really?" said Minou, giving Tibble such a vicious look that he stepped back out of range of her nails.

"In any case, it's not something for the paper," he said. "And that's all there is to it."

Whenever Minou was angry, she got into her box to sulk. She was about to do that now, but Fluff came in through the kitchen window with a long-drawn-out meow.

"What's he saying?" Tibble asked.

"The fishmonger?" cried Minou.

"*Rwo . . . wwieeu . . . row . . . ,*" Fluff continued. He told her an ecstatic story in Cattish, then disappeared again, back on the roof.

"What about the fishmonger?" Tibble asked.

"He's in the hospital!"

"Really? I thought it sounded like Fluff had good news."

"The fishmonger got hit by a car," Minou said. "It ran right into his fish stall. All the local cats are going straight there because there's fish spread all over the road."

"I'm on my way," Tibble said. "I can write an article about this." And he grabbed his pad.

"I'm going too," Minou said. "Over the roof, that's faster."

She tried to climb out of the window, but Tibble stopped her. "No, Miss Minou. I don't want my secretary scrounging around an upset fish stall like an old alley cat!"

Minou gave him a haughty look.

"What's more," said Tibble, "there's bound to be a lot of people there, and you don't like that."

"Fine, I'll stay here," said Minou. "I'll hear the news on the roof."

* * *

There *were* a lot of people in Green Square. A real crowd. The police were there, there was glass on the street from the broken windows, and the fish stall was completely wrecked; there were slats and boards all over the place, the bunting had been trodden underfoot, and the last cat was running off with the last herring.

Mr. Smith was looking around too.

"They just drove off with the fishmonger," he said. "They're taking him to the hospital. He's got a broken rib."

"What happened?" Tibble asked.

"A car! But the weird thing is nobody knows *which* car. It was a hit and run. Outrageous!"

"Weren't there any witnesses? Right in the middle of the day?"

"No," said Mr. Smith. "It was twelve noon exactly. Everyone was having lunch. They all heard the smash, but by the time they'd come out to have a look, the car had gone round the corner."

"And the fishmonger?"

"He doesn't know either. One moment he was gutting some herring, the next thing he's upside down, stall and all. The police have questioned everyone here in the neighborhood, but no one saw the car. It must have been a stranger, someone from out of town."

Tibble looked around. There was a cat eating something on the corner of the square. The cats must have seen who it was, he thought. And I bet Minou has already been informed.

He was right.

"We've known who it was for ages," she said when Tibble

arrived back upstairs. "Everyone's told everyone else up on the rooftops. It was Mr. Ellmore's car. He was in it too. It was him."

Tibble could hardly believe it. "Come on," he said. "Why would a man like that keep driving after an accident? He'd report it straightaway."

"The cats saw it," Minou said. "You know how there's always cats hanging around the fish stall. Cross-Eyed Simon was there, and so were the School Cat and Ecumenica. They all saw it. Now you can put it in the paper."

Tibble sat down and started chewing his fingernails.

"That's right, isn't it?" asked Minou. "This can go in the paper, can't it?"

"No," said Tibble. "I'll write an article about the accident. But I can't say Ellmore was the driver. There's no proof."

"No proof? But *three* cats—"

"Yes, *cats*! But what good's that? There wasn't a single witness."

"There were three witnesses."

"Cats aren't witnesses."

"No?"

"No. I can hardly write in the paper: 'According to information we have received from several cats, the vehicle that smashed into the fish stall was driven by prominent Killenthorn resident Mr. Ellmore.' I just can't. Don't you understand that?"

Minou didn't understand. She left the room and got into her box without a word.

* * *

At night on the roof Cross-Eyed Simon said, "There's someone waiting for you at the town hall."

"Who?"

"The Deodorant Cat. He's got news."

Minou went straight there. It was three in the morning and very quiet on the square. Two marble lions were crouched in front of the Town Hall, each with a marble shield between its knees.

Minou waited. A mixture of strange smells was wafting out from the left lion's shadow. She could smell cat *and* perfume. And now the Deodorant Cat emerged.

"Nosey-nosey first," he said.

Minou held out her nose.

"Sorry about the apple blossom," the cat said. "It's our latest fragrance. I've got something to tell you, but you mustn't tell anyone you got it from me. You have to keep my name out of the papers. Promise?"

"I promise," said Minou.

"Well . . . remember I told you about Billy? The boy who worked in our cafeteria and got fired?"

"Oh, yes," said Minou. "What about him?"

"He's back. He got his job back."

"He must be pleased," Minou said. "But is that all? It's not really newspaper material."

"Don't interrupt," said the Deodorant Cat. "I'm not finished. Listen. This afternoon I was sitting on the ledge. Outside on the wall there's a ledge, and when I sit on it, behind the creeper, I can hear and see everything that goes on in the owner's office. Our owner is Mr. Ellmore. Do you know who that is?"

"Of course I do!" Minou exclaimed. "He crippled your mother!"

"Exactly," said the cat. "That's why I hate him. Not that I see much of my mother these days. She smells a little too vulgar to my taste. I'm used to more refined fragrances. But that's not the point. I was sitting there on the ledge and I saw Billy in Ellmore's office and I thought, let's have a little listen, you never know."

"Go on," said Minou.

"I heard Ellmore say, 'That's agreed, then, Billy, you get your old job back. Just run along straight to the cafeteria.' And Billy said, 'With pleasure, sir, lovely, sir, thank you very much, sir.'"

"And that was the end of it?" asked Minou.

"I thought so at first," said the cat. "I thought it was over and I dozed off a little . . . because the sun was shining and you know what that's like . . . sitting on a ledge in the sun. . . ."

"Yes, I know," Minou said. "Go on."

"Well, all at once I heard Ellmore whispering something at the door: '. . . and don't forget . . . if anyone happens to ask you what you saw this afternoon on Green Square . . . you didn't see a thing. Understood? Not a thing.'

"'No, sir,' said Billy, 'Not a thing.' And he left the office. And that was that."

"Aha," said Minou. "I get it. Billy must have seen the accident."

"That's what I thought too," said the cat.

"Now we finally have a human who saw it," Minou told Tibble. "A real witness. Not just a cat witness."

81

"I'll go see Billy right now," said Tibble. "Maybe he'll admit to seeing something if I ask him straight out."

He left.

While Tibble was gone, Minou had a conversation on the roof with the cat from the hotel. The Metropole Cat.

"Tell me," Minou said. "I hear that Ellmore sometimes eats at the hotel. Is that true?"

"Yes," said the Metropole Cat. "He and his wife have dinner in our restaurant once a week. On Fridays. That's tonight."

"Could you sit close by?" Minou asked. "To listen in on what he says?"

"Not likely," said the Metropole Cat. "He kicked me once under the table."

"It's just that we'd really like to know what he's saying in private," Minou explained, "but none of us dare go to his house to eavesdrop. Because of his dog . . . Mars . . . So if you could, try to get close to the table."

"I'll see what I can do," the Metropole Cat promised.

Tibble came home much later, worn out and disheartened.

"I went to see Billy," he said. "But Billy says he didn't see anything. He insists he wasn't even in Green Square when it happened. I'm sure he's lying. He's too scared to say anything, of course. I went to see the fishmonger too, in the hospital."

"How is he?" Minou asked. "Did he still smell good?"

"He smelt like hospitals," Tibble said.

"How sad."

"I asked him, 'Could it have been Mr. Ellmore's car?' But

the fishmonger just got angry and shouted, 'What a stupid idea! Ellmore's my best customer, he wouldn't do something like that.' And . . ." Tibble hesitated. "I went to the police too. I asked them, 'Could it have possibly been Mr. Ellmore's car?'"

"And what did they say?" Minou asked.

"They burst out laughing. They thought I'd gone mad."

—11—

THE PUMP CAT AND
THE METROPOLE CAT

"Hasn't your human written about Ellmore in the paper yet?" the Tatter Cat asked.

"No," Minou said. "He says he doesn't have any proof."

"What a coward! How gutless can you get! Humans are the most useless animals around! They're as spineless as dogs," the Tatter Cat cried. She was so wound up, she forgot to keep an eye on her babies. One of the little tortoiseshell kittens had walked almost all the way to the camper door. When the mother cat saw it, she shouted, "Hey, look at that! Someone's ready for the great outdoors! Come here, you dope!" She grabbed the baby cat by the scruff of the neck and pulled it back to the blanket and the rest of the litter. "They're starting to be a real handful," she said. "The little whippersnappers."

The kittens had their eyes open. They kept tumbling over each other and playing with each other's tails. And with their mother's tattered, stringy tail.

"How's your leg?" Minou asked.

"It's a bit better. I'm still limping though. It's probably permanent. Every day I go out to drink from the puddle under the tap and it takes me ages to get there."

"Can you leave the children alone that long?" Minou asked anxiously. "Is it safe?"

"Nobody ever comes here," the Tatter Cat said. "Just you and Bibi. She brings me something every day too. And today she took photos of the little riffraff. Pictures of all those ugly little monsters! Weird, huh? Oh, yeah, before I forget . . . their father, the Pump Cat, asked if you could drop by on your way past. He's got something to tell you. Don't ask me what, but it's probably something to do with the fishmonger's accident."

Minou said goodbye and walked over to the gas station. The Pump Cat said a friendly hello.

"I don't know if it's worth bothering about," he said, "but I thought . . . it can't do any harm to mention it."

"Mention what?"

"Ellmore was here. He had a big dent in his bumper. And a smashed headlight."

"Ah!" said Minou.

"He's got two cars," the Pump Cat said. "It was the big one, the blue Chevy. You know we've got a garage here as well as a gas station. So he says to my human, the mechanic, 'I ran into my own garden wall. Could you fix it today?' And my human says, 'That's gonna be difficult.'"

85

"And then?" Minou asked.

"Then Ellmore gave him some money. I couldn't see how much, but it must have been a lot because my human looked very happy. And then Ellmore said, 'If anyone should ask any questions . . . about dents in my car or anything like that . . . I'd rather you didn't mention it.'"

"*Aha*," said Minou. "Thanks. I'll see you later."

While she was heading off, she turned and called back, "You've got some lovely kids there."

"Who?" asked the Pump Cat.

"You."

"Me? Who says so?"

"The Tatter Cat."

"She says all kinds of things," scoffed the Pump Cat.

The Metropole Cat was a gleaming, pitch-black tom with a white chest. He was also extremely fat from the luxurious life he led in the hotel dining room. At mealtimes, he wandered slowly from table to table, looking up at the hotel guests with pitiful, pleading eyes, as if to say, can't you see I'm starving to death? Most people gave him something, and gradually he'd grown fatter and fatter. He waddled.

It was Friday evening around six-thirty, and the dining room was fairly full. Waiters were walking in and out; knives and plates rattled; people were eating and chatting; it smelt of roast beef and roast potatoes.

Sitting in a corner by the window, a little to one side, were Mr. and Mrs. Ellmore.

The Metropole Cat made a tentative approach. He'd promised Minou to listen in, but because Ellmore had once kicked him under the table, he was being cautious. He sat down a few feet away and didn't go any closer. They were arguing, he could tell that from their gestures and faces, but unfortunately they were arguing under their breath.

I'm definitely not going to sit under the table, thought the cat. I'd get a boot straightaway. But if I go and sit next to *her* chair, I'll be safe enough.

Now he was close enough to hear what they were saying.

"So incredibly stupid of you," said Mrs. Ellmore. "You should have reported it immediately."

"You're not going to start all over again, are you?" said Mr. Ellmore. "Stop nagging."

"I still think you should have reported it," she persisted. "You still can."

He shook his head fiercely and stabbed a piece of meat with his fork.

The Metropole Cat took another step closer.

"Get lost, you nasty little monster," Mr. Ellmore hissed. But the cat stayed where it was and looked up at him with a very innocent and very hungry expression.

"Don't talk rubbish," Mr. Ellmore continued. "It's too late now. Of course you're right. . . . I *should* have reported it at once . . . but I didn't. And now it's too late."

"But what if it gets out?"

"It can't. Nobody saw it, except for a dim-witted ex–cafeteria assistant from the factory, and I gave him his job back right away."

"And the garage where you're getting the car fixed?"

"The mechanic will keep his mouth shut. He's a buddy of mine. Through thick and thin."

"I *still* think you should go and report it," Mrs. Ellmore said stubbornly.

"Will you just give it a rest? You think I'm mad? I've gone to so much trouble to get people here in town on my side. I've donated money left, right and center, one charity after the other. All to make people like me, all to get *in*. I've joined associations, I'm the president of this, that and the other, I'm on committees . . . I've done everything I can to make people trust me. And I've succeeded!"

The Metropole Cat took another sneaky step forward.

"Psst, scat!" hissed Mr. Ellmore. "That cat's enough to put you off your dinner!"

The black cat waddled off, did a small circuit of the dining room, and returned to the same spot. He heard Ellmore saying, "What if it got in the paper! My good name would be ruined. And then I wouldn't be voted onto the council committee. And the expansion of the factory wouldn't go ahead. I'd have everyone against me. And now let's change the subject. What are you having for dessert?"

"Cassata ice cream," said Mrs. Ellmore.

"And if I ever bump into that disgusting cat in the dark, I'll strangle it," her husband said, glaring at the fat black tom.

The Metropole Cat had heard enough. He strolled out through the door and dragged himself up to the rooftops to report back to Minou.

* * *

88

"Another *cat* who's overheard him," Tibble complained. "We still don't have a real witness. How can I write an article without proof? And the two people who could help me, Billy and the mechanic, refuse to speak up. They both claim they don't know anything about it."

"But you do believe the cats now, don't you?" Minou asked.

"Yes," said Tibble. "I believe you."

"I hope one day I'll get to give Ellmore a good scratch," said Minou.

"I hope so too," said Tibble.

It made him feel very despondent. He was convinced the cats were telling the truth, but he didn't dare write about it without any evidence. Besides being despondent, he was also angry. Angry and indignant. And all that anger made him less shy. It made him brave enough to approach people and ask them all kinds of questions.

But whenever he casually said, "I've heard that Mr. Ellmore caused that accident with the fish stall," people were outraged. "Where'd you get that idea? Who's spreading stories like that? Mr. Ellmore would *never* do anything of the kind! First of all, he's a careful driver, and second, he'd have owned up to it straightaway. He would *never* drive off like that. . . ."

"No, Tibble," Mr. Smith said. "You're talking complete and utter rubbish. That's nothing but cheap gossip."

—12—
THE TATTER CAT'S BABIES

Mrs. Van Dam said to her husband, "I used to have a small green teapot. Whatever did I do with it?"

"I haven't got a clue," said Mr. Van Dam. But a little later he said, "Didn't we used to keep that teapot in the camper? In our old camper."

"Oh, yes . . . that's right. Well, it's gone, then, with the camper, to the wreckers. Because that's what we did with that old camper, we took it to the wreckers!"

"Now that you mention it," said Mr. Van Dam, pondering the question, "I think it's still at the back of that parking lot. Remember?"

"After all these years?"

"It's been a while."

"I'll go have a look," said Mrs. Van Dam. "Maybe the teapot's still there. . . . It was such a handy little thing. There might be other things we can use too."

And so it was that Mrs. Van Dam walked into the parking lot just when the Tatter Cat had gone for a drink. Like every day, the Tatter Cat dragged her crippled leg along behind her on her way to the puddle under the tap. She'd always left her babies behind by themselves and nothing had ever happened; they'd never come to any harm because it was such an out-of-the-way spot where there were never any people.

But now Mrs. Van Dam pushed the door open and stepped inside.

The first thing she saw was the whole gang of kittens on the old blanket.

"Well, I never!" She scowled. "In my camper! A whole litter of kittens . . . and neglected, filthy kittens at that. And they're on *my* blanket."

It was a very old blanket. Torn and dirty. But Mrs. Van Dam still thought it was too good for the kittens. She grabbed an old floral pillowcase and dumped the six little kittens into it.

Then she picked up the green teapot and a tablecloth and a torn mat and said, "There."

She left with a bag in one hand and the pillowcase full of kittens in the other.

The Tatter Cat saw her leaving the caravan, but she was still a long way away. And she couldn't run. She limped home as fast as she could, dragged herself up the steps, and saw that her babies were gone. A mournful, howling caterwaul rang out over the parking lot, but no one heard it because the radio was playing in the gas station. And Mrs. Van Dam would have ignored it anyway, even if she had heard it. She stood next to the gas pump and looked down uncertainly at the heavy bag of kittens in her hand.

What on earth am I going to do with these cats? she thought. I can't take them home with me. What do I want with six dirty little kittens?

Now she saw that there was a car next to the pump. A big blue car. Mr. Ellmore was buying gas.

Mrs. Van Dam went over to him. She bent over and said, "Oh, hello, Mr. Ellmore," through the open side window.

"Hello, Mrs. Van Dam."

"I have a litter of kittens here. I found them in my old camper. I've got them in an old pillowcase. May I give them to you?"

"To me?" Mr. Ellmore asked. "What would I do with a litter of kittens?"

"Well," said Mrs. Van Dam, "I read that you're the president of the Animal Lovers' Association. You are, aren't you?"

"Yes, that's right," said Mr. Ellmore.

"Well, what that association is for . . . I mean . . . the aim of that association is to make sure the little creatures have a home. That's what I read."

"Yes, but right now I don't have much time," said Mr. Ellmore.

"And if there's no home available," Mrs. Van Dam continued, "you'd take them somewhere where they could be put down painlessly. It said that too. . . . So could you take care of that for me? I'll put them in the back."

She laid the bulging floral pillowcase on his backseat, gave him a friendly nod, and hurried off.

Leaving Mr. Ellmore sitting there with a bag of kittens in his car.

"The woman thinks I run a cat shelter," he growled. "What am I supposed to do with a bunch of kittens?"

He drove off.

The poor Tatter Cat stayed in the caravan moaning and mewling for a moment, and by the time she came out again, Mrs. Van Dam was gone. But the Pump Cat walked up to her.

"They've taken your kids," he said. "In a bag. In Ellmore's car. He drove off with them."

The Tatter Cat sat down and started whimpering.

She knew now that her little ones were lost, that there was no point in looking for them, that they might already be dead. And to make things worse, she could hardly move. She was totally helpless.

"I'll pass the news on," the Pump Cat said. "To the Cat Press Agency. I don't know if it will do any good."

The Tatter Cat couldn't speak. She whined softly.

"Well, good luck," said the Pump Cat. "It's a tough break."

As he walked off, the Tatter Cat called out after him, "They're your babies too."

The Pump Cat turned back for a moment. "That remains to be seen," he snarled.

The Cat Press Agency was always very fast. But no news had ever come through this fast. In less than ten minutes, Minou had heard it from Fluff.

"Where did Ellmore take them?" she asked quickly.

"His car's in front of the post office."

"Are the kittens still in it?"

"No," Fluff said, shaking his head sadly. "They're not there anymore. Simon looked in through the window. The car's empty."

"Where are they then?" Minou asked. "What's he done with them?"

"No one knows," Fluff said. "The Pump Cat saw him drive off and Ecumenica saw him drive past the church. And later a few cats spotted the car at the post office. But nobody saw what he did with the kittens."

"Maybe he drowned them somewhere," Minou cried. "Oh, this is terrible. The poor Tatter Cat. She was always calling them names, but she was so proud of her children. Let's get all the cats searching and tell them to keep their eyes and ears open. . . . I'll go out and start searching too."

She went down to the street and headed off in the direction of the post office. The cats she met on the way couldn't tell her any more than she'd already heard. Not a single cat had seen what had happened to the pillowcase. They'd only seen the car driving around and, later, parked and empty.

Minou didn't know where to look and wandered aimlessly through the back lanes until finally Muffin, the Bakery Cat, came running up to her.

"They've found them," she called. "The School Cat heard them squeaking!"

"Where?"

"In a rubbish bin near the post office. Hurry, we can't get them out."

Minou was there in less than a minute.

All six kittens were still alive. They were still in the floral pillowcase; they'd been dumped, pillowcase and all, in a big gray rubbish bin. The little tykes squeaked and trembled as Minou pulled them out one by one, but they were alive.

Just up the road the rubbish truck had started its round. . . . If Minou had arrived just a few minutes later, the bin containing the Tatter Cat's children would have been emptied into the back of the truck. They would have been crushed.

Carefully, she put the six kittens back into the pillowcase to take them with her. And she stroked the School Cat, who had found them. "That was brilliant," she said. "Thanks. Just in the nick of time . . ."

"I've got some news too," the School Cat said.

"Tell me. . . ."

"Henry the Eighth got divorced."

Minou didn't take the kittens back to the caravan. She took them to the attic and laid them in her own box for now.

"What's the idea?" said Fluff. "You're not planning on keeping them here, are you?"

"Absolutely," said Minou. "And the Tatter Cat too. I'm going to go get her now."

"I'm not sure I approve of that," said Fluff. But Minou had already climbed out through the kitchen window.

The Tatter Cat hadn't heard the news yet. She kept circling the camper, going in every now and then as if the babies might have reappeared inside in the meantime. And she kept meowing helplessly. No matter how rumpled and grimy the Tatter Cat had been . . . she'd never been *pathetic*. She'd always remained proud and cheerful. But not anymore. Now she was a sad little stray, miserable and inconsolable.

Until Minou suddenly appeared on the camper step.

"We've found them," she said. "All six. They're at our house. In the attic."

The Tatter Cat didn't show any signs of being happy. She just sat up a little straighter.

"Get them back here, then," she snapped.

"No," Minou said. "It's not safe here. You know that now. I've come to get you."

"Who? *Me?*"

"Yes, you."

"I don't let anybody *come and get* me," the Tatter Cat said with icy contempt. "Nobody *comes and gets* me."

"It's only temporary," Minou said. "In a few weeks we'll look for homes for your children. Until then, you're coming with me."

"Over my dead body."

"Your children still need you. They need to feed."

"Bring them here and I'll feed them."

There was no point in trying to argue with the Tatter Cat. And you couldn't take her anywhere against her wishes. She'd fight you tooth and claw.

But Minou was just as stubborn. "If you want them, come and get them," she said. "You know where I live."

The Tatter Cat shouted something at her as she left. It was the worst insult she knew: "Human!"

Minou made a soft nest for the kittens in the corner of the junk room. Tibble wasn't home, he was off wandering around town in search of evidence.

"I don't know that I'm really happy about this," Fluff complained. "I can't say I'm pleased. Six howling strangers in my attic . . . but yeah, just go ahead, make yourself at home."

"It's only temporary," Minou said.

"All we need now is for the mother to show up too," Fluff said. "You needn't think I'm going to put up with *that*."

Minou didn't reply. She stood at the kitchen window and looked out over the rooftops.

An hour later the Tatter Cat did show up. Slowly and with great difficulty, she'd climbed up to the rooftops with one lame leg. With her last bit of strength, she dragged herself through the gutter and let Minou lift her down through the window.

She didn't say anything. Minou didn't say anything either. She just put the Tatter Cat down next to her babies, who squealed with delight, squirmed, and began feeding at full speed.

"What did I say?" said Fluff. "The mother too. And now I know I'm not going to put up with it."

He fluffed up his tail, put back his ears and let out a horrific growling sound.

"Behave yourself, Fluff," Minou said. "And keep out of the junk room."

As long as the Tatter Cat stayed close to her children, everything went well, but as soon as she stepped away for even a

97

moment, on her way to the kitchen or in search of the litter box . . . it was all-out war.

And just when Tibble came in, a furious fight was in full swing. A screeching tangle of fur rolling over and over on the floor with big tufts of hair flying everywhere.

"What's going on, for goodness' sake? Have we got *another* cat?" Tibble cried.

"We've got another *seven* cats," said Minou, pulling Fluff and the Tatter Cat apart.

She told him what had happened.

"You mean Ellmore dumped live kittens in a rubbish bin?" Tibble asked.

"That's exactly what I mean," said Minou. And now, finally, Tibble got really angry.

—13—

TIBBLE IS WRITING!

"Eight cats in the house," Tibble mumbled. "Nine, really . . . if I count Minou. Talk about crowded."

It was crowded. The kittens were already quite mobile. They crawled around everywhere, they climbed up on chairs, they scratched the couch and curtains, they sat on Tibble's paper and played with his pen. But he didn't mind. He even felt honored that the Tatter Cat was willing to live in his flat. He knew the old stray had never wanted to live with people ever . . . and now she was even sitting on his lap and letting him scratch behind her ears.

"You can stay here with us for the rest of your life," Tibble said.

"That's what you think!" the Tatter Cat cried, leaping off

his knee. "As soon as the brats are big enough, I'm back on the street."

Tibble didn't understand her. He was just glad that the fighting had stopped. The two big cats hissed and spat at each other now and then, and sometimes spent half an hour glaring and growling, but they kept themselves under control.

Suddenly Tibble said, "And now quiet, everyone. I've got some writing to do."

He sat down at his desk with a fierce look on his face.

Minou asked hesitantly, "Are you going to write an article?"

"Yes," said Tibble.

"Oh," said Minou. "Are you going to write *the* article? About Ellmore?"

"Yes," said Tibble. "And I couldn't care less if I don't have any proof. Witnesses leave me cold."

He tapped away on his typewriter. Now and then he disentangled a kitten from his hair and put it down on the floor. Now and then he slid two kittens off his sheet of paper. He kept typing away.

Fluff and the Tatter Cat forgot to feud. They sat watching him quietly and respectfully and the news passed from cat to cat over the roofs of the entire neighborhood. "Tibble is writing! Tibble is finally writing! Have you heard the news? It's going to be in the paper at last. . . . Tibble is writing!"

When Tibble had finished the article, he took it in to the paper.

In the newspaper building, he met the Editorial Cat. For the first time the cat looked up at him with respect and appreciation.

And after he had delivered his article and was crossing Green Square on the way home, he noticed a lot more cats than usual out on the street. They came up to him, brushed past his legs affectionately and called out, "Well done . . . finally!"

He didn't understand them, but he got the meaning.

Mr. Ellmore was sitting in the office of the editor of the *Killenthorn Courier*.

The morning newspaper was open on the desk and Ellmore was pointing at an article.

"What's the meaning of this?" he asked. He was pale, and his voice was trembling with anger.

Now it was the editor who was biting his nails nervously. "I'm afraid I didn't know anything about it," he said. "I've only just read it. . . . It got into the paper without my knowing."

"That doesn't make any difference!" Ellmore shouted. "This is slander. And it's *your* newspaper."

The Editorial Cat sat on the windowsill listening with big, shocked eyes and its ears up.

"I'm terribly sorry," the editor sighed. "The young man who wrote this is always extremely reliable. . . . He writes excellent articles. It's never just rumors, it's always the truth, and—"

"Are you claiming *this* is the truth?" Ellmore screamed.

"Oh, no, no, most definitely not . . ."

My editor is a coward too, thought the Editorial Cat.

"I just meant that I've never needed to read his articles beforehand. . . . They've always been correct. That's how this got in the paper without my knowing."

"I demand," said Ellmore, pounding the table with his fist, "I *demand* that this young man write a new article today setting this straight."

"An excellent solution," said the relieved editor. "I'll make sure of it."

The Editorial Cat had heard enough. He jumped down from the windowsill and hurried up to the roof to tell Minou.

"Listen . . . ," said the cat.

Minou listened.

"Thanks," she said.

And she went inside to tell Tibble.

"So," said Tibble. "Now I know what to expect."

The telephone rang. It was Tibble's boss.

"I have to go into work," Tibble told Minou a little later. "He wants to talk to me right away."

Nine pairs of cats' eyes watched him walk down the stairs.

"I'm making a very reasonable request, Tibble," said the editor. "You've made an enormous blunder. You've written something that has offended one of Killenthorn's best-known and most respected citizens. Your article's not just offensive, it's also *untrue*. Where on earth did you get such a ridiculous idea? That it was Mr. Ellmore who crashed into the fish stall!"

"It's true," said Tibble.

"What proof have you got? Where's the evidence? Who are your witnesses? Who saw it happen?"

"A few people know about it," Tibble said.

"Really. Who? And why haven't they said anything?"

"They're scared of Mr. Ellmore. He's got them under his thumb. They don't dare to speak up."

"Well," his boss sighed. "It all sounds extremely unlikely to me. But, as I said, you've got a chance to make up for it. All you have to do is write a nice article about Mr. Ellmore. Stating clearly, of course, that it was all your fault and a stupid mistake. And that you're sorry. And besides that, he asked if you could write something nice about the Deodorant Factory. How great it is to work in the factory. And about all the lovely fragrances you can get in a spray can. And how terrible it would be if we didn't have any deodorant . . . how much everyone would stink . . . Anyway, you get the idea. . . . And how essential it is that the factory be expanded. So you're going to do that today, Tibble. Agreed?"

"No," said Tibble.

It went quiet for a moment. The Editorial Cat was back up on the windowsill and winked at Tibble to encourage him.

"No? What do you mean, *no*? Are you refusing?"

"Yes, that's exactly what I'm doing," Tibble said.

"This is getting serious," the boss said. "You've been going so well recently. And now your pigheadedness is going to cost you your job. Be sensible, Tibble."

Tibble looked the Editorial Cat in the eyes.

"I'm sorry," he said. "But I'm not doing it."

"It's a shame," his boss sighed. "But you're not leaving me any choice. You're finished here, Tibble. You can go."

And Tibble left.

*   *   *

On the street he met Mr. Smith.

"What have you done now, Tibble?" he asked. "I just got the paper out of the letter box and what do I read? Gossip! Lies! Mr. Ellmore, the president of our Animal Lovers' Association . . . dumping kittens in a rubbish bin? And knocking down the fish stall . . . and not reporting it . . . and just driving off? Tibble, where do you get this nonsense? Bah! And I was going to ask you if you'd like to come to my reading. I'm holding a reading next week about 'The Cat Through the Ages.' I wanted to ask if you'd like to write an article about it. But now I'm not sure you're the right person for the job. . . ."

"I can't do it anymore anyway," Tibble said. "I'm no longer with the newspaper."

And he walked on with his head hanging.

"Now I've been fired after all, Miss Minou," he said. "First I was able to keep my job because of the cats; now I've lost it again because of the cats. But I'm not in the least bit sorry."

He sat down on the couch and the cats sat around him looking serious. Even the little ones could feel how serious things were—they hardly played with his shoelaces at all.

"We haven't given up yet," Minou said. "We've got something planned for tonight. As soon as it's dark, all the cats from the whole neighborhood will come to meet on our roof. We're going to have a Meowwwow."

That evening Tibble stayed home with the kittens, who were too little to go to a meeting. He could hear the Meow-wow perfectly, though.

He couldn't guess how many cats there were, but, going by the sound, it must have been at least a hundred. They screeched, they squealed, and every now and then they sang the Yawl-Yowl Song.

At about eleven o'clock the doorbell rang.

It was Mrs. Van Dam. She came panting up the stairs in her fur coat and snapped, "Mr. Tibble, I've talked to my husband about it and we think enough's enough."

"What do you mean?" Tibble asked.

"This is no longer a respectable house, not with you living in it. It's become a hotbed of cat activity. Just listen. . . . Listen to them."

On the roof the caterwauling started up again.

"It's unbearable," Mrs. Van Dam continued. "And here . . . What's this I see? Six kittens as well. If I'm not mistaken they're the little beasts I found in my caravan. Six kittens plus those two big cats, plus that strange lady who's more cat than person . . . that's nine! Plus another hundred on the roof, that's a hundred and nine . . . ."

"Plus twenty dead cats," said Tibble, "that's a hundred and twenty-nine."

"*What do you mean?*"

"I mean your coat. There's twenty in that."

This made Mrs. Van Dam absolutely furious. "The cheek of you," she yelled. "My mink coat! Are you claiming it's cat fur? Are you trying to insult me, like you insulted poor Mr. Ellmore in the newspaper? Because I read it! It's a disgrace. And that's why my husband and I agree that you have to go. Out of *my* attic. With all your kitties and caboodles. I'll give you until the end of the month. After which I shall rent my attic out to someone else. Good day, Mr. Tibble."

I shouldn't have said that about the fur coat, thought Tibble once she was gone. Not that it makes any difference. She would have kicked me out anyway. But it still wasn't very nice of me. And now I'm going to bed.

Tibble went to bed. He was so exhausted he slept right through the Meowwow and didn't even feel the six little kittens tickling and scratching his face. He didn't hear Fluff come home. And he didn't hear the Tatter Cat either, screeching for her children to come to her. And he didn't notice Minou getting into her box.

When he woke up it was eight o'clock in the morning. What was the horrible thing that had happened? he thought. Oh yeah, I lost my job. *And* I got kicked out of my flat. What do I do now? Where can I go with nine cats . . . and how am I supposed to bring home enough fish for such a large cat family? He wanted to talk to Minou about it, but she'd already gone out.

She was sitting in the park with Bibi.

"The cats of Killenthorn have a plan," she said. "And we wanted to ask you if you'd help us, Bibi."

"Sure," Bibi said. "How?"

"I'll tell you just what you need to do," Minou said. "Listen carefully."

—14—
FAR TOO MANY CATS

Mr. Ellmore was walking down the street. He had parked his big blue car, which was once again completely free of dents, and now he was on his way to the shoe shop to buy a pair of shoes.

For the first time he noticed how many cats there were in Killenthorn. He couldn't take a step without a cat getting in the way. Some of them even shot through between his legs. Twice he stumbled over a cat.

We really need to get rid of some of these cats, he thought. It's a cat plague, that's what it is. Next time I'll bring Mars with me.

And after a while he noticed that the cats were following him. First it was just one trailing along behind him, but when he looked again a little later there were eight of them.

And by the time he made it to the shop there were more than ten. They all followed him in.

"*Kssss!*" hissed Mr. Ellmore angrily. He chased them out of the shop, but they came back in again with the very next customer.

And when he was trying on shoes and standing there defenseless in his socks, they circled around him.

"Are these your cats, sir?" asked the shop assistant.

"What do you take me for?" Mr. Ellmore shouted. "They just followed me in."

"Shall I chase them away again?"

"Yes, please!"

The shop assistant chased the cats out for a second time, but as soon as the door opened again for a new customer, the whole horde came back in and crowded around Mr. Ellmore's legs.

He would have loved to kick them. He would have loved to catch one of them on the head with a heavy boot, but there were quite a few customers in the shop by now. And everyone knew him. Everyone knew he was the president of the Animal Lovers' Association. And that meant he wasn't allowed to kick any cats.

At least, not while people are looking, he thought grimly. But just wait. . . . I'll get my chance.

He got his chance. On the street all the cats trooped along behind him. As long as people were watching, he didn't dare do a thing, but when the street was quiet for a moment close to the school, he looked around quickly, saw that the coast was clear, and gave the Butcher's Cat a good kick.

The cats shot off in all directions.

"That's that taken care of," smirked Mr. Ellmore. But when he got to his car and opened the door he found eight or so cats sitting inside it. He was so furious he was about to bash them right out again when a voice behind him said, "Oh, look . . . how lovely."

He turned around and saw Mr. Smith beaming at him.

"A car full of cats," he said. "You're such an animal lover."

"Absolutely . . . ," said Mr. Ellmore with a strained smile.

"You *are* coming to my reading tomorrow, aren't you?" Mr. Smith asked. "I think *you* will find it particularly interesting: 'The Cat Through the Ages: A Feline History.' With beautiful colored slides. You'll be there, won't you?"

"Yes, definitely," said Mr. Ellmore.

The cats emerged sedately from the car. Mr. Ellmore drove to his factory. He had an important meeting in his office with the councillor. To discuss expanding his factory. But because of all the cats, he was late. When he walked into his office the councillor was already there.

Mr. Ellmore apologized, offered the councillor a cigar, and started talking about his expansion plans.

"There are a lot of people who aren't so keen on an expansion," the councillor said. "They're afraid the town will get too smelly."

"Oh, but our fragrances are wonderful," Mr. Ellmore said. "Our latest is apple blossom. . . . I'll just let you smell it."

But when he turned around to get the spray can, he saw three cats slipping out through the open window.

He suppressed a curse.

"Just smell how wonderful it is," he said.

The councillor sniffed.

"Apple blossom," said Mr. Ellmore. He sniffed too. But what they smelt wasn't apple blossom at all. The whole room reeked of tomcats.

"Cat pee," the councillor wanted to say. But he was a well-mannered man and said politely, "Mmmm, that smells good."

That afternoon Mr. Ellmore took his dog in the car with him, in case a troop of cats tried to follow him again.

And there they were. Standing around the parking spot. Some were close by, others at a distance. The whole street was crawling with cats.

Mr. Ellmore held the door open and said, "Come on out, Mars. Look, Mars . . . kitty-cats . . . come on, boy, get 'em!"

But to his surprise, Mars stayed in the car, quietly whimpering. He didn't want to get out.

"What are you doing? You're not scared of a few cats, are you?"

But Mars didn't stir. He growled viciously, but he was too scared to get out of the car.

He could see the Tatter Cat. She was the closest of all, and although she had a limp now and couldn't move that quickly, she was the bravest of all as well. She looked so mean, so devilish, with such a bloodthirsty expression on her dirty cat face. . . .

Mars suddenly remembered how she'd clawed him in his own backyard. And now there were all those other cats too. There were too many—he couldn't take them on. He was staying in the car.

"Call yourself a dog!" Mr. Ellmore said contemptuously.

He looked around. Lots and lots of cats . . . not very many people . . . and no one watching.

He grabbed the dog leash from the back of the car and lashed out left and right. He caught the Church Cat Ecumenica, who shot screeching into the church; the others disappeared in all directions, like a swarm of hornets when you spray them with water.

But just like hornets, they came back. The Tatter Cat leading the way. And they trailed along behind Mr. Ellmore until he drove off again.

That evening they went to his garden as well.

Until now Mars had always kept all the cats away. None of them had ever dared go into the garden, except now and then when the dog was shut in the garage. Like the time that led to the Tatter Cat's lame leg.

And now all of a sudden . . . cats in the garden.

"Mars . . . kitty-cats!" Mr. Ellmore called. "Get 'em, boy. Go on, get 'em!"

Mars jumped around excitedly in front of the french doors, but didn't dare go out into the garden.

"I don't understand what's got into the dog," Mr. Ellmore said. "He's scared of cats! Have you ever heard anything so ridiculous? A German shepherd that's scared of cats!"

"If I'm not mistaken, they're attacking our rosebushes," his wife said. "Chase them away! Here, take this bottle. Last time you hit that filthy stray with it."

Mr. Ellmore ran out with the bottle.

The cats were hard at work scratching the flowers and leaves off the roses Ellmore was so proud of.

They looked up at him triumphantly as he approached.

"Dirty rotten cats! Now there's nobody around to watch! Now I'm in my own garden. . . . I'll get you. . . ."

He lashed out left and right but stamped on his own roses in the process and stabbed himself with a thorn. And the cats were gone, disappearing between the bushes and trees.

"And you know what you'll get if I see you here again!" Ellmore roared at the bushes.

He went back inside and his wife said, "They're back."

"Where?"

"In the rose bed. They're going to destroy all our roses."

"That's it," her husband said grimly. "This is too much. And fortunately there aren't any people around here, so I don't have to restrain myself. Get me my hunting rifle!"

She fetched it for him.

He stood next to the terrace with the gun in his hands. Although it was already evening, the spring sun was shining down through the branches of the trees onto the rose bed, where no fewer than ten cats were ripping up the rosebushes with delight in their eyes.

"Now I'll get you . . . you scum . . . ," Mr. Ellmore said softly.

He raised the gun up to his shoulder.

Simon the Siamese was the closest. He looked at Ellmore with his eyes completely crossed but didn't budge.

Seven cats ran off in fright; three stood their ground. The Councillor's Cat, the Tatter Cat, and Cross-Eyed Simon.

Seconds before the shot rang out, they sped off—just in time. Only the Tatter Cat was still limping on the lawn, but before Mr. Ellmore could take aim again, she ducked into the shadows.

He turned around to go back inside but saw a girl standing there. A little girl in his garden. She tried to slip away, but he saw that she was laughing. She was laughing at him.

"What's the idea? What are you doing here?" Mr. Ellmore cried.

She was laughing so hard she couldn't answer.

Mr. Ellmore was beside himself with rage. He grabbed the girl by the arm and shook her hard.

"Now get out of my garden, you little brat."

At first it looked like Bibi was crying. But as soon as she was through the gate, she started laughing again.

She waited for a moment on the other side of the fence, on the street. Then Minou came out of the garden through a hole in the hedge. And behind her came the Tatter Cat . . . and all the other cats, one by one.

The rest of the evening they left the roses alone.

—15—

THE CAT
THROUGH THE AGES

"The reading's on tonight," Minou said. "Mr. Smith's talk. In the Metropole Hotel."

"I know," Tibble said. "I don't need to go anymore."

"They'll be showing slides," Minou said. "Of all kinds of special cats. In color."

"Maybe," Tibble said. "But I'm not going. I don't need to write any more articles. I don't work for the newspaper anymore. And anyway, I've got enough cats right here. Thanks, but no thanks."

"Everyone's going to be there," Minou said.

"Exactly," said Tibble. "And that's why I'd rather not go. Mr. Ellmore will be there too, of course, as the president of the association. And if I never see him again it will be too soon."

"I'm going," Minou said.

He looked up with surprise—Minou, who was so shy and so scared of going anywhere crowded.

"And I would like it very much if you could come with me," she said.

And now there was something about her voice that made him realize something special was going on. He couldn't imagine *what*, but after a slight hesitation he said, "All right, then."

Outside there was a poster saying:

ANIMAL LOVERS' ASSOCIATION
TONIGHT: *THE CAT THROUGH THE AGES: A FELINE HISTORY*.
A READING WITH SLIDES BY MR. W. SMITH

Tibble and Minou were the last to arrive. The hall was packed because Mr. Smith was extremely popular and a gripping speaker. And of course, the people of Killenthorn were crazy about cats.

Sitting in the front row was Mr. Ellmore, who was going to say a few words of welcome.

As it hadn't started yet, people were chatting among themselves, and when Tibble and Minou began looking for somewhere to sit, people around them whispered and pointed.

Two elderly ladies just behind them spoke softly to each other.

"That's the young man from the newspaper, you know. With his secretary."

"He's not with the paper anymore, though."

"No?"

"No, he wrote that outrageous article about Mr. Ellmore!"

"Was that him?"

"Absolutely, his name was at the bottom. And it said that our own Mr. Ellmore had run into the fish stall."

"Yes, and it also said that he'd dumped live kittens in a rubbish bin. Disgraceful things to write. Without a shred of evidence."

Tibble could hear every word. He felt more and more miserable and wished he'd stayed home. Next to him sat Minou, who was in an extremely catlike and inscrutable mood. And very calm . . . She seemed completely oblivious to everyone around her.

A little bit closer to the front sat Bibi, next to her mother.

Now Mr. Ellmore rose to speak a few words of welcome. He was met with enthusiastic applause.

While clapping, people kept sneaking backward looks at Tibble. It was as if they were trying to say: Even if you write nasty gossip, we don't believe you. We trust our Mr. Ellmore.

Mr. Ellmore gave a friendly smile and nodded. He kept it very short and handed the microphone over to Mr. Smith.

It was a fascinating reading. Mr. Smith spoke about cats among the ancient Egyptians. He spoke about cats in the Dark Ages and he showed slides.

The lights in the auditorium were off, and every time he tapped on the floor with his stick a new cat appeared on the screen.

"We will now have a fifteen-minute break," Mr. Smith said

after he had been talking for an hour. "In that time refreshments will be available at the buffet. But before we stop, I'll just show you *one* more slide of a most extraordinary pedigreed cat from the Renaissance."

He gave a tap with his stick. That was the sign that the boy operating the slide projector should show the last slide before the intermission.

A cat did appear on the screen. But it wasn't a pedigreed cat at all. It was a slide of the Butcher's Cat fetching a good kick on Green Square. And the person giving him the kick was Mr. Ellmore, who was clearly visible. It was true that the photo wasn't beautiful and it was very wonky, but there was no mistaking its content.

Tibble sat up straight. He looked at Minou. She smiled.

"That's *my* cat!" shouted the butcher from the second row. Mr. Smith tapped angrily with his stick and cried, "That is not the correct photo."

People started mumbling in the auditorium. And now the next slide appeared. This one showed Mr. Ellmore hitting the Church Cat Ecumenica with a dog whip. He was enjoying it very much, you could see that clearly.

"That's *our* cat!" cried the vicar, but the next slide had already popped up. And now Mr. Ellmore was standing next to the terrace in his own garden holding a gun. He was aiming at three cats.

"That's *my* Simon!" Mr. Smith cried indignantly.

"Our cat . . . ," whispered the councillor's wife.

The Tatter Cat was in the photo too, but no one worried about that except Tibble, who looked at Minou in dismay. She

117

gave him another friendly nod, and suddenly he understood the cats' plan. He realized that Bibi had taken the photos on the street and in Ellmore's garden with her new camera. Only Bibi could take photos *that* crooked.

The mumbling and whispering in the auditorium grew louder.

Everyone looked at Mr. Ellmore. It was fairly dark, but everyone could see that he'd stood up and walked to the front.

"It's not true," he shouted. "That's not me!"

But now the next slide appeared. Even more crooked than the others, but just as clear. Mr. Ellmore holding a girl by her arm and shaking her. The girl was Bibi.

"That's a fake!" Mr. Ellmore shouted. "I can explain everything. It's a trick!"

But by now the audience was talking so loudly that nobody heard him.

He walked to the back of the auditorium and the slide projector.

The boy who was showing the slides was Billy, the canteen assistant.

"Stop it at once!" Mr. Ellmore shouted.

"That was the last one," said Billy.

"You—" Ellmore said furiously. "You—where did you get those photos?"

"I'm just working through all of them," Billy said, "like I'm supposed to."

"But how did those last ones get in there?"

"How should I know?" asked Billy.

There was now an enormous uproar in the hall. Mr. Smith

118

tried to calm things down. "Ladies and gentlemen, this is all based on a regrettable misunderstanding," he said. "I suggest we all just have a quiet cup of coffee, after which I will resume my talk."

"You're fired!" Mr. Ellmore hissed quickly at Billy.

He went back into the middle of the hall, where the lights were back on and people were standing around in groups, talking as they pushed up to the buffet. Wherever Mr. Ellmore went, they suddenly fell quiet.

He'd wanted to explain, but there was nothing to explain. The photos had been all too clear. Mr. Ellmore shrugged helplessly and left.

No sooner had he left than the conversation picked up again on all sides.

"Unbelievable," said the councillor's wife. "The president of the Animal Lovers' Association. Shooting at cats! He shot at *my* cat!"

"He grabbed *my* daughter," said Bibi's mother. "That's much more serious. And to think that he's head of the Child Welfare Commission."

Bibi was sitting there very sweetly, as if none of it had anything to do with her.

"Why didn't you tell me?" her mother asked. "About that man grabbing you?"

But Bibi kept quiet. She looked at Tibble over her Coke bottle and whispered, "Good, huh?"

"Fantastic," he said.

"Minou took that one of me," she said. "She was in a tree." Tibble looked around to see if he could see Minou. He'd been

119

separated from her in the crowd. He walked around and heard scraps of conversations everywhere.

The two elderly ladies were talking again.

"It's quite possible that it was true after all, at least partly."

"What?"

"That article in the paper. About Ellmore dumping kittens in a rubbish bin."

"Yes, of course, a man like that is capable of anything. And that bit about the fish stall is sure to be true too."

Nearby, Mr. Smith was talking to Billy.

"How on earth did that happen, Billy?" Mr. Smith asked. "Those photos at the end . . . that wasn't the idea at all. How did they get in there?"

"Miss Minou gave them to me," said Billy. "She asked if I could show them before the break. I didn't know why, but she was *so* friendly. And she was *so* sweet when she asked me."

"I see . . . ," said Mr. Smith. "Well, well . . ."

"And now I've lost my job anyway," Billy went on, "so I can tell everyone too."

"Tell everyone what?" Mr. Smith asked.

"That I was there," said Billy.

"Where?"

"In Green Square. When Mr. Ellmore crashed into the fish stall."

"But, my boy!" Mr. Smith exclaimed. "Why didn't you say so before?"

Someone else came over to join them. The mechanic from the garage. "Then I might as well tell you what I know too," he said. "Mr. Ellmore's car was badly damaged."

"You shouldn't be telling *me* that," Mr. Smith said. "You have to tell the police. And there just happens to be a policeman here in the hall right now."

He went over to Tibble, who was still walking around by himself.

"Tibble," said Mr. Smith. "I'm afraid I misjudged you. I'm sorry. I believe you were right all along. You should write an article about this evening now."

"I'm no longer with the newspaper," said Tibble.

Minou, too, was walking around among all the people who were talking away and drinking their coffees. Now and then she caught snippets of conversation: "That Tibble fellow was telling the truth after all. . . . His article wasn't just gossip."

"You really think so?"

"I'm sure of it!"

And she felt very contented. This was just what the cats had hoped for when they made their plan.

She was about to return to her seat when she saw something black behind a glass door. It meowed.

Minou pushed open the door and stepped out into the hotel lobby.

The black shape was the Metropole Cat.

"I've been standing here calling you for hours," he moaned. "I was too scared to go in with all those people there. It went well, didn't it?"

"It went exceptionally well," Minou said. "Thanks to all the cats."

"Excellent," said the Metropole Cat. "But I called you because there's someone waiting for you outside."

"Who?" Minou asked.

"Your sister. Outside the revolving doors, in the shadow of the linden tree. If you have a moment."

Minou felt warm and cold all at once. Just like in Aunt Sooty's garden . . . Thinking about her sister made her throat throb strangely.

"I can't," she said. "I have to get back. There's a reading."

"Come off it," said the Metropole Cat. "What's that reading to you? What do you care about 'The Cat Through the Ages' when today's cat is out there waiting for you?"

"I'm not going," Minou said.

"Why not? You're not scared of your own sister, are you?"

"No . . . or . . . maybe," Minou said. "Tell her I can't come right now."

And when Tibble made it back to his seat, Minou was already there, on the chair next to his.

Mr. Smith finished his talk without any more unusual developments.

—16—

THE EDITORIAL CAT

The next morning there was a constant stream of cats up on the rooftops.

They'd all been informed. The cats had passed the word on from one to the other that very night.

"This is the best news since Dunkirk," said the School Cat

They were sitting on the roof of the Social Security Building Minou had never been in the middle of such a large group of cats before, and definitely not in broad daylight. She'd brought a bag of meat with her and was sharing it out on all sides Ecumenica was so wild with joy that she burst into a fit of harsh screeching—quite unseemly for a Church Cat. "We're going to celebrate!" she screamed.

"Yeah, let's celebrate," the Tatter Cat said. She was proud

that she could climb up to the highest rooftop again despite her leg.

"There's nothing to celebrate," Minou said. "My human is still fired, and in a few days he'll have to move out of his flat."

"Wait and see," said Cross-Eyed Simon. "Anything could happen today. The mood's changed. People don't like Ellmore anymore. *My* human's furious with him."

"*Mine* too," said the councillor's cat.

"The whole town's talking about it," said the Metropole Cat. "And this time, I mean the people."

Meanwhile Tibble was stuck in the attic with the six little kittens. His big cats were out on the roof, including Minou.

He'd hardly seen her since the reading, and there were all kinds of things he was dying to ask her.

He wandered around the flat and didn't really know what to do with himself. Then the doorbell rang.

It was Mr. Van Dam, his downstairs neighbor. When he finally made it to the top of the stairs, he seemed a little bashful and didn't want to sit down.

"This won't take long," he said. "I've heard that my wife has given you notice to leave. That she wants you out of our attic. She did that without telling me. And she shouldn't have. I don't agree with it."

Tibble said, "Please, have a seat."

Mr. Van Dam sat down on the edge of a chair.

"Sometimes she overdoes things," he said. "She was angry because there were so many cats on the roof. But I told her right away, 'Tibble can't help that. That's just what this

neighborhood's like. There happen to be a lot of cats around here.'"

Tibble nodded.

"And you having cats yourself," Mr. Van Dam continued, "that's not a problem for us at all. She says it is . . . but I disagree."

"Thank you," said Tibble.

"And otherwise she was very angry about that article of yours in the paper," Mr. Van Dam said. "But now we all know that you were absolutely right. It was true. I just heard that it was Ellmore who ran into the fish stall. And the police have finally found a couple of witnesses."

"Oh," said Tibble. "Great. I can't offer you a cigarette because I don't smoke, but would you like a peppermint?"

"I'd love one," said Mr. Van Dam. "You also had a . . . um . . . a secretary . . . somewhere." He looked around vaguely.

"Yes," said Tibble, "but she's not here right now. She's out on the roof."

"Cute little kittens," said Mr. Van Dam. "I'd love to have one."

"Oh," said Tibble, "you can. When they're a little bigger."

"No, I can't. My wife doesn't like cats, you see. There's no way round that. But there's *one* thing I want to tell you, Tibble: this is your home, and you can rent it from us as long as you like. That's all there is to it."

"That's fantastic . . . ," Tibble sighed.

He would have loved to tell Minou straightaway, but she wasn't there. And right after Mr. Van Dam went downstairs again, the phone rang.

It was Tibble's boss.

Asking if he could drop by shortly.

Half an hour later he was back in that old familiar spot, sitting in front of his boss's desk. And the Editorial Cat was there too and winked at him.

"By the looks of things, you were right, Tibble," the editor said. "That article you wrote was *true*."

"Of course it was true," Tibble said. "Otherwise I wouldn't have written it."

"Not so fast . . . ," his boss said. "That doesn't alter the fact that you didn't have the slightest bit of evidence. And you mustn't ever write something without evidence to back it up. What you did was wrong. Let's hope you never do it again."

Tibble looked up. "Again?" he asked.

"Yes. Because I hope you're willing to carry on here with us at the paper. You are, aren't you?"

"Oh, yes," said Tibble. "I'd love to!"

"Good, that's agreed, then. And . . . oh, yeah, Tibble . . . one last thing before you go: it's been a long time since you wrote anything about cats. It's all right if you want to write about them again sometimes. As long as it's not too often."

"Great," said Tibble.

As soon as the conversation was over, the Editorial Cat slipped out of the window and hurried up to the roof to tell Minou the news.

"Your human's back with the newspaper!"

Minou sighed with relief.

"So now you can go away again," the cat said.

"Go away? Where?"

"Well," said the Editorial Cat. "Your sister wants you back,

126

doesn't she? You're allowed to go back to your old house now, aren't you?"

"I don't know . . . ," Minou said, very flustered all of a sudden. "Where did you hear that?"

"On the way here . . . from a couple of different cats. Haven't you spoken to her yet?"

"No," said Minou.

"You'll see her soon, then. She's coming to get you."

"But I don't want to move," Minou said. "I've already got a human. And he still needs me. How else is he going to get news?"

"He doesn't need you anymore," the Editorial Cat said. "He's changed so much! He's not shy anymore, not at all. He's not scared of anything. Haven't you noticed?"

"Yes," Minou said. "It's true. He's brave enough to go up to anyone and ask anything now. He was so angry at Ellmore, he stopped being scared. He Learnt to Dare."

On their way back to the attic, Minou talked a little with the Tatter Cat, who immediately brought up the subject of her sister.

"Your sister wants you to drop by," the Tatter Cat said. "I haven't spoken to her myself, but that's the message going round. I'd get over there if I were you."

"Yes . . ." Minou hesitated.

"I hear she's found some remedy that will cure you. That would be a real blessing," the Tatter Cat said. "The *bliss* of being a cat again . . . don't you think?" She peered at Minou with her yellow eyes.

"I . . . um . . . I don't know anymore . . . ," Minou said.

127

She found Tibble in the living room, over the moon about all the things that had been happening.

"I've got my job back, and my flat!" he shouted. "We're going to celebrate with fish, fried fish, and lots of it." But because he was so happy, he didn't notice how quiet Minou was. Quiet and thoughtful and not happy at all.

—17—

A CAT AGAIN?

Tibble was woken by a downy paw stroking his face.

It was Fluff.

Tibble looked at his alarm clock. "Quarter past three . . . Fluff, why are you waking me up in the middle of the night? Go back to the end of the bed and lie down."

But Fluff meowed insistently.

"Have you got something to say? Are you trying to tell me something? You know I don't understand you. Go and tell Minou. She should be in her box."

But Fluff kept meowing until Tibble got up.

Minou wasn't in her box. Apparently she was still out on the roof. It was already starting to get light. The kittens were playing in the junk room and Fluff kept meowing at Tibble until he followed him over to the kitchen window.

"What is it? Do I have to look out?"

Tibble leant out of the window and looked out over the rooftops. There were two cats sitting nearby on the slanting roof. One was the Tatter Cat. The other was a beautiful ginger cat with a white chest and a white-tipped tail.

Tibble leant out farther and the window squeaked. The ginger cat looked at him.

He was so shocked he almost lost his balance and had to grab hold of the window frame. It was Minou.

The eyes he knew so well. Minou's eyes. And Minou's face, totally, but now *all* cat.

He wanted to call out, *Minou!* but the shock had made him hoarse and taken his breath away. It only lasted a moment anyway. The ginger cat turned and disappeared over the edge of the roof with a few quick jumps.

The Tatter Cat stayed where she was. She just flicked her tail and looked at him with her mysterious yellow eyes.

Feeling a little dizzy, Tibble went inside, sat down on the couch, and started to chew his nails.

"Ridiculous," he said. "Nonsense. I'm letting my imagination run away with me. Miss Minou will come back any moment now."

Fluff kept circling around him and trying to tell him something. Never before had Tibble *so* wished he understood Cattish. . . . *Something* was going on. . . . That was all he knew.

"What are you trying to tell me, Fluff? Has she changed back to a cat?"

"Ah, nonsense," he said again. "I'm still half asleep. I'm dreaming. I'm going back to bed."

He tried to go back to sleep but couldn't. He just lay there waiting. . . . Usually Minou came home as soon as it got light. Then she'd get in her box. Now she didn't come, and he grew more and more worried. In the end he got up to make some coffee.

It was six o'clock. And Minou still hadn't come home.

Tibble went to see if her things were still there.

Her washcloth and toothbrush and things. They were all there. Her case was still in the junk room too. That was a relief.

A relief? Why should it be a relief? Tibble thought. If she's changed back to a cat, she won't need any of that anymore.

I'm going mad. What kind of rubbish have I gotten into my skull?

At quarter past six the doorbell rang.

It's her! thought Tibble. She's coming up through the front door.

But it wasn't Minou. It was Bibi who came up the stairs.

"I know it's really early, Tibble," she said. "But I got such a fright. I looked out of my window this morning . . . I have a view out over the rooftops too, just like you . . . and I saw Minou. She went past."

"Yes?" said Tibble. "And?"

Bibi was silent for a moment and looked distraught.

"Go on, Bibi. . . ."

"She's turned back into a cat again," Bibi said. She said it hesitantly. She was afraid that Tibble would laugh at her. But Tibble stayed serious. He did say, "Bibi, come on . . . don't be silly. . . ." But he said it without any conviction.

"It's really true," Bibi said.

"I think I saw her too," Tibble said. "I went to call her, but she ran off. She could be anywhere now."

"I think she's gone back to her old house," Bibi said. "To her garden."

"Which garden?"

"On Victoria Avenue. She told me once that her real home was in Victoria Avenue. A house with a golden chain tree next to the patio. That's where she lived when she was still a cat."

Fluff started meowing again.

"I don't understand what he's saying," Bibi said. "But he's probably agreeing with us. What should we do, Tibble?"

"Nothing," Tibble said. "What can we do?"

"Go there," Bibi said. "To Victoria Avenue. To see if she's there."

"No," said Tibble. "That's ridiculous."

But ten minutes later they were walking down the street together in the early-morning light.

It was a very long way, and it took them a while to find Victoria Avenue. It was a short, winding street with white houses and big front gardens.

"I can't see a ginger cat anywhere," said Tibble. "I don't see a golden chain tree anywhere either."

"It must be at the back," Bibi said. "I'll go round and walk through the gardens. Nobody will be up this early."

It was very quiet on the street at this hour. Birds were singing and the blossoms were swaying in the breeze. Tibble sat down on a garden wall to wait for Bibi to come back. In front of one of the houses there was a big rubbish bin. The house itself wasn't being used as a home anymore; it looked more like offices. A sign on the gate said *Institute for Biochemical Research* in black letters.

And that reminded Tibble of something Minou had told him: that as a cat she'd eaten something from a rubbish bin that had changed her. He'd laughed about it at the time, but now he thought, who knows . . . with all these modern scientific experiments . . . They must have thrown out something that went wrong.

Bibi had reappeared next to him.

"It must be that one," she said, pointing at the house next door to the institute.

"There's a golden chain tree out the back. But I didn't see any cats. Maybe she's gone inside. *Oh, look!*"

Tibble looked.

The ginger cat was standing in the front garden. Under a lilac bush.

She turned her head to look at Tibble and Bibi, staring straight at them. And again they both saw Minou's eyes.

But the most horrific thing of all was that the cat had a thrush in her jaws. A freshly caught, live, fluttering thrush.

Bibi yelled and waved her arms and in a flash the cat ran off through the bushes at the side of the house with the bird in her mouth.

"I'm going after her!" Bibi cried, but Tibble stopped her.

"Don't," he said. "That bird's probably wounded and half dead . . . it's best to just leave it."

They stood there at the hedge. Minou had disappeared round the back of the house with her prey and Bibi started to cry.

"Don't cry," Tibble said. "It's just the way things are. You can't stop a cat from being a cat. And cats catch birds."

"I saw that expression on Minou's face a lot," said Bibi. "When we were in the park and a bird landed near us. I thought it was creepy. I'd shout out, 'It's not allowed.' And then she was always so ashamed of herself. But now she's not ashamed anymore. And that's why I'm crying."

Tibble was only half listening. He was wondering whether he should ring the doorbell. He wanted to ask, excuse me, ma'am, but was your ginger cat missing for a while?

But he thought about it and realized that the lady who lived here wouldn't even be up yet. It was still so early. And anyway . . . what difference did it make? She'd probably say, yes, she was gone for quite a long time, but now she's back.

What good would that do him?

"Come on, let's go," he said.

"Don't you want to take her with you?" Bibi asked.

"No," said Tibble. "She's someone else's cat. And I've still got eight cats left."

Slowly and silently they walked back through the streets.

It hadn't been a pleasant sight . . . their own Minou with a live bird between her jaws.

—18—

THE GINGER SISTER

It was still nighttime and pitch-black when Minou met her sister on the roof of the Social Security Building.

The Bakery Cat had come to tell her, "Your sister's waiting for you. It's urgent. You have to come at once."

Even before Minou saw her sister, she smelt the family smell. A very distinctive and very familiar smell of Home . . . and that was why she immediately said, "A quick nosey-nosey?"

"What do you take me for?" Her sister scowled. "Not until you're a proper cat again."

"I don't know if that's ever going to happen."

"Don't worry about that. It will. Tonight. The opportunity is *there*."

"Where?" Minou asked.

"I mean it's possible *now*. It wasn't possible before. And later it won't be either. This is your last chance. So come with me."

"You mean to your house?"

"I mean to *our* house. To *our* garden."

The enormous sky over the roofs seemed to be growing a little lighter in the east. Minou could now make out all of her sister's body. It didn't make her look any friendlier.

"You chased me away," Minou said. "You said you never wanted to see me again. You were angry about me taking the Woman's case and clothes. Even though I really couldn't leave without anything."

"Forgive and forget," her sister said quickly. "The Woman didn't even notice. She's got so many cases and so many clothes . . . you know that."

"But you were most furious about me not being a cat any more. You chased me out of the garden with your claws!"

"That was *then*," her sister said. "Tonight you can recover. Tonight or early tomorrow morning at the latest."

"How can you be so sure?"

"Perhaps you've heard," her sister said, "that I *almost* had the same thing?"

"Yes, Aunt Sooty told me."

"It wasn't as bad as with you. But I'd eaten out of that rubbish bin as well. And terrible things started happening. My whiskers disappeared and my tail grew smaller and smaller. And I got some very strange urges. I wanted to start walking on my hind legs. And I wanted to have a shower. Instead of washing myself properly with spit."

"And then?" Minou asked.

"A dusk thrush cured me," her sister said. "I ate a dusk thrush, that's all. You know how rare they are in our gardens. You hardly ever see them. They only pass through. But I just happened to catch one. And that reversed it. It cured me. . . . I know that dusk thrushes eat certain herbs that are good for all kinds of diseases. Yours too."

"And? Are they there now?" asked Minou.

"Only tonight. And maybe very early in the morning. That's why you have to come with me right away. It's already starting to get light."

Minou stayed sitting there and thought about it.

"Come on," said her sister. "Come home."

"But I've got a home," Minou said. "A home and a Man . . ." She fell silent. The attic and the Man seemed so terribly far away. And so unimportant. Her sister smelt so warm and so *close*.

"Remember how we used to catch starlings together in the garden?" her sister asked. "And how fabulous our garden is in spring? Think of the golden chain tree . . . it's in flower now. . . . Soon, when you've got your tail back, you can walk under the golden chain tree. You can sit on the Woman's lap and purr. You'll be able to do everything that's cattish and normal. What is there to think about? You're shivering, you're cold. Come with me, and soon you'll have your coat back."

Minou *was* cold. It would be lovely to have fur again, she thought. To stretch out on the paving stones in the sun in thick ginger fur. The bliss of licking yourself with one paw up in the air . . . and then gnawing between your toes. The pure bliss of having claws you can retract or put out, whichever you choose.

And spending ages scratching and scratching away at the leg of a brand-new chair.

"I'm coming," Minou said. "Just wait a moment. . . ."

"No, I'm not waiting . . . it's almost dawn. What else do you need?"

"I just wanted . . . I thought . . . I have to get my case . . . and my washcloth and that . . ."

"What?" her sister cried. "What do you need all that for? What good's a case to a cat?"

"I thought . . . maybe I could return it . . . just leave it somewhere," Minou spluttered.

"Don't make things difficult," her sister said irritably.

"But I have to at least say goodbye, surely?"

"Say goodbye? Who to? Your human? Are you crazy? He might not let you go. He'll lock you up."

"Let me at least say goodbye to the Tatter Cat," Minou cried unhappily. "And explain what's happening . . . It's only four roofs away."

"You stay here," her sister hissed. "*I'll* take care of it . . . otherwise you'll just let him talk you into staying. Wait for me here. I'll see the Tatter Cat there in your gutter."

And off she went, over the dimly lit rooftops, passing Bibi's attic window on her way to Tibble's gutter.

When she came back she said, "I have to wish you luck."

"Who from?" Minou asked quickly.

"Not your human," her sister said. "I did see him. He came to the window and I left in a hurry. But the Tatter Cat wishes you luck. She said she hopes you'll drop by soon when you have a tail again. She said I look just like you!"

* * *

Now it was morning and sunny.

For hours, Minou had been sitting in a toolshed in the back garden of the house on Victoria Avenue. Next to the lawnmower. She was still shivering a little, more from excitement than from the cold. But soon I'll have fur, she thought. Soon . . . with any luck.

They hadn't had any luck yet. Her sister hadn't been able to catch a dusk thrush.

"Is it going to take much longer?" Minou asked through the half-open door of the tool shed. "The sun's already up."

"Yes, great, just *hurry* me, will you?" her sister snapped. "It's a tremendous help, you hurrying me. . . . But I'll go and check the front garden."

From the toolshed Minou could see the back of the house where she had been born and where she had lived as a young cat.

Soon she'd be allowed to go back inside and get a saucer of milk and be patted. And when she started purring, no one would say, "Shame on you, Miss Minou!"

Here in the garden, she knew every tree and every shrub. In the old days she had caught frogs here on the lawn and once she had even caught a mole. She had scratched in the flower beds. Digging a little hole between the begonias and then sitting over it with a quivering tail and thoughtful eyes, the way cats do.

And then scratching the soil to cover it up again when she was finished. She was starting to feel more and more cattish.

It was going to work, she could feel it in her bones. Very soon now . . .

Then she was shocked by a terrible cheeping sound.

Her ginger sister was running toward her. She had nabbed one of the dusk thrushes from the front garden. In that same instant, Tibble and Bibi were standing at the front hedge, but Minou didn't know that. Her sister trotted up triumphantly.

She couldn't say anything with her mouth full of thrush, but in her eyes you could see her thinking, Who's the best hunter around?

The bird chirped and cheeped and fluttered hopelessly between her sister's cruel jaws. For a second, Minou thought, Mmmm, yummy!

But when her ginger sister came closer, Minou hit her hard and yelled, "Let go!"

Her sister jumped and released her prey. The dusk thrush immediately flew off, wobbling and unsteady at first . . . then straight up into the sky, twittering its way to freedom.

"*That* is the last straw," her sister said in a quiet voice full of menace.

"I . . . I'm sorry . . . ," Minou said. She was utterly ashamed of herself.

"*This* really is the end," her sister hissed angrily. "I've been running around all night for you . . . all night. Finally, using all my strength and all my cunning, I catch a rare dusk thrush for you. Because I know that it's your last chance . . . because you're my sister. And *look what you've done!*"

"I couldn't help it," Minou spluttered. "I didn't stop to think."

"You didn't stop to think! That's a fine remark. After

140

everything I've done for you . . . You knock the bird out of my mouth. *Bah!*"

"I'd done it before I even realized," Minou moaned. "And there is *another* one—didn't you say there were two of them?"

"You don't think I'm going to go hunting for you again, do you?" Her sister was now beside herself with rage.

"You know what you are? You're a *human*! You're just like that Woman of mine. That Woman of *ours*, because she used to be yours too. She eats *chicken*, but if we catch a bird it's, *Oh, no!* Then she knocks the birds right out of our mouths. Remember? When you lived here . . . Remember? We used to talk about it often. It made you furious. 'The hypocrite,' you said. 'Eating chicken herself and taking our birds off us.'"

"I remember," Minou said.

"So why did you just do exactly the same thing?"

"I don't know. I think I've changed."

"You've changed *too much*," her sister said. "You'll never recover. And now it's over. You're not my sister anymore. Go away. Get out of my garden for good. And watch out if I ever see you here again!"

She hissed so viciously that Minou fled . . . farther into the back garden. And then through a hole in the hedge into the next garden and farther, through garden after garden, with her sister's hissing screech still audible far behind her.

As she wandered on, she thought about what had happened.

How could something like that even be possible? All the while she had longed to hunt and catch birds again. Why had she done something so unnatural? So *uncattish*?

Saving a bird . . . what an idiotic thing to do.

As she walked she tried to work it out. I could *imagine* the bird's pain, she thought. I could *imagine* how frightened it was. But if you can imagine something like that, you're not a cat anymore. Not at all. Cats never feel sorry for birds. *Ever.* I think I've let my last chance slip by.

—19—

CARLO THIS TIME

The weather changed while Tibble and Bibi were still on their way back to their own neighborhood. The wind got up, big clouds drifted over, and raindrops started to fall.

"Will you be on time for school?" Tibble asked.

"Easy," said Bibi. "It's nowhere near half eight yet."

They had reached Green Square and Tibble said, "Let's shelter from the rain for a bit. That bench under the trees is dry." They sat down and sucked their peppermints, feeling a little sad.

I've got my job back, thought Tibble. And I don't have to move out of my flat anymore. So everything's worked out. I've just lost my secretary. And I don't have a Cat Press Agency. No more news from cats. I'll have to do it myself. Am I up to it? Am I brave enough?

"Of course I am," he told himself sternly. "I'm not even that shy anymore. I'm brave enough to go up to all kinds of people to ask them questions. And having to do it myself will actually be good for me. But I'm still not happy. You'd think I'd be a tiny bit happy, but I'm not."

Miss Minou . . . he thought. There were so many things I wanted to ask her. Before she changed back to a cat. And did I ever actually thank her? No, never. I always told her off for acting too cattish. And I never even paid her either. Not that money would be any use to her now.

That thought didn't make him any happier. Just a pair of gloves . . . that's all I ever gave her . . . and that was only because I was scared she'd scratch someone. If she ever comes back—as a person, even if she's a very cattish kind of person—I'll never get angry again. She can hiss sometimes if she likes. And purr too. And rub up against people. She was actually sweetest of all when she was purring. *Purrfect*, thought Tibble. And then a dog barked just behind their bench.

It was a Great Dane. It was standing under a tree and barking at something in the branches.

Without a word, Tibble and Bibi jumped up and went over to look. The dog was making an enormous racket and leapt up against the trunk like a wild thing until its master called it. "Carlo!" he called. "Here, boy. Sit!"

Carlo whimpered for a moment, then obeyed.

Tibble and Bibi stood there looking up in the rain that was dripping down from the leaves, and there, very high up in the branches, they saw a leg and a shoe. The milk van came round the corner to Green Square.

"Excuse me, could you help for a moment?" Tibble asked. "My secretary is up a tree. And she's too scared to come down."

"It was a dog, I suppose," the milkman said. "It happens all the time. We're used to it round here. Hang on, I'll park the van under the tree."

Two minutes later Minou was down at street level again and the milkman had driven off. She was wet and her clothes were covered with green smudges, but that didn't matter. Tibble and Bibi were both grinning with relief, and they both wrapped an arm around her wet shoulders.

"How wonderful," Tibble said. "It's fantastic! It was all just our imagination! It wasn't true at all! We just let ourselves get carried away!"

"What wasn't true?" Minou asked.

The rain had grown heavier and they were getting wetter and wetter, but none of them felt it.

"We saw you early this morning, Miss Minou," Tibble said. "At least, we thought it was you."

"A ginger cat," Bibi said. "First on the rooftops!"

"That was my sister," said Minou. "My quintuplet sister. We're very similar."

"And then in Victoria Avenue," Tibble said. "We went there and we saw that cat again. With a thrush."

"Yes, that was her too. My sister."

"But we're all getting drenched! Let's go home!" Tibble cried.

And when he said that—"Let's go home!"—he felt so enormously happy that he wanted to burst into song right there in the middle of the street.

"I can't come with you," Bibi said sadly. "I have to go to

school. And now I won't hear about everything that's happened."

"Come to our place as soon as school's finished," Minou said. "Then I'll tell the whole story all over again."

Sopping wet, Tibble and Minou arrived at the attic, where all the cats were waiting for them. Fluff and the Tatter Cat and the little kittens all crowded around their feet, meowing and purring.

"We'll put on some dry clothes first," Tibble said. "Then you can tell me everything."

Minou told him what had happened. About her sister. And about why she'd left without saying anything first.

"After all, I'd always been so desperate to turn back into a cat," she said. "At least, I thought so. And when it finally came down to it, I didn't want to anymore. I spent an awfully long time shilly-shallying."

"And that's over now?" Tibble asked.

"I think so," said Minou. "My shilly-shallying is over. I want to be a human. But I'm afraid a lot of my cattish traits are here to stay. I just shot up that tree, for instance. When the dog came."

"That's fine," said Tibble.

"And I can feel that I'm going to start purring again."

"It's all fine," said Tibble. "Purr away. And you can hiss and rub up against people too."

"Hissing's not necessary at the moment," said Minou. "But a nice little head rub . . ."

"Be my guest," said Tibble.

Minou rubbed her head against his shoulder. It was a very wet head, because her red hair was still far from dry.

"I . . . I was s-so scared," Tibble stuttered. "So scared I'd never see you again, Miss Minou. It's only just sinking in how terrible I felt when you were gone. Don't run away again like that. Please! Promise me that!"

"I won't run away again," Minou said. "But I was worried you didn't need me anymore. Now that you've got over your shyness."

"I need you so much, Minou," Tibble said. "Not just as a secretary, but also . . ." He blushed. "Well . . . I just need you," he said. "Here in the house, with me. Do you understand what I'm saying, Minou?"

He noticed that he'd grabbed hold of her hand. And that he'd stopped calling her *Miss* Minou. He let go again and looked away nervously. Until now she'd always insisted on that *Miss*. And she'd always called him *Mr.* Tibble. But now she just smiled and said, "I'd love some breakfast, Tibble. A whole tin of sardines. And after that I'll just pop out onto the roof for a second. The Tatter Cat says she'd like to talk to me in private for a moment."

"Do that first, then," said Tibble. "And in the meantime I'll get a big breakfast ready with all kinds of yummy things." He set to work in the kitchen, and Minou and the Tatter Cat went out through the window and onto the roof.

"Something's wrong," said Minou. "What is it? You look like you're not glad to see me back."

"Of course I'm glad you're back," said the Tatter Cat. "That's not it at all. It's just . . . Look, I don't respect you anymore. . . . What can I say? This latest thing is just too much."

"What? Coming back here?"

147

"No, I'm talking about this business with that thrush and your sister! I've seen plenty in all my years as a stray, but nothing like this. Feeling pity for a thrush! It makes me want to puke! Next thing you'll pity a fish. You'll go up to the fishmonger and knock the fish right out of his paws . . . sorry . . . his hands. Never mind me, I'm a bit upset."

"Yes, you could tone things down a little," said Minou.

"And I wanted to tell you that I'm heading off again too," said the Tatter Cat. "I'm going back to being a stray. My kids are already eating from saucers. As far as I'm concerned, you can start giving them away. They don't need me anymore. Oh yeah, I've got some news for you too. Just heard it from the Deodorant Cat. The perfume factory expansion is off. The councillor refused to approve it. Tell your human."

"Thanks," said Minou.

"Because the Cat Press Agency will be continuing as normal, won't it?" the Tatter Cat asked.

"Sure, everything will continue as normal."

"And you'll be back in your box?" the Tatter Cat asked. "To sleep?"

"Of course," said Minou. "Why not?"

"Oh . . . I don't know." The Tatter Cat stared at her mistrustfully with her yellow eyes. She was looking very battered and grimy again. "You know," she said softly, "I suddenly had a feeling you were going to marry him."

"What gives you *that* idea?" Minou asked.

"It was just a feeling . . . ," the Tatter Cat said. "And I'm just warning you. If you do that, you'll have blown it completely. You'll never be able to turn back into a cat. And maybe it'll get so bad that you won't be able to talk to us anymore. You won't understand Cattish. You'll even forget the Yawl-Yowl Song."

"We'll cross that bridge when we get to it," said Minou.

Tibble leant out of the kitchen window and called, "Breakfast is ready! For cats and people!"

"Come on," said Minou. "Let's go inside."

ABOUT THE AUTHOR

ANNIE M. G. SCHMIDT (1911–1995) was regarded as the Queen of Dutch Children's Literature and her books have been an essential part of every Dutch childhood for the last fifty years. She trained as a librarian but burst onto the literary scene when the newspaper she was working for discovered her gift for children's verse. Having won numerous awards during her lifetime, including the 1989 Hans Christian Andersen Award, Schmidt is now included in the canon of Dutch history taught to all Dutch schoolchildren, alongside Spinoza, Anne Frank, and Vincent van Gogh.

DAVID COLMER has won several international awards for his translations of Dutch and Flemish novels, poetry, and children's books. He has translated much of Annie M. G. Schmidt's work.

A HISTORY OF
SLOVAKIA

Also by Stanislav J. Kirschbaum

La coopération France-Canada et la sécurité maritime *(editor)*

East European History *(editor)*

Reflections on Slovak History *(editor with Anne C. R. Roman)*

La sécurité collective au XXIe siècle *(editor)*

Slovak Politics *(editor)*

Slovaques et Tchèques. Essai sur un nouvel aperçu de leur histoire politique

A HISTORY OF SLOVAKIA

The Struggle for Survival

Stanislav J. Kirschbaum

St. Martin's Press
New York

First published in the United States of America 1995

Printed in the United States of America
Book design by Acme Art, Inc.

ISBN 0-312-10403-0

Library of Congress Cataloging-in-Publication Data

Kirschbaum, Stanislav, J.
    A history of Slovakia : the struggle for survival / Stanislav J.
Kirschbaum.
        p. cm.
    Includes bibliographical references and index.
    ISBN 0-312-10403-0
    1. Slovakia—History. I. Title.
DB2763.K57 1995   94-22501
943.7'3—dc20   CIP

To my beloved wife Agnes,
our daughters Olga, Sophia, and Alexandra,
and in memory of
Maria Kapsanova Loydl

CONTENTS

LIST OF MAPS

PREFACE

The idea for this book originated with St. Martin's Press in 1992. It looked as if a new state called Slovakia was about to appear on the map of Central Europe, and no major history was available in the English language. I felt that it was a challenge worth picking up. But it was only when Simon Winder, senior editor of the Scholarly and Reference Division, accepted my proposal that I fully realized what a daunting task I had given myself. A political scientist who ventures into the bailiwick of historians does so at his own peril. In this case, the peril is all the greater as the works I could rely upon are limited, as the reader will discover in the introduction. If I aimed to write a history of Slovakia and the Slovaks, then it was preferable that I pursue a theme, according to the precepts of my own discipline.

For the last quarter of a century my professional specialization has been Slovak politics in Czechoslovakia. I came to realize that in the twists and turns imposed by Communist politics, the Slovak people were determined to survive. Intuitively, I also concluded that the members of this small Central European nation had acquired a sense of survival that most likely had a history to it. As my research progressed, the historical evidence justified my intuition and indicated that the Slovaks had been locked in a struggle for survival.

This study traces the struggle for survival of the Slovak people since their ancestors appeared on the territory of today's Slovak Republic. The story I tell is one that shows how they have individually and collectively over the centuries developed and faced the challenges of invasion, foreign statehood, and, in the later periods of their history, also assimilation. This struggle appears first in the social and economic development of Central Europe, later in a political conflict with state authorities. The focus changes as the struggle is redefined. From chapter 5 on, it is therefore far more a political than an economic and social history. But the focus is not on the history of the states in which the Slovaks found themselves; that I leave to Hungarian, Czech, and Slovak historians. I can only hope that the perspective I offer will find an echo in their writings.

I had the good fortune to be able to do some of the research for this book at the Bundesinstitut für ostwissenschaftliche und internationale Studien in 1986–1987 in Cologne, Germany as part of another project. I wish to thank the Volkswagenwerk Stiftung for having awarded me an International Fellow-

ship from their International Fellowship Program for Advanced Soviet and East European Studies which made the research possible. I am particularly grateful to the head librarian, Stefan Mardak, and to Dr. Karin Schmid for their help during that extraordinary year in Cologne.

The writing of this book could not have taken place without the help of a number of people. My thanks go first to those who have either lent me sources or drawn my attention to them: Frantisek Lisy; Thomas Barcsay; Gerald Sabo, S.J.; Ada Böhmerova; Mark Stolarik; Jozef Hvisc; Vincent Danco, S.J.; Peter Sugar; Anton Pacek; Janos Bak; David Daniel; Marian Reisel; Roman Martonak; Stefan Fano; Milan Bucek; Jan Bobak; Jozef Markus; Nandor Dreisziger; and Igor Jurisica. Part of the manuscript was read by colleagues to whom I would like to express my appreciation and absolve of any and all errors found in the text. The responsibility is entirely mine. They are Peter Petro, Susan Mikula, Janos Bak, Anton Hykisch, Milan Melnik, and from the Historical Institute of the Slovak Academy of Sciences in Bratislava Dusan Kovac, Alexander Avenarius, Eva Kowalska, and Jan Lukacka. Two colleagues were my constant reading companions and advisors. I eagerly awaited their comments and advice on each chapter and I owe them a heartfelt debt of gratitude: Walter Beringer and Louise Hammer. They too are absolved of errors in the text. I also wish to thank most sincerely Jozef Suchy, who so kindly helped me with many a translation from Slovak to English; our regular telephone conversations often enabled me to clarify my thoughts. All translations from Slovak, German, Czech, and French to English are my own. The five maps were drawn by Carolyn King of the Cartographic Drafting Office, Department of Geography, York University to whom I extend my thanks. Finally, I would like to acknowledge the help of Jaromir Lukac and Frances Bukovec where the electronic aspect of this endeavor is concerned; they were very helpful when the C-drive on our computer at home crashed.

The writing of the chapters dealing with the nineteenth and twentieth centuries was facilitated by the use of my own material first published elsewhere. Passages were used from the following articles: "National Self-Assertion in Slovakia" in George Simmonds, ed., *Nationalism in the U.S.S.R. and Eastern Europe in the Era of Brezhnev and Kosygin* (Detroit: University of Detroit Press, 1977): 380–400; "Federalism in Slovak Communist Politics," *Canadian Slavonic Papers* 19, no. 4 (1977): 444–67; "The Cooperative Movement in Socialist Slovakia" in A. Balawyder, ed., *Cooperative Movements in Eastern Europe* (Montclair, NJ: Allanheld, Osmun & Co., Publishers, 1980): 49–75; "The Slovak Republic and the Slovaks," *Slovakia* 29 nos. 53–54 (1980–1981): 11–38; "The Slovak People's Party: The Politics of Opposition, 1918–1938" and "The Revolt of 1944" in Stanislav J. Kirschbaum, ed., *Slovak Politics*

(Cleveland: Slovak Institute, 1983): 157–187, 286–313; "The Slovak Republic, Britain, France and the Principle of Self-determination," *Slovak Studies* 23 (1983): 149–70; "Slovak Nationalism in the First Czechoslovak Republic 1918–1938," *Canadian Review of Studies in Nationalism* 16 nos. 1–2 (1989): 169–87; and "Turciansky Sväty Martin and the Formation of the Slovak Nation," *Slovak Review* 2, no. 1 (1993): 113–23.

My lifelong interest in Slovak history and politics is the result of the careful nurturing I received in my parents' home. Although I was born in Bratislava, I left with them at the age of three months and eventually emigrated to Canada, where I was raised and educated. It is they who taught me Slovak and gave me a sense for the country the Communist regime forbade me to visit. This book is in many respects the fruit of their love. Last but not least, my thanks go to my wife, Agnes, who is also my colleague at York University, and our three daughters, Olga, Sophia, and Alexandra, who always willingly gave up the family computer so I could write my book, and who watched me in amusement as I reorganized their lives, and in particular our summer holidays, when the pressure was on. I thank them for their love and understanding from the bottom of my heart.

SJK
Toronto
August 1994

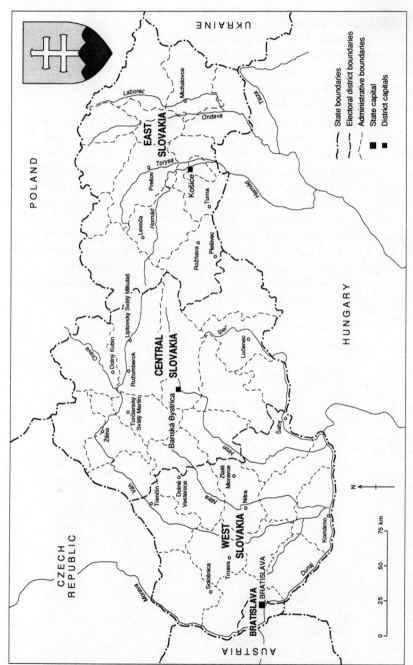

1. The Slovak Republic of 1993

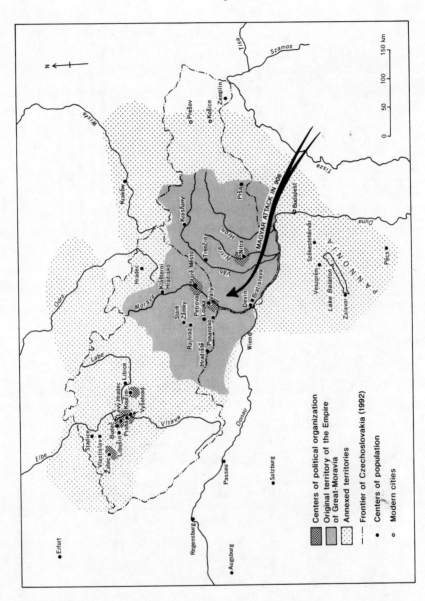

2. The Great Moravian Empire

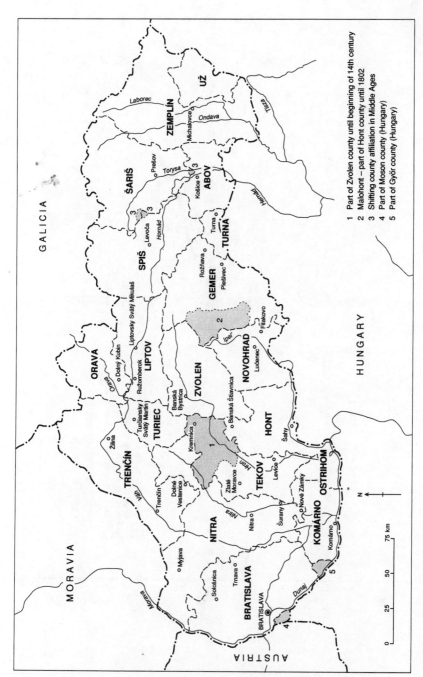

3. Slovak counties *(župy)* in Hungary

1 Part of Zvolen county until beginning of 14th century
2 Malohont — part of Hont county until 1802
3 Shifting county affiliation in Middle Ages
4 Part of Moson county (Hungary)
5 Part of Györ county (Hungary)

that the misunderstanding arose from "the manipulation of public opinion in the West concerning Slovakia and the Slovaks."[3] This manipulation was the result of two factors; first the role of misinformation in politics, which Mikus argues "has always been a component of internal and international politics"; and second a deliberate Czech policy to have "Slovakia and the Slovaks . . . not identified as such, but simply labelled as Czechs."[4] He points to many works by Czech scholars abroad, though the list is by no means exhaustive, who have pursued this policy. He traces its origins to the writings and political activities of Czechoslovakia's first president, Tomas G. Masaryk.[5]

In the face of this kind of political, but also scholarly, approach, one can well understand that there developed a particular interpretation of Slovak history in the West. However, Mikus also indicates that certain Czech scholars did not accept their colleagues' approach.[6] They are a minority, but they opened the door to the possibility of another interpretation, to a refutation of the commonly accepted theses. Indirectly, they forced Western scholars to ask what Slovak history is and what role it plays in Slovak national life.[7] This is not unimportant, for as is the case in other parts of Eastern Europe, the writing of history represents more than merely the recording of past events and people. Alexandru Zub writes: "Historiography in this area has played a prominent role in shaping both the consciousness of the people about themselves and of a certain region-wide collective consciousness."[8]

If the writing of history is important to the nations of Eastern Europe, one may well ask why Mikus refers to Czech scholars where Slovak history is concerned? Are there no Slovak historians? Could it be that Slovak history was misunderstood in the West because it is unknown? It is to these questions that we now turn.

The writing of the history of the Slovaks is not a recent phenomenon, but its impact has been limited because of domestic as well as external developments. The first works were published in the seventeenth century and were written in Latin. As a result, they reached a small audience. Unlike the Czechs, for whom Frantisek Palacky wrote a history—it was first published in German and later translated into Czech—that had a profound impact at a crucial moment in their national development in the nineteenth century, the Slovaks did not have historians of equal stature until well into the twentieth. A strong oral tradition celebrated in song and poetry heroes and happy events and deplored villains and disasters. However, little, particularly of a scholarly nature, was written.

Late in the nineteenth century, at the height of Magyarization, a handful of Slovak scholars set out to write about various aspects of their nation's past. Not surprisingly, the output was not phenomenal. The first general outlines of Slovak history were published by Anton Bielek in his *Dejepis Slovakov od*

Introduction

SLOVAK HISTORY: MISUNDERSTOOD, MISINTERPRETED, OR UNKNOWN?

The events in the autumn of 1989 in Central Europe did more than just put an end to the Cold War and bring down the Iron Curtain; the collapse of the Communist regimes meant the end of the exclusive hold of Marxism in the social sciences there. This is a welcome development for the nations of the region whose academics, researchers, and writers can once again study their societies, especially their history, openly and not along ideologically and politically dictated lines. In many instances, this means a serious revision of what has been for the last four decades the official history of those nations. And for no nation can such a perspective be more welcome than for the Slovaks.

In the last forty-five years in Slovakia, history was written under serious constraints and limitations. A similar situation also existed in the West; there were and, now to a lesser degree, still are particular conditions that affect the writing of Slovak history. However, just as in Slovakia, scholarship in the West on the Slovaks is undergoing change, not only because of the new situation, but above all because of the status it had in the past. To understand why this change is taking place, it is important to understand how, until the recent events in Eastern Europe, Western scholarship approached Slovak history. Our aim is to assess this situation and its problems rather than to offer an exhaustive examination of the literature on Slovak history in Western languages.[1]

In 1979, the Nestor of Slovak historians abroad, Joseph A. Mikus, published an essay entitled *Slovakia, a Misunderstood History*.[2] In it he argues

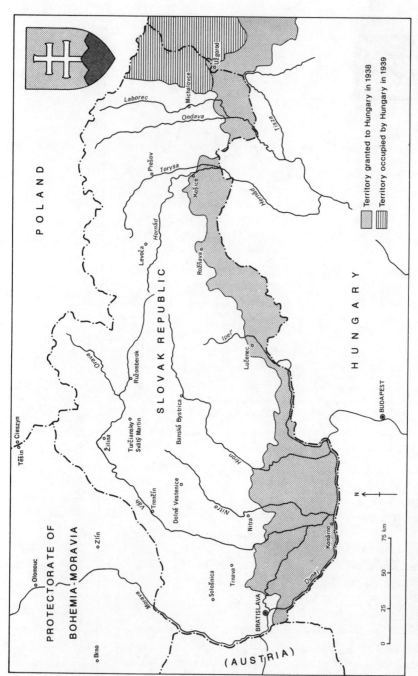

5. The Slovak Republic of 1939

Territory granted to Hungary in 1938

Territory occupied by Hungary in 1939

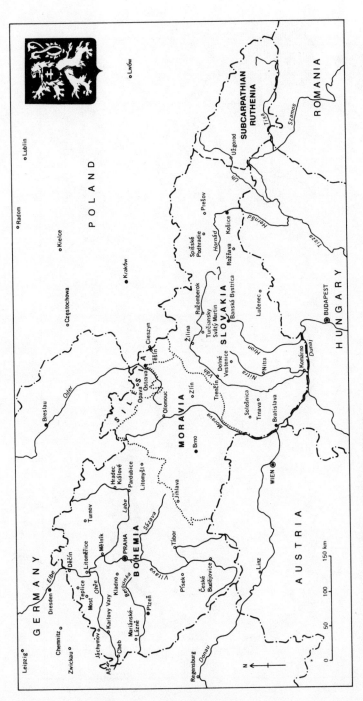

4. The First Czechoslovak Republic 1918-1938

najstarsej doby do dnesnych cias (History of the Slovaks from the Oldest Times to the Present) in 1897 and by Frantisek V. Sasinek in his *Slovaci v Uhorsku (Slovaks in Hungary)* in 1905. A year later, Thomas Capek published in the United States a small volume destined for the general public.[9] Another historian from that generation, Julius Botto, published his major work, *Slovaci. Vyvin ich narodneho povedomia (The Slovaks. The Development of their National Consciousness)* only after the Great War.[10] As a result, the first surveys by non-Slovaks published in this century, by Robert W. Seton-Watson[11] and Ernest Denis,[12] had little to rely upon. It would take a generation before the Slovaks could point to major works, researched and written by their own historians. Therefore, it would not be inaccurate to say that when the Slovaks joined the Czechs in their common state in 1918, Slovak history and national goals were basically unknown in the West. At a time when the principle of national self-determination was applied to Central Europe to break up the Habsburg, Ottoman, and Romanov empires, this Western ignorance of Slovak goals enabled the Allies to bypass the Slovaks when redrawing the map of Europe.[13]

The creation of Czecho-Slovakia had a definite but paradoxical impact on the writing of Slovak history. Unlike the situation in Hungary, where educated Slovaks had been subjected to Magyarization, the new state allowed the development of education and scholarship in Slovakia. Yet at the same time, the writing of Slovak history was not encouraged. The reasons for this will be discussed. Nevertheless, despite a number of difficulties, a generation of Slovak scholars was being trained under Jozef Skultety's leadership to research and write the history of their nation. Specific and sectoral work was done by people such as Daniel Rapant,[14] and by the end of the 1930s, two major surveys were nearing completion. Frantisek Hrusovsky's work is entitled *Slovenske dejiny (Slovak History)*[15] and Frantisek Bokes's work was published after the war as *Dejiny Slovenska a Slovakov od najstarsich cias az po pritomnost (The History of Slovakia and the Slovaks from the Earliest Times to the Present).*[16] In the aftermath of World War II, however, their work had little or no impact.[17] As far as foreign-language publications are concerned, in the twenty years of the First Republic, only one monograph appeared in English, written by Skultety and entitled *Sketches from Slovak History.*[18] It was aimed at the general public, in particular Americans of Slovak origin, and is not a scholarly work. Despite these efforts, Slovak history continued to be unknown in the West.

The Communist seizure of power in 1948 had a peculiar impact on the writing of Slovak history.[19] Slovak education and scholarship continued to develop but in order to be published, all studies had to be ideologically and politically acceptable. Many of the established scholars, such as Rapant, were seriously restricted and controlled or forbidden to pursue their work. Still, over

the years, the output of essays, articles, and books grew and was impressive, although the same cannot be said of its scholarship and scientific quality.[20] The division of Europe into two camps had the further result that very few works written by the new Slovak Marxist historians were translated into Western languages.[21] Once again, the West learned little of Slovak history from native Slovak historians.

Fortunately, Slovaks abroad were able partially to fill the void. They too, however, suffered the consequences of the ideological division of Europe. They were denied access to Slovak archives and libraries and became embroiled in a major ideological battle. Nevertheless, this postwar generation of Slovak emigres managed to do remarkable work, not just as scholars, but also as organizers of scholarly conferences and editors of journals. They launched three scientific journals, *Slowakei* for articles in German, *Slovakia* for the English-speaking public, and *Slovak Studies* with articles in Slovak as well as in Western European languages. Last but not least, thanks to the support of the Slovak World Congress, which many of them helped found in 1970, they organized conferences and published the proceedings.[22] Among the publications worthy of note are the surveys of modern Slovak history published by Joseph M. Kirschbaum and Mikus,[23] who have also written extensively on other aspects of Slovak history and culture,[24] a study of the first Slovak Republic's foreign policy by Milan S. Durica,[25] and aspects of Communist politics by Frantisek Vnuk, written in Slovak.[26] Their work was complemented by the publication of additional surveys by non-Slovak scholars such as Gilbert Oddo[27] and Kurt Glaser[28] and by studies on specific topics such as the creation of the first Slovak Republic by Jörg K. Hoensch[29] or the political program of Jozef Tiso by Lisa Guarda Nardini.[30] A particularly noteworthy contribution is the history of the Slovaks from the Middle Ages to 1918 by Ludwig von Gogolak.[31]

Over time, a younger generation, the sons and daughters of the postwar emigres, began to show interest in Slovak history and politics. In 1977, they created the Slovak Studies Association in the United States and took over the publication of *Slovakia. Slovak Studies,* the journal published in Rome, Italy, since 1961, also experienced a changing of the guard. Whereas *Slovakia* is an English-language publication, *Slovak Studies* remains multilingual. As for *Slowakei,* it merged in 1991 with the Slovak scholarly publication *Slavica slovaca* to become the biannual *Slovak Review,* published in Bratislava. Like *Slovak Studies,* it is multilingual with short résumés in Slovak. In 1984, a group of younger scholars, continuing a series of conferences initiated and sponsored by the Slovak World Congress, met in New York to discuss Slovak history. Their deliberations resulted in the publication of the monograph *Reflections on Slovak History,*[32] the first English overview since Skultety's 1930 book. Many from this

generation have published scholarly papers and some enjoyed access to Slovak archives in Prague, Bratislava, and Martin during the Communist period.[33]

Alongside these scholarly efforts in the West, various Slovak associations, fraternal or otherwise, particularly in the United States, have published annual calendars or almanacs containing essays on Slovak history and the Slovaks. The Slovak press in North America also has opened its pages both in Slovak and English to articles and reviews generally found in scholarly journals.

This general overview would seem to suggest that Slovak history has its scholars and writers, especially since the end of World War II. In addition, even if little of Slovak Marxist scholarship was translated into Western languages, scholars in the West used, generally judiciously, the research and publications of their colleagues in Slovakia. A reading of this literature indicates that even with many interpretations, which were to be expected, the general lines of Slovak history are known: The Slovak people have struggled successfully to survive despite all of the challenges they have faced as a result of living at the crossroads of Central Europe. In the process, they have sought to determine their own destiny and, what is more significant, also have made a contribution to European civilization. To suggest, as the century ends, that Slovak history is unknown might be considered something of an exaggeration. Unfortunately, however, it is not an exaggeration.

If Slovak history still remains unknown in the West, even with the output just outlined above, is it because, rather than being misunderstood, it has been misinterpreted? This is a delicate question, yet it must be asked. In 1968, Stanley Z. Pech wrote:

> Although Western specialists in Eastern European history have usually regarded it as their task to make the West familiar with the entire ethnic panorama of the polyglot region, they have in practice often been selective in the favours they bestowed on each nation. They have incorporated in their work, in modified form, the outlook and the prejudices of the nations which they "adopted." To give the most conspicuous examples, they viewed Slovak history through Czech eyes and Ukrainian history through Polish (or Russian) eyes. In so doing, they have in fact created a second-class status for certain nations. The history of the Slovaks in the West has usually been presented from the point of view of "Czechoslovakism" and has appeared as hardly more than a postscript to Czech history.[34]

The origins of this "adoption" go back to the creation of the Czecho-Slovak Republic in 1918. On the morrow of a war as devastating as the Great War, the principle of the self-determination of nations was accepted at the Peace

of Versailles as the solution that responded to the needs of most Central European nations. That it was a flawed solution was clearly indicated by Germany's challenge within two decades, yet, it still was deemed adequate. Indeed, in 1945, when the German challenge was beaten back again, the Versailles solution was maintained except for some territorial adjustments.

The states that had arisen out of the ashes of the three defeated empires in 1918 had faced the difficult task of consolidation. For two states, Czecho-Slovakia and the Kingdom of the Serbs, Croats and Slovenes, later to become Yugoslavia, there was also the additional problem of its multinational composition. The solution of the Czech elite was to put into effect, despite the problems and contradictions, the principle of self-determination rather than to recognize and establish a balance between the constituent nations of the new state. The result was the creation of a "Czechoslovak" nation living in an unhyphenated Czechoslovak Republic. Inevitably this had a consequence on the writing of Slovak history.

The application in Central Europe of the principle of self-determination brought about a fusion of state and nation. In Czechoslovakia, this meant that the history of the new state was the history of the majority nation. Only those elements that strengthened the new state's history—Czechoslovak history—were incorporated from the history of the other nations, in this case the Slovaks. Thus, a state created in 1918 suddenly had a history going back to the beginning of time, as Jaroslav Prokes points out in the first Western-language monograph on the subject, which he called not surprisingly *Histoire tchécoslovaque*.[35] Even Seton-Watson became partial to this approach.[36] Slovak history was subordinated to Czechoslovak history. Was Slovak history being reinterpreted or misinterpreted?

This is not the place to outline the works that present Czechoslovak history. They are numerous, and, as Mikus points out, many authors are also of Czech background. What must be pointed out is the consequence they have had on the writing and acceptance of Slovak history.[37] Many works published in the interwar years were not just reinterpreting but clearly misinterpreting history. By denying the existence of a Slovak nation, they were also denying Slovak history. The fact that this ran against the historical evidence and record seems to have bothered too few historians, in Czechoslovakia and abroad.[38] Since Czechoslovakia was recognized as the only democracy in Central Europe in the interwar years, and was perceived as the country that successfully applied the principles of the Peace of Versailles, Czechoslovak history, as Pech points out, gained predominance in Western historiography. Slovak history, which was a challenge to the state and its ideology, met with vigorous opposition in Czechoslovakia and was ignored or belittled abroad. Only a Czechoslovak approach to Slovak history was deemed acceptable.

The events that led to the breakup of the First Republic, Slovak independence in 1939, World War II, the re-creation of Czechoslovakia in 1945, and the Communist takeover in 1948, all of which are examined in this book, modified only marginally the Western perception of Slovak history. Indeed, the Slovak involvement in some of these events, whether for or against, strengthened the thesis in favor of a Czechoslovak history, to which the continued existence of the state also gave some justification. On the other hand, these events also produced the acknowledgment of a Slovak component to Czechoslovak history.[39] With the recognition of the existence of a Slovak nation by the Prague government in 1945, scholars accepting the Czechoslovak approach gave new interpretations and direction to the history and politics of the state and of both nations: Czechoslovak history and politics were no longer the history and politics of the Czechoslovaks, but that of two peoples living and destined to live in a state whose integrity and policies had to be defended, the events of 1938 to 1945 notwithstanding. This postwar approach was strengthened by a new attitude appearing in both Western and Marxist writings that may be described as triumphalist. For example, the Slovak involvement in the events of 1938 to 1945 was presented as an aberration[40] or as an unfortunate aspect of the history of Czechoslovakia.[41] Slovak interpretations that did not condemn outright these events were either ignored or disparaged; those that did were deemed authoritative.[42]

Marxist scholars, especially in the 1950s, brought a proletarian twist to the Czechoslovak approach, often sinking to new depths in ideological and political partisanship and amnesia. To understand how bad this situation became and especially its consequences, suffice it to quote a short passage from a samizdat letter written by Bishop (now Cardinal) Jan Ch. Korec that circulated in Slovakia in April 1989: "Rare are the small nations which today can maim and defame their own history and in this way destroy the national consciousness in future generations as we know how to do in Slovakia."[43] Nevertheless, despite official ideological pressure, works appeared by the late 1960s that showed serious scholarship and also greater detachment.[44] Slovak scholars published a multiauthored history[45] and also concentrated on many specific Slovak subjects. The exception was the history of the state and their own regime; for such works guidelines were set by Communist Party ideologues: Czechoslovakism remained de rigueur.[46] It was up to Western scholars to offer a critical evaluation. The adherents of the Czechoslovak approach focused on the attempts of the regime to modernize the state and considered the Slovak question as nothing more than one of political culture and minority management.[47]

It is not easy to avoid the conclusion that the Czechoslovak approach to Slovak history represents a misinterpretation rather than a reinterpretation of

Slovak history. Most of its adherents, whether Western or Marxist, have too often been guilty of facile explanations or else of the virtual dismissal of events and interpretations that put in doubt their own approach. By the sheer volume of their publications, they gained acceptance in the postwar period. This acceptance is also the result of the continued existence of Czechoslovakia, a state that was sanctioned by international rather than internal politics, a fact that further helped the "adoption" to which Pech refers. The challenges to the Czechoslovak approach to Slovak history were few.[48] On balance, it would not be incorrect to suggest that as a result of the influence of the Czechoslovak approach, Slovak history remained unknown in the West.

The seventy-four years between the creation and the dissolution of the Czechoslovak Republic were a short period in the history of both nations. The Slovaks have a past that goes back centuries; quite a few themes beg investigation. Western scholarship has some catching up to do in areas where Marxist scholars were at work: social and economic history, education, art and architecture, and emigration. On the other hand, Western scholars can help with those topics that have been the object of one-sided interpretations in Marxist and Western scholarship, among others, the first Slovak Republic, the 1944 uprising, the Slovak involvement in the tragedy of Europe's Jews, the political system of the First Czechoslovak Republic, and the socialist system.[49]

These seventy-four years were also the longest period of direct relations between Czechs and Slovaks, which, with the exception of the war years, were conducted according to the politics and constitutional rules of their common state. Until 1993, minority management was the favored approach for examining these relations; Carol Skalnik Leff's study of Czech-Slovak relations is the most sophisticated analysis from this perspective.[50] The focus will now have to be on the reasons for the state's failure to maintain itself and in particular on the roots of its dissolution,[51] which spelled the end of the legitimacy of the Czechoslovak approach to Slovak history.

There are no longer any valid reasons for Slovak history to be misunderstood, misinterpreted, or unknown in the West. All that is required is a change of focus in Western scholarship. The task has been rendered easier by the publication, since the fall of communism, of three surveys of Slovak history in Slovakia;[52] among them, the volume by Anton Spiesz, entitled *Dejiny Slovenska: na ceste k sebauvedomeniu (History of Slovakia: On the Road to Self-Consciousness)*, stands out as the first survey in the post-Communist era by a Slovak historian.[53] In the West, there are two new publications, one by Renée Perréal and Joseph A. Mikus which emphasizes cultural history,[54] and another by Josef Spetko which looks at Slovak-German relations through the centuries.[55] In addition, archives are now open and accessible, and a body of

scholarship on various topics offers opportunities for research. What is lacking is a history of Slovakia for non-Slovak readers. In the pages that follow, we offer such an account, based primarily, but not exclusively, on the work of Slovak scholarship.

The term *Slovakia,* as a geographical and political concept, is relatively recent; it appeared for the first time in the nineteenth century, in a petition to the Habsburg emperor in 1849. It has had greater currency in the twentieth century. Yet, for the Slovaks, the land on the northern shore of the Danube and in the Tatras has always been their home, even when the political and geographical boundaries were not always clear. Some may object therefore that there is no history of Slovakia as such. This argument would have validity if there were no history of the Slovak nation. As there is one, simply put, the history of the Slovak nation is the history of Slovakia. Furthermore, the Republic of Slovakia, which appeared on the map of Europe on 1 January 1993, covers the territory that the Slovaks have always inhabited.

One of the consequences of the demise of communism was the creation of a number of new states in Europe. Slovakia is by no means the smallest among them. In area and population, it is greater than Albania, Denmark, Estonia, Iceland, Liechtenstein, Lithuania, Luxembourg, Malta, Moldavia, Monaco, San Marino, and Slovenia; in area alone, it is larger than Belgium, the Netherlands, and Switzerland; and in population, bigger than Croatia, Finland, Ireland, and Norway. Of Europe's thirty-nine states, it ranks twenty-sixth in area and population combined and twenty-second in population alone.[56] Slovakia may not have always been on the map of Europe; the Slovaks, on the other hand, have always been in Europe and involved in its history and civilization.

The history of the Slovaks is one of survival, self-determination, and contribution. The first two themes are often treated separately because each has its own imperatives and is also dependent on different internal as well as external factors. This applies to every national history in Central Europe. However, it is our contention that survival is the salient aspect of the Slovaks' history and self-determination is simply an expression of it. For this reason, survival and self-determination are examined and treated together. Otherwise, it becomes difficult to explain how a nation, which did not have an opportunity to create its own state for most of its history, resisted the efforts to become the object of other national agendas and political ambitions.[57] Yet it also can be said that the Slovaks sought in this process to determine their own destiny regardless of the political configuration in which they found themselves. In the modern era, this is also what their history is about, especially where challenges to state authority are concerned.

In a comparison with other nations, particularly those whose national state was involved in the course of European history and may even have shaped it, some may be tempted to think that the Slovak struggle to survive is not deserving of attention because it is not very heroic. Yet there is heroism here, the type that is identified with the struggle for the existence of individuals, where the refusal to be assimilated or beaten is the supreme victory. As Archbishop Giovanni Cappa, Vatican ambassador to Slovakia, stated on the morrow of Slovakia's independence, the Slovaks are

> tried and tested, but [have] never [been] broken over long centuries of adversity; humble and simple people, clever, bound to their land and traditions, as expressed in their poetry, their music, and the colors of a rich folklore; a people as hard and tenacious as their Tatra mountains, as serene and optimistic as the green expanse of their valleys and forests; a people, above all, deeply attached to the values of their European civilization: honesty, hard work, family and religious faith, as witnessed by so many popular shrines and stupendous churches.[58]

There is more. In their struggle to survive, the Slovaks also have made a modest contribution to European political history and a major one to European civilization. What makes Slovak history interesting and worth knowing, therefore, is more than simply learning the reasons and the circumstances that allowed this nation to survive and to refuse to become a mere footnote in European history. It is learning about the role and position of a small nation in European history and civilization; this is the story that we tell in the chapters that follow.

1

The Land and
Its People

GEOGRAPHY AND POPULATION

Slovakia covers an area of 49,036 square kilometers (18,922 square miles) in the heart of Central Europe. Its most remarkable physical attributes are its mountains, which make up the northern part of the Great Carpathian Bow. They cover some 30 percent of the territory and are divided into three parallel ranges, the High Tatras, the Low Tatras, and the Slovak Ore Mountains (Slovenske Rudohorie). A smaller range in the West, the Small or White Carpathians, forms the border with Moravia, continuing into Austria where they join the Alpine system. The tree line is found at 1,500 meters (4,875 feet). The highest peak, Gerlachovsky stit, at 2,655 meters (8,710 feet), is part of the High Tatras, a small area of rugged but breathtaking mountain peaks with lakes that were formed during the Ice Age. They form part of the border with Poland. The Low Tatras boast more flattened summits between 1,800 and 2,000 meters (5,900 and 6,500 feet). Finally, the Slovak Ore Mountains, stretching from Zvolen in Central Slovakia to Kosice in the east for some 145 kilometers (90 miles), are an important source of silver as well as high-grade iron ore and nonferrous metals such as copper, magnesium, lead, and zinc.

The mountains have given rise over the centuries to the development of forestry and mining industries while their slopes, peaks, lakes, and valleys make up singularly magnificent landscapes for the modern hunter, the nature lover,

and the tourist. More than two-fifths of Slovakia is forested. There are five national parks in Slovakia's mountains: Low Tatras, Mala Fatra, Slovensky Raj, Pieniny, and Slovensky Kras. The Slovensky Raj National Park boasts an area called "Antarctica" for its wintery scenery, narrow passages, and cliffs, while the Slovensky Kras National Park is full of caves and chasms replete with stalactites and stalagmites, some covered with ice, others with calcium-covered deposits. The mountain ranges are of the metamorphic and volcanic type, offering narrow passages and mountain torrents, bubble and hot springs of curative and mineral waters, and underground streams and waterfalls. In strategic areas, usually on mounds or rises, at the entrance of valleys, in mountain passes, or overlooking expansive plains, stone fortresses and castles, some in ruins, as well as chapels, roadside crosses, and shrines mark the human contribution to this magnificent temperate landscape, to which each of the four seasons gives its special emblem. In Slovak folklore and literature, the mountains, valleys, and forests are the subject of innumerable songs and poems, praising heroes and heroic deeds and lamenting natural disasters and human tragedies.

Flora and fauna abound and not just in the five national parks. The botanical wealth corresponds to the various microclimatic conditions in all stages of vegetation while some 25,000 species of animals roam the parks and the countryside. In addition to Tatra chamois and Tatra marmot, both unique to the country, there are bears, boars, deer, lynxes, martens, and golden eagles, falcons, and the biggest European bird, the bustard. The European bison is one of the protected species found in the Topolcianska Velka Zvernica; beavers also have begun to make an appearance as have elks, straying from the north. Well-preserved and groomed hunting areas along with clear rivers and streams offer sportsmen exceptional opportunities not found anywhere in Europe.

The Danube is Slovakia's major waterway. It flows through Bratislava, the capital city, and forms part of the border with Austria and, for 175 kilometers (109 miles), with Hungary. After passing through Bratislava, it breaks into two channels, the Danube proper, flowing southeasterly, and the Little Danube, which rejoins the Danube farther east at the river Vah. At each end of the country is a river; the Morava in the west acts as a border with Moravia, and the Uh in the east serves the same purpose with Sub-Carpathian Ruthenia. Another major river that constitutes part of the border with Hungary is the Tisza in the southeast. Between these rivers are the Vah, Nitra, Hron, Ipel, and Orava rivers, which flow in a southwestern arc into the Danube, and the Slana, Bodrog, Laborec, and Hornad rivers, which flow into the Tisza in a southeastern arc. Another river, the Poprad, drains northward. The Vah, Slana, Orava, and Hornad, along with the Danube at Gabcikovo, are also sources of hydroelectric power.

Lowlands, where agriculture predominates, make up part of the Greater Danubian Plain in the southwest, where there are also brine swamps, moors, and forests as well as prairies and alpine meadows, particularly in the northern part of the plain. Lowlands are found again in the southeast, at the other end of the country. Slovakia's two largest cities lie in the lowlands: Bratislava in the southwest and Kosice at the center of the lowland plain in the southeastern part of Slovakia. Only about one-third of Slovakia is cultivated, producing wheat, rye, barley, corn (maize), sugar beets, and vegetables. Cattle and hogs are the primary livestock. Fruit trees and orchards are found in the river valleys, in particular the Vah, and vineyards on the slopes of the Small Carpathians produce some excellent wines.

The rivers and mountains of Slovakia combine to divide the country into a number of geographical compartments of different dimensions and shapes. Of significance for population settlements are the Vah, Orava, and Hron valleys; the Bratislava, Liptov, and Kosice basins, the Presov plain; and the Nove Zamky depression. While mountains have acted as ramparts against the invaders of yesteryear, the valleys enabled penetration of foot and mounted armies.

The majority of today's inhabitants of Slovakia are called Slovaks and speak Slovak, a Slavic language that belongs to the Indo-European language family. According to the latest census, they account for 85.63 percent of a total population of 5,287,080 inhabitants. There are also national minorities, the largest of which is the Magyar, making up 10.76 percent of the population. The remaining 5.64 percent of Slovakia's inhabitants are divided among Romanis (1.53 percent), Czechs (1.01 percent), Ruthenians (0.32 percent), Ukrainians (0.26 percent), Germans (0.11 percent), Moravians (0.07 percent), Poles (0.06 percent) and others (0.25 percent).[1] Except for the Magyars, the Romanis, and the Germans, the rest of Slovakia's inhabitants—the Slovaks together with the other minorities—are members of the Slavic group of European nations.[2]

Slovakia's population is relatively well distributed across the country. The biggest city is the capital Bratislava with 450,000 inhabitants. In Eastern Slovakia, the major cities are Kosice (population 237,000) and Presov (population 90,000); in Central Slovakia they are Banska Bystrica (population 86,000) and Zilina (population 85,000); and in Western Slovakia they are Nitra (population 91,000) and Trnava (population 72,000). For electoral purposes the country is divided into four regions, each with a regional center: Western Slovakia with Bratislava; Central Slovakia with Banska Bystrica; Eastern Slovakia with Kosice; Bratislava as the capital city is the fourth region. Administratively, Slovakia is divided into thirty-seven districts each with a designated district capital; these districts act as the middle level between government and municipal authorities, with the exception of Bratislava and Kosice. (See Map 1.)

PRE-HISTORY

The original homeland of the Slavic people is not known with certainty,[3] given the few references on the Slavs that are found in the writings of historians from antiquity. They were first noticed before our era by the Greek Herodotus (484–425 B.C.). Pliny the Elder (A.D. 23–79) and Tacitus (A.D. 55–120) were the first Romans to refer to them, calling them Wends *(Venedi, Veneti,* or *Venedae),*[4] and they appeared in the writings of the Roman historians Velleius Paterculus, Cassius Dio, and Ammianus Marcellinus. In the second century A.D., Claudius Ptolemy (A.D.?–148) indicated on his map that the Slavs inhabited the Carpathian Mountains. Ptolemy, an Egyptian who wrote in Greek, also called them Wends. These references are too sparse and insufficient to determine their exact location and above all their activities and role in Europe before the sixth century. Nevertheless, it is generally thought that the ancestors of present-day Slovaks settled and established permanent residence on the territory that is known today as Slovakia between the sixth and eighth centuries after migrating from their original homeland. This territory, however, was inhabited long before they settled it.

The first traces of human presence in today's Slovakia go back to the Paleolithic age (ca. 200,000 B.C.); archaeological research indicates that there was a habitation near Nove Mesto nad Vahom and in the museum in Poprad there is a travertine molding of a skull of a Neanderthal man from Ganovce. Settlements appeared during the Middle Paleolithic period (200,000–35,000 B.C.) while the first cultural artifacts were created during the Upper Paleolithic age (35,000–8,000 B.C.). The climatic conditions and the area seemed propitious for organized human activity, in fact to such an extent that, as John Wymer writes: "The Upper Palaeolithic peoples in western Europe, from the Atlantic coast to the Ukraine, between about 33,000 and 9,000 B.C., had achieved the most efficient and organized communities known in the world at that time."[5] The Slovak National Museum in Bratislava Castle contains a magnificent little artifact from this period—the Venus of Moravany—"which belongs to the best product of European Upper Paleolithic art, and according to radio carbon dating (C14), is 22,800 years old."[6]

Farming was introduced in Europe in the Mesolithic period (8,000–6,000 B.C.), but it is during the Neolithic age (6,000–2,900 B.C.) that human economic activity intensified when agriculture replaced gathering and hunting as primary occupations.[7] There is ample evidence that such a development also occurred in Slovakia. According to Alasdair Whittle: "In the north Carpathian basin (northern Hungary and Slovakia) agricultural settlement begins with the Linear pottery culture in the mid fifth millennium bc [*sic*], classically seen as the result of

colonization from the northern Balkans but possibly the result of indigenous transformation."[8] Material cultures such as the Linear pottery one not only made their appearance, but succeeded one another as prehistoric people refined tools and increased activities; "Neolithic man proceeded in the development of implements. He not only knew how to split and form instruments, but also to sharpen and drill them to such a degree that they suited perfectly his working environment."[9] In Slovakia, the archaeological evidence indicates the presence of many European material cultures that followed one another. Some of the cultures found include the Lengyel, Baden, Polgar, Jevisovice cultures, and some unique to the area, as defined by modern Slovak historians: Madarovska, Mosonska, Uneticka, Severopanonska,[10] Stara Dala-Hurbanova, Hatvantska, and Cacianska.[11] One example of the archaeological evidence found in Slovakia is a burnt-burial grave from the Baden culture in Vcelince.

These developments had an impact on the activities and the evolution of prehistoric people. As they advanced from the Neolithic to the Bronze Age (1900–700 B.C.), they domesticated many animals and in particular tamed the horse in order to use it as a mode of transport and a beast of burden. At this time, too, particularly in the area of the Middle Danube, people built more permanent settlements, like the one in Spissky Stvrtok, where archaeologists found circular bastions, walls, and houses made of stone. In addition, they left evidence of burgeoning commercial as well as cultural activities. As T. G. E. Powell writes:

> In all this region vigorous Bronze Age cultures came into existence, but their distribution is seemingly selective to areas of industry and trade. Information is somewhat constrained by the nature of archeological research so far conducted in this great region, but large, and long surviving, Bronze Age communities were established at many places along the Middle Danube, including the foothills of the Slovakian mountains, as well as in Transylvania and the drainage area of the Tizsa tributaries. . . . There are three points of perhaps special significance to be borne in mind about the Middle Danubian populations in their full Bronze Age. The people were settled village dwellers with an implicit agricultural food supply, their burial rite was predominantly that of urn cremation contributing to very large flat cemeteries, and their metal industry was particularly open to Mediterranean influences so that new types of weapons and tools had been most easily absorbed therefrom.[12]

Finally, as prehistoric people entered the Iron Age (700–300 B.C.), their social organization became more defined with indications of the development of a military democratic system. Their activities also began to be recorded.

CELTS, GERMAN TRIBES, AND ROMANS

There is no written history about the peoples in the area until the Celts arrived. They made their first appearance on the territory of today's Slovakia in 500 B.C., although they did not settle until the latter half of the second century B.C. They came from eastern France, the Alps, and Central Germany. Arriving at the time of the late Hallstatt culture, they brought, as a result of commerce with the Etruscans and the Greeks, the artistically rich La Tène culture into the Danubian area, including today's Slovakia. They were the first to mint coins in this area and they built military settlements, better known in Latin as *oppida,* not just for protection, but also for economic and cultural activity. The settlement in Bratislava, which was destroyed some time before the first half of the first century B.C. by Dacian attackers, "was a separate political center which was supported by the surrounding hinterland, as the discoveries in the entire Bratislava area point out."[13] The indications that coins were minted in Bratislava and that wine was produced in the region suggest that this *oppidum* was a dominant center. The Celts left behind a great deal of archaeological evidence that give us many clues as to their style of life and social organization. In the words of Anton Spiesz: "We know about the Celts who inhabited the territory of today's Slovakia during the last centuries before Christ that they lived not too far from one another in small organized settlements and courtyards where they developed precise craft production."[14]

As the pre-Christian era came to a close, the Celts, in particular the Boii tribes that had settled on Slovak territory, were challenged and chased away by German tribes from the north and Roman legions from the south. As our era unfolded, Slovak territory, particularly in the southwest, became the battleground between the German tribes known as Marcomanni and Quadi and the Romans. In A.D. 6 the Romans attacked the Quadi kingdom of Marobud but did not defeat it until around A.D. 19. Part of the reason why the Romans had difficulty in pacifying the German tribes was due to the fact that Slovakia was divided into four parts, thereby presenting dangers on many fronts: In the southwest were the German settlements of the Quadi and Marcomanni; the Romans established themselves along the Danube in the south as part of the *Limes Romanus,* a series of fortified towers and settlements that defend the empire from barbarian attacks; native inhabitants lived in the north and center, and the east was peopled by surviving Celtic-Dacian populations "assimilated during the Roman period, at first by a German (Vandal) wave, and, as it ended, probably infiltrated by Slavic peoples."[15]

Frequent incursions from Northern Europe forced the Romans to make peace with the Quadi. In A.D. 21 they supported Vannius, a Quadi king who established the "Regnum Vannianum," which lasted until A.D. 50. It is possible that Bratislava was the center of his kingdom, especially as the Romans did not

establish themselves there—the two main Roman centers in the area were Vindobona and Carnuntum. However, after Vannius's death, the Romans and the German tribes again fought wars off and on. Under Emperor Trajan (A.D. 98–117), the Roman province of Dacia was formed to protect the empire from the Danubian German tribes. But the Marcomanni were stopped when they sought to expand into the Roman province of Pannonia during the reign of Emperor Marcus Aurelius (A.D. 161–180), provoking the Marcomanni wars of 166 to 172 and 177 to 180. These wars happened on Slovak territory and form one of the few, but nonetheless interesting, links between Roman civilization and Slovakia:

> It is during this campaign that he [Marcus Aurelius] wrote his philosophical *Meditations* and on the sculptured column in Rome [in his honor] one can see etched the miraculous rain which saved his troops on our territory and which, according to tradition, was made possible by the prayers of the Christians fighting in his legions. In A.D. 179, Roman units reached as far as the contemporary city of Trencin (Laugaricio) where they carved on a rock a significant inscription about their presence there.[16]

During the first four centuries of our era, cultural as well as military clashes arose between the more developed Roman civilization and the more primitive world of the Quadi and Marcomanni and "Roman elements which existed previously only on imported objects began to fuse in Slovakia with domestic patterns."[17] The consequences of this interaction were not without significance: "This period left behind many beautiful artifacts and thoroughly prepared the country to become the scene of the new human activity which would shortly also involve our undisputed predecessors—the Slavs."[18] However, these new developments took place only when Roman imperial power started to wane, allowing new peoples to migrate into the area.

The migrations of nations began in the third quarter of the fourth and continued well into the first half of the sixth century. During the reign of Attila the Hun (A.D. 435–453), Central Europe experienced the greatest wave, which, for the better part of a century, brought various peoples and tribes into the area. The Slavs, coming from the east, made their definitive appearance roughly around A.D. 500. Still, the Goth historian Jordanes noted their presence in Hungary as early as Attila's reign. They were the last in this series of migrations of peoples, and, according to Francis Dvornik, these Slavs represented a second wave in the Slavic migrations.[19]

If the Huns reached Central Europe during their invasions of Europe in the fourth and fifth centuries, they disappeared with Attila's death, giving way

to the Gepids and the Langobardii (also called Lombards), who evicted the Quadi and the Marcomanni. Their stay was short-lived, for they too were chased away by another nomadic people, the Avars. The arrival of the latter marked a turning point in the history of the area: "The flight of the Langobardii from Pannonia into Italy in the face of the Avar danger in 568 marks the end of the previous colonization of southwest Slovakia by German tribes."[20] Only during the Middle Ages would German colonization resume on Slovak territory.

SLAVS AND AVARS

It is important to note that Slovakia had not been an area of permanent settlement prior to the fifth century. Only at the end of the migration of nations did the Slavs, of all the peoples who passed through or chased others away, settle in the area. In addition, "the most recent research clearly indicates that the Slavic colonization of Slovakia was profound and that Slavic tribes, already toward the end of the fifth and the beginning of the sixth centuries, that is to say long before the arrival of the Avars, had occupied a great part of Slovakia where they established a solid base for the later independent development of the western Slavic tribes."[21] However, three more centuries would pass before they organized themselves and created their own political entity. First they had to contend with the nomadic Avars who appeared in Central Europe shortly after them and created a kingdom under the leadership of Khagan (King of kings) Bajan.

Not much is known about the Avars. They were "warring nomads and cattle herdsmen, their state organization had neither a common culture, nor a common language, and it sustained itself only through crude force."[22] It would seem that they were also drinkers of wine, in fact to such an extent that "their unquenchable thirst was the main cause of their [eventual] downfall."[23] On the other hand, they seemed to have little difficulty in subjugating the Slavic tribes. Byzantine historians tell us that these Slavs were relatively primitive, that they were not particularly accomplished in warfare, that they did not have a strong central authority to rule over them, and that their social organization was patriarchal. Nevertheless, under the Avars they acquired some form of tribal autonomy. It is perhaps because of Avar power, rather than despite it, that the Slavs also were able to enjoy their first experience of organized political power and a state structure, the Kingdom of Samo, whose history was recorded in the Chronicle of Fredegar, author unknown.[24]

Samo was a Frankish merchant who was involved in trade and other commercial activities between Byzantium and the Kingdom of the Franks. In

A.D. 623, in order to defend himself and other traders against Avar attacks, he organized the Slavic tribes around the western part of the territory of Slovakia, but also parts of Moravia and Lower Austria, and ruled over them for thirty years until his death in A.D. 658. His success in establishing a kingdom may also have been due to the fact that the Slavic tribes sought at this time to loosen the grip of the Avars, who had just been defeated by Byzantium on their southeast borders. His kingdom is thus considered to have been an alliance of clan chieftains *(Fürstenbund)* and certainly a defense federation of the Slavic tribes.

Paradoxically, it was against the Franks, rather than the Avars, that Samo had to defend his kingdom. In A.D. 631 and 632, King Dagobert (600–638) made two unsuccessful attempts at conquest.[25] This was the only major threat to a state that we can assume by inference from the Chronicle of Fredegar, Samo ruled quite successfully. Inexplicably, it disappeared with his death. This mystery is all the more puzzling when one considers how favorably the Chronicle of Fredegar speaks of the Kingdom of Samo:

> a certain Frank named Samo, from the district of Soignies, joined with other merchants in order to go and do business with those Slavs who are known as Wends. The Slavs had already started to rise against the Avars (called Huns) and against their ruler, the Khagan. . . . When they took the field against the Huns, Samo, . . . , went with them and his bravery won their admiration: an astonishing number of Huns were put to the sword by the Wends. Recognizing his parts [*cernentes utilitatem*—usefulness?], the Wends made Samo their king; and he ruled them well for thirty-five years. Several times they fought under his leadership against the Huns and his prudence and courage always brought the Wends victory. Samo had twelve Wendish wives who bore him twenty-two sons and fifteen daughters.[26]

Samo is the first in a series of individuals in Slovak history whose contribution is quite singular. The fact that none of his sons was able to take over from him in ruling the Slavs suggests that his reign was very much a tribute to his own talents as warlord and political leader. It is also possible that after his death the Slavic tribes no longer felt the need to be united under strong leadership and that new conditions prevailed. Clearly, the Avars did not threaten their survival anymore and new political arrangements were countenanced and arrived at, which probably gave the Slavs some form of autonomy. Indeed, after Samo's death, Avar power was reestablished for another century and a half. The consequences were not without some benefits. There are indications that at this time the Slavs abandoned their tribal principality organization and underwent

economic, especially agricultural, and demographic development. But this is all conjecture:

> Unfortunately, we do not have written sources that tell us more about Samo's kingdom and the developments [in the area] after its disappearance; in fact there are no sources for the [subsequent] decades. Just as we do not have any news about the Slavs, there are also none as far as the Avars are concerned. We meet them again only at the end of the eighth century when Emperor Charlemagne, having destroyed Bavarian independence, sought to reach the territory of the Slavs and the Avars.[27]

In A.D. 792 the Avars were attacked by the Franks. They sued for peace in 796 after having been defeated first by Charlemagne's son Charles (772–811) during a three year campaign and then by another son, Pepin (773–810) a year later. As King of the Franks, Charlemagne (742–814) let the Avars settle in an area that extends in today's Austria from the Vienna Woods to the Hungarian border. Avar power was thus finally broken and gave way to Frankish influence, with which the Slavs would have to reckon for a little more than a century.

With the disappearance of the Avars, what might be termed the prehistory of the Slovaks comes to an end. The available historical record does not permit us to draw any other conclusion: "For the period prior to the ninth century, we have on the one hand only archeological evidence from a time before the ages and before history and on the other a few generally broadly formulated reports by writers from Antiquity."[28] Perhaps equally important in explaining this lack of knowledge is the fact that those Slavs who were the last to settle in the northern part of the Great Danubian Plain and in the valleys and mountains of Slovakia had not had the time, or perhaps the opportunity, to establish a historical tradition that could be later considered national. At this point, it still is too early in Central European history to consider any sort of national differentiation. As Dvornik writes:

> All these Slavic tribes which had established themselves in the whole of the territory stretching from the Alps to the Adriatic and to the Dobrudja on the Black Sea were very similar. Their idioms, at the same stage of evolution, were, in fact, dialects of one common language. If they had been able to find a common political center, they would have formed one immense nation of which all branches would have spoken the same language. All these tribes called themselves Slovenes, which the Latins translated as Sclavini, Sclavi, Slavi and the Greeks as Shklavenoi (Shtlavenoi), Sklavoi.[29]

They remained separated, even fought one another, and none established any sort of political and state structure that dominated the others or that stood out and with which their descendants could identify. The Kingdom of Samo is a case in point. Although it existed on Slovak territory, unlike its successor four centuries later, the Empire of Great Moravia, it did not enter into oral tradition or into the folklore of the Slovaks and did not give substance to the national awakening of the modern Slovak nation. Were it not for the Chronicle of Fredegar, written in fact to celebrate Dagobert's reign, it was an episode in the history of Central Europe that might have even passed unnoticed.

Additional archaeological discoveries may tell us more about this period of prehistory, but they are not likely to change the perception that the history of the Slovaks and Slovakia begins only with the creation of the Great Moravian Empire. On the other hand, it is possible that they will give substance to the conclusions suggested by a Slovak author:

> Not possessing another rallying figure similar to Samo, under unfavourable circumstances, this empire broke up once more into national units, which had originally formed the federation, the "Fürstenbund." These units absorbed from their common heritage as much as each one's spiritual, physical and moral capacity would allow. These national entities—hidden for a certain time under the surface of the sea and after a period of maturation—when pushed by the power of the energy accumulated in them, emerged again in the form of the Great Moravia[n Empire] to create the conditions for the epochal work of the great scholars and saints: Cyril and Methodius.[30]

2

The First State

THE EMPIRE OF GREAT MORAVIA

At the time when the Franks defeated the Avars, two Slavic principalities had already emerged on the territory found on both sides of the Morava River, particularly on the east side. They made up the core of what became in less than half a century the Empire of Great Moravia, the name given by Byzantine Emperor Constatine Porphyrogenet (A.D. 913–957) to this new Slavic state situated on the northern Danubian Plain and extending into the Slovak mountains. The term *Great Moravia* is purely geographical. As used in his *De administrando Imperio*, it was based on the name Moravians *(Sclavi Marahenses)*, found in the *Annales Regni Francorum* (822) and especially in the *Annales Fuldenses* (822–897).[1] This brief but nonetheless significant historical account of Great Moravia describes the activities of those who created, interacted, and ultimately destroyed it.

The state was composed first and foremost of two Slavic principalities: Morava and Nitra. The former encompassed territory in western Slovakia and in today's Moravia in the Czech Republic. Nitra, on the other hand, covered an area in western and central Slovakia. They were separated by the White Carpathian mountain range; as Jan Dekan writes, this meant that they represented two different tribal Slavic societies: "At the beginning of the [Great] Moravian state we find two independent political centres, Morava and Nitra, and it is quite likely that these two centers represented independent tribal entities, different from each other not only in terms of economics and geography but also dialect."[2] A third principality that would play an important role was

Pannonia, situated on the south shore of the Danube, in today's Hungary. Its territory was a part of what had been the Roman province of Pannonia. Each of these areas was ruled by a prince who was lord and military leader of the populations inhabiting his territory.

Great Moravia's immediate neighbors to the northwest, north, and northeast were mostly Slavic tribes, some of whom would be subjugated for a time; to the west and southwest the neighbors were the Franks, whose presence and influence would be felt throughout the whole history of the empire. This influence would manifest itself either through direct royal interest or through involvement by the Margrave of the Ostmark, vassal of the Frankish king. After Charlemagne's empire was divided between his grandsons in the Treaty of Verdun in 843, these Franks gradually became known as Germans. To the southeast lay the kingdom of the Bulgarians and the Byzantine Empire. Only the latter was involved openly in the history of Great Moravia. The papacy in Rome also played a role, as did the Frankish clergy in the dioceses of Salzburg, Passau, and Regensburg. Finally, there were the Magyars, a nomadic people from the east, who would ultimately destroy Great Moravia, and who arrived in force in the Great Danubian Plain at the end of the ninth century.

THE FIRST PRINCES

The genesis of the Great Moravian Empire dates from the first half of the eighth century when Irish missionaries from Bavaria sought to Christianize the Slavic tribes.[3] They brought to these pagans the strength of their unifying faith, yet they had only limited success among them. Nevertheless, the missionaries opened up the area for further religious and political activity. The dynamic relationship between church and state that would mark the politics of the Middle Ages began to play itself out fully in this area at this time:

> Abbots and bishops became powerful landlords, dependent upon the will of the king. They became the strongest supporters of the royal and imperial idea, but were at the same time completely entangled in the secular affairs of the Empire. At first controlled by the state, the Frankish Church rapidly gained an immense influence, until by the end of the ninth century, it was itself controlling state affairs. This situation could not fail to be reflected in the missionary activities of the Frankish Church.[4]

In 798, Charlemagne commissioned Archbishop Arno of Salzburg to study the situation in the land of the Slavs. But it is only after his visit to Arno

in 803 that Frankish missionaries started to make serious inroads in the area with well-defined goals: "the extension of Church authority into the Slavonic lands was an integral part of Frankish-Slavic politics, which had as its primary aim the strengthening of the imperial power of the Franks over the Slavs."[5] In pursuit of this policy, Archbishop Adalram, who had succeeded Arno in 821, consecrated a church in Nitra in 828.[6] With this consecration, the territories east of the empire entered in the sphere of interest of the Frankish church and the kingdom of the Franks. However, the full expansion of the Frankish sphere of interest in the area proceeded only after the death of Charlemagne, more specifically with the breakup of his empire in the Treaty of Verdun in 843. Louis the German (804–876) inherited the eastern *(Francia Orientalis)* or Germanic part of the Carolingian Empire. He decided to expand eastward and encouraged the Christianization of the Slavs.

Pribina (?–861) was the ruler of the Principality of Nitra when the church in Nitra was consecrated. It is not likely that this could have happened without his consent. It suggests, therefore, that there had been commercial relations between the Slavs and the Franks for some time already. But more important is the significance that this act had for the Slavs: Pribina not only recognized the importance of Christianity in the politics of the region, but he also felt that his people were cohesive and strong enough to engage in discourse with Frankish missionaries and countenance conversion.[7] Some Slovak historians are of the opinion that these activities indicate that the inhabitants of the Principality of Nitra were conscious of their identity; if so, this makes them the ancestors of today's Slovaks:

> This is the beginning of Slovak history based on concrete historical evidence. Even if at that time the name Slovieni [Slovenes] referred to all the Slavs who had not created or received their own name *(etnonymum)*, we have to consider the Slavs inhabiting Pribina's principality as a specific group of Slavs who lived in the area above the middle Danube. . . . For this entire area, we have to accept that the nation-creating process *(etnogenesa)* of its inhabitants was complete and we can speak of a Slovak nation from that moment on.[8]

In their desire to extend their influence, Frankish rulers, in particular Ratbod, the Margrave of the Ostmark, not only encouraged missionary activity, but may also have played the rulers of the Slavic principalities against each other. In any event, in 833, Mojmir (833–846) of Morava managed to drive Pribina out of Nitra and unite the two principalities to form a new state—the Empire of Great Moravia—and become its first ruler as Mojmir I. As for Pribina, after

first finding refuge with Margrave Ratbod, who presented him to Louis the German in Regensburg, he and his followers accepted Christianity and for a number of years wandered in Central and southeastern Europe before settling in Pannonia in 839. He set up a principality there, was its ruler from 839 to 861, and undertook to Christianize the population and build churches. Whether by design or by accident, Frankish activities in this area not only created a new state in the Danubian Basin but, more significantly, launched the Christianization process of Central Europe.

RASTISLAV AND SVÄTOPLUK

The history of Great Moravia, like that of many states of this period, was one of wars of defense and conquest, personal alliances and betrayals, consolidation and, in this case, ultimate dissolution. The brevity of this history, less than three-quarters of a century, adumbrates to some degree these activities and distracts from the accomplishments and from the fragility of the new state. In oral Slovak tradition, its existence takes precedence over its short history; expressed in another way, this means that the Slovaks remember that they had a state in the ninth century but they hardly know its history. Subsequent developments may have something to do with this: For almost a millennium the Slovaks were without their own state and were ruled by another people, the Magyars. Great Moravia had not left a state tradition upon which the Slovaks could have relied. But the historical record also contributes to the type of legacy the Great Moravian Empire bequeathed to the Slovak nation: "From the ninth century on, there are written sources for the territory of Slovakia, but the number falls in the tenth and remains small also for the eleventh and twelfth; only in the thirteenth century does it grow considerably, with some 3000 documents which concern the history of Slovakia and the Slovaks."[9]

Great Moravia was a vassal state of the Germanic Frankish kingdom and paid an annual tribute to it. Some of the Slavic nobles in Nitra resented paying this tribute. This may be the reason why the reign of Mojmir I was not without major internal problems, in particular in the relations between the two constituent principalities. These conflicts were serious enough for Louis the German to be informed of them by representatives from Morava during a royal council meeting in Paderborn in 845. He traveled to Great Moravia a year later to resolve them. In connivance with Mojmir's nephew, Prince Rastislav of Nitra, Louis had Mojmir arrested and deposed. Rastislav (846–861) became his successor.

It was during Rastislav's reign that Great Moravia underwent a process of expansion and consolidation. First, he acquired more territory in the east,

namely the Slanske Mountains near Kosice, and established a border with the Bulgarian kingdom. This precipitated an alliance between the Frankish and Bulgarian states, which kept him in check for a while and ensured his fealty to the Frankish ruler. But in 853–854, during an internal Frankish power struggle, Rastislav supported Margrave Ratbod against Louis the German with the result that the Frankish king invaded Great Moravia in 855 and attempted to overthrow him. Hostilities lasted until 859 when a peace treaty was signed. The inability of the Franks to achieve anything more than a stalemate was an indication of the increasing strength and independence of Great Moravia.

In order to increase his maneuverability, Rastislav attempted to curtail the activities of the Frankish missionaries whose presence and role among the Slavs was already quite entrenched. To achieve his objective, he decided to ask Rome to create an ecclesiastical province on Slav territory, independent of the German dioceses that vied for influence and control in the area. Toward the end of 861 or in early 862, he wrote to Pope Nicholas I and asked for teachers who were familiar with the Slavic tongue. He received no answer to his letters, seemingly for the simple reason that the Holy See did not have such teachers to send.[10] He then turned to Byzantium and in 862 requested of Emperor Michael III not just teachers, but also a bishop. His request was granted when Constantine (Cyril) and Methodius, two Greek brothers who had learned the Slavic dialect spoken in Thessaloniki, arrived with a few disciples in Great Moravia in 863. More is said below about these two brothers who are known today as the "Apostles of the Slavs."

Rastislav's request had not been merely a religious one, it had political objectives as well: "Rastislav had detailed information about Byzantium and imperial policies toward the Bulgarians, his neighbors who had become his enemies, and it is absolutely logical that he made use of this information and asked Constantinople to give him the help that he needed."[11] In fact, by turning to Byzantium, Rastislav introduced a new factor in the political situation in Central Europe. The first to understand Rastislav's move and feel the change were the Frankish clergy, who did not approve of the presence of clergy from Byzantium in their sphere of interest. Rome also became interested; Pope Nicholas I, one of the most remarkable popes of the Middle Ages, acquiesced to the Byzantine mission because he saw it as serving the interests of the papacy: "Pope Nicholas I had long watched with suspicion the growing ambitions of Salzburg and the other Bavarian sees. He was aware that an East Frankish or German Church was rising in the eastern part of the Carolingian Empire and that if it were allowed to assume great importance, it would prejudice the rights of the Roman See, as he conceived them."[12] Rastislav's policies proved successful with the mission of the two Greek brothers in Great Moravia. The Frankish

clergy complained to the king, and Louis the German put into effect his alliance with the Bulgarians by attacking Great Moravia in 864. However, Byzantium in turn attacked the Bulgarians, and Louis's campaign brought him only limited success: In return for peace, Rastislav accepted Frankish suzerainty.

Undaunted by this minor setback, Rastislav carried on with his policy to establish an independent ecclesiastical province in Great Moravia. In 869, Pope Hadrian II, who succeeded Nicholas I, consecrated Methodius bishop, named him archbishop of the new archdiocese of Great Moravia and Pannonia, and approved the use of the vernacular in the liturgy. Frankish reaction was not long in coming. Under the leadership of Carloman (859–876), the new Margrave of the Ostmark, Frankish armies invaded Great Moravia in 870. However, Great Moravia had not consolidated enough to withstand this new onslaught. Rastislav's nephew, Svätopluk (870–894), Prince of Nitra, quickly sought Carloman's protection and had Rastislav arrested. Methodius, who was on his way back from Rome to assume his new episcopal duties and other ecclesiastical responsibilities, was arrested by order of the Frankish clergy. Great Moravia now had a third ruler, one who had also been put there by the Franks. However, not unlike his predecessor whom he had deposed, Svätopluk would eventually shake off Frankish influence and become Great Moravia's greatest ruler.

The first years of Svätopluk's reign, not unexpectedly, were taken up with his relations with the Frankish kingdom. Although Svätopluk had overthrown Rastislav, Carloman appointed two Frankish lords, Engelschalk and Wilhelm, to rule over Great Moravia. Svätopluk resisted and was arrested in 871 and taken to Bavaria to stand trial for treason. In Great Moravia, Slavomir of Morava led revolts against the brutal rule of the two Frankish lords. However, Slavomir was unable to overthrow them. In the meantime, Svätopluk was found innocent of the charges against him and agreed to lead Carloman's armies against Slavomir. Once on the battlefield, he bolted from the Frankish ranks, joined forces with Slavomir, and defeated the army he had just led. Engelschalk and Wilhelm were both slain, and Svätopluk became the undisputed ruler of Great Moravia. In the wake of his duplicity, Frankish pressure was maintained on Great Moravia. Even if Svätopluk successfully repelled a Frankish attack in 872, he understood that it was in his interest to sue for peace. In 874, he signed the Peace of Forchheim, which, "although a humiliating experience for Svatopluk [sic]— who was forced to make an annual payment or tribute to the Franks—was nevertheless a compromise, for the Frankish ruler on his side agreed to avoid any hostile acts of aggression against his Slavic neighbor and vassal."[13]

The Peace of Forchheim lasted until 882. During this period, Svätopluk was able to expand in areas that the Frankish kingdom did not consider to be in its sphere of interest. He thus extended his power to the north and to the

west in parts of today's Poland; he incorporated much of what is today the Czech Republic; and in the south, he went as far as the borders of Bulgaria, thereby also extending his control over parts of Pannonia. During his reign, Great Moravia achieved its maximum extension and power and exercised its greatest influence in the region. (See Map 2.)

Svätopluk's successful conquests allowed him to pursue an independent policy, much like his predecessor Rastislav had done. However, in matters of religion, he abandoned the policy of establishing an independent ecclesiastical province because, unlike Rastislav, he "did not grasp the full significance of the need for an independent Church province."[14] On the other hand, he appreciated the necessity of maintaining good relations with Rome and especially of obtaining papal protection, which he requested in 879. He received it from Pope John VIII in 880 with the bull *Industriae tuae*. This document had wide-ranging political consequences: "With this protection, Great Moravia and its ruler became equal in rank to the other contemporary states and rulers of Christian Europe and the international position of Great Moravia was also strengthened."[15] There were also ecclesiastical consequences. According to the papal bull: "by the decision of our apostolic authority we give him [Methodius] the privilege of his archdiocese and we affirm and state, that with the help of God, the privilege of his office as archbishop will remain forever valid."[16] It confirmed the decision taken by the Holy See during Rastislav's reign to create an archdiocese for the Slavs of Great Moravia. For all intents and purposes, we can speak of an ecclesiastical province "because the bull explicitly mentions that as far as church administration is concerned, all priests in Great Moravia are subordinated to Methodius regardless of their origin."[17]

The power and independence of Great Moravia, now fully acknowledged by the papacy, were not without consequences for Svätopluk in his relations with the Frankish kingdom; the result was that both states were engaged in a struggle for influence and control. Many of the conflicts that arose centered around Methodius and his followers, about which more is said below. But from 882 to 885, Svätopluk also had to withstand attacks from Arnulf (881–899), who first ruled Pannonia after Kocel (861–881), son of Pribina, died in 881. Arnulf was also the son of King Carloman (876–881), successor of Louis the German. He himself became king in 887 when he succeeded Charles the Fat (881–887). He attacked Great Moravia again in 892 but, like the previous time, failed to defeat Svätopluk. Arnulf found it necessary to involve roving Magyar tribes, the Bulgarians, and other Slavs in southeastern Europe in this attempt, an activity that led Slovak historians to conclude: "The broad diplomatic activity of King Arnulf in his struggles with Svätopluk indicates that Svätopluk was a powerful ruler who controlled vast territories."[18]

If Svätopluk controlled vast territories, his state, on the other hand, was a fragile political entity, weak as a result of his conquests and the relative autonomy of the Slavic tribes and principalities that constituted it. Its fragility became manifest when Svätopluk died in 894 and his conquests were undone relatively quickly and easily. In June 895, "Czech princes, through their diplomatic representatives in Regensburg, submitted themselves to East Frankish King Arnulf, [an action] which marked the beginning of the breakup of Svätopluk's empire."[19] Other subjugated tribes and peoples revolted, contributing thereby to the further weakening of Great Moravia. It also has been suggested that Svätopluk's "kingdom was weakened considerably by his failure to consolidate the authority of the Slavonic ecclesiastical province."[20] One of the paradoxes of the history of Great Moravia is that its greatest ruler, Svätopluk, was also the one who inhibited rather than encouraged and fostered the work and activities of two Greek religious scholars and priests, Constantine (Cyril) and Methodius, whose contribution to the establishment and development of Central and East European civilization and culture is second to none.

CYRIL AND METHODIUS

Prior to their arrival in Great Moravia in 863, the brothers Constantine and Methodius had created a basic alphabet for the Slavic language. This alphabet is called glagolitic. A second alphabet was devised, probably at the beginning of the tenth century, in Bulgaria. Its author may have been St. Konstantin Presbyter, a pupil of Constantine and Methodius. Using Greek letters whenever possible, this alphabet adapted the glagolitic symbols for typically Slavic sounds. This is the alphabet long associated with Constantine-Cyril, called Cyrillic, and it is used with a number of modifications specific to each by some of the Southern and the Eastern Slavs (Serbs, Macedonians, Bulgarians, Russians, Ukrainians, and Bielorussians).[21]

The two brothers were the sons of Leo, a Greek battalion commander in Thessaloniki of noble birth. Constantine was an outstanding scholar and grammarian who had studied under patriarch Photius, "the chief ecclesiastical and intellectual light of Byzantium in his day."[22] He was also a diplomat and had led a Byzantine diplomatic-religious mission to Samarra, near Baghdad, and to the Khazar Khan near the Black Sea. When he was chosen to go to Great Moravia, he translated passages from the Holy Scriptures into the new Slavonic language. In Great Moravia, he established a seminary for the training of priests with Slavic as the language not just of instruction but also of liturgy. His older brother Methodius, a lawyer by training, was his principal assistant.

The Frankish clergy soon came to realize that the activities of the two Byzantine brothers represented a threat to their vocation and influence. In particular, they viewed the use of the vernacular in the liturgy not only as politically dangerous—it gave those who used it a decided advantage over the local populations—but was also not in accordance with the policies of Rome. When they realized that Constantine and Methodius had the support of Rastislav, they turned to the Holy See. The internal politics of Great Moravia now acquired a religious dimension that two rulers, Rastislav and Svätopluk, used in different if not contradictory ways, as we saw above, to enhance the power and independence of Great Moravia.

In 867, the two brothers left for Rome to have some of their seminarians consecrated priests. Their journey took them through Pannonia, where they visited Kocel, staying three months. During this time, Kocel assembled fifty young men whom he recommended for religious training. The brothers also stopped in Venice, where they defended publicly the use of a specific alphabet for the Slavs and the vernacular in the liturgy. Although Pope Nicholas I had invited them, especially when he had learned that they were in possession of the remains of Pope Clement I (92–101), which they had found near Cherson, they were welcomed by his successor, Pope Hadrian II, when they reached Rome. He examined their translations of the Holy Scriptures and liturgical texts, approved them, and authorized their use in the liturgy. Methodius and a number of seminarians received holy orders. Their mission for Rastislav accomplished, they decided to return to Byzantium. However, the political situation there did not allow them to make the journey to Constantinople and they remained in Rome. Constantine entered a monastery, where he took the name of Cyril and died three months later on 14 February 869. Before his death he asked Methodius to return to Great Moravia and carry on with the work that they had begun.

In the meantime, Kocel of Pannonia requested of Pope Hadrian II that he send Methodius to him. Methodius was given letters from the Supreme Pontiff for Rastislav of Great Moravia and Svätopluk of Nitra as well as Kocel. In the summer of 869, Methodius arrived in Pannonia. He returned to Rome when Kocel decided a bishop was needed, a request that had to be made to the Holy See. Again Hadrian II agreed to the request, consecrated Methodius bishop, and named him archbishop as well as plenipotentiary papal legate of all the Slavs living in the territories ruled by Rastislav, Kocel, and Svätopluk. Methodius left Rome once more for Great Moravia but stayed with Kocel for some time when war broke out between Great Moravia and the Frankish kingdom. When he tried in 870 to reach Great Moravia after Svätopluk had deposed Rastislav, he was arrested by Frankish soldiers at the behest of the

Frankish clergy, and taken to Regensburg. It is likely that the document *Libellus de conversione Bagoariorum et Carantanorum ad fidem christiana (Booklet about the Conversion of the Bagaori and the Carantani to the Christian Faith)*, one of the first documents to shed light on the activities of Pribina and Kocel, was written at this time to defend the rights of the archbishopric of Salzburg.[23] Methodius was released only in 873, when Pope John VIII, appraised by Kocel of Methodius's imprisonment, threatened the Frankish clergy who were holding him with excommunication. Methodius was finally allowed to return to Great Moravia. To placate the German clergy, John VIII forbade Methodius to use the Slavic liturgy, although he could preach in the vernacular. Methodius, however, disobeyed and continued the work that he and his brother had begun.

The Peace of Forchheim gave the Frankish missionaries new opportunities to oppose Methodius's activities: "The Peace of Forchheim, which they [the Frankish clergy] interpreted as a defeat of Svatopluk, was the occasion for making a comeback in order to make use of a political setback to block the establishment of the new Slavonic province."[24] The battle lines were drawn on the question of the use of Latin and the vernacular in the liturgy. The Frankish clergy complained once more to Rome, accusing Methodius of heresy, and in 880, Methodius, together with a Great Moravian delegation, traveled once again to the Eternal City. As the bull *Industriae tuae* indicates, the use of the vernacular was approved, although the Gospel first had to be read in Latin. In addition, an ecclesiastical province was created and a Swabian monk, named Wiching, was consecrated bishop of a new see in Nitra and made suffragan of Methodius. Last but not least, the Supreme Pontiff took Great Moravia under his protection.

In political terms, as we have seen, Methodius's visit to Rome was a success for Great Moravia. However, it was only a mitigated success for him personally because he now had as a suffragan someone who clearly had the support of Svätopluk. Wiching's appointment had been made at the latter's request. Not surprisingly, the earlier conflicts between the partisans of the vernacular and those who supported the use of Latin, namely the Frankish clergy, were renewed. Wiching led them in these attacks. Almost immediately upon his return, Methodius was in correspondence with Pope John VIII, as was Svätopluk, but the problems Methodius raised about Wiching were not solved; "Pope John VIII during his entire pontificate took an active interest in and manifested a sympathetic attitude towards Archbishop Methodius and his apostolate and at the same time maintained cordial relations with the Slovak ruler, Svatopluk."[25] John VIII died in 882. The two popes who succeeded him, Marinus and Hadrian III, were not in a position to do anything, as their pontificates were of too short a duration. The situation reached crisis propor-

ıns only during the pontificate of Stephen V in 885, when Wiching sent the Holy Father a letter charging Methodius once again with heresy along with other accusations.

Methodius had gone into retirement in 882 after a journey to Bulgaria and Constantinople. In the three years since his retirement, he had spent the time completing the translations of the Holy Scriptures, the lives and teaching of Christian ascetes called *Nomokanon,* and the collection of canon law acts entitled *Paterikon* which he had begun around 873. Even though he was no longer involved in church activities, the conflict between him and Wiching had not abated. In fact, it had become so serious that Methodius used the ultimate weapon at his disposal in order to get his suffragan to obey him: excommunication. Wiching, with the support of Svätopluk, left for Rome. However, on 6 April 885, shortly after his departure, Methodius died. Before his death, he had named Gorazd, one of his disciples, and probably a native of Nitra, his successor. This nomination did not resolve matters by any means. On the basis of Wiching's testimony against Methodius who, unbeknownst to the Holy See, had already passed away, Pope Stephen V prohibited the use of the vernacular in Great Moravia. Svätopluk then intervened in the matter of Methodius's succession by writing to Rome on behalf of Wiching, who was granted the position of administrator of the church in Great Moravia but was never elevated to the rank of archbishop. He stayed in Nitra until 893, when he was named later chancellor in King Arnulf's court. As for Gorazd, he was summoned to Rome. It is not known whether he did go there, but it is known that Methodius's other disciples were forced to flee into exile: "The unrelenting pressure and subsequent series of tensions caused by the Latin clergy . . . finally resulted in the removal of all forms of Slavonic liturgy from the lands ruled by Svatopluk. That left the Latin Church triumphant."[26] For all intents and purposes, it also meant the end of what had characterized the apostolate of Methodius, namely Slavic ecclesiastical activity in Great Moravia.

THE END OF THE LEGACY OF GREAT MORAVIA

According to Emperor Constantine Porphyrogenet, Svätopluk had made a deathbed request to his sons that they remain united and not fight one another. Legend has it that he took three twigs in his hand to show how difficult it was to break them when they were held together and how easily one could break each one individually. Mojmir II (904–907), the oldest, became his successor while the other two, Svätopluk II, was given Nitra, and Predslav or Preslav, other territory. But Svätopluk's death, as we indicated, also had encouraged

the secession of conquered peoples, and Mojmir II found himself having to defend the integrity of the core of his father's empire, the Slavic principalities. This he sought to do first by putting order in the ecclesiastical affairs of the kingdom. According to Francis Hrusovsky: "Following the precedent set by his predecessors (Rastislav and even his illustrious father Svatopluk, who failed to follow up his earlier advantages in this respect), Mojmir II communicated with Rome and informed the Holy See that he could not recognize the claims of the Bishop of Passau, who, after Wiching's departure from Nitra, showed every determination to secure ecclesiastical authority. . . ."[27] Pope John IX, who had succeeded Stephen V, dispatched around 900 an archbishop and two bishops to Great Moravia, where they consecrated an archbishop and three bishops from among the native priests. There is no record in any historical source of their names or sees. Nor is it known whether John IX approved the use of the Slavonic liturgy. Nevertheless, it can be assumed that the Holy See was seeking to renew the ecclesiastical province of Great Moravia. There was reaction from the Bavarian episcopate, but subsequent political developments rendered their objections void.

The Magyars, who during the migrations of nations had settled in an area near the Dniestr between the Don and Danube rivers, started moving westward toward the end of the ninth century. In 896, they established themselves in the eastern part of the Danubian Plain. In addition, the Czech tribes, who just two years before had sworn fealty to Arnulf, complained to him in 897 that Mojmir II was seeking to dominate them. Finally, a power struggle broke out between Mojmir II and his brother Svätopluk II. As a result, on two occasions, in 898 and 899, Arnulf's armies invaded Great Moravia and in the end made Svätopluk II prisoner. Mojmir II still refused to be a vassal of the German king. After Arnulf's death in 899, the Germans attacked again. But shortly afterward, war broke out between the Magyars and the Germans, and it is likely that Mojmir II fought on the Magyar side. However, Magyar victories had made them so powerful that in 901 Mojmir II signed a peace treaty with the German Empire. The Magyars then turned against Great Moravia and, in 907, Mojmir II was slain during an engagement with them. With his death, Great Moravia ceased to exist as a state in Central Europe and its Slavic territories became the sphere of interest of the Magyars. Before long they would establish themselves permanently in the Danubian Plain, in the area south of the Danube.

At first glance, the legacy of the Great Moravian Empire would seem very small, almost in the measure of its very short history. Other than the documents pertaining to the relations between Rome and the Great Moravian Empire, there are the translations of the Holy Scriptures and other sacred and liturgical texts by Cyril and Methodius. The latter make up a far greater legacy than the

former, one that belongs to the entire Slavic world. As Michael Lacko writes: "The most important achievement of the missionary brothers, the one which has endured through the ages and from which millions of Slavs draw spiritual sustenance, is the introduction of Slavonic into the liturgy."[28] Also, there are two literary works, *Life of Constantine-Cyril* and *Life of Methodius,* most likely written by their disciples, which may be said to constitute an embryonic history of the life and activities of the two brothers and the Great Moravian state that they served. They too reached other Slavs and seem to have played a not unimportant role in their Christianization.[29] It would seem, therefore, that the legacy of the Great Moravian period is at one and the same time quite vast and specific, as Joseph M. Kirschbaum points out:

> Slavists and literary historians consider the Cyrillo-Methodian literature as the heritage of all the Slavs. Others claim that it is the heritage of the Slavs who laid the bases of the Empire of Great Moravia, namely the Slovaks, the Moravians and the Slovenes. Slovak scholars have been saying for three centuries that the literature created in Great Moravia or translated by Sts. Cyril and Methodius and their disciples for the ancestors of the Slovaks are rather part of the Slovak cultural heritage.[30]

In order to appreciate what both the Great Moravian Empire and Cyril and Methodius mean for the Slovaks, it is essential first to deal with two rather curious claims. Throughout a good part of this century, when the Slovaks and the Czechs lived in a common state, it was suggested that the Great Moravian Empire was the equal legacy of both nations. George Vernadsky, a leading Russian historian, came to the conclusion that it is the legacy only of the Czech nation.[31]

These claims, apart from the political imperatives that brought them about, were based on the difficulty in establishing an adequate definition and identification of the inhabitants and the territory of Great Moravia. As we have seen, the historical record is anything but precise on this question. The structure of the state itself does not provide better answers, for it is quite likely that it was a loose structure of federated principalities that also included, under Svätopluk, conquered territories. The latter broke away upon his death, reducing Mojmir II's state to more historical and, to some degree, also more ethnic (i.e., original Slavic) dimensions. Therefore, in answer to both claims (the answer to the second is in fact given in the first), contemporary Slovak historians suggest that "It is not correct to label Great Moravia as the first common state of the Czechs and Slovaks for the simple reason that the membership of the Czechs in this state had been short-lived and they themselves had considered it as forcefully imposed."[32]

Was it a Slovak state in that case?[33] Here, geography and ethnography provide a partial although not entirely satisfactory answer.[34] The Principality of Nitra was located in what is today Slovakia, as was part of the Principality of Morava, in the area east of the Morava River. Their inhabitants were likely Slavs, but there is no indication of the duration and the exact nature of their relationship with the two principalities. As for the Slavs who lived west of the Morava River, by geographical definition they are the ancestors of the Moravians of the Margraviate of Moravia of the Middle Ages and of today's Czech Republic. They are not Slovaks, neither as a result of subsequent historical development nor through language (although there is a Moravian dialect, spoken in southern Moravia, which is close to Slovak). There is, therefore, some basis to what contemporary Slovak historians suggest, namely that Great Moravia "cannot be considered as the state belonging to the Slovak-Slavs. To put it in modern terms, we have to define Great Moravia as a Moravian-Slovak state. It is, however, also true that of the two ethnic groups which had Great Moravian statehood, only the Slovaks have kept their own national (and not only) territorial identity to this day."[35]

For the many Slovaks who accept the Slovak claim to the legacy of Great Moravia, a more powerful argument than the geographical and ethnographical ones is found in the roles Great Moravia and Cyril and Methodius played in the oral and cultural traditions and in the politics of the Slovak nation.

The importance of tradition is, in many respects, a very subjective phenomenon. It is often determined by the political objectives of the day. For example, under the Communist regime, anything that predated their accession to power usually was given short shrift (unless it could be shown to be tied directly to the struggles of the working class and their eventual victory) and otherwise made to serve their ideological and political objectives. This was certainly the case of Great Moravia, which was defined as the first common state of the Czechs and Slovaks.[36] Likewise, the mission and activities of Cyril and Methodius were given more of a political than a religious connotation.[37] At the very best, Marxist historians acknowledged that both Great Moravia and Cyril and Methodius became part of the Slovak literary tradition, appearing in written form, beginning in the seventeenth century.[38]

In the non-Czechoslovak and non-Marxist tradition, Great Moravia and Cyril and Methodius play an important role because they occupy a central position in Slovak history. This is particularly the case of the Cyrillo-Methodian tradition. Of it Jaroslav Pelikan writes: "Whenever the Slovak people sought to identify themselves within the history of the nations, they turned to this tradition as the warrant of their national identity."[39] For example, during the Middle Ages, it formed the basis for Slovak oral culture. The legacy is, therefore,

more than just literary; this tradition gave substance to the Slovak national renaissance of the eighteenth and nineteenth centuries, and underpinned and to some degree even defined Slovak political activity during the period of Magyarization, in the First Czechoslovak Republic and in the first Slovak Republic. During the Communist period, it was kept alive in the cultural and political activities of Slovak emigre groups and organizations.[40]

The importance and the legacy of a historical period like that of Great Moravia is best judged in the light of subsequent developments. After its disappearance, the Slovaks were not in a position to form a state, whether feudal or national, until the twentieth century. To the extent that the history of a people is defined in terms of the creation and the activities of their own state, then Great Moravia was, for a millennium, the only state to which the Slovaks could point. Its legacy, like that of Cyril and Methodius, could not therefore be anything but fundamental for the Slovak nation. In addition, the Slovaks also played a brief but important role in European history and contributed to its development and civilization through Great Moravia and Cyril and Methodius. What this means for the Slovak people is best expressed by the Slovak man of letters, Jozef Skultety, who writes:

> As long as there will be souls capable of becoming enthused with sublime things, so long will the memory of the Slavonic apostles Cyril and Methodius remain revered, and there will be always found people who will know that the Slavonic Church had been instituted for our Slovak ancestors, and that it all emanated from the mind of their great ruler Rastislav. The Slovak state of the ninth century did not survive, it became extinct in the maelstrom of the world, but the Slavs have a great heritage from it.[41]

With the disappearance of Great Moravia, the Slovaks lost their main unifying bond. Yet they did not disappear, they were not assimilated, nor were they dispersed; the question is: What unified and united them, what factors allowed them to withstand many of the challenges to their identity and existence that came their way? Three factors, already present when Great Moravia fell served the Slovaks throughout the centuries: language, geography, and history. The population living on the territory of today's Slovakia never ceased to speak Slovak, the language that developed from the Slavonic spoken by their ancestors. The geography of their homeland, with its mountains, rivers, and valleys, facilitated this maintenance of their language. The area was cohesive enough to stave off all attempts to dislodge the Slovaks, except perhaps in the southern parts, on the north shore of the Danube. This area was also settled by Magyars,

who are to be found there to this day. Last, but not least, as already discussed, there is the history of Great Moravia from which an important tradition developed, a memory that gave the Slovaks the basis for their national consciousness and to which they returned time and again as they defended their homeland. In the words of Matus Kucera and Bohumir Kosticky: "In the nation building process of the Slovaks, the Great Moravian period produced a many sided tradition which from the eleventh century on accompanied the fate of the nation right up to the period of national liberation."[42] These factors, which identified and unified the Slovaks, are also the ones that their elites used to nurture and develop their culture and to defend the nation and its territory after it became a part of Hungary.

The history of the Slovaks after the fall of Great Moravia became interlocked until the twentieth century in the history of the Hungarian state. The loss of political power means that their destiny was not entirely in their own hands. As a result, a new leitmotif appeared in Slovak national life, that of survival. The focus thus changes from primarily political to economical, cultural, and social history. However, it is far from an uninteresting history, even when compared with the attractiveness of state history.

3

The Middle Ages

UNDER THE ARPADS

When the Magyars defeated the Great Moravian state in 907,[1] the Slovaks found themselves in a situation not unlike that of their ancestors when the Kingdom of Samo disappeared: As a result of a forced migration, they would be ruled by a people who appeared in the area in search of a homeland. Only this time, unlike the earlier Avar invaders, the Magyars settled down and created a state in which the Slovaks would live until the twentieth century.

The British historian C. A. Macartney writes that their settlement in the Danubian Plain was due to the "favour of fortune." He suggests that had the passes in the Carpathians been defended, the Magyars, who were being forced out of their homeland on the right bank of the Don River by the Pechenegs, might have seen the end of their national existence.[2] Nothing, however, impeded their migration: "A German source dating from the late ninth century speaks of an uninhabited desert between the Moravian and the Bulgarian borders. The plains between the Danube and the Tisza, as well as the northern, steppe-like half of Transylvania, stood empty when the conquering Hungarians appeared in 896."[3] Great Moravia had ceased to be a political factor in the Danubian area after Svätopluk's death, so the power vacuum that resulted offered the right conditions for a well-led group of nomadic tribes not only to create a new homeland, but to become a force to be reckoned with as well.

Prior to their arrival, the Magyar tribes, who were composed of clans linked by family or a real or imaginary common ancestry, had formed a sort of loose federation. However, because of their defeat at the hands of the Pechenegs

and their westward migration, the seven tribal chieftains elected the strongest among them, Arpad (A.D.?–907), son of Almus, to lead them in the search for a new homeland. He became their first prince. As they moved westward, the Magyar tribes became embroiled in the disputes of the Danubian area. In 892, the Frankish king, Arnulf, enlisted one of their contingents to help him against Great Moravia's ruler, Svätopluk. In 896, under the leadership of Arpad, they crossed the Carpathian Mountains. Then they attacked Great Moravia, and in 907, after defeating the Germans near Bratislava, they settled and became the main political force in the Danubian Plain. Encouraged by their military victories and conquests, their mounted (cavalry) units became for almost half a century "the scourge of Europe, which they raided far and wide, striking terror into the hearts of their victims with the suddenness of their descents—for their little, lithe horses outdistanced any news of their coming—the ferocity of their attacks, their outlandish and, to Western eyes, hideous appearance, their blood curdling battle-yells."[4] Finally in 955, the Germans handed them a crushing defeat on the Lechfeld, near Augsburg, forcing these nomadic tribes to adopt a completely new way of life. By doing so, they became permanent settlers.

After the fall of Great Moravia, the principalities of that former Slavic state were allotted to various Magyar clans: "the Hungarian chieftains with their armed retainers and bondsmen moved into the fortresses of the Slavic zhupans or else they built strongholds of their own. Those Slavic leaders who surrendered to the Hungarians were probably allowed to retain their property but the land of those who resisted passed into the hands of the Hungarian chieftains."[5] The main core, especially the Principality of Nitra, was given to Arpad. During the time when the Magyars were launching raids throughout Europe, taking them as far as Bremen in the north and Constantinople in the south, it is quite likely that Nitra and the other Great Moravian principalities enjoyed a certain degree of freedom. But after their defeat on the Lechfeld, when the Magyars ceased being nomads and turned to agriculture, the clan system underwent a modification: "The majority of the native Slavs, who were engaged in agriculture, were subjected to the Hungarian chieftains, a fact which was decisive in the final transformation of the clan from an organization based on kinship into a social organization based on territory."[6]

Although the Slavic principalities continued to exist, they also became the object of royal donations and until the beginning of the twelfth century, during the reign of Kalman (1095–1116), they served as the power base for pretenders to the throne. The Magyars set up a political system that granted the principalities autonomy. As Macartney suggests, they managed to establish "a nation in a new home, not, as the Normans did in England or Russia, to impose the rule of a relatively small band of conquerors on a subject people. . . . The polity was

exclusively that of the Magyars and their confederates."[7] Until the twentieth century, the political history of this new state would be that of the Magyars. Except for a short period of time toward the end of the tenth and the beginning of the eleventh century, for the Slovaks, the question was one of the relations between themselves and their rulers. The answer would determine their social and national development.

One of the factors that influenced the relationship of the Slovaks to the state as well as to other peoples in it was the maintenance and development of their own language. The Slavic tribes were incorporated into the Hungarian state without having to abandon their idioms. Slovak linguists believe that Slovak acquired the status of an independent Slavic language sometime in the tenth to the eleventh centuries.[8] The consequences were not without importance for the Slovak people as well as their language, as Eugen Pauliny writes: "In the period from the tenth to the fourteenth centuries, the foundations were laid for the origin and the formation of Slovak nationhood; this developing Slovak nationality created . . . the basic conditions for the origin of all of the social forms of its language."[9]

The consolidation of the Hungarian state began to take place with Gejza (?–977), great-grandson of Arpad, whom most of the clan chiefs recognized as prince. He defeated those who opposed him, took their lands, made peace with the Germans, and allowed Christianity to spread in his territory through the efforts of German clergy. His son Vajk, who was granted the principality of Nitra, was baptized under the name of Stephen (Istvan)[10] (970?–1038), and married Gisela, sister of Henry, Duke of Bavaria. When Stephen succeeded his father, he was opposed by the Koppany clan whose rebellion he put down with the help of the Poznan and Hont clans. He applied to Rome for recognition as king, a recognition that not only Pope Sylvester II but also Emperor Otto III (980–1002), granted him in the year A.D. 1000. Hungary now belonged to the Christian family of nations with a national church answering only to Rome. Under Stephen's leadership, "thanks to the substantial help of the Slavic magnates Poznan and Hont,"[11] the new kingdom consolidated as a medieval state that, in time, also ruled among its peoples the Slavic populations of the defunct Great Moravian Empire.

If the disappearance of Great Moravia had favored Hungarian territorial consolidation in the Danubian Plain, it also encouraged the renewal of the quest of the German clergy to extend their influence eastward. Stephen's request for a national church may well have been motivated by a desire to limit their influence.[12] Otto III's approval of Stephen's request to Rome would seem therefore to have been in contradiction with German policy. In fact, it was part of a new imperial conception that was bold and innovative for its time:

He [Otto] planned to give all new nations and States in Europe the freedom to regulate their own affairs in return for their membership of his renovated Roman and Christian Empire. The conception was at once idealistic and realistic; it was the only scheme ever conceived by a German King for Central Europe and one that could have been accepted without fear by any new State, whilst to the German element in that part of Europe it allotted the place it deserved at the time as being the most vigorous and cultural power in Central Europe.[13]

In addition to Stephen of Hungary, Duke Boleslav the Great (992–1018) of Poland also gave an enthusiastic response to the German plan. However, it did not survive the premature death of its author. His successor, Henry II (1002–1024) sought instead the destruction of Poland. But Boleslav turned out to be a formidable opponent who was also given the opportunity to intervene in Czech dynastic disputes. As a result, in 1003, the Polish state extended into Bohemia, Moravia, and Slovakia.[14] This Polish expansionism, however, was short-lived.

No documentary evidence sheds any light on this period, on the conquest of Slovakia by Boleslav or on the events that enabled Stephen to wrest it back from Poland. It would seem that the latter happened immediately following Boleslav's death[15] or later: "All we know is that modern Slovakia was in Hungarian hands in 1031, though it is impossible to tell in which period of Stephen's reign this happened."[16] The date is unimportant; what is important is the fact that for a short period of time Slovakia was the object of dispute between the two principal states in the area. The Magyars prevailed and the Slovaks found themselves finally and definitely in Hungary sometime in the second or third decade of the new millennium.

The Arpad kingdom, not unlike other European medieval kingdoms of its time, experienced dynastic disputes, especially as no definite rules for succession had been laid down when Arpad was elected the first prince. A new ruler had to be approved by the Royal Council. Among the descendants of Arpad who ascended the throne, three rulers made major and significant contributions to the consolidation and development of the Hungarian state: Stephen, Ladislas (Laszlo) I (1077–1095), and Bela IV (1235–1270). The early Hungarian monarchy reached its fullest development and the limits of its possibilities under Bela III (1173–1196) who managed to collect revenues equal to those of his English and French counterparts. Between these reigns, the succession was marred by dynastic challenges that, in the case of Andrew II (1205–1235), resulted in 1222 in his having to sign the Golden Bull, a document not unlike the Magna Carta that his English counterpart, King John,

signed at Runnymede in 1215, which seriously limited royal power by giving the landed nobility a *jus resistendi* (right to resist royal power).

Stephen's reign was characterized above all by his decision to allow Christianity to spread in the Danubian Plain. An archbishopric was established in Ostrihom (Esztergom)[17], which became the see of the Hungarian province, and parishes were created and churches built throughout his kingdom. The Catholic Church was given large tracts of land while the king retained vast properties. He also created large estates through donations to followers and laid thereby "the roots of a new society. . . built on the new landowners and the members of the court."[18] The head of the royal household, the count palatine, was appointed by the king and was the most powerful official in the kingdom after the king. It is likely that Samuel Aba was the first count palatine. Stephen further strengthened the medieval system by dividing royal lands—during his reign 85 percent of land in Slovakia belonged to the crown—into units called counties *(zupy)*, headed by an administrator named by the king called *zupan* (*comes* in Latin, *ispán* in Hungarian) who "received the dues in kind and the taxes, was in charge of fairs and collected the tolls and customs from traders. He received one third of the income; the remaining two thirds went to the royal treasury. The *comes* [*zupan*] also administered justice in the county; freemen could appeal from his court to the king."[19] All inhabitants owed obedience to the *zupan*, and the male population was obliged to bear arms when called upon to do so. Counties were not just administrative, but also ecclesiastical units; the archdeacons were expected to cooperate with the *zupan*. Over time, the *zupan* exercised authority over the clan lands, especially when the head of a clan became the *zupan*. In 1030, Stephen I withstood attacks from German Emperor Conrad II (1024–1039) who sought but failed to destroy the Hungarian kingdom. Conrad's successor, Henry III (1039–1056), intervened in the succession after Stephen's death and also attacked Hungary unsuccessfully on two occasions, in 1050 and again two years later.

Ladislas I continued the consolidation of the state begun by Stephen by strengthening his rule; he established a legal system and introduced a code of laws dealing with criminal offenses and commercial transactions, and created further bishoprics. In 1083, he reestablished in Nitra the sole episcopal see to be entirely on Slovak territory until the eighteenth century and established another one in Jager (Eger) which also served eastern Slovakia. Like Stephen, Ladislas was later canonized for his exemplary Christian life. During his reign, by becoming its king, he united Croatia with Hungary in a personal union; "Croatia was a dynastic acquisition. How far the Hungarian-Croat union was real (in later phraseology), and how far only personal, is a question which the historians of the two countries argue and can never resolve, since they are talking

in terms to which the Middle Ages assigned no precise and immutable meaning."[20] The result, however, was that Hungary had become a major political power in Central Europe, destined not to escape the attention of its neighbors.

In the thirteenth century, during Bela IV's reign, Hungary was attacked by the Mongols. Up to that point, Hungary's political and military activities had not involved Slovakia. With the Mongol defeat of the Magyars at Muhi in April 1241, towns and villages throughout the kingdom were pillaged and plundered, including Slovakia, in particular the southwest, the eastern lowlands near Kosice, and the Hron valley up to Zvolen. However, the situation was not as bad as in Hungary where the consequences of their twelve-month invasion were disastrous, as Macartney points out: "That year, with the plague and starvation which followed it, cost Hungary something like half its total population."[21] The disappearance of the Mongols in 1242, as sudden as their appearance the year before, allowed Bela IV to start getting the country back into shape. He rebuilt towns and dotted the countryside with fortifications and castles to defend the kingdom against any other attacks; to do so, however, he gave the landed nobility a free hand on their domains, thereby weakening royal power. He also invited German colonists to engage in mining; he gave them special privileges in the towns where they settled. These two decisions had immediate as well as long-term consequences for Hungary: "The final dissolution of the old order based on the county castles and royal estates was brought about not only by the emergence of a landed oligarchy but also by the development of the middle layers of feudal society: the burghers of the towns and the smaller landowners (the so-called 'nobility')."[22] His death in 1270 triggered a struggle for succession that brought forth in Slovakia a noble whom many view as a ruler who united the nation.

MATTHEW CAK

The Mongol raids had so weakened Hungary that Friedrich Babenberg of Austria took the opportunity to attack western Slovakia in 1242. But the combined forces from the Nitra and Trencin counties beat him back. Friedrich died during a second attempt in 1246, thereby also ending the Babenberg line and launching among his neighbors a struggle for his succession in Austria. For close to a quarter of a century, the Arpads and the Czech Premyslides battled for Austria; during this time parts of western Slovakia fell under Czech control. Finally, in 1278, the Premyslides were defeated when Rudolf of Habsburg joined forces with Ladislas IV (1272–1290). The Babenberg succession, however, did not go to the Arpads; it went to Rudolf of Habsburg, who started a

dynasty that in time would play a major role in Central European politics as well as in the life of the Slovaks.

The struggle for the Austrian succession had further weakened royal power while strengthening that of half a dozen noble families who "made meteoric rises to near-sovereign state."[23] They formed a new oligarchy. Among them were the Caks of Trencin; Matthew (1260–1321) would rule an area that corresponds more or less to today's Slovakia. His power became evident when Andrew III (1290–1301), the last of the Arpads, died and a successor had to be found.

The succession to the Arpad throne involved the Premyslides, to whom the throne was offered by some of the nobles, and the Angevins, who by virtue of the marriage of Maria, daughter of Stephen V (1270–1272), to Charles II of Anjou, had a legitimate claim to the Hungarian throne. At first Cak supported the Premyslide Vaclav III (1301–1305), who reigned under the name of Ladislas, but then he switched to Charles Robert (1307–1342) when Ladislas abdicated to succeed to the throne of Bohemia upon the death of his father and Otto of Bavaria made a claim for the Hungarian throne. Cak's support of Ladislas earned him more power and territory. When Cak threw his lot behind Charles Robert, he was made one of the three palatines of the kingdom in 1309, with his authority extending to much of what is contemporary Slovakia.

The accession of the Angevins on the throne of Hungary opened a new chapter in the country's history. Medieval Hungary, which had always had contacts with Western Europe, became receptive to new influences, and its political life took on new directions: "French culture and mores, the arrival of foreigners at court, and the preponderance of French influenced the intellectual life of Hungary."[24] In addition, Charles Robert decided to strengthen royal power and diminish that of the oligarchs: "Charles had to fight long and hard before the country had not only a king, but also a real master. His task was difficult: he had to end the anarchy that had prevailed for decades and liquidate the power structure of the dreaded oligarchy, which was in the process of becoming institutionalized."[25]

Cak did not go along with Charles Robert's plans and within two years, in 1311, turned against him. The monarch also had difficulties with another oligarchical family, the Amadei, who ruled parts of eastern Slovakia. In 1312 they combined with Cak, who provided them with some military formations, to challenge the king; they were defeated at Rozhanovce on 15 June. As a result of this defeat, Cak issued no further challenges to Charles Robert. However, he allied himself with Friedrich III (1308–1330) of Austria and led some incursions into Moravia in 1314. Until his death in 1321, he ruled Slovakia from his castle in Trencin. He was known as the Lord of the Vah and the Tatras. Cak

left no son to succeed him. Slovakia therefore returned to the royal fold after his death, and the power of the oligarchs also came to an end. A year later, Charles Robert also reconquered Bratislava and its surrounding areas, which the Austrians had acquired at the beginning of the struggle for the succession to the Arpad throne.

Was Matthew Cak a Slovak potentate, a national hero as older Slovak historiography describes him? Many historians consider him to have been merely a Magyar oligarch.[26] Marxist historiography suggests that "it is just a coincidence that his domains were in Slovakia and that this enabled him to become a personality who played an important role in the life of Slovakia and the Slovaks."[27] On the other hand, it is quite likely that most of his troops were composed of Slovaks and that many of his officials were Slovak; he also had the support of important Slovak groups such as the Diviacky and Ludanicky families. Given the nature of his rule—feudal and centralized—and the area over which it extended—most of Slovakia—his reign could not have been without some direct impact on the life of the Slovaks. Kucera and Kosticky suggest that his reign resulted in "the strengthening of Slovakia in the conscious-ness of the people as a territorial-political entity in its own right which contemporaries called Terra Mathei—Land of Matthew."[28]

The rule of Matthew Cak was not unlike that of the Frankish king Samo some 700 years before; for a period of time a non-Slovak was able to unite the inhabitants of Slovakia under one rule. And like Samo, the political entity that he ruled disappeared after his death. This time, however, this Magyar oligarch was remembered in Slovak oral history and tradition as "Matias Trenciansky"— that is to say "Matthew of Trencin"—perhaps the clearest indication of the estimation with which he was held among the Slovaks. Both the city of Trencin and the county of Trencin are deep in Slovak territory.

With Cak's death, Charles Robert was able to consolidate royal power. He confiscated Cak's lands as well as that of the Ludanicky family for having sided with Cak and, for almost a century, Slovakia enjoyed relative peace and prosperity while undergoing a process of urbanization. He was succeeded by Louis I (1342–1382), who accorded the Slovak inhabitants of many towns the same voting privileges that his predecessors had granted German colonists. As the document *Privilegium pro Slavis (Privilege for the Slavs)*, granted to the town of Zilina in 1381, indicates, such towns had to accept official bilingualism. It is worth noting that the Hungarian city of Buda became officially bilingual, in this case German and Hungarian, only in 1438.

Louis I's death brought about another struggle for the succession to the Hungarian throne, involving foreign royal houses, and resulting in three monarchs in a period of five years: Marie of Anjou (1382–1385), followed by

Charles II of Naples (1385–1386), succeeded by Sigismond of Luxemburg (1387–1437), who also became later Emperor of the Holy Roman German Empire (1410–1437) and King of Bohemia (1419–1437). Sigismond played a significant role in the history of Bohemia with the condemnation to death of the religious reformer Jan Hus in 1415. He is remembered in Slovakia for the sale of twenty-four villages from Spis county to Poland in 1412 in return for a financial loan. They remained under Polish administration until 1769.

HUSSITISM IN SLOVAKIA

After the boom that Europe experienced from the eleventh to the thirteenth centuries, social and economic conditions deteriorated slowly in the next 200 years. Epidemics such as the Black Death ravaged towns, cities, and the countryside. Social unrest was not uncommon; there were many revolts and rebellions. In addition, since the beginning of the fourteenth century, the papacy was beset by problems resulting from its involvement in temporal as well as religious matters. In 1309, the French city of Avignon became the seat of the Holy See; while the Supreme Pontiff returned to Rome in 1377, it was not until 1429, when Martin V, in the aftermath of the Council of Constance, was acknowledged the only legitimate pope, that the history of what is also known as the Babylonian captivity came to an end. The wealth that church institutions had been accumulating along with the disintegration of ecclesiastical authority led to the decadence of the clergy. Among the first to raise his voice against this state of affairs was the Englishman John Wycliff. Declared a heretic by the Catholic Church, his voice was nevertheless heard in Europe, in particular in Bohemia, where a movement for religious reform soon appeared. As Ernest Denis, the eminent French historian of the Hussite period, writes: "Even if Wycliff hadn't written a word, the reform movement in Bohemia would nevertheless have given the signal to attack the religious system of the Middle Ages because in no other country had the faith corrupted the Church more by making it richer and the people more sensitive to its abuses."[29]

The chain of events that resulted in Hus's condemnation was a mixture of religious idealism,[30] political considerations, national struggles,[31] and social movements. His death did not by any means put an end to the movement he launched; rather Hussitism spread. Its appearance in Slovakia was less due to the fact that the inhabitants were Slavs than to the fact that the emperor, Sigismond, who had allowed Hus to be condemned, was also king of Hungary.

Opinion is divided, depending on national or religious leanings, on the influence of Hussitism in Slovakia. Hussite armies appeared on Slovak territory

in 1428.[32] They established garrisons in towns such as Trnava, Skalica, Topolcany, and Zilina and remained in Slovakia on and off—they left in 1434 but returned in 1440—for about four decades. Their leader was Jan Jiskra z Brandysa, who in 1440 became one of the seven captains of Hungary. He was involved in the succession struggles for the Hungarian throne. Sigismond was succeeded by the Habsburg Albert I (1437–1439), later followed by his son, Ladislas V Posthumous (1444–1457), who was born after his death. Albert I's succession, by a vote of the Diet, was given to Wladislaw Jagellio I of Poland (1440–1444) and was challenged by Elizabeth, mother of Ladislas V, who had him crowned with St. Stephen's crown. In the civil war that ensued, Jiskra sided with Elizabeth while the other nobles, led by Janos Hunyadi, supported Wladislaw I. Wladislaw's death at the battle of Varna against the Turks in 1444 resulted in an interregnum during which Hunyadi was regent, from 1446 until 1453, when the nobles and the Hungarian Diet finally recognized Ladislas V Posthumous as the legitimate king of Hungary.

Jiskra left Slovakia in 1453, exhausted from his struggles with Hunyadi. Many of his followers, however, remained and became known throughout Slovakia as the Brethren, attacking abbeys and monasteries as well as merchants who travelled throughout the Hungarian kingdom. Jiskra was called back in 1454 to liquidate the Brethren. He succeeded partially in doing so when he defeated them at Trebisov in November of that year. They were finally defeated in 1467 by the son of Janos Hunyadi, Mathias I "Corvinus" (1458–1490), who succeeded Ladislas V Posthumous after he died under mysterious circumstances in 1457. Jiskra, who once again found himself in a struggle with the Hunyadi clan, refused to leave Slovakia, and because of his power became a noble and remained in Hungary until his death in 1469.

Did Hussitism win adherents in Slovakia, were the Hussites soldiers of the faith and did they find support among the population? Hussitism might have spread in Slovakia had there existed an intellectual center similar to Prague that would have allowed for the new faith to be debated, for adherents to be won. As it was, "new ideas were limited to a few individuals in [church] chapters, which was insufficient for the spreading of Hussitism among the broad masses of ordinary people."[33] They found support only in the lesser nobility. Therefore it is likely that the influence of the Hussites who came to Slovakia was felt in those areas where they established garrisons, particularly as they were intolerant of opposition. On the other hand, their behavior, according to Frantisek Bokes, was not likely to win them many supporters[34] so that whatever influence they had gained was most probably dissipated once they were chased out of Slovakia. At best, as Branislav Varsik suggests, they brought about social transformations in many Slovak towns and villages.[35]

Mathias "Corvinus," whose army and administration contained Slovaks, chased the last of the Brethren out of Slovakia. He was succeeded by two Polish Jagellios, Wladislaw II (1490–1516) and Louis II (1516–1526) who fell on the battlefield at Mohacs where the Turkish forces defeated the Hungarian ones. The Turks, who since the fall of Constantinople in 1453 were slowly moving northward, were now poised to push farther into Europe. The mission to stop them fell to Austria's Ferdinand I of Habsburg (1526–1564) who acquired in the process the crowns of Hungary and Bohemia. A new era opened that would differ markedly from the one that was ending. From the fall of Great Moravia until the accession of the Habsburgs on the throne of Hungary, Slovakia had on the whole enjoyed the opportunity to undergo social and economic development. It was also an era of relative tranquillity, except during the short-lived Mongol invasion and the Hussite episode.

SOCIAL AND ECONOMIC DEVELOPMENT

The incorporation of Slovakia into the Arpad kingdom had brought benefits to the Magyars, especially once they ceased to be nomads and became agricultural settlers. In the first century after the fall of Great Moravia there was some reduction in the standard of living in Slovakia because of the Magyar raids, but after the defeat of the Magyar armies near Augsburg in 955, the Slovaks were able to live relatively freely on the north side of the Danube and in the valleys of the Tatra Mountains. Judging from the many Slavic terms that entered the Hungarian vocabulary, especially in agriculture and craft production, terms that nomads would not use, it is clear that the relationship between the two nations produced a "Magyar-Slovak symbiosis."[36] It is also suggested that "at the beginning of the twelfth century Hungary had the character of a Slavic state, a fact confirmed by the Chronicler Helmold in the *Cronica Slavorum* from 1172."[37] However, Helmold is not universally acknowledged as a reliable source. Politically the Magyars controlled the state and ruled over the Slovaks. This would never change. It does not mean that the Slovaks could not and did not have some influence on the political life of the state. That there was such influence was evident from the beginning.

After the fall of Great Moravia, Wiching's victory over Methodius and Gorazd ensured that German missionaries carried out the Christianization of Hungary. While there is also evidence of similar activity from Byzantium, in the end Hungary accepted Christianization from missionaries who quite likely came from the principalities of Nitra and Morava. There is nothing surprising in this development as Slovakia was the most advanced part of the kingdom,

especially since Christianity and feudal institutions had already taken root in the Great Moravian state.

The main task of spreading the Christian faith in Hungary was given to abbeys and monasteries, whose numbers would increase dramatically over the next two centuries. They reported to the archbishopric in Ostrihom and the bishoprics of Nitra and Jager. The Benedictine monastery of Zobor, near Nitra, which was probably founded during the reign of Svätopluk in the ninth century, was most likely the main center of religious activity in the early years of the Hungarian kingdom. It later became a place of pilgrimage because of two saints who sojourned there, Svorad-Andrew and Benedikt, "the oldest and first, in the true and full sense of the word, Slovak saints."[38] In 1075, Gejza I (1074–1077) founded a Benedictine monastery in Sv. Benadik nad Hronom. At about the same time another was erected in Krasna nad Hornadom by the same order; "the abbey of Krasna was in its time [from the eleventh to the sixteenth centuries] one of the religious, economic and cultural centers of Eastern Slovakia."[39] There were Benedictine abbeys also in Janosovce, Ludanice, and Kliz. Other orders also were active in Slovakia, namely the Cistercians, who founded abbeys in Lipovnik in 1141, in Stiavnik in 1223, and a nunnery in Bratislava in 1235. The Premonstratensians established monasteries in Jasov near Kosice in 1220, and in Klastor pod Znievom in 1251. Among the mendicant orders, the Dominicans erected a monastery in Kosice at the beginning of the thirteenth century while the Franciscans appeared in Bratislava in 1228 and at about the same time also in Nitra and in Trnava. Likely some of these monasteries were destroyed during the Mongol invasion.

In addition to abbeys and monasteries, ecclesiastical authority, which remained unchanged throughout the Middle Ages, "was superseded only by the developing practice of governing very extensive sees through authority delegated by the presiding bishop to provosts and archdeacons. In the main this was the form of administration that was introduced throughout most of the Slovak territory."[40] As a result, chapters were established in major cities such as Bratislava and Nitra. Although no records indicate the date of their creation, documents show that there existed a chapter in Nitra in 1111, one in Spisske Podhradie in 1275, and one in Bratislava in 1302. Their importance is confirmed in the case of the Spis chapter, which was made the official residence of the provost and the headquarters of the council of canons. Another institution of some significance was the prepositure, something akin to a diocese, to whom the Holy See granted comprehensive privileges and prerogatives. Prepositures in Nove Mesto nad Vahom, Jasov, and Leles came into being toward the close of the twelfth century; in Spis, at the beginning of the thirteenth century; in Sahy, in 1238; and in Klastor pod Znievom, in 1251. Many of these monas-

teries, prepositures and chapters functioned as centers of culture because of their libraries and schools.

The reconstruction that took place after the Mongol invasions brought about changes in the economic and social life of the Slovaks even if they had come off relatively better than the inhabitants of the plains by hiding in the mountains when the Mongols attacked. The survivors of these raids were employed in agriculture and lived in the vicinity of castles and fortified towns. The German colonists who accepted the invitation of Bela IV to settle in Hungary became involved in mining, and they settled in or created new mining towns throughout Slovakia, towns that also attracted native inhabitants. To encourage German colonization, the king granted them and their towns special privileges, which the Slovaks eventually also claimed for themselves. By the end of the thirteenth century some thirty towns in Slovakia had such privileges.[41] Bratislava received its *Privilegium* in 1291, most likely because of its economic importance as a wine producing town: "This *Privilegium* refers to old vineyards and indicates that the citizens of Bratislava did not have to pay fees on new vineyards."[42] Of a legal and economic nature, these privileges were granted not just by the king but also by a noble if the settlers had been invited by him. The towns could elect their own municipal council as well as a reeve who had to be approved by the king or noble. The same pattern was followed in villages. The reeve and his council were also the court of first instance with appeals going not to the *zupan* but rather to the king or noble or his representative. By the beginning of the thirteenth century, there were towns in Slovakia with either complete (Banska Bystrica, Bratislava, Nitra, Krupina, Trnava) or limited legal jurisdiction (Babina, Dobra Niva, Jasov, Kosice, Sväty Kriz nad Hronom). This made Hungarian political life interesting because, according to Spiesz, "from the thirteenth century on, the constitution of old Hungary was very original, it did not copy any other; all offices and positions were elected, including the palatine, the highest representative of the country."[43]

The inhabitants of the towns were for the most part free artisans, merchants, and miners and enjoyed many rights, including the right to own property and to dispose of it in their wills as well as the right to move. Villages were inhabited by peasants and sharecroppers who owned their own land, which they cultivated on a crop rotation basis. Townspeople and villagers also had the right to choose the parish priest, to hunt and fish, to cut wood in the forests, and to get stone from quarries. Perhaps the most important right was that of holding a market with the profits going to the town. These markets were often held on specific days with the town named accordingly, for example, Dunajska Streda (Dunajska Wednesday), Plavecky Stvrtok (Plavecky Thursday), or Rimavska Sobota (Rimavska Saturday). On the other hand, towns paid taxes

to the crown, welcomed and hosted the king or noble when he came for a visit, and made an annual gift to the lord. To obtain revenues, town councils levied taxes on bridges and also at the entrances to the town.

Of equal importance at this time, along with the growth of town markets, is the development of commerce, not only within Hungary, but also with other parts of Europe. In the west, Bratislava became a major center for trade with Germany, Austria, Dalmatia, and the Adriatic coast; while in the east Kosice served Poland in the north and the Balkans in the south. Other towns such as Trnava and Levoca also were involved in international trade. Among the goods exported from Slovakia were wine, cattle, horses, and raw materials; imports included luxury goods, furs, salt, and artisanal products. However, when Constantinople fell to the Turks in 1453, the flow of international commerce through the eastern part of Slovakia came to a halt. The region never had another opportunity for the economic and cultural development international trade brings.

Slovakia's administrative infrastructure, the county system, evolved slowly from the tenth century onward. The southeastern and southwestern counties were in place by the end of the twelfth century while counties in northern and central Slovakia came into being later. By the fourteenth century, the county system was fully in place and was not altered until the twentieth century when Slovakia was no longer a part of Hungary.[44] (See Map 3.) Since the time of King Stephen, the counties were headed by a *zupan*. His deputy, the *podzupan,* did not make an appearance until the thirteenth century. The control of the counties remained for a long time the object of a struggle between the ruling class and the lesser nobility for whom the county meant the protection of their property and their status. This nobility thus became the driving force behind the autonomy of the counties and their transformation into administrative sees. The first step in this process was reached in many counties by the end of the thirteenth century: "The royal decrees of 1290 and 1298 which codified the right of the nobility to elect four noble administrators *(iudices nobilium)* . . . completed the process of creating sees."[45] These administrators not only oversaw the administration of the county, but also had jurisdiction in judicial matters. The next step came about in the second half of the fifteenth century during the reign of Mathias "Corvinus": "County autonomy was again recognized with the stipulation that the baronial *ispán* [*zupan*] should appoint his deputy from the local well-to-do nobility, and not from his own retainers. This was the first step towards making this *alispán* [*podzupan*] the representative of the nobility and not of the barons."[46] Also at this time, the palatine was elected by the Diet for the first time.

These developments were taking place at a time when the feudal structure of the country was also undergoing change. At the top of the social ladder was

the nobility, descendant initially from the original Arpad warriors, also known as "freemen—that body which later usage knew as the 'Hungarian nation'."[47] This class underwent many changes, in particular in "the areas inhabited by non-Hungarians [where it] was formed of Hungarian feudal lords enfeoffed from royal lands, free Hungarian soldiers and local leaders rising into the land-holding ruling class."[48] Although all nobles were equal in rank, there was a differentiation determined either by the extent of landholding or by the function at court. Bishops and abbots also belonged to this class. The power of the nobility depended on the internal political situation; under the Angevins, for example, it had given rise to an oligarchy whose preponderance, however, ended up being short-lived. Still, a precedent had been set and for the Slovaks there had been an episode not without interest, the reign of Matthew Cak. Under Sigismond in the fifteenth century, there was an enormous concentration of landed property at the expense of the royal domain.

The changing political fortunes of the nobility had a direct impact on the constitutional development of Hungary. The succession crisis following Albert I's death in 1439 "witnessed the maturing of the idea of a noble-aristocratic polity and the establishment of a number of institutional frameworks."[49] Since the reign of the Arpads, councils composed of the nobility, later to become Diets, had always been convoked for the election or coronation of a king. By the fifteenth century, "they came to be virtually annual meetings of the upper stratas of the nobility, with secondary roles assigned to county delegates, the urban deputies and churchmen."[50] Yet it was the county system that under-pinned the administration of the country and in times of civil disorder, such as 1382 to 1397 and 1440 to 1445, the county nobles virtually ran the state. While the upper nobility retained their privileges, the pressure from the country nobles brought about what Janos Bak calls a "corporate polity"[51] where the deputy head of the county, the *podzupan (vice-comes)*, was elected by these lesser nobles. The *zupan (comes)* continued to be appointed by the king, but the *podzupan* ran the county's affairs. Given that the lesser nobility were also landed gentry, they represented a force with which the king and the upper nobility had to reckon. Not surprisingly, the lesser nobility opposed the growth of towns to which the next strata in the population eventually gravitated.

The next group were the peasants, a class politically nonexistent, most of whom were craftsmen or were involved in agriculture but were also free to move as long as they had fulfilled their obligations to their lord. Prior to the arrival of the German colonists, they had no claim on the land they worked. The anarchy that followed the Mongol invasion made it possible for them to acquire the right to own land, but they also had to meet a series of obligations, including financial ones, depending on the type of work they were involved in and their

relationship to the lord; the result was that "In exchange they owned their hereditary village plots, were entitled to the hereditary use of the lands beyond the village borders, and, most importantly, acquired the most cherished privilege of the guests [*hospites*], the right of free migration. The peasantry now became known as *jobbágy*."[52] They also paid a tithe to the church.[53]

Between the nobility and the peasant were foreigners, known as *hospites*, whose status was defined in law and could not be altered arbitrarily by anyone. Some lived in towns while others worked on the land, particularly in vineyards, where those who owned land formed a "new patrician group."[54] Originally, these people had moved into forts and castles for protection where

> Under Bela IV and his successors, they formed new communities, joining the few remaining original inhabitants. Thus was born the *civis (Bürger, polgár)* urban class, protected by privileges. Signs of its double origin survived in documents, which still refer to them as "*cives et hospites.*" The soldiers were usually Hungarian [or Slovak in Slovakia] and the merchants and artisans German; thus amalgamation did not take place easily.[55]

Jews had special standing except in Bratislava which was "the only city in Hungary which expressly mentioned in its charter that the Jews should enjoy the same civil rights as the other citizens."[56] They usually lived in towns and engaged in commercial activities and financial transactions. In towns such as Bratislava, Nitra, and Trnava they formed their own communities. As was the case elsewhere in Europe, the Jews were on occasion the victims of attacks from the population. Finally, there were the serfs, usually prisoners of war, who were the property of the nobility and could be sold. However, by the end of the thirteenth century, slavery had disappeared from Hungary.

At the beginning of the fourteenth century, Slovakia had some thirty towns and its population, which had grown during the previous century by one-third, totalled around 300,000 inhabitants; this increase was due to a great extent to the influx of German colonists. Sixty more towns were founded by the end of the century. Their average population was around 3,000; the two biggest were Bratislava and Kosice, each with some 5,000 inhabitants. By the time a Habsburg ascended the Hungarian throne in 1437, the population of Slovakia exceeded the half-million mark, spread throughout some 2,000 localities. The towns' legal status differed, depending on whether they were royal free or towns founded by the nobility. The former jealously defended their freedoms, joining together to do so. Thus we see at the end of the fourteenth century mining towns (Banska Bela, Banska Bystrica, Banska Stiavnica, Kremnica, Lubietova, Nova Bana, Pukanec) forming a union, as did eastern

Slovak towns (Bardejov, Kosice, Levoca, Sabinov, and Presov) in the fifteenth century, which was given the name "Pentapolitana."

Agriculture developed throughout this period, in particular viticulture in the southwest, yet the most important single economic development was the mining of precious metals, copper, and iron. Much of this mining activity took place in Central Slovakia, and towns such as Banska Stiavnica, Kreminca, and Banska Bystrica became major mining centers. There were also smaller ones in the Spis, Gemer, and Liptov counties. It is estimated that in the fourteenth century the mines of Kremnica produced around 400 kilograms of gold and over 1,000 kilograms of silver annually, a level of production unequalled elsewhere in Europe. In Smolnik, in Spis county, around 180 tons of copper were mined annually; as for iron ore, most of it was extracted in the Slovenske Rudohorie. It is worth noting that this mining production decreased somewhat in the fifteenth and sixteenth centuries. The extraction of precious metals was under royal control, as were the mints in Kremnica and Smolnik, which struck coins for the realm. The gold ducats struck in Kremnica around 1330 were among the most sought-after coins in Europe.

Miners were organized in societies; one of the best known and best run was the one created by Jan Turzo from Betlanovce in Spis county. In addition to being a mining entrepreneur, Turzo was also a citizen of Levoca and of Cracow in Poland. Toward the end of the fifteenth century he merged his enterprise with the German firm Fugger from Augsburg; thereafter the Fugger-Turzo concern controlled mining in Central Slovakia and also around Cracow. It was headquartered in Banska Bystrica and proved to be a mining enterprise without equal in Europe, exporting minerals to Germany, Poland, the Low Countries, and Portugal. For example, in the years 1494 to 1526, the concern's mines produced 2,550 tons of copper ore annually. Last but not least, Turzo's enterprise offered working conditions for miners that were quite exceptional for the period, as Spiesz indicates: "Not only the level of production, but also the social conditions of the employees of this enterprise were very high. The workers were employed eight hours a day, they had sickness and old age insurance and their widows and orphans had guaranteed pensions."[57]

One of the first things that the German colonists did when they arrived in Slovakia was to set up guilds. Their main objective was to represent the economic interests of the artisans, rather than to elect representatives to the town council, as was the case in Western Europe. On the other hand, artisans were represented in these councils by successful candidates in town elections. Guilds appeared in Slovakia later than in Western Europe; the first recorded case, complete with statutes, dates back to 1415 in Podolinec, a shoemaker

guild. While some towns had only one guild, bigger towns such as Kosice, Presov, and Bratislava had as many as eight.

When King Louis I issued to the Slovak inhabitants of Zilina the *Privilegium pro Slavis* in 1381, he set into motion a system that gave Slovaks and Germans equal representation in the town council. There is in fact a progressive affirmation by the Slovaks of their equal rights during the Middle Ages. However, the granting of these rights and privileges was not always achieved without resistance. For example, in the case of the election of the parish priest in Trnava, King Mathias "Corvinus" had to intervene and threaten with the death sentence anyone who provoked national dissension. Another right that had been granted to the German colonists, namely the purchase of a house, was also given to Slovaks in Kremnica in 1518. In some towns, the vernacular was also used in civil administration, although not systematically. An interesting situation of multilingualism arose. Latin was the official language of administration in Hungary during the Middle Ages. However, Slovak, Czech, and German were also in use. For example, the town of Skalica has a charter in Czech dating back to 1422. In 1473, we find in Zilina the *Zilinska kniha,* a translation of the Code of Magdeburg from the German into a Slovakized form of Czech. The utilization of Czech as a written (literary) language by the Slovaks is not surprising; Slovak was a vernacular but not yet a literary language. On the other hand, the Czech literary language had been codified by Hus and brought to Slovakia by the Hussites. During the Reformation, in the seventeenth century, Slovak Lutherans adopted the Czech *Kralicka Biblia* (Bible from Kralice) for use in their liturgy.

In the Middle Ages the situation of Slovak town dwellers, as well as that of the peasants on the land, saw steady improvement. When the lord parcelled out land for cultivation, he did so in exchange for rent. Over time this influenced ownership, which came more and more to be identified with the peasant, a situation that advantaged the predominantly agricultural Slovak population. As Spiesz writes: "In Hungary, this right [to own land] was available only to Germans and Slovaks, it was unknown among the Ruthenians, the Rumanians, the Croats and other nations and among the Magyars, it was available only on lands west of the Danube."[58]

The accession of the Angevins to the throne of Hungary had opened the kingdom to Western cultural influences as never before. During the reign of Mathias "Corvinus," Slovakia began to feel the influence of the Renaissance, not just in architecture, but also in art and education. Macartney writes:

He [Mathias "Corvinus"] was, as his panegyrists never tire of repeating, a true Renaissance prince. He was exceedingly talented in every respect: a

brilliant natural soldier, a first-class administrator, an outstanding linguist. Speaking with equal fluency half a dozen languages, a learned astrologer, an enlightened patron of the arts and himself a refined connoisseur of their delights. His library of "Corvina" was famous throughout Europe. . . . Scholars of European repute lived and worked at his court and in the circle of the Archbishop-primate, János Vitez.[59]

The most important contribution of Mathias "Corvinus" to the intellectual life of Slovakia was the founding in 1465 (with the official opening taking place in July 1467) of the Academia Istropolitana in Bratislava under the jurisdiction of Jan Vitez, Archbishop of Ostrihom. Its administrator was the vice-chancellor, Juraj Schomberg, who was the provost of the Bratislava chapter of canons. The choice of Bratislava for a university may well have been due to Schomberg's influence and determined by the availability of a building and the library of the chapter.

This institution, often designated in documents of the period as "Universitas Histropolitana,"[60] consisted of four faculties, arts, law, medicine, and theology. The curriculum in the Faculty of Arts centered on the *septem liberales* (the seven liberal arts), as defined at the time, namely mathematics, geometry, music, astronomy, Latin grammar, dialectics, and rhetoric. Little is known about the other faculties and even less about the student body. Poor financing from the king, the Hungarian conquest of Vienna in 1485 (where there was a well-established university), the decreasing involvement of Vitez and Schomberg, and a lack of interest by their successors resulted first in the university's decline and then in its closing in 1490. Another two centuries would pass before another institution of higher learning would appear on Slovak soil.

There were also primary and secondary schools in Slovakia, connected mostly to chapters, convents, and parishes. At the request of citizens and corporations, town and village schools began to appear. The first village school was founded in 1342 in Diviaky nad Nitricou. However, unlike their religious counterparts, village schools often used the vernacular as a language of instruction rather than Latin. In addition, Slovak students studied abroad, initially in some Western European universities, later in Vienna (founded in 1365) and Prague (founded in 1348); those from northern and eastern Slovakia usually studied in Cracow (founded in 1364). Even with all this evidence of educational activity, there is little that is known about the impact and influence of humanism at this time in Slovakia.[61] Much of the literature was religious, yet there were a number of secular writers, in particular poets, who wrote in Latin; in the early phase none stands out. Outstanding writers appeared later, in particular during the Reformation. Had Central Europe not been menaced by

the Turks, with Hungary in the direct line of invasion, intellectual life in Slovakia might have experienced an even greater development than it did.

It is in architecture and art that the Middle Ages left their most magnificent and lasting imprint in Slovakia. Commensurate with the development of warfare and weapons, the larger towns (Bratislava, Bardejov, Kezmarok, Kosice, Levoca, Trnava) strengthened their fortifications, replacing wood palisades with stone walls and adding gates with watchtowers. Gothic architecture, in the Swabian-Lower Danube style, took over in the building of churches and monasteries, later also in the homes of rich citizens, in particular those situated around the town square. Among the most outstanding examples of sacred Gothic art are the Church of Sv. Mikulas in Trnava (early fourteenth century), the Benedictine Monastery Church of Sv. Benadik nad Hronom, the Chapel of Sv. Jan next to the Franciscan Church in Bratislava, and the parish Church of Sv. Jakub in Levoca (all three late fourteenth century). Construction on the Cathedral of Kosice, based on the style of French Gothic cathedrals, also began in 1385. In the fifteenth century, the Gothic style came into its own, not just in major towns, but also in smaller ones such as Zehra and Spisska Sobota.

Art, in all its aspects, also underwent major development. Toward the end of the fifteenth century, there were three art schools in Slovakia: the Central Slovak one (in mining towns), based on native art and perhaps the most vivid; the Spis one (in Levoca and Spisska Kapitula), which was more experimental; and the Kosice one (in Bardejov) with its lyrical approach. It is in wood carving, however, that Slovak artistic genius was expressed, in particular early in the sixteenth century. The best example is the Gothic altar in the Church of Sv. Jakub in Levoca, completed in 1517, by the artist known to Slovaks as "Majster Pavol". As a Slovak art historian writes: "The main altar of Levoca constitutes a synthesis of architecture, sculpture, painting, and decorative art. But it is clearly the work of the sculptor, with his sense of proportion and harmony, which gives the immense altar piece its perfect unity."[62]

Just like the towns of Carcassonne in France and Rothenburg ob der Tauber in Germany which have remained excellent examples of Middle Ages town planning and organization, Levoca has offered over the centuries a unique testimony to the Gothic artistic talent in Slovakia for very specific reasons: "Levoca is the richest city in Slovakia for late Gothic treasures. What gives it exclusiveness is not only the richness of its artistic treasures but also their chronological continuity."[63]

In the last two centuries of the Middle Ages (the fourteenth and fifteenth), Slovakia underwent rapid and major change. Its social structure was transformed, there was economic growth, and intellectual and cultural life reached an exceptionally high level of creativity. These developments confirmed what

had already begun to take place in Great Moravia, namely Slovakia's orientation toward Western Europe. As Spiesz writes:

> One should note that here is a country and a people who can be categorized as Western European, a people who have a Western European mentality, who own land and property as other Europeans do and who have a European way of thinking. This is all the more meaningful as it concerns a country on the eastern border of Western civilization where part of the Slovak nation did not practice a Western, but rather an Eastern, type of Christian faith and where both of these types overlapped and complemented each other in the easternmost regions of our country.[64]

As the Middle Ages drew to a close and a Habsburg ascended the throne of Hungary, the first half of Slovak history in the Hungarian kingdom came to an end. The fight for survival had been relatively easy; there had been no major threat to the existence of the Slovak nation, and therefore no need to challenge authority, whether that of the king or of the ruling class. The Hungarian political system had heeded the motto attributed by some historians to its first king, St. Stephen, to respect the multilingual and, by extension, multinational composition of the kingdom: "Nam unius lingue uniusque moris regnum inbecille et fragile est."[65] (A kingdom is weak and fragile if it has only one language and only one set of customs.)

The Magyar system, because it was more open and more adaptable to local needs than in many areas of Europe, had allowed for the growth of Slovak national consciousness, in particular in towns and cities. It was the presence of German colonists, their economic activity and the rights that they were granted by the king, more than anything else, that reinforced and helped it to develop. The granting of the same privileges to the Slovaks precluded major confrontations, strengthened national consciousness, and ensured the loyalty of the population. Last but not least, the role of the Catholic Church, through its monasteries and abbeys, chapters and prepositures, schools and libraries, further ensured a degree of social and political stability and development that enabled the arts to flourish. When one considers what awaited the Slovaks in the next 500 years, the Middle Ages almost seem like a golden era. As Spiesz indicates, it was a period that had a positive impact on both the Slovaks and the Hungarian kingdom: "At the end of the Middle Ages, we notice generally the development of Slovak consciousness in the villages, towns and cities, in other words on the territory where the Slovak nation lived, even though it could not rely on a Slovak political formation. Inevitably, along with this Slovak consciousness there existed the consciousness of belonging to the Hungarian state."[66]

This double consciousness would be severely tested in the following centuries as a result of the Turkish advance through Central Europe, royal absolutism, the process of modernization, and the age of nationalism.

4

The Habsburg Empire

THE TURKISH OCCUPATION OF HUNGARY

The Ottoman victory at Mohacs on 29 August 1526 had many consequences for Hungary and its inhabitants. For the Magyars, it was "the prelude to the most miserable period"[1] of their history. Their state was divided into three parts; one part, the Hungarian plain, came under Turkish rule, notable "at its best . . . [for] barren unconstructiveness, and at its more frequent worse, savage destructiveness."[2] Another, Transylvania, acquired some form of autonomy under Turkish suzerainty, allowing thereby its *voivode* (later elevated to the rank of prince) to play a role in the politics of the region. The third was Slovakia, which was connected to a corridor extending southwest from Bratislava and a point east of Ostrihom to the Adriatic coast, just south of Rijeka (Fiume) down to the other side of Senj to form a territory that Hungarian historians call royal Hungary. As a Slovak historian writes: "After Transylvania became a vassal principality of the Ottoman Empire, Slovakia became the center of the Hungarian state. All important Hungarian offices, all central administrative, cultural and Church institutions moved here. The Hungarian parliament met in Bratislava and Trnava became the seat of the archbishopric of Ostrihom."[3] Bratislava, called Pozsony (Preßurg in German) at that time, was thus a de facto capital of Hungary, and its kings were crowned there. This arrangement suited the Habsburgs because of Bratislava's proximity to Vienna. The Slovaks, like the Transylvanians, were spared, for the most part, the worst aspects of the Turkish penetration in Central Europe. However—and this is the most direct consequence of the Turkish presence in the Hungarian plain—Hungarian and

Slovak history were henceforth not merely juxtaposed, as they had been up to that point, but interwoven. The Slovak battle for survival entered a new phase.

Another consequence of the Turkish advance into Central Europe was the accession of a Habsburg to the throne of Hungary. When after the death of King Louis II in the battle of Mohacs his brother-in-law, Ferdinand I of Austria, made his claim, it was contested by many Hungarian magnates and the lesser nobility, who preferred Jan Zapolsky (Janos Zapolyai), Voivode of Transylvania and the biggest landowner in Hungary, as a national king. Both men were in fact crowned King of Hungary. The resulting stalemate lasted for years as Zapolsky turned for support to the sultan, who installed him in Buda. When Zapolsky died in 1540, Ferdinand I tried but failed to regain Buda a year later. The sultan in the meantime acknowledged Zapolsky's son, Janos Sigismond, as king and vassal. In 1547, when Ferdinand I concluded a peace with the sultan, he was recognized as de facto ruler of what was now royal Hungary. Janos Sigismond retained Transylvania, "which in 1566, the Sultan formally declared an autonomous principality under his own suzerainty."[4] But it was only Ferdinand's successor, Maximilian II (1564–1576), who recognized this arrangement in 1568 along with the new frontiers of royal Hungary. The Habsburgs were now the sole rulers of Hungary. Their mission: to defend Europe against the Turks, with whom they remained in a state of war until 1606.

The struggle for the succession to the throne of Louis II facilitated the Turkish advance into Central Europe and the partition of Hungary. As Macartney writes: "the partition did not come about immediately, and but for the disastrous accident of the young king's death, it might not have come about at all."[5] When the Turks marched into Hungary in September 1529 during their advance on Vienna, the population of Slovakia met them for the first time. A year later, Turkish attacks first devastated Slovak territory along the valleys of the Nitra and the Vah, in particular the areas around Trnava and Nitra and along the Hron valley to Levice and Sv. Benadik nad Hronom. It was harvesttime and the population had not been warned of the attacks; as can be expected, they had "catastrophic consequences."[6] Those who escaped did so by seeking refuge in forests and mountain valleys. The next onslaught of this magnitude took place in 1599, when the Tatars, who were in alliance with the Turks, entered Slovakia. In 1666, the plight of the Slovaks, especially those taken prisoner by the Turks, was described most vividly in *Sors Pilarikiana* by Stefan Pilarik. This epic poem in Slovakized Czech describes Pilarik's two-month incarceration in a Turkish jail, his sale into slavery to a Romanian, and his escape.

For the Slovaks, their prolonged misery during the Turkish presence in the Hungarian plain came primarily from the fact that the Hungarian-Ottoman frontier was located in their southern regions, which the Turks occupied during

the years 1541 to 1568. Another factor added to the misery of the Turkish occupation. At this time the economy of Central Europe was entering a process of slow decline, due in part to the Turkish penetration but above all to the consequences of the discovery of the New World. New patterns of international commercial activity were developing, and many overland routes from Central to Western Europe ceased to be important; the result was that "much of Eastern Europe [was] consigned to an alien pattern of development after a long period of continuous association with the rest of the continent."[7] The rise of capitalism in Western Europe that accompanied the intellectual movements of the Renaissance and Reformation played a role in changing the feudal system. While the system disintegrated in Western Europe, the stagnation in Central Europe contributed to its continuation, allowing multinational empires characterized by the centralization of power rather than national states to emerge.

The consequences of these developments were most evident in the mining towns of Slovakia. The gold and silver brought back from the Americas was more abundant, cheaper, and more easily accessible to Western Europe than that produced in the mines of Central Slovakia. The economy of the mining towns suffered, and because of incessant warfare, the towns were not always able to handle the influx of refugees, for whom there were few opportunities. The poverty they brought with them often provoked unrest and revolts.

In agriculture, the social situation was not much better; in fact, it deteriorated slowly. Central Europe continued to benefit from the grain and livestock trade with Western Europe; however, "profits obtainable in the grain trade stimulated East European feudal landowners to increase the obligations of the peasantry."[8] Laws were introduced that curtailed the migration of the indentured population on the land. In addition, war regularly disrupted the trade patterns, adding to the social and economic unrest. In the end, the rulers and the population of royal Hungary recognized that the greatest threat came from the Turks and that a system of defenses had to be erected to protect the population against their incursions.

To achieve some coordination of defense activities, Slovakia was divided into two military captaincies, one in the east, in Kosice (from 1564 on), covering the northeast of Slovakia, and the other in the west, covering primarily the southwest, whose headquarters changed with the fortunes of war: Nitra (1564–1568); Surany (1568–1581); Levice (1581–1589); and Nove Zamky (1589–1663). Efforts were made constantly to shore up defenses. In 1564, for example, the western area captain met with military and political representatives in Banska Stiavnica to establish a line of defense of Slovak mining towns from an anticipated three-pronged Turkish advance in the Hron valley. Military fortifications were

also organized with a system of fire signals that warned of the enemy's presence. However, as this was neither a constant nor an impermeable frontier, the result of unceasing Turkish and Magyar sorties was the devastation of the land by both parties. Over time, until the Turks left, these border areas developed into a "condominium system—the joint government of Magyar and Turkish land-owners."[9] Moreover, towns such as Esztergom (Ostrihom), Nograd (Novohrad), and Szecseny (Secany) in Hungary and Filakovo in Slovakia were transformed into Ottoman *sandjaks* (military administrative units).

The border area was also one where Hungarian magnates owned property, a situation not necessarily disadvantageous for the population; the magnates were responsible for the castles and fortifications erected to defend royal Hungary against the Turks. There were in fact some unexpected benefits. Developments in warfare, in particular the musket and the cannon, brought about important innovations in the defense of towns. Renaissance fortifications, often surrounded by wide moats, were built and located not just on high but also on low ground; "Nove Zamky became, for instance, a unique example of a fortified renaissance town, whose builders were Italians, the brothers Baldigari."[10] Moreover, the towns offered protection to the Magyar aristocracy who then built their palaces in them. It is estimated that two thirds of the Magyar nobility sought refuge in Slovakia despite the declining economic situation of the towns. Over time, the country became more urbanized. Some 160 localities in Slovakia can be considered to have had an urban character by the end of the Turkish occupation.

The Turkish wars had two immediate consequences on the life of the Slovaks. The first was specific to those who lived in the border areas, in the Novohrad, Hont, Tekov, and Nitra counties; peasants in these counties created peasant committees to help in the defense against the Turks. As Ludwig von Gogolak notes: "the peasants fought under their own captains and then delivered the captured Turkish robbers to the area administration which in turn gave the peasants part of the booty."[11] These peasant committees disappeared once the Turks left Hungary. The second consequence was the co-optation of an increasing number of Slovaks into the lower nobility by virtue of their involvement in the defense against the Turks. This nobility, perhaps more accurately defined as gentry, was the intermediary between the people and the major landowners. However, unlike purely Magyar areas where there was linguistic homogeneity, there were important differences among magnates in Slovakia, due not only to land ownership but also location. This influenced the gentry because "the lower and middle nobility, where the Slovak language and the solidarity with the people was strongest, was completely dependent on this upper aristocracy, proprietors of vast estates."[12] The importance of this gentry

as interlocutors or intermediaries depended therefore on the magnates and the degree to which they themselves identified with the Slovak people. Religion and literary language, as we shall see later, were determining factors.

In the years preceding a period of intense fighting known as the Fifteen Years War (1591–1606), when the Turks sought to push further into Central Europe, Slovak territory was subjected not just to sporadic Turkish attacks but also, where the Turks were in control, to the rigors of the Ottoman administration. Heavy taxes were imposed and their payment was exacted in money and in kind, in particular agricultural goods and household or precious objects. When taxes were not paid, the Turks retaliated with raids against the population. One of the major causes of the Fifteen Years War had been the increasing refusal of the population to pay taxes. The war ended in a stalemate, emptied both treasuries, and cost both sides heavily in men and matériel.

If the wars with the Turks provoked the economic decline of the towns and cities of royal Hungary, they had, on the other hand, some specific consequences on the status and organization of these towns and cities. Apart from those that were destroyed by the Turks, most noticeable was the decrease in importance of royal free towns and the growth of new ones in which guilds established themselves. By the end of the sixteenth century, there were some 150 towns in Slovakia with over 1,000 guilds. The character of many towns changed as Magyars, fleeing the Turkish occupation of the Hungarian plain, moved into them. In 1551, for example, the Nitra town council agreed to have equal representation from the German, Slovak, and Magyar parts of the population. Far more important, however, was the intensification of a process that had begun when Germans began to settle in Slovakia in the thirteenth century, namely the growth of a nationally conscious Slovak citizenry. As Spiesz writes: "Even if at this time they did not possess their own state, the Slovaks were the only nation in Central Europe which had higher social classes than just the peasantry. One cannot speak of a Slovak consciousness among the aristocracy, on the other hand, Slovak citizens played an important role in the history of Slovakia at that time."[13] If anything good came out of the Turkish presence in Central Europe, it was the enhancing of this process, which helped to maintain, if not strengthen, Slovak national consciousness.

In addition to fighting the Turks, the Habsburgs had to contend with many rebellions, such as the 1604 magnate rebellion led by a Calvinist, Stefan (Istvan) Bocskay, who in 1605–1606 controlled most of Slovakia; these rebellions either influenced or constrained the ability of the Habsburgs to defend royal Hungary. Nevertheless, it became clear to the Habsburgs that if they attempted at one and the same time to dislodge the Turks and defeat Bocskay they would fail in both attempts. It was in their long-term interest to come to

an arrangement with the Sublime Porte. They signed the Peace of Zsitvatorok of 1606, which regulated the relations between the Habsburg and Ottoman empires for the next half century and brought a modicum of peace to the region. Bocskay, who was elected Prince of Transylvania in 1605, was instrumental in arranging it.

Hostilities were renewed in the 1660s and Slovak territory bore some of the brunt of the incursions from Ottoman forces. In the summer of 1663, the Ottomans invaded Central Slovakia. The unsuccessful attack against a Turkish vanguard by forces led by Adam Forgac of Nove Zamky on 17 August 1663 resulted in deep Turkish penetrations and the devastation of Slovak territory. The Ottomans occupied Nove Zamky, Nitra, and Levice, turning each into *sandjaks* and unifying them into the westernmost *ejalet* (province) of the Ottoman Empire; "the occupation of Nove Zamky, Nitra, Levice, and Novohrad was the greatest military expedition on Slovak territory during the entire period of Ottoman presence, almost one hundred fifty years."[14] They were beaten back a year later. The Turks continued to be a factor in Slovakia until they were finally driven out of Hungary toward the end of the seventeenth century, with a second battle at Mohacs in 1687 as the determining engagement, one that was not devoid of symbolism. In 1699, the sultan signed the Peace of Karlowitz, "under which he relinquished all Hungary except the Maros-Tisza corner and the long-lost Croat territories across the Save."[15]

The Turkish occupation of Hungary had many consequences on the life of its inhabitants, in particular the Magyars. They suffered the devastation of the Hungarian plain and the destruction of their towns and villages. In addition to the population movements that this provoked, they saw the national balance tip in favor of the non-Magyars, who lost fewer people.[16] As far as the Slovaks are concerned, the Turkish occupation not only hastened the process of urbanization but, by virtue of its duration and at times its intensity, also had another impact on their national development: "The long occupation of the southern parts of Slovakia and the danger to much of the territory behind the line of border castles left profound traces in the material and spiritual culture of our people. To this day we can see the [traces of the] rebuilding of many fortifications or churches. In oral tradition, this [occupation] theme is found in legends, ballads and songs."[17]

Royal Hungary and other Habsburg domains were threatened not only by the Turks; an equally serious challenge came from the Reformation. Martin Luther's dispute with the Catholic Church, which came to a head in 1530, had political consequences across Europe. In the power alignment that took place on the continent, the Habsburgs (in Spain and Austria) became defenders of the Catholic faith. By acceding to the Hungarian throne, they brought with

them a second mission to Hungary, that of preventing the spread of Protestantism. The Reformation found fertile ground in royal Hungary, where the power of the magnates was still great, and many of them were sympathetic to its message. In addition, as Ferenc Szakaly writes: "The spread of religious reforms was the major intellectual event in sixteenth-century Hungary."[18] What made the Reformation such a challenge to the Habsburgs was the fact that the wars with the Turks helped the spread of Protestantism: "Great concessions to the Protestants in the Empire and in other countries were closely connected with the military activities of the Ottoman armies in Eastern Europe."[19]

THE REFORMATION AND COUNTER-REFORMATION IN SLOVAKIA

The Reformation initially made deep inroads in Slovakia, in particular in the mining centers of Banska Bystrica, Banska Stiavnica, Kremnica, and Zvolen, where German colonists were especially receptive to its message. Some of this success is also due to the fact that in 1526 at Mohacs, two Catholic archbishops and five bishops had lost their lives. In addition, from 1522 to 1564, some 200 Slovaks studied at the University of Wittenberg, so among the Protestant pastors in Hungary, Slovaks predominated. Also, many parish schools passed into the jurisdiction of the towns during the sixteenth century. The Protestant faith spread from the mining centers to the landed gentry through the efforts of such people as the brothers Peter and Nicholas Kostka, Francis Revay, and the Turzo, Radvansky, and Balas families. At the same time, cultural contacts between Bohemia and Slovakia intensified with the presence of many Hussite refugees who brought with them a Czech bible prepared by the Czech Brethren in the 1450s. Slovak Lutherans adopted it in their liturgy. One result of these contacts, according to Spiesz, was that "many Slovak Lutherans truly considered themselves to be Czech and assumed that their Church had been established by the Hussites in the fifteenth century."[20] The seeds of a conflict important in the nineteenth and twentieth centuries had been sown.

The spread of Reformation ideas in Hungary was not a sudden or a homogeneous process and proceeded within existing institutions: "The Lutheran leaders were able to work within and utilize the structures and institutions of the Catholic Church as they moved to fill the vacuum in ecclesiastical leadership at the local and regional levels."[21] Among the other denominations that attracted followers were the Lutherans, the Sacramentarians, the Calvinists, the Anabaptists, the Zwinglians, the Trinitarians, and the Antitrinitarians. Whereas Calvinism took hold among the Magyar population, in Slovakia it

was Lutheranism of the Augsburg Confession.[22] Yet not all Lutheran teachings from Germany were accepted; in particular, a conflict developed between the partisans of moderate reforms and those favoring more radical ones. Over time, the Slovak Lutherans, to defend themselves against charges of radicalism from government as well as religious quarters, and to demonstrate that their theology was truly catholic and orthodox, formulated their own confessions of faith. The *Confessio Pentapolitana,* prepared by Leonhard Stoeckel of Bardejov, was agreed to by five eastern Slovak towns (Bardejov, Kosice, Levoca, Presov, and Sabinov) in 1549 and the *Confessio Montana* (also known as *Heptapolitana*) by seven central Slovak towns (Banska Bela, Banska Bystrica, Banska Stiavnica, Kremnica, Lubietova, Nova Bana, and Pukanec) in 1559. A decade later, in 1569, 24 parish priests in Spis county proclaimed the *Confessio Scepusiana.*

The gradual acceptance of the Protestant faith by many Hungarian magnates in Slovakia created enough pressure for the Lutherans to be granted religious freedom in 1606, in the wake of the Bocskay rebellion. Under the authority of Palatine Juraj Turzo, they convoked a synod in Zilina in 1610 and organized western and central Slovakia into three regions, each with a superintendent. At another synod in Spisske Podhradie in 1614, eastern Slovakia was organized into two regions, each also with a superintendent. David P. Daniel writes: "Two superintendencies were created for Spis and Saris counties and the Book of Concord was established as the doctrinal standard for the Lutherans in the region. . . . [The activities of this synod] mark the end of the Reformation era in Slovakia as a whole and in eastern Slovakia in particular."[23] A Slovak Lutheran Church had also come into being.

The spread of Reformation ideas must be seen in the context of humanism, which, as we saw in the last chapter, had reached Hungary in the fifteenth century and given Slovakia its first university, the Academia Istropolitana. In the words of Szakaly: "The Reformation was to some extent inspired by humanism and carried its traditions further, while the Hungarian Catholic intelligentsia continued to build on its ideals."[24] In Slovakia, the link between humanism and Reformation was such that both "left deep traces in the spiritual life of society and brought about changes which generated and determined the development of culture in Slovakia right up to the end of the eighteenth century."[25] However, before long Slovakia also experienced the full force of the Counter-Reformation. It would bring about an even more profound cultural revolution that would mark the religious, social, and political life of the Slovak people to this day. In this maelstrom of competing religions and cultural influences, the Slovaks continued to make a contribution to European civilization, much in the same way as they had been doing since Great Moravia.

At the beginning of their reign, the Habsburgs tried to carry out simultaneously their double mission against the Turks and the Reformation. However, only once they were firmly in power could they begin to concentrate on the Reformation and launch the Counter-Reformation. Its beginnings in Slovakia can be traced to the appointment in 1553 of a Romanian, Nicholas Olah, as archbishop of Ostrihom. In 1560, he sent some Jesuits to Trnava, where they established a seminary the following year;[26] it carried on its academic mission until 1567, when its buildings were destroyed by fire. The Jesuits left Trnava and in 1585 established themselves in the Turiec prepositure, in Klastor pod Znievom and Sala. These initial efforts, however, did not seriously prevent the spreading of the Reformation message, but merely set the stage for later activities as the Habsburgs were still very much involved with the Turks.

When Rudolf II (1576–1612) successfully sued for peace with the Ottoman Empire in 1606, the way became clear to concentrate on countering the expansion of Protestantism. The death of three Jesuit priests—Marek Krizin, Stefan Pongrac and Melicher Grodecky—at the hands of supporters of rebel magnate Gabor Bethlen on 7 September 1619 in Kosice was one of those incidents that proved a catalyst: "The year 1619 may be considered as marking a turning point for the Church; thereafter she began to revive and move forward."[27] Under the leadership of Peter Cardinal Pazmany, a Catholic convert from a Calvinist family, appointed bishop of Ostrihom in 1616, the Counter-Reformation came into its own in Slovakia. Cardinal Pazmany was an energetic man with exceptional organizational abilities. He was a gifted preacher, able to speak to the ordinary people, yet he concentrated specifically on education and the training of priests, particularly from the aristocracy. In Slovakia, he reopened the Trnava seminary and, in 1635, founded the University of Trnava from which the Jesuits carried on their activities throughout royal Hungary. The university also had a printing press, which, during its existence, published some 5,000 titles in Latin, Greek, German, Slovak, Magyar, Romanian, Croatian, Ukrainian, and French.[28] Religious books dominated. While the Lutheran hymnal, *Cithara Sanctorum,* had been published by Juraj Tranovsky in Levoca in 1638, the *Cantus Catholici* of Benedikt Szölösi was printed in 1655 at the university press. In it Szölösi affirmed the strength of Slovak national consciousness. This hymnal, written in Slovak and considered by Slovak Catholics to be part of their national heritage, testifies to the importance of the university and the town during the Counter-Reformation. The university thrived for over a century until it was moved to Buda in 1777 after the Society of Jesus had been dissolved in 1773.

The Counter-Reformation quickly spread also as a result of the activities of many religious orders among the people of the cities and towns. In addition

to the Jesuits and those already established since the Middle Ages, orders appeared in Slovakia whose aim was to reestablish the primacy of the Catholic faith and the authority of the Catholic Church; in Bratislava, for example, the Capucins and the Brothers of Mercy arrived in 1672, the Ursuline Sisters in 1676. Two other orders that played an important role were the Franciscan Conventuals (Friars Minor), who established themselves in Levoca in 1668, and the Piarists, who settled in Podolinec in 1642, in Prievidza in 1666, in Brezno in 1673, and in Sväty Jur in 1685. In this period, Orthodox Catholics also acknowledged the authority of the Bishop of Rome in the Union of Uzhorod of 1646. Their rite, known as the Byzantine rite, which uses Old Church Slavonic in the liturgy, became predominant in Eastern Slovakia.

These orders also had a major impact on primary and secondary education in Slovakia. Generally, wherever they went, they established schools, not just for boys but also for girls, as did the Ursuline Sisters in Bratislava, Trnava, and Kosice. No order, however, was as active as the Jesuits, who, in addition to Trnava, founded *gymnazia* (secondary schools) in Bratislava, Trencin, Skalica, Banska Bystrica, and Levoca. In addition, they created a second institution of higher education in 1657 in Kosice, which also offered a *studium generale* (university curriculum), making it equal to the University of Trnava in all but name. The Protestants were also involved in education. Many Lutheran magnates established schools for the aristocracy in the royal free towns, in the mining cities, and on their lands; for example, the Turzo family did so in Velka Bytca, Hlohovec, Banovce, Ruzomberok, and Ilava. By 1600, sixteen city and eight noble schools were *gymnazia*. Four decades later, their number had grown to seventy. It is estimated that there were 132 Lutheran schools on Slovak territory in the second half of the seventeenth century.

The opening of so many schools produced some interesting developments in education. Pedagogical goals and methods were improved both in Catholic and Protestant schools. As David P. Daniel writes: "The Protestant Reformers and, following the Council of Trent, leaders of Catholic reform, urged that local institutions be established to inculcate pure doctrine and to foster piety as well as to train students in the so-called 'studia humanitatis.'"[29] Many of these developments were due to the work and efforts of Lutheran educators like Daniel Tissenbach in Bratislava, Andreas Graff in Trencin, Jan Duchon and especially Matej Bel in Banska Bystrica, a pioneer of pedagogical realism and "the foremost representative of pietism in Slovakia."[30] These men were *gymnazium* teachers or directors. Many *gymnazia* enjoyed an excellent reputation, none more so than the *Collegium scholasticum* established in Presov in 1665. However, as the Counter-Reformation gained ground, "the political events in the last decades of the seventeenth century interfered with Protestant schools.

From the great number of Lutheran *gymnazia* established before the year 1640, there were only ten left in Slovakia at the beginning of the eighteenth century."[31] Among them was the *Collegium scholasticum,* which was closed in 1711 and its properties handed over to the Catholics.

The emphasis on education also extended to university education. Students attended foreign universities, notably Prague, Vienna, and Wittenberg and a number in Italy; in many of these institutions, there were also professors from Slovakia. A pattern begun in the Middle Ages had simply continued to develop. In addition, with a university in Trnava, intellectual life in Slovakia was on par with that of other European countries. Among those in this institution who made a significant contribution to the scholarship of their time were Henrich Berzevici in mathematics and trigonometry and Martin Sentivani (Szentivany), whose publication *Curiosa et selectiora variarum et scientiarum miscellanea* (An assortment of interesting and rather select items of general and academic knowledge) (1689–1702) was a major work in astronomy, meteorology, botany, zoology, geography, history, and geology. The first atlas of Hungary appeared in 1689 in Trnava, where Samuel Timon also published the first topographical work on the cities and towns of Hungary. Others who made an important contribution but were not at the university were the geographers Mikulas Olah and Lazar Rosseti, the botanist Jan Lipai, the astronomer Jakub Priebitzer, and the philosopher Martin Rakovsky.

At this time the first works making specific reference to the Slovaks and their history began to appear. The most influential was from Peter Revai, a Slovak at the University of Strasbourg, who published in 1656 *De monarchia et sacra corona regni Hungariae centeniae septem* (Seven centuries of the Hungarian kingdom and holy crown), a work that looked at the history of the Slavs in Hungary and throughout Europe. An important defense of the Slovaks appeared in the writings of a Czech exile, Jakob Jakobeus, who arrived in Slovakia after the battle of White Mountain and settled in Presov. In 1642, he published in Slovakized Czech *Viva gentis Slavonicae delineatio* (A living outline of the Slovak nation) and also a poetic work entitled *Gentis Slavonicae lacrumae, suspiria et vota* (The tears, sighs and demands of the Slovak nation) (Levoca, 1642), which complements his history of the Slovaks. Finally, Daniel Sinapius-Horcicka, a Lutheran pastor, wrote a defense of the Slovaks and their language in *Neo-forum Latino-Slavonicum* (A new Latin-Slovak market) published in 1678.

By building on the ideals of humanism, the Counter-Reformation, just like the Reformation, also brought with it a renewal of the arts, new directions in architecture, and a major output of literary works. There was the flowering of secular poetry from the pens of Valerian Mader, Jan Bocatius, Pavol Rubigallus, Valentin Balasa, the brothers Juraj and Leonard Mokosini, Andrej

Mudron, Jan Sambucus, and others, all of whom wrote in Latin. Ondrej Sklenar-Banovsky, Jan Pruno-Frastacky, Ondrej Cengler, Matus Urbanovsky, and Elias Lani were among those who composed religious poetry. Another important art form was the epic song. Among those describing the anti-Turkish and anti-Habsburg struggles are "*Pisen o Sigetskom zamku*" (Song about Siget Castle), "*Pisen o Modrom Kameni a Divine*" (Song about Modry Kamen and Divin) and "*Pisen o zamku Muranskom*" (Song about Muran Castle). Catholic and Protestant authors also performed plays in schools, with Lutherans appearing in the towns of Presov, Prievidza, Kezmarok, and Roznava and Catholics appearing in Trnava and Skalica. The Jesuits were particularly active in the theater arts; "in the years 1601–1773, in all of Hungary the Jesuits produced over 10,000 school plays, the majority of which were in Slovakia."[32]

In architecture, new developments were made possible by the appearance of a new social institution, that of "cultural patron of the arts."[33] Three such outstanding patrons in Slovakia were Bishop Anton Vrancic, Zacharias Rohoznik-Mosovsky, and Nicholas Olah. Renaissance and early baroque styles dominated that which the Counter-Reformation encouraged, namely "expensive and luxurious churches, imposing monasteries and shrines that were not only holy, but also spectacular. All were built in great numbers. It was the palatine, Miklos Esterhazy, who built the first baroque church modeled on Rome's *il Gesu*. This church, at Nagyszombat [Trnava], was followed by several others which he and his son Pal, also a palatine, founded."[34] The orders benefited particularly from this cultural phenomenon. The Jesuits built churches in the Slovak towns of Sväty Jur, Banska Stiavnica, Banska Bystrica, Levoca, Spisska Kapitula, and Bratislava. The Franciscans had their churches in Hlohovec, Nizna Sebastova, Malacky, and Trnava, where the Paulinians also had a church erected. In addition, Protestant churches built at this time bear witness to the new art and architecture in Bratislava (1636–1638), Sväty Jur (1651–1658), Pezinok (1655–1659), Stitnik (1636), Puchov (1643), and Dolne Strhare (1654), the last three inspired by the Dutch baroque style. Among other buildings erected in the Renaissance style were the town halls of Levoca (1615) and Banska Bystrica (1564–1565) and the Marriage Palace of the Turzo family, built in 1601 in Velka Bytca. Fortifications also underwent changes, in particular those in Leopoldov and Komarno and the Bratislava Castle, which experienced major renovations from 1635 to 1649.

The most meaningful consequence of the Counter-Reformation's significant enrichment of the cultural life of Slovakia was the acceptance and development of religiosity in the population. This characteristic remained with the Slovaks right up to the twentieth century; its strength and importance can be gauged by the fact that religiosity was, during the Communist regime, one

of the more successful ways to express individual as well as national opposition to a totalitarian regime. It deeply influenced the social and political life of the Slovaks, even in the age of modern mass communications. Moreover, as we shall see later, clergy of both the Catholic and Protestant faiths became political leaders, a situation that was not necessarily without some drawbacks. Nonetheless, from the time of the Counter-Reformation until the advent of modern government in the twentieth century, the religiosity of the population testified to the Catholic Church's ability, with its organizational structure and the social, medical, educational, and caritative activities of its various orders, to sustain not only social but also national cohesion. In different ways, this was also the case of the Lutheran Church. In the absence of a native aristocracy—the magnates who owned land and built residences in Slovakia were for the most part Magyar—these two churches provided leadership which the Slovak population accepted to face the challenges that awaited them. One of these challenges was absolutism, and it was strongly opposed by the Hungarian magnates. Even if the Slovak people would have little if nothing to say in the struggle between the king and the Magyar aristocracy, they were nevertheless directly affected because it was fought out mostly on their soil.

SLOVAKIA AND THE MAGNATE REBELLIONS

The evolution of the Hungarian political system, as we saw in the previous chapter, mirrored primarily the political fortunes of the aristocracy but also the ability of the king to play off the high nobility against the lower one. In addition, the king also had the right to ennoble defenders of the crown. Charles Robert, after defeating the oligarchs, had strengthened royal power by either confiscating the land of his enemies or using it to reward his supporters. He thereby created an important landowning aristocracy. By appointing other loyal supporters to administer royal lands, he also established a court aristocracy whose elite "was formed by the highest lay and ecclesiastical officeholders. Sources refer to them as the prelates and barons of the realm *(praelati et barones regni)* . . . who were the members of the king's permanent council, which decided all political issues and represented the country in foreign affairs."[35] As this system developed, other kings made their own contribution. Mathias "Corvinus," for example, strengthened royal power by a reform of the administration of revenues and the judicial system. However, Mathias knew, for he came from among their ranks, that power ultimately rested in the landowning nobility, many of them old baronial families. He never challenged them. Still, less than a century later, in 1514, the Diet adopted the *Tripartitum,* a

document that "laid down in explicit terms the complete legal equality of all nobles, as enjoying 'one and the same liberty.'"[36] Even so, the power of the magnates did not wane; in time they formed the Upper Table ("Upper House") in the Hungarian Diet. When the Habsburgs ascended the throne of Hungary after Mohacs, the challenge to their power came from this landed aristocracy who used both the Turkish menace and the Reformation to make good their opposition. In the words of Katalin Peter: "It was typical that in royal Hungary all anti-Habsburg movements were organized by mighty magnates."[37]

The tug-of-war between the magnates and the Habsburgs, which lasted throughout the seventeenth century, took place in the context of the appearance and growth of absolutism in Europe. Hobbes published *Leviathan* in 1651, and Louis XIV's long reign on the throne of France began in 1643. If European sovereigns increased their power by refusing to convoke the estates, in Hungary the magnates held back royal power by retaining the right to elect their own palatine. In addition, the sovereign never acquired an automatic right of succession, and each new king had to swear an oath to uphold the Hungarian constitution. When all else failed, the magnates instigated armed rebellion against the king; there were five such rebellions. However, with one exception, the rebels did not seek to oust the Habsburgs. This was an important benefit for Hungary, which, as a result, "escaped almost entirely the inhuman enforcement of the Counter-Reformation under which Bohemia suffered so terribly, and was also spared the worst ravages of the Thirty Years War."[38]

Many of these rebellions must be seen in the context of the wars of religion that were enveloping Europe at this time. The first one, that of Bocskay, started when the Lutheran Church in Kosice was taken over by the Catholics in January 1604. Protestant representatives in the Diet in Bratislava objected, but Rudolf II simply reaffirmed the validity of earlier laws against non-Catholics and forbade the Diet to discuss henceforth religious questions. The unrest that this provoked spread and led to an open rebellion under the leadership of Bocskay. By the fall of 1605, the rebels controlled all of Slovakia except Bratislava. Finally, on 23 June 1606, a peace was signed in Vienna between Bocskay and the king whereby the magnates retained all their hitherto acquired privileges, elected their palatine, and ensured that major Hungarian offices would be occupied only by Hungarians in the future, irrespective of religion. Religious freedom was granted to the population and an amnesty was given to those who had participated in the rebellion. As we saw earlier, Bocskay then helped the king to sign the Peace of Zsitvatorok with the sultan a few months later. For the rest of Rudolf II's reign and that of his successor, Matthias (1612–1618), royal Hungary enjoyed a period of relative tranquility.

The second rebellion was led by Gabor Bethlen, Prince of Transylvania. It was linked with the Thirty Years War and the rebellion of the Czech magnates in Bohemia, whose defeat at the hands of the Habsburgs at White Mountain in 1620 spelled the end of what Denis calls "Bohemian independence."[39] In August 1619, Bethlen occupied Kosice and from there his supporters proceeded to occupy the rest of Slovakia. This rebellion was motivated primarily by the desire of Protestant magnates to put their hands on property confiscated by the Catholic Church and not by a desire to overthrow the Habsburgs. When the Diet, meeting in Bratislava in 1620, proclaimed anew religious freedom and approved the expulsion of the Jesuits from Hungary, Bethlen signed an agreement with Ferdinand II (1618–1637) in September of that year. However, after the battle of White Mountain in November, hostilities were resumed until a peace was signed in Mikulova in January 1622. Bethlen abandoned Slovakia in return for Ferdinand's reaffirmation of the terms of the Peace of Vienna. He died in 1629.

The third rebellion took place during the reign of Ferdinand III (1637–1657). At issue was the question of churches, in particular the right of Protestants to build them for themselves. By this time, many magnates, under the efforts of Cardinal Pazmany, had reconverted to Catholicism, so that "disputes about the churches were basically a fight on the part of the Protestant magnates to gain political power."[40] They were led by Juraj Rakoci (György Rakoczi) I, who in 1630 had become Prince of Transylvania and from 1638 on was in contact with the Swedes and the French. In June 1644, he opened hostilities in Slovakia and occupied towns in the central and southeastern parts of the country. A stalemate ensued that resulted in the signing of the Peace of Linz in the summer of 1645. The freedoms of 1606 were reaffirmed, but the Protestants did not get the return of all the churches they had demanded. Only with the intervention of Ferdinand III in the Diet in 1647 did they receive 90 of the 400 churches whose return they claimed.

In 1657, Juraj Rakoci (György Rakoczi) II, Prince of Transylvania, decided without consulting the Ottomans to join the Swedes in their war against Poland. As a result the Turkish army invaded Transylvania. The Prince's forces were beaten by the Turks at the battle of Oradea in 1660; this defeat ended the Principality's role as a European power. A new prince, Mihaly Abafi, was installed by the Sublime Porte. The Habsburgs could not be indifferent to this Ottoman victory, and hostilities were renewed. In 1663, Ottoman armies, led by Grand Vizier Mohammed Köprülü, reentered Hungary. Once again, Europe seemed threatened and the Habsburgs were reminded of their first mission. Leopold I (1657–1705) received military aid from Spain, Italy, Germany and France and the Turks were defeated near St. Gotthard, on the Austrian frontier,

on 1 August 1664. Rather than exploit this victory, on 27 September Leopold I signed the Peace of Vasvar, "which would have been more appropriate had Austria been the defeated party: under it, he recognized the Sultan's gains in Transylvania, ceded him a fortress in west Hungary, and even submitted to paying an indemnity."[41]

The Hungarian magnates, Catholics as well as Protestants, reacted to the terms of this peace by organizing a conspiracy against the Habsburgs. They sought help from the Sublime Porte, France, and other powers. Led by Palatines Frantisek Veseleni (Ferenc Wesselenyi) and Peter Zrinsky (Peter Zrinyi), the conspiracy failed as a result of betrayal; some leaders were executed and large-scale reprisals took place against other participants. During the 1670s, in the aftermath of this conspiracy, one of the less edifying episodes of the Counter-Reformation took place. Not only were churches taken from the Protestants, but their pastors and teachers, accused of fomenting anti-Habsburg opposition, were forced to renounce their faith or else be sent to the galleys. Revolts flared on and off throughout Slovakia, culminating in the fourth rebellion, led this time by a magnate from Slovakia, Imrich Tököli (Imre Thököli). By the end of 1680, he was master of Slovakia. He forced Leopold I to convoke the Diet, which met in Sopron in April 1681. An amnesty was declared, some degree of religious freedom restored, and some properties returned; however, neither Tököli nor the Protestants of Hungary were satisfied with these terms.

Opposition to Leopold I did not abate and the Turks, encouraged by Tököli's success and assured of his support, invaded Hungary on 31 March 1683. Europe rallied once more to Hungary's defense under the leadership of the Polish king Jan Sobieski. The Turks were defeated near Vienna on 12 September when Charles of Lorraine came to the aid of the beleaguered defenders of that city. As Macartney writes: "This time the victory was not squandered. By the end of the year, all Royal Hungary was free."[42] In January 1684, Leopold I announced a general amnesty; as a result, many magnates, abandoned Tököli. By the end of 1685, Slovakia was liberated of Leopold's forces. The Diet, which met in Bratislava in October 1687, recognized the hereditary right along the male line of the Habsburgs in Hungary, abolished the *jus resistendi* that the Golden Bull had given the nobles in 1222 (which Veseleni had used to justify his conspiracy), confirmed the Catholic Church's dominant position, and reaffirmed the rights Protestants had obtained from the Diet in Sopron in 1681. However, a commission created in 1690, called the *Neoacquistica Commissio*, challenged the property rights of many Protestants. As a result, opposition to the Habsburgs continued unabated and led in 1703

to the last of the magnate rebellions, that of Frantisek Rakoci (Ferenc Rakoczi) II, *zupan* of Saris county.

The outbreak of the War for the Spanish Succession in 1701 gave Rakoci an opportunity to challenge Leopold I. Rakoci, "one of the most reluctant rebels in history."[43] battled him for seven years, mostly on the territory of Slovakia, with local help. According to Gogolak, "the evidence clearly shows how very involved the majority of the Slovak people was in the Rakoci movement."[44] The cost in lives and property was great; cities such as Trencin, Krupina, and Presov payed a heavy price for their support of the rebels. Slovak folk culture later celebrated them in songs and ballads. The magnates convoked a Diet in Onod in 1707, which deposed Joseph I (1705–1711). Yet Rakoci was not able to unite the magnates, and, when Joseph I confirmed their tax-free status and other privileges and royal forces won a victory near Trencin in 1708, they began to abandon Rakoci. With the capitulation of Kosice, the last rebel stronghold, the Peace of Szatmar was signed on 20 April 1711, putting an end to a century of magnate rebellions in royal Hungary.

These rebellions had proven costly not only to Hungary but also to the Slovaks. For the latter, the seesaw between rebel and royal authority on their territory had not been conducive to good government; rather lawlessness and brigandage were prevalent. This situation gave rise to the legend, based on fact, of Juro Janosik, a Slovak Robin Hood who fought local authorities and came to the aid of their victims. He was born in 1688 in Terchova and had initially served in the royal army. In 1711, he became leader of a group of brigands who roamed the valleys and mountains of Slovakia, at times going into Poland and Moravia as well. Arrested in early 1713, he was condemned to death by the county tribunal in Liptovsky Sväty Mikulas and executed. The ballads and songs that soon immortalized him recount the miseries and sufferings of the Slovak population at that time. In the nineteenth century, he became the darling of Romantic writers, in particular poets such as Janko Kral in *Vylomky z Janosika* (Excerpts from Janosik) (1844–1847); Samo Chalupka in *Janosikova naumka* (Janosik's meditation) (1845), *Likavsky väzen* (The prisoner of Likava) (1860), and *Kraloholska* (The song of Royal Mountain) (1868); and Jan Botto in *Piesen Janosikova* (The song of Janosik) (1846) and *Smrt Janosikova* (The death of Janosik) (1862), among others. In our time, Jan Cikker composed an opera entitled *Juro Janosik* (1953), and four films were produced about him, in 1921, 1936, 1962–63, and 1977.[45]

As far as Hungary was concerned, the rebellions had weakened the power of the nobility and ensured that Habsburg authority could be opposed only with the greatest difficulty. The Habsburgs also would embark on the

road to absolutism. A new era in the politics of Hungary and the life of the Slovaks began.

THE BEGINNINGS OF HABSBURG ABSOLUTISM

The main challenge facing individual Slovaks in the sixteenth and seventeenth centuries had been that of personal survival. The most direct threat had come from the Turks, particularly in the southern parts of Slovakia, yet the competition for men's souls between the adherents of the Reformation and the Counter-Reformation had also not been without violence and risk to personal safety. Then there were the magnate rebellions, which, together with the Turkish wars, brought the inevitable bouts of famine, disease, epidemics, and pestilence. Still, individuals, villages, towns, and cities survived and even thrived, as the building of Renaissance churches and residences indicates, as did the Slovak nation. Much of this national survival must be ascribed to the Catholic and Lutheran Churches, whose religious and educational establishments provided not just the leadership but above all the link between individuals and local communities. Due to the presence of biblical Czech in its liturgy, the Lutheran Church encouraged the use of the vernacular. Where the Catholic Church is concerned, the evidence of the use of the vernacular is even more compelling, as Szölösi's hymnal *Cantus Catholici* indicates. Its Slovak text, which is known as "Jesuit Slovak" and which, according to Slovak linguists, later developed into "Cultural Western Slovak," testifies to the Catholic Church's involvement in nurturing national cohesion and Slovak national consciousness. Clearly the Catholic Church used Slovak in its interaction with the population; "Jesuit Slovak" shows that there was already "Slovak linguistic consciousness during the one hundred fifty-odd years before the codification of that language by Anton Bernolak."[46]

This consciousness was further enhanced by two political developments. The first was the national representation in city and town councils, a phenomenon that had started in the early Middle Ages, as we saw in the Chapter 3. In addition, as Spiesz writes: "The period from 1681 to 1781 is an era when the Slovaks strengthened their position in towns. It is not merely a question of the numerical strengthening of the Slovak element, but also the fact that Slovaks in the eighteenth century showed considerable national consciousness."[47] Except for the superintendencies in the Lutheran Church, this experience in self-government, even if it was limited in form, was the only political experience the Slovaks enjoyed in the Hungarian state. (The appointment to and administration of the counties was under royal control and more often than not under

local magnate influence.) Nevertheless, combined with the leadership and support it received from the churches, the experience of municipal politics gave the Slovak body politic some of the wherewithal necessary for survival and continued development.

A second factor of equal importance arose from the Turkish occupation of the Hungarian plain. As we indicated earlier, the Slovaks had been less affected by it than the Magyars; they experienced population growth as a consequence. While this demographic increase produced a greater cohesiveness in the geographic and linguistic distribution of the Slovak population, it did not result in immediate political consequences for them. Nevertheless, as Szakali indicates: "The ethnic changes of this period had a tremendous influence on political developments of Hungary in subsequent centuries, and, finally, became critical in determining her fate."[48]

One factor that had become important at this time for the inhabitants as well as the political system of Hungary was the growth of state power and the competition it provoked between the monarch and the political classes. The magnate rebellions had not been able to resist this development and had the opposite effect than the one intended; namely, in the end they tipped the balance in favor of the crown. By the beginning of the eighteenth century, little stood in the way of the growth of royal absolutism. As far as the Slovaks were concerned, once again, at least initially, they were bystanders in this development; later they would be dragged into it as the state progressively interfered with their lives and the question of who would control the state became one of the main issues in the political struggle.

Absolutism came about as the cumulative result of the policies of three Habsburgs, Charles VI (1711–1740), Maria Theresa (1740–1780), and Joseph II (1780–1790). All three were involved in many European adventures, the most important of which were the two wars for the Austrian succession (1740–1742) and (1744–1748) and the Seven Years' War (1756–1763). However, none of these had serious consequences for the empire, so we must turn to the rulers' domestic policies. The Peace of Szatmar had been signed at the beginning of Charles VI's reign, and the Hungarians were "more than ready to accept the terms—which, indeed, were generous enough in the situation."[49] While Charles VI had sworn to respect the national laws of Hungary, two problems had to be resolved. In the end each moved the Habsburg political system closer to royal absolutism. The first concerned the succession; Charles VI had no son and wished to have his eldest daughter, Maria Theresa, succeed him. In 1723 the Hungarian Diet accepted the Pragmatic Sanction, which established the succession in the female line and also linked Hungary "indivisibly and inseparably" to the Habsburgs. This was a fundamental point, for, as

Macartney points out, "Only if the line became entirely extinct did the nation recover its right to elect its monarch, and the automatic connection with 'Austria' come to an end."[50]

The second problem concerned the organization of government in Hungary and the creation of a standing army. A *Consilium Locumtenetiale* became the highest administrative body, sitting in Bratislava under the presidency of the palatine, assisted by twenty-two councillors appointed by the king from among the Hungarian nobility. In addition to the noble levée, Charles also had the Diet agree to the creation of a standing army, which was to be one-third Hungarian and two-thirds foreign, stationed in Hungary, at Hungarian expense, with the amount of tax to be decided by each Diet. However, the army was to be under the control of the *Hofkriegsrat* (Imperial War Council) in Vienna with a promise of Hungarian representation in that body.

The solution of both of these problems made Hungary a part of a bigger political unit with minimal influence on the politics of that polity, except in matters directly concerning Hungarian interests. The margin for maneuver was limited because "the standing army developed into a permanent and powerful instrument for the enforcement of the monarch's will in any case in which it conflicted with that of the nation."[51] Having acquired a foot in the Hungarian door, Charles VI pressed his advantage by exercising freely the crown's financial prerogatives and by claiming every matter within its competence for which there was no earlier law. The powers and influence of the Diet receded; even the *Consilium* in the end reported to chancellery in Vienna rather than to it. When Palatine Miklos Palffy died in 1734, the office was left vacant and Charles VI appointed instead a viceroy. When the Diet refused that same year to renounce the nobility's tax exemption, he did not convoke it again. Maria Theresa used similar measures during her reign.

Hungary's subordination to the Habsburgs was also manifest in the economic policies of the empire. The kingdom retained its agricultural character, and the overwhelming majority of the population derived its meager living from the land. As of 1754, Hungarian exports were controlled by a tariff wall that discriminated in favor of Austria. Likewise, in industrial development, Hungary was a producer of raw materials, with additional internal tariffs that favored Austrian manufactured goods. These measures were in part a reaction to the opposition of the Hungarian nobility to proposals to tax them. Adam Frantisek Kollar, a Slovak ex-Jesuit, had published in 1764 a booklet entitled *De originibus et usu perpetuo potestatis legislatoriae circa sacra apostolicum regum Ungariae* (About the origins and perpetual use of the legislative power of Hungary's Holy Apostolic King). Maria Theresa used it to demand from the Diet a drastic increase in the war tax. Another Slovak, Jozef Bencur, had argued

similarly in his work *Ungaria semper libera* (Hungary is always free), published the same year. The Magyar nobility refused to accede to Maria Theresa's demands, and she did not convoke the Diet again. In addition, she enacted in 1767, as a result of peasant revolts in 1735 and 1753, an Urbarial Law which defined the normative size of a peasant holding, forbade further conversion from peasant to demesne land, and codified the exact sum and nature of peasant obligations. While given free use of forests, the peasants payed their landlords rent for their lands in cash, one-ninth of their products and fifty-two days of compulsory labor service (which became known as "robot") if animals were to be used, otherwise one hundred four days per year. Children of peasants were free to chose their education and profession without obtaining the lord's permission. This law did not please the landed nobility.

The success of the Counter-Reformation was confirmed at this time, especially with an empress who was as devout a Catholic as Maria Theresa. Her father had settled the status of the Protestants in the *Resolutio Carolina* of 1731, which upheld the restrictions imposed by Leopold I; it limited worship, allowed only Lutheran grammar schools, forbade conversion, and required the swearing of a Catholic oath upon entry into the public service. The Protestants' situation improved only half a century later, when Joseph II issued his Edict (Patent) of Toleration in 1781; with it, these restrictions were eliminated and Protestants, along with members of the Greek Orthodox faith, achieved civic equality with Catholics. The Jews were granted freedom of worship but did not receive full civic rights. Joseph II also introduced a Livings Patent, which dissolved a number of contemplative monasteries and founded new schools.

The greatest changes in the administration of the empire, extending to Hungary and Slovakia, took place in the reign of Joseph II. He was "a firm believer in the absolute power of monarchs and was, therefore, vehemently opposed to the nobility's privileges and all regional rights and institutions."[52] He enacted the Peasant Patent in 1785 in Hungary, which gave the peasantry the liberty to leave their holding upon payment of their dues and forbade the expropriation of their land without adequate compensation. He had divested the counties (the *zupy* in Slovakia) of their autonomy, made the *podzupan* a government employee, replaced Latin with German in 1784 as the language of administration, and in 1786 made German the sole language of instruction in schools above the primary level except during religion classes.

When Joseph II went to war with the Ottoman Empire between 1787 and 1790, he encountered resistance and provoked opposition that extended to most of his reforms. Just before his death, he revoked all measures except for the Edict of Toleration and the Livings and Peasant patents. In Hungary, he had already reactivated the county assemblies to obtain financial support for

the war. He also promised to convoke a Diet and to return St. Stephen's crown to Hungary from Vienna, where he had it kept after refusing also to be crowned King of Hungary when he ascended the imperial throne in 1780. Still, in a decade of reign, Joseph II had "so successfully broken into pieces the old feudal edifice that after him it was impossible to put them back together."[53] A new age was about to begin.

The reforms of Maria Theresa and Joseph II had important consequences for the population of the empire, in particular the Magyars and the Slovaks. The Magyar magnate class had been so changed that many no longer spoke Magyar and were looking to Vienna or Paris for culture; some had also married into German-Austrian or Bohemian nobility. By becoming supporters of the monarchy they decreased thereby the ranks of the Magyar high nobility. As Macartney writes: "This was enormously important politically, for few as they were—the families bearing hereditary titles at the end of the eighteenth century numbered only 108 (two princely, 82 of counts and 24 baronial)—they owned between them about one third of the soil of Hungary."[54]

As a result, the leadership of the nation accrued to the middle nobility in the counties that felt Magyar and spoke Magyar, a living tongue that had not yet been raised to the level of a literary language. Latin was still used by the bureaucracy and in the debates in the Diet, and education above the primary level was in Latin, with German as the preferred second language. Nevertheless, this noble class spoke Magyar and "when the time came for the full political national revival, the Magyar people, like the Polish, had to hand a class which was already fully national."[55] However, Macartney also points out that this class had a well-defined attitude of superiority to the other inhabitants of Hungary, in particular the peasantry.[56] Evidence suggests that they felt similarly toward the other nationalities, especially the Slovaks. In 1722, Michal Bencik (Bencsik), a professor of Hungarian law at the University of Trnava, submitted a report to the Diet in Bratislava in which he suggested that the Slovak inhabitants of Trencin were the descendants of the subjects of Svätopluk who allegedly had sold his country to the Magyars for a white horse. In the words of Slovak historians: "Bencik was not alone in holding such views."[57] These attitudes among the Magyar nobility indicate that Hungary was in the process of undergoing major change. Above all, they point to major transformations in the composition of the non-Magyar population.

After the Turks withdrew from the Hungarian plain, the land had to be resettled.[58] The eighteenth century witnessed an important population growth in Hungary, achieved in part by bringing people in from other parts of Europe, in particular from Germany. Some areas were also settled by landowners moving peasants by from their properties in the north to ones in the south, with

promises of better working conditions. Many peasants left Slovakia for Hungary in this manner. Macartney writes that "it was in this way, . . . that the Slovak colony round Békescsaba, still in existence [in 1962], came into being."[59] However, by the end of Maria Theresa's reign, the Magyars had lost their majority, numbering about 3.25 million and representing 35 percent of the total population, while the Slovaks were the biggest minority, totaling about 1.25 million.[60] This growth in the Slovak population had been accompanied by a number of important changes in Slovakia during the reign of the Habsburg reformers.

The eighteenth century was the century of the baroque and the Enlightenment. Hungarian magnates and landowners continued to build magnificent residences throughout the country, while "comfortable homes of burgesses, and many new churches and other public buildings, adorned Pozsony [Bratislava] and Buda."[61] This outward manifestation of cultural activity was matched by new developments in education. Although the school system was still divided along denominational lines, it came under the control of the crown after 1723. Mining schools were opened in Banska Stiavnica in 1735 and Smolnik in 1746, and the University of Trnava was reorganized in 1753 on the model of the University of Vienna. A year later, the teaching of natural sciences began, an astronomical observatory was opened, and in 1769, the university acquired a faculty of medicine. In Banska Stiavnica, in the meantime, an institution of higher learning in mining opened in 1763 and was given the name of *Bergakademie* (Mining Academy) in 1770. Its faculty was in contact with the École Polytechnique in Paris. As Kucera and Kosticky write: "There were first class instructors of Slovak origin among the faculty and for the purposes of instruction, the first, and for a long time, only textbook, *Anleitung zu der Bergbaukunst* (Introduction to mining), was written there and translated into French. Slovakia, after a long period of time, was once again contributing knowledge and experience to neighboring states and nations."[62] A school of administrative studies, called *Collegium oeconomicum,* had also opened in Senec in 1763. However, when the University of Trnava was transferred to Buda in 1777, the educational system in Slovakia was severely affected. There would not be another Slovak institution of higher learning like it until the twentieth century. The Hungarian education system was reorganized that year, establishing a new system of village schools[63] on the basis of a document known as the *Ratio Educationis* (Education Act), to which Kollar contributed. Eva Kowalska writes: "The Ratio Educationis is exceptional in that it crated conditions for the development of truly national elementary and, up to a point, also secondary schools. It came about as a result of the conditions in multinational Hungary where each nation was to have, in addition to primary schools in the villages

and towns, also model basic schools and many teacher's colleges where future teachers would be trained in their mother tongue."[64]

Perhaps the most important development for the Slovaks in the eighteenth century was the debate about them that appeared in various writings. The theses and arguments of Revai, Jakobeus, and Sentivani had carried over from the previous century and fueled the arguments needed to answer Bencik's attack on the Slovaks in 1722. Jan Baltazar Magin published in 1728 *Murices Nobilissimae et Novissimae Diaetae Posoniensis Scriptori Sparsi, sive Apologia* (The leg traps which the writer of the most distinguished and most recent Diet in Bratislava distributed here and there or an Apology) which defended the citizens of Trencin, whom Bencik had maligned in his work. Timon published *Imago antiquae Hungariae* (Images of ancient Hungary) in 1733, which described the origins of the Slovaks and suggested that they, like the Magyars, were equally members of the "natio hungarica," what we would call today the Hungarian political nation. Magin's *Apologia* was a particularly powerful document, as Gogolak points out: "The *Apologia* already attracted a great deal of attention when it was published; it was the first articulation of the opposition of the Slovak people to the early Magyarisation attempts of the Hungarian state, and a reinstatement of their right to national freedom."[65]

Another staunch defender of the Slovaks, especially of their origins, was Bel, one of the leading Lutheran pedagogical reformers. In his publication *Hungariae antiquae et novae prodromus* (Herald of ancient and new Hungary), Bel showed that Slavs had arrived in the Danubian plain long before the Avars and the Huns. Bel also advanced the theory that Czech Hussite refugees had strengthened the Slovak nation by assimilating into it; this would explain the Slovaks' acceptance of the Czech language. The political ramifications of this theory would become clear in the next two centuries. Another important publication by Bel is his history of the Slovak counties in Hungary, *Notitia Hungariae novae historico geographica* (A historical and geographical description of the new Hungary), published in Vienna in 1736. But perhaps the most important history was written in 1780 by Juraj Papanek. His *Historia gentis slavae—De regno regibusque Slavorum* (History of the Slavic people—about the kingdom and government of the Slavs) traces the history of the Slovaks back to Great Moravia and Cyril and Methodius. Four years later Juraj Sklenar strengthened Papanek's argument in *Vetustissimus magnae Moraviae situs* (The greatest site of Great Moravia), a study of Great Moravia, which, according to Sklenar, had been a Slovak creation. None of these histories was a work of scholarship in the modern sense and the audience for all was not a broad one, reaching only government officials, the nobility, clergy, and literate lower classes who read Latin. However, their impact, was anything but insignificant. Pananek's his-

tory, according to Slovak historians, "closes the period which saw the maturing of the Slovak nationality."[66]

Whereas most of the writings defending the Slovaks were written in Latin, the Slovak language was gaining ground and continuing to affirm itself in municipal administration, primary schools, church services, at the University of Trnava, and in private correspondence. Its use came about as a result of a slow but steady evolution. As Izidor Kotulic writes: "From the tenth century onward, the Slovaks developed, along with [different] dialects, 'Cultural Slovak' in which all religious texts were translated (for those who did not know Latin)."[67] As a written language, Cultural Slovak was structurally and functionally weak because its use was limited to social and cultural functions, yet at the same time it was a language that was linguistically more complex than spoken Slovak and its dialects. But Cultural Slovak did not develop into a literary language as Czech did and toward the end of the fourteenth century Slovak writers began to use Czech, modified to suit their needs. The result was "a hybrid linguistic formation—Cultural Slovak in which stable or dynamic and indiscriminate Slovak and Czech linguistic elements were included. Czech influence was the greatest on orthography."[68]

As Cultural Slovak evolved, it was also influenced by two language integration areas that had developed by the seventeenth century. One was in Central Slovakia, whose dialects "became a basis for a new regional koine,"[69] which was used in occasional poetry and some religious and nonliturgical functions. The second language integration area was in Western Slovakia where the University of Trnava was located. Both Cultural Central and Cultural Western Slovak were used there. However, by the eighteenth century, the latter had overtaken Cultural Slovak to such an extent that even texts written in Cultural Central Slovak had to be rewritten in Cultural Western Slovak in order to published. The court also accepted Cultural Western Slovak as the language of the Slovaks and used it in the publication of such documents as the Urbarial Law of 1767.

It should also be noted that the Slovak language was the object of an interesting contribution from Romanian, from nomadic Wallachs, dating as far back as the fourteenth century, but which became particularly evident during the Turkish presence in Central Europe. As Gogolak writes: "The Wallachian vocabulary and terminology of pastoral life influenced Slovak popular poetry from the sixteenth and seventeenth centuries onwards. This Wallachian popular element retained certain peculiarities in spite of mixing with the Slovak environment and often created particular Slovak social organizations that influenced Slovak consciousness in an important way."[70] These Wallachs were nomadic shepherds. Their descendants, known as *valasi* in Slovak, obtained special

privileges in matters of taxation, self-administration, military duties, and even judicial processes. These privileges were at times of short duration, but where they persisted, in the Orava region of Central Slovakia for example, they became elements of "Wallachian law."

The most outstanding example of the influence of the *valasi* on Slovak culture is found in the didactic poem "*Valaska Skola*" (The shepherd's school) by the Franciscan monk Hugolin Gavlovic. Although born in Poland, he lived most of his life in the Orava region of Central Slovakia and wrote some twenty or so works in Slovak. "*Valaska Skola*" was completed in 1755 but not published until 1830, and then not in the original form, but "according to the norms of the Slovak codified by Anton Bernolak."[71] The poem was composed for Franciscan Tertiaries (lay people who live according to the Rule of St. Francis of Assisi), offering a Christian-Catholic moral perspective on their lives and their interaction with God and society. Three themes dominate the poem: Slovak national consciousness, eighteenth-century religious and secular culture, and pastoral life. It is in the third theme that the Wallachian legacy appears, giving the poem particular significance. As Gerald J. Sabo writes: "Inclusion of the *valach* and his culture contributes to the down-to-earth, everyday character of *Valaska Skola* and has its own special associations. . . . the *valasi* represented a distinctive type in Slovak society with their various advantages and freedoms that stood in contrast to the restrictiveness of the feudal society around them."[72] The language of the poem is traced to the Western Slovak integration area.

There are two major indications of the prestige Cultural Western Slovak enjoyed in the eighteenth century. A Camaldolese monk, Romuald Hadbavny, prepared in 1763 in Cerveny Klastor in Eastern Slovakia a Latin-Slovak dictionary *(Syllabus Dictionarii Latino-Slavonicus)* based on the dialects of the Western Slovak integration area. Unfortunately, the *Syllabus* was never published. When Joseph II banned all contemplative monasteries, including Hadbavny's, his manuscript was confiscated and later given to the Hungarian Academy of Sciences. The same fate awaited his translation into Slovak of the Holy Scriptures. As Ada Böhmerova writes: "Had Hadbavny's dictionary and his translation of the Bible been available to Slovak scholars and intelligentsia, Cultural Western Slovak would have had better chances for an earlier codification and our Slovak lexicography could have advanced much quicker."[73] The other indication was the publication of the first novel in Cultural Western Slovak in 1783 by Ignac Bajza, entitled *René mladenca prihodi a skusenosti* (Adventures and experiences of a young man called René).[74] Bajza's novel was the first sign that Slovak literature was fast approaching the end of what Joseph Kirschbaum calls its multilingual period.[75]

Despite the absence of national political institutions, on the eve of the modern era the Slovak people found themselves relatively cohesive and, up to a point, ready to confront new challenges. The experience of the past 275 years had not been without trials, yet also not without opportunities and rewards. Slovakia had been home to most of royal Hungary and had given refuge to the Hungarian government; there were tangible benefits associated with having the seat of government in Bratislava. Most of the magnates spoke Slovak and even encouraged Slovak culture and language. The Slovak language continued to thrive, and, thanks to the activities of the churches the social fabric was not destroyed and national cohesion was maintained. The Slovaks had experienced the Reformation but in the end had come out stronger as a result of the Counter-Reformation. The Slovaks belonged to Western civilization, kept in step with it, and even contributed to it.

In the economic and social spheres, however, the situation was less favorable. The Turkish wars and the discovery of the New World had relegated Central Europe to a secondary position in the economic development of Europe. As a result Slovakia lost some of the economic advantages that it had acquired in the early Middle Ages, particularly in mining. On the other hand, agriculture retained its importance but at the same time brought about certain social changes, namely increased obligations for the peasantry. In the towns and cities, the Slovak population fared better and enjoyed freedom and some of the guilds prospered. However, the Slovaks did not have a very strong middle class and lacked a nobility ready to defend their national interests. The aristocracy in Slovakia was part of the political class that made up the "*natio hungarica*" and defended its interests, despite the fact, as von Gogolak writes, that "the North Hungarian nobility . . . in language and custom was very closely tied to the Slovak population and the North Hungarian political strata spoke Slovak."[76] The result was that the Slovaks were disadvantaged politically. It would not be long before they would feel the consequences of their situation.

The Slovaks belonged to the Hungarian state and were aware of this. The political history of Hungary was also their political history; on the other hand, they had their own cultural history and language, and they also were very conscious of their national individuality. The Germanization policies of Joseph II challenged them as much as the Magyars. Absolutism provoked a national renaissance among the nations of the empire but it was the activities of past generations and the degree of national cohesion that determined how each would evolve. As Robert W. Seton-Watson writes, "the revival of national sentiment and literary effort was not the monopoly of any one race in Hungary, but a very general phenomenon, stirring the Croats, Serbs and Slovaks quite as early as the Magyars."[77] The Slovaks were on the starting line with the other

Central European nations when the winds of nationalism blew through the region. Many challenges, some quite unexpected, awaited them, challenges that first appeared as they launched their national awakening.

5

The National
Awakening

THE CODIFICATION OF THE SLOVAK LANGUAGE

The national awakening of the Slovaks had been in preparation for some time. Even before the publication of Szöllösi's *Cantus Catholici* in 1655, Slovak intellectuals, many of them clerics, had been publishing their works not just in Latin but in the vernacular, either a form of Slovakized Czech or more often Cultural Western Slovak. Their efforts had been facilitated to some extent by the publication in 1648 of *Verborum in institutione grammatica contentorum translatio* (Translation of words used in elementary education), also known as the *Trnavsky slovnik* (The Trnava dictionary), where Latin words were translated into Magyar and Slovak (based, however, on a Central Slovak dialect). The increasing use of the vernacular also was enhanced by two important developments that would give impetus and substance to the national awakening. The first can be traced directly to Josephinian reforms, in particular the decree of 1786 that obliged government officials to explain legislation in the language of the various peoples of the monarchy. The corollary of this decree was education in the vernacular, which Joseph II encouraged; in its wake would come the spread of literacy. Without a reading public, the national awakening had few chances to survive, let alone flourish. The emperor also decreed the Germanization of the administration, a measure that provided a political

argument in favor of the use of national languages that the leaders of the various nations, Magyar and non-Magyar, would exploit in due time.

The second development was the French Revolution. It had a double-pronged effect as its ideas spread throughout Europe and left no political system untouched. Monarchies were particularly vulnerable, since monarchs, the nobility, and the clergy were frightened by its antimonarchism, antifeudalism and anticlericalism. This reaction was especially evident in the Habsburg lands. Joseph II had been succeeded by Leopold II (1790–1792,) who was equally determined to transform the monarchy into an enlightened polity with the emperor at its head and the main agent of transformation. However, his reign was too short to have any real impact and his successor, Francis II (1792–1835), who ascended the throne as the French Revolution was in its most radical phase, ensured that the Habsburgs, "in the eighteenth century a reforming dynasty, became the champions of conservatism; and the defence of their family position was merged in the general interest of European stability. Once more, and again unintentionally, the Habsburgs found themselves with a mission: to defend Europe against revolution, as they had once, supposedly, defended it against the Turks."[1] The nations in the Habsburg Empire thus faced a new political reality with which each would have to deal in its own way. The Slovak reaction is examined in Chapter 6.

The second effect of the French Revolution was the spread of nationalism. Nationalism was a product of the Enlightenment, with philosophical roots in the eighteenth century, which underpinned the national awakenings in Central Europe. However, as a political concept, it has eluded a generally acceptable definition. It has had as many manifestations as there are nations or collectivities that so define themselves. The dependent variable of nationalism is self-determination; yet nations can define and pursue self-determination in a multiplicity of ways. The efforts at arriving at a classification of these ways make fascinating reading[2] and lead to the conclusion that each nationalism must be judged on its own merits and in its own time; nationalism can be considered both a disease and a cure, especially in Central Europe.

The Slovaks soon discovered that these new cultural and political conditions gave political life in Hungary an additional dimension that directly influenced their national development. One of the last measures enacted by the dynasty before it abandoned the path of political reform was the passage of a law by Leopold II in 1790 that made Hungary "a wholly independent kingdom, not subject to any other land or people and to be ruled by its own lawfully crowned kings and in accordance with its own laws and customs."[3] This was a reversion to the *status quo ante* in matters of internal Hungarian politics, especially where the Slovaks were concerned. While the emperor refused to

allow Magyar to replace Latin, he did make it possible for it to be taught at the university and in all *gymnazia*. This gave the Magyars an opportunity to develop their culture and literature to such an extent that they, as Seton-Watson describes it, "though they had no great start, very rapidly outdistanced the other races. . . . in the first half of the nineteenth century they produced a rich crop of poets, dramatists and other writers, who would have been an ornament to any language and threw the Slovaks, Serbs or Romanians completely into the shade."[4] This judgment on the Slovaks is a bit harsh, although not devoid of substance. The Slovaks were not held back by the absence of means similar to those of the Magyars, as Seton-Watson suggests[5]; rather a particular historical situation directly influenced both the direction and intensity of the national awakening and as a result left the Slovaks lagging somewhat behind. The codification of the Slovak language presented a challenge not so much in terms of the exercise itself—Hadbavny had already done that, even if his efforts reached no one—but in the choice of dialects from which a literary language would be created. There were two language integration areas during the seventeenth century, a Central Slovak and a Western Slovak one. Given the importance of Bratislava as a political center and of Trnava as a cultural and economic center in the last two centuries, it is understandable that the first attempt was made on the basis of the Western Slovak dialects spoken in and around these two cities. Cultural Western Slovak also had developed from these dialects.

The person responsible for the codification of this Slovak language was Anton Bernolak. He was born in Slanica in Orava county on 3 October 1762 in a family of landed gentry. He attended the *gymnazia* in Ruzomberok and Bratislava, enrolled at the seminary in Trnava, and then studied theology in Vienna and Bratislava. He received Holy Orders in Trnava in 1787, and served in Ceklis, Trnava, and from 1797 in Nove Zamky until his death on 15 January 1813. A General Seminary had opened in Bratislava in 1784 (it was closed in 1790), and there Bernolak was able to codify the Slovak language; the seminarians had set up a *Societas excolendae linguae slavicae* (Society for the Cultivation of the Slavic Language) whose objective was to translate the Bible into the vernacular. His codification emanated from his involvement with this group.

Bernolak believed that Slovak "was the purest of the Slav languages, and the only one to have remained close to the original speech of the Slavs since it was still uncontaminated by outside accretions."[6] His first work, published in 1787, was the *Dissertatio philologico-critica de litteris Slavorum* (A philologico-critical dissertation of the letters of the Slavs) in which he formulated the principles of a literary language. Three years later, he completed a *Grammatica slavica* (Slavic grammar), based on a 1746 Czech grammar. In the introduction,

he indicates that he thought that the literary language ought to be based on Central Slovak dialects, but did not believe that it was useful to stray too far from what was already in existence. In 1791 he published *Etymologia vocum slavicarum* (The etymology of Slavic words) while working on a dictionary that was published only after his death, the *Slowar slovenski cesko-latinsko-nemecko-uherski* (Slovak Czech-Latin-German-Hungarian dictionary) (Buda, 1825–1827). This dictionary is a monumental work of scholarship and erudition, "an example of unbelievable persistence and love for his native tongue. Not only did he introduce words, but he also pointed out incorrect phrases, and to explain the meaning of words, he used complete sentences from the living language of the people."[7]

In order to propagate the new literary language and encourage its use, Bernolak founded a society called *Slovenske ucene tovarisstvo* (Slovak Learned Society) which was launched in Trnava in 1792. Its members numbered 581, the majority were Roman Catholic priests. It was, in the modern sense of the word, a literary society that organized meetings and published the works of its members, and was deeply involved in education. The society also gave the Slovak nation two exceptional men, Juraj Fandly, who might be termed a Slovak encyclopedist, and Jan Holly, considered to be one of Slovakia's greatest poets. It also "gave a significant impetus to the creation and development of an independent Slovak literature based on the language of the people."[8] Fandly and Holly, among others, were instrumental in bringing this development about.

Juraj Fandly was born in Casta, near Trnava, on 21 October 1750. He studied theology in Buda, was consecrated a priest in 1776 and served in Sered and Nahac as a chaplain. As a result of illness he retired to Dolany in 1807 where he died on 7 March 1811. Fandly organized Bernolak's society and it was also he who published the first work in Bernolak's literary Slovak, the *Duverna zmluva medzi mnichom a diablom o prvnych pocatkoch, o starodavnych, aj o vculajsich premenach reholnickych* (A confidential agreement between a monk and the devil about the beginnings and the ancient and contemporary changes in religious orders), which appeared in 1789. It is a satirical work that defends the policies of Joseph II toward the contemplative monasteries. He was an extremely well read man with a well-developed sense of social responsibility. His attitude toward the peasants and his desire to come to their assistance distinguished him from his contemporaries. Beginning in 1792, he published a series of writings, some known simply known as *Hospodar* (Economist), which together make up an agricultural encyclopedia that "educates the farmer to a new life, to a national consciousness, to human pride and dignity, to hard work, to a rational understanding of life and to a democratic coexistence. . . . Fandly's

books do not merely give dry advice to farmers, they also offer examples taken from history, they speak enthusiastically of nature, of the beauty of a farmer's life and of its healthy natural state."[9]

In 1793, he completed a history, based on Papanek's and Sklenar's works, entitled *Compendiata Historia Gentis Slavae* (A short history of the Slavic nation). It was aimed at the members of the society in order to encourage them, through a knowledge of the Slovak past, to work for the Slovak people. He wrote and published untiringly on a vast variety of subjects, but many of his ideas were too progressive for his time. He was silenced by the reactionary policies of Francis II and died a broken man, abandoned even by his friends.

There were two persons whose support of Bernolak and the society were of paramount significance. The first was a Slovak born and Slovak-speaking prince of the Catholic Church, Alexander Cardinal Rudnay, who in 1819 became the archbishop of Ostrihom; he gave financial assistance for the publication of Bernolak's *Slowar*. The other was another priest, a professor of theology, Canon Jur Palkovic, who from 1802 to 1808 taught Holly at the Trnava Seminary and after Bernolak's death worked toward the preparation and publication of the *Slowar*. He himself published a translation of the Bible (Ostrihom, 1829–1832) and gave Holly financial assistance to publish his poetry. The consequences of this support were not insignificant, as a Slovak literary historian indicates: "The Bernolak school reached its zenith in the poetry of Jan Holly. After 20–30 years of efforts to create a Slovak literature and the convenient intermezzo following the Napoleonic wars, the Slovak language produced a [body of] work that would have also honored the great literatures [of the world]."[10]

Jan Holly was born on 24 March 1785 in Borsky Sväty Mikulas in a peasant family. He studied in Skalica, Bratislava, and Trnava and entered the priesthood in 1808. His pastoral work was in the parishes of Pobedim, Hlohovec, Madunice, and Dobra Voda. He died on 14 April 1849. Holly first caught the attention of his contemporaries by using Bernolak's newly codified language to translate the classics, including Homer, Horace, Ovid, Theocritus, and especially Virgil's *Aeneid,* which "was received with enthusiasm, because no one before him had translated so much material, so easily captured the metric verse and used to such an extent the poetic possibilities of the language."[11]

In 1833, Holly published the first of a series of epic poems that dealt with the past of the Slovaks. Entitled "*Svätopluk,*" this work in twelve cantos describes the glorious reign of Great Moravia's most famous ruler. Two years later, he sang the glories and accomplishments of Cyril and Methodius in an epic poem in six cantos entitled *Cirilo-Metodiana.* The past of the Slavic people, both mythical and real, was celebrated in the six canto epic poem *Slav,* published

beginning in 1839 in the society's publication, *Zora,* which appeared irregularly between 1835 and 1840. Perhaps his greatest work is *Selanky* (Idylls), a collection of twenty-one rhythmic poems about the appeal and meaning of pastoral life in every season of the year, which he published from 1835 on in *Zora.* These poems are considered by many to be his best creative writing.

Despite the society's activities, Bernolak's Slovak failed to catch on; it did not have enough support among the intelligentsia, among the citizenry who spoke local dialects, and among the Protestant clergy, who were still using biblical Czech in their liturgy and in their writings. Within a half century, it would give way to a reform based on Central Slovak dialects, itself an indication that the lack of support among the educated was merely one of the problems with Bernolak's Slovak. In addition, poor communication due to the geography of Slovakia hampered the society's work. In the 1834, Martin Hamuljak established, in the tradition of the society, the *Spolok milovnikov reci a literatury slovenskej* (Association of Friends of the Slovak Language and Literature) in Pest and launched *Zora* in an attempt to bring both groups together. The association was dissolved in 1850. Even if Bernolak's Slovak failed to catch on and become permanent, it cannot be said to have been a total failure. It gave Slovak literature the poetry of Holly, whose contribution to Slovak national life was seminal. In the words of Joseph M. Kirschbaum: "He not only created in his works a Slovak national poetry and ideology, but in urging the Slovaks to regard their past with pride, he revived the present and exhorted them to look with hope to the future."[12] His exhortations were not without cause; Slovaks of the Protestant faith were pushing the national awakening in other directions.

THE CHALLENGE FROM BIBLICAL CZECH

One of the consequences of the wars of religion in Slovakia was linguistic dualism. When the Czech Hussite clergy came to Slovakia in the fourteenth century, they not only brought with them the Bible translated in Czech but also used their own language in their pastoral work. In the seventeenth century, the Czech *Kralicka Biblia* (Kralice Bible), published in six volumes in 1579–1593, was adopted by Slovak Protestants; it was the clearest way to indicate their break from Rome (the adoption of German might have been another option, but given the centuries-old rivalry between Germans and Slovaks, especially in mining towns, this was quite unlikely), and this choice of language also embodied what they thought was an important historical dimension, the link with the Brethren, those precursors of the Reformation who had carried on their fight in Slovakia. In addition to its religious usage, Czech also was employed in

municipal correspondence since the fifteenth century and was therefore not unknown to the educated strata of the Slovak population, Catholic as well as Protestant, particularly those who did not know German. Its durability in Slovakia was made possible by the absence of a major cultural or economic center that would have provided a nucleus for the development of a Slovak literary language, as Prague did for Czech. The Turkish wars and the magnate rebellions also provided a inhospitable environment for the development of a Slovak literary language.

Although Czech was used as a written language, the spoken language in Slovakia was Slovak. The presence of Slovakisms in written Czech already in the fifteenth century—for example, in the town book of Zilina of 1451—offers compelling evidence of this fact. Slovakisms continued to creep into biblical Czech over the centuries. Still, biblical Czech developed as a literary medium to such an extent that the first Slovak newspaper in Bratislava, *Prespurske noviny* (Bratislava News), was published in that language. The editor was Stefan Leska, a friend of the Czech *savant* Josef Dobrovsky. However, despite many attempts, Leska did not succeed in getting a wide readership and the publication lasted only half a decade, from 1783 to 1788. In 1792, after Bernolak codified the Slovak language, Lutheran pastor Juraj Ribay, also a friend of Dobrovsky's, proposed the creation of a society to study *biblictina,* the name given to the language of the *Kralicka Biblia.* His efforts resulted in the creation of a chair of Czechoslovak language and literature at the Protestant *lyceum* in Bratislava in 1803. Another Lutheran pastor, Juraj Palkovic, a scholar in his own right, was appointed first chairholder. Two years earlier, in 1801, he had become president of a society founded by Lutherans, the *Spolok literatury ceskoslovenskej* (Society for the Study of Czechoslovak Literature) and, from 1812 to 1818, he was editor of *Tydennik,* a Slovak weekly periodical. It was in this *lyceum,* through the activities of the *Spolok* and in the pages of *Tydennik,* that pressure was maintained to have biblical Czech become the literary language of the Slovaks.

Similar efforts to encourage the use of *biblictina* also were made in other parts of Slovakia, namely in Levoca, Kezmarok and Banska Stiavnica. In 1810, Bohuslav Tablic created the *Ucena spolecnost banskeho okoli* (Learned Society of the Mining Region) to support a chair of *biblictina* at the *lyceum* in Banska Stiavnica, a town that also claimed to have a significant cultural life. It was there that Samuel Ambrosius published a Latin annual publication, the *Annales novi ecclesiatico-scholastici* (New church-school annals) from 1793 to 1803. It was an all-purpose religious review written for the students who came from all over Austria, Hungary, and Slovakia to attend the *Bergakademie.* In Nizny Skalnik in Central Slovakia, thanks to the efforts of Jan Fejes, the *Ucena spolocnost malohontska* (Malohont Learned Society) was founded and from 1810 to 1832,

with a final special issue in 1842, it published the *Solennia Bibliothecae Kis-Hontanae* (Yearbook from the Kis-Hont county library), a general-interest publication that had articles in four languages, Latin, Czech, Magyar, and German.

These efforts to have biblical Czech accepted as a literary language, intensive and far-reaching as they were, might have been very short-lived had it not been for the efforts and publications of Jan Kollar and Pavel Jozef Safarik, two Slovak men of letters whose writings embraced and influenced the whole of Slavdom. Jan Kollar was born on 29 July 1793 in Mosovice. He studied in Bratislava and in Jena, Germany. From 1819 to 1849, he was pastor of the Slovak Lutheran community in Pest, and from 1849 until his death on 24 January 1852, he was professor of Slavic archaeology at the University of Vienna. While in Jena he became imbued with German Romanticism, taking to heart the vision of a bright future for the Slavs described by Johann Gottfried Herder in the sixteenth chapter of his *Ideen zur Philosophie der Geschichte der Menschheit* (Thoughts on the philosophy of history of mankind) (1784–1791). He also participated in the huge student demonstration at Wartburg Castle in 1817, commemorating the tercentenary of Luther's challenge to Rome. It is at this time that he started writing what would become his most famous epic poem, *Slavy dcera* (The daughter of Slava), published in Pest in 1824. The 151 sonnets divided into three cantos are written primarily in Czech with a mixture of Slovak, which explains why the Czech national awakening also claims Kollar as one of its own. The poem had immense success among the Slavs because, as Denis writes, it "lights up by fragments with a warm and radiant beauty, and to the ears of the Slavs, some of his sonnets vibrate much in the same way as *La Marseillaise* in the hearts of Frenchmen. . . . Eliminate Kollar and the contemporary Slavic soul drowns in a vaporous and smoky shadow."[13]

Kollar's reputation among the Slavs and the contacts he maintained with Czech scholars and men of letters made him an influential figure in the debate on the creation of a Slovak literary language. He was persuaded that the future of the Slovaks lay in a union with the Czechs, and he opposed all attempts, not just Bernolak's codification,[14] to create a separate Slovak literary language. He wanted both languages to come together and in 1824 he published a *Citanka* (Reader) where he set out the norms for a Czechoslovak language. However, it was not well received by the Slovaks and the Czechs.

Kollar's motives in wanting to create this new literary language were of an ideological and personal nature. Influenced by German Romanticism, he equated nation with language. As far as he was concerned, this could mean only the language of the educated.[15] For a Slovak Lutheran pastor who had attended university, this was Czech. To it he was ready to add contributions from Slovak, thereby creating the new language, Czechoslovak. His literary success among

the Slavs added a personal dimension to his endeavor: "Kollar was a man of great ambition, for whom 19th century Slovakia seemed too small. The Slovaks seemed to him doomed to denationalization unless they united with the Czechs. He wanted to be a great Slavic and European poet, and wished to belong to the ruling strata of society. The Czech language apparently seemed to him a better vehicle than the Slovak to achieve his literary ambitions at the very least."[16]

Kollar found an ally to oppose Bernolak's Slovak in the person of Pavel Jozef Safarik, another Lutheran who had a major impact on the Slavic world of his time. Safarik was born on 13 May 1795 in Kobeliarovo, a village north of Roznava where his father was the Lutheran pastor. He also studied in Jena and stayed for two years in Bratislava in the employ of *podzupan* Gaspar Kubiny, where he became friends with Kollar and the great historian of the Czechs, the Moravian Frantisek Palacky. Palacky was studying at the Bratislava *lyceum* at that time. In 1819 he left for Novi Sad in Serbia to teach in the local Serb *gymnazium*. In 1833, at Palacky's invitation, he moved to Prague, where he lived until his death on 26 June 1861.

In 1814, as a young man, Safarik had published in Levoca a collection of poems entitled *Tatranska muza s lyrou slovanskou* (The Tatra muse with a Slavic lyre), but it is for two major scholarly works that he became well known in the Slavic world. He published in 1826 the first survey of the languages and literatures of the Slavs, *Geschichte der slawischen Sprache und Literatur nach allen Mundarten* (History of the Slavic language and literature in all dialects) and in 1837 a major work on Slavic ethnography entitled *Slovanske starozitnosti* (Slavic antiquities). Both works had a direct impact on the awakening national consciousness of the Slavic peoples in Central Europe, because they showed, particularly the survey of Slavic literatures, that "after the Greeks and Romans, the Slavs had a culture as ancient as that of other European nations."[17] Like Kollar, Safarik wrote in Czech. After he moved to Prague he was also required to Czechize his family name by adding a diacritic sign on the letter r, thereby using a consonant that does not exist in Slovak. The Czechs also consider him to have contributed to their national awakening. The Southern Slavs acknowledge a debt to him for his publications *Über die Abkunft der Slawen* (On the origins of Slavs), which appeared in 1828; *Serbische Lesekörner* (Serbian manual), in 1833; and especially *Geschichte der süd-slawischen Literatur* (History of South Slavic literature), which was published after his death in three volumes in 1864–1865.

Kollar and Safarik also had an impact on the growth of Panslavism in the nineteenth century. The term *Panslavism* was coined by yet another Slovak, Jan Herkel, in a Latin treatise on Slavic philology published in 1826. There Herkel proposed the creation of a common Slavic literary language. Such was not the objective of the two Slovak men of letters. However, what Kollar and Safarik

did, the first through poetry and the second through his scholarship, was to influence the development of a Slavic consciousness and cultural community. Kollar also preached Slavic reciprocity in the literary and cultural field as a way for the Slavs to unite and face the political challenges of the times. He advanced his ideas in a treatise entitled *Über die literarische Wechselseitigkeit zwischen den verschiedenen Stämmen und Mundarten der slawischen Nation* (On the literary reciprocity among the various tribes and dialects of the Slavic nation), published in 1837. As for Safarik, his contribution to Panslavism, though as important as that of Kollar, was more by way of consequence than direct involvement. His scholarship had the same effect on the Slavs as did Kollar's *Slavy dcera.* In the words of Joseph M. Kirschbaum, "the influence of Safarik's works, namely his *Slav Antiquities,* on the formation and development of Slav national consciousness cannot be valued too highly."[18]

What makes Kollar and Safarik such fascinating participants in the Slovak national awakening is the fact that their writings had effects other than those intended. First of all, each published a collection of folk songs "exactly as we speak"[19] that were very well received by young Slovaks and did more than just awaken their enthusiasm for their own people. Safarik published the first and second volumes of *Pisne svetske lidu slovenskeho v Uhrich* (Popular songs of the Slovak people in Hungary) in 1823 and 1827, and Kollar his *Narodnie Zpievanky* (National songs) in 1834 and 1835. As the most these songs were written in Central Slovak, "Kollar's collection of folk songs fulfilled an important mission in the cultural consciousness of the Slovaks, it strengthened the tendencies to slovakize the literary language, increased Slovak ethnic consciousness and had a profound influence on our poetry in its later stages of development."[20] As far as their better-known writings are concerned, Safarik and Kollar brought to the Slovaks "the notion of the modern cultural and linguistic nation and planted it firmly in Slovak soil."[21] This message was picked up by the younger generation, Catholic and Protestant. Given the political conditions in Hungary which required unity and leadership of the non-Magyars if they were to resist attempts to denationalize and assimilate them, the new Slovak leaders quickly realized that they needed popular support; to achieve this they had to have a literary language that was acceptable to all Slovaks. This meant the rejection not only of biblical Czech, but also of Bernolak's Slovak.

THE REFORM OF THE SLOVAK LANGUAGE

The impulse to reform the Slovak language arose out of two factors that were influencing the national awakening. The first was not unfamiliar to Kollar and

Safarik although they preferred to overlook its significance: the indifference in Prague to their attempts at creating a new Czechoslovak language. Both men noted that the Czech language itself was evolving, and they complained in their correspondence of the rebuff they kept receiving from their Czech colleagues when they proposed modifications, taken from Slovak, in order to form the new Czechoslovak language. The younger generation, particularly those studying at the Bratislava *lyceum,* also came to realize that the Czechs were neglecting Slovak interests. Faced with the second reality of the radicalism of Magyar nationalism, which threatened the national survival of the non-Magyars, this generation understood the need to unite all Slovaks. What stood in their way was a literary language acceptable and accessible to all.[22] They proceeded to create one with consequences that were far-reaching:

> The resolution of the question of a literary language at once solved many other problems which prevented the development of the national move-ment; for example the question of a single Slovak nationality, the question of a common approach by the Catholic and Protestant intelligentsia, the question of relations with the Czechs and other nations, the question of the character of [Slovak] literature and various other questions concerning the organization of cultural and political life. Suddenly, everything be-came clear.[23]

The leader of this young generation was Ludovit Stur, a Lutheran and a man of talent, vigor, and exceptional intellectual and political energy. He was born on 19 October 1815 in Uhrovec, in a house almost within the shadow of the castle of a Hungarian magnate, Count Imre Zay, whose son Karoly would be one of his fiercest opponents. He studied theology at the Lutheran *lyceum* in Bratislava, where in 1828 he became one of the founding members of a student organization called *Spolecnost cesko-slovanska* (Czecho-Slav Society). Similar societies were founded in other *lycea* across Slovakia, and the students in Bratislava kept in touch with them. He published in 1836 *Plody zboru ucencu reci ceskoslovenske prespurskeho* (Harvest of those studying the Czechoslovak language in Bratislava), a publication that marks the appearance in Slovak literary and political history of what is known as *Sturovci,* Stur's group. He studied in Halle from 1838 to 1840 and when he returned to Slovakia, he resumed his lectureship at Palkovic's chair at the Bratislava *lyceum* to which he had been appointed in 1837. As a result of Magyar intrigues, he was dismissed in 1843. He was also one of the founders in 1844 of *Tatrin,* a society whose aim "was to rally all Slovaks who wished to work actively on the basis of the new literary language for the social and cultural development of their people."[24]

He remained in Slovakia, active as a writer, publicist, and political leader until his death on 12 January 1856 as a result of a hunting accident. He is buried in Modra.

When Stur arrived in Bratislava and became active in the *Spolok,* he wrote in Czech like other young Lutheran Slovaks. A number of publications were at their disposal. Among them was a literary journal called *Tatranka,* edited 1832 to 1847 by Palkovic. At the same time, in Banska Bystrica, another Lutheran pastor, Karol Kuzmany, edited from 1836 to 1839 another literary journal, *Hronka.* Stur was also in contact with the other men involved in the national awakening and was swept in their enthusiasm for Slavic solidarity. He was among the students who met in Devin on 27 April 1837 where they vowed to devote themselves to the cause of Slavdom and their people. At the *lyceum,* he lectured on the Slavs. It was from his study of the history and culture of the various Slavic nations that he concluded that the Slovaks were entitled to their own national culture and language.

However, the project of language reform was delayed for a few years when a struggle broke out within the Lutheran Church in Slovakia that united the older and younger generations against Count Karoly Zay. In 1840, Zay was appointed inspector general of the Lutheran Church in Hungary. Soon thereafter he decided to make Magyar the official language of the church and to unite with the Calvinists. In the wake of the struggle that developed, Stur, together with two Lutheran pastors, Jozef Miloslav Hurban and Michal Miloslav Hodza, decided at a meeting on 14 February 1843 to abandon Czech in favor of Slovak. In June of that year, the *Sturovci* met with Holly, who gave his approval for the use of Central Slovak. When in 1844 the Hungarian Diet replaced Latin with Magyar as the sole language of administration and instruction in Hungary, the need to reform the Slovak language became even more compelling. A public announcement was made at a meeting of *Tatrin* on 26–28 August 1844 that Central Slovak would become the Slovak literary language.

In 1846, Stur published *Narecja slovenskuo alebo potreba pisanja v tomto nareci* (The Slovak language or the need to write in this language), a treatise defending the need for a Slovak literary language. In it he also took issue with the classification of the Slavic languages into four categories—Russian, Polish, Czecho-Slovak, and Serbo-Croatian—an idea very dear to Kollar. His *Nauka reci slovenskej* (Study of the Slovak language) came out later that year; in it he set out the principles of the new Slovak grammar. He accepted Bernolak's phonetic orthography but switched from the Western Slovak language area to the Central Slovak one and based the language on the dialects from Liptov, Orava, and especially Turiec county. His decision, as Pauliny writes, arose from the fact that "Cultural Central Slovak was a supra-dialectical linguistic form that predominated

in the eighteenth and at the beginning of the nineteenth century."[25] Stur knew, as did Bernolak, that Cultural Central Slovak already enjoyed a great deal of prestige as the main vehicle of popular oral culture, something that Kollar's and Safarik's folk song collections confirmed. It was also understandable to those speaking Eastern as well as Western Slovak dialects. As a result, he not only completely rejected and removed Czech as a literary language in Slovakia, but by basing himself on Bernolak's work, he crowned a linguistic development that had been centuries in the making. In the words of Joseph M. Kirschbaum: "Stur had grasped the true basis of the Slovak language by a careful analysis of the fundamental roots of the Czech and Slovak languages and by a comparative study of their development. He knew that the claim that Slovak is but a dialect of older Czech was not based on facts of history or philology."[26]

The reform was not accepted immediately. Czech intellectuals were categorically opposed to it because it resulted in what Palacky termed a "separation." Stur was then attacked by Safarik, Palkovic, and, particularly severely, by Kollar. In 1849, Kollar moved to Vienna where, in addition to his professorship at the university, he became an advisor to the imperial government on Slovak questions. He tried unsuccessfully to introduce a corrected form of Czech, which he called "Old Slovak." Stur also had difficulties with his own people. In 1847, Hodza, in *Epigenes slovenicus,* (A Slovak rejoinder) criticized Stur's orthography for not taking into account other Slavic languages. Martin Hattala in *Grammatica linguae slovenicae, collatae cum proxime cognata Bohemica* (The grammar of the Slovak language compared with the closely related Czech language), published in 1850, sought to find middle ground between Stur's and Bernolak's literary Slovak. It was not until 1851 that a compromise was finally reached. The results were published in 1852 in *Kratka mluvnica slovenska* (A concise Slovak grammar), written by Hattala and signed by three Catholic and three Lutheran leaders. While biblical Czech was not given up so easily by many Lutherans, the new language almost immediately produced a literary output of very high quality that anchored it definitely. No longer did any endogenous factor hamper the national awakening; the time was ripe for the flowering of Slovak literature.

SLOVAK ROMANTICISM

The literary production of the *Sturovci* was the result of a combination of factors and not just the consequence of the reform of the Slovak language. The resolution of the literary language issue certainly did make it possible for Slovak writers, in particular poets, to participate in one of Europe's greatest literary

movements, Romanticism. However, the national awakening was also a potent motive and inducement to express the values and feelings of a people who, like other peoples in Central Europe, were seeking to affirm themselves, to take their place in the family of nations. Last but not least, the writings of the *Sturovci* were strongly influenced by the revolutionary events in Slovakia in which some of them were directly involved. In the words of Peter Petro, this period "represents truly the best that Slovak literature produced, . . . [and] is unlikely to be repeated with similar magnificence, range and power."[27]

The group was led by Stur, who was not only a scholar and a revolutionary leader, but also a poet. He published in 1853 a collection of poems entitled *Spevy a piesne* (Chants and songs), considered to be one of the best from this period. They express his disillusionment after the 1848–1849 revolution. This theme is taken up again in the epic poems *Svätoboj* and *Matus z Trencina* (Matthew from Trencin), the first dealing with the fall of Great Moravia and the second with the reign of Matthew Cak. In both works Stur also expresses the conviction that the nation will one day be free. However, Stur is not remembered so much for his poetic works as for his reform of the Slovak literary language and the fact that he was "the first modern Slovak publicist and journalist who fought for the existential and political rights of the nation."[28]

Another person whose literary contribution is second to his leadership and organizational qualities is Jozef Miloslav Hurban. He was born on 19 March 1817 in Beckov, son of a Lutheran pastor. He studied in Trencin and Bratislava and in 1840 became chaplain in Brezova, where two years later he began editing the almanac *Nitra*. In 1843, he became pastor in Hlboke. The second issue of *Nitra*, which he published that same year, was the first publication in the new literary language. In 1846, he began publishing a literary and cultural journal. He turned to literature after the failure of the 1848–1849 revolution; he and Stur had been among its leaders. He wrote novels, literary criticisms, satires, and poems. The epic poem *Osudove Nitry* (The fate of Nitra) and the collection of verses called *Spevy* (Chants) are from this period and express his love for his country and the need to fight for its freedom. Hurban was one of the few to adopt a Czechoslovak orientation in the 1870s after the closing of Matica slovenska, going so far as to publish two issues of *Nitra* in Czech in 1876 and 1877. He died in Hlboke on 21 February 1888. It was as editor of *Nitra* that he contributed to Slovak Romanticism, publishing the poetry of Botto, Chalupka, Kral, and Andrej Sladkovic, the greatest writers of this period.

Jan Botto was one of those who took to heart Stur's exhortations to young Slovaks to fight for freedom and social justice. He did so in his writings. He was born on 27 January 1829 in Vysny Skalnik, attended the *gymnazium* in

Levoca and studied law in Presov and engineering in Pest. He became a land surveyor in Turciansky Sväty Martin, Banska Stiavnica, and Banska Bystrica. A life-long bachelor, he did not partake in the revolutionary events of the 1840s but devoted his life to literature and writing. He died on 28 April 1881. A number of themes recur in his writings, especially that of sacrifice in *Baj na Dunaji* (Baj on the Danube) (1846) and *Vojenske piesne* (Military songs), which he published from 1847 to 1850. His epic poem *Svetsky vitaz* (World conqueror) (1846) is an allegory on yet another theme, heroism. However, he is best known for *"Piesen Janosikova"* (The song of Janosik) (1846) and *Smrt Janosika* (The death of Janosik), written in 1858, the romantic epic poem that celebrates through the life and death of Janosik the people's fierce desire for freedom. It was published first in 1862.

Another poet of this period, Samo Chalupka, also picked up the Janosik theme. Chalupka did not partake actively in the revolution of the 1840s, yet he did fight in the Polish rebellion of 1830. He was born on 27 February 1812 in Horna Lehota. He went to school first in Kezmarok and Roznava, and then studied theology in Bratislava and Vienna. In 1835, he became pastor of the Lutheran Church in Jelsavska Teplica, moving in 1840 after the death of his father to Horna Lehota, where he died on 5 May 1883. His three poems *"Janosikova naumka"* (Janosik's meditation) (1845), *"Likavsky väzen"* (The prisoner of Likava) (1860) and *"Kraloholska"* (The song of Royal Mountain) (1868) celebrate the fight for liberty. This theme is also found in his poems about the Turkish wars on Slovak soil, in particular *"Boj pri Jelsave"* (The battle near Jelsava) (1861) and *"Turcin Ponican"* (The Turk from Poniley) (1863) in which he sings his love for his country. His most famous poem, *"Mor ho!"* (Vanquish him!), deals with the period of the Roman presence on Slovak soil and reverberates with sentiments of freedom and equality.

Another poet to celebrate Janosik was Janko Kral, the first poet of the new language who is best known for his ballads. A lawyer by training, he was born on 24 April 1822 in Liptovsky Sväty Mikulas. He studied in the *lycea* of Kezmarok and Levoca before going to Bratislava where he joined the *Sturovci*. Stur suggested that he go to Pest to work in a lawyer's office to acquire legal training. Kral was involved in the revolution of 1848–1849, was jailed for his activities, and after the revolution found employment in the civil service in Zlate Moravce until 1867, when he was dismissed by the Magyars. He opened a law office and continued to write until his death on 23 May 1876. Much of Kral's creative writings were not published until after his death. Initially he wrote in Czech but then switched to the new Slovak literary language and published in *Nitra* ballads such as *"Zakliata panna vo Vahu a divny Janko"* (The cursed virgin in the Vah and Crazy Janko) (1844) in which he romantically describes his place

of birth and the peregrinations of Crazy Janko along the Vah. However, he is best known for his epic poem *Vylomky z Janosika* (Excerpts from Janosik) (1844–1847) in which he expresses openly his antifeudal feelings. Yet his influence was greatest among his peers, as Milan Pisut, a Slovak literary historian, points out: "The poetic works of Janko Kral, even if only a few of them were published during his lifetime, created the standard for a new style in lyrical, ballad and epic form and expressed the sentimental feelings of the revolutionary period of the national movement."[29]

The Slovak poet who perhaps best expressed the sentimental feelings of this period was Andrej Braxatoris-Sladkovic. While his poetry has been compared to that of Kollar and Holly, it also is seen as being much closer to the Slovak homeland and the people. He was born on 30 March 1820 in Krupina, the son of a teacher. He attended the *lycea* in Banska Stiavnica and Bratislava, where he studied theology. Like many others of his generation, he went to Germany to study and stayed in Halle from 1843 to 1844. It is there that he started to write his most famous poem, "Marina," named after a young woman with whom he had fallen in love a few years before but whose parents would not allow them to marry. When he submitted the poem to the literary society *Tatrin* in 1844, the board refused to publish it because it was deemed to be too personal and too amorous. It was published in Pest in 1846. In 1847, Sladkovic became pastor in Hrochot and later in Radvan, near Banska Bystrica, where he stayed until his death on 20 April 1872.

"Marina" is probably the best-known Slovak poem. It celebrates the apotheosis of womanhood and love. This lyrical work is "figuratively speaking, the daughter of Kollar's *Slavy dcera.*"[30] Sladkovic extended his love for Marina to his country in the epic poem *Detvan,* (The man from Detva) published in 1853. It is organized in five songs that express his opposition to violence, his feeling for justice, his strong emotional life, and his willingness to fight for freedom. The poem is often compared to Holly's *Selanky.* Sladkovic's literary output was quite extensive, and he was also a translator of works by Voltaire, Racine, Goethe, and Khomiakov. When he died, his funeral was a national event, the like of which was not seen for any other Slovak poet of that period.

The national awakening was not a timid or a frivolous period in the life of the Slovak nation. It may have started out as little more than a *querelle de chapelles* between clerics of two denominations in the matter of a literary language. However, it turned into a debate with far-ranging consequences that cost the nation half a century of popular education and political development. The religious dimension cannot in fact be dismissed; at times the language debate seemed to be a substitute for and prolongation of old religious quarrels. The Lutherans' insistence on having Czech accepted as a literary language is

understandable only in confessional terms. As a political calculation it made little sense; most Slovaks were Catholic. And regardless of how close Lutheran pastors were to their flocks and how comfortable they were with biblical Czech in their liturgy, they surely realized that this language had little if no currency beyond the sanctuaries of their temples. Their resistance also cannot be explained away by pointing to the influence of Kollar and Safarik, two Slovaks who actually lived most of their lives outside Slovakia. These two merely strengthened a conviction that was deeply rooted and gave it justification in poetry and scholarship.

As for Slovak Catholics, they had no theological reason for using, let alone preserving, biblical Czech. They had turned to the Slovak vernacular during the Counter-Reformation as the best way to reach the illiterate masses; it followed that a literary language had to develop from it. When it came to the final codification, the Catholics adopted a practical and realistic position. Most abandoned Bernolak's Slovak relatively early and showed their willingness to come to some agreement with the Lutheran intelligentsia in order to develop an acceptable literary language. Had Bernolak followed his own instincts and chosen Cultural Central rather than Cultural Western Slovak at the outset, the debate might have perhaps been avoided altogether. Still, the Catholic clergy accepted sooner and without afterthought the need for linguistic reform and did so because they were the beneficiaries of the Catholic Church's centuries-long involvement in the life of the people.

This was a time when the Habsburg lands were caught in a maelstrom of ideas that included absolutism, nationalism, democracy, and industrialization. The Slovaks were no longer bystanders. The politics of the new age formed the background of the national awakening. This presented a problem for the Catholic Church. The nineteenth century was not the Middle Ages, and the new politics precluded the Catholic Church from openly entering the political arena. Moreover, in the wake of the French Revolution, the Catholic hierarchy was more likely to support legitimate authority, especially in Austria. The paradox of the Slovak national awakening is that the Lutherans, who were not tied by religion to the Habsburgs, were freer to provide political leadership at this time. They also acted because they were forced to do so by the Magyars, if only to protect their own confessional interests. When they did take the inevitable step, it was with an enthusiasm and a creativity that has no parallel in Slovak history. The Slovak nation was united at a time when disunity would have had far-reaching negative consequences on its struggle for survival, which had already entered a new phase.

6

The Politics of Survival

THE PREPARATORY YEARS

It was sheer happenstance that the deaths of Joseph II and Leopold II coincided with the French Revolution and the advent of a new political age in Europe. It was also unfortunate because their successor, Francis II, ended their experiment in political reform and launched the dynasty on the course of conservatism and reaction. As a result, the politics of the Habsburg lands pitted the people against the ruler. In Hungary, the ideology of nationalism added a new dimension, one that brought the nations on a collision course with the ruling class and with each other. The politics of the nineteenth century and early twentieth, not only in the Habsburg lands but also elsewhere in Central Europe, became a series of interwoven two-way fights in which each party had a well-defined objective: the people wanted democratic liberties and the end of feudalism, the nations strove for self-determination, while the ruling classes sought to keep unlimited and unhindered political power. At different times and for different reasons, the nations and ruling classes advanced and retreated tactically in their strategy to achieve their objectives. If leadership was the ultimate determining factor for success, it was the population's political consciousness that defined the outcome. Events also contributed to the shaping of that consciousness as well as to the outcome.

One often underestimated important factor that shaped the politics of the new era was the history of a people, in particular the role it assumed in defining nationalist goals. The image of a nation's past is one of those subjective elements from which nationalist leaders draw inspiration and the justification

for their actions.[1] Their opponents from other nations often challenge these images in order to bolster their own national aspirations. This is particularly the case in situations in which the history is shared as a result of conquest, cession, or a dynastic or political union. The claim to have historic rights assumed major importance in the definition of each nationalism in Central Europe at this time; that is to say, the possession of a state at one time or another in the area's history, preferably in fairly recent times. For those who could not make such a claim—such as the Slovaks who had not formed their own state after the demise of the Great Moravian Empire—this approach implied that they had no historic rights. Their presence in the Hungarian kingdom was perceived as an absence of legitimate historic rights. To counter such assertions, successive Slovak writers emphasized that their people's past was not devoid of any significance and should not hinder the Slovaks from being involved in the new politics. Slovak leaders knew that their people's history was one of survival and development, but also one of involvement in and contribution to European culture and civilization, and this formed a sufficient basis from which to espouse new ideas and challenge the established order. Their claim was based on natural rather than historic rights. In an age that held democracy and self-determination as the new political values, they argued that their demands were not any less legitimate than those of any other nation and there was nothing to bar their nation from involvement in the movements that characterized political life at the end of the eighteenth century. Gogolak is correct, if somewhat patronizing, to suggest that "the history of the amorphous Slovak nation which lacked sovereignty before 1790/91, that is to say before the outbreak of national struggles in Hungary, was the history of certain social groups, and was similar to the history of all of the states and nations of Europe before the French Revolution."[2] The question was whether it could define national objectives and pursue them as successfully as those nations that did enjoy historic rights.

While the Slovaks were eager to enter the new age that began on the eve of the nineteenth century as new politics, industrialization, modernization, and exponential economic, social, and cultural development, burst on the scene in Central Europe, they were not as prepared as some of the other nations, especially the Magyars, since they lacked an organizational and administrative center and a unified national movement. They entered the political arena slowly. For half a century they were involved in discussions and disputes regarding what form the Slovak literary language should take. These debates wasted valuable time and political experience. Second—and this is far from being unimportant at the onset of the age of nationalism—the population and social organization in Slovakia were quite heterogeneous and decentralized, "composed of the nobility which was

slowly but also emotionally influenced by the Slovak base and which in its majority also spoke Slovak, of the rural Slovak people which in time of war was led by the nobility and finally also of the German townspeople and peasants."[3] In the face of such heterogeneity, which was not just social but above all political, the Slovaks needed leaders who could meet the daunting challenge of establishing a consensus, in particular a national one.

One of the fundamental problems that made the task ahead difficult was the position and role of the Hungarian nobility in Slovakia. However much it felt itself to be Slovak and even spoke the Slovak language, it identified with and responded to the interests of its class, a class that held political power and defined itself as the "*natio hungarica.*" There was also a problem with town and city dwellers who, unless they were German, were "without political rights, dispersed, hardly in a position to take action and thus unable to become the unequivocal leaders of the new national revival movement."[4] The Slovaks were at a disadvantage by not being able to count on either group when it came to defining and especially pursuing their national objectives. They had to create a political class, which could come only from the people in the villages and on the land. Besides taking time, there were difficulties involved in raising people's political consciousness.

The third and certainly not least important drawback was the absence of political experience and political goals from which new objectives could be drawn and defined. No longer was it enough simply to carry on with the old way of life, which at its very worst meant barely eking out an existence and at its very best meant entry into the Hungarian nobility if one was willing to speak Magyar. The new age demanded of the nation not just new human, intellectual, and spiritual resources, but above all clearly defined political goals, especially when its very survival was about to be challenged dramatically.

Leopold II convoked the Diet in 1790 and recognized Hungary as a free and independent kingdom in a law known as Law X, which "was thereafter counted by the Hungarians as the fundamental guarantee of their national status."[5] This set into motion the process that would facilitate the development of Magyar nationalism in a manner that Peter F. Sugar calls aristocratic nationalism.[6] In addition, as Macartney indicates: "The new Magyar nationalism agreed with, and in its turn helped to reinforce the assumption that the Hungarian polity must be the preserve, as it had been at the creation, of the Magyar element of the country."[7] In time, to avoid any equivocation on its validity, this assumption developed into a policy of assimilation of the non-Magyar peoples of Hungary, a process that became known as Magyarization. Whether this was justified, in political and moral terms, is a question best left to Hungarian historians. Suffice it to remember that the Turkish occupation

of Hungary had brought about demographic changes favoring the nationalities and had put the Magyars in the position of not having an absolute demographic majority in the kingdom: "The increasing awareness of national differences suggested to Magyar leaders that something should be done to repair the numerical inferiority of the ruling people."[8] The Slovak leaders had to respond to the consequences of this situation as well as face other challenges. France was already in the throes of the French Revolution.

While the French Revolution produced only a faint echo of political reform in the Habsburg lands, it had interesting consequences in Slovakia. The ideas of the revolution were the object of commentary in the pages of the *Preßburger Zeitung* (Bratislava Journal) and were discussed among intellectuals. In 1790, Juraj Alojz Belnay presented a petition to the Diet entitled *Reflexiones cunctorum Hungariae civium* (The thoughts of Hungarian citizens) in which he attacked the unjust demands and privileges of the Hungarian estates. As Jozef Simoncic writes: "Belnay was not alone to have such thoughts. His ideas were developed in even more concrete forms in pamphlets that were distributed throughout Hungary."[9] The distribution of pamphlets, in particular to the peasants, was but one of many revolutionary activities in Slovakia during the 1790s. There were also Jacobin clubs and secret societies.

The most interesting activity was the attempt to transform Hungary into a republic. The conspiracy was quickly uncovered and its participants were arrested and tried. The leader was a former Franciscan from Pest of Serbian origin, Ignac Martinovic, who, when he failed to get a chair at the University, turned informer for the Viennese government. He then became involved revolutionary activity and created two societies, the *Societas reformatorum* (Society of Reformers) for the nobility and the *Societas libertatis atque equalitatis* (Society of Freedom and Equality) for radical democrats and Jacobins. For each society he prepared and published a catechism. His conspiracy included a number of Slovak participants, among them Jozef Hajnoci, a lawyer from Modra. Martinovic worked out a democratic constitution which included the nationality principle; its application would have turned Slovakia into an independent administrative unit called Slavonica. In the words of Slovak historians: "It is in fact the first proposal to include Slovakia as an independent national administrative unit within the framework of Hungary."[10] The conspiracy not only cost the lives of five conspirators, including Martinovic and Hajnoci, but above all "ended all plans for reform and silenced all opposition in Hungary."[11]

Apart from this event which had no political consequences, Slovaks barely remembered the reign of Francis II. Europe was at war at this time, and Napoleon's campaigns directly involved the Habsburgs—the emperor convoked the Diet in Bratislava regularly to ask for subsidies and recruits—but

otherwise "touched Hungarian territory only twice, and each time only for a few weeks, and in other respects brought the country actual gain, for the land-owners were able to make high profits out of the wheat for which there was an almost unlimited demand, at high prices."[12] Despite the challenge from the ideas of the French Revolution, the aristocratic order of Hungary seemed secure; the Diet met every three years, as had been agreed to in 1790, and in 1805 the emperor granted it the request that correspondence with the chancellery and the *Consilium* be written in Magyar.

The relations between the emperor and the Diet became strained over the cost of the wars; the Diet was dissolved in 1812 because it refused to vote Hungary's part of the state debt. It was not convoked again for thirteen years. Once the Napoleonic wars were over, the Habsburg lands were subjected to the conservative regime of Prince Clemens Metternich. In many respects, this suited the Diet, whose "members were as anxious as Metternich himself that revolution should not spread."[13] On the other hand, the Diet achieved another linguistic concession in 1830 by making Magyar a requirement for those wishing to work in the public service in Hungary and for admission to the bar. Otherwise, the monarchy weathered the ripple effects of the July Revolution, which saw the restoration of the Bourbons in France and the Polish anti-Russian uprising of 1830–1831.

The end of the Napoleonic wars had brought about some negative economic consequences in Hungary. The price of grain had fallen sharply, and in 1817–1818, famine had struck a number of Eastern Slovak villages where some 40,000 people died. Some relief was brought through the cultivation of the potato and the export of wool to Western Europe, especially to England, Holland, and Germany, which replaced the previously lucrative wheat export. Nevertheless, a cholera epidemic broke out in 1831 and the government was forced to suppress the resulting peasant revolts in Eastern Slovakia, among other areas. The government could not, on the other hand, contain the need for reform, a need that these revolts brought out only too plainly. The catalyst turned out to be the scion of one of Hungary's great historic families, Count Istvan Szechenyi. He was the first in a series of new actors on the Hungarian political scene who took the kingdom out of medievalism into what Hungarian historians call the Reform Era.

In 1830, Szechenyi published a book entitled *Hitel* (On credit). In it he attacked the Hungarian political system and in particular the social and economic policies of the landed nobility. Published at a time when liberal ideas were reappearing in Europe, this book, together with two others by him, *Vilag* (Light) and *Stadium,* published in 1831 and 1833 respectively, had such a profound impact on Hungarian society that "henceforth, national life was to

center on political questions rather than literary debates, as it had in previous decades."[14] Another man who made a singular contribution to this new atmosphere was Lajos Kossuth, a flamboyant orator and gifted journalist born of a Slovak mother. Less than two decades later, he would take Hungary down the path of aborted revolution and independence. Three other important liberal personalities of the period who exerted their influence in the Diet were Ferenc Deak, Baron Jozsef Eötvös, and Count Lajos Batthyany, who became prime minister. Until revolution broke out in Paris in February 1848, an event that completely changed the political climate in the Habsburg lands, these men dominated Hungarian political life. Kossuth was especially important. In 1841 he became editor of *Pesti Hirlap* (The Gazette of Pest), in whose pages he "reflected the frustrations and ambitions of a younger generation of lesser noblemen open to Western ideas, eager to challenge an ossified absolutist system, and, above all, ready to take over the government of a country."[15] Francis II died in 1835 and was succeeded by Ferdinand V (1835–1848). This change in rulers did not bring about any change in Vienna's conservative policies; Metternich remained in power.

The Hungarian Diet took two measures during the Reform Era that were of significance for the Slovak people. The Diet of 1839–1840 passed a new urbarial law that allowed peasants to become landowners by the payment of a fixed sum as manumission compensation. While this law did not free all of the peasants from their obligations, or *robot* to give some of their time to the lord, it made it possible for some to acquire their freedom. This breach in the old medieval bond had two consequences: By being incomplete, it thrust upon this hitherto politically dormant but also economically disfavored class, some of whom were now freed of the consequences of statutory economic dependency, the need to acquire political consciousness that not only involved individual rights and liberties, but also alerted them to the national struggle. Second, the Slovak and Magyar national agendas now competed for the peasantry. The other measure was passed three years later, when the Diet of 1843–1844 finally reached its long sought for goal of making Magyar the official language of all government institutions and schools in the kingdom. The road that led to a policy of official Magyarization was now completely free. These two measures were but a prelude to the issues that would put Magyar and Slovak leaders on a collision course, especially as two eminent men, Kossuth from Pest and Stur from Zvolen were elected to the Diet in the fall of 1847. The fall of Louis Philippe in Paris in February 1848 was the spark that put both nations on the path of revolution and confrontation and altered their relationship forever.

THE MAGYAR-SLOVAK RELATIONSHIP

During the half century preceding the "Spring of Nations," as the year 1848 is generally described, the Slovak intelligentsia was caught up in a language debate that was also a kind of religious proxy fight, a leftover from the Reformation and Counter-Reformation eras. When the challenge from the Magyars became clear, the need to unite became paramount. The Lutheran community produced leaders who were successful in achieving this objective not just on the language issue but also on the political level. However, the Slovak leaders were hindered by the fact that their nation lived in a polity that gave power exclusively to the Magyar element. While the Magyars ruled, they had always been willing to accept and even give positions of prominence to non-Magyars who acquired Magyar language and culture. This was certainly the case of many Slovaks.

In the 800 years or so of coexistence between the Slovaks and Magyars, their relationship, at least until 1790, had not been fundamentally confrontational. Both groups had in fact given and accepted much from each other. Their histories had interlocked and together they made up, along with that of the other constituent nationalities, the history of the Hungarian kingdom. Until the Turkish occupation of the Hungarian plain, the two nations lived side by side. When Slovakia became the core of royal Hungary after the battle of Mohacs in 1526, the histories of the two nations became interwoven. The political class had always been Magyar, but it ruled over a population that was now in its majority Slovak speaking. While the latter accepted the medieval order and identified with the Hungarian state—a fact that, until the nineteenth century, no Slovak writer ever questioned—the Magyar nobility in Slovakia not only learned to speak Slovak but also identified with the Slovak core, encouraged its culture, and often defended its interests. It was a reasonable *modus vivendi* in a medieval society, and it seemed to benefit both parties. However, Slovak historian Daniel Rapant is right to caution that this was not an idyllic situation, for if there was no nationality question, as there would be henceforth, there was also no national or linguistic equality.[16] For individual Slovaks, the path to personal and social advancement was a one-way street, one that led ultimately and inevitably to a form of Magyarization. The Slovak environment imposed a reverse process but generally only for the peasantry and in some instances the inhabitants of towns and cities. Rarely did it result in significant individual social advancement. All of this changed in the nineteenth century when a Magyar national agenda was imposed on the country and Magyarization became the result of an official policy rather than merely the consequence of a personal decision.

The reforms of Maria Theresa in 1777 and Joseph II in 1781 and especially the language laws passed by the Hungarian Diet in 1844 altered the balance between Magyars and Slovaks that the medieval order had been able to maintain. The reforms had slowly brought about the national awakening of both the Slovaks and the Magyars. The latter realized that the new consciousness among the Slovaks and other non-Magyar nationalities had the potential of becoming a threat to their survival. The nobility understood this threat particularly well; they were the class that held political power in the kingdom and who also saw that foreign powers could use the nationalities to interfere in Hungarian affairs. Their first response was the language laws, an act of self-defense as much against Vienna and Germanization as against the non-Magyars. Gogolak is right to point out that "it would be a mistake to regard the Slovak-Magyar relationship . . . merely from the overall perspective of a racial or national struggle."[17] It was a struggle for the definition of the Hungarian state and for its control, one that pitted the Magyar ruling class against the Slovak (and other non-Magyar) political leadership. As Magyarization proceeded, the Hungarian nobility in Slovakia simply became completely Magyar. Each side invoked rights, historic ones for the Magyars and natural ones for the Slovaks; however, "the natural rights that it [the Slovak political class] traced to its existence as the representative of the nation were diametrically opposed to the historic rights of the Hungarian state which since 1790/91 and 1825 was becoming more and more Magyar."[18] In this type of confrontation, Magyarization was the inevitable by-product of the historic rights claim.

When Magyarization became official policy, non-Magyars discovered that it was no longer the consequence of a personal choice; rather it was a requirement not just for membership in the Hungarian state but above all for participation in its political life. Magyarization was all-pervasive in its application, affecting social and personal relations and exerting moral and existential pressure on individuals. It was the fulfillment of the nation-state equation whose consequences were fully understood by both Magyars and Slovaks. For the former, it meant no political compromise; for the latter, given their history and social and political situation, it meant the search for a way to ensure survival. During the 1840s, both groups defined their objectives and set out their strategies. As far as the Slovaks are concerned, Rapant writes, "after almost a thousand years, this is the first time that the Slovak nation as such finally makes political history."[19] As events began to unfold swiftly in the spring of 1848, both nations also ended up taking up arms to achieve their goals.

The Slovak leaders evolved a survival strategy that was directed on three fronts. The first, examined in the previous chapter, was the national awakening, a process that in time "changed these unconscious creators and bearers of Slovak

nationality into a modern, self-conscious and fully legal nation."[20] It was in fact a precondition for the second approach, which consisted in raising the national consciousness of the people by direct involvement in their life, a concept the *Sturovci* called *drobna praca* (menial tasks), and which meant the creation of reading circles, temperance clubs, credit unions, and self-help groups. One of the first reading circles, called *Spolok Pohronsky* (Circle of the Hron Valley), was created in September 1845 by Canon Anton Tilesa in Banska Bystrica. According to Rapant, *drobna praca* was "the best defence at that time against the new process and the new methods of Magyarization (indirect pressure)."[21] It is also worth noting that the first cooperative movement in Central Europe was founded in Slovakia in 1845 by Samuel Jurkovic when he created the *Spolok gazdovsky* (Farmer's Union) in Sobotiste; it played an important role in improving the economic lot of the rural population, especially in the second half of the nineteenth century.

The third approach involved contacts with other Slavs who were also experiencing their awakening and whose political importance, were they to unite, could transform the political landscape in Central Europe. Croats, Czechs, and Serbs were among those Slavs from whom the Slovak leaders sought assistance in 1848 for support in their struggle with Budapest. This Panslavism, especially if there was a suggestion of Russian interest or involvement, and even though it actually never had a chance of becoming a serious political movement, frightened the rulers in Vienna and Budapest and became the catchall accusation used against all the national demands of the Slovaks.

In the application of their strategy, the Slovaks had to get around one major structural problem, namely the fact that the political system in the Habsburg lands was not set up to deal favorably with the demands formulated by the nationalities. The only channel for these demands was to submit them to the Hungarian authorities or, failing that, to imperial ones. In either case, they were assessed and subjected either to the interests of the Magyar polity or to those of the imperial court with consequences that were not always favorable to the petitioners. The Slovak leaders discovered this in 1842 when they submitted their first petition to Prince Metternich; it concerned the protection of their language in their schools and the setting up of a chair of Slovak language at the University of Pest. While it was not a politically offensive document, in addition to indifference in Vienna, it produced a violent negative reaction from the Magyar authorities and especially from the Magyar press. As a consequence, the Slovak leaders became convinced of the need for linguistic as well as political unity. To counter the mounting negative pressure from the Magyar press, despite the limited means at their disposal, the Slovaks began publishing in August 1845 *Slovenskje narodnje novini* (The Slovak National Gazette) with a

supplement called *Orol tatransky* (Eagle of the Tatras) with Stur as editor. A year later, Hurban produced a cultural publication called *Pohladi na vedi, umenja a literaturu* (Perspectives on science, art, and literature) which was printed in Skalica. It ceased publication after two issues but reappeared in 1851. Slovaks also ran for the Diet. Stur was elected in the fall of 1847, thanks to the voters of Zvolen. However, when the suffrage was broadened in 1848 and new elections were held, no Slovak was elected.

During his tenure as a member of the Hungarian Diet, Stur presented and defended the program that he had published already in *Slovenskje narodnje novini*; he spoke on behalf of the Slovak peasant, advocated the end of all forms of serfdom, and emphasized the need for social and economic reform. In this, he did not differ from the more liberal Magyar representatives such as Kossuth. However, his proposal for a Slovak national program did not find any support in the Diet. His dilemma was basically the one that defined the national struggle of the Slovaks: "On the positive side, of all the Hungarian nations, they were the least hindered by some sort of state formation based on an older ideology while on the negative side, they lacked sufficient protection arising out of past experience and were forced to create their own national defensive shell as soon as possible."[22] It took events in Budapest and Vienna in March 1848, which brought down the Metternich government, to prod them into action, under the leadership of Stur, Hurban, and Hodza.

THE REVOLUTIONARY YEARS 1848–1849

The Diet was meeting in Bratislava when the news of Metternich's fall of reached it. Kossuth immediately proposed a series of liberal measures, including the abolition of the *robot* as well as a declaration of Hungary's autonomy that stated that the nation's tie to Austria would be only through the person of the emperor. In April, during a visit to the Diet in Bratislava, Ferdinand V approved these laws. In the context of the period, they were revolutionary yet they were also half-measures, in particular the law abolishing serfdom. Not all peasants were freed from their obligations; the nobility were promised reparations and kept their vast estates; and many questions concerning the use of forests, common pastoral, non-urbarial and terraced land were left unanswered. The Diet also did not vote any laws that favored the nationalities. On the contrary, the Magyar nobility, led by Kossuth, announced its intention to create an entirely Magyar state. The stage was thus set for a confrontation with the dissatisfied peasants and with the nationalities.

The Slovak reaction to these laws took on various forms. During the spring and summer, there were many signs of discontent in just about every county in Slovakia, especially among the peasantry. The poet Janko Kral led a peasant revolt in Hont county that cost him and the teacher Jan Rotarides many months in jail. In Banska Stiavnica, the miners manifested their discontent on 22 March by threatening to strike. In the face of the Diet's stand toward the nationalities, Stur, Hodza, and Hurban prepared and circulated petitions for signature, which they then submitted to the Hungarian government. They also organized meetings. The first one of significance took place on 27 March in Liptovsky Sväty Mikulas under Hurban's leadership. He formulated a series of demands that were submitted to the county offices the next day. After the offices demanded their withdrawal, they were published in *Slovenskje narodnje novini*.

In April, Hurban published anonymously an article entitled *"Bratia Slovaci"* (My Slovak brothers) that did not go unnoticed. In it, he expressed the worry "that the Slovaks, for whom, like other nations, the 'bells of freedom tolled,' would miss the opportunity for revolutionary transformations, and he urgently demanded that they raise a decided and just voice for national freedom."[23] The demands outlined in this article became the basis for other meetings, in Myjava, Brezova, and finally in Liptovsky Sväty Mikulas on 10 May. There, two lawyers, Stefan Marko Daxner (1822–1892) and Jan Francisci (1822–1905), helped Hurban draft a national program entitled *Ziadosti slovenskeho naroda* (The Demands of the Slovak Nation) which he proposed the next day to those assembled. In fourteen points, the Slovak nation demanded the recognition and guarantee of national identity; the transformation of Hungary into a state composed of equal nations, each with its own parliament and equal representation in the Hungarian Diet; and the use of Slovak in all Slovak county offices. In addition, it insisted on democratic rights, including universal and equal suffrage, the total abolition of serfdom, the return of the land to the peasants from whom it had been taken away, and the release of Kral and Rotarides from prison. These demands went far beyond anything that the Diet had approved in March. The Hungarian government's response was to post a warrant for the arrest of Stur, Hodza, and Hurban.

This response forced the Slovak leaders to establish contacts with other Slavic nationalities. Hurban and Stur first traveled to Vienna to meet with Croatian and Serbian representatives. Then Hurban traveled south while Stur left for Prague in April to "probe the question of Czecho-Slovak cooperation and also to propagate the idea of a Slavic Congress—an idea of which he had been one of the leading originators, having broached it in Vienna at the beginning of April."[24] The Slav Congress was held in June 1848 in Prague. Stur attended as the unofficial leader of the Slovak delegation, which included

Safarik, who gave the keynote speech at the opening of the congress. The Magyar authorities had forbidden Kollar from attending. The congress was divided into three sections: The Czechs and Slovaks formed the Czecho-Slovak one; the South Slav was comprised of the Slovenes, Croats, Serbs, and other Slavs from the region who were designated geographically as Dalmatians and Slavonians; and the Polish-Ruthenian section was comprised of the Poles and the Ukrainians.

Stur soon discovered that there were important differences between the Slovak and Czech political objectives. The latter pursued a policy of Austro-Slavism, which, in its goal to federalize the empire, meant a political union between Czechs and Slovaks. The Slovaks, not yet ready to make a complete break with Hungary, did not favor such a union but did need help in their struggle with the Magyars. The outbreak of revolution in Prague in which Stur participated brought about the indefinite adjournment of the congress. When it became clear that the revolution would fail, he returned to Slovakia to lead the fight against the Magyars. As for the idea of a Czech-Slovak union, it made no further headway among the Slovaks but did reappear on the Czech side, in Palacky's second constitutional draft which was presented to the imperial Parliament's constitutional committee and was discussed in January and February 1849. It did not find favor either with the imperial authorities and the Germans of Austria or the Slovaks: "This proposal provoked misgivings among Slovak leaders. Stur and some of his colleagues feared that it would establish a Czech hegemony over the Slovaks and other Slavs of Austria, while others, who felt that even such a basic reorganization would still leave the Slovaks in the Magyar sphere of influence, preferred to see Slovakia directly administered from Vienna."[25]

The unfolding of events in the Habsburg lands greatly determined the opportunities available to Slovak leaders to make political headway. The appointment in March of a Croat army officer, Colonel Josip Jellacic, "an enthusiastic 'Illyrian' and fanatical anti-Magyar,"[26] as Ban (governor) of Croatia had not necessarily been unwelcome news to the Slovaks. It did, however, create serious frictions between Hungary and Croatia, with Vienna caught in the middle. On 11 July the Diet, spurred on by Kossuth, voted men and money for Hungarian defense. On the other hand, the victory of Field Marshal Count J. W. Radetzky in Custozza against the Piedmontese armies on 25 July made his units "available for 'restoring order' in the interior of the Monarchy."[27] In the meantime, a constituent imperial assembly met in Austria and passed legislation in September abolishing the *robot*. There were also numerous national meetings and congresses of Romanians and Saxons in Transylvania. Many of the Serbs, like the Slovaks, were making demands of Budapest for

national and territorial autonomy. The situation finally came to a head in September, when the imperial authorities decided to act; Jellacic was authorized to move against Hungary. His forces, badly led, were defeated by the newly formed Hungarian army, the *Honved*.

Having failed to get anywhere with Budapest during the spring and early summer of 1848, Slovak leaders began meeting in Vienna in August and September. They took two important decisions. On 16 September they created the Slovak National Council. It was the first modern Slovak political institution, which, according to Slovak historians, "symbolized the hopes of the Slovaks for national self-affirmation and represented their national sovereignty."[28] Led by Stur, Hodza, and Hurban, its task was to coordinate all Slovak political and military activity. They also organized a volunteer force of 600 men, mostly students, led by two Czech officers, Bedrich Bloudek and Frantisek Zach. When Jellacic entered Hungary, this volunteer force crossed into Western Slovakia, collecting more volunteers along the way. On 19 September in Myjava, the Slovak National Council declared Slovakia's separation from Hungary and called upon the Slovak nation to join in a national uprising. Their leaders believed that such an uprising would convince Hungarian and imperial authorities that their demands had broad mass support.

The Myjava declaration provoked a number of military engagements between Slovak and Hungarian forces. On 22 September, the Slovak volunteers registered their first victory near Brezova. The Slovak National Council did not, however, exploit the opportunity it offered due to a number of factors. In the first place, the Slovak volunteers, among whom were also students from other nationalities, were not all that well equipped militarily, lacking above all artillery. Even their footwear was a problem. Moreover, the Slovak leaders failed to establish an infrastructure of representatives across Slovakia to coordinate their political and military activities. The leaders worked on the premise—naive as it turned out—that their proclamations and initial victories would have a snowball effect. Moreover, although they counted on being able to sweep from Western into Central and Eastern Slovakia, whatever fighting there was took place in Western Slovakia. The emperor condemned the uprising on 25 September. The Slovak forces were defeated the next day in Senica and proceeded to withdraw westward. By the end of October, Hungarian forces pushed the Slovak volunteers into Moravia. As Spiesz concludes, the "first independent armed stand of the Slovaks in their history ended unsuccessfully. This failure was also due to the fact that the imperial armies were on the side of the Hungarians."[29] The Hungarian government declared the Slovak leaders to be traitors and deprived them of their citizenship. Throughout this entire period, Hungarian authorities showed little clemency; as Macartney writes, "the

Slovaks long remembered, under the name of 'Kossuth gallows', the trees from which itinerant Commissioners had hanged the leading [local] insurgents."[30]

The emperor's decision in early October to crush the Hungarian rebellion provoked unrest in Vienna, forcing him to flee to Olomouc and the imperial Parliament to Kromeriz in Moravia, where it proceeded to draft a new constitution. In the meantime, General Alfred Windischgrätz, who had put down the Czech rebellion in Prague in June, brought about the capitulation of Vienna on 28 October. On 2 December, the abdication of Ferdinand V in favor of his young nephew, Francis Joseph (1848–1916), resulted in further Hungarian resistance. Jellacic and Windischgrätz combined forces to enter into Hungary. On 4 March 1849, an imperial manifesto announced that Hungary belonged to "an indivisible and indissoluble constitutional Austrian Empire." The manifesto accompanied the new Stadion Constitution, named after minister of the interior, Count Franz Stadion, which superseded the one drafted in Kromeriz.[31] On 14 April, the Hungarian Diet proclaimed the independence of Hungary after Batthyany had resigned as prime minister. Kossuth became Hungary's provisional head of state.

The Viennese rebellion had prodded the Slovak leaders into preparing a second military involvement, although this time in coordination with imperial forces. In December 1848, a group of volunteers headed for Zilina. For a while they controlled much of central and eastern Slovakia under the leadership of General Karl Götz. They successfully pushed back the Hungarian *Honved* forces of General Artur Görgey. Another group established itself in southwestern Slovakia. In the territories they occupied, the imperial armies established royal administrative councils, which took over from county offices. In these councils, "for the first time in the public administration of Slovakia in greater numbers, non-aristocrats and active Slovak patriots enjoyed real success."[32] The Slovak leaders also had decided in October 1848 to abandon the program outlined in the *Ziadosti*. On 29 January 1849, they met in Turciansky Sväty Martin to formulate new demands. On 20 March, the leaders of the Slovak National Council were received by the emperor in Olomouc. To him they submitted a petition requesting the creation of an autonomous territory called Slovakia, free of Hungarian control, which would have its own parliament and an administration answering directly to Vienna. Slovak would also be the official language. While the young emperor made vague promises concerning the Slovak demands, Minister of the Interior Stadion was inclined to consider them seriously. Vienna was willing at this time to make use of the requests from the smaller nationalities as a way of putting pressure on the Hungarians to end their resistance.

The Hungarian declaration of independence, however, brought about a change of policy in Vienna; the decision was taken to end Hungarian secession.

With the help from Russian czar Nicholas I, who sent troops in June, the Hungarian forces were finally defeated at Vilagos on 11 August 1849. It was the end of all military activities in the Habsburg lands. Conservatism and reaction were back on the agenda. A conference was called in September to determine the status of Hungary in the empire. The Slovak leaders took this opportunity to make one final attempt to have the imperial authorities accept their demands. They also launched a mass movement whose aim it was "to persuade the distrustful conservative Imperial ruling circles, the government, the dynasty and the conference, all objects of one-sided information, that the Slovak national demands for the separation of Slovakia from Hungary was not proposed only by a small group of 'Panslavs' and national radicals but that a broad section of the population supported them."[33] Not surprisingly, the Slovak demands were ignored. Slovakia was divided into two administrative units with centers in Bratislava in the west and Kosice in the east. This arrangement was part of the reorganization of Hungary, announced on 17 October, which in effect put the entire country under military control. The Habsburg lands were ruled by the centralist provisions of the Stadion Constitution until 31 December 1851, when it was abrogated by imperial decree. However, the Slovaks were not completely disadvantaged under these provisions; their language was allowed in primary schools as well as in county offices. Slovaks were also named to administrative positions, among them Kollar, who tried but failed to introduce his own form of yet another Slovak literary language, based on Czech, which he called Old Slovak.

In the space of two generations, the life of the Slovaks was transformed. The revolutionary changes that took place affected them as individuals as well as a nation. The peasants were the greatest beneficiary of the "Spring of Nations." For them, the abolition of the *robot* meant they achieved that long sought for freedom from obligation even if in practical terms their situation was barely altered if they remained on the land. In the flow of the revolutionary transformations that marked the nineteenth century, the abolition of the *robot* was an important milestone but hardly a final outcome. There were more rights to be fought for, yet paradoxically this first success was also the factor that caused the process of change to ground almost to a halt. As A. J. P. Taylor points out: "Until September 1848, the peasantry were in an aggressive revolutionary spirit throughout the Empire; once sure of emancipation, they lost interest in politics and watched with indifference the victory of absolutism."[34] Many peasants, in particular poor ones, sold their lands to wealthier ones and moved into towns, thereby strengthening their national character by numerically swamping the German town dwellers. As the process of industrialization intensified, they formed the pool from which the working class developed. The wealthier

peasants and magnates benefited most from the peasant emancipation. They were now free to run their agricultural holdings economically, and the magnates, with the compensation they received, were able to invest in capitalistic enterprises. Further revolutionary change was not in the interest of either group. Yet both groups would bring it slowly about with their attention to and need for industrial development. In the political life of the empire, however, they represented conservative forces.

If the struggles for national emancipation were effectively halted in 1848–1849, national development, on the other hand, had certainly not been hindered. The Slovaks, it could be said, had taken a quantum leap forward. They had failed to achieve their political goals and their uprising had not been one of epic proportions, yet at the same time they had given notice that they were no longer an "amorphous nation" but a force to be reckoned with. The Slovak revolutionary leaders, however disappointed they were by this failure, could take some satisfaction in knowing that they were the representatives of a nation whose existence could no longer be put into question and, what is more, a nation that would fight for its survival. The Magyars were also served notice that the inhabitants of Slovakia were not willing to accept the Magyar-Hungarian equation, that is to say the transformation of Hungary into a purely Magyar state (the name *"Felvidek"*—Upper Hungary—for Slovakia appears at this time in Magyar circles). The one constant in the Slovak political program was the Slovaks' desire to run their own affairs. They submitted this demand to Budapest and, after the Hungarian declaration of independence, also to Vienna. Their inability to achieve this goal cannot be ascribed just to their political weakness; more powerful forces, in particular the Magyars and conservative dynastic interests in Vienna, controlled the game and decided the outcome. There was no universal suffrage yet to act as a counterforce; the nationalities were pawns in a broader political game.

Their failure to make political headway was, on the other hand, a portent of the difficulties they would face in the years ahead as they pursued their national goals. Their lack of success had not been the result just of certain drawbacks, or the consequence of inexperience and insufficient leadership; rather it was also the outcome of the changed political balance brought about by the events of 1848–1849. The most important political class in Slovakia, the nobility, had been totally unavailable to the national movement. Since 1790 it had been in the process of becoming completely Magyarized, and during the events of 1848 and 1849 identified its interests with those of the Hungarian state. The lesser nobility, especially those who occupied positions in the counties, took their cue from the magnates and used their offices to obstruct the Slovak national movement and crush the uprising. They became the

instruments of Budapest's policy of Magyarization, the most formidable opponents of the Slovak national movement.

The situation of the peasantry also gave cause for concern from a national point of view. During the upheavals of 1848–1849, many joined Hungarian rather than Slovak forces when they were told that their social liberties were granted by the Magyars and not the Slovak revolutionary leaders. As Gogolak points out, the behavior of the Slovak peasantry was very much influenced by a "patriarchal-patrimonial estates past"[35] that made them deferential to the nobility and respectful of its authority. This explains to some extent the absence of major bloody encounters between Slovak and Hungarian forces. Slovaks did not fight with the ferocity that Hungarian forces encountered in other parts of the kingdom. For Budapest this meant that there was room to maneuver and opportunities to exploit. Hungarian politicians did so on many occasions and would not miss a chance to do so in the future.

Nevertheless, through these events, the Slovak leaders made a twofold contribution to the development of the nation. In the first place, they were able to minimize the confessional differences of the two previous centuries and begin to unite all Slovaks. While it took the challenge of Magyar nationalism to reach a degree of unity, their success can be measured in their refusal to accept the Czecho-Slovak option of their Czech colleagues, an alternative that nevertheless appealed to many in the Lutheran community. They forged a common approach because they had understood that the struggle for survival required overcoming religious differences and demanded unity.

Their second contribution is even more significant, not merely because it formed the basis for the first one, but because it left a legacy that inspired later generations. They gave the nation the gift of its own written language, bolstered its literature, and enriched its culture. Gogolak sums up its relevance when he writes: "The young Slovak leaders served their nation superbly with their romantic national engagement and gave it the gift of an enchanting poetry in their own language. They raised the Slovak language to the level of an independent Slavic poetic language and with it helped the still undeveloped sense of Slovak national independence to become a future political force."[36]

These revolutionary years had been but a prelude to and a preparation for a new phase in the Slovak struggle for survival. The Slovak nation had come out of them transformed, but so had Hungary. Their leaders knew that the unity they had achieved was fragile. The future was uncertain; the nation had to face the challenge of ever-increasing Magyarization. Now that the matter of the literary language had been settled, they were better prepared than before. The demands of industrialization and the need for political development also had to be addressed in a state that was not, on the other hand, willing to share

political power and to give the Slovaks the political tools to do so. The Slovaks learned from the events of 1848 and 1849 that they would have to carry the struggle on their own and that the challenge to the survival of their nation they now faced was the most serious one yet.

7

The Struggle for Nationhood

NEOABSOLUTISM AND THE AUSTRO-HUNGARIAN COMPROMISE

The aftermath of the revolutions of 1848 and 1849 had shown that the Habsburgs and the imperial ruling classes were the overall winners of the first round of the interwoven two-way struggles that had characterized the events of those years. They managed to retain power, even to consolidate it, while at the same time legally emancipating the serfs and giving the nationalities certain rights, which may be seen as victories of sorts as well. Nevertheless, the net result was the imposition of neoabsolutism in the empire. In Hungary, Macartney points out, "the regime was not in every respect unbeneficial especially to the poorer classes and the nationalities. . . . But for the backbone of the [Magyar] nation, the middle and smaller nobles, the times were ruinous."[1] While some economic factors explain the difficulties of the nobility, this situation also can be explained by the fact that the Magyars were severely punished for their revolution. The punishment was meted out by Field Marshal J. J. Haynau. Former Prime Minister Batthyany and the leading generals of the *Honved,* except for Görey, were given death sentences. Kossuth escaped into exile, where he remained until his death in 1894. He continued to seek international support for the separation of Hungary from the empire, and almost received it in 1860 from Napoleon III of France. Hungarian politics,

under the leadership of Deak, entered a period of passive resistance, with the political class biding its time until the moment was ripe not just to regain earlier rights for Hungary but above all to forge ahead with the national agenda.

Francis Joseph and his officials, in particular Prime Minister Felix von Schwarzenberg and Interior Minister Alexander Bach, were determined to create a centralized imperial political system where German was the official language of administration. Military control was maintained until 1853 when civilian rule was restored, meaning in effect that the generals were replaced by appointed civilians. There was no constitutional change, and as far as Hungary was concerned, Bach had simply declared its constitution null and void. Schwarzenberg's death in 1852 had resulted in the emperor becoming his own prime minister. Bach was in charge of the internal matters of the empire, and this first period, which ends in 1859, is known as the Bach era. He brought about a reform of the judicial services, creating in the process a class of central administrators whom Szechenyi dubbed, ironically but not inaccurately, "Bach Hussars" because of their special uniforms.[2] He also required Hungary to pay for its entire share of the central services of the empire and a proportionate share of the national debt. Still, during this time Hungary enjoyed an economic boom in agriculture and manufacturing and also saw the growth of the railroad network.

The end of the Bach era came about as a result of Austrian foreign policy adventures connected with Italian nationalism and involving France and Piedmont and indirectly also England and Prussia. In the war that resulted, the imperial forces were defeated at Magenta on 4 June and at Solferino on 24 June 1859. Bach resigned in July and was replaced by Count Agenor Goluchowski. Bach's departure did not bring about an immediate constitutional change but did initiate the process. Throughout 1860, in particular after the meeting of the *Reichsrat* in May, Hungary's representatives, the Old Conservatives, produced a report that proposed among other things the reactivation of the nation's former self-governing institutions. The representatives exerted pressure on the emperor to accept their proposals, and on 20 October he issued the "October Diploma," which turned the empire into a sort of federal state. However, it satisfied no one—not the Czechs, Poles, Germans of Austria or the Magyars. Hungary regained its "historic constitution," but, as Macartney points out, "half-heartedly, for while restoring the chancellery and the *Consilium,* it [the October Diploma] still provided for a strong central executive and a *Reichsrat* with competence extending to all questions affecting the Monarchy as a whole."[3]

These reactions provoked additional discussions, which resulted in the 1861 "February Patent"; it put the October Diploma into operation but

centralized the organization of the legislature even more, which favored the Germans. The *Reichsrat* was composed of two chambers, the Upper House *(Herrenhaus)*, a sort of imperial House of Lords, and the House of Deputies *(Abgeordnetenhaus)*, dominated by Germans, in which Hungary was alloted only 85 out of a total of 343 deputies. As Taylor writes: "The Germans received an artificial majority in a sham parliament; in return they gave up their liberal principles, barred the way against cooperation with the other peoples of the Empire, and committed themselves to support the dynasty whatever its policy."[4] When the Hungarian Diet refused to recognize the February Patent, it was dissolved and the Magyars returned to their policy of passive resistance. Goluchowski was succeeded by Count Anton von Schmerling, the author of the patent. Schmerling's system was in effect until July 1865, when he was replaced by Count Richard Belcredi. Constitutional negotiations between Austria and Hungary started up again. However, their outcome was once more determined by the results of imperial foreign policy adventures, but this time very much in Hungary's favor.

Since the Napoleonic wars, there had been many proposals and attempts to unify the plethora of kingdoms, principalities, duchies, and states that ruled over the German people. Although a multinational state, the emperor and Vienna's ruling circles felt that Austria was entitled to bring unification about and then assume the leadership of the new united German nation. This approach was known as the *grossdeutsche* solution. The alternative, called the *kleindeutsche* solution, proposed by Prussia, projected in effect excluding the empire from involvement in German unification. Austria and Prussia went to war over the issue. The Prussian victory at Sadova (Königgrätz) on 3 July 1866 put an end to the Austrian dream and in the process brought about a change in the balance of political forces in the empire.

This military defeat, along the indemnity paid to Prussia and the loss of Venetia, was very expensive for Austria and increased its already large deficit. The war also dealt a psychological blow to the Germans of Austria and brought about a realignment of political power in the empire. Once again the nationalities felt that they had an opportunity to pursue their national agendas. Yet, not unlike 1848–1849, the only two credible players were the imperial government and the Hungarians—"the only nation . . . which offered the Government a firm foundation on which it could build."[5] In the ensuing negotiations by Prime Minister Count Gyula Andrassy, Hungary recovered its right to self-government. The agreement, reached in May 1867 with Vienna, became known as the Austro-Hungarian Compromise *(Ausgleich)*. The Empire, now called Austro-Hungarian, not Habsburg, had three "common subjects": foreign affairs, defense, and the financing of both, which was to be conducted by a "common" minister in Vienna.

Otherwise, all other enactments by the emperor pertinent to Hungary had to bear the countersignature of the responsible minister. After the Diet approved Law XII, Francis Joseph was crowned king on 8 June in Buda. Hungary had recovered its independent royal status.

Not surprisingly, the nationalities, including the Slovaks, were not at all satisfied with the compromise. It forced them to deal directly with the Hungarian government rather than allowing the possibility of recourse to the emperor. It was not a felicitous situation, especially after the adoption of the Nationalities Law on 1 December 1868, which defined their status in Hungary. No Slovak had won a seat in the elections to the Diet in 1865, and thus the Slovak leaders had no opportunity to make any sort of parliamentary representation except through representatives of other nationalities. The deputy who took over this responsibility was a Ruthene, Adolf Dobriansky, and he joined Rumanian and Serb deputies in defending the rights of the nationalities. When the Diet met in 1866, it appointed a committee under the leadership of Eötvös to prepare the law. Its work was based on a draft report initially formulated in 1861, which expressed Eötvös's personal philosophy concerning Hungary's nationalities problems. That report had recognized that all the citizens of Hungary formed politically a single unit, the unitary and indivisible Hungarian nation, and that national claims could be made on the basis of freedom of the individual and of association. While Magyar was the official language of the state and the university (Hungary had only one university at that time, which had to have chairs of the non-Magyar languages and literatures), national languages could be used at lower levels of the administration and also in church-run schools.

The Law of 1868 did not modify substantially these clauses except to liberalize somewhat the language provisions by allowing local instruction in the mother tongue where numbers warranted. On the other hand, the Diet remained firm in denying the corporate recognition of the nationalities; a proposal along these lines made by Eötvös himself, which would have allowed "national" districts to form administrative units was rejected. The reaction of the nationalities was hardly surprising:

> The history of Hungary's relations with the nationalities after 1867 is the same dismal hen-and-egg story as before 1848, embittered on both sides by the memories of the intervening years. . . . the nationalities had accepted the Law of 1868 only under *force majeure*, and few of them thereafter showed any wish to make a success of it; the majority continued to hope openly for a situation to arise in which at least their old programmes could be revived.[6]

Thus the Slovaks suffered another setback. Up to that point, their leaders had tried, despite the failure of their efforts in 1848 and 1849, to acquire political rights for their people.

THE SLOVAK AGENDA

When the Slovak leaders decided to support the Habsburgs against the Magyars in the fall and winter of 1848–1849, they opted for a policy by which they would stick until the Compromise of 1867. It was a logical policy, in some respects even a realistic one, for it brought them some dividends. They might have achieved a measure of greater success if imperial circles had shown genuine interest in the nationalities and worked with them. Instead, Vienna used the Slovaks either for imperial purposes or against the Magyars and, once their usefulness was over, abandoned them to whatever fate awaited them. The Slovak leaders knew that they were not exactly in a strong position, yet, in order to ensure the survival of their nation, they also knew that they had no other option to pursue. In fact, their decision to support did not prove to be without benefits to the development of the Slovak nation.

As we saw earlier, after the events of 1848–1849 the imperial authorities tried to gain some measure of control over the Slovaks by appointing Kollar, who had moved to Vienna in 1849 to take up a professorship at the university, as advisor on Slovak questions. They also sponsored a newspaper in Vienna called *Slovenske noviny* (Slovak News), edited by Daniel Lichard and published in Czech. They offered Stur and Hurban government positions but, when they declined, both were put under police surveillance. Nevertheless, the *Sturovci* continued the work begun in the 1830s and the 1840s, in particular getting the Slovak people to see that "what was at stake was above all that Slovaks understood and realized that they are a nation."[7] However, in Slovak circles, the matter of a literary language was uppermost at this time. It was settled only in 1852 when Hattala published his *Kratka mluvnica slovenska* (A concise Slovak grammar).

While many Lutherans were involved in ensuring the acceptance of Stur's codification, it also came about as the result of the activities of many Catholics. among them a priest, Andrej Radlinsky. He was born on 8 July 1817 in Dolny Kubin; his mother was Bernolak's niece. He began his schooling in Ruzomberok, continued in Kremnica and Buda, then went on to Bratislava, Trnava, and Vienna to pursue theological studies. He earned a doctorate in Pest in 1841 and entered the priesthood in the same year. Radlinsky was appointed parish priest in a number of towns throughout Slovakia during his lifetime. He

was one of the founders of *Tatrin,* and, from 1856 on, editor of *Katolicke noviny* (Catholic News). During the 1850s, he traveled throughout Slovakia to see how the new language was being received. On his recommendation it was adopted as the administrative language of the city of Kosice in Eastern Slovakia. He died on 26 April 1879 near Senica.

Another Catholic clergyman who played an important role at this time was Stefan Moyses. He was born on 19 October 1797 in Vesele. He studied in Trnava, Pest, and Ostrihom. In 1821 he received Holy Orders and was granted a doctorate in 1829. In addition to a number of positions as chaplain, he was professor of philosophy and Greek at the Royal Academy in Pest from 1829 to 1847. He was elected, along with Stur, to the Hungarian Diet in 1847. In 1851, he was appointed bishop of the diocese of Banska Bystrica. In this position, he exerted a great deal of influence on the Slovak national movement. He died on 5 July 1869 in Ziar nad Hronom, which he had chosen as the seat of his diocese.

Civilian rule returned to the Habsburg lands in 1853, the year an imperial decree officially ended the serfdom that had been abolished in 1848. There were some disturbances as a result of this act of emancipation in Spis and Saris counties in Eastern Slovakia. The year before, the Society of Jesus had returned to Hungary when a novitiate was opened in Trnava in the presence of the cardinal archbishop of Ostrihom, the Slovak Jan Scitovsky. There was some respite from Magyarization, but not from centralism and the Germanization policy of the government, especially in the school system, which had consequences for secondary education. By 1857, there were no purely Slovak schools left in Slovakia because, as Spiesz writes, "not all the inhabitants of Slovakia were Slovaks and not all families, where Slovak was spoken, were interested in a Slovak education for their children. In a state, where German was the language of administration, many opportunities for a good position were available to those who had received their education in the German polytechnical institutes of Vienna and Prague."[8] If the Bach era was one of political paralysis, it was also the period when the *Sturovci* continued to be involved in *drobna praca* and the most talented among them produced the works that defined Slovak Romanticism. Gogolak feels that Sladkovic's poetry "reflected painfully the political pessimism of the Slovak middle class."[9] The *Sturovci* were active throughout Slovakia and were not necessarily unsuccessful in their endeavors. In the words of Vladimir Matula: "Slovak social and cultural life was for the first time influenced by an ideologically and organizationally uniform compact group having a common and broadly conceived nation-wide program of democratic restructuring of the society characterized by [a] purposeful intertwining between cultural activities and [the] vital interests of the broadest layers of [the] Slovak folk."[10] The one leader who stands out as an exception at this time was

Stur. In 1853, under the Bach regime, when he was under police surveillance and had lost any hope for his people, he wrote *Das Slawenthum und die Welt der Zukunft* (Slavdom and the world of the future), a political manifesto of Panslavism that proposed salvation for his people by Russian intervention. It was not published until 1867 in Russia. Like most of Stur's work, this idea would leave a legacy in the political life of the Slovaks.

In the decades that followed 1848, one town experienced firsthand all of the contradictions, twists and turns and successes of the Slovak national movement as no other and in the process also played a role in defining it. It was there that the Slovak leaders made one more attempt to obtain a political solution for their nation and that a national institution, Matica slovenska (Slovak Cultural Institute), was established. For these reasons, the town of Turciansky Sväty Martin deserves special consideration.

THE MEMORANDUM AND MATICA SLOVENSKA

Seton-Watson, one of the first Western scholars to write on the history of the Czechs and Slovaks, makes some comments that are instructive for an understanding of the formation of nations and the role of locality in that process. Examining the beginnings of the Czech revival in the late eighteenth century, he writes: "To this early stage of the Czech revival belongs the famous anecdote, so often dismissed as fictitious, but most certainly symbolic of the facts. A small group of patriotic *savants* was accustomed to foregather once a week at the *Stammtisch* (table reserved for regular guests) of a Prague inn; and one of its leaders, looking around the room, is alleged to have exclaimed: 'If this ceiling were to fall, there would be an end to the national revival.'"[11]

In the chapter devoted to examining of the life and activities of the Slovaks under Hungarian rule, especially in the latter half of the nineteenth century and the early part of the twentieth, Seton-Watson concludes that "the Magyarization of Slovakia was advancing by leaps and bounds, and . . . in another generation, especially if the Central Powers had been victorious, assimilation would have been virtually complete."[12]

In both passages Seton-Watson refers to the fragility of national survival and development and also to locality. Of course, neither hypothetical event took place. The ceiling did not fall, the Czech national revival happened, developing especially in Prague, a predominantly German city at that time, and prepared the ground for the "resurrection of a state" as Tomas G. Masaryk, an eminent Czech political figure in the twentieth century, later called the French version of his memoirs.[13]

As for the Slovaks, the Central Powers did not win the war and the process of Magyarization, as Seton-Watson indicates, ended. Moreover, his conclusion about the virtual assimilation of the Slovaks cannot be substantiated. Yet we have seen that the Slovaks had become slowly locked in a process of Magyarization that they were fighting with whatever means at their disposal. In this fight the town in question, located in central Slovakia and nestled in the plain that leads to the Tatra Mountains, played a fundamental role in the development of the Slovak nation.

There was absolutely nothing that predestined Turciansky Sväty Martin for the role it would play from the 1860s on. It has been called alternatively "no more than a provincial town,"[14] a "little town,"[15] a "secluded small town,"[16] and a "small centre."[17] Its population did not exceed 2,000 souls. As one Slovak literary historian writes: "[Turciansky Sväty] Martin became a literary and political center more or less by chance."[18] It is the urban composition of Slovakia that gave it this chance: "Only eleven towns in Slovakia in addition to Bratislava and Kosice had populations of more than 10,000, the largest being the solidly Magyar Komarno. Clearly, the Slovak urban presence was insignificant. This weakened any potential national movement. Slovak political activities, such as they were, focused on changing centers—Banska Bystrica, Ruzomberok, Liptovsky [Sväty] Mikulas, or [Turciansky Sväty] Martin."[19]

Until 1861, no historical event had given this little town any special significance, only its geographical location. Stur used the dialect around it in his codification of literary Slovak; in addition, the *Sturovci* developed a myth about the centrality of the Tatra Mountains both for the Slovak language and in Slovak national consciousness.[20] In the words of Ivan Kusy, a Slovak literary historian: "The Tatras were without doubt eternal, Devin had great Slovak and Slavonic historical meaning and cities not far from these symbols, Bratislava and Levoca, started to be important centers of national activity; yet they were on the periphery of Slovak ethnicity and were centers only for a given period of time. There was an obstinate desire to have a center."[21] Still, Turciansky Sväty Martin was but one possible location for national activities. Nevertheless, and even if it was perhaps coincidence, there Stur launched his *Slovenskje narodnje novini* in 1845, which was then published in Bratislava. In 1846, Hurban founded in the town the longest-running Slovak literary review which is still published today, *Slovenske pohlady* (Slovak Perspectives) (initially called *Pohladi na vedi, umenja a literaturu* [Perspectives on science, art, and literature]); it was, however, published in Skalica. The town had acquired in this manner *titres de noblesse* that made Slovak leaders choose it as the meeting place where they drew up the Memorandum of the Slovak Nation on 6 June 1861. It was a turning point in Slovak national life: "the national gathering in [Turciansky Sväty]

Martin and its memorandum accelerated Slovak life to an extent that no one had been able to do before."[22]

The Bach era had given way in 1859, as we saw, to a return to constitutional changes in the Habsburg Empire. In the October Diploma, there was a disposition "insisting that the non-Magyar languages must enjoy adequate facilities under the new Hungarian regime. Francis Joseph had also declared that he would set his face against any action of nature to provoke or aggravate inter-national feelings. During the later exchanges he formally demanded legislation safeguarding the rights of the non-Magyars."[23] The Slovaks became mobilized thanks to Radlinsky, who collected signed petitions demanding the use of Slovak as the language of education and administration in Slovakia. Slovak leaders used the opportunity offered by the October Diploma to prepare new demands, ones that, however, would be less far-reaching than those of 1849. Hurban was the first to prepare a document that he submitted to Vienna but which became dead letter when the February Patent was issued.

The Slovak leaders realized that they had to proceed differently if they were to gain any political rights for their nation. In March Daxner published a brochure entitled "*Hlas zo Slovenska*" (Voice from Slovakia), which he circulated widely. In it he rejected the theory of a single Hungarian political nation and demanded the recognition of the Slovaks as a nation. That same month, Francisci became the editor of *Pestbudinske noviny* (Budapest news), a publication that initially was meant to help Slovaks get elected to the Diet (the first issue did not appear until after the elections and no Slovak was elected), but that in the end was used to whip up support for a national meeting in Turciansky Sväty Martin in June.

The meeting that took place on 6–7 June was an exceptional event; Slovaks came from all parts of Hungary, and some of the most important leaders and writers of the period were present: Hurban, Francisci, Daxner, and Sladkovic among others. Unable to be present were Moyses, Hodza, and Radlinsky. Also in attendance, but whose signatures did not appear on the final document, were Baron Simon Revay and Martin Szentivanyi, the *zupany* from Trencin and Liptov, and Jozef Justh, the deputy from an electoral district in Turciansky Sväty Martin. Using Daxner's brochure as a basis, the Slovak leaders put together the Memorandum of the Slovak Nation, "which became the basic Slovak constitutional program even if it was not worked out in detail and contained merely basic principles about a certain Slovak autonomy within the framework of Hungary."[24] More specifically, they sought equal rights with the Magyars, the recognition of their national individuality by law, the formation of a North Hungarian Slovak District (*Okolie* in Slovak), Slovak as the official language of administration of this district, a Slovak Academy of Law and a chair

of Slavonic studies in Pest, and the repeal of all Hungarian laws that infringed on the principles of the equality of the nationalities. Francisci led a sixteen-man delegation to Budapest and handed the Memorandum to the president of the Diet, Kalman Tisza, at his home on 26 June.

The Memorandum was not submitted to the Diet, but it was examined by a committee under the presidency of Eötvös. He and Deak were "convinced that both justice and expediency called for the enactment of legislation of a nature to satisfy the 'justified demands' of the nationalities."[25] However, the committee rejected the territorial solution and instead focused on individual rights and the ability of individuals to achieve what the report defined as "the possible corporate development of the individual nationalities, through free association." As we saw earlier, the report reflected Eötvös's personal philosophy on the place of the non-Magyar nationalities in Hungary. The Diet approved the report, but because the Diet's was dissolved a few days later, it was never given legislative sanction. Instead, it became the basis for the Nationalities Law of 1868.

The Slovaks were clearly disappointed on a number of fronts. Not only had the Hungarian Diet not received the Memorandum, but the committee's report was anything but satisfactory for them. In addition, county offices had been instructed to start an anti-Memorandum campaign. On the other hand, the National Committee, created at the meeting in Turciansky Sväty Martin under the leadership of Francisci, translated the Memorandum into Magyar and prepared the statutes for a new cultural institution, yet to be created, called Matica slovenska. The dissolution of the Diet in August as a result of conflicts between Vienna and Pest and indications from the emperor that he was willing to consider language rights for the nationalities gave the Slovak leaders a chance to renew their efforts to have the Memorandum accepted. On 11 December, Moyses led a Slovak delegation to Vienna where he presented the document, somewhat revised, to the emperor. Among the main differences between the June and the December documents were the establishment of a parliament in the *Okolie* whose capital would be Banska Bystrica and the fact that the demands were not made to the Hungarian Diet but to the emperor himself, as King of Hungary. The Slovaks were asking in effect to bypass Pest. Although they failed once again, the trip was not in vain, as Seton-Watson writes: "For some years to come help from Vienna enabled the Slovaks to breathe rather more freely."[26]

Education was the first great beneficiary of the Slovak initiatives of 1861. Teaching in the Slovak language spread in Catholic secondary schools, in particular in Trnava, Trencin, Skalica, Levice, and along with German in Banska Bystrica, Levoca, Nitra, Banska Stiavnica, and Presov. Banska Bystrica

became a particularly important center thanks to the pedagogical professionalism of a Catholic priest, Martin Culen (1823–1894). According to Gogolak: "Under his leadership, a strong Panslav movement of national Slovak and self-sacrificing idealists developed among the students who propagated the Cyrillo-Methodian idea which was benevolently supported by the equally embittered 'Slavic bishop' Stefan Moyses."[27] Starting in 1862, three new Slovak *gymnazia* were opened; two were Lutheran, in Turciansky Sväty Martin (1867) and in Revuca (1862); a Catholic one opened in Klastor pod Znievom (1869). In addition, with a donation of 1,000 gold florins from the emperor, Matica slovenska was finally opened in 1863 in Turciansky Sväty Martin. "The authorization to create Matica slovenska brought forth enthusiasm throughout Slovakia," writes Bokes.[28] This institution more than any other consecrated this little town as the main center of Slovak national development and resistance to Magyarization in the last half century of Hungarian rule; Matica slovenska "was not just a cultural society, it became everything for the Slovaks. It also fulfilled the role of an academy, a museum, a library, [and] a publisher."[29]

Kollar and Karol Kuzmany (1806–1866), the Lutheran superintendent from Banska Bystrica, had proposed a cultural organization like Matica slovenska in 1851, but it had taken more than a decade for permission to be granted. Turciansky Sväty Martin had not been the first choice of location for Matica Slovenska; the town of Brezno, had been chosen, but had turned it down as a result of pressure from Magyar authorities. Liptovsky Sväty Mikulas, home of *Tatrin,* had also shown interest, but free land offered by the mayor of Turciansky Sväty Martin settled the choice. In 1865, a building was erected which, in 1908, was still the second largest in town.

The year 1863 represented the millennium of the arrival of Cyril and Methodius in Great Moravia, and the Slovaks wanted to celebrate. However, church authorities in Hungary did not allow for a national celebration. Instead, diocesan ones took place at different times. As part of these Cyrillo-Methodian celebrations, Matica slovenska was formally opened on 4 August 1863 in the presence of Bishop Moyses of Banska Bystrica as well as Kuzmany. The opening "was attended by many hundred educated Slovaks and 4,000 or 5,000 of the peasantry. . . . No one can doubt that the enthusiasm was genuine and lasting."[30] Moyses was elected its first president; Jan Orszagh (1816–1888) for the Catholics and Kuzmany for the Lutherans became the first vice-presidents. In 1864, Matica slovenska began publishing the *Letopis Matice slovenskej* (Annals of Matica slovenska) under the editorship of Frantisek Sasinek, who later wrote one of the first modern histories of the Slovaks.

Matica slovenska, and with it the town, became the hub of Slovak cultural and literary endeavors. When created, it had 984 members but it was not

allowed to establish branches throughout Slovakia. Its activities were divided into six research departments: language, history, ethnography, law and philosophy, mathematics and natural science, and economics and industry and two arts departments, music and theater. In 1874 an educational department was also proposed. It was supported financially by all Slovaks with periodic collection campaigns made throughout Hungary. It quickly became a success: "Matica slovenska successfully united all groups of the Slovak population, regardless of religious affiliation, embodied the Slovak nation and its culture and became the unifying force on the basis of the living literary language which the entire nation accepted."[31] However, four years after its creation, the political landscape in the empire changed dramatically and Slovak politics began to adjust to the last, but also the most demanding, survival phase of Slovak history in the Hungarian state.

THE IMPERATIVES OF SURVIVAL

The main consequence of the Austro-Hungarian Compromise of 1867 in the life of the Slovaks was the renewal of Magyarization. They were familiar with this policy, which, however, with the compromise, underwent modification. As Macartney writes:

> The Magyarization of the educational system, . . . was at first justified by its authors, as it had been in the 1830s, as the necessary means of producing a Magyar administrative class, but the target was soon enlarged as, by natural transition, it came to be assumed that all members of society above the peasant-worker level should at least speak and understand Magyar, and before long chauvinists were again dreaming of a day when the whole population should be Magyar.[32]

Not surprisingly, Matica slovenska was soon targeted; along with the three *gymnazia* created in 1862, it was closed down in April 1875. The building was taken over by the Hungarian government and the "property of Matica slovenska, which according to the statutes belonged to the Slovak nation, was confiscated by the Prime Minister's office, with the justification that, according to Hungarian laws, there did not exist a Slovak nation."[33]

The activities of Matica slovenska during the twelve years of its existence had anchored the importance of Turciansky Sväty Martin as a leading national center.[34] After its dissolution, its cultural activities were taken over by a number of groups and organizations. Slovenska omladina (Slovak Youth), a student

organization that lasted only five years, and Zivena, a women's organization, both founded there in 1869, carried on cultural activities, while the Spevokol (Choir), founded in February 1872, put on plays and organized other cultural events. *Slovenske pohlady* renewed publication in 1881 under the editorship of Pavol Mudron (1839–1914). The Narodny dom (National Home), founded in 1887, took over from 1890 on some of the repository activities of Matica, especially the collection of literary works and manuscripts. A Slovak museum was opened in 1890, "a haunt . . . of peasant life and manners."[35] In 1893, a Muzealna slovenska spolocnost (Slovak Museum Society) was founded to coordinate the various activities. It published in 1898 the *Casopis Muzealnej slovenskej spolocnosti* (Journal of the Slovak museum society) and in 1899 the *Sbornik Muzealnej slovenskej spolocnosti* (Review of the Slovak museum society). A publishing house, the Knihtlaciarsky ucastinarsky spolok, had also been created in 1869 and carried on throughout this period. All these activities were necessary to combat the pressure of Magyarization as Michal Elias writes: "During the period when Magyarization intensified, social entertainment was the main tool for the preservation of national consciousness—theater, choirs, interest groups, publications. In this respect [Turciansky Sväty] Martin was a model for the remaining Slovak towns, outdistancing them with the number of organizations and the content of their activities."[36]

The importance of Turciansky Sväty Martin can be seen in other ways. In February 1885, the Tatra Bank was opened there with 8,290 shareholders and a capital of 800,000 florins. On 3 August 1887, there was an exhibition of Slovak embroidery "which showed Slovaks and Magyars and the rest of the world that a Slovak nation does exist and that these artistic creations testify to its developed culture."[37] In July 1893, the town was chosen to put on the main celebrations for the centenary of Jan Kollar's birth. However, Hungarian authorities forbade these events and sent "such a number of policemen that the little town looked as if it were overwhelmed by them."[38] Authorities even forbade the construction of a large factory along the Turiec River to manufacture cellulose "allegedly because the liquid waste from the machinery, emptied into the river, would poison the fish."[39] It was built in Transylvania. Perhaps the importance of Turciansky Sväty Martin is best illustrated from a passage in the *Pest Encyclopedia,* which presented the town as the "rallying place of Panslav agitation of the Hungarian Slovaks."[40] In fact, Turciansky Sväty Martin compared very well with other national centers in Central Europe, and, as Jozef Hvisc shows, its cultural and political elite sustained particularly strong links with Polish scholars and intellectuals.[41]

The most important consequence of the Austro-Hungarian Compromise was to bring into sharper focus the need for the Slovaks to be politically active

and set an agenda if they were to counter Budapest's policies. The ideas of the *Sturovci* had run their course and Magyarization was seriously challenging the goals of the Slovak national program. For the next few years, there were "struggles for a new orientation of the national movement."[42] A number of options were proposed. Already in 1859, Jan Palarik (1822–1870) had suggested cooperation with the liberal Magyar nobility in its opposition to Viennese centralism as a way of advancing Slovak national objectives. He was a Catholic priest, politician, and writer, founder of the publication *Cyrill a Method,* and editor of *Katolicke noviny* from 1852 to 1856. His ideas had gained little support and were superseded by the proposals of the Memorandum. However, in 1868, they reappeared when a new group in Pest called *Nova skola* (New school), under the leadership of Jan Bobula (1844–1903), advocated cooperation with the Magyars. It published a newspaper called *Slovenske noviny* (Slovak News), and in it proposed the abandonment of the idea of a Slovak *Okolie* and the acceptance of the integrity of the Hungarian state in exchange for language rights. The group members faced, however, an insoluble paradox: "Their pro-Hungarian approach could not be successful because Magyar politics was possessed by the achievement of the idea of a united Hungarian political nation; in the name of this idea, the Hungarian government and the opposition supported linguistic and cultural Magyarization."[43] In 1872, they sought to cooperate with the Deak government and changed their name to *Slovenska strana vyrovnania* (Slovak Party of Settlement), but by the mid-1870s they ceased to be a political force.

The Memorandum of 1861 had turned Turciansky Svätý Martin into a political center. In 1868, the *Slovenska narodna strana* (Slovak National Party, or SNP), under the leadership of Viliam Pauliny-Toth (1826–1877) was founded there, and a year later the *Pestbudinske noviny* moved there from Pest, changing its name to *Narodnie noviny* (National News). It became the party's official organ and "helped make [Turciansky Svätý] Martin a leading national center."[44] Its political program was based on the Memorandum and its members were referred to as adherents of the *Stara skola* (Old School). In 1869, Pauliny-Toth was elected to the Hungarian Diet along with two other Slovaks from the *Nova skola*.

The role that Turciansky Svätý Martin played as a national cultural and political also made it a center for most of the personalities of the national movement of the Lutheran faith. Catholic activities were centered on Trnava and the Spolok Sv. Vojtecha (St. Adalbert Society), established in 1869. *Katolicke noviny,* which renewed publication in this period under the editorship first of Radlinsky and, from 1880, of Martin Kollar (1852–1919), were published in Trnava as were many other Catholic publications. Catholics

created organizations in other towns as well, in particular Ruzomberok and Bratislava. Catholics and Lutherans remained in contact and corresponded with Slovaks throughout Slovakia as well as with foreigners and Slovaks abroad.

However, this was the era of the government of Kalman Tisza, who, as minister of the Interior, had ordered the closing of Matica slovenska on 6 April 1875. Until 1890, Tisza "brought the Slovaks . . . many other measures which prevented them from keeping pace with the progress of other European nations."[45] Slovaks failed in 1875 to send a representative to the Diet, and in 1878, Hurban tried unsuccessfully to get an audience with the emperor in Vienna. In 1879, the Diet accepted a proposal from the Zvolen *podzupan,* Bela Grünwald, to make the teaching of Magyar obligatory in all non-Magyar schools. Author of an anti-Slovak booklet entitled "*A felvidék*" (The upper Hungarian land) which Gogolak describes as "pathologically prejudiced and typical for the inhumanity and perversity of Magyarization,"[46] he was also unrelenting in his search for "Panslav agitators" in the cultural institutions, *gymnazia* and seminaries of Slovakia. In addition, societies were founded to propagate Magyar values and Magyar education. One such society, *Felvidéki magyar közművelődési egyesület* (North Hungarian Magyar education society), better known by its initials, FEMKE, was created in 1883.

Pauliny-Toth died in 1877. A new generation of leaders arose in the 1880s headed by Hurban's son, Svetozar Hurban Vajansky (1874–1916), as well as by Pavol Orszagh-Hviezdoslav (1849–1921) and Mudron, who took over the leadership of the Slovak National Party. The failure of the previous generation to achieve a political solution and the need to resist Magyarization provoked a reassessment and readjustment of Slovak national development and politics that would mark Slovak nationalism for over a century.

In his examination of East European nationalism, Sugar writes: "Nationalism was born in western Europe as part of a general trend and with political meaning. Moving eastward its emphasis became cultural-linguistic in Germany, reverting, once again, to politics when it moved out of Germany into the lands of the Slavs, Greeks, Turks, Romanians, and Magyars."[47] Until the national awakening, the Slovaks fought for linguistic and cultural rights. Thereafter, the Slovaks' nationalism became a mixture of a cultural-linguistic emphasis and politics. The *Sturovci* had been writers, poets, and social workers as well as political leaders; their successors would be no less. This combination of culture and politics, the need to define and elevate the Slovak core as well as ensure its survival, meant that Slovak nationalism avoided the extreme manifestations that, according to Sugar, became the by-product of its development elsewhere in Eastern Europe.[48] Instead, the pendulum of Slovak activity swung between

culture and politics, its movement determined by the assessment of the political options available, both internally and internationally.

After it failed to get any members elected to the Hungarian Diet in the late 1870s and early 1880s, and in the face of mounting Magyarization, the leadership of the Slovak National Party decided in 1884 on a course of electoral passivity, which it maintained until the end of the century. Some of the politicians in Turciansky Sväty Martin turned to Slav unity and a certain Russophilism. Known as the Martin group and led by Vajansky, in particular after the Russo-Turkish war of 1877–1878, they became convinced that only Russia could come to their aid. Stur's Panslav ideas, expressed before his death, had come full circle. Mudron, for his part, participated in the Nationalities Congress in Budapest in August 1895 and joined other non-Magyar representatives in a joint program demanding that Hungary become a multinational state where the counties were delimited along national lines with the language of administration and justice in the national language; they also demanded universal suffrage and other democratic reforms. The response of Budapest was to intensify the Magyarization of the nationalities. However, according to Macartney, the Congress may be taken as "the first sign of that turn of the tide, which, ten years later, was flowing forward visibly and purposefully, particularly among the Slovaks."[49]

This political passivity was more than compensated by the outburst of cultural activity that, perhaps because of its richness, probably also sustained it. As Gogolak points out:

> The ideology of language and natural rights that supported Slovak independence vis-à-vis the Czechs and Magyars, the belief in an independent Slovak nation, equal to the other Slavic nations, the idealizing of the simple, good-natured Slovak peasant and the glorification of the backward Slovak village idyll as an old Slavic phenomenon—these and other similar theories were at that time the basic ideas of the Slovak opposition.[50]

Not all writers, however, did fit this mold or propagated all of these ideas. As the question of a literary language was no longer at issue, efforts were concentrated on didactic literary production, in particular religious publications, and amateur theater where the plays of Palarik were particularly well received. Amateur choirs also were successful; this meant that Slovak folk songs were the object of interest as were the early compositions of the first Slovak professional composer, Jan Levoslav Bella (1843–1936), notably his "Sväto-Martinska Kadrylla," "Staroslovansky otcenas," and the cantata "Cyrilo-Methodiana." However, now, as half a century earlier, secular literature best

expressed the vitality and strength of Slovak culture. In the words of Petro: "The period that followed the closing of Matica slovenska seems less dark than at first glance, when we realize that it marked the arrival of Pavel Orszagh Hviezdoslav (1849–1921) and Martin Kukucin (1860–1928); the first an unequalled poet of lyric and epic poetry, the second the greatest Slovak novelist."[51]

Pavol Orszagh was born in Vysny Kubin on 2 February 1849. After attending the *gymnazia* in Miskolc and Kezmarok, he completed his law studies in Presov and Budapest. He practiced law until 1904, when he devoted himself entirely to writing until his death on 8 November 1921. He adopted the pseudonym Hviezdoslav in 1877. He was a prolific poet; his first collection of verse appeared in 1878 and was entitled *Jesenne zvuky* (The sounds of autumn). Other collections followed, namely *Oblaky* (Clouds) in 1879, *Sonety* (Sonnets) from 1882 to 1886 and his most extensive lyrical collection, presented in three cycles, *Letorosty* (Growth rings) from 1885 to 1896. He also translated world literature into Slovak, including works by Shakespeare, Goethe, Schiller, Slowacki, Mickiewicz, and Petöfi. He brought the literary convention of realism into Slovak literature. In the words of a Slovak literary historian: "The struggle of our literature to achieve realism is reflected in the entire creative effort of Hviezdoslav. We find all the fundamental problems of contemporary man and humanity in the many themes of his lyrical and epic writings. He turned to the people as the healthy core of the nation, and fought against its oppression, whatever form it took."[52]

Martin Kukucin reflected the other side of Slovak life toward the end of the nineteenth century, namely emigration to foreign lands. Born Matej Bencur in 1860, he became a physician and after his medical studies in Prague (1885–1893) emigrated first to Dalmatia and then to Chile. He returned to Slovakia only in 1922, left again in 1925, finally moving in 1926 to Yugoslavia, where he died in 1928. While his literary production reflects to a great extent his life abroad, in his early works, namely *Na hradskej ceste* (On the castle road) (1883), he depicts the village life of the Slovak peasant. In this period he wrote a series of tales that achieved great popularity because of their humor, a humor "unusually affectionate, full of feeling and often also compassionate."[53]

The third literary giant of this period was Svetozar Hurban Vajansky. The son of Jozef Miloslav Hurban, one of the leaders of the *Sturovci,* he was born on 16 January 1847 in Hlboko. He studied law, practiced for a short time in Skalica, and in 1878, when he moved to Turciansky Sväty Martin, he became editor of *Narodnie noviny* until his death on 17 August 1916. He adopted the pseudonym Vajansky in the mid-1870s. His collection of poems, *Tatry a more* (The Tatras and the sea), published in 1879, was considered by his contemporaries as "the beginning of a new epoch in the development of Slovak poetry."[54]

It marked a break with the romanticism of the *Sturovci*. Other collections that followed were *Spod jarma* (Under the yoke), published in 1884, which describes the life of the country people, and *Verse* (Verses) published in 1890, which expresses the tragedy of his nation and the hopeless wait for change. He was also a prolific prose writer who sought to describe the life of the different classes in those difficult times, notably in *Lietace tiene* (Flying shadows) (1883), *Sucha ratolest* (Dry twig) (1884), and *Koren a vyhonky* (Root and sprigs) (1895–1896). He produced many works of literary criticism and, as editor of *Narodnie noviny*, gained a reputation as a sharp political commentator. All three of these writers continued their literary production into the twentieth century.

The paralysis of Slovak politics in Hungary and the pressure of Magyarization in the last two decades of the nineteenth century brought forth the beginnings of political activity abroad, in particular in Prague. Some Slovaks began to look for support among the Czechs. The initial signal was given by the elder Hurban in 1876 when he published the first of two issues of *Nitra* in Czech. Two years later, Hviezdoslav, Vajansky, and Jozef Skultety travelled to Prague to participate in the celebrations commemorating the Czech *savant* Josef Jungmann. Then in 1882, Slovak students pursuing their education at Charles University in Prague founded a club they called Detvan whose purpose, according to its statutes, was primarily social and educational, but which in fact would play an important role in helping to define new directions for Slovak politics. As Edita Bosak writes: "Detvan's contribution to the rebirth of Slovak nationalism both inside and outside Slovakia was considerable. . . . [It] acted as a springboard and nursery for the young Slovak intelligentsia which returned home to re-activate the national movement."[55] Tatran and Narodny spolok, similar clubs, were founded in Vienna and Budapest respectively, and all three maintained regular contacts with each other.

The presence of Slovak students in Prague and the situation of the Slovaks in Upper Hungary *(Felvidék),* as the Magyars defined Slovakia at that time, brought forth a positive echo among some of the Czech intelligentsia from the 1890s onward. Yet their "overall view of the Slovaks tended to be a rather sentimental and romantic one."[56] In the provincial ethnographic exhibition of 1895, the Slovaks were given two rooms and were identified as "Part of the Czechoslav Nation." This definition reflected less the nature of contemporary Czech-Slovak relations, than the evolution of Czech politics. In the light of subsequent developments, the Czech approach to the Slovaks warrants a closer examination.

The origins of this particular Czech perception goes back to the writings of the Czech philologist Josef Dobrovsky at the beginning of the nineteenth century. In his philological approach to the modernization of the Czech

language, "Slovakia appears at that time, as does Moravia—including the differences in historical development—only as a more defined region speaking a dialect of the Czech Slavs. This is the source of his first negative, often also ill-disposed attitude to Slovakia's own attempts to revive its language, namely Bernolak's literary language."[57] Slovak men of letters such as Kollar and Safarik supported this approach to create a single literary language for the Czechs and Slovaks (at times defined as "Czechoslav," at others as "Czechoslovak") and also rejected the efforts to create a Slovak literary language. However, two developments stood in the way of this ambition. As we saw earlier, the need to defend themselves against Hungary's Magyarization pushed the Slovaks into creating a literary language understandable to all Slovaks, which is what Stur and the *Sturovci* did.

The second development was the role that Prague began to assume in the Czech national movement early in the nineteenth century. This magnificent Central European city, in addition to being the capital of the Bohemian kingdom and at one time also the capital of the German Holy Roman Empire, became what Slovakia still lacked, a national center. In no time, Czech intellectuals began to gather there. They set the tone and direction of the Czech national movement, influencing in particular the evolution of the Czech language. This brought about a growing gap between the Czech and the Slovak national movements. As Jaroslav Solc writes:

> Prague as a center became the stimulant and basis for innovation. The formation of a new Czech language was a sort of first and natural linguistic "separation". . . which we may identify in the history of Czech-Slovak relations. . . . From the point of view of the organic and speedy development of the Czech national movement and its language, this "separation" was a positive and stimulating factor, but from the point of view of a "Czechoslavic" language, it meant the petrification of the differences between the movement in the Czechs lands, in Moravia and especially in Slovakia.[58]

Paradoxically, it was Czech intellectuals who accused the Slovaks of "separating" when they created their own literary language in the 1840s, and this accusation reappeared at the end of the nineteenth century when Slovaks went to the Czechs for support. It was still a hollow accusation, because after the 1848–1849 revolutions, the Czech decision to claim "historic rights" in the Habsburg Empire brought about a second "separation," a political one; "In its program, Czech politics abandons political unity with them [the Slovaks], accepts their integration into Hungary, gives up the vision of a 'Czechoslavic'

or better said 'Czechoslovak' nation and Czech-Slovak relations are reduced to a non-political level of literary reciprocity."[59] As a result, during the second half of the nineteenth century, both sides buried the idea of the creation a "Czechoslovak nation." However, the Slovak search for support in the 1880s rekindled interest among the Czechs. By 1896, there was sufficient interest for Frantisek Pastrnek, a Czech Slavist, to found in Prague an association called Ceskoslovanska Jednota (Czechoslavic Unity), whose aim, according to its constitution, was to "cultivate Czechoslav interest" and maintain contacts between Slavic peoples, including the Slovaks. While some Slovak students in Prague were influenced by its goals and activities, and its annual meetings from 1908 to 1914 in the Moravian spa of Luhacovice enabled various topics of mutual interest to be aired, the contribution of the Jednota to both nations was in the end negligible and even deleterious:

> Ceskoslovanska Jednota had been founded by a minority, based on an idea rather than as the result of a political and economic evolutionary process. Thus, much of the misunderstanding which resulted after 1918 can be attributed to a mutual lack of awareness. The Czech intelligentsia sought to change basic Slovak society along the lines of their own but they did not take into account the growth and differentiation of the other.[60]

This very limited Czech interest in the Slovaks also must be understood as reflecting only one of the many options that Czech politics was examining at this time. As Solc writes: "At the moment when Czech politics started looking beyond its historical boundaries, their sight could not but fall on neighboring, related Slovakia which an old tradition of cooperation tied to the Czechs."[61] However, the Slovak interest in the Czechs was much greater and was due, in addition to the tradition of cooperation, to a conviction on the part of some Slovaks that the Czechs were the only neighbors who would cooperate with them in the pursuit of their national development. The accuracy and pertinence of this option would occupy Slovak politics for the better part of the twentieth century. Its foundations were laid in the two decades preceding the outbreak of the Great War.

NEW POLITICAL OPTIONS

The attraction of Czech politics is understandable in the context of the unrelenting policy of Magyarization that was being imposed on the Slovaks and the consequences that it was having. Peter Brock writes that

Slovak nationalism in the last quarter of the nineteenth century suffered a series of almost fatal blows. The small nationalist intelligentsia succeeded in maintaining itself then only with great difficulty. It was unable to prevent the increasing denationalization of the younger generation, chiefly by means of the school system, and it exercised scarcely any influence among the peasant masses who nevertheless preserved their Slovak language intact. From the beginning of the twentieth century the tide slowly began to turn.[62]

The change of centuries was like the breaking of a psychological barrier and an encouragement to seek new directions, to experiment with new ideas and approaches. Joining the ranks of Hviezdoslav, Vajansky, and Kukucin in literature were Ivan Krasko, Bozena Slancikova-Timrava, and Jozef Gregor-Tajovsky; in music, Mikulas Schneider-Trnavsky; and in the socials sciences, Samo Czambel (linguistics), Jozef Skultety (literary criticism), and Julius Botto and Frantisek Sasinek (history). In 1897 Anton Bielek had founded *Ludove noviny* (The People's news), and as the new century began, there were thirty-two newspapers and periodicals published in the Slovak language. By the outbreak of war, this number had doubled. Even in politics there were new developments; the Catholics separated from the Hungarian People's Party created in 1895 to form in 1905 the *Slovenska ludova strana* (Slovak People's Party, or SPP), and Social Democrats did likewise the same year to create the Slovak Social Democratic Party. However, it lasted only one year.

The reaction of the Hungarian authorities was not just to increase the intensity of Magyarization as the language laws of 1896 and 1907 indicate, but above all to defend a political system that was quite particular, as Gogolak points out: "For the Magyars, the entire period of the Compromise and with it their nationality policy stood under the ill fated star of an anachronistic, and in Hungary a completely peculiar and deformed, middle estates hegemony."[63] Nevertheless, as pressures for democratic changes mounted, Slovaks succeeded at different elections in sending representatives to the Diet, and Slovak politics began to bear the imprint of three men who would play an even greater role after the Hungarian connection was severed. Each represented an option that sought to improve the conditions of the Slovak population and enable its representatives to speak on behalf of the nation.

The option that spoke directly to and for the Slovak people was embodied by Andrej Hlinka, a Catholic priest who, unlike many of his illustrious religious predecessors, decided not to pursue advanced theological studies after his ordination. He was a man of the people, a superb and fiery orator and a tireless social worker and organizer. He was born in Cernova on 27 September 1864.

After attending the *gymnazia* in Ruzomberok and Levoca, he studied theology at the diocesan seminary in Spisska Kapitula and was ordained in 1889. He began to show interest in politics in 1895 in the Hungarian People's Party. Two years later he founded with Bielek the *Ludove noviny,* but in 1898, as a candidate for Ruzomberok, he failed to get elected to the Diet. He joined the Slovak National Party in 1901, and as a member of the Ruzomberok city council, he attacked the local Magyar political establishment. Due to his political activities, church authorities suspended him in June 1906 on a charge of simony; in December he was found guilty under section 172 of the Criminal Code of "instigation against the Magyar nationality" and was sentenced to two years imprisonment and a fine of 1,500 crowns. He served his sentence in Seged.

The event that brought Hlinka into prominence was the massacre of Cernova on 27 October 1907. This tragedy, which cost fifteen lives, encouraged Seton-Watson, then a young British academic, to condemn Budapest's policies toward the nationalities in the book *Racial Problems in Hungary,* which he published under the pseudonym of Scotus Viator in 1908. A picture of Hlinka is on the frontispiece of the book. The massacre happened around the consecration of the village church in Cernova, where Hlinka was born. The parishioners wanted Hlinka to attend the consecration because he had helped build this church, but ecclesiastical authorities would not consider this. (Hlinka was in jail at this time.) On the day of the consecration, the people tried to stop the Magyar clergy who came to Cernova, and, in the words of Seton-Watson:

> Without even resorting to the bayonet, far less to the butt-ends of their rifles, the gendarmes fired indiscriminately into the crowd, packed together as it was in the narrow roadway, and some are said to have reloaded and discharged again. Nine person were killed on the spot, including two women; three more succumbed to their wounds in the course of the day; twelve more were seriously wounded, and three of their number have subsequently died. . . . The number of persons slightly wounded is said to have exceeded sixty.[64]

The news of this massacre received worldwide attention not only through Seton-Watson's book, but also thanks to the reports of the Norwegian author and journalist Björnsterne Björnson.

After serving his sentence, Hlinka toured Moravia. When he returned to Slovakia, he continued to be active politically, although he never was elected to the Diet. He was in touch with the Martin group but did not share their Russophilism. He did not develop a particular political platform and merely demanded the respect of the 1868 Nationalities Law. In July 1913 in Zilina,

the Slovak People's Party sought a new lease on life when it elected him president of the party, but, in fact, this did not make way for a renewed political force. He spent most of the war doing pastoral and social work. In the summer of 1917, he opted for a political union of Czechs and Slovaks. In his capacity as party leader, he was invited by the president of the Slovak National Party, Matus Dula, to Turciansky Sväty Martin on 24 May 1918 to participate in a meeting to consider "the future of the Slovaks and the untangling of the entire Slovak problem."[65] It is there that he pronounced the famous sentence: "Our thousand year marriage with the Hungarians has failed. We must part ways."[66] He was also present at the meeting of 30 October of the same year when the men assembled in Turciansky Sväty Martin signed the Martin Declaration, which signaled the end of the Slovak presence in Hungary and the political union of Slovakia with the Czech lands in a new state. Hlinka accepted this solution. His biographer, Karol Sidor, sums up his approach to the old and the new in the following terms: "Andrej Hlinka did not want autonomy from the Magyars because he knew that they would misuse it against the Slovaks. He wanted a common state with the Czechs but he left the autonomous organization of Slovakia in the new state to later developments and in particular to the time when the Slovaks would have the means to guarantee the permanence of Slovakia's autonomy and in this way also the Czechoslovak state."[67]

The second personality to play a dominant role in Slovak politics was Milan Hodza, nephew of Stur's companion in arms, Michal Miloslav Hodza. He was born on 1 February 1878 in Sucany. He attended the *gymnazia* of Banska Bystrica, Sopron, and Sibiu, and studied law at the University of Budapest and later philosophy at the University of Vienna, where he earned a doctoral degree in 1918. His education explains in part why his political style was so very different from that of Hlinka. He was not insensitive to the needs of his people, but as Susan Mikula explains, "He, more than any of the other Slovak national leaders, recognized that the Slovaks could not think and act in isolation, that they had to understand and operate within the political realities of their broader situation."[68]

He began his career as a journalist in Budapest and, in 1903, founded and edited *Slovensky tyzdennik* (Slovak Weekly), which he used to establish his political credentials. He was elected to the Diet in 1905 along with Frantisek Skycak and became instrumental in creating a Nationalities Party for the non-Magyar peoples. His approach to the future of the Slovaks was based on their acquiring democratic rights and improving their economic condition through agrarianism. The acquisition of these rights, he argued, would liberate them from Hungary's medieval oligarchical system. Hodza was reelected in the 1906 elections, which saw seven Slovaks sent to Budapest. He did not run

in 1910 in return for a better Slovak representation in the Diet; in fact, however, only three Slovaks were elected then, Ferdinand Juriga, Pavol Blaho, and Skycak.

In 1908, Hodza moved to Vienna, convinced that the transformation of the empire into a multinational state could be achieved from the top. He became a member of the Belvedere Circle, a group of politicians, particularly from among the non-Magyars, advising the heir to the throne, Francis Ferdinand. He had contacts throughout the empire. Prior to the Great War, thanks to Czech financial support, Hodza established a Central Cooperative for Economic and Commercial Activity in Slovakia. He supported Czech-Slovak cooperation because of the economic and cultural benefits it would give the Slovaks. During the war, he opted for a common state of the Czechs and Slovaks, worked to create a Czechoslovak Agrarian Party, and in October 1918 was one of the signatories of the Martin Declaration.

The third person to play a dominant role in Slovak politics was the one whose option for the Slovaks would in the end carry the day. Vavro Srobar was born on 9 August 1867 in Liskova. He attended the *gymnazia* in Ruzomberok, Levoca, and Banska Bystrica, but because of "Panslav activity" was expelled before graduation and excluded from all secondary institutions in Hungary. He completed his education in the Czech lands, finishing his medical studies in Prague in 1898. He practiced medicine in Ruzomberok from 1898 to 1918.

He joined the student organization Detvan during his studies in Prague. Under his presidency in 1894–1895, it gained a political purpose by accepting the concept of *drobna praca*. This was similar to what the *Sturovci* had been doing half a century before. It was propagated by a Czech academic Tomas G. Masaryk. Srobar also accepted the latter's vision of close cooperation between the Czechs and Slovaks and began developing this idea in the pages of *Hlas* (The Voice). He had been one of the journal's founders in 1898, and he edited it from 1903 to 1904. The Slovaks around him who also accepted Masaryk's conceptions became known as Hlasists. When *Hlas* ceased publication in 1904, it was replaced by another journal called *Prudy* (Currents), to which Srobar contributed regularly. In 1906, along with Hlinka, he was jailed for one year for "instigation against the Magyar nationality" after unsuccessfully running for a seat in the Diet. He spent the war years pushing Masaryk's ideas of a common state. On 28 October 1918, he happened to be in Prague and was invited to attend the session of the Czech National Committee that declared the creation of a new state. The proposal to create a new state came about as a result of new ideas that had begun circulating in Czech political circles in Prague in the second decade of the new century.

THE CZECHOSLOVAK ORIENTATION

In 1910 Czech politics had entered into a phase that would have important consequences for the Slovaks. Up to that point, the Czech approach to the Slovaks had been superficial, either paternalistic or at best benignly interested. However, one of the active Czech Slovakophils of the Ceskoslovanska Jednota, Karel Kalal, published an article that signaled a change in the Czech perception. He laid the basis for what would become an ideology. It stated that the future of the Czechs was bound up with that of the Slovaks. As Solc indicates: "The appearance of this ideology, whose intellectual content grows out of initially non-political ideas of Czech Slovakophils, is above all a reflection of a new phase in the Czech struggle, the growing strength and development of the Czechs."[69] This ideology began to make its way slowly among the Czechs. *Prudy* circulated a questionnaire in 1914 on a union of the Czechs and Slovaks; it was received far more positively by the Czechs surveyed than the Slovaks, the majority of whom were not favorable to it. In 1915, Masaryk made the union of the Czechs and Slovaks an objective of Czech politics. He submitted a memorandum to the British Foreign Secretary, Sir Edward Grey, in which he made the unsubstantiated claim that "The Slovaks are Bohemians in spite of their using their dialect as their literary language. The Slovaks strive also for independence and accept the programme of union with Bohemia."[70] In this way the Czech agenda took on a Czechoslovak orientation. All that was left was to persuade enough Slovaks to accept this idea so that the creation of a new state could be seen as the work of both nations.

The *Prudy* questionnaire had shown that among the Slovaks, "those who welcomed political cooperation with the Czechs were former Hlasists and Prudists, the liberal-progressive stream in the Slovak National Party."[71] Srobar was one of those Hlasists, and he worked to have it accepted. Another influential Slovak was Milan Rastislav Stefanik, a man whose role in the creation of the new state would be singular in every sense of the word. Born on 21 July 1880 in Kosariska, like Srobar, he studied in Prague and became president of Detvan. He left Central Europe in 1904, acquired French citizenship, worked as an astronomer, traveled the world, and became a general in the French army. Masaryk sought him out and together with a young Czech graduate student, Edvard Benes, they formed the triumvirate that worked abroad to create the new state. Stefanik's importance to the Czechs was at the heart of an interesting incongruity, as Solc points out: "The first Slovak in the struggle against the Habsburgs was a Czechoslovak—this was not only a definite paradox from the Slovak point of view, but also one of the formative conditions of the Czech approach!"[72]

The outbreak of war in 1914 brought Slovak politics virtually to a standstill, especially as martial law was declared in Hungary. The search for a new option could take place only abroad, and for a while this was happening in two centers, Russia and the United States. Slovak exiles in Russia accepted the Martin group's policy of relying on their stronger Slavic brethren from the East; however, this option completely lost ground as Russia disintegrated. In the United States, where there were strong Slovak communities and the Slovak League of America was a force to be reckoned with, the idea of a common state of the Czechs and Slovaks made some headway. In October 1915, Czech and Slovak American organizations signed a document called the Cleveland Agreement, which, however imprecise its wording and concepts, proposed the creation of a federal state of two territorially independent nations. It specified, in addition to universal, direct, and secret suffrage, that Slovakia would have its own Diet, government, and financial and political administration, and that Slovak would be the official language. The implementation of this agreement depended very much on the outcome of the war in Europe, where many Slovaks had been pressed to fight in the ranks of the Austro-Hungarian armies.

As the war dragged on, there were some interesting developments on the military front. Stefanik traveled to the United States in April 1917; he tried to organize military units, but met with little success, primarily because the Americans had entered the war. On the other hand, Masaryk, who left for Russia in May 1917, was able to organize Czecho-Slovak military units into the Czecho-Slovak Legion, which, by the end of the year, had grown to 40,000 men as a result of defections from the Austro-Hungarian armies. The October Revolution and the signing of the Brest-Litovsk Peace in March 1918 brought about a plan to move the legion to the Western Front. It crossed Siberia, the Pacific Ocean, and Canada to do so, successfully engaging the Red Army in Siberia. As Slovak historians write: "This military success brought the Czecho-Slovak army to the attention of the world."[73]

While these activities were taking place abroad, some Slovak politicians became active in Austria-Hungary. On 1 May 1918, at the May Day celebrations in Liptovsky Sväty Mikulas, Srobar called for a union of the Slovaks and Czechs in a common state, a declaration that had been coordinated with Czech politicians as a way of giving open support to Masaryk's efforts abroad. Throughout that month, Hodza and Srobar were involved in discussions with Czech deputies in the *Reichsrat* who, on 30 May 1917, proposed a union of the Czech Lands and Slovakia within a federated empire. The 24 May meeting in Turciansky Sväty Martin had also shown the need to re-create the Slovak National Council. Hodza made it a public issue in *Slovensky tyzdennik*. Seven members of the Slovak National Party met in Budapest on 12 September 1918

and proposed twelve representatives from Slovak parties as members of the council. However, the council had to be circumspect in its activities: "In the way of constituting the Slovak National Council publicly and especially openly under the gaze of the Hungarian Government was the fear by its organizers that there would be persecution and that it would be misused for a forced declaration of loyalty and the maintenance of Hungary as a whole."[74] It was officially constituted only on 30 October in Turciansky Sväty Martin.

In the meantime and more significantly, the struggle abroad had entered a new phase. It centered around the implementation of the Czech agenda, as articulated by Masaryk and Benes and accepted by Stefanik. The formation of new state, which included Slovakia, became a matter that concerned primarily Czech politics. Not surprisingly, there was Slovak resistance. To seek to neutralize it, at least initially, the official organization abroad, the Czech National Council in Paris, changed its name to Czecho-Slovak National Council under pressure from Stefanik and an envoy from the Slovak League of America, a young lawyer named Stefan Osusky, who became an active member of the council.[75] Masaryk handled the more tenacious resistance in the United States, by despatching Stefanik to persuade the League to accept the Czechoslovak orientation, and by traveling there himself. In May 1918, together with representatives of Czech and Slovak organizations in America, Masaryk signed the Pittsburgh Pact, whose terms were different from those of the Cleveland Agreement. The new pact promised only a degree of linguistic and administrative autonomy for Slovakia in a common state: Slovakia would have its own administration, Diet, and courts, and Slovak would be the official language in public offices and public life generally.

The April 1918 failure of the Congress of Oppressed Nations in Austria-Hungary in Rome to bring about the international recognition of the Czecho-Slovak National Council by the Allies had led its representatives to seek recognition from individual states. They were successful; on 29 June, the French government recognized the Czecho-Slovak National Council as the Czecho-Slovak government, a recognition that Great Britain and the United States extended on 9 August and 3 September respectively. Finally, on 28 October, the Czech National Committee met in Prague and declared the creation of a new Czecho-Slovak state.

There was also movement in Slovakia. On 30 October, the Slovak National Council was finally constituted at a meeting in Turciansky Sväty Martin; the council was composed of twenty representatives from Slovak parties with twelve Executive Committee members. Dula was elected president and Karol Medvecky secretary. It issued the Declaration of the Slovak Nation, the document that officially rejected the right of the Hungarian government to

speak on behalf of the Slovaks, gave the council the right to do so, and proposed a political union with the Czechs in a common state. This document, as laconic and imprecise as the Cleveland Agreement and the Pittsburgh Pact, was nonetheless decisive. Slovak historians write: "The Declaration of the Slovak Nation had the character of an independent constitutional document which by an official resolution broke the union with Hungary and created as well as sanctioned a new union with the Czech nation."[76] With no precise idea of what the future held in store, this declaration took the Slovaks out of Hungary, a state where since the 1870s Slovaks had begun to experience the transformations that industrialization and modernity cause.

ECONOMIC AND SOCIAL DEVELOPMENT

Although Slovakia's natural resources were always abundant, after the Turkish occupation of Hungary they were never fully exploited. As a result, Slovak economic development did not attain anywhere near the proportions that would have brought about major transformations in Slovak society. The population of Slovakia remained basically agricultural, and subsistence farming was the lot of the overwhelming majority of the people. A comparison of the population distribution between the years 1869 and 1900 shows only a small change in the composition of the work force. The number of farmers dropped from 80 percent to 68.3 percent, workers and artisans increased from 14 percent to 25 percent, shopkeepers went from 2 percent to 3,4 percent, and office and self-employed workers remained steady at 3.2 to 3.3 percent. As for the distribution of land, the statistics of 1869 indicate that 84.60 percent of farmers owning land had less than 6 hectares. In 1896, the figure had fallen to around 80 percent (the statistics are for lots of different sizes from those used in 1869) and include 9.44 percent who did not own land. Just above 1 percent of the farmers were "rich." The fact that one-third of Slovakia was forested and owned by the magnates justifies Spiesz's observation that "Slovakia was in essence a country of great landowners and agriculture."[77]

The 1870s saw massive emigration to the United States and Canada due not only to the boom in these countries but also to the slow pace and alienating conditions of industrial development and employment in Hungary. On average, for the half century preceding the Great War, some 30,000 people emigrated annually. Often the departure was shortterm to make money in order to purchase property back home later, and a third of the emigrants throughout this period are deemed to have returned. There was growth in banking, in industry (especially the production of iron, gold mining, wood products,

cotton, and textiles), and in agriculture, in the sugar beet industry. Of the 4,091 kilometers of railway tracks built by 1873, 890 were on Slovak soil. However, the government in Budapest did not support industrial development directly; to a great extent foreign capital accounts for the development that took place. In addition, the work conditions were often very primitive. As was the case elsewhere in Europe, workers' movements developed and the 1870s saw the first industrial strikes in Slovakia, in Zvolen, Lucenec, and Kosice. Equally important was the fact that the industrial workplace was yet another place to Magyarize the Slovaks. This was the drama, as we have seen, that was imposed on Slovak society, and it was the one that defined the struggle for survival.

Populations statistics show that in 1869, there were 1,818,228 Slovaks in Hungary (in Slovakia around 1,570,000); in 1900, that figure rose 2,008,744 (in Slovakia around 1,750,00); and in 1910, the figure fell to 1,946,357 (in Slovakia 1,684,681). The last set of figues indicates that Magyarization was having some impact, in particular among the educated segments of Slovak society. The Nationalities and various education laws had taken care of that. Literacy increased from 35 percent in 1880 to 50 percent by the turn of the century. Those who acquired an education beyond the primary level sought good employment and social advancement. Even in Slovak towns, especially in county offices, such possibilities were not accessible without a knowledge of Magyar and, at times, the total acceptance of Magyar values. The churches were also involved in Magyarization, although the degree and the intensity of the process could be and often was attenuated by local authorities, namely Catholic bishops and Lutheran superintendents. Where Magyarization was less successful was among the peasantry, and given that group's proportion in the total population of Slovakia, Macartney is justified in suggesting that "It is doubtful whether the Magyarization of the school changed the ethnic character of a single village. The little Slovak or Ruthene who spent his schooldays painfully acquiring a few scraps of Magyar (and often acquiring precious little else) forgot them happily and completely as soon as the school door closed behind him."[78]

What defined the Slovak's struggle for survival in the last century of their existence in the Hungarian kingdom and influenced their individual as well as collective behavior was not just Magyarization, the slow pace of economic change, and industrial development, but above all the political system and politics of the Hungarian state. To the very end, the control of Hungarian politics remained in the hands of the magnate class, a class that completely supported the Magyarization process. It was backed by the small and middle nobility, the backbone of the counties, people like Grünwald who were uncompromising in its implementation and used the full extent of state power to achieve it. The election process was anything but beyond their reach. Moreover,

as Gogolak points out, "the new Magyar rulers, no matter how high they stood above the Slovak people, tried to isolate the middle ranking stratum of the Slovak political *literari* from their own people—and until around 1900 [did so] with some success."[79]

In these circumstances the attempts and achievements of the Slovak leaders appear remarkable. In many respects they were often the result of a great deal of personal courage, and it is difficult to imagine that they could be otherwise. The leaders sought to make progress for their people in a political system that did not give the Slovak people much opportunity to develop political activity, practice political dialogue, learn political compromise, or acquire a consensual societal and even national ethos. The growth of newspapers and other periodicals and the creation of political parties, especially at the beginning of the twentieth century, indicate that this process was getting under way. But it would require some time before it could overcome the one characteristic that imprinted Slovak political life, namely the habit of opposition. As long as the Slovaks were forced to struggle for their survival, then this habit was their greatest weapon. We saw that the conditions surrounding the creation of the common state with the Czechs carried with them elements for a new struggle. Without anticipating its politics, we may accept as an epitaph on the history of the Slovaks in Hungary the following observation by the Hungarian historian Gogolak: "Without the school of opposition in Hungary, the Slovak leadership would never have been able, after the revolution of 1918–19, to impose its unwavering oppositional attitude on the new Czechoslovakia."[80]

The struggle for survival of the Slovaks was about to enter a new phase.

8

The First Czechoslovak Republic 1918–1938

IN A NEW STATE

The severing of Slovakia from Hungary to become a part of the Czecho-Slovak Republic happened under quite exceptional and difficult circumstances. The Slovaks were literally catapulted from one political system into another with very little preparation, no public debate, and few experienced political leaders to facilitate the transition. In addition, they were called upon not only to help build a new state, but above all to abandon many of the habits and perceptions acquired in Hungary, and develop new ones. This daunting challenge was aggravated by three problems arising out of their life in Hungary, which enabled the leadership of the Czech Lands to impose on the new state the Czech agenda that they had worked out before and during the Great War.

The first problem was political. Although the Slovak National Party, the Slovak People's Party, and a branch of the Social Democratic Party had existed in Hungary none was a mass party, certainly not in the modern sense of the word. The roles of all had been quite limited, with little opportunity to educate their electorates in the usefulness and necessity of party politics. They were elite parties, grouping together members of the intelligentsia, most of whom were involved primarily in the struggle against Magyarization. They did not consider a radical change like the breakup of Austria-Hungary and the entry of the Slovaks into a new state until May 1918, when their representatives met in

Turciansky Sväty Martin. However, in the following months, they took certain measures to facilitate this outcome and prepare for the new situation; they created some 350 national committees and other similar organs, including units of a national guard. The Slovak National Council, which was created at the October Turciansky Sväty Martin meeting, also issued some 200 directives. The reaction of Budapest was swift and brutal: Turciansky Sväty Martin was occupied by Magyar troops in November and the president of the Slovak National Council, Matus Dula, was arrested. All in all, very little could be and was done to make the transition possible.

Equally troublesome was the absence of political leadership. Of the three leading political personalities in the last years of Hungary, none was instrumental in preparing the ground for the forthcoming change. Hlinka remained in Slovakia, involving himself primarily in pastoral duties, while Hodza traveled constantly between Vienna and Budapest as a member of the Belvedere Circle where he also became involved with Czech politicians. He did enter into negotiations with Budapest for a new status for Slovakia in Hungary, but in the end his efforts came to naught. As for Srobar, he stayed in touch with Czech political leaders, informed the leadership of the Slovak National Party in Turciansky Sväty Martin of developments in the Czech Lands, argued for a political union of the Czechs and Slovaks, but otherwise did nothing to prepare the latter even for the solution that he was advocating. These circumstances explain the absence of any plan that defined Slovak objectives for the future. The only documents that gave any inkling of Slovak goals were prepared in the United States, namely the Cleveland Agreement and the Pittsburgh Pact.

The second problem was administrative. Slovakia had been governed through a system of nineteen counties under the authority of a *zupan* and a *podzupan,* both of whom were appointed by Budapest. Moreover, these officials were usually under the influence of the local landed nobility, which, like them, was Magyar, and whose primary interest it was to maintain the estates system. When Austria-Hungary ceased to exist, the majority of these officials left Slovakia for Hungary. As very few Slovaks had been given the opportunity to acquire county administrative experience, the system almost collapsed. The posts of *zupan* and *podzupan* were given to young Slovaks, mostly lawyers and notaries. Many had been involved in the struggle against Magyarization, which probably was their only political experience. This county system was maintained until 1 January 1923 when it was replaced by new reorganized counties and a devolution of power to district *(okres)* offices.[1] Slovakia also lacked a main administrative and political center similar to the one Prague had become for the Czechs in the nineteenth century. For all that it represented in the life of the nation, the town of Turciansky Sväty Martin had not been able to take over

that role. Bratislava eventually became the capital of Slovakia; however, the organization of the state ensured that all political and administrative power remained in Prague. (See Map 4.)

The third problem was psychological. The generation that was about to change states had experienced the Hungarian political system, the slow economic and urban development of Slovakia, the influence of the landed nobility in the life of the counties, and Budapest's policy of Magyarization toward the non-Magyar nationalities. As Gogolak writes: "Slovak peasants lived almost until the revolution of 1918/1919 under the influence of a patriarchal-patrimonial estates past; these were entirely in the hands of the North Hungarian nobility which was politically alienated from the Slovak population, but which always used the Slovak language in their homeland and thereby influenced the ordinary people."[2] The Magyar social and political system had inculcated in the population an attitude of deference toward authority and respect for social rank. As a personal mechanism for the preservation of language and national identity, this attitude was not an unsuccessful way of handling external pressure; as a collective pattern of behavior, however, it bred passivity, resignation, suspicion, and almost always also opposition. These were not social characteristics that would facilitate a transition as radical as the one the Slovaks were about to undergo.

However, these three problems, important as they were, only partially influenced and determined Slovakia's integration into the new state. Far more significant was the international context that made possible its creation and directed its organization. In fact, the common state of the Czechs and Slovaks was created because of fortuitous international conditions. It had not been clear until January 1918, when U. S. President Woodrow Wilson announced his Fourteen Points, that Austria-Hungary would be broken up and replaced by a series of small Central European states.

THE INTERNATIONAL CONTEXT

The political union of the Slovaks and the Czechs in 1918 was the consequence not just of the activities abroad of Czech and Slovak politicians who were determined to create a new state, but also of a radically changed international situation. States were created by the Treaties of St. Germain and Trianon that, despite the contradictions and the problems, came to represent the fulfillment of the principle of self-determination. They became the basis for the new European order on the morrow of the Great War. The political life of the Slovaks in Czecho-Slovakia was influenced by this context, especially as the new

state quickly adopted a democratic regime and thereby acquired international sanction and support. What was not clear to them when they agreed to join the Czechs in a common state was the extent to which their own national goals would find fulfillment in it and what international support they could count on if the government proved unwilling or incapable of acceding to their needs. Some of the answers were given at the time of the new state's creation.

Ignorance in the West about the Slovaks turned out to be the most important factor in the creation of Czecho-Slovakia. The Czech political leadership exploited this ignorance to their benefit as Taylor writes: "Masaryk revived the radical idea of 1848 and proposed to create a single 'Czechoslovak' nation by will-power. Masaryk knew little of the Slovaks; others knew even less. That was his strength in dealing with the allied leaders."[3] It was also his strength that the Czech agenda had support in the West, in particular among academics; for example, Ernest Denis, who exerted great influence in French government circles and who wrote the only monograph on the Slovaks to be published by a foreigner for the Paris Peace Conference, enthusiastically endorsed the union of the Slovaks with the Czech Lands, primarily for reasons of French security. His book openly supported the Czech agenda.[4]

The Slovak leaders were not unaware of the international context and its emphasis on the principle of self-determination, but they were ignorant of the degree of international support for the Czech agenda. They expected that Czecho-Slovakia would not only give them every opportunity to develop economically, socially, and politically, but that it, unlike Hungary, also would allow them to participate fully and equally in governing the state. However, this was not to be. In addition to the problems outlined earlier that made governing Slovakia difficult, the plight and resistance of the Slovak people before the war had left the impression that their political passivity and inactivity were signs of national fragility. Masaryk and other Czech believed this to be true. It not only reinforced and justified the imposition of the Czech agenda on Slovakia, but also underpinned the claim about the existence of a Czechoslovak nation.

In the context of the international situation, this claim was neither far-fetched nor unacceptable; it could be justified on the basis of considerations pertaining to the fulfillment of the right of self-determination. Of all the nations and nationalities that were to be included in the new state—according to the 1921 census this added up to 13,874,364 people and included Czechs (6,818,995), Germans (3,123,568), Slovaks (1,941,942), Hungarians (745,431), Ruthenes (Ukrainians) (461,849), and Poles (75,853)—none commanded an absolute majority and thereby a claim to create a nation-state.[5] The Czechs were the only ones with accepted historical rights. But they required, in addition to these rights, also an absolute majority. A

fusion with the Slovaks was the solution to this dilemma; together the two peoples would form a Czechoslovak nation that would make up an absolute majority of the population (8,760,937 people, or 65.13 percent).

The new leaders met the challenge of the principle of self-determination by setting out to create a nation-state that designated the Czechoslovaks as a state people *(Staatsvolk)* and relegated the other nationalities to the status of national minorities. This was in contradiction with the declarations Benes had made before the New States Commission of the Paris Peace Conference that Czecho-Slovakia would be a sort of Switzerland,[6] that is to say, a federated state of many nationalities. Inevitably, the minorities reacted: The Germans looked to Berlin for support, while the Magyars turned to Budapest despite the fact that Czecho-Slovakia signed (and throughout its existence respected) treaties that guaranteed the protection of the linguistic and national rights of the minorities.

As for the Slovaks, there was confusion at first, and indeed for some time afterward. At the two meetings in Turciansky Sväty Martin in 1918, reference had been made to a Czechoslovak nation, particularly in the Martin Declaration, yet no effort was made to specify what was meant by it.[7] The only frame of reference that the Slovaks had was a Hungarian one, and there Budapest had used the term nation, as in *natio hungarica,* to mean those who made up the body politic of the state. It is quite likely that the authors of the Martin Declaration had in mind a similar definition of a Czechoslovak nation, a definition that did not invalidate their own national identity and individuality. Yet as a result of the Czech agenda, they discovered that they were not recognized as a nation per se nor as a national minority protected by the League of Nations but as a branch of a nation that had hitherto not existed. The elite of the new state had created the conditions for many potential conflicts not just at home but also abroad.

Could the leadership in Prague have acted otherwise? The statements made during the war and at the peace conference and the many agreements and accords signed, especially with the Slovaks, indicate that other options were available. The Czech leaders had needed the Slovaks to create the state, and Slovak representatives had met with them in good faith to achieve this objective. But once the state came into being, the Prague leaders produced excuses to ignore the promises made to the Slovaks. Consider Masaryk's reaction to the Pittsburgh Pact: "I signed the Convention [the Pittsburgh Pact] unhesitatingly as a local understanding between American Czechs and Slovaks upon the policy they were prepared to advocate."[8] Only a determination to pursue the Czech agenda explains the disappearance of any flexibility to consider honoring some of the discarded wartime agreements. Secure in their knowledge that they had

international support, the Prague leaders proceeded to build a centralized nation-state of the Czechoslovak people. The manner in which it was launched and organized became crucial for the definition and development of Slovak politics. Once again it proved to be a struggle for survival.

SLOVAKIA AND THE FORMATION OF THE STATE

The leadership of Czecho-Slovakia faced a difficult task of administrative as well as political consolidation that required skill and, at times, even daring. This was particularly true in the case of Slovakia. Yet, instead of seeking to bring all Slovak political leaders together to meet the new challenges, the founders of the state gave full authority to a single individual, Vavro Srobar. He was the one Slovak political personality in Hungary who had been absent at the 30 October meeting in Turciansky Sväty Martin. He had been in Prague on 28 October, was co-opted as a member of the Czech National Committee, and signed the proclamation of the Czecho-Slovak state. He was then appointed head of a "Slovak government" by the committee and left for Slovakia on 4 November. He arrived in the town of Skalica with three companions, and from there this group began to administer Slovakia. Soon after he returned to Prague. Faced with the problem of maintaining control in a difficult situation, Pavol Blaho, his closest collaborator, wrote: "Vavro, only an iron centralism will get us out."[9]

Srobar concurred and he was able to introduce an iron centralism in Slovakia as a result of a combination of factors. Representatives of the Czech National Committee and the Czecho-Slovak National Council (but not the Slovak National Council) had met in Geneva on 31 October to set down the practical steps to get the new state started. They agreed that Czecho-Slovakia would be a democratic parliamentary republic with a bicameral legislature (House of Deputies and Senate) with Prague as the capital, and that Masaryk would be its first president. They also formed the first government: Karel Kramar, president of the National Committee, became prime minister; Benes, secretary of the council, became foreign minister, and Stefanik, the leading Slovak on the council, became minister of war. Other portfolios were given to political leaders at home: Srobar was named minister for Slovakia.

The confirmation of Srobar's appointment was neither fortuitous nor the result of his having been in Prague on 28 October. He had been a leading student organizer of the Detvan club in Prague and a close follower of Masaryk before the war. He was one of the Hlasists who were convinced that the future of the Slovaks could be assured only in a union with the Czechs. They were the only Slovaks with whom the Czech leadership was acquainted and, what is more

important, whom it trusted. They also approved of the Czech agenda so that their involvement was a foregone conclusion. Ferdinand Peroutka writes: "The revolution put the Hlasists in the forefront in Slovakia. They received every position of responsibility because the Czechs trusted them. Slovakia was now literally governed by the Hlasists."[10]

However, Srobar's appointment also concerned a number of people, in particular Hlinka, because of the way he defended the government and its handling of certain developments. The overwhelming majority of the Slovak population—more than 75 percent—was Roman and Greek Catholic, and Hlinka and other priests who had been members of the Slovak People's Party before the war were keeping a close watch on events to ensure that the interests of their constituents were taken into account. One particular incident troubled them: the destruction by a mob of the statue of the Virgin Mary in Prague on 3 November 1918. It also became apparent that the new state was about to adopt measures that were not perceived to be in the interest of Catholic Slovaks. In addition, within a very short time, the Czechs sent by Srobar to Slovakia to take up posts for which there were no qualified Slovaks began to attack publicly the religiosity of the people. Hlinka and his colleagues lost no time in voicing their misgivings and in insisting that they be given representation in the government. On 28 November, the Executive Committee of the Catholic Clerical Council met in Ruzomberok under the leadership of Hlinka and made a number of demands, including Catholic schools, a Slovak ecclesiastical province under a Slovak bishop, and the elimination of civil marriages. The committee also gave Srobar a list of twenty-nine priests to be named to the Revolutionary National Assembly.

But Srobar was not interested. When it came to appointments, he chose those whom he wanted, and in his memoirs he writes: "As one can see from the list of names, for the second Slovak government I chose exceptional men who could evoke trust and authority."[11] As it turned out, they were mostly Slovak Lutherans. In choosing Slovak representatives to the Revolutionary National Assembly, he was a little more careful, but certainly not much more judicious. Of the fifty-four representatives that Slovakia was allotted—proportionate to its population, it should have received seventy—there were thirteen Czechs, thirty-one Slovak Lutherans, and ten Slovak Catholics. In addition, in the counties most of the *zupany* were appointed from the Lutheran community. The result was that "in probably the most complete way, they [the Lutherans] excluded Catholic representatives from public service and the enjoyment of glory."[12]

There is no doubt that these appointments were a major error in judgment on Srobar's part. Conditions in Slovakia were far from settled, and a Hungarian

invasion looked likely. Yet Srobar chose not to call upon the leaders of all the Slovak political forces to join him in ensuring cohesion in the face of external danger, the consolidation of Slovakia, and its rapid integration into the new state. Much has been made of the animosity that is said to have existed between him and Hlinka[13] to explain the denominational and political division that appeared in Slovakia. Sidor suggests, however, that this was not a major factor; nor in any strict sense was the religious aspect. Srobar had known Hlinka for a long time and had even spent time in jail with him in 1907. He knew how strong were Hlinka's religious convictions; perhaps it was these convictions and their consequences that he feared.[14]

It seems more likely that Srobar considered it his first duty to ensure the rapid integration of Slovakia into the republic along lines and conditions acceptable to Prague. At stake was the implementation of the Czech agenda. Although he cautioned the Czechs about taking lightly the religiosity of the Slovaks, he also knew that the mood in Prague was anti-Catholic and that he risked the opposition of his Czech colleagues if he relied on Slovak Catholics, especially as they had begun to voice their misgivings of government policies. It was simpler to rely on the Lutherans who, in any event, had historically shown an affinity for the Czechs.[15] To neutralize opposition from the Catholics, Srobar put them on the defensive by branding Magyarone many of them who had worked for the Budapest government in Slovakia before the creation of Czecho-Slovakia and removing them from the positions that they held.

The Magyarone accusation was another error of judgment of major proportions. In addition to fueling the opposition of the Catholics, it deprived Slovakia of many qualified people by making the accused ineligible for administrative positions. It also opened the way for the influx of Czech personnel to fill the vacancies. Problems arose when the government began to treat these people in a special way, granting them higher salaries than their Slovak counterparts and handing out positions on a partisan basis. As Sidor would remark some years later: "It was already clear after barely ten months of life in common . . . that it would be impossible to find a settlement and maintain peace between the Czechs and the Slovaks without interested external intervention in the formation and the consolidation of the Czecho-Slovak Republic."[16]

This difficult situation was not helped by Srobar's political style. Peroutka dubs him "the dictator of Slovakia."[17] Indeed Srobar ruled as he pleased, imposing censorship on the Slovak press and incarcerating people who opposed him or refused to carry out his orders. He not only alienated an important segment of the Slovak population, but through the appointments he made, he also accentuated the religious division. Peroutka notes that "A number of Lutheran families filled the majority of influential positions with their relatives."[18]

On 10 December 1918, government control was officially extended in Slovakia when a ministry for Slovakia was created. At this time leaders in Prague were aware that Masaryk had been one of the signatories of the Pittsburgh Agreement of 30 May. However, in Slovakia the agreement's existence was still unknown. Czech leaders wanted Czecho-Slovakia to be a centralist state and the ministry was created for practical purposes rather than for reasons of Slovak individuality. No Slovak political organization, in particular the Slovak National Council, nor any leader in Slovakia was consulted. Hodza wrote many years later: "Without consulting the Slovak National Council, it [the Czech leadership] reached an agreement with some Slovaks who accepted a centralistic system."[19] Inevitably, there was a reaction.

The response of the Catholics, under the leadership of Hlinka, was to re-create the Slovak People's Party on 19 December 1918 in Zilina. Sidor points out that "Hlinka's democratic thinking—flowing also from Catholic doctrine—was insulted whenever anything was done against the democratic principle, that is against the rule of the majority, against Slovak Catholics."[20] Srobar was immediately informed of the re-creation of the party. The message was clear, as Peroutka indicates: "The founding of the People's Party was the first public sign that not all were happy with the government of the Hlasists in Slovakia."[21] It also signaled the first, albeit still imprecise, Slovak challenge to the Czech agenda.

In the months that followed, Slovak political life began to get organized. In addition to the Slovak People's Party, other parties reappeared or began forming. This was also a period of great social unrest in Slovakia. Economic conditions were very unsettled, Bela Kun's bolshevik regime in Hungary invaded parts of Slovakia, and there was a short-lived Soviet Republic in Eastern Slovakia. Czech troops were sent to Eastern Slovakia to deal with Kun's bolsheviks. In May 1919, Stefanik, one of the three founders of Czecho-Slovakia, died under mysterious circumstances as he was landing his airplane near Bratislava. His tragic death as well as his activities during the war turned him into a national hero. Finally, in the summer of 1919, the Slovak People's Party learned of the text of the Pittsburgh Agreement. This marked a turning point in Slovak politics. There now existed an alternative to the Czech agenda. However, it would take some time before the Populists made it the focus of their political program.

SLOVAK AUTONOMY

The men and women appointed to represent Slovakia in the Assembly organized themselves in a Slovak Club. These deputies were also representatives of the

major parties in Slovakia. The club was dominated by Hlasists, who were to be found in every party except the Slovak People's Party. Its membership stabilized toward the end of 1919, and it was composed of thirty-two Agrarians, ten Social Democrats, nine Populists, and three National Socialists. The Slovak People's Party did not find support and understanding for its policies in the club. When Hlinka was attacked in his absence in the assembly by the Czech Social Democrat Rudolf Bechyne, no member of the club rose to defend him; rather they too joined in the attack. His defense was taken up by Jan Sramek, leader of the Czech People's Party. This was the beginning of a rapprochement between the two parties; in the 1920 elections, they appeared as a single Catholic party, the Czechoslovak People's Party led by Sramek.

Until the moment when it became aware of the Pittsburgh Pact, the Slovak People's Party directed its efforts at protecting the interests of Slovak Catholics. For example, in January 1919 Karol Kmetko insisted that the teaching in primary and secondary schools in Slovakia be in a Slovak and Catholic spirit, that a Slovak university be founded in Bratislava, and that church property remain in church hands even when it was made available for public purposes, such as schools and hospitals. The Pittsburgh Pact gave the party a new basis on which to fight, not only for the Catholics, but for the entire Slovak nation. Knowledge of the existence of the pact also precipitated an action on the part of Hlinka that would have negative consequences for him and his party in its efforts to achieve Slovakia's autonomy.

In the summer of 1919, Hlinka wrote an open letter to Prime Minister Vlastimil Tusar, who had replaced Kramar, to complain about the situation in Slovakia and to advise him that he had no choice but to go to Paris to see that the Pittsburgh Pact was put into effect, especially as it bore the signature of president Masaryk. When Hlinka received no answer, he left for Paris on 27 August using a Polish passport, traveling through Romania, Yugoslavia and Italy with three companions to reach France. He was not given a hearing at the peace conference, and when he returned to Czecho-Slovakia, he was arrested and interned in Mirov, Moravia and, elsewhere. He was never brought to trial and was allowed to return to Slovakia only after he was elected to the Czecho-Slovak Parliament in the elections of 1920.

Hlinka paid dearly for his trip to Paris. Not only was he disowned by the Slovak Club and divested of his parliamentary mandate in the Assembly, but by being held in detention, he was excluded from any further political activity. These were critical months, especially as the constitution was being debated. As a result, the Slovak People's Party's demand for autonomy was weakened not only by his absence, but by his failure in Paris as well. The representatives of the Slovak People's Party voted unanimously for the constitution when it was

tabled in the assembly on 29 February 1920. It abandoned the spelling of Czecho-Slovakia in favor of Czechoslovakia and confirmed the centralist system that had existed since October 1918. Populist participation in the debate had met with mixed success. On the one hand, in concert with the Slovak Club, the Slovak People's Party's deputies prevented the inclusion of a clause on the separation of church and state; they failed, on the other hand, to have a clause accepted that recognized the right of the Slovaks to have autonomy at some future date. As a result, six Populists signed a declaration stating that although they voted for the constitution, it did not mean that they had given up the fight for autonomy. However, during the election campaign that followed the adoption of the constitution, the question of Slovakia's autonomy barely figured at all.

Elections were held in April 1920. While twenty-three parties fielded candidates, four were major ones competing for the support of the electorate. These parties had platforms that reflected philosophical and social options as well as electoral calculations. The oldest party was the Slovak National Party. Its president was Emil Stodola, and shortly before the elections, the party formed a coalition with the *Narodna republikanska strana rolnicka* (National Republican Farmer's Party) led by Hodza; it became the *Slovenska narodna a rolnicka strana* (Slovak National and Farmer's Party). Its electoral program was a compromise between the nationalism, democracy, and self-rule platform of the Slovak National Party and the social and economic program of Hodza's party which put emphasis on the need for land reform and the interests of farmers and farm workers. The second party with roots in the prewar period was the reborn Slovak People's Party. Led by Hlinka, the Populists fought the election together with its Czech equivalent as the Czechoslovak People's Party. It had a conservative platform that dealt with religious issues, church schools, the education of youth, and social and economic problems. The Populists along with the Slovak National Party counted on their record in Hungary to win support among the voters.

The third major party was the Social Democratic Party and it could also trace its origins to the prewar period. At a congress in Liptovsky Sväty Mikulas on 26 December 1918, Slovakia's Social Democrats voted to join their Czech colleagues in the Czechoslovak Social Democratic Party. Led by Ivan Derer, the party offered the electorate a socialist program and stressed the need to improve the conditions of the working class. The fourth party was the National Socialist Party. It was organized in Slovakia by representatives of the Czech National Socialist Party and was led by Igor Hrusovsky. It had the most developed social program, with demands of an eight-hour work day, unemployment insurance, increased social insurance benefits, and better housing. It took a critical stand

toward clericalism as well as bolshevism. Its influence was due more to the strength of the party in the Czech Lands and its representatives in the government than to its electoral successes in Slovakia. There were also parties representing the Germans and Hungarians living in Slovakia as well as specific interest groups.

The Czechoslovak Social Democratic Party was the main winner in Slovakia and in the Czech Lands, obtaining 38.1 percent of the vote and twenty-three seats from Slovakia in the Chamber of Deputies. The Slovak National and Farmer's Party and the Populists received 18 percent and 17.5 percent of the vote respectively and twelve seats each. One seat was awarded to the National Socialists, who polled 2.2 percent of the vote. Another twelve seats went to the Hungarians and the Germans, who gave 18.5 percent of the vote to the German-Magyar Christian Socialists. The election campaign was not without incidents. In Rumanova, Czech gendarmes had fired into a crowd, killing two people.

The election results reflected the difficult economic and social conditions existing not only in the new state, but throughout Europe. As Victor S. Mamatey writes:

> Strikes and riots were widespread and demands for reform or revolution were commonly voiced. The phenomenon was not unique to Czechoslovakia but was widespread in Europe. Undoubtedly, it represented an outpouring of social discontent of the working class that had built up during the war and the immediate postwar period, but had been stifled by the emergency measures then in force in most European countries. A catharsis of this pent-up feeling may have been precipitated by the triumphant advance of the Red Army toward Warsaw in July, 1920, during the Polish-Soviet War, and the militant propaganda emanating from the Second Comintern Congress in Moscow in July and August.[22]

Tusar remained prime minister, thus maintaining the "Red-Green" (Social Democrat-Agrarian) coalition with some small alterations as a result of the elections. There was one significant change for Slovakia; Derer replaced Srobar as minister for Slovakia. Srobar was given instead the portfolio of minister of unification which up to that point had been held by Hodza. This ministry had been created on 22 July 1919 to unify all laws and codes; Hodza had been named its first minister on 6 December 1919.

There were changes in a number of parties after the elections. The Social Democrats split when the radicals in their own ranks decided to join the Comintern. They created the Communist Party of Czechoslovakia (CPCS) in

May 1921, which thereafter became a player on the Slovak political scene. The Slovak People's Party became a member of the Populist Club in Parliament and a supporter of the government. But its members did not feel that they were subordinated to Sramek's leadership. One deputy declared that their role was to represent the Slovaks. As Sidor writes: "This declaration is very important. It shows that the [Slovak] People's Party considered its union with Sramek to be tactical and not ideological. The Party stands and wants to stand on those ideas which led to its creation."[23] On 30 March 1921 the coalition that formed the Slovak National and Farmer's Party broke up. The Slovak National Party regained its original name and platform while Hodza's Agrarians joined the Czech Agarian Party to form the *Republikanska strana polnohospodarskeho a malorolnickeho ludu* (Republican Agricultural and Farmer's Party).

In September 1920, Tusar government was replaced by a cabinet of officials led by Jan Cerny, provincial president of Moravia. Occuring as a result of the right-left split in the Social Democratic Party, the change marked a new phase in Czechoslovakia's history, in particular for Czech-Slovak relations. Cerny's government was led by an informal institution called the Petka (Committee of Five). As Mamatey writes:

> The origin of the committee was fortuitous. The non-party Cerny cabinet resembled a ventriloquist's dummy: it had no political will or voice of its own. To give it political direction and to provide it with parliamentary support, representatives of the five major parties or parliamentary blocs— Antonin Svehla (Agrarian), Alois Rasin (National Democrat), Rudolf Bechyne (Social Democrat), Jiri Stribrny (National Socialist) and Jan Sramek (Populist)—began to meet informally and discuss and decide political measures for the Cerny cabinet to take, which their parties supported in the National Assembly.[24]

Once the crisis that had brought about the Cerny cabinet passed, negotiations opened for the formation of a new government. Manfred Alexander shows that the possibility of the Slovak People's Party entering the government was considered, the quid pro quo being the inclusion of a clause on Slovak autonomy in the constitution.[25] But nothing came of it, and a government under Benes was formed in September 1921.

It may well be that the reason Benes was chosen was the international situation, which "made it desirable to have an experienced diplomat at the helm."[26] However, there were equally valid domestic reasons. Local elections were scheduled to take place in February 1922; no party wanted to take the responsibility for granting the Slovak People's Party its request for autonomy.

The request risked being misunderstood by the Czech people as a threat to the unity and stability of the state and prompting similar demands from the national minorities, especially the Germans. Even the Communists, whose leader, Bohumir Smeral, had attacked the government in Parliament in January 1921 for not treating the Slovaks as equal partners and granting them autonomy, recognized the strength of Czechoslovak nationalism among the Czechs. Faced with such considerations, the Petka felt it inadvisable to give in to the Slovak Populists and thus begin a process of constitutional revision. As a gesture to them, Benes named Martin Micura, a Slovak member of Sramek's party, minister for Slovakia. Benes also named Srobar minister of education. Srobar immediately reneged on a promise that had been made by the Cerny government to give the Catholic Church in Slovakia three secondary schools. This refusal to honor the commitment made by the previous government provoked a reaction from the Slovak Populists. Up to that point, as partners in Sramek's Party, they had been supporters of the government; they now broke with Sramek and the Slovak People's Party became an opposition party.

Initially the Slovak People's Party had merely reacted to the centralism of the government on political and religious grounds. It had fought Srobar, its main spokesman in Slovakia, and demanded autonomy. Yet, it had not chosen to go in open opposition because it had welcomed the creation of the new state and had continued to hope that its main demand, the autonomy of Slovakia, might be met. But in Prague, that was not even an option:

> The government hesitated between the plan of introducing a tough regime against the [Slovak] People's Party and the plan of winning them through kindness. Srobar counselled in favour of the first . . . he was given a plan to put down the autonomist movement, but unfortunately this plan occasionally disgusted even those who gave him the responsibility. They were not sure whether it was the proper method [to use] in a brotherly land and they became less certain as it showed itself to be less and less successful.[27]

Even if the government had changed its strategy toward the Slovak People's Party, it had other reasons going into opposition. The principal one transcended all political considerations, as Hlinka explained in Parliament: "The first reason for this step is that the Slovak nation does not have in Parliament even one completely Slovak party . . . none had even a Slovak name in Prague."[28] The second reason was equally compelling, namely the need to combat Czechoslovakism, the state's ideology, examined in the next section. Third, the Pittsburgh Pact had given it a platform that could appeal to all

segments of the Slovak nation. Finally, through its activities and its growing popularity among the Slovaks, the Slovak People's Party had shown that it had "won its right to be the party it wanted to be."[29] By the fall of 1921, when the Petka's choice of Benes signaled to the Slovak Populists that the Czech parties were unwilling to consider autonomy for the Slovak nation, the Slovak Populists left the Czechoslovak People's Party and registered in the Czechoslovak Parliament as the Slovak People's Party. It became the party that influenced, and at times even defined, political life in Slovakia during the remainder of the First Republic. No other party in Slovakia, even with all the power they had in Prague, played as important a role in the First Republic as did the Slovak People's Party.

CZECHOSLOVAKISM AND SLOVAK NATIONALISM

The first years in the new state had been critical for Slovakia. In addition to internal instability, the Slovak people had been called upon to acquire a new political culture, to participate in the building of a new state, and to use the new opportunities to further their own development. But the blunders committed by Srobar, the difficulty of resolving certain internal issues concerning Slovak political development, and the direction in which Prague was steering the state, had made it difficult to forge a consensus in Slovakia to achieve these objectives. What further worsened the situation and galvanized the opposition was the introduction of the ideology of Czechoslovakism. Out of these initial circumstances a definitive form of Slovak nationalism emerged.

From a Czech point of view, the ideology of Czechoslovakism was a natural development arising from the extension of the Czech agenda to the new state. Its aim was the fusion of both nations into a single one. The first signal was given with the passage of the Language Law, which, in Article 1, stated:

"The Czecho-Slovak language is the state (official) language of the Republic." This clause of course represents a legal fiction, since there is no such thing as a Czecho-Slovak language, but two intimately related dialects, enjoying full parity in the administration, justice and education. As, however, the name "Czecho-Slovak" had won general recognition and already stood as the symbol of unity, it appears to have been felt that to refer to the "Czech and Slovak language" or "languages" would have been not only a contradiction in terms, but actually a step away from fusion.[30]

If this law was acceptable to the Czech nation, it created serious problems for the Slovaks. Slovak nationalism in Hungary had concentrated to a great extent on the protection and development of the Slovak language and of Slovak culture. This was the reason why the defense of the language along with national recognition and political rights had come across so clearly in the political demands of 1848–1849 and 1861, and also in the Pittsburgh Pact; one of its clauses stipulated: "The Slovak language shall be the official language in the schools, in governmental offices and in public life generally." The creation of Czecho-Slovakia should have eliminated the threat to the Slovak language. However, what the Language Law signaled, despite the fact that Slovak could be used as the working language in Slovakia, was another threat to it and to the culture of its people as well.[31]

Another characteristic of Czechoslovakism was the political structure of the state, which also created a problem for Slovak individuality. The founders of Czecho-Slovakia based the political system of the new state on the Third French Republic. The Czechs took a unitary democratic political system from a classical nation-state, introduced it into a multinational society, and imposed on it their own agenda. The system contained many factors of stability, but also of rigidity that permitted attacks on its integrity. The most serious of these factors was "the structure of the Czechoslovak Republic as a *Czech* national state [which] proved to be the greatest danger to democracy."[32]

The appointment of the Benes government demonstrated clearly that the fusion of the two nations was the ideological cornerstone of government policy toward Slovakia. It was pursued relentlessly during the two decades of the First Republic. It legitimized the refusal to consider any propositions for the autonomy of Slovakia. Benes best summed up the government's position when he declared in Nove Zamky in December 1933: "I am neither for separatism, nor for political autonomy because it would simply be a new and major *artificial* political obstacle to the normal and inevitable biological and sociological evolution of our nation, a measure that would not have the anticipated results but which would only complicate further our regular evolution."[33]

However, Benes's approach created a problem, namely that it did not allow for a dual loyalty, to either a Slovak or a Czech nation and to the Czechoslovak state. Unlike in other states, notably France, where nation and state had fused as a result of a long historical evolution, in Czechoslovakia the unified nation was an artificial creation. Few understood this in 1918 and indeed for years to come. Commenting on a declaration made by a Czech delegate at the Paris Peace Conference that the Czechs had received "an international mandate to create a Czechoslovak political nation with the entry of the Slovaks in the Czech political nation," Peroutka writes: "This [the

declaration] was true, but otherwise nothing else was true. If you read carefully the quotation, it is clear that there did not exist a Czechoslovak nation. The subsequent astonishment toward Slovak events resulted from the fact that this had been forgotten."[34]

The Catholics of the Slovak People's Party and the Lutherans in the Slovak National Party voiced the Slovak opposition to Czechslovakism and raised the banner of Slovak nationalism. Fortunately, the relations between Czechs and Slovaks never deteriorated to the point that an external intervention was required; the government was careful enough to make sure that Slovak concerns were not completely ignored. Yet, they were not completely met either, and conditions remained that could only lead to an increase in Slovak disenchantment. As early as 1921, Seton-Watson recognized the existence of these conditions, which he defined as the *imponderabilia* of Czech-Slovak relations.[35] More than a decade later, Macartney also acknowledged that there were still "intangible and difficult to describe" factors that had created serious problems in Czech-Slovak relations.[36] What these observers were sensing was the Slovaks' refusal to identify with the Czech conception of the state. As Hlinka stated shortly after his party went into opposition: "[The] Prague [government] doesn't understand Slovakia, nor it is trying to understand it. It does not want to grasp that Prague centralism means the ruin of Slovakia. We want institutions which will defend our Slovak interests completely and will not be dependent on Prague capriciousness."[37]

The Social Democratic leader Derer suggested that "the political differences which exist in the matter of the demands for autonomy are not differences between Czechs and Slovaks, or between Czech parties and Slovak parties, but are a matter rather of differences among the Slovaks themselves."[38] This statement is true to the extent that the discussion was principally among the Slovaks in Slovakia or in parliament. As far as the Czechs were concerned, they went on with the matter of governing the state, indeed, from their perspective, the nation. There were Slovak representatives in all their parties, and to the extent that they were elected in Slovakia, they thus fulfilled the criterion of electoral representation. Even so, the Czechs were present in the discussions, though not directly. The parliamentary form of representative government in Czechoslovakia favored the Czech nation, both geographically and demographically. The government had to respond to the pressure of its constituents. As the Czech nation did not approve of Slovak autonomy or, for that matter, even decentralization, it determined the outcome of the argument. Slovaks who accepted and echoed the policies of the government became known as Czechoslovaks in Slovakia.

These Czechoslovaks identified with the ideology of Czechoslovakism out of a conviction that it offered the best opportunity for the Slovaks to catch up

economically and socially with the Czechs. By accepting this ideology, they participated in governing the state; in every government there were two or three Slovak ministers. In the two decades of the First Republic, fourteen Slovaks occupied sixty-three different government positions. They also ensured themselves political power in Slovakia. However, not all of them shared the extreme views of union with Derer who, in 1922, stated in the National Assembly: "All Slovak classes are at present inferior to Czech classes. It is impossible to conceal the fact that the present Slovak generation is inferior to the present Czech generation."[39] These Czechoslovaks were found in the National Socialist, Social Democratic, and Agrarian parties and they offered the Slovaks no specific national program, only the platforms that were part and parcel of the partisan and electoral process.

All of these parties were united, however, in their opposition to the Slovak People's Party and its demand for Slovak autonomy. They backed Hlinka's internment in the Czech Lands in 1919 and 1920 after his unsuccessful attempt to present the Slovak case for autonomy at the Paris Peace Conference, and instigated the arrest and conviction in 1929 of Vojtech Tuka, editor of *Slovak*, the newspaper of the Slovak People's Party, for his article about a legal vacuum *(vacuum juris)* in Slovakia. These parties successfully used what was otherwise a minor issue to embarrass the Slovak People's Party.[40] The attitude of the Czechoslovaks toward not only the SPP but also its political program had forced the Slovak People's Party—renamed the Hlinka Slovak People's Party in 1925 to honor its leader—to be an opposition party most of the First Republic. It was a constant, at times even strident, commentator and critic in parliament and in its press of Czechoslovak politics and opponent of the ideology of Czechoslovakism. It was also the only major party in Slovakia that consistently fought for Slovakia's autonomy.

THE SLOVAKS AND THE CZECHOSLOVAK STATE

During the two decades of the First Czechoslovak Republic, the Slovaks benefited from many government policies. Overall, Prague successfully built a modern state while trying to create a Czechoslovak nation. It established an efficient and, for the period, modern administration, built an infrastructure of east-west roads and railways to complement the north-south ones created in Austria-Hungary, and laid the basis for the development of a modern economic system. Progressive social legislation was enacted including an eight-hour week, unemployment, and medical insurance and old age pensions. On the whole, the standard of living of the population rose. However, such overall consider-

ations hide some of the imbalances in the economy, in particular in Slovakia. The economy experienced three crises, in 1921 to 1923, 1930 to 1934 (the Depression), and 1937. All three hit Slovakia particularly hard, for Slovakia had less industrial development than the Czech Lands. Moreover, as a result of the economic liberalism at the time, Slovak economic activity and the prospects for development were not only limited, but in many cases curtailed. In the republic's first decade and a half, 260 enterprises in various industrial branches in Slovakia were shut down as a result of the competitive pressure from Czech industries; by 1937, another 680 enterprises in heavy industry experienced the same fate. Where there was capital investment, it was in old rather than new industries. By 1930, Slovakia's share of industrial labor was only 19.4 percent compared to 42.1 percent in the Czech Lands. As Slovak historians write: "Some busy industrial areas, in particular in mountainous regions, were literally transformed into 'valleys of hunger.'"[41]

Slovakia's economy was the object of a specific policy that ignored its needs, capabilities, and potential, and relegated it instead to the role of an agricultural adjunct of the industrial economy of the Czech Lands. The Agrarians, under Hodza's leadership, proposed the theory of "agrarian Slovakia," which became the cornerstone of government policy. However, rather than establishing a beneficial division of labor, this policy created an economic dualism that disadvantaged Slovakia. The land reform of 1919, although radical when proclaimed, in fact set the tone and did little to improve the situation of those working in agriculture. Although the law stipulated that 1,407,000 hectares were to be parceled out, through exemptions (church lands, for example) and patronage, only 247,000 hectares were made available to farmers. Other policies were equally infelicitous. For example, land improvement took place from 1919 to 1927 on 87,263 hectares in the Czech Lands, but only on 9,323 in Slovakia. Of the investment costs for rural modernization, 95.1 percent went to the Czech Lands and only 4.3 percent to Slovakia. (The rest to Ruthenia, which was in an even worse situation than Slovakia.) Electrification was another sector where the imbalance was particularly flagrant: whereas 31.7 percent of the agricultural enterprises were electrified in the Czech Lands, only 1.9 percent of these in Slovakia were. As Mikula indicates: "Throughout the 1920s, Slovak agriculture remained essentially stagnant and less productive and in the 1930s the world agricultural crisis had a greater adverse effect on the Slovaks. In the industrial sector there was a whole battery of problems, so much so that it was referred to as the 'complex of industrial woes.'"[42]

However economically disadvantaged Slovakia was, it was part of a country that had a parliamentary form of government and regular elections, was governed according to the rule of law, and generally gave its citizens the freedoms of a

democracy. One of the major achievements of the government was its emphasis on education, in particular the establishment of secondary schools throughout Slovakia. During the life of the First Republic, there were in all eighty-four secondary schools that included fifty-three *gymnazia,* five industrial, and seven commercial schools, one agricultural, and one forestry school. Sixteen of these schools began operation only in the last four years of the republic. While Bratislava had nine such schools, Kosice had eleven, and every city with more than 20,000 inhabitants had at least two schools, except for Komarno. Catholic seminaries were also important educational institutions with more than half of the total located in Slovakia. Lutherans had only one institution, the Bratislava Theological Academy which opened in October 1919 but changed its name to Theological College in 1921. There were also twelve Jewish yeshivas that offered advanced religious training which led to rabbinical ordination.

After Elizabeth University, created by the Magyars in Bratislava during the war, had moved to Hungary, a Slovak one was founded with three faculties: law, medicine, and philosophy (humanities). It was named after Amos Comenius, a Czech humanist reformer of the seventeenth century. Most of its professors, appointed by the government, were Czechs, and they were among those who "in practical terms, even though they were in their great majority supporters of a 'Czechoslovak nation', helped to make Slovakia Slovak."[43] However, Slovak students who wanted to pursue higher education in fields other than those offered at Comenius University had to go to the Czech Lands where there were three universities, one agricultural, one mining, one veterinary, and four technical colleges. A Slovak Technical University, located in Kosice, was created only in 1937.

Matica slovenska also reopened on 1 January 1919 and began immediately to establish local branches to encourage cultural and social life among the people. It supported writers and researchers through its publishing house and press, and also "played an important role in the development of national consciousness and the protection of the purity of the Slovak language."[44] Many other social organizations, among them Zivena, Sokol, Scouts, and many institutions run by the Catholic and Lutheran churches, also helped in the explosion of cultural and social life that Slovakia experienced in the new state. Amateur theater groups and organizations for cultural enlightenment were established in many towns and villages. Bratislava housed the Slovak National Theatre and in 1920 became the home of the Slovak Philharmonic Orchestra. The press benefited particularly; in 1918, there were 23 Slovak newspapers and journals, a decade later there were 186.

The Czechoslovak Republic made it possible for the Slovak nation to meet the challenges of a new state as well as those of modernization. Many of the

problems that had made the integration of Slovakia in the new state so difficult when it was created were overcome. Political parties, whether they were in government or in opposition, were also active in the promotion of various cultural and social activities. The link between Slovak People's Party and the Catholic Church enabled it to reach all strata of the population. As for the other parties, especially the Agrarians and Social Democrats, they too had links with social and economic organizations; their participation in the government enabled them to deal with many problems in Slovakia and generally to promote growth and development. They were unable, however, to protect Slovak industries and the Slovak economy from the more powerful Czech competitors. Consequently, they bore the brunt of criticism for Slovakia's lagging economy, especially in the years following the Depression, during which time thousands of Slovaks emigrated to other European countries and North America.

Slovaks participated actively in its political life. Many did so to be involved in the life of the state; others aimed to combat Czechoslovakism and achieve Slovakia's autonomy. The former were the ones who voted for the centralist parties, the latter for the Slovak People's and the Slovak National parties. This political process strengthened the sense of Slovak national identity. Ironically, so did the government despite its avowed intention to create a Czechoslovak nation. This occurred as the unexpected result of some of its social and economic policies. For example, the government continued to send Czechs to Slovakia long after there were enough trained and educated Slovaks to fill positions in the state administration, education, and the economy. Whereas in 1921, 71,733 Czechs lived in Slovakia, by 1938, their number had risen to 120,926. As a result, from the first years of the First Republic, emigration proved to be the only alternative to unemployment for many Slovaks. According to available statistics, out of 400,193 persons who left Czechoslovakia in the years 1920 to 1938, 213,185, or 54 percent, were from Slovakia.

The consequences of these policies became even more evident in the second decade of the First Republic. By the mid-1930s, a new generation appeared on the scene demanding not only jobs, but also the equitable participation of Slovaks in areas such as the foreign service, the armed forces, and other state ministries. Here again, the available statistics give a particularly clear picture: in 1938, out of 7,470 civil servants in seventeen ministries and departments, 131 were Slovaks. Out of 139 generals in the Czechoslovak armed forces, only one was Slovak, and Slovaks totaled only 33 out of the 1,246 officials in the Ministry of Foreign Affairs.

It is not surprising, therefore, that there were numerous instances of a public affirmation of Slovak nationalism, especially in the second decade of the First Republic. Three examples suffice to show the depth of Slovak sentiment.

In 1932, Czech scholars presented a new Slovak grammar to the Matica slovenska. According to Macartney: "Protests poured in from nearly all the leading figures in Slovak literature, journalism and cultural life; the Czechophiles were ousted from the Committees, and a new and purely Slovak body was entrusted with preparing a different and more acceptable grammar."[45] On the occasion of the festivities to celebrate the eleven-hundredth anniversary of the founding of the first Christian church at Nitra in August 1933, the Slovaks publicly humiliated the government delegation for not having invited Hlinka to join them. He was spotted in the crowd and urged to speak. As he had done many times before, Hlinka demanded that the Slovaks be given autonomy. Mikus notes: "Before 150,000 wildly enthusiastic people, Hlinka pronounced in a tone at first calm and cool, then more ardent and excited, one of the greatest discourses of his life. The spectators listened to him in recollected silence. The representatives of the government, humiliated, left the gallery, and the foreigners present tried to get an explanation of what had taken place."[46] Finally, in the summer of 1938, a massive demonstration organized in Bratislava, Slovakia's capital, commemorated the twentieth anniversary of the signing of the Pittsburgh Pact. The original copy from the United States was displayed to the assembled throng. Hlinka pronounced what was to be his last public speech; with the document in hand, he demanded that Prague honor this agreement, which Masaryk himself had signed.

Political life in Slovakia, in particular the voting patterns at election time, reflected the benefits obtained and the problems experienced in the state. In the 1920 elections, the Social Democratic Party with 23 seats and 38 percent had obtained the greatest number of votes. In the 1925 elections, compared to the twenty-three seats and 34.3 percent of the vote for the Slovak People's Party, the Social Democrats received only two seats and 4.2 percent of the vote. The Agrarians received twelve seats and 17.4 percent of the vote, thus holding their own from the previous poll. The Communist Party of Czechoslovakia was a newcomer and, by appealing to former Social Democratic voters, received eight seats and 13.9 percent of the vote. The National Socialists retained one seat for 2,6 percent of the vote. Hungarian and German parties obtained together nine seats in the Chamber of Deputies and 16.1 percent of the vote.

The 1929 elections, held on 27 October, were considerably affected by the Tuka trial and Hlinka's refusal to disavow him. The vote for the Slovak People's Party fell to 28.3 percent and nineteen seats, the Agrarians again held their own with 19.5 percent and twelve seats, the Social Democrats made a modest comeback with 9.5 percent and five seats, while the Communists scored only 10.7 percent and five seats. The National Socialists obtained 3.1 percent and two seats. The Hungarians and Germans remained stable at 15.9 percent

and nine seats. The Slovak People's Party, in the government since 1927, left it and went back into opposition. The fourth and last elections of the First Republic were held on 19 May 1935 in the aftermath of the Depression and saw somewhat different political configurations seek the support of the electorate. The People's Party joined with the Slovak National Party, the Polish Party from Silesia, and the Ruthenian Autonomist Agrarian Union to form an "Autonomist Bloc," which polled 30.1 percent and twenty-two seats in Slovakia. The Agrarians fell to 17.6 percent and twelve seats, the Social Democrats increased to 11.4 percent with six seats, the Communists went up to 13 percent and seven seats, the National Socialists maintained themselves at 3.2 percent and two seats, while the Germans and Hungarians dropped to 14.2 percent and nine seats. Ominous for the survival of the republic was the landslide victory of the Sudeten German Party, which polled 15.2 percent of the total vote in the state and 66 percent of the German vote, receiving forty-four seats.

The economic crisis resulting from the Depression brought about some modifications in the platforms of Slovak parties. After the June 1932 Congress of the Young Slovak Generation in Trencianske Teplice, the Slovak People's Party accentuated social and economic questions, adopting a demand for the reindustrialization of Slovakia in its program in 1936. As Dorothea El Mallakh writes: "the party's platform included, in addition to autonomy, strong economic and social planks in such areas as food prices, employment, and religious education, subjects all involving a greater degree of local decisionmaking and power of implementation."[47] The Agrarians continued to emphasize agricultural development and use their position in the government to avail themselves of many opportunities to support agricultural organizations and cooperatives. However, they suffered from a major liability, as Slovak historians indicate: "The obstacle that the Agrarians were never able to overcome and which prevented them from becoming the biggest party in Slovakia was their great dependence on Prague."[48] Its two most prominent members were Hodza, its leader who became prime minister of Czechoslovakia in 1935, and Srobar. During the 1930s, there were indications of opposition to centralism, especially among the younger members, yet none ever dared to express publicly the word *autonomy*. The Social Democrats, led by Derer, had to compete with the Communists, who broke away in 1921, for support among industrial workers. After their initial success during the 1920 elections with 46 percent of the vote and their drop to 4.3 percent in 1925, the Social Democrats steadily began to improve their standing with 9.5 percent in 1929 and 11.4 percent in 1935. The party's platform changed little over the years, especially on the question of Slovakia's autonomy. The Communists maintained a following that obtained

for them 10 to 14 percent of the popular vote throughout the First Republic. One of their main organizers in Slovakia was a Czech, Klement Gottwald, who became leader of the party in 1929 and bolshevized it. In 1937, the party adopted a platform that stressed the industrialization of Slovakia.

The constant pressure from the two Slovak opposition parties in favor of Slovak autonomy brought some dividends after the elections of 1925 when the Slovak People's Party came out as the strongest party in Slovakia with twenty-three seats. The government agreed to move in the direction of greater decentralization. On 14 July 1927 a law was passed that abolished the county system and reorganized the administration along provincial lines. A *Slovenska Krajina* (Slovak Province) was brought into existence. The province had an assembly, with two-thirds of its members elected and one-third appointed by the government; however, its jurisdiction was quite restricted. The assembly was presided over by a public servant appointed by the government. The ministry for Slovakia was abolished. Although a far cry from the autonomy of the Pittsburgh Agreement, this reorganization was seen as a step in the right direction; Hlinka declared it a "first flash of autonomy."⁴⁹ The Slovak People's Party agreed to leave the opposition and was in the government from 1927 to 1929. The Populists were given two portfolios: unification and health. Marek Gazik took over unification, while Jozef Tiso obtained health. Another positive development from the Slovak point of view was the Concordat signed with the Vatican on 20 January 1928. Catholic ecclesiastical boundaries coincided henceforth with those of Czechoslovakia and thus ended the centuries-old jurisdiction of the archbishop of Ostrihom in Slovakia.

But there was no constitutional reform. After its failure in January 1922 to have the National Assembly consider a bill for the autonomy of Slovakia, the Slovak People's Party made two additional submissions; the first was made in the wake of the 1927 reform and was submitted in May 1930, and the second in June 1938. Each time the submission met with failure. Masaryk resigned as president on 21 November 1935. The 1938 attempt had been preceded by the party's support for the election of Benes to the presidency. Although he was opposed to Slovak autonomy, the party had preferred him to his opponent, Bohumil Nemec, an Agrarian. The prime minister was Hodza, also an Agrarian, and the Slovak People's Party was not willing to have the same party hold both positions. Benes proved himself unwilling, however, to reward this support by granting the Slovaks autonomy. While he did embark on a series of negotiations with the Slovak People's Party they never led to anything.

Although the Slovak People's Party failed to achieve Slovak autonomy, support for the party did not diminish. Whether it would have increased under continued normal circumstances is moot. What this support indicates, however,

is that relations between Czechs and Slovaks were inevitably headed for a new modus vivendi, and not merely because Czechoslovakism had not taken root among the Slovaks. The problem was a fundamental one, influencing the entire history of Czechoslovakia, as Carol Skalnik Leff points out: "Slovakia is too small and closely related a nation not to provoke Czech efforts to bring it into line. It is, however, too large and distinct a nation to suffer such attentions gladly or docilely."[50] The search for a new balance between the two nations was derailed when the international situation took on a radical turn when the National Socialists took power in Germany in January 1933.

THE BREAKUP OF THE FIRST REPUBLIC

Of all the aspects of political life in Czechoslovakia, foreign policy was the one area where Slovak parties had no influence. Until 1935, it was, for all intents and purposes, the personal preserve of Benes, Czechoslovakia's foreign minister. It was he who made policy, and he never hesitated to claim that his policy included Slovakia. Slovak historians write: "Benes, as minister of foreign affairs and later also as president, proclaimed many times that Slovakia was important for the defense of the state, yet he never understood the consequences [of this position]."[51] The Slovak People's Party did. However, like the other Slovak parties, it could do no more than comment on or criticize it, in particular during parliamentary debates. Speakers from the Slovak People's Party made a point of linking their approbation or opposition to the needs, and above all the survival, of Slovakia and the Slovak nation. During the 1920s, Hungarian revisionism was the single most important threat to the stability of Central Europe. Thanks to the international support Czechoslovakia enjoyed and also the creation of the Little Entente, Slovakia was protected from it.

The situation changed dramatically in the 1930s when Germany, under Adolf Hitler, sought to revise the Versailles Treaty. Czechoslovakia, with its important German population, became a target of German interests, in particular Hitler's determination to unite all Germans in Europe in one state. It became one of the main objects in a diplomatic game. The Western powers, unwilling to counter Hitler's aggressive diplomacy, forced Prague to cede the German parts of the Czech Lands, known as the Sudentenland, to Germany during the Munich Conference of September–October 1938. The results were catastrophic for the survival of Czechoslovakia: "Munich meant, for all intents and purposes, that the Great Powers recognized that the CSR [Czechoslovak Republic] was in the German sphere of interest. The fate of the republic was thus entirely in the hands of Hitler."[52]

It is not just Germany's aggressive diplomatic moves that were of concern to the Slovak parties; equally worrying was the rise of radical ideologies, in particular communism and fascism, which had achieved power in the two most powerful, although at that time self-absorbed, states in Europe, the Soviet Union and Germany. Both were universalist ideologies, motivated to conquest, certainly in the ideological sphere, but also territorially in Europe. Both were opposed to liberal democracy, but each was also the mortal enemy of the other. They represented extreme responses to the uncertainties and problems of industrialization. These ideologies influenced European political life and found supporters who formed parties in most other European countries. As a result, European interstate relations took place along two tracks: official diplomacy and international ideological solidarity. The Soviet Union had launched the second with the creation of the Comintern in 1921, and Nazi Germany had quickly understood its usefulness. The classical European state order was thus subverted first by Germany, which used both diplomacy and ideological solidarity to achieve its aims. Czechoslovakia became one of its victims in Munich as a result of a judicious use of internal pressure by Konrad Henlein, leader of the Sudeten German Party, and diplomatic demands pertaining to the revision of the Versailles Treaty.

The Slovaks were bystanders when this drama was being played out. The Slovak People's Party was nevertheless considering various options to save the Slovak nation if the government could not guarantee the survival of the state and to avoid international isolation. The result was that in the days preceding the Munich Conference, the party proposed the union of Slovakia with Poland. As the Munich Agreement did not result in the disappearance of Czechoslovakia, this option was never put into execution. However, the Munich Agreement brought home one unpleasant truth: The government was unable to protect the integrity of the state. As a result, the government parties lost credibility, leaving the political arena in Slovakia open for the Slovak People's Party. The party quickly recognized the obverse of Benes's maxim about the importance of Slovakia for the defense of the state: If the state could not defend itself, then it could also not defend Slovakia. This would have to be done by the Slovaks, and for this they needed their own government. The party moved quickly after the Munich Conference; it invited other Slovak parties to a meeting on 5–6 October 1938 in Zilina, where it produced the Zilina Agreement, which worked out the autonomy of Slovakia. The government accepted the agreement the next day, and nominated an autonomous provincial government, led by Tiso, who had succeeded Hlinka as leader when he died on 16 August in Ruzomberok. A constitutional project was prepared and submitted to Parliament, which approved it on 19 November; it entered

into effect four days later, on 22 November. The spelling of the name of the state returned to its original form: Czecho-Slovakia.

At Munich, the First Czechoslovak Republic, the centralized nation-state of the Czechoslovaks, created by Masaryk, Benes, and Stefanik, had been destroyed. Its president, Benes, resigned shortly thereafter on 5 October. The succeeding Second Republic was an asymmetrical quasi-federal state consisting of the truncated territory of the Czech Lands governed by the central government, and an autonomous Slovakia and Ruthenia. Its life was short as Germany continued to press for major changes to the Versailles Treaty. In the vortex of the diplomatic and ideological game that Berlin was playing in Europe after Munich, Slovakia was no longer a bystander but rather an actor, albeit not a very important one. The test of its status and strength came when Poland and Hungary also made territorial demands after the Munich Agreement. Direct negotiations with Hungary in Komarno on 9–13 October proved unsuccessful, and Budapest appealed to the British, French, German and Italian signatories of the Munich Agreement. The German and Italian foreign ministers met in Vienna on 2 November and redrew the frontiers of Slovakia. Hungary obtained 10,390 square kilometers; 854,217 inhabitants, among them a 250,000 Slovaks; and the cities of Nove Zamky, Surany, Levice, Lucenec, Rimavska Sobota, Roznava, and last but not least, Kosice. Poland acquired, in addition to Tesin from the Czech Lands, territory in Kysuce, Orava, and Spis. Germany occupied Devin, which gave it strategic control over the area where the Morava and Danube rivers meet near the Austrian (by that time German) border.

Germany's successful diplomatic offensives had consequences in the ideological sphere. Fascism was winning adherents in Europe, and authoritarian methods were also not without their appeal. Some in the Slovak People's Party were attracted by Italian fascism and German national socialism. The party did not, however, accept the tenets of either ideology. The exclusion of some representatives from other parties from the provincial elections of 19 November was a response, albeit not a very good one, to attempts to create political unity and cohesion. Although renamed the Party of Slovak National Unity after the Zilina conference to underline the participation of other parties (the Communists and Social Democrats had not been invited), the Slovak People's Party was in effect the main political actor in Slovakia with a near-monopoly on power. Its list won the elections and Tiso was confirmed as head of the provincial government. When the Slovak Provincial Assembly met for the first time on 18 February 1939, it elected Martin Sokol as its president.

The Second Republic was never given a chance to consolidate, nor was Slovak political life offered the opportunity to stabilize. German territorial ambitions had not been appeased in Munich despite British Prime Minister

Neville Chamberlain's assurances of "peace in our time." Farsighted commentators and politicians such as Winston Churchill sensed that Berlin would continue in its offensive against Czecho-Slovakia, although it was not clear in what manner or what the outcome would be. Some were members of the People's Party who sensed that the days of the Second Republic were numbered and who considered that the best way to ensure the survival of Slovakia was to declare its independence. Among the adherents of this viewpoint were Tuka, who had been released from prison, Alexander Mach, and Ferdinand Durcansky. Rumors that the only other alternative was the parceling out of Slovakia among Hungary, Poland and Germany gave impetus to this option. As Ladislav Deak points out, during the 1930s Slovakia's southern and northern neighbors were playing a "game over Slovakia."[53] With no recourse to Western support against further German moves in Central Europe, the only avenue of action was to deal directly with Germany. Tuka, Mach, and Durcansky contacted German officials; Tuka personally traveled to Berlin on 12 February 1939, where he met with Chancellor Hitler and indicated that independence was what the Slovaks wanted. His trip had not been sanctioned by the Slovak government. For their part, Tiso and other members of the government were not yet willing to see Slovakia secede from Czecho-Slovakia. Like the rest of the world, they were playing a wait-and-see game.

The dénouement came as a result of a combination of intrigues, misperceptions, and precipitate actions. Prague watched the activities of the Slovak government which it perceived as no more than a subordinate provincial government, uneasily. Yet it also realized that Slovak independence was a possibility. There was thus confusion in Prague on how to deal with Slovakia. On 12 February, without the knowledge of the prime minister and the ministers of foreign affairs and defense, a secret plan was drawn by senior Czech officials to have Czech troops occupy Slovakia. On 1 March, Berlin was informed of the plan. When Berlin sent signals to Prague on 9 March that Germany had no interest in an independent Slovakia, the Czecho-Slovak government, which had nervously followed Durcansky's earlier trip to Berlin to discuss matters of economic cooperation, dismissed Tiso and the Slovak government the next day, declared martial law, sent in the army, and arrested Slovak officials. As Solc writes: "After long months of concessions and manoeuvres, the Czech politicians of the Second Republic decided at the last moment to opt for a desperate reversal. They tried to secure the basic unity and existence of the state with the use of extreme means of power."[54]

On 11 March, Emil Hacha, who had succeeded Benes as president, named Karol Sidor as head of the Slovak government. Prague's sudden move in Slovakia not only took the Slovaks by surprise, but also provoked German

activity. Third Reich officials approached Sidor to declare Slovakia's independence; he refused. Berlin then invited the former Slovak premier, Tiso, to Berlin on 13 March to let him know that the time had come for Slovakia to make up its mind about its future or be left to an uncertain fate. Tiso was also offered the opportunity to declare Slovakia's independence on Berlin radio; he declined, indicating that only the Slovak Provincial Assembly could take such a decision.

After his meeting with Hitler, Tiso telephoned Hacha and asked him to convoke the Slovak Provincial Assembly; Hacha acceded to the request. When Tiso returned to Bratislava on 14 March, he outlined to the deputies the options that Slovakia faced. A motion for independence was proposed and the Slovak deputies voted for it unanimously; the Hungarian deputies abstained. Tiso was chosen to become the head of the first government of independent Slovakia. Thus in 1939 the common state of the Czechs and Slovaks ceased to exist.

9

The Slovak Republic
1939–1945

THE INTERNATIONAL CONTEXT

Although the Slovak Provincial Assembly proclaimed the independence of Slovakia in time of peace, its fate became tied to the world war that broke out five and a half months later. Britain declared war on Germany on 3 September 1939 to put a stop to German territorial aggression in Europe. However, the war was also part of the three-way ideological contest among liberal democracy, fascism, and communism. Since the end of the Great War, these three ideologies had been competing in parliamentary elections across Europe in states that had not succumbed to either of the two radical ones. After signing an alliance with the Soviet Union in August 1939, Germany sought to ensure the victory of fascism by going to war. But when Germany launched an invasion of the Soviet Union in June 1941, a new alliance was created between the liberal democratic states and the latter. It sealed Germany's fate and also discredited the ideology that it represented and sought to impose on European society.

It took almost six years of bitter fighting in Europe to achieve this outcome. During that time, the states caught in the vortex of Berlin's territorial and ideological objectives were faced with the task of survival. Germany, from the time of the Munich Conference until final defeat, determined not only the territorial organization of Europe but also the ideological context. For those

states that were not taken over outright by Germany (as were the Czech Lands, which became the Protectorate of Bohemia-Moravia on 15 March 1939), or that were not the object of military operations and occupation (as was Poland), the way to ensure survival was to have a regime run by fascist parties or by political leaders not unaware of the interests of Berlin.

Resistance was also an option. The Allied powers, in particular the British and the Soviets, encouraged Central European political groups and parties to organize resistance movements and thereby contribute to their war effort and the defeat of Germany and fascism. Official resistance in the countries in the German sphere of interest was a complicated, if not impossible, matter. The governments that opted for such a policy invited overthrow and occupation. Each was thus faced with a decision to situate itself somewhere between collaboration and tolerable resistance. As Germany's fortunes changed, so did the policies of the governments in its sphere of influence. However, at the end of hostilities, it was the resistance movements and governments-in-exile that were permitted to participate in the decisions on the organization of postwar Europe.

The Slovak Provincial Assembly proclaimed the independence of Slovakia in order to ensure the survival of the nation. Its leaders knew that the policies of their state also had to be determined by this need to survive, especially as the country's geopolitical position was not a felicitous one. In terms of Germany's strategic objectives, Slovakia was nowhere near a peripheral theater of war, which would have made it available to the Allies; rather it was in the middle of the German sphere of military operations. Only toward the end of the war, as the German armed forces were retreating back to Germany, did Slovakia offer opportunities for Allied involvement. Slovak domestic politics thus came under the shadow not only of German power but also of the Third Reich's ideological program. Just two options were available in the pursuit of the politics of survival: The first was to use the opportunity to organize the state according to the traditions and needs of the Slovak people while at the same time avoiding a German intervention; the second was to accept fascism so as not to give Germany a reason to end Slovak independence. These two options were articulated by two men who had been prominent in the Slovak People's Party before independence: Tiso represented the first one while Tuka favored the second. These men determined politics in the Slovak Republic.

After independence, the Slovak Parliament chose Tiso to become prime minister of Slovakia. When the constitution was passed on 21 July 1939, giving Slovakia a republican form of government, he was elected president of the republic. With these positions, he became a central figure in Slovak politics during the entire life of the Slovak Republic. He was born in Velka Bytca on 13 October 1887, went to school in Zilina and Nitra, and completed his studies

for the priesthood at the Pazmaneum in Vienna. He was ordained in 1910. In Vienna he became acquainted with the Christian Socialist movement, in particular with such men as Ignac Seipel and Franz Martin Schindler. He also became familiar with the Catholic social encyclicals, notably Pope Leo XIII's *Rerum Novarum* and Pius XI's *Quadragesimo Anno*. He entered politics at the end of the Great War, when he joined the Slovak People's Party. In 1921, he was appointed personal secretary to the bishop of Nitra, Karol Kmetko, who was also a Populist member of the Czechoslovak Parliament. He was elected to Parliament in 1925. Like many Slovak priests in politics, he continued in his duties as parish priest in Banovce.

In 1927, Tiso was one of the two Populist deputies who became ministers when the Slovak People's Party decided to join the government coalition. The trial and imprisonment of Tuka in 1929, which ended the Populist participation in the government, gave him a chance to play an even more important role in the party. He became vice president and its principal ideologue. Basing himself on Slovak thinkers of the preceding century, he saw the nation as having a purpose in God's scheme of things. He accepted a hierarchy of values in the world, beginning with the individual, the family, and finally the nation. He rejected the existence of a Czechoslovak nation because he did not accept the notion that Slovakia and the Slovak people were just a topographical unit, an economic or a cultural entity. He was persuaded that the Slovaks would eventually achieve statehood.

When Hlinka died in August 1938, Tiso was one of the two main contenders for the leadership of the party. Although his rival, Sidor, controlled the party's newspaper *Slovak* as well as the Hlinka Guard, the party's paramilitary wing, Tiso, with the support of a majority in the party presidium and the backing of the church, inherited Hlinka's mantle. He was thus thrust in the forefront of Slovak politics and became one of the main actors in the events that would lead to Slovakia's autonomy and six months later its independence. In his efforts to safeguard Slovak national interests, he had to contend with the proponents of an alternative approach professed by Tuka that aligned itself with the fascist ideologies of Italy and Germany.

When Tiso was elected president of the republic, Tuka became prime minister. Tiso knew that he could not keep Tuka out because Germany would not have tolerated such a situation. Tuka was born in 1880 in the mixed Slovak-Hungarian village of Kremnicke Bane in southern Slovakia. Throughout his life whether he was Slovak or Hungarian was questioned due to the fact that he spoke Slovak with a Hungarian accent. His father, a teacher, was considered to be a nationally minded Slovak. On his mother's side, he was related to the Slovak bishop Stefan Moyses. But like most young people of his

age and his area, he received his education in Hungarian. He was a brilliant student who attended several European universities. In 1914, at the age of thirty-four, he was appointed professor of legal philosophy and international law at the Magyar Elizabeth University in Bratislava. He had earned this appointment as a result of a treatise published in 1910 entitled *A Szabadsag: politikai tanulmany* (Liberty: a political study). It was one of two major works he published in his life. The other, *Die Rechtssysteme. Grundriß einer Rechtsphilosophie* (1941), was written while he was in prison.

When Elizabeth University closed in 1919, Tuka did not follow his colleagues to Budapest, but stayed in Slovakia. Nor did he become active in a Hungarian minority party. He joined the Slovak People's Party and in 1922 became the editor of its daily newspaper, *Slovak*. In 1925, he was elected to the Czechoslovak Parliament and soon became embroiled in one of the major historical and constitutional controversies of the First Czechoslovak Republic. Tuka was in fact an extraordinarily versatile and flamboyant figure. Fluent in a number of languages, he kept abreast of international events and enjoyed personal as well as political contacts throughout Europe. He was attracted to Italian fascism. In 1923, he organized in Slovakia the paramilitary organization *Rodobrana,* which he modeled on the Italian Black Shirts. Although it grew from 5,000 to 30,000 members by 1926, the *Rodobrana* never engaged in activities similar to those of the Black Shirts or the German Brown Shirts.

In 1928, as we saw in the preceding chapter, Tuka achieved both national and international prominence with his article about a *vacuum juris* in Czechoslovakia resulting from an alleged secret clause in the 1918 Martin Declaration that allowed the Slovaks to review their position in Czechoslovakia ten years later. Despite his parliamentary immunity, he was brought to trial. As a result of evidence that indicated that he was receiving funds from Hungary, he was found guilty of treason and condemned to fifteen years imprisonment. When he was released in 1938, he was in many ways a broken man, half blind from his ordeal and bitterly anti-Czech. Nevertheless, he reentered Slovak political life. Whatever personal reasons influenced him to return to political life, Tuka also had concluded that the balance of power in Central Europe was rapidly shifting toward Germany and that the fate of Czecho-Slovakia would most likely be decided by the Third Reich. He took it upon himself to go to Berlin and speak with the German leaders. On 12 February 1939, he was received by Hitler, from whom he sought support for the Slovaks. Historians still debate whether this visit was instrumental in developing German policy toward Slovakia; it did draw German attention to him. Once German policy toward Slovakia crystallized, Tuka clearly was one of the Slovak politicians favorably inclined toward Germany on whom Berlin could count.

From the moment the Slovak Republic was created, Tiso and Tuka became involved in its political life. The first five months were crucial for Slovakia as well as Central Europe, since these were the months that preceded the outbreak of war when the European powers could still consider all options. Even if Britain and France had signaled noninvolvement in the affairs of Central Europe after the Munich Conference, they were interested in the manner in which the new state was organizing itself and becoming a member of the European family of nations. They gave it de facto recognition by the appointment of consuls in Bratislava and in London's case also by giving an exequatur to a Slovak consul in the British capital. British recognition was granted on 4 May and French on 14 July 1939. These diplomats sent regular reports, which give a unique view not only of Slovak politics during the first six months but also paint the background that led these two powers, and in the end also the Allies to eliminate Slovakia as an actor from postwar Europe.[1]

THE FIRST SIX MONTHS

The two consuls who had been accredited to Czechoslovakia initially, were Milon de Peilion, born in 1890, and Peter Pares, who was born in 1908. The French representative, de Peilion, served longer in Bratislava, arriving on 30 September 1935, while his British colleague, Pares, took up his post on 12 December 1938. Both left within a month of each other, de Peilion on 19 August 1939, Pares on 2 September. However, Pares went to Budapest, where he still could keep a close watch on Slovakia. On 6 January 1940 he filed his last report.[2] The British and French archival material on Slovakia is not voluminous. Cross-checks into related archives have not produced additional information. Yet what is available is both detailed and comprehensive.

In his first report after independence, de Peilion had little positive to say about Slovakia. He was interested primarily in determining the exact degree of Slovak independence: "The question can now be asked to what extent is Slovakia an independent state and whether the situation she finds herself in differs from the 'protectorate' imposed on Bohemia and Moravia." Referring to an unpublished article that was to have appeared in *Grenzbote*, Bratislava's German newspaper, he indicated that it was felt Slovakia would have a status similar to that of the states of the British Empire. In the end, however, he felt that there was one overriding factor that defined Slovak independence: "It is certain that the occupation of a great part of the country by troops from the Reich allows one to doubt about the independence of this state, an independence that appears more like fiction."[3] Pares concentrated more on the situation

in Bratislava and the population's reaction to independence: "The reception given to the declaration on Tuesday [14 March] by the people of Bratislava was lukewarm indeed. There were no manifestations of joy and the townsfolk went about their normal business as if nothing had happened." He also noted that "a week after the declaration of independence the inhabitants of Bratislava are still unable to show great enthusiasm for the present state of affairs. The general impression is one of apathy or pessimism."[4]

With the proclamation of Slovak independence on 14 March 1939, the Slovak Provincial Assembly had transformed itself into a full-fledged Parliament and proceeded to approve a new government with Tiso as prime minister. Tuka became deputy prime minister, Sidor was given the Interior Ministry, Durcansky Foreign Affairs, while other portfolios, namely education, national economy, transport and public works, justice and treasury, and national defense were handed out on the basis of expertise, political weight, regional, or confessional representation. The Head of the Information Office, Mach, was also allowed to sit in cabinet meetings. They were all civilians; Tiso was the only priest. Most retained their portfolios throughout the life of the state; Sidor was the first to resign. In May 1939, he took up the post of Slovak envoy to the Vatican.

The most pressing issue that faced the new state was the question of security. Since only Germany could provide it, the Slovaks requested a treaty between the two states. When German troops entered the Czech Lands on 15 March, some units crossed the Slovak border and established themselves in the western part of the country, as far as the Vah River, creating surprise and consternation in the population. Negotiations began on 17 March and were concluded when German Foreign Minister Joachim von Ribbentrop signed a *Schutzvertrag* (Treaty of Protection) on 23 March. Tiso had signed on 19 March. As a result of this treaty, Slovakia's foreign and defense policies were aligned with those of Germany. The troops that had entered Slovakia drew back to a small well-defined zone near the border agreed to in the treaty. A secret clause also indicated close economic cooperation between the two states. However, the independence of Slovakia and the signing of the treaty had not prevented Hungary from trying, with German knowledge and consent, to acquire more territory at Slovakia's expense which the Hungarians expected Slovakia would not be able to defend. On 17 March, the Hungarians proposed to Bratislava a revision of the frontier between Slovakia and Ruthenia, which they had occupied on 15 March. Bratislava refused and Hungarian troops crossed into Slovak territory on 23 March to effect this revision; the Slovaks counterattacked the next day. Germany intervened and when negotiations opened on 27 March, Berlin backed the Hungarian demands. As a result,

Slovakia ceded an area of 1,697 square kilometers and 69,639 inhabitants, according to the 1938 census. (See Map 5, p. xvi).

Both consuls sent analytic reports on the political situation in Slovakia less than a month after independence. The difference in the reporting is once again striking. De Peilion reached a categorical conclusion about the meaning of these events: "Totalitarian methods current in the Third Reich govern henceforth the activities of the Slovak government leaders who find exclusive inspiration in them to set up the political, administrative and economic framework of the state." He concluded that these policies "are leading the country rapidly into ruin and university youth is so aware of this that it is now beginning to regret the past while the powerless and resigned rural mass gives itself up to its fate."[5]

Pares drew a different conclusion: "A review of the present state of affairs in Slovakia, after nearly a month of independence, seems to indicate that, in spite of the manner in which the declaration of independence was brought about and of the disturbing effects of the Hungarian invasion of Eastern Slovakia, conditions are more stable than anybody expected."[6] He foresaw problems with the German minority, whom he judged correctly as opposing the single-party proposal of the Populists and the influence of this party on every form of activity in the state. The German minority numbered some 126,000 people, represented by the Deutsche Partei, led by Franz Karmasin. They received recognition for their party, as did the Hungarians, and both retained parliamentary representatives.

Not long after independence and over the course of the next three years, the Slovak Republic received diplomatic recognition, either de jure and/or de facto, from twenty-eight states. The United States was not among them. Three of them, Britain, pre-Vichy France, and the Soviet Union, later withdrew it. In terms of diplomatic relations, representatives were exchanged primarily with the European states, in particular those like Switzerland, with whom Slovakia maintained important commercial relations throughout its entire life. However, this diplomatic recognition did not provide Slovakia with any significant room to maneuver; in terms of foreign policy, it was bound by its alliance with Germany. Pares reported that Tuka, in a declaration at a banquet given in honor of a German general, "said that in the event of Slovakia being obliged to take part in a war to defend European civilization, she would fight on the side of Germany."[7] He also outlined a speech Durcansky made before the Committee for Foreign Affairs of the Slovak Parliament and remarked: "The speech was much what one would have expected." It dealt with the Slovak-German Treaty which "Dr. Durcansky endeavored to prove by a number of not very convincing arguments that its provisions do not constitute a diminution of Slovak sover-

eignty"; with Slovak-Polish relations, which the minister saw as being able to develop to the mutual satisfaction and advantage of each country; with Hungarian aspirations "after the restoration of the Kingdom of St Stephen"; and with Italy and the Vatican. Slovak foreign policy, according to Durcansky, flowed from a national tradition and was based "on two ideas, the defence of the independence of the Slovak people and the protection of European culture against destructive foreign influences, first against the Turks and latterly against Bolshevism."[8]

The Slovak Constitution, which gave Slovakia a presidential form of government, was promulgated on 21 July 1939. The Slovak Parliament elected Tiso president of the republic on 26 October 1939. He appointed Tuka prime minister. Both consuls sent in lengthy reports to their respective ministries. Each describes in detail the Constitution's major provisions, with Pares occasionally expanding on certain clauses. De Peilion's overall evaluation was as laconic and categorical as his previous assessments of political life in Slovakia: "Although this text was enclosed in a liberal-like framework, it finally consecrates the transformation of Slovakia into an authoritarian republic."[9]

Pares, for his part, noted a strict one-party system was not created "due to the opposition of the German party which objected even to the formal incorporation of their organization in the Hlinka Party." He did not see the corporations whose existence is acknowledged in the Constitution as likely to "play much part in the development of the national life," but rather thought, on the other hand, that the presidency, Parliament, the Council of State, and the cabinet "may provide a certain guarantee against the abuse of power by one or the other." Finally, he foresaw the opposition of Slovak Lutherans who "appear in the nature of things to be excluded" from the Hlinka Party: "The insignificant position into which they have been thrust is sure to arouse their bitter resentment, all the more since, as it is admitted even by their Catholic critics, they possess proportionately greater wealth and social influence than the Catholic part of the nation."[10]

After war broke out, Pares was asked to respond to the analyses Bruce Lockhart of the Political Intelligence Department was submitting to the Foreign Office. In one report, Lockhart relayed the views of Rudolf Viest with whom he had been in contact. Viest had been the only Slovak general in the Czechoslovak army and had gone to London after the declaration of Slovak independence to work for Benes. Viest claimed that there was general discontent in Slovakia with German domination, that the intelligentsia and the Lutherans were in revolt, that the clergy was opposed to "autonomous government," and that the vast bulk of the people were for the restoration of Czechoslovakia with new rights for the Slovaks. The conclusion of all this was that "the political

administration is, if anything, harsher than in the Protectorate. Economic conditions are worse . . . the Slovaks are politically immature and the establishment of complete Slovak political unity will be difficult, not so much in sentiment as in practical realization."[11]

Pares's response was necessarily careful. Nonetheless, he made it quite clear that one could not accept reports like the one from Viest at face value. However, the Foreign Office was not interested in the accuracy of information; rather it needed to know what role the Czechs and the Slovaks could play in the war against Germany. F. K. Roberts of the Central Department commented: "Our information from both sources is insufficient to form any definite judgment, but it is at least clear that we cannot count upon Slovak support to the same degree as upon Czech support. The reason for this seems to be that the Germans have behaved with sufficient tact not to disgust the Slovaks with their new-won independence from Prague and they have kept Slovakia busy if not economically unprosperous."[12] By June 1940 the Foreign Office accepted Benes's claim that he spoke for both the Czechs and Slovaks, and that he could organize in due course both peoples into helping the Allied war effort. Slovakia as such ceased to be an object of British as well as international interest.

Benes had in fact perceived as soon as war broke out that political and military exigencies would encourage Britain and France to recognize a Czechoslovak government-in-exile. But as his personal secretary and legal advisor writes: "Benes's endeavors to obtain British and French recognition of a Czechoslovak government-in-exile were strongly rebuffed."[13] In December 1939, the British and the French granted recognition to a Czechoslovak National Committee whose main task was to reconstitute a Czechoslovak Army. On the French side, there was also strong opposition to Benes's participation in a Czechoslovak movement. French Premier Edouard Daladier wanted Benes to retire to private life. Only after Daladier and British Prime Minister Chamberlain resigned in March and May 1940 respectively could Benes proceed with his plan for the recognition of a Czechoslovak government-in-exile. The recognition accorded on 21 July 1940 was however "marred by three serious flaws"[14]: The British recognized a *provisional* government-in-exile; the recognition did not imply recognition of or support for future boundaries in Central Europe; there was no acceptance of Benes's thesis of the legal continuity of the 1920 Czechoslovak Republic. It took political intervention on the part of Prime Minister Winston Churchill for full recognition to be granted. Nevertheless, as the note of 18 July 1941 indicates, the last two points—future boundaries and the question of legal continuity—were not accepted.

On the French side, with the fall of France on 23 June 1940, the question of recognition "became moot."[15] Nevertheless, Benes entered into negotiations

with General Charles de Gaulle's French National Committee. In an exchange of letters dated 29 September 1942, the French repudiated the Munich Agreement and all the territorial changes that had taken place since September 1938. The British refused to repudiate Munich. During meetings in the first half of 1942 they refused both to recognize unconditionally Czechoslovakia's pre-Munich boundaries and to declare the Munich Agreement invalid *ab initio*.

Benes's diplomatic maneuverings were important for the Slovaks in two respects. The recognition of his government-in-exile gave an indication of the kind of postwar arrangements that awaited Slovakia once the war was over, namely that the Slovak Republic was condemned to disappear despite the fact that it was diplomatically recognized by twenty-eight states. Moreover, this loss of international recognition gave encouragement as well as support to those intent on creating a resistance movement in Slovakia, which is discussed in the next chapter. Second, it rendered the task of governing Slovakia more difficult for Tiso and the moderates around him by giving indirect support to those who favored the complete alignment of Slovakia's political life on Germany's. This latter group could count on Berlin's support. The experiment in statehood and not just political life thus became dominated, and in the end also marred, by ideological considerations.

SLOVAK POLITICAL LIFE

As had happened two decades earlier, the Slovaks found themselves catapulted into a new state when independence was declared. However, this time they had behind them two decades of democratic and parliamentary experience in the Czechoslovak Republic. They also had the memory and a mild taste of uncompromising politics. The battle for the autonomy of Slovakia had not taken place without the occasional excessive use of power by the Czechoslovak government. Some members of the Slovak People's Party who had been the victims of some of the excessive measures were ready to emulate such excesses when their party achieved power. The first indication came when the Slovak Provincial Assembly passed a government decree on 23 December 1938 that transferred some 9,000 clerks and employees of Czech nationality out of Slovakia. Other measures followed. However, the most important influence on Slovak political life was the international environment: Politics in Central Europe were dominated by radical and undemocratic measures. Moreover, the international situation after independence changed so rapidly that the Slovak Republic did not get an opportunity to achieve democratic legitimacy by calling elections to the Slovak Parliament. Political life was thus determined by the sudden and extraordinary

conditions that brought about independence and Slovakia's inclusion in the German sphere of interest.

As the reports from the two consuls in Slovakia indicate, the elite in power made haste to organize the new state, ensure its stability, and above all anchor its international security. The outbreak of war in September 1939 modified the tenor of Slovak political life. The *Schutzvertrag* had left no doubt that Slovakia would be on the German side during hostilities. The Third Reich did not tolerate any suggestion of an independent Slovak foreign policy. Slovak forces participated in the war on Poland mainly to recover the twenty-five villages in Spis and Orava counties that Slovakia had lost in 1918 as well as those given away in the Vienna Award of 1938. In April 1940, Slovakia joined the Axis Powers, and when Germany attacked the Soviet Union in June 1941, two Slovak divisions of 20,000 men went on to fight in Ukraine and the Caucasus.

In domestic politics, the war gave the Tuka group the opportunity to launch an offensive against the moderates in the Slovak People's Party who, since independence, had held most of the important positions in the state and the party. In January 1940, the Tuka group attempted to dislodge Durcansky from his two portfolios of foreign affairs and interior. The attempt failed. What this incident did do, however, was to clarify the differences between those who wanted Slovak politics to align entirely with Germany and those for whom independence meant an opportunity to pursue objectives and goals in line with Slovak needs and national traditions.

When Berlin became aware of Durcansky's attempts to pursue a policy of neutrality, Tiso was summoned to Salzburg on 28 July 1940. Hitler told Tiso that Foreign Minister Durcansky and his supporters had to be replaced by people more acceptable to him. Tuka, in addition to being prime minister, became foreign minister and Mach, the head of the Information Office, moved to the Ministry of the Interior. The secretary general of the Slovak People's Party, Jozef Kirschbaum, was forced to resign his post. Germany became more involved in Slovak political life as it entered a new phase.

The consequences of the Salzburg meeting were twofold: First, it clarified the options available to Slovak politicians. Those who had seen independence as an opportunity to foster national development realized that their efforts had to be directed partly if not primarily at restraining those who were willing to do Germany's bidding unconditionally. This latter group, while motivated to some degree by ideological affinity, argued above all that Slovakia's size and geopolitical position obliged it to align itself closely with Germany in order to survive. Thus for the Tuka group, the politics of survival dictated alignment; for Tiso and the moderates, the politics of survival required the prevention of

such an alignment, so as not to lose the opportunity for the Slovaks to benefit from independence.

The second consequence of the meeting was to bring the struggle for power between the two groups to a head. Emboldened by Hitler's intervention on his behalf, Tuka proceeded to challenge Tiso for control of the country. Tiso had the support of the Slovak People's Party, even after Kirschbaum's departure; Tuka could rely on the Hlinka Guard, the party's paramilitary wing. But Tuka also had the backing of the German minister in Bratislava, Manfred von Killinger, and together they planned a coup d'état to overthrow Tiso. Once again Berlin intervened, but this time to foil the attempt. Von Killinger was recalled in January 1941. While Tiso's position was secure and he would not be challenged again, he achieved this goal at some costs. One was a change in the style of Slovak political life; some historians take it as proof of Slovakia's total subservience to Germany. The Führer principle was adopted; Tiso became *Vodca* (Leader) when Slovak People's Party Statutes were amended in October 1942. This title did not alter his personal style—"he continued to do as he pleased"[16]—but it did deflect criticism from the Tuka group, who henceforth could not attack him for not being sufficiently pro-German. This clever political move enhanced Tiso's freedom to pursue his policy of restraint but also tainted him with the fascist ideology that he was trying to keep out of Slovakia. Another decision had tragic consequences for thousands of Slovak citizens and cast a dark shadow on his stewardship of the Slovak Republic.

THE JEWISH TRAGEDY

One of the saddest episodes in the history of the Slovak Republic was the Slovak participation in the German efforts to find a solution to what the Third Reich considered to be the Jewish problem in Central Europe. In terms of the political struggle between the two groups, the Tuka faction endorsed such efforts and saw they were carried out in Slovakia. Tiso was personally opposed to such measures but as head of state his position was complex, reflecting political pressures, and he used his office to oppose them only when it was clear what the consequences of the German Final Solution were.

The Slovak government began considering limiting the role of the Jewish community in Slovakia as early as January 1939. A commission was created on 23 January composed of leading members of the Slovak People's Party, among them Sidor and Durcansky, to look at the Jewish question in Slovakia. At its only meeting, on 5 March 1939, it examined a proposal for the definition of a "Jew" and limitations on Jewish participation in Slovak life. Ladislav Lipscher

writes that it was the only proposal "which was not influenced by the ideology of National Socialism."[17] No action was taken on it. After independence, on 30 March, a chain of events occurred that testifies both to German pressure and to Slovak willingness to comply. On that date, the Slovak government enacted the first decree that targeted Slovakia's Jewish population; it forbade Jews from involvement in the manufacture of Christian symbols of faith. As the pressure to take action continued to mount, the government passed a decree on 18 April that curtailed Jewish participation in Slovak life. In addition to limiting the number of Jews in the liberal professions, it also proceeded to define who a Jew was. While other decrees dealt with economic relations that also directly affected Slovakia's Jews, the April decree ended the first phase of anti-Jewish measures.

The Constitution of the Slovak Republic, in its preamble and article 81, guaranteed the protection of life, freedom, and possessions to all its citizens, regardless of origin, nationality, religion, or occupation. However, according to a Slovak historian, "the Slovak constitution denied constitutional protection to the Jews" primarily because it did not secure it specifically as had the peace treaties after the Great War.[18] Subsequent legislation indicated that this comment is not inaccurate. A law on land reform, dated 22 February 1940, made it virtually impossible for a Jew to own agricultural land. On 24 April, another law was passed that initiated the "arianization" of Jewish firms, that is to say the transfer of 51 percent ownership to non-Jewish owners. Decrees passed in October and November of the same year further specified the terms of arianization, giving the government the necessary powers to enforce it.

For the next ten months, while there was no additional major legislation against the Jews, their property was progressively taken from them. It is estimated that 44,371 hectares of agricultural land and 2,100 enterprises mostly in light, luxury, and consumer goods industries changed ownership while another 10,000 enterprises were simply shut down. There were fewer changes in heavy industry because the holdings of Jewish investors were usually found in foreign banks, in particular in Budapest. Shops, homes, and offices also changed owners. These measures intensified when the Codex Judaicus was passed on 9 September 1941. Based on Germany's Nuremberg Laws, it worsened the already difficult situation of Slovak Jews and made them "a clearly segregated group from the rest of the population."[19] Moreover, Berlin sent two advisors to Bratislava at this time: Dieter Wisliczeny and E. Gebert.

The Tuka faction in the government was not satisfied with such measures and throughout 1941 showed its willingness to cooperate with the German advisors on additional steps against Slovak Jews. In July of that year, two Slovak officials accompanied a German delegation to occupied Poland (in an area in Upper Silesia) to look at labor camps and ghettos. As Ivan Kamenec writes: "The

delegation, naturally, did not see much, nevertheless the impressions received by the Slovak members were upsetting."[20] The warnings of one Slovak official about the unsatisfactory conditions in the camps went unheeded, especially as pressure from the Germans began to mount. The Germans had started to look at more radical ways of dealing with Europe's Jews. When Tiso visited Hitler at his headquarters on 23 October 1941, Tuka and Mach were told by German officials of their plans to concentrate Europe's Jews on occupied Polish territory and invited Slovakia to participate in this policy. Upon his return to Bratislava, Tuka negotiated with the Germans for the deportation of 20,000 Slovak Jews. He also agreed that the Slovak government would pay Germany 500 Reichmarks for each deported person to cover "settlement costs." But the Slovak government was not told of the decision German officials took in Wannsee on 20 January 1942 to organize the extermination of Europe's Jews, a policy that became known as the Final Solution. The Slovak public was equally unaware of it.

From December 1941 until the first deportation began on 25 March 1942, Tuka first sought to keep the preparations secret and then to obtain legislative consent for the deportations. The Slovak Parliament refused to discuss the matter. When Mach proposed a government bill on an emigration law concerning Slovak Jews on 25 March, the presidium of Parliament did not allow for debate to take place. As Kamenec writes: "The government, however, did not take it [the refusal] into consideration and began the deportations in accordance with §22 of the Jewish codex concerning the work duty of the Jews."[21] The evacuation of what was a total of 57,628 men, women, and children, which represented "two-thirds of the Jewish population in Slovakia"[22] began that same day and continued until 20 October. The evacuation was carried out by the Hlinka Guard and the *Freiwillige Schutzstaffel* of the German community in Slovakia.

The deportations did not take place without provoking serious opposition in Slovakia. In the first place, the Jews themselves began organizing when the rumors of deportations started to spread, creating within the Jewish Central Office a "Shadow Government" (also known as Working Group) "to start a wide-ranging movement to prevent deportations."[23] Shortly after the deportations began, there were reactions from all levels of the population, from Catholic and Lutheran clergy, from the Vatican, and from deputies and members of the Council of State. Slovakia's bishops sent many memoranda to Tiso and the government and on 12 April 1942 issued a pastoral letter protesting the measures that were being applied to Slovakia's Jewish population. In addition to public expressions of revulsion at the deportations, there were also expressions of anger at the breaking up of families since the first selected were men between the ages sixteen and thirty-five. However, the Slovak government did not back

down and sought assurances from the Germans that families would remain together. On 10 April, Reinhard Heydrich, head of the Reich Security Office, assured Tuka in Bratislava that the Jews would be treated humanely. The deportations continued. But opposition also continued to mount. On 15 May, Parliament passed legislation to limit the application of the codex, and specifically confirmed the right of the president to grant exceptions to individuals and to extend them to family members. The result was a temporary halt to the deportations during June. In a dispatch to Berlin, German envoy Hans E. Ludin noted: "The process of evacuation of Jews from Slovakia is presently at a standstill. Due to the influence of the Church and the corruption of individual officials, approximately 35,000 Jews were given special identification papers. On these grounds they are not required to be evacuated."[24] Before long, German officials applied further pressure and additional deportations took place until October, when they were halted completely. In the summer of 1943 Tuka secretly attempted to resume the deportations but failed when his plan was uncovered by a member of parliament.

Tiso's role in this tragic episode was complex and interpretations of his involvement have varied considerably and even been diametrically opposed. When the Slovak Parliament passed the Codex Judaicus in September 1941, Tiso let it be known that he wanted to resign because he "did not approve of the legality of the Jewish Code."[25] He was persuaded to stay on as a result of pressure from many quarters,[26] in particular from Bishop Kmetko, Tiso's religious superior. Three Jewish representatives had paid Kmetko a visit to ask him to convince Tiso to remain in his post.[27] On the other hand, just before the deportations began, Tiso received two memoranda, one on behalf of Slovakia's Jewish communities, the other on behalf of Slovakia's rabbis, warning that the deportation of Jews to Poland would mean their extermination. He never sent a reply and the memoranda were filed away. Tiso did speak in public about what was happening to the Jews, and, according to Kamenec, "he publicly approved the deportations, his reasons being the nation's highest interests."[28] His speech in Holic on 16 August 1942 in which he said that Slovak life was threatened by the Jews is cited as an example of his policy. Yet, at the time he made this speech, the frequency of the deportations was diminishing while the pressure from the Germans was mounting.[29] Similarly, he took no action in December 1943 after promising Heinrich Himmler's special envoy, Edmund Veesenmayer, that the deportations would resume. In fact, when Tiso learned that the Slovak Jews sent to Poland were being murdered, he allowed the extensive use of presidential exceptions to save as many as he could. According to Milan S. Durica: "Although accurate figures are not available, it would seem that anywhere from 30,000 to 40,000 Slovak Jews were saved through the

application of Presidential exceptions."[30] However, when the 1944 uprising against the Slovak Republic broke out (see Chapter 10 for details), Tiso was unable to prevent the resumption of the deportations. Jews were among the first victims of the end of Slovak independence.

These deportations represent an episode in the life of the Slovak Republic which provoked tragedy, heroism, and also courage. Two-thirds of Slovakia's Jews were deported, and most perished in the German death camps in Poland. Personal heroism helped save many individual Jews and their families. In the face of pressures from the Germans and the Tuka group, Tiso's political courage allowed him, for a time at least, to spare many Jews through official action and bring about an end to the deportations until the outbreak of the 1944 uprising.[31] The evidence certainly suggests that the history of the deportations in Slovakia "is the story of the first outright failure of the 'Final Solution' and a failure at a time when there was no glimmer of hope for Jewry in Axis-controlled Europe."[32] From October 1942, when the last transfer took place, to August 1944, Slovakia, as a result of the activities of the Jewish Central Office in Bratislava, became a haven also for other Central European Jews, according to the findings of the International Committee of the Red Cross after the war. Slovakia was a safe haven because there was stability in the country, and the Slovaks were using every opportunity to improve their social, economic and cultural situation even while the tragic episode of the deportations was taking place and a war was raging around them.

SOCIAL, ECONOMIC, AND CULTURAL POLICIES

Slovak historians write that "the political ideal of Dr. Jozef Tiso and the majority of Populist politicians was a conservative, paternalistic and authoritarian system with a special emphasis on 'the protection of the poor.'"[33] The regime was, in fact, successful in taking the Slovak people far down the road of modernization, and, until the uprising of 1944, it looked after its non-Jewish citizens through planned economic and social development. The major achievements of the Slovak Republic were in the economic and sociocultural fields despite the stringent diplomatic and military conditions imposed on the government. As Gustav Husak, a Communist, wrote in 1944, distinguishing between regime and state: "If this state had another content and were led by another regime, not to say anything about a change of ally, there would be nothing to say against it from a Slovak point of view."[34]

Although there were difficult periods during which there was a shortage of foodstuffs, in particular in 1940 and 1941, Slovakia experienced general

economic growth, with improvement in most sectors at a time when the rest of Europe was at war. Husak wrote that there had been a definite advancement over the situation that had existed in Czechoslovakia. He added that in the first seventeen months of the Slovak Republic, "it also became evident that Slovakia could take care of itself economically, there was neither economic nor monetary chaos, the standard of living did not go down, quite the contrary, a good number of people, especially the intelligentsia, got ahead. . . . "[35] The following eyewitness account cited in a report in the Foreign Office files dated August 1943 also confirms the progress made: "A traveller who has recently returned from Slovakia was amazed to find how normal things were, not only in Bratislava, but also in other towns. There was no blackout and practically no restrictions. Food and clothing were plentiful and prices reasonable. There was little war talk. Life went on as usual everywhere, but there was a shortage of servants and indeed a general shortage of labour."[36]

Much of the Slovak economy was dominated by Germany as a result of the secret clause in the Treaty of Protection, which called for an increase of Slovakia's industrial and agriculture output. Other treaties followed that spelled out in detail economic arrangements between Slovakia and Germany, and the Reich also sent advisors to help in various ministries. In 1938, the share of German and Austrian capital totaled only 5 percent in Slovakia; by 1944, it had grown to 64 percent. This phenomenal growth is due to the fact that Germany took over the shares of Czech and foreign capital in Slovakia as the Germans occupied European financial centers. At the same time Slovak capital grew from 2 percent in 1938 to 6 percent in 1944, and the number of companies in which Slovaks held a controlling interest rose from forty to seventy-four. Furthermore, from 1942 on, Slovak banks were successful in obtaining additional shares, especially in industry, that enabled them to transfer controlling interest from Germany to Slovakia. This capital inflow allowed for the development of Slovak industry. Some 4,855 million Slovak crowns (Ks) were invested in five years, allowing for the creation of 250 new enterprises and the enlargement of 80 existing ones. The railways benefited from 95 kilometers of new tracks, while 184 kilometers were rebuilt or repaired. Road paving, repair, and reconstruction were done on 1,100 kilometers, with 282 kilometers of new roads laid; telephone links, under- and above ground, were greatly improved, adding 291 communities to the existing network, while 470 villages were electrified. The 12,000 kilowatts of hydroelectric power built between 1918 and 1939 was increased to 90,000 kilowatts between 1939 and 1945.

British Foreign Office files also give some statistics worthy of note. In 1942, the investment in chemical, textile, mining, metallurgy, and electrical industries represented close to half of that year's investment. The Slovak National Bank net

profit in 1941 was 21.86 million Ks., rising to 30.83 million Ks. in 1942.[37] Trade statistics also show that Slovakia was by no means restricting the variety of goods and services available; in January–February 1942, Slovakia exported 400 million Ks. worth of goods while it imported 575 million Ks. For the same period in 1943, exports increased to 570 million Ks., and imports rose to 730 million Ks. A Slovak-Italian agreement valued at 800 million Ks., with 60 million Ks. in Slovakia's favor, was signed in 1943.[38] Very few agricultural statistics are available; apparently this sector did not encounter too many problems, even though the promised land reform of 1939 was not carried out. British reports note good fruit crops in 1942 and 1943, and 1943 was also reported as a good vintage year for Slovak wines.

The social groups that benefited most from the economic expansion and growth in Slovakia were the middle and upper-middle classes. The lot of workers also seems to have been satisfactory, except perhaps early on when worker discontent culminated in a strike fomented by Communists in Handlova in October 1940. The Slovak Parliament passed a number of bills to improve the social conditions of the working class, and salaries and wages showed a steady increase, while unemployment virtually disappeared.

After Slovakia's autonomy and later independence, positions in the state as well as tertiary sectors became available that previously had been occupied primarily by Czechs. Education was another area that showed considerable activity and enabled educated Slovaks to move ahead. Comenius University in Bratislava changed its name to Slovak University and added two new faculties. A Slovak Technical Institute was created in July 1939, replacing the one created in Kosice in 1937 (but by then under Magyar control), and a Slovak School of Commerce also was founded. By 1943, there were more than twice as many students enrolled in Slovak institutions of higher learning than there had been in 1938. An educational reform also was announced in July 1939, and church-controlled schools were reestablished. The founding of the Slovak Academy of Arts and Sciences and the modernization of the publication facilities of the Matica slovenska gave additional impetus to scientific and literary work. For the period 1939 to 1944, literary output, for example, totaled 709 works: 437 prose, 169 poetry, and 103 plays. Access to such works was made possible by a chain of bookstores operated by Matica slovenska across the country. Among the writers who achieved prominence at this time were Jozef Ciger Hronsky and Rudolf Dilong as did Janko Jesensky, Boleslav Lukac, and Margita Figuli, who were not supporters of the regime. In music, Alexander Moyzes, Eugen Suchon, Jan Cikker, and Gejza Dusik were the most prolific composers.

In five of the six years of the Slovak Republic's existence, while a European war was raging around them, the Slovaks dispelled any doubts about their ability

to handle their own affairs. There is no better testimony to this fact than Husak's report, where among other things he writes:

> In general one can say that on the basis of the experience of six years, Slovakia is able to exist as an independent unit economically and financially, can hold out on its own, has even today the necessary forces (including technical ones) and conditions of production for international competition. . . . The Slovaks are an independent nation, they have the same rights and expectations as any other nation. Today Slovak is the exclusive language of administration, all the formal attributes of a nation are there, and for this reason anyone who would like to return to the old conception of a united Czechoslovak nation will meet with opposition. . . . In these last six years, the development of a national consciousness and the completion of this development on the formal level are the most remarkable achievements that will not disappear with the fall of the regime. . . . It is a fact that this state is independent and has as much independence as a small state can have especially in time of war.[39]

Despite these achievements, those who had opposed the breakup of Czecho-Slovakia in 1939 were not persuaded to accept the existence of the Slovak Republic. In any event, the outbreak of war had sealed the new state's fate; the Slovaks would not enjoy their independence at the end of hostilities. In preparation for this outcome, which some foresaw as soon as the war began, opposition groups developed that began to prepare the ground for Slovakia's reincorporation into Czechoslovakia after the war.

OPPOSITION TO THE SLOVAK REPUBLIC

The appearance of a group opposing the Slovak Republic came to the attention of British consul Pares almost immediately after independence. In his July report on the Constitution of Slovakia, where he noted the unique position of the Slovak People's Party in the political system, he pointed out that the Catholic origin of this party probably meant the virtual exclusion of Slovak Lutherans within it, as well as their relegation to the background of public affairs. In fact, this did not happen. A number of Lutherans occupied key positions in the state, the economic influence of the Lutheran community in Slovakia did not diminish but in fact increased, and their leaders publicly proclaimed their adherence and loyalty to the Slovak Republic. Nevertheless, the Slovak Lutheran community did form an opposition group, whether for

sectarian or political reasons, especially after Benes began to regroup his political partisans in London. As Pares noted in his last dispatch on Slovakia, the Lutherans formed an opposition link at home and abroad and lent Benes support for his goal of re-creating the Czechoslovak Republic. Together with some Catholics, they formed the Democratic Party. By 1943, they were actively involved in seeking to restore Czechoslovak authority in Slovakia and helped a second opposition group, the Communist Party of Slovakia (CPS), formed in May 1939, to prepare an armed uprising, which is examined in Chapter 10.

The role of the Communists in Slovakia mirrored well the turgidity of their movement until the German attack on the Soviet Union in June of 1941. Soviet diplomatic recognition of Slovakia had invalidated the slogans of national self-determination that the Slovak Communists propagated in 1939, and the leadership of the CPCS, by then resident in Moscow, ordered that the slogan of a "Slovak Soviet Republic," which had begun to appear in 1940, be abandoned. The Communist Party had been declared illegal in Slovakia in 1938, so its activities as well as the creation and organization of the CPS were clandestine. The security services of the Slovak Republic occasionally rounded up Communists, but not only were they quickly released from prison, they also were allowed to resume their positions in economic and state institutions. Not until late 1943 and 1944 did Communist activity become a major factor in Slovak political life, in part because the Communists were in touch with Soviet partisan units operating out of Kiev and in part because they had worked out a new political program for Slovakia in the future of Czechoslovak Republic. This program determined the postwar future of the Slovaks.

The German defeat at Stalingrad in February 1943 marked the turning point of the war. In Slovakia, many began to think about the postwar period and what lay ahead for the nation as it faced reincorporation in Czechoslovakia. To counter Benes's determination to return to the republic of 1920, the two opposition groups joined forces and in December 1943 hammered out a political program that became known as the Christmas Agreement. Resolving to take power at the first opportunity, they created the Slovak National Council (SNC), a legislative organ, and the Board of Commissioners, an executive one, as the two institutions that would wield power until Slovakia's position in the renewed Czechoslovak Republic was determined. They began organizing in earnest in 1944.

10

The Uprising of 1944

A MILITARY ACTION

For the better part of five years, the people of Slovakia were able under Tiso's presidency to avoid the war that was raging in Europe. The country's geopolitical position and the Treaty of Protection with Germany forced Slovakia to accord free passage to the German armed forces, but by the same token spared it the consequences of German military operations. Yet Slovakia was also at war; as a member of the Axis powers, its troops fought in the Soviet Union. Some also assert that Slovakia was at war with Britain and the United States; this assertion is based on a press report from Germany alleging such a declaration by Tuka in December 1941. No text of this declaration was quoted and none was ever found in State Department archives.[1] Since Germans challenged the European order by the force of arms, the Western Allies made the unconditional surrender of Germany their objective when they met in January 1943 at Casablanca. Therefore only the victorious powers would have a say in deciding the future of Germany and its allies. The diplomatic recognition of the Czechoslovak government-in-exile in 1941 by Britain, the Soviet Union and the United States had already signaled that the Slovak Republic would disappear at the end of hostilities. Thus the Slovaks found themselves once more struggling for survival, looking for a way to assure their own future.

The Allied armed forces, in particular British and Soviet ones, gave individual Slovaks the opportunity to fight on the Allied side and help defeat Germany and its allies. The situation in Slovakia for anti-German Slovaks was different. Even if there was, in the words of Lubomir Liptak, a certain

liberalism[2]—no death penalty was carried out and Tiso did not need a personal bodyguard—the press was censored and the presence of the security forces and the Hlinka Guard made opposition activity, in particular the military kind, hazardous. Yet, if the Slovaks were to be found among the victors, they had to earn their place through some anti-German military action. The extent to which they would have a say in determining their future depended on its nature and scope. The opposition groups that had begun to form understood this well and slowly started to take the necessary measures to see that military activity eventually occurred in Slovakia.

The two main opposition groups were distinguished in Slovakia not only by ideological differences, but also by dissimilar organizational principles. The first group, the Democratic Party, was led by Jozef Lettrich and Jan Ursiny, owed its allegiance to the Czechoslovak government-in-exile, and represented a variety of political interests. The second group was an all-Slovak Communist organization, the CPS; it was in constant touch with the leadership of the CPCS in Moscow and was led by Karol Smidke and Gustav Husak, a man who would experience in his career torture and prison as well as the highest positions in the CPS, the CPCS, and the Czechoslovak Republic. Husak was born on 10 January 1913 in Dubravka, on the outskirts of Bratislava. He studied law at Comenius University where he also was active in left-wing student organizations. After graduation, he practiced law until 1944, when he devoted himself entirely to politics. He had joined the Communist Party in 1933 and during the war he quickly assumed a position of leadership, particularly in the resistance movement. By signing the Christmas Agreement in December 1943, both groups made preparations for an armed uprising possible, although their different allegiances had a serious bearing on the success of the action.

The launching of an armed uprising was a problematic affair. It required more than just arms and men; it demanded above all the complicity from many who worked for the Slovak Republic. However, as Slovak historians write: "For the first time in [Slovak] history, the newly acquired independent statehood fascinated many, and potential opponents of the regime were often employed in the building of new economic and cultural institutions, schools, offices and their own careers."[3] Still, others, such as Imrich Karvas, governor of the Slovak National Bank, kept their positions while at the same time becoming involved in planning the military action. Likewise, many officers in the Slovak armed forces who had begun their careers in the Czechoslovak ones, either crossed to the Allied side or became involved in the military plans of the opposition groups, perhaps with an eye on the future. These people worked underground; used couriers to communicate with each other, with the Czechoslovak government-in-exile, and with the leadership of the CPCS in Moscow; had contacts with

resistance groups in the Protectorate of Bohemia-Moravia, Hungary, and elsewhere; were organized in groups, taking names such as Demec, Obrana naroda (Defense of the Nation), and the most important, Flora. Finally, the opposition groups benefited from desertions from the Slovak armed forces, not an unusual occurrence among the troops fighting in the Soviet Union after the battle of Stalingrad.

The preparations were monitored by the Czechoslovak government-in-exile. The objective, in addition to overthrowing the government of the Slovak Republic, was to make Slovakia accessible for strategic actions in the Danubian plain by using two Slovak divisions to open the front while other ones in Central Slovakia engaged German forces. Operational headquarters were in Banska Bystrica under the leadership of Lieutenant Colonel Jan Golian, who at that time was chief of staff of the Slovak land forces there. Finally, it was essential to coordinate these activities with the Soviet High Command. On 4 August 1944, Smidke flew to Moscow with the plans for a military action, yet the hoped-for coordination did not take place. The action was launched before all preparations were finalized. The result was an event whose meaning is equivocal in Slovak history.

A QUESTION OF THE FUTURE

The uprising that broke out in Slovakia in 1944 spelled the end of the Slovak Republic. Yet it became the object of many conflicting interpretations, not only by those who condemn it and those who justify it, but also by those who led it. There is no doubt that from 1941 on, when the Allies recognized the Czechoslovak government-in-exile, the future of the Slovak nation was at best uncertain. The leadership of the Slovak Republic knew that the alliance with Germany had to be maintained if Slovak national life was to develop further and Slovakia spared involvement in the war. This decision also represented a gamble on the foreign front: If the republic could remain cohesive and united, there was a chance that the future of the Slovak people might avoid falling into the hands of Benes and his Czechoslovak government-in-exile in London. In 1943, for example, a group of Slovak politicians met in Ruzomberok. There they reaffirmed not only their belief that the Slovaks must remain independent, but that this message must be relayed to the American Slovaks, who, it was hoped, might play a role similar to the one Czech and Slovak emigres had played during the Great War in the creation of Czecho-Slovakia.

While the future of the Slovak nation lay primarily in the hands of the Allies, it also lay in the activities of individual Slovaks when they joined the

opposition groups. Since these groups were dedicated to the destruction of the Slovak Republic and they enjoyed Allied support, their activities had a direct bearing on the future of the Slovak people. In linking up with these groups, the Slovaks in opposition to Bratislava were mortgaging the life of the nation; they were asking their countrymen to turn the clock back to 1920 and accept the Czechoslovak option once more, an option that meant a state organized strictly on Czech terms. The London broadcasts to Slovakia during the war indicated that more than two decades after the creation of Czecho-Slovakia, the situation had remained unchanged. In his second broadcast to the Slovaks during the war, on 13 March 1943, Benes clearly stated that "even after what happened in the years 1938 and 1939, the Czechoslovak Republic was not destroyed, it continued to live and still lives legally, politically and internationally."[4] However incorrect this statement may be, it relayed the unequivocal message to the Slovaks that they would be brought back into the same state in which they had been denied both national recognition and political autonomy.

Had Benes taken into account the evolution of the Slovak nation, much of the tragedy that befell the Slovak people from 1944 on might have been avoided. Those Slovaks who decided to collaborate with Benes knew that they were accomplices in the imposition of a state structure and system that was fundamentally inimical to the survival of the Slovaks as a nation. In addition, Benes made no concessions during the war, for example, on the question of the existence of a Slovak nation versus a Czechoslovak one, so that the Czechoslovak option that he represented and that the Slovaks were asked to accept contained more than just the choice of a political future at the end of the hostilities. It was loaded with elements dangerous to the material as well as the national well-being of the Slovak people. Was the game worth the candle? In other words, would a military action against the Slovak Republic bring about a better future in Czechoslovakia than the one they could have in their own state?

Some Slovaks thought so; it is important to note, however, that the only Slovak political personality in the First Republic to collaborate with Benes in London was Juraj Slavik who had been a deputy in the Czechoslovak Parliament and a diplomat. In Slovakia, Benes was able to count on Srobar. The two most eminent Slovaks abroad, Hodza, former prime minister of Czechoslovakia, and Osusky, former Czechoslovak Ambassador to France, did not accept Benes's Czechoslovak option, broke with him, and left for the United States, where Hodza died in 1944. Benes was therefore able to impose his own views upon his Slovak coterie. The Slovak people soon became acquainted with them from the broadcasts he and his Slovak associates made during the war to Slovakia.

The London broadcasts give us a general outline of the ideas, arguments, messages, exhortations, warnings, and threats that were transmitted to the

Slovak people in an effort to bring them back into Benes's Czechoslovak Republic. These broadcasts were freely and widely listened to. In addition, Bratislava radio regularly broadcast commentaries and counterarguments by Konstantin Culen. The Slovaks in Slovakia thus had the opportunity to ponder and discuss their future. What London was saying and promising must have often puzzled them to say the least. Particularly when Benes was speaking, listeners must have been struck by his vocabulary and imagery when referring to the Bratislava leaders. In his Christmas broadcast in 1942, he exclaimed: "You are ruled by a few criminals who, gambling, have put their money on a false card. They see now that they have lost and they will be obliged to make retribution. They are therefore capable of any crime which they think might save them at the last moment."[5] In March 1943, he referred to the declaration of independence as an "infamous act of treason [perpetrated] on the common Czechoslovak homeland and on the Czechs" and to the independence anniversary as a day commemorating the "crime of Jozef Tiso and his helpers."[6] In February 1944, he affirmed that the Slovak people had been "betrayed by numbers of unworthy and traitorous politicians, Magyarophile renegades and uneducated Fascists, who will certainly have to suffer fully for their crimes."[7] Benes returned to the theme of punishment again in his broadcast of 27 October 1944, when he made it clear that there would be a "settling of accounts with all the collaborators."[8] He discussed this theme with the foreign officials, and he was determined that more Slovaks than Czechs would be punished after the war.

Among the arguments used in the broadcasts to convince the Slovaks to betray their own state, four had a direct relationship to the survival of the Slovak Republic. The first and, by 1943, the most evident argument was the fact that the Allies would win the war. This meant, as Benes stated in his March 1943 broadcast, that Slovakia, "as a state separated from the Czech lands . . . *will never be recognized by the victorious Allies.*"[9] This affirmation was further strengthened by a second argument, aimed especially at those who felt that the Germans might still help the Slovaks at the end of war: The war would end only with the unconditional surrender of Germany in accordance with the decision taken by U. S. President Franklin D. Roosevelt and British Prime Minister Churchill at the Casablanca Conference. In the light of this inevitable outcome, Benes used a third persuasive argument, extrapolated from the first two, that the Slovak people had been spared the consequences of being in a defeated state because of the "Czechoslovak government, the Czechoslovaks abroad who, thanks to their struggles and their work carried on in your name, defended the rights of pre-Munich Czechoslovakia and renewed the international position of the Czechoslovak Republic and its government and obtained its general

international recognition."[10] His fourth argument referred to rumors of Hungarian intrigues against Slovakia, in which he accused Slovak Prime Minister Tuka of being involved.[11]

Benes also spoke of the renewed republic. He made it clear that it would "automatically come to life as a unit once more on the day when Germany and Hungary collapse. Its *de jure* existence, based on the constitution of 1920, will become *de facto*." But he added that he was willing to allow some decentralization "decided in a free and democratic spirit by our people themselves, and this particularly applies to the Slovak people."[12] He refused to commit himself to anything more. Whatever the future held, the Slovaks were also told that the Germans would destroy Slovakia when the time came for them to retreat to the East. It was an argument used particularly by Vladimir Clementis, a Slovak Communist and former deputy of the Czechoslovak Parliament, who broadcast regularly from London. Clementis often referred to this theme in broadcasts to special groups, such as farmers. He argued that this fate was certain if the Germans found "an uninterrupted transportation network, secure roads, stock of provisions and if they were not threatened with partisan warfare."[13] All of these arguments offered in the London broadcasts, in particular the last one, led to one conclusion, articulated by Benes as well as Clementis. It can best be illustrated by quoting from a broadcast by Jan Becko, one of Benes's Slovak unknowns: "I am calling you, Slovak workers; leave your factories, do not work for Germany, take up arms and fight an open fight against the traitors, the Germans and the Hungarians. It is in such an open battle that you will save the most lives, for in this way you will help to shorten the war."[14] Was it in the interest of the Slovak people to accept these arguments and to follow these instructions?

THE SITUATION IN SLOVAKIA

Husak's 1944 report, referred to in Chapter 9, not only gives a broad summary of the economic and social conditions in the Slovak Republic, but also accurately depicts the political situation of the Slovaks. Usually the line between a regime and a state should not be blurred. In the case of the Slovak Republic, however, this distinction was not always clear. That fact explains to some extent the opposition that some Slovaks felt toward the Slovak Republic. Political life in Slovakia until 1944 was devoid of any major public political battles. Germany ensured that the Bratislava government did not deviate seriously either in ideological or policy matters from general guidelines that Berlin found acceptable. However, in the period following the Soviet victory at Stalingrad in 1943,

the Slovaks became confronted with two realities. The first and the most evident was the success of independent statehood. The regime may not have been palatable to everybody, but it protected the country and provided the conditions for the expression of national aspirations. Moreover, under most difficult circumstances, the Slovaks proved that they were able to govern themselves. On the other hand, there was the prospect of the reincorporation of Slovakia into the Czechoslovak Republic that was to be re-created after the war. The London broadcasts made it clear that there was much in this option that was unacceptable to the nation. As a result the Slovaks faced two options; neither offered assurances as to the final outcome.

The first was to remain true to their state and hope that, by the end of the war, international conditions would have changed enough for the victorious powers to realize that the Slovaks desired independence. This option did not exclude the taking of whatever means were necessary, including changing the regime and the political system, to guarantee that the ultimate message remained clear. It was an option that called for an acute sense of timing, exceptional diplomacy, and above all luck. It presupposed not only faith on the part of the people, but also capable leadership at the top. The second option, for which many in the Lutheran community had opted already in 1939, was the return to the Czechoslovak Republic. By 1943, however, it was clear to the people favoring this option that Slovakia's position in Czechoslovakia would have to be on a different basis from that of the pre-Munich republic. This option also involved good timing, great political skill, and luck. But an additional element also was essential for its success: overt support from the Slovak nation. Leadership in this case was an extremely critical factor, as it was imperative to find a way that made returning to Czechoslovakia not only nationally acceptable, but also genuinely welcome.

Nothing in the program and the actions of opposition groups that favored the second option, especially in 1944, suggests that it was acceptable to the nation, that it was indeed genuinely received, and that it could sweep away independence at a single stroke. During the late spring and summer of 1944, the political and military situation became so confused that, while not necessarily consecrating the second option, it eliminated the first one. Partisan warfare was waged in various parts of Slovakia. The Slovak government did not take adequate measures to protect people. The Slovak leadership was in fact split: One group, including Tuka and Mach, was willing to collaborate with the Germans and sought their help; the other group, with Tiso, expected the Slovak army and security forces to deal with the partisan problem.

As a result of this situation, partisan warfare intensified during the late spring of 1944. The mood, especially in the villages and small towns of Central

and Eastern Slovakia, progressively deteriorated to the point that "where people have helped the partisans, it was far more from fear than sympathy for their cause."[15] But by whatever means support was solicited and for whatever reasons it was given, partisan activity was challenging the government's authority. As it became clear that the Slovak military and police forces were unwilling to deal with the partisans, Tiso felt he had to request German help. This decision precipitated prematurely what has since become known as the "Slovak National Uprising" in Communist historiography. Tiso later said that he was taken by surprise when it broke out.

At the same time as partisan warfare was escalating, some Slovak politicians sought alternatives that would ensure the first option and the continued viability of the Slovak Republic. Documentation exists for only one plan, prepared by the minister of national defense, General Ferdinand Catlos. Several Slovak officials were aware of the plan, although it is not known whether the president was informed of it. Catlos hoped to deliver the plan to Soviet authorities in time to help their advance in the Danubian plain. The plan had two major aspects, military and political. Catlos's military propositions consisted of having the Slovak armed forces clear the passage for Soviet troops through Slovakia on their way to Hungary and Austria. The moment military operations began, the Slovak government would be overthrown, and a military dictatorship would be installed that would at the same time declare war on Hungary in order to gain popular support. In time, political figures would be found, although power would remain in military hands. Contact with Soviet authorities would be maintained through a Permanent Commission, and Slovak Communists would be informed, though not involved, especially at the very beginning when the military took power. Slovak statehood would thus be maintained.

The acceptability and viability of this plan was never tested. Catlos contacted the leadership of the CPS; in return for their taking his plan to Moscow, he put an aircraft at their disposal. The plan became known to Soviet authorities in early August when Smidke left for Moscow. But a copy had already been sent to Czechoslovak officials in London, who in turn had it sent to their military representatives in Slovakia with instructions not to deal with Catlos. The military representatives used it as the basis of their first—the so-called offensive—alternative in their plans for an armed uprising against Germans: The uprising would start when the Soviet forces reached the vicinity of Cracow. The other alternative—the so-called defensive—plan involved continued harassment of German forces in Slovakia through partisan activity. The way was thus clear for the second option, for a return to the Czechoslovak Republic.

THE PREPARATIONS AND OUTCOME OF THE UPRISING

To carry out successfully this option, the opposition groups had to work out a credible Slovak counterweight to Benes's Czechoslovak option. Moreover, they had to make it clear that Slovakia would return to the Czechoslovak Republic on a different basis from the one London was constantly referring to in its broadcasts. There is no evidence to suggest that either of these stipulations was met, even though it is clear that the opposition groups in Slovakia were fully aware that London's Czechoslovak option was basically unacceptable to the Slovak people. As a 1944 report to the Czechoslovak government-in-exile indicates: "The idea of a Czechoslovak nation will find ground with difficulty, even among the former representatives of this idea at home. It would be dangerous to want to put into effect at one stroke through legislation something against which current developments and circumstances have worked."[16] Moreover, there was the problem that Benes and his people were insisting on directing the opposition in Slovakia from London.

This latter problem was also not a simple one to resolve. Benes's claim for control was made in part through his token Slovaks, who said they spoke on behalf of the nation. But as Husak points out: "The Slovaks around Benes are highly unpopular and no one wants to hear anything about Slavik and Becko. [Jan] Lichner and [Viliam] Pauliny, [Jan] Caplovic and other starlets do not mean anything here [in Slovakia]."[17] Whether Benes knew this is only marginally important, for he also knew that he had organizational support in Slovakia in the person of Srobar, who organized a National Committee. Srobar stayed in constant contact with Benes through his special emissary, Captain Jan Kratky. The fact that Srobar accepted Benes's authority may have been enough to convince Benes that it was he and the London government who directed the opposition movement in Slovakia. He therefore adopted an authoritative attitude toward all opposition groups, including the Communists. But as Husak points out, his attitude was creating problems for the entire resistance movement: "The London emigration behaves much too imperiously toward the home movement, it gives assignments and commandments, does not ask for opinions even about such important matters as the nomination of people for 'the liberated territory', sends here immature and often impossible people so that in this way an impression is developing that Benes wants to swindle away, to dictate the Slovak question."[18]

The two resistance groups, while continuing to keep in touch with London, joined in December 1943 when they signed the Christmas Agreement and created the SNC. Its task was not only to lead the resistance movement in Slovakia but above all, "to take over all political, legislative, military, and

administrative powers in Slovakia and exercise them according to the will of the people until freely elected representatives of the people are able to assume all power." What had prompted them to join forces were the rumors that Benes wanted to impose a military dictatorship in Slovakia after the war. As Husak writes: "reports come from London that, for a time, there will have to be a military dictatorship here in order to suppress all traitors, and above all, to screw on correctly the heads of the Slovaks."[19]

Despite their differences, there were frequent contacts between Benes and the resistance movements in Slovakia. The Slovak population became aware of these contacts when Benes boasted in his February 1944 broadcast that "underground organizations in Slovakia have been working with us successfully from the very beginning of 1939." Moreover, he claimed: "We have more than sufficient proof of the real, truly Czechoslovak outlook of the wide masses of the people, workers, peasants and also of the main nucleus of Slovak intellectuals."[20] What Benes did *not* tell the Slovak people, on the other hand, was that a Slovak National Council had been created, that it meant to take power and see to it, as the Christmas Agreement indicates, that "the relation between the Slovak and Czech nations as assured by the Constitution—is to be decided by the freely elected representatives of the Slovak nation."

The Slovak people were asked in the London broadcasts to overthrow their own state in order to return to the pre-Munich Czechoslovak Republic. There is no evidence that the Slovak population could have had evidence of any other plan except that of the government-in-exile. The Christmas Agreement was a well-guarded secret, known only to the Communists and some non-Communist leaders of the resistance movement. And when the agreement was finally made public at the outbreak of the uprising on 1 September, there were no indications from London that the Czechoslovak government was accepting it. In fact, a serious conflict developed between Benes's government and the SNC. Only after the visit of three SNC representatives in London in October 1944 did Benes agree to announce: "There is agreement between us and the Slovaks, who with such determination and valour have manifested their support for the Republic, that the State shall be changed into a widely decentralized Republic governed by the people and rebuilt on a national basis."[21] But by the time he made this declaration, much harm had come the way of the Slovak people for them to take notice.

The political option of the resistance movements was in fact mired in confusion and contradictions. First they had to contend with Benes's Czechoslovak option which was not without serious problems for the Slovaks. As British officials noted: "It seems probable that unless the degree of autonomy given to Slovakia in the future Czechoslovak Republic is considerably greater

than we have evidence that Dr. Benes intends it to be, the Slovaks will unite on their only common ground—the struggle for complete independence."[22] Second, even if the contents of the Christmas Agreement had been publicized before the uprising, it is not certain that the foreign policy option in it was wholly acceptable to the Slovak nation especially as an amendment of the Czechoslovak option. The agreement, while stressing the importance of applying the ideas of democracy, also stated that Czechoslovakia would "lean on the U.S.S.R." to the exclusion of the Western Allies. Many Slovaks recognized this contradiction. Finally, there was no indication as to how Czech-Slovak relations would be handled, except, as the agreement states, on the principle of national equality and by the freely elected representatives of the nation. Since the agreement postulated the return of the Czechoslovak Republic, with the Slovaks a minority nation in that state, many may well have asked what the chances were that the promised equality could be achieved or that the wishes of the representatives of the Slovak nation would be met. Given what the London broadcasts were saying, the aims, tasks, and principles enunciated in the Christmas Agreement look like pious hopes and not a program that the Slovak people could trade for self-government and statehood. Even the federal proposals that Slovak Communists propagated some months later had the same built-in problems. The Christmas Agreement did not guarantee that the Slovaks reentered the Czechoslovak Republic on the basis of national equality or, if they did, that this equality would be implemented and protected. It was an option all the less acceptable as it was tied to an uprising that had tragic consequences for hundreds of thousands of Slovaks.

While the goals of Benes's Czechoslovak government-in-exile in London and the resistance movement in Slovakia were in conflict, both groups recognized the need for some sort of military action that would destroy the moral, political, and judicial authority of the Slovak Republic. Each group had different reasons for such an action; for Benes, it was imperative that he have something to show to the Allies as evidence that the citizens of the republic he represented abroad were contributing to the war effort. Except for the assassination in May 1942 of Reinhard Heydrich, *Reichsprotektor* in Bohemia-Moravia, and the resulting tragedy of Lidice, Benes could produce no action as proof of widespread Czech and Slovak participation in the war. On the other hand, the Slovak resistance movement needed a mass action to justify its claim to the leadership of the Slovak nation and the acceptance of its program to enable it to forestall any decision by Benes that might be prejudicial to it. Whatever their differences, Benes and the resistance movement collaborated in the military preparations in Slovakia that brought the Slovaks fully into the war and the war into Slovakia. In the summer of 1944, conditions became propitious for such actions.

Although the Slovaks knew since July 1941 that the Allies had agreed to restore Czechoslovakia after the war and since early 1943 that the Germans would be vanquished, they had not judged it necessary to take any actions against their own government and their state. It was generally known that there were opposition movements, but it was also clear, as a Foreign Office document of August 1944 testifies, that "the nation is by no means united in opposition against the present administration."[23] There were, however there had also been signs that the situation was changing. By the end of 1943 many units of the Slovak Army had crossed to the Allied (Soviet) side. The defections to the Soviets were not kept secret, and very likely they helped the growth of anti-German feeling that by 1944 was quite open. For example, when Franz Karmasin, the leader of the Slovak Germans, spoke on the fifth anniversary of Slovakia's independence, not only was his speech not welcomed, but many left the Slovak National Theater while he spoke.

In the spring of 1944 the domestic situation began to worsen. Slovakia underwent occasional air bombardments; London broadcasts even announced that one would take place to coincide with the date of the fifth anniversary of Slovakia's independence. On the other hand, a clandestine radio transmitter operating in Slovakia promised that no further bombardments would take place if the Slovaks destroyed all bridges and other useful means of transportation. German reports constantly refer to a growing sense of fear, especially as the successes of the Allies in Italy and on the Western Front became known. The attempt on Hitler's life in July 1944 further influenced this growing sense of uncertainty and apprehension in Slovakia, as did the Romanian change of camp from the Germans to the Allies in August. It was the growth of partisan activity, however, that brought about the outbreak of an uprising. Most of the partisan units had been parachuted from the Soviet Union and had been sent in to harass German forces. The units quickly realized that Germany had hardly any forces in Slovakia, and none in Central and Eastern Slovakia. They then turned against any Germans they could find, all the while recruiting Slovaks to join their ranks. The Bratislava government also played into their hands indirectly, for as one German report states: "The Slovak government does not take these reports tragically as the partisans until now have attacked and murdered exclusively Germans."[24] After the murder of a German military mission in the night of 27/28 August 1944, however, Ludin, the head of the German legation in Bratislava, spoke to Tiso about German help to fight the partisans. Tiso agreed and Catlos went on the air on 29 August to announce that German troops were coming to Slovakia. This was one of the signals to start the uprising. Jozef Styk, a member of the SNC, broadcast the call to arms in Srobar's name in Banska Bystrica on 30 August. Unaware of Styk's broadcast, the leaders of the SNC had not realized that

the uprising had started and only when the news was brought to them later did they rush from Bratislava to Banska Bystrica to coordinate the actions they had been preparing for some time.

The outbreak of the uprising brought to a head the sense of confusion that had reigned over Slovakia during the preceding months. The call to arms was interpreted by many people as a call to defend Slovakia against the Germans. Rumors immediately abounded, the most important of which was that Tiso had been murdered. He went on the air on 30 August, not only to reassure the Slovak people that he was indeed alive, but also to offer a pardon to all those who immediately left the partisans. His speech was followed by that of General Augustin Malar, commander of the two Slovak divisions in Eastern Slovakia that Catlos had earmarked for his plan. Malar had promised to hand them over to the military commander of the resistance movement at the proper moment. But Malar now judged the moment to be inopportune, for he declared: "If we preserve order so that we can act as one organized entity, we shall be respected and maybe things will develop according to our will. If we smash to pieces, if we destroy our dearly bought values, be they moral or material, we shall lose respect and represent nothing at all. . . . Up to now we have been masters of our own home. Are we certain that the same will also be the case in the future?"[25] This speech prevented a vast number of soldiers from joining the uprising, but it did not take the wind out of its sails. Now that the uprising had begun, the resistance movement came out into the open and the SNC proceeded to carry out the tasks it had laid down in the Christmas Agreement.

For the better part of two months, partisan groups and military units fought the Germans in Central Slovakia. The latter were part of the First Czechoslovak Army, numbered some 60,000 men, and were led by Golian, who was replaced by Viest on 7 October. Supplied primarily with light arms, they did not have antitank weapons, armor, or airplanes. The Germans had immediately impounded most of the supplies of the Slovak Army, which were located in Western Slovakia. Likewise, the two divisions that Catlos had promised the Allies were quickly disarmed and confined to barracks. However, a commando unit and two parachute brigades were flown in from the Soviet Union along with tons of equipment and arms. American aircraft also flew supplies into partisan territory, into Sliac airport, from Bari, Italy. In addition to military units, the partisans groups totaled about 18,000 men and included fighters from other countries, especially France. Some under Soviet commanders, mostly NKVD officers, they roamed the Slovak countryside and were merciless in their search for enemies. There was fierce fighting and many towns and villages changed hands a number of times.

The Germans began bringing in reinforcements after a major offensive by Czechoslovak and Soviet units in September. The final German counter-offensive against the uprising took place on 17 October with some 35,000 troops, launched from the south in Hungary. Banska Bystrica, the center of the uprising, fell ten days later; Golian, who had been promoted to general in the Czechoslovak Army, and Viest were captured and later perished in German concentration camps. Whereas the remaining Czechoslovak and Soviet units were disarmed, the partisan groups continued to harass the Germans and also relay intelligence to the Allies until the end of the war. At the beginning of 1945 they numbered 13,500 men in seventeen brigades and twenty-two units.

Thousands of people became involved in the uprising, whether by design or accident, willingly or unwillingly, out of political conviction, anti-German feeling, opportunism, or fear. Based on memoirs of the uprising's leaders, it is clear that individual Slovaks had many reasons for becoming involved in the uprising. And once the uprising broke out, it was also clear that it signaled the existence of another anti-Fascist resistance movement similar to those operating in other parts of Europe. Likewise, those who opposed the uprising had numerous reasons for doing so, not just the maintenance of independence and statehood. As Tido J. Gaspar, a member of the Slovak government, explains in his memoirs:

> It wasn't fear of the future, but fear of a renewed past. A return to the disgusting "Benesiada." We were afraid of it. Benes was threatening us with revenge and promised to renew everything which had previously oppressed us Slovaks. . . . He did not recognize for us any national rights. In fact he did not even recognize us as a nation. We were afraid of that. For this reason we did not see the Uprising as liberation from the path of fascism, but rather as an unenticing overture to a new process of enslavement.[26]

The uprising spelled tragedy not only for untold Slovaks, often killed on mere suspicion, but once again also for Slovak Jews. Three special German units were brought in to seek them out; when they were not executed on the spot, they were rounded up and deported to Poland and Germany. In the period from 30 September 1944 to 31 March 1945, eleven transports carried 11,532 persons. Also many Czechs who lived in Slovakia, especially those who had taken up Slovak citizenship, were among the first singled out by the Germans for specific action, as one report suggests: "A radical solution of the Czech question in Slovakia will have a positive political effect on all Czechs living in Bohemia and Moravia."[27] While the uprising was put down within two months,

both the SNC and Benes benefited from it. The SNC was recognized in due course by the Czechoslovak government-in-exile as speaking for the Slovaks; Benes could now point to pro-Allied activity in "Czechoslovakia." With this uprising the Slovaks were brought back into Czechoslovakia. What still had to be decided was their role and position in the state.

WHAT STATUS FOR SLOVAKIA?

Although the Christmas Agreement had established a common basis for political and military activity, both resistance groups had different agendas for the future. The Democratic Party wanted Slovakia to have autonomy and had a flexible approach to Czech-Slovak relations. The Slovak Communists, on the other hand, opted for a federal solution, and this decision influenced the course of postwar Slovak politics, especially Communist politics. It was taken a few months before the uprising when the plenum of the Fifth illegal Central Committee of the CPS accepted the report Husak had written. Smidke had taken it to Moscow in August 1944 to present to the Soviet and Czech Communist leaders. In addition to describing the situation in the Slovak Republic, Husak indicated that if Czechoslovakia had to be restored, it must be on a federal basis. The leadership of the CPCS neither rejected nor accepted this proposal. On 6 December 1944, Georgi Dimitrov (former secretary-general of the Comintern) told Gottwald, leader of the CPCS, and some Slovak Communists that the only possible solution of the national question in Czechoslovakia was a federation. This opened the way for the Slovak Communist leadership to seek to have its solution implemented.

What Husak and his colleagues achieved was at best a compromise that did not favor their federal plans. One of their major errors was not to have worked out a detailed constitutional project and a solid ideological justification. They harbored the illusion that the declaration of intent embodied in the Christmas Agreement was sufficient to convince not only their Czech colleagues but also the Czech bourgeois politicians around Benes who were opposed to any solution of this sort. They had some success at first with the former; the leadership of the CPCS in Moscow prepared a text in January 1945 that projected a federation, but they quickly abandoned this plan under pressure from the Czech bourgeois parties. From this moment on the struggle was uneven.

Nevertheless, in 1945, the CPS, through the SNC, used all available means to seek to have the federal solution implemented. The first official declaration of the SNC was made on 4 February 1945 in Kosice, which had

been liberated from Hungary in January of that year. On the future arrangement between Czechs and Slovaks, it stated: "In accord with the representatives of the Czech nation, we shall arrange the relations between Czechs and Slovaks in the new Republic on the basis of total equality, in such a way that in Slovakia the Slovaks and in the Czech Lands the Czechs will administer their own affairs, while the central parliament and government will administer only the common affairs of a united and indivisible state."[28] This declaration, known as the Manifesto of the SNC, was the first and clearest expression of federalism. The CPS reiterated this stand at its meeting on 28 February and 1 March in Kosice. The next day, the SNC met and published the "Memorandum" of 2 March. This document indicated that the SNC expected the president and the government to make an official declaration upon their arrival on Czechoslovak territory concerning the equal rights of both nations in a united and indivisible republic. It also defined the respective powers of the central and Slovak institutions (thought not of Czech ones) and included some foreign policy elements from the Christmas Agreement as well as some social principles from the manifesto. There was, however, no mention of a federal solution. Instead, the memorandum stated that the SNC "expects a promise which will tie the new government to a future constitutional solution of the relations between the Czech and Slovak nations on the principle of equality and agreement between both nations."[29] The spirit of the memorandum indicated that a federal solution was being sought. At the same time, Husak published a pamphlet entitled "*Za narodnu slobodu a ludovu demokraciu*" (For national liberty and a people's democracy) in which he clearly came out in favor of a federation.

Delegates from the SNC left for Moscow in March 1945 with the memorandum in hand, hoping to have the Czechoslovak government-in-exile, which had moved from London to Moscow, accept their federal plan. Yet as Laco Novomesky, one of the Communist leaders, notes: "The word federation was not used. When we began to work, we never spoke of federation or autonomy, we never used a specific terminology which might complicate the situation in the Czech Lands where we did not know how they might see it; we made every effort not to be misunderstood in the Czech Lands."[30] The Moscow conference was not a success for the SNC or the CPS. If anything, it showed how weak the SNC really was and how little political power it would enjoy in Czechoslovakia. The governmental program had been prepared *in their absence,* and their presence in Moscow was really meant to achieve two goals: to have the SNC accept the governmental program and to reach some agreement concerning the future relations between Czechs and Slovaks. The manner in which the SNC had been invited and was treated during the two days of discussion on the Slovak question indicated that from the outset that it had lost the battle over federation.

The first surprise that awaited the SNC in Moscow was Gottwald's opposition to the creation of Czech national organs. As Husak writes: "We don't know what awaits us, he kept repeating. What you have today in Slovakia [i.e., the SNC], you will keep. For the moment, this is how the position of the Slovaks is being solved. Later we shall see what the situation is like and can come back on this question."[31] Gottwald knew that the Czech non-Communist parties were unequivocally opposed not only to a federal solution, but also to a special status for Slovakia. For this reason, he suggested the compromise of dropping the federal solution in order to have the SNC recognized. Husak writes: "We gave in, but we demanded a constitutional commitment on the part of the government and the political parties that the given situation would also be acknowledged in the new constitution."[32] The unrelenting opposition of the National Socialists, particularly Benes, and the Czech Populists forced the SNC to abandon Gottwald's compromise and to return to the stronger demands of the memorandum. This tactic succeeded and on 26 March all parties accepted Gottwald's compromise. In the end nine Slovaks, rather than six as the Czech parties had insisted upon, were appointed to government. In this manner, the government program granted Slovakia a measure of autonomy. It was made public in Kosice, in Eastern Slovakia, and became known as the Kosice Program. The Slovaks were back in Czechoslovakia where an old battle for survival was renewed.

EPILOGUE AND PROLOGUE

The uprising ended Slovak statehood. When Tiso turned to the Germans to put down the partisans, he did so not to save the regime but rather to minimize the suffering and destruction that partisan warfare brought in its wake. He knew that the future was not his to determine anymore. No European power was willing to guarantee the survival of the first modern state of the Slovaks. There was also no possibility of switching allies, as Romania had done because Slovakia was not recognized by the Allied camp; when the Slovak chargé d'affaires in Bern, Jozef Kirschbaum, sought to establish contact with the Allies he was told to go through the Czechoslovak representative in Switzerland. Even Catlos was rejected by the partisans when he sought to join them. Slovakia's postwar fate was sealed, and none of the politicians identified with the Slovak Republic was allowed to speak on behalf of the nation among the Allies.

The Slovaks had acquired their statehood in 1939 under circumstances that were not of their own making; Tiso was one of the political leaders who

accepted the challenge of independence because he knew that it was the only way to ensure the survival of the nation. He not only presided over the new state, but also made certain that it was not dominated by a foreign ideology. Inevitably, he became identified not only with its creation and ultimate fate but also with the regime's policies. While his supporters grant him his due for his leadership during statehood, his detractors point to the negative policies of the regime. As a result, as Liptak writes, "Tiso was metamorphosed from the position of a real historical person into the function of a symbol."[33] Whatever view one may have of him, the fact is that it was under Tiso's leadership that the Slovak nation, at a time when most of Europe was at war, saw the process of national development reach its final and natural outcome, the establishment of its own state. The Slovak Republic also laid to rest the claim often made in the nineteenth century but particularly in the First Czechoslovak Republic that the Slovaks needed the Czechs to complete their national development. In this respect, the uprising was an epilogue, a tragic one in the eyes of many, to a historical evolution that had its origins in the 1848-1849 revolution but that was not allowed to continue.

If the uprising signaled a Slovak contribution to the war against Germany and an acceptance of the new European political order, it was also a prologue in the new phase of Czech-Slovak relations. Solc writes that "when the uprising broke out, the government[-in-exile] in London acted as if it were 'its' uprising, an action inspired and organized by it which made it possible for the Slovaks to redeem their sins and return home like prodigal sons to the Czechoslovak Republic."[34] The uprising actually earned its leaders and not the government-in-exile the right to speak on behalf of the Slovak nation in a restored Czechoslovakia. What was not clear to the Slovak leaders was whether they could successfully negotiate a new role and position for Slovakia in the postwar common state, different from what it had been in the interwar years.

They failed in their objective to turn Czechoslovakia into a federal state that would guarantee political autonomy and national equality to the Slovaks. They were unable to bring about a change in the Czech approach to the common state. Their failure in Moscow was the first step in a process that saw the complete subordination of the Slovaks to the Czech agenda by the end of the 1940s. The deformation of their objectives and even the historical record by the Communist regime in the 1950s was the paradoxical, but not illogical, culmination of this process. It is only when Czechoslovakia became a federation in 1968 that the uprising received its *titres de noblesse,* only to see them seriously tarnished and devalued in the "normalization" that followed.

The uprising belongs to the annals of World War II and defines the Slovak participation in the victory against Germany and fascism; it saved the Slovaks

from being treated as a defeated nation. As for Slovakia's position in the renewed Czechoslovakia, it is not at all clear that the uprising made a significant contribution to a better future for the nation.

11

Communism and Federalism

SLOVAKIA IN POSTWAR CZECHOSLOVAKIA

When Central Europe underwent another reorganization in 1945, the Slovak people were, for the third time in a little more than a quarter of a century, denied the option of deciding their own future. Slovakia was reincorporated into Czechoslovakia by a decision of the Allies to reconfirm the order of Versailles. With the exception of Germany, Poland, and the Baltic states, the status quo ante bellum was restored with some territorial modifications in favor of one of the victors, the Soviet Union. Czechoslovakia lost Ruthenia, which was annexed to the Ukraine. Slovakia, for its part, recovered the territory that had been given to Hungary in the Vienna Award of 1938 as well as that occupied in March 1939. However, certain other changes, in addition to those brought about by the war, modified the prewar order. The Czechoslovak government ordered the expulsion of its German citizens, denied citizenship to the Hungarians, and effected a population transfer between Hungary and Slovakia. After extended negotiations with Budapest, 74,000 Hungarians crossed into Hungary and 73,000 Slovaks left Hungary to settle in Slovakia in 1946. Another 44,000 Hungarians were moved from Slovakia to the Sudetenland, into the areas formerly inhabited by the Germans. Over the years, thousands of Slovaks would be sent to populate the former German areas. There was also a campaign to "reslovakize" the predominantly Hungarian areas

of Southern Slovakia by the granting of citizenship to those Hungarians who declared themselves Slovaks. However, of the over 400,000 who came forward, only about half became citizens. Only when the Communists came to power were the remainder granted Czechoslovak citizenship. By the end of 1945, these measures had turned Czechoslovakia into a binational state of the Czechs and Slovaks. Still, the Slovaks were not spared another fight for their survival.

The fate of Slovakia was decided during the nine months that preceded the end of the war. The uprising of 1944 had destroyed the link existing between the government and the population. Tuka had been replaced by Stefan Tiso, a relative of the president, as prime minister, and his government did its best to maintain order while German forces hunted the partisans. As the Allied advance forced the retreat of the Germans, Slovakia, in the language of the time, was liberated by Soviet and Czechoslovak forces, but not without cost. The Germans destroyed much during their retreat; for their part, Soviet NKVD officers rounded up some 10,000 alleged and real supporters of the Slovak Republic, especially in Eastern Slovakia, as well as many Hungarians who had opted for Hungarian citizenship during the Horthy regime, and had them deported to Soviet camps. Those who survived returned only in the 1950s. Tiso and the Slovak government fled to Austria on 1 April 1945, precipitating an exodus of some 5,000 officials of the Slovak Republic. National committees were organized throughout Slovakia, and many were completely in the hands of the Communists. On 3 April, Benes landed in Kosice in Eastern Slovakia. Two days later, he made public the Kosice Program, which confirmed the new status of Slovakia in Czechoslovakia that the opposition leaders had negotiated in Moscow. The CPCS leader Gottwald referred to it as the "Magna Carta" of the Slovak nation. Soviet forces entered Bratislava on 4 April, and after their arrival on 11 April, the SNC and the Board of Commissioners took over the governing of Slovakia which began to experience yet another style of political life: "The political regime that was established in 1945 brought with it uncertainty for broad sections of the population. In its efforts to distance itself from the first Slovak Republic, the SNC accepted legislative norms that especially affected state and public employees."[1]

Despite its failure to have the federal solution accepted in Moscow, the SNC attempted twice more to have it brought back on the agenda. The matter was raised on 24 April 1945 at a joint session of the presidia of the SNC and the government and then on 26 May, the morrow of the only meeting of the ministerial commission created to examine it. On both occasions the SNC failed. On 30 May, at a joint session of the presidia of the CPS and the CPCS, the Slovak Communists agreed to abandon the fight for the federalization of Czechoslovakia. This decision marked the starting point of the process that

brought about the complete subordination of Slovakia to the Czech agenda in postwar Czechoslovakia.

The CPS abandoned the federal solution for a number of reasons. In 1939, Slovak Communists had organized themselves into a party, the CPS, while remaining under the control of the CPCS. However, they acted independently during the war, and in 1944 constituted themselves formally into a party separate from the CPCS. But in 1945, with the disappearance of Slovakia as an independent political entity and the need for party discipline put the CPS once again in a subordinate position to the CPCS. In addition, as we saw in Chapter 10, the CPS leaders had not worked out a comprehensive constitutional program and theoretical justification for their federal proposal. They failed to convince their CPCS colleagues, most of whom had been raised and trained in the prewar republic with its ideology of one "Czechoslovak nation," of the importance of a new constitutional approach. As Solc writes: "the Czech Communists—with the assistance of V. Siroky who travelled to Moscow—although they clearly accepted the recognition of Slovak national individuality and equality and also the position the SNC had during the uprising, did not accept federalism."[2] The result was not only the failure to achieve their goals, but above all the creation of a division within their own ranks that would ultimately have tragic consequences for many of them.

This division goes back to the 1944 uprising. Not all Slovak Communist leaders had participated in it. Those who had not did not consider themselves bound by the policies of Husak and the *povstalci* (i.e., those who had been actively involved) and constituted themselves into a centralist wing of the party.[3] They supported the policies of the Czechoslovak government and openly opposed their rivals with the backing of the CPCS. In mid-1945, after Gottwald severely criticized the activities of the CPS in Slovakia, Viliam Siroky, a Communist of Hungarian origin, became president of the CPS and moved to Prague rather than stay in Bratislava.

The CPS's abandonment of the federal project had repercussions on both the constitutional and political levels. The autonomy of Slovakia, while perceived as a solution, had in fact created an imbalance in the state; the Czechs did not have national organs and were entirely under the jurisdiction of the Czechoslovak government. The Slovaks enjoyed administrative and political autonomy but also had representation in the Czechoslovak government. None of the Czech parties was comfortable with this situation. As far as the Czech Communists were concerned, their position in constitutional matters "was not, as it would seem, unambiguous, nor worked out in all of its consequences."[4] As for the non-Communist parties, they were determined to correct this situation as soon as possible. As Hubert Ripka writes:

neither the National Socialists, the Populists nor the Social Democrats were disposed to recognize the Czech-Slovak dualism which had in fact existed since the liberation. All these parties were defending the traditional doctrine of national unity, and it was only grudgingly that they had to recognize the doctrine of two independent nations, with the hope that the experiment, both on the political and economic plane, would end in an attenuation or a progressive suppression of the dual system.[5]

The Czechoslovak National Socialist Party, led by Benes, prepared an internal document, entitled Memorandum on Slovakia, that went even further. It outlined a policy to achieve the "spiritual assimilation of the Slovak people" through the church and their "forceful assimilation" by economic, political, military, national, and preventive means.[6] The Communists put many of these policies into effect when they came to power.

The autonomy of Slovakia outlined in the Kosice Program gave the SNC legislative powers and the Board of Commissioners executive ones. Both were sovereign in matters pertaining to Slovakia, while the board, which was subordinate to the SNC, also was given executive power in the name of the central government in matters of central competence. This type of arrangement became known as the "asymmetrical model." However, the Kosice Program did not specify the areas of Slovak and central competence; this was settled during negotiations between the Presidium of the SNC and the Czechoslovak government on 31 May and 1 June 1945. From these negotiations came the First Prague Agreement of 2 June; it defined twenty areas of central competence. The remaining areas were reserved for the SNC. The Constituent National Assembly ratified these arrangements in April 1946, pointing out that the SNC was also competent to issue regulations in Slovakia except when the Assembly decided otherwise. However, the First Prague Agreement did not satisfy the Czech parties, and two more negotiations further defined and, in fact, severely limited the powers of the SNC and the board. The Second Prague Agreement of 11 April 1946 stated that consultation with the concerned minister of the Czechoslovak government was mandatory on all resolutions of the SNC and the Board of Commissioners. It also gave the president of the republic the right to nominate all university professors, high-ranking judges, and public servants in Slovakia. But it was the Third Prague Agreement of 27 June 1946, negotiated after the May 1946 elections, which caused the greatest diminution in the powers of the Slovak national organs. The Czechoslovak government was given the right to decide what the SNC was empowered to discuss and could also order it to pass resolutions. Likewise, the Board of Commissioners was seriously weakened: A government minister could bypass his colleague in the board by

acting directly through his ministry; the government had final say in the composition of the board; and the government could suspend the execution of a decision by the board.

The SNC was forced to sign the Third Prague Agreement not only as a result of pressure from the Czech parties, but above all because of the electoral failure of the CPS. Until the elections, which were held on 26 May, the Slovak Communists, even after abandoning the federal project, strongly backed Slovakia's autonomy. To gain votes among Catholic voters, they even referred to themselves as Red Populists. However, Catholic politicians publicly supported the Democratic Party after signing an understanding with its representatives just before the elections. The results were mortifying for the CPS. While in the Czech Lands, the CPCS obtained 40.17 percent of the votes, the National Socialist Party 23.6 percent, the Czech Populist Party 20.24 percent, and the Social Democratic Party 15.58 percent, in Slovakia, the Democratic Party obtained 62 percent, the CPS 30.37 percent, the Labour Party 3.11 percent, and the Freedom Party 3.73 percent. The latter two parties were created on the eve of the elections to split the non-Communist vote. For the whole of the republic, the Communists had 37.94 percent of the votes, which made them the largest party in the state. Gottwald became prime minister of Czechoslovakia. As a result of their electoral failure, the Slovak Communists made an about-face and aligned themselves with the CPCS. In the struggle for power with the non-Communist parties, unity of action was imperative. An autonomous Slovakia led by the Democratic Party presented problems that centralization easily avoided.

Ever since the creation of the SNC at the time of the Christmas Agreement of 1943, the CPS had shared power with the Democratic Party. For a short period of time—from 5 September to 27 October 1944 and from 11 April to 14 September 1945—there were two co-chairmen of the SNC: one Communist, Smidke, and one non-Communist, first Srobar, then Lettrich. From 1945 until the coup of February 1948, Lettrich of the Democratic Party was its only chairman. On the other hand, the chairman of the Board of Commissioners was a Communist, at first Smidke and later Husak. The results of the elections of 1946 concerned specifically the board, where the Democratic Party had a majority of the commissions, although the chairmanship remained in Communist hands. This created an unfavorable situation for the CPS and also explains its decision to opt for centralism.

After the elections, the struggle between the Communist and non-Communist forces in Czechoslovakia became acute. One of the main tests of strength came with the trial of Tiso before a Slovak court. It began on 2 December 1946 and lasted until 15 April 1947. In the aftermath of the war, people's courts

tried 20,550 people and found 8,058 guilty of collaboration. Among them were Tuka and other officials of the Slovak Republic. However, Tiso's trial was the most important because of its meaning and multiple repercussions. He was accused of two counts of treason, against the Czechoslovak Republic and the 1944 uprising, and of collaboration. The accusation of treason was a signal that not only confirmed the subordinate position of Slovakia in the state but also acted as a deterrent to any future Slovak attempt to secede. The collaboration accusation was ideological. Anything connected with fascism, in whatever form and for whatever reason, had to be denounced. The past had to be forgotten and eradicated. Tiso was found guilty on all three charges and condemned to death. The Democratic Party promised clemency. When the Presidium of the SNC met on 16 April to consider the clemency demand, the Communists voted against it and, by putting pressure on other members, prevented a majority vote in favor. The demand was then sent to the Czechoslovak government, which also rejected it. Tiso was executed on 18 April. Lettrich had remarked in 1946: "Political processes are underway. . . . We are living through a period of bloody purification."[7] Tiso's trial had been just the beginning.

The political situation became more critical in Czechoslovakia after the United States announced the Marshall Plan in the spring of 1947 and the government agreed to participate in it. Moscow forced Czechoslovakia to withdraw. In the fall of that year the Communist parties of Central Europe decided at a meeting of the Cominform in Warsaw to make an all-out effort to take power. In Czechoslovakia, where the CPCS was in a more delicate position than its sister parties in the rest of Central Europe, a coup was attempted in Slovakia. The Democratic Party enjoyed little support from the Czech non-Communist parties, and the Communists felt that its position, despite the election results, could be challenged. In November 1947, the CPS, through public pressure manipulated by its organizations, sought to obtain a change in the composition of the Board of Commissioners after some of its Democratic Party members were accused of being involved in an antistate conspiracy. In the crisis that ensued, the Communists succeeded in eliminating the Democratic majority by having representatives of two small parties included, but they themselves did not gain additional commissions. Although this may be considered a victory for the democratic process in Czechoslovakia, the Democratic Party was nevertheless seriously weakened. This crisis also turned out to be a rehearsal for the February 1948 coup.

Throughout the entire period from 1945 to 1948, there was no suggestion of resurrecting the federal project. The struggle for power dominated political life in Slovakia and the Czech Lands, and everything was subordinated to it. However, the Communist coup in February 1948 raised the possibility of

reopening the federal question. Gottwald had said to Husak during the Moscow discussions of 1945 that the question could be renegotiated once the party came to power. In fact, no renegotiation took place and the Constitution of 9 May 1948 merely confirmed the asymmetrical model. The temporary compromise that the Slovak Communists had been forced to accept, namely an autonomous status for Slovakia, became permanent. However, this status bore little resemblance to the autonomy Slovakia had enjoyed immediately after the war; the three Prague Agreements had reduced Slovak autonomy to little more than a measure of self-administration in areas of purely Slovak interest. The Communist regime eliminated even that, and after the coup of 1948, concentrated on a totally different task, the transformation of Slovakia.

COMMUNIST SLOVAKIA

The imposition of communism in Slovakia is one of the greatest tragedies of its history. The population was forced to accept a totally different political regime and a way of life that had little to do with Slovak traditions or for that matter with the socio-economic needs of the people. In the elections of 1946, Slovak voters had clearly rejected this radical solution to industrialization. However, like other Central European peoples, they became trapped in the bipolar struggle between the Western liberal democratic world and the Eastern international proletarian Communist one. The war had placed them in the Soviet sphere of interest. The Communist parties, inspired by the historical determinism of their ideology, were resolved to win the ideological struggle and stopped at nothing to achieve their goal. They introduced a Stalinist regime that touched all aspects of political, social, and personal life. As Slovak historians who experienced the regime write:

> The dictatorships of the Stalinist type are different from other European dictatorial systems of the twentieth century by being even more "total," more complete. In contrast to the dictatorships of Hitler, Mussolini, Franco or Salazar, they interfere more profoundly in the economy, they bind each citizen to the governing system not only with an ideological chain and political organization, but also in his daily life, his livelihood, [and] his family existence.[8]

The expulsion of Yugoslavia from the Cominform in June 1948 brought about the implementation of a series of radical measures in the Soviet bloc. The Yugoslav leader, Josip Broz Tito, had resisted the attempts of the Kremlin

to subordinate his country to Soviet interests. The Soviet leader, Joseph Stalin, fearing that other satellites would follow Tito's example, assured himself of their obedience through a series of purges, show trials, and executions of high-ranking Communists that lasted until his death in 1953. The trials were also staged to gain support among Arab states against the newly created state of Israel. Gottwald's proposal of a "Czechoslovak road to socialism" came to an abrupt end. Fourteen top-ranking officials were arrested. Eleven were Jews. The Slansky trial of December 1952 was turned into a showcase for Eastern Europe. Eleven of the fourteen accused, including CPCS First Secretary Rudolf Slansky, were executed after being convicted of partaking in a conspiracy against the state and of Zionism. There were only two Slovaks among the condemned: Clementis, who was executed and Eugen Löbl, who was given a life sentence.

The small number of Slovaks confirmed that Slovakia had ceased to be a matter of concern in Czechoslovakia. Although the centralists had many of the *povstalci* arrested after they were accused of bourgeois nationalism at the Ninth Congress of the CPS on 24–25 May 1950, none figured in the Slansky trial. The centralists therefore were determined to ensure that their victory over the *povstalci* was complete. Some, like Husak, were still being held in jail. They were brought before a tribunal in Bratislava in April 1954, one year after Stalin's death and the end of the purges in Eastern Europe. Husak and his companions were found guilty of "Slovak bourgeois nationalism" and sentenced to prison terms. With their conviction, the federal solution was discredited and the Slovak question considered solved.

The defeat of the *povstalci* allowed the centralists to occupy key positions not only in Slovakia but also in Czechoslovakia. Karel Bacilek, a worker of Czech origin, who had lived in Slovakia most of his life, became first secretary of the CPS while Siroky was named prime minister of Czechoslovakia. Under their leadership, in the words of Liptak, "Slovak politics" was replaced by "politics in Slovakia."[9] Once more the Slovaks found themselves in a situation similar to the one they had experienced in the First Czechoslovak Republic. Despite the existence SNC and the Board of Commissioners, they were governed from Prague and subject to the Czech agenda. The Czech objective of unifying the Czechs and Slovaks had not changed although it was modified by an ideological imperative: this was to be a unification into a socialist people, and was to be accomplished by reducing, if not eliminating altogether, the economic and social differences between them. To achieve this objective, the Communists invaded all sectors of society, subordinated all social institutions to the Communist Party, created their own organizations, and eliminated anything that represented what they saw as a threat to their monopoly of power.

Among the first to be targeted was the Catholic Church: "In Slovakia, the church represented the only serious danger for Communist ideology. It received definite support from the population, was more successful in reaching the consciousness of the Slovaks, and what for the Communists was the most humiliating, it had a definitely long tradition."[10]

The process that led to radical measures against religion in Slovakia began on 16 May 1945, when the SNC decided to transfer all church schools to the state. In 1949, all the churches of Czechoslovakia were put under state control, and in Slovakia all religious newspapers except *Katolicke noviny* (Catholic News) and *Duchovny pastier* (Spiritual Pastor) were banned and all presses taken over. In February 1949, the CPCS created a commission to look at ways of exercising complete control on church activities. It recommended the creation of an Office for Church Affairs, which came into existence on 14 October. The stage was set for additional measures.

On 16 March 1950 the regime ordered the closing of all seminaries; four days later, the apostolic nuncio in Prague, Monsignor Ottavio di Livio, was asked to leave and the regime broke diplomatic relations with the Vatican. The next step took place at Easter 1950, on 13–14 April, when the security forces and people's militia invaded all monasteries, rounded up the monks and brothers, and held them first in selected monasteries and later in camps. All religious orders were ordered dissolved, and their members were sent to various places of work, usually to other parts of Slovakia or the Czech Lands, forbidden to exercise their vocation, condemned to manual labor and often subjected to personal humiliation and ridicule. Those who refused to cooperate were arrested. From the nineteen orders that were dissolved, out of a total of 1,326 members, 171 were brought to trial. The same fate was reserved for the twenty-one female orders; 4,219 religious sisters were taken from their convents and nunneries on 28–30 August. Out of that number, 244 were brought before a tribunal. On 28 April the regime had also ordered the dissolution of the Greek Catholic Church in Eastern Slovakia and forced its members to join the Orthodox Church.

Since the Constitution of Czechoslovakia proclaimed the freedom of religion, the regime did not seek to abolish religion, merely to curtail it severely. Many churches were closed, the faithful were openly discouraged from attending services, and those who proclaimed their faith faced loss of employment and loss of educational opportunities for their children, in particular university studies, and any other punitive measures that local Communists could think of. The priests who were allowed to exercise their ministry were made employees of the state and were kept under strict control. As Anton Hlinka writes: "Priests who performed pastoral duties inside the church or in groups outside it without

permission from the Office for Church Affairs could be condemned for up to five years."[11] In addition, organizations such as the student group Rodina (Family) were disbanded and its founder, Tomislav Poglaven Kolakovic, brought to trial. The initial campaign against the Catholic Church reached its apex on 10 January 1951 when bishops Jan Vojtassak, Michal Buzalka, and Pavol Gojdis were tried and condemned to prison sentences.

The Catholic Church responded to the policies of the regime with passive resistance and also underground activity. Many monks and priests condemned to manual labor became secretly active in their places of work, carrying on with their ministries and preparing candidates for ordination. Two bishops were secretly ordained in 1951, Pavol Hnilica on 21 January and Jan Ch. Korec on 24 August. Hnilica, realizing that he was the object of police surveillance, managed to flee to the West in the fall of that year. Korec carried on for a number of years until he was arrested in 1960 and brought to trial on 17–21 May. His condemnation had a boomerang effect on the regime. According to Frantisek Miklosko: "The elevation of Korec to the rank of bishop and his activities, secret up to that point, became public. The trial and judgment were transformed into an inaugural celebration. Bishop Korec set out on a new life path. . . ."[12] His condemnation to twelve years was announced shortly after President Antonin Novotny proclaimed an amnesty. The regime used a carrot-and-stick policy toward the Catholic Church, supporting in particular those clergy who joined the Peace Movement of the Catholic Clergy, an organization created in 1951 and funded by the state, and arresting those it considered dangerous or disobedient.

Another way that the regime sought to achieve the transformation of Slovakia was by imposing a policy of rapid industrialization. In order to do so, it first had to turn its attention to agriculture, which it proceeded to collectivize. On 23 February 1949, the Czechoslovak Parliament passed a law on the creation of United Agricultural Cooperatives. Three types were created. The first was the Unified Agricultural Cooperative (UAC) Type I, which did not abolish ownership of the land but encouraged collective work and sharing in machinery and other ancillary services such as communal laundries, chicken hatcheries, and calf stations. Soviet-style Machine Tractor Stations were also created and made available to these cooperatives. In order to encourage the farmers to join, propaganda teams that included people who had been to the U.S.S.R. to study Soviet collective farming were sent to the countryside. The regime also initiated a campaign against rich peasants, who, in imitation of Soviet terminology, were called *kulaks*. The decision to exclude the rich peasants from the cooperatives was taken by both the Central Committee of the CPCS and the government on 26 May 1952; it was one of eight measures destined to strengthen existing

cooperatives and create new ones. Ladislav Feierabend calls this campaign a "war of extermination," because the designated victims could not even join a cooperative to save themselves.[13]

New types of cooperatives were created when the regime proceeded to abolish private property. Absence of ownership signaled the difference between Type I and Types II and III cooperatives. In the UAC Type II, crops were cultivated collectively, boundary lines were eliminated, and border strips were plowed out. The fields were united and the only activity that remained in private ownership and care was animal husbandry. However, private ownership of the land by the members was legally recognized, and the absence of collective management gave the former owner a say in production. But the individual farmer's freedom was circumscribed by a system of labor units that determined renumeration. UACs Type III were characterized by collective management and the collective organization of animal husbandry. A small family holding was allowed, and at season's end members of these cooperatives received a percentage of profits as compensation for the contribution of their land. UACs Type IV, were the same as Type III but with no percentage paid for use of land and remuneration was based entirely on labor units.

The campaign to collectivize agriculture turned out to be far more problematic in Slovakia than the Communists expected. The initial campaign was almost unsuccessful; "the overwhelming majority of initial cooperators was recruited from former landless agricultural workers, small farmers and industrial workers who lived in villages (their wives joined in fact the cooperatives)."[14] Not only did people resist joining Type I UACs, but they also refused to give up private property. In 1952, the regime resorted to more radical measures. It launched a drive into the cooperatives by using economic and psychological pressure rather than persuasion to achieve maximum results. Even writers and poets were employed to ensure the success of collectivization. The results were not what the regime expected. Instead of increasing, the number of UACs, fell, although some of this was due to the amalgamation of UACs. The radical measures were abandoned in September 1953 in favor of material support and increased financial investments in existing UACs. This policy achieved a measure of success. In 1957, collective and state ownership finally superseded private ownership, reaching 54.4 percent. By 1960, it rose to 80.5 percent of which the UAC's represented 65.8 percent. What private property remained was found mostly in mountainous regions that had not been targeted for collectivization. Likewise, the rural population fell from 41.9 percent of the total population in 1950 to 27 percent in 1960. Agricultural productivity increased by 47 percent in the same period. Slovak agriculture was transformed, becoming large-scale and mechanized. Villages also experi-

enced modern life-style improvements, with indoor plumbing and heating, electricity, telephones, and a network of paved roads.

The collectivization of agriculture created the labor force that was essential for the industrialization of Slovakia. Between 1948 and 1983, the number of people employed in industry increased from 216,884 to 809,928. The industrial development of Slovakia was based entirely on the needs of the Czechoslovak economy and, above all, the Warsaw Pact's strategic requirements. It was integrated in the central planning system. The plans and the tempo of plan fulfillment were worked out in Prague, were adjusted annually, and underwent only minor modifications over the years. As Jozef Markus writes: "In its basic characteristics, the management of the Czechoslovak national economy retained the features of the management system of the period of industrial growth (from the beginning of the fifties)."[15] In Slovakia, the plans called for the development of mining, smeltering, and chemical industries, and for the fulfillment of production quotas, but otherwise for little else. As Slovak historians note: "These factories, often built without regard to the cost of production, for strictly strategic-military reasons, with old technology, seriously affected the ecology of many areas."[16] Most of Czechoslovakia's military industries, which produced tanks, munitions, rockets, and all types of weapons, were found in Slovakia because of its proximity to the Soviet Union. Such factories employed 10,000 to 12,000 workers. There was little consumer goods or light industry, other than what was needed for internal consumption, and raw materials extracted in Slovakia were usually sent to the Czech Lands for processing and finishing. Still, Slovakia became industrialized, a development that also brought with it urbanization. By the 1980s, half the population lived in cities. But the price that Slovakia paid for industrialization brought about a reaction and in the process raised anew the question of Slovakia's role and position in Czechoslovakia.

Nikita S. Khrushchev's de-Stalinization campaign in the Soviet Union in 1956 offered the first opportunity for change. Czechoslovakia had at that time the highest standard of living in the Soviet bloc, so the leadership had little difficulty in preventing outbreaks like those in Poland and Hungary. Nevertheless, there were student demonstrations in Prague and Bratislava in May. In June, there were reactions from Czech and Slovak writers and intellectuals at the second Czechoslovak Writers' Congress; many participants publicly voiced their opposition to the regime. It marked the beginning of a new role that intellectuals would play in Communist Czechoslovakia and bring about in the 1960s what is termed an intellectual revolution.[17] The regime in Czechoslovakia took no notice of these protests; on the other hand, it did augment the power of the Slovak national organs on the grounds that political and economic

conditions had changed and that the Slovak working class had increased in numbers. A constitutional law was passed in June 1956 that gave the SNC the right to act independently of the government and reestablished the link with the Board of Commissioners, which still remained subordinated to the Czechoslovak government. Although the law was hailed as granting Slovakia extensive powers, in the end the changes were more formal than real.

The constitutional law of 1956 turned out to be nothing more than a brief episode in the wake of Khrushchev's de-Stalinization. The regime returned to its centralizing policies when the Soviets launched a campaign against revisionism in the aftermath of the Hungarian Revolution. There was a series of purges during 1957 and 1958 in Slovakia, particularly against writers and educators. The aim of these trials was to prepare the population in Slovakia for yet another measure of centralization. In 1960, the leadership of the CPCS, headed by Gottwald's successor, Antonin Novotny, announced that Czechoslovakia's development had reached the stage where a new socialist constitution could be promulgated. The Czechoslovak Republic (CSR) became the Czechoslovak Socialist Republic (CSSR). The powers of the Slovak national organs were further diminished so that very little remained of Slovak autonomy. Slovakia was divided into three administrative regions with regional committees at their head, thereby diminishing the authority of Bratislava. The Board of Commissioners was abolished and the SNC Presidium was given executive powers. Some of the members of the SNC Presidium were appointed commissioners of various sectors or commissions. The 1960 Constitution reflected the basic approach of the CPCS leadership toward Slovakia in Czechoslovakia. It also underscored the CPCS approach to socialist development in a binational state.

LIBERALIZATION AND FEDERALIZATION

The policy of de-Stalinization that Khrushchev had encouraged in Eastern Europe after his second attack on Stalinism at the Twenty-second Congress of the CPSU in 1961 made way for Stalinism's condemnation in Czechoslovakia and a reform movement that sought to divest socialism of its sectarian and dogmatic aspects. Beginning 1963, some of the more Stalinist measures were relaxed, travel outside the Soviet bloc was possible, foreign newspapers became available and generally the regime tolerated a certain degree of liberalization. In Slovakia this opened the way for a process of national self-assertion that would lead to the reexamination of the asymmetrical model, and to its rejection and ultimate replacement by a federation. What had become evident to Slovak

Communists, although this was not articulated openly until 1968, was the fact that the asymmetrical model had failed to achieve its goals. Rather than being used to ensure the economic development and equalization of Slovakia with the Czech Lands, the Slovak national organs were instead systematically stripped of their powers. This process had begun under Gottwald, and his successor Novotny, who later also became president, had merely taken this process to its logical conclusion in 1960. In addition, in terms of economic development, the industrial gap between Slovakia and the Czech Lands, rather than narrowing, had in fact widened.

The reexamination of the federal proposal of the wartime era became possible with the release from prison of the "Slovak bourgeois nationalists" and their rehabilitation in 1963, the development of an opposition movement against Novotny among Slovak intellectuals, and the reform movement during the years 1963 to 1968. Husak's return to Slovakia added a dimension of continuity from which the new generation of Slovak Communists benefited. A new style of political life began to take shape and a consensus developed on the goals the Slovaks should pursue. The Communists learned from their mistakes in the immediate postwar period and not only developed a strategy but also ensured for themselves the support of their Czech colleagues. The opposition to federalization did not manifest itself on strictly national lines as in the past, but rather on ideological ones, although occasionally national overtones crept in. In the end, federalization overcame the liberal-conservative split in the CPCS.

The formulation of Slovak goals began to take shape after the Twelfth Congress of the CPCS in December 1962. Czechoslovakia was in the throes of an economic crisis and the continued destalinization of the Twentieth Congress of the CPSU was adding fuel to the criticisms of the policies of the leadership, in particular Novotny's opposition to any major constitutional change. Two issues surfaced as the motive force of Slovak demands: The rehabilitation of the Slovak road to communism through the rehabilitation of the Slovak bourgeois nationalists and the constitutional guarantee of the equality of the Slovak nation with the Czechs that the Slovak Communist leaders bad fought for in the 1944 uprising.

The rehabilitation of the Slovak bourgeois nationalists turned out to be a complicated affair. As the Piller Report of 1968 indicates, the CPCS leadership received enough signals even before the Twentieth CPSU Congress that "something was seriously wrong."[18] Yet its two commissions did not alter many verdicts and rehabilitated even fewer persons. It was not until 1962, as a result of continued destalinization at the Twenty-Second CPSU Congress, that "a considerable number of Czechoslovak Party members turned again to the

question of Stalinism and its consequences in Czechoslovakia. The subject of the trials became once more a foremost issue in the Party."[19] In September, the party appointed a rehabilitation commission, known as the Kolder Commission, and its findings were reported to the April 1963 plenum of the Central Committee. While Czech Communists were rehabilitated, Clementis, Husak, and other Slovak bourgeois nationalists were only rehabilitated partially and the accusation was not withdrawn. The immediate result was, as the Piller Report indicates, that the rehabilitations became "a national issue in Slovakia."[20] Another commission, the Barnabite Commission, was established by the presidium of the CPCS in June 1963 to look specifically into the accusation of bourgeois nationalism in Slovakia. Its report to the Central Committee in December indicated that the charges had been unjustified: "Novotny and other members of the Presidium who had tried to prevent the complete rehabilitation of the Slovak Communists convicted of bourgeois nationalism, . . . were gradually compelled by the pressure of public opinion in Slovakia and the hard facts amassed by the "Barnabite Commission" to change their standpoint."[21]

The regime publicly admitted that the trials of the Slovak bourgeois nationalists had been unjust, and Novotny jettisoned his two lieutenants in Slovakia, Siroky, who was prime minister of Czechoslovakia and who had been chief accuser of the *povstalci,* and Bacilek, first secretary of the CPS and minister of interior at the time of the purges. They were replaced by two Slovaks, Jozef Lenart, who became prime minister, and Alexander Dubcek, who took over the leadership of the CPS. Dubcek was born on 27 November 1921 in Uhrovec. In 1925, his family moved to Kirghizia in the Soviet Union and in 1933 he began his schooling in Gorky. They returned to Slovakia in the summer of 1938. Dubcek joined the illegal CPS in March 1939 and in August 1944 the partisan brigade Jan Zizka. He began his career in the party in 1949, becoming secretary of the Banska Bystrica region in 1953. During the years 1955 to 1958, he attended the CPSU High Party School in Moscow, was named secretary of the Bratislava party organization upon his return, and was elected to the presidium of the CPCS in 1962. His election as first secretary of the CPS in 1963 was the beginning of his rise to national and international prominence.

The constitutional question also made its first appearance in 1963, although not yet in public. A Slovak historian, Milos Gosiorovsky, presented to the leading members of both the CPCS and CPS a well-argued case for the need for a federation in Czechoslovakia. Looking at CPCS policy toward Slovakia since the early 1920s, he showed how it had been inadequate and how the centralist wing of the CPS after World War II, under the leadership of Siroky, with the tacit agreement of the CPCS, had in fact pursued a program that affected Czech-Slovak relations in a negative way. He drew attention to

the federal arrangements in Yugoslavia and the Soviet Union and indicated that the Slovak nation was the only Slavic nation in the socialist camp that did not have national organs of socialist state power. He submitted this report to the Communist journal *Nova Mysl* (New Thinking) for publication in March of that year. However, when the partial rehabilitations of the bourgeois nationalists were made public, he withdrew the report. He sent a second, revised, and enlarged version to President Novotny and other party leaders in July. This action angered Novotny, and it was only through the efforts of Dubcek and other CPS leaders that Gosiorovsky avoided major punishment. Novotny remained opposed to any major constitutional change. However, he agreed to minor adjustments in 1964, which, as in 1956, formally gave Slovak national organs additional powers.

As soon as they were rehabilitated, the former Slovak Communist leaders reentered Slovakia political life. They were not permitted to occupy party or government positions, but they could write in Slovak periodicals and newspapers. As former leaders of the CPS they also exerted influence behind the scenes and in the Slovak press, especially in the weekly *Kulturny zivot* (Cultural Life), with the tacit consent of the leadership of the CPS, especially Dubcek.[22] These former leaders concentrated on the rehabilitation of the 1944 uprising in central Slovakia. It was not merely a case of setting the record straight or even of permitting Husak to contradict the official interpretation of that event. They forced the regime to make a public demonstration of its importance. In August 1964, in Banska Bystrica, in the presence of president Novotny and CPSU First Secretary Khrushchev, the regime officially celebrated the twentieth anniversary of the uprising. Other aspects of Slovak history also came in for reevaluation. This historical revival "had a cathartic effect which enabled Slovakia as a whole to recapture a national initiative and spirit which would later find a vigorous political expression in the drive for federation and constitutional reform."[23]

Dubcek, who at the time of his election as first secretary of the CPS had not immediately come out for federation, made the issue of Czech-Slovak relations public for the first time in 1965. During the celebration of the 150th anniversary of the birth of the nineteenth-century Slovak leader, Ludovit Stur, Dubcek, who was born in the same town, linked Stur's activities with subsequent developments; "this was a fascinating and most important speech, for it was the first time on which he [Dubcek] could be seen to champion in public the cause of Slovakia and to recognize that the nationality problem was vital."[24]

Other aspects of the regime's policies were also the object of attack from the Slovaks, in particular Prague's economic policies toward Slovakia. The criticisms of the Slovak economists were aimed at the rate of growth and on other aspects economic activity.[25] In 1950, for example, the regime had

forbidden the calculation of the Slovak national income, and from that moment on it argued that, in view of the statistical methods used, it was impossible to establish it. Three Slovak economists took up the challenge and proved the regime wrong.[26] In the pages of the journal *Ekonomicky casopis* (Economic Review) and in Slovak newspapers like *Pravda, Smena, Praca,* and *Rolnicke noviny* (Farm News), the regime was assailed for its inadequate economic policy toward Slovakia.

Novotny did not let the Slovak challenge go unanswered. He held Dubcek responsible for these attacks. In 1966, Novotny attempted at the CPS congress to replace Dubcek by a more compliant Slovak Communist at the head of the Slovak party, but failed. His position secure, Dubcek could now put his weight behind the Slovak national demands. In March 1967, he raised publicly the constitutional question when he spoke once again on the subject of Stur. He stated: "Stur's ideas on the development of Slovakia were reborn in the Slovak Revolt . . . [when] the national and international aspirations of Slovakia were clear—soldiers and partisans fought not only for the rights of the Slovak nation, but also for the renewal of Czechoslovakia as a state of two equal nations, as a home of Czechs and Slovaks and built on nationally and socially just principles."[27] In November, Dubcek urged the rejection of the existing constitutional system: "Thus the challenge from the Slovaks was placed upon Novotny by the highest authority and representative of the party in Slovakia."[28] Novotny responded with a couple of faux-pas, one at Matica slovenska in (Turciansky Sväty) Martin in 1967,[29] and the other at the December 1967 plenum of the Central Committee where he accused Dubcek of acting as a "bourgeois nationalist"; this second faux-pas acted as the catalyst for his ouster.[30]

Novotny was replaced as first secretary of the CPCS by Dubcek in January 1968. General Ludvik Svoboda, commander of the Czechoslovak forces in the Soviet Union during World War II, became president two and a half months later. Czechoslovakia was in a period of liberalization. The aim was the creation of "socialism with a human face," for which Dubcek became the symbol in Czechoslovakia and abroad. Censorship was abolished, an unprecedented measure in a Communist regime. The federalization process also got under way. The Slovak Communists worked simultaneously at the state level, where Husak was vice-premier and chairman of the commission created to prepare the federation, and at the public level, where a press campaign was launched to rally support for the project. Articles appeared in Slovak newspapers and journals not only to show the extent of Slovak support, but also to explain the difficulties that the project involved. The federal project went through three stages before the law was voted in Parliament. The first stage, which lasted until June, was the most important; the idea of a federation

had to take shape not only in Slovakia but above all in the Czech Lands, where the creation of Czech national organs would be the most important sign of its acceptance as well as its real starting point. But the major effort had to come from Slovakia. On 6–8 March 1968, leading Slovak intellectuals asked for the federalization of the state for the first time in public. The SNC met on 14 March (the anniversary of Slovakia's independence in 1939) and the next day published a similar declaration.

The publication of the Action Program of the CPCS on 6 April put the whole problem in a new perspective since it emphasized the need to take a fresh look at Czech-Slovak relations. On 9 April the CPS created a commission to prepare for the federation. On 16 April, the SNC created a commission, headed by Karol Laco, to examine a *symmetrical* federal proposal. Laco's article in *Pravda* a few days later, in which he condemned the asymmetrical model, indicated that the Slovaks would not accept anything less than a symmetrical federation. These developments and a Czech suggestion to create a federation of three states (Bohemia, Slovakia, and Moravia-Silesia) as well as some opposition in the Czech Lands brought about a crisis in Communist ranks over the fulfillment of the federal project. Husak dealt with it and defused the crisis in public at the extraordinary conference of the CPS on 4–5 July.

The importance of federalization for the Slovaks did not mean that they ignored or opposed the democratization process. Slovakia indulged in all of its manifestations, from the free examination of their Stalinist past, including interviews with some of the actors like Bacilek, to the creation of *Slovenska organizacia na ochranu ludskych prav* (Slovak Organization for the Protection of Human Rights), the Slovak equivalent of K–231 (from a clause in the criminal code) in the Czech Lands. Catholic laymen came together in an organization called *Dielo koncilovej obnovy* (Action for [Vatican] Council Renewal), and cooperated closely with other opposition groups. The Slovak attitude toward liberalization was also reflected in public opinion surveys. In a June poll, 92.9 percent of the respondents gave their support to the reform movement by agreeing that the Action Program would positively influence the development of Czechoslovakia; in another poll taken a month later, 86 percent of the respondents were in favor of broadening the measure for individual freedom. The most telling poll was an April one on the men to whom the respondents gave greatest confidence: in Slovakia Dubcek obtained 67.5 percent (28.0 percent in the Czech Lands) while the next Slovak figure, Gustav Husak, received only 18.8 percent (1.7 percent in the Czech Lands). In the whole of Czechoslovakia Dubcek enjoyed 39.7 percent of popular support, followed by the Czech Josef Smrkovsky with 17.1 percent (23.1 percent in the Czech Lands but only 2.7 percent in Slovakia), with Husak third, receiving 6.7 percent.[31]

The federalization-democratization dichotomy did, however, have repercussions in Slovakia that did not exist in the Czech Lands.[32] The weekly *Kulturny zivot,* which had been the standard-bearer of Slovak intellectuals in the Novotny era, took the position that it was important to achieve democratization before federalization rather than the other way round. Three regular contributors to that journal, one a former bourgeois nationalist, resigned from it. They accused *Kulturny zivot* of publishing anti-socialist views. They joined *Nove slovo* (New Word), a paper founded by Husak, which was in the forefront of the federalization campaign.

The Czech National Council (CNC) was created on 24 June. This event inaugurated the second stage, during which the details of the federation were worked out. Many problems were dealt with, such as whether the parliament would be unicameral or bicameral, the relationship between the houses of a bicameral parliament, the voting procedure in parliament, the decision-making process at the federal level, and the distribution of powers between the federal and republican levels. There were two basic ideas behind these problems: how to achieve parity and how to implement democratic principles, such as representation, without creating injustices. For the Slovaks, the latter was important since they were outnumbered by the Czechs.

On 26 July, the government accepted the general principles of federalism, a bicameral parliament, and parity in the House of Nationalities, making it possible thereby to move to the third stage. This was the most difficult stage as there was little time to prepare the necessary constitutional texts. The objective was to have them ready before 28 October, the date of the fiftieth anniversary of the creation of Czecho-Slovakia. The Warsaw Pact invasion on 20 August, which ended the process of liberalization, compounded the problem as some felt that there were more important matters to deal with than the federalization of Czechoslovakia. On 26 September, the government published its *Stanovisko k federalizacii CSSR* (Stand on the federalization of the CSSR) in order to allow the public to familiarize itself with the project. The bill passed, despite many gaps, on 27 October and was proclaimed in Bratislava by President Svoboda the next day. On 1 January 1969, Czechoslovakia became a federal state of two socialist republics, Czech and Slovak, which, according to the preamble of the Constitution, enjoyed the right of self-determination, including secession, and possessed identical national institutions in the CNC and the SNC. There was parity in the House of Nationalities and in all federal institutions.

The Constitution was a compromise of opposite approaches to the federalization of Czechoslovakia. As Carol Skalnik Leff writes: "The federal solution that emerged from the consultation of 1968 embodied a theoretically inconsistent

compromise on the question of representation: a modus vivendi rather than a logically coherent blueprint of power distribution."[33] The Slovak approach had been more confederal in nature and had stressed the need to give the constituent republics vast powers whereas the federal organs would have limited exclusive powers. The Czech approach, on the other hand, was to give the federal organs greater powers, especially in areas of "common affairs" for both republics. The Constitution in fact gave the federal organs exclusive powers in four areas: foreign affairs, defense, federal state material reserves, and the protection of federal legislation and administration. Article 8 outlined sixteen common areas of federal and republican jurisdiction which were not broken down into ministries and committees. Such a breakdown was drawn up in the period between the promulgation of the Constitution and its coming into effect on 1 January 1969. Early in October, agreement was reached that there would be five federal ministries (defense, foreign affairs, exclusively federal; planning, finance and foreign trade, common) and five federal committees (labor and social affairs, prices, transport, post and telecommunications, and internal affairs). By December, when the constitutional law on federal ministries and committees was passed, seven ministries were established, each with a state secretary, and seven committees. Remaining areas were left to the republics; the CNC created seventeen ministries whereas the SNC created fifteen.

NORMALIZATION

The invasion of August did not put an immediate end to the liberalization process of the Prague Spring but it did introduce new constraints. Dubcek and other political leaders were flown to Moscow and forced to sign the Moscow Protocol which legitimized the stationing of Soviet armed forces in Czechoslovakia. The domestic political scene also had to be stabilized along lines acceptable to the Kremlin. On 26–29 August, the CPS met in an Extraordinary Congress in Bratislava and elected Husak first secretary; in this position he influenced the subsequent course of events, although not in the way expected by those who voted for him. He persuaded the CPS not to recognize the Fourteenth Congress of the CPCS—the Vysocany Congress—that was held on the morrow of the invasion (from 22 to 27 August) because of the absence of Slovak representatives and also because of a clause in the Moscow Protocol. A new Fourteenth Congress was eventually held in May 1971. The most outspoken reformers in the CPCS were also ousted from leading positions and on 17 April 1969, Husak replaced Dubcek as first secretary of the CPCS. On 28 April, Dubcek was elected chairman of the Federal Assembly, a position he

resigned from on 15 October. In December, he was named Czechoslovak ambassador to Turkey. In June 1970, he returned to Czechoslovakia where he learned that he had been expelled from the party. In December 1970, he accepted a position as mechanic in the local Office of Forest Administration in Krasnany, on the outskirts of Bratislava. Until 1989 the entire Dubcek family remained under constant police surveillance.

A more radical course was imposed on Czechoslovakia after the savage repression of the mass demonstration against the regime in Prague on 21 August 1969, the first anniversary of the invasion. A process of "normalization" was pursued that was modified in December 1970 to allow neo-Stalinism to be implemented; "in Slovakia, the blow of the consolidation ax was not as unconditionally brutal as in the Czech Lands."[34] Nevertheless, there were modifications in the federal system. It became, therefore, identified with a specific political course. Even if the "normalization" policy had not been pursued by Husak, the monopoly of power by the Communist Party could not, by definition, have made the federation work. What the Czechs and Slovaks had created was a system that was federal in form and centralist in substance.

The Marxist literature published in the postinvasion period on federalization praised the 1968 transformation of the Czechoslovak state. Federalism was hailed as representing a new solution to the nationality problem in Czechoslovakia while maintaining unity at the same time. But federalism also allowed the regime to pursue what might be termed neo-Czechoslovakism. As one commentator put it:

> On the basis of the recent history of mutual relations, it is evidently only a question of time, under these new and most favorable conditions, for the prerequisites to develop which will lead to the acceleration of the total development and rapprochement of the Czechs and Slovaks and the nationalities living in the republic, and to the attainment of such a synthesis that the notion of a "Czechoslovak people" will be the symbol of a new qualitative unity of all the citizens of the CSSR.[35]

The federal model emphasized cultural and economic development in Slovakia. Sensitive to the fact that economic development had been the intent of the discredited asymmetrical model, the federal government favored Slovakia with massive investments; by the end of the Fourth Five-Year Plan in 1970, despite the economic crisis of the late 1960s, Slovakia reached the goals set for it in the plan; there was an increase of per capita contribution to the gross national product of 50.8 percent (49.8 per cent had been forecast in the plan), and an increase in the national income of 60.8 percent (61.0 percent had been

forecast). In 1966, the Slovak contribution to the national income had been 24.8 percent; by 1970 it had reached 27 percent. The regime also liked to emphasize the progress that Slovakia made, especially since 1948. Slovakia's participation in the gross national income when compared to that of the Czech Lands was calculated at 61.2 percent in 1948, 74.4 percent in 1960, and 78.9 percent in 1971; in gross industrial production, it represented 39.7 percent in 1948, increased to 55.8 percent in 1960, and 69.8 percent in 1971; and in gross agricultural production Slovakia accounted for 105.2 percent in 1948, and had gone up to 110 percent in 1960 but down to 108.3 percent in 1971. According to a Slovak economist, by 1974 "Slovakia had overcome her economic, social and cultural backwardness and become a country with a developed economy," and was well on its way to reaching equalization with the Czech Lands.[36] The policy of favoring Slovak development was renewed in the Fifth Five-Year Plan (1971–76). Communist statistics indicate not only that industrial production in Slovakia increased dramatically—namely twenty times since 1948—but that Slovakia's share in the overall volume of industrial production, for example, rose from 20.8 percent in 1965 to 26.6 percent a decade later. At the CPS Congress held in 1976, first secretary Jozef Lenart spent the bulk of his report dealing with Slovak economic achievements, stressing that the basic goals of the just-completed plan had been reached and in some cases even surpassed. There was also noticeable activity in the cultural sphere, in the arts, museums, literature, the press, and radio and television during the Fifth Five-Year Plan. One analyst claimed that this activity "ranks among the greatest achievements of this period."[37]

The one area where the regime was having some difficulty was religion. The party made serious efforts not only to break the traditional attachment of the Slovaks to the Catholic faith but to avoid the recurrence of a phenomenon that manifested itself in 1968, namely spiritual revival as a result of the return to Slovakia of members of the orders that had been disbanded in 1950. They were allowed to live together in communities. A sociological study carried out in 1970 on the religiosity of the Slovaks showed 70.7 percent of the population to be believers, 14 percent atheist, and the rest undecided.[38] Shortly thereafter an article appeared in *Pravda* attacking religion as constituting a "breach in our society and a conservative element in the people's consciousness."[39] In 1971, the Slovak government created an Institute for Scientific Atheism at the Slovak Academy of Sciences with the objective of offering an alternative to religion. In addition, the regime replaced the Peace Movement of the Catholic Clergy with a new organization called *Pacem in Terris* (Peace on Earth). The results were not the ones the regime expected: "There was movement in Slovakia. Many parish priests paid particular attention to young people as did members of

various orders, namely Salesians, Jesuits, Piarists and Franciscans who gave up part of their time to work with the youth."[40]

The carrot-and-stick policy toward the Catholic Church was maintained; in 1972 a number of seminarians were expelled from Bratislava's Theological Faculty, which the regime had created in 1950, and in 1975 priests were physically attacked after Czechoslovakia signed the Helsinki Final Act. Yet the regime also finally settled a question that dated back to the creation of Czechoslovakia, namely the establishment on 30 December 1977 of an archbishopric in Trnava and a Slovak ecclesiastical province with Trnava as the see:

> If for some 20 years, *via facti,* Slovakia was no longer under the jurisdiction of the Primate in Ostrihom, legally its status had not been settled; nor had it been in the First Republic—because of the lack of interest of the Prague central government who saw in ecclesiastical independence a danger for the unitary state; nor in the Slovak Republic [of 1939 to 1945]—because Slovakia did not have its southern territories which were given to Hungary in 1938; nor in the first years of the second Czecho-Slovak Republic—for reasons similar to those of the twenties and thirties.[41]

By the mid-1970s, the regime recognized that its policies were not having the expected results in Slovakia. It started to issue warnings and threats about the recurrence of bourgeois nationalism, reminiscent of those uttered in the 1950s. These attacks signaled a move away from the earlier enthusiastic recovery of the national heritage in cultural and academic publications. Leff writes: "It is unlikely that this noticeable shift reflects a diminution of Slovak national sentiment—quite the contrary, it suggests a concern that such sentiment was getting out of hand."[42] The regimes's policy of neo-Czechoslovakism was producing results opposite to what it intended.

The regime's pursuit of "normalization" since 1969 made the political system in Czechoslovakia one of the most conservative and repressive in Central Europe in the late 1970s and the 1980s. Yet it was this same regime that signed the Helsinki Final Act in 1975. A reaction to the government's neo-Stalinist policies and its refusal to honor the act's Basket Three provisions was inevitable. In the Czech Lands this reaction manifested itself in the creation of the dissident movement called Charter 77, which Dubcek described as "a courageous initiative in the tradition of Czech political and cultural defiance going back to Austria-Hungary."[43] But Charter 77 failed to take root among the Slovaks not only because of the fact that it did not correspond to a Slovak reaction to the regime, but above all because of the constraints chartists placed on Slovak followers: "Slovak intellectual dissidence was not independent, did not even

take a step without the consent of Prague, was Czechoslovak, and in its political consequences, it was even Czechoslovakizing."[44] The Slovak reaction to the regime was displayed in totally different ways. There were no organized political groups, but there were people who were patiently waiting for change: "The men—and, of course, also the women—of the year 1968 were certainly not organized as a movement, nor even half-organized as the chartists, but they knew one another. . . . In contrast to the chartist dissidents, these Slovak reformers concentrated on their own country. . . . they were prepared for changes, awaited them, and tried to be ready for them."[45] There were also public manifestations of opposition and they came from an entirely different quarter.

Historically a religious people, the Slovaks turned to the practice of their faith as a way of showing their opposition. Regular religious events bear this out, in particular the annual pilgrimages to Levoca, usually in early July and to Sastin, normally in mid-September in the late 1970s and 1980s. Some 150,000 people attended the Marian celebrations in Levoca; in Sastin, around 50,000 pilgrims attended similar celebrations. By their very nature of bringing people together of all ages and from all parts of Slovakia, these pilgrimages also became nationalist demonstrations. In 1985, the Catholic Church and the religious movement in Slovakia received a moral boost when Bishop Jozef Tomko was elevated to the rank of cardinal, the first Slovak to be so named in modern times. He was appointed by the Supreme Pontiff to head the Congregation for the Evangelization of Peoples. The regime did not publicly react to this nomination, especially as Cardinal Tomko was an emigre; but the faithful in Slovakia became aware of it.

In the 1988 signature campaign in Czechoslovakia demanding the freedom of religion, from the 500,00 signatures collected, 300,000 were from Slovakia. The regime felt threatened by this action and reacted accordingly. On 25 March 1988, it repressed brutally a peaceful candlelight religious rally organized by Frantisek Miklosko of 2,000 people on one of Bratislava's main squares. It reacted with an equal lack of discrimination a year later in a television program. On the fiftieth anniversary of the 1939 Slovak declaration of independence, Czechoslovak Television in Bratislava showed a six-part series beginning on 6 March 1989, entitled "The Cross in the Shackles of Power." The program was prepared by the Institute for Scientific Atheism of the Slovak Academy of Sciences without the collaboration of professional historians. Not only was it an attack on the events that had taken place a half century before, but the program clearly implied that the Catholic Church was responsible for all the evil that had taken place not only in the Slovak Republic but also in the two decades preceding its creation and in the events of 1944. The crudity of the message was not repeated in an editorial on the anniversary of Slovak independence in the pages of the Slovak Communist

daily *Pravda.* The program also brought forth a letter from Bishop Korec that circulated in samizdat. This extraordinary document took issue not only with the blatantly antireligious message, but also with the distortions of Slovak history in the program and in contemporary historiography generally.[46] To a Slovak reader, the message was clear, as clear as the meaning of religious dissidence in Slovakia was to the regime.

In 1985, the Soviet Union experienced a change of leadership that was to have profound effects on the Communist regimes of Eastern Europe. The new Soviet leader, Mikhail Gorbachev, realized that the neo-Stalinist policies of his predecessors were not only counter-productive for the Soviet economy, but prevented the enactment of much needed reforms and other modernization measures that would allow socialism to remain a credible ideology and the Soviet Union a super-power. He set out to restructure the Soviet economy in a policy called *perestroika,* and he ended the regime's restrictions on the freedom of expression in another policy called *glasnost.* The Communist leaders of Eastern Europe, especially those of Czechoslovakia, reacted negatively to the new Soviet course. Nevertheless, in December 1987, Husak was ousted from his position as secretary general of the CPCS and replaced by Milos Jakes, another conservative. Husak remained president of the Czechoslovak Republic. As for the East European populations, they were becoming receptive to the Gorbachev message; their reaction was voiced primarily through various dissident movements which demanded change. The tension that developed between the East European Communist leadership and the people was broken when Gorbachev decided in 1989 that Eastern Europe was no longer a Soviet sphere of interest and that each regime was henceforth free to deal with the question of reform as it pleased.

During the summer and fall of 1989, the Central European states abandoned their Communist regimes, either as a result of elections, as in Poland, or as a result of mass demonstrations, as in East Germany. Czechoslovakia's regime fell after the government ordered the brutal repression of a student demonstration in Prague on 17 November. The demonstration was called to commemorate the murder of a Czech student by the Nazis on the same day in 1939. During the course of the week that followed, Czech dissidents organized themselves in a movement called *Obcanske forum* (Civic forum) under the leadership of the Czech dissident and playwright, Vaclav Havel. The Velvet Revolution was launched. The regime fell a week later; on 10 December Husak resigned from the presidency—he died two years later, on 18 November 1991—and on 29 December Czechoslovakia had its second non-Communist president in the postwar era in the person of Havel. On 28 December, Dubcek had also reentered the political scene as chairman of the Federal Assembly.

In Slovakia, there were public protests in the wake of the Prague events and they took on a specific Slovak flavor: "The individuality, the difference of the Slovak movement became evident from the first mass meeting on the Square of the Slovak National Uprising with the unforgettably original moderators Milan Knazko and Jan Budaj. . . . it is these two men who caused the temperature of the nation-wide democratic movement in Slovakia to be comparable to that in the center [Prague]."[47] However, unlike Prague, where people like Havel and Dubcek addressed the crowds and gave the meetings a very political tone, in Bratislava the atmosphere was more relaxed and more social, without being less serious. The banned Slovak flag of the pre-Communist era was also in evidence. In those initial days, a movement called *Verejnost proti nasiliu* (Public against violence) was formed, bringing together former Communists, dissidents, Catholics, intellectuals, and writers. Its formation marked the first stirrings of new political life in Slovakia.

A new era opened for the Czechs and the Slovaks. They faced new challenges, and above all, the need to resolve the question of their relations in a common state: another chapter opened in Slovakia's struggle for survival.

12

Democracy and
Independence

A NEW POLITICAL SETTING

With the fall of the Communist regime of Czechoslovakia in November 1989, the Slovak people entered a period of political dialogue and activity that ended with the proclamation of the second Slovak Republic on 1 January 1993. This declaration happened under circumstances unprecedented in Slovak history: There was an absence of external pressure or threats. On the other hand, the political situation in Czechoslovakia, as in the rest of Central Europe, after almost a half-century of Communist rule, was anything but stable. The rapidity with which the Communist regimes had fallen was an indication of fundamental opposition to the Communist system not just of dissident groups, but also of the population; it had not been an indication of consensus on what should replace it. The need to create a new political system and to define political priorities and goals thus became paramount in all countries, particularly in Czechoslovakia. The absence of political parties in the single-party system of the Communist regime, and also of an organized dissident group in Slovakia,[1] resulted in an unusual situation: In the initial stages of the post-Communist era individuals, rather than parties, defined priorities and goals. Many were new politicians who faced the task of learning not only the art of political maneuvering, but above all that of public discourse in a

democratic society. They were the ones who dealt with the issue of Czech-Slovak relations which found resolution in the dissolution of Czechoslovakia.

Although the events that brought about independence are described below, it is still too soon to conclude with any degree of certainty which ones were catalysts and which ones were determinant in bringing about the final outcome. Similarly, it is not possible to describe and evaluate the role and influence of all political actors involved. Only when archival material is available, in particular the memoirs of those who were at the center of political life in this period, will an accurate account of the chain of events that led to independence be available. What is feasible at this time is a presentation of the main features of Slovak political life and above all the debate on the future of Slovakia that took place in the three years that preceded independence.

The new phase in the life of the Slovaks began in November 1989 with mass demonstrations in Bratislava against the Communist regime. One analyst has suggested that the revolution was brought to Bratislava from Prague.[2] There is perhaps some truth to this, especially as it was unlikely that any public activity in Slovakia would have had any effect in Prague in Czechoslovakia's post-1968 neo-Stalinist system. In addition, the Slovak dissidence movement, as we pointed out in Chapter 11, unlike Charter 77 in the Czech Lands, concentrated on the freedom of religion. Yet, once the regime fell, the Slovaks lost no time in getting involved in politics. For the first time since February 1948, they were free of imposed slogans and impossible dreams and had the opportunity to take a good look at the past that they just left behind, and consider their future. The press and media were no longer censored and commentators and analysts wasted no time in assessing the condition of Slovak society. There were some troublesome symptoms:

> Even from the point of view of a historically very short period as that of the last forty-six years, the consequences of the most recent developments are very evident. There is a moral decline and a national schizophrenia in Slovak society that shows itself in a split into two implacable camps. This catastrophic situation is the result of the "normalization" attempts of the Czech-Marxist regime which carried out Benes's aggressive anti-Slovak chauvinism even more effectively by imposing the idea of a united Czechoslovak state with all available means, in other words, [through] state Czechoslovakism. In short, with the Communist hammer, they succeeded there where they had failed in the inter-war years, namely to change our national essence. The Czechoslovakization of two Slovak generations, thanks to Communist jails, eliminated to some degree not only national, but also human dignity in Slovak society.[3]

This mordant comment provides an accurate reflection of the state of Slovak society which, after four decades of communism, was still very different from Czech society.[4] It also sums up the two closely related themes that would dominate political life in Slovakia in the period after the elections of 1990: Slovakia's position in the common state and the renewal of Slovak national life. However, in the months that followed the fall of communism, there was an explosion of political activity and debate that preceded the elections of June, and celebrated the end to the brutality, political conservatism, and intellectual turgidity that had characterized the Communist period since 1968.

FREE ELECTIONS

The people who took over from the Communist hard-liners, a mixture of middle-rank Communist bosses suddenly converted to democracy, Communist dissidents, and non-Communists, set out to seek a popular mandate to govern. Thanks to the federal system, not just Prague and the Federal Assembly, but also Bratislava and the Slovak National Council (SNC) were centers of Slovak political debate and the enactment of legislation. A new Slovak government under Milan Cic took over in December 1989 from the previous hard-line Communist one, while different political groups began forming around certain personalities. The first two groups to emerge were Public Against Violence (*Verejnost proti nasiliu,* or VPN) and the Christian Democratic Movement (*Krestanske Demokraticke Hnutie* or KDH). The VPN was formed by a group of intellectuals, writers, actors, and ecologists and it was led by Fedor Gal. Among the political personalities to figure early in it were Dubcek and Cic. As the VPN sought to broaden its base, new people became active in it, namely a lawyer from Trencin called Vladimir Meciar, who was made minister of the Interior in the Cic government, and Miklosko, leader of the March 1988 candlelight demonstration in Bratislava. In its platform, the VPN stressed democratic and pluralistic values. In many respects, it was the Slovak equivalent of the main Czech political group, Civic Forum *(Obcianske forum).* It should be noted that neither Gal, nor those around him, stood for election; Meciar did and he led the VPN in the SNC. The KDH was formed in Nitra on 22 February 1990 and was led by Jan Carnogursky, a Catholic dissident lawyer from Bratislava. He had become deputy prime minister of Czechoslovakia shortly after the Communists were ousted. Like the group's name indicates, its platform stressed Christian values and it established contacts with Western European Christian Democratic parties. But it was also split into two wings, a nationalist and a moderate one.

Other political groups were created during the spring of 1990. The first to call itself a party was the Democratic Party (*Demokraticka Strana,* or DS). It was created from the Slovak Freedom Party that the Communist National Front had tolerated, and was led by a Slovak who had lived in exile during the Communist period, Martin Kvetko. He had been a leading member of the post-war Democratic Party that had won the 1946 elections. Its platform stressed democratic values in a strong Czechoslovakia. Another party that took its name from the past, the Slovak National Party (*Slovenska narodna strana,* or SNS), under the leadership of Vitazoslav Moric, was created shortly before the June 1990 elections. It was the only party to advocate openly the independence of Slovakia. None of the other parties had yet developed a well-defined platform regarding Slovakia's position in Czechoslovakia, except for the Democratic Party which stressed that Slovakia's future lay in a democratic Czechoslovakia. The CPS, though ousted from power, regrouped and remained a political force with a left-wing program under a new leader, Peter Weiss. Smaller groups were also formed but none assumed any importance.

Elections were held on 8–9 June 1990. Out of an electorate of 3,622,650 people in Slovakia, 95.39 percent voted with less than 3 percent of the ballots spoiled. The voters gave political power to a coalition of political groups. Twenty fielded candidates, but only seven polled enough votes to have representation in the SNC. These elections were an unequivocal expression of the rejection of communism: "the people voted above all for successful movements, they gave their votes to those whom they assumed would get rid of the 42 years-long Communist totalitarian past. For this reason, these were votes more against communism than for any concrete specific program. . . . there was still a certain aversion against [political] parties and a preference for movements."[5] In the local elections on 24 November 1990, the electorate also voted in coalitions, although this time many Communists won mayoralties.

The first post-Communist elections produced two surprises: First, the results did not correspond to the public opinion polls that preceded the voting. Throughout May, the KDH, which led the polls with a high of 38.0 percent on 8 May, brought down to 29.1 percent at the end of the month, obtained only 19.2 percent of the vote on polling day. The VPN, with a low of 5.0 percent at the beginning of May, was polled at 17.3 percent in the third week and obtained 29.3 percent of the votes on election day. The electorate was clearly not yet willing to express itself openly outside the secrecy of the ballot box. The story is much the same for other parties, in particular the SNS, which produced the second surprising factor about the elections.

The SNS was the late comer on the political scene, with a program of Slovak independence. While public opinion polls gave it only 3.8 percent of

popular support at the end of May, on election day it polled a surprising 13.9 percent, making it the third party in Slovakia, just ahead of the CPS. The success of the SNS and its subsequent activity in the SNC indicated that "the Slovak question" was still on the political agenda even though the party did not have in its ranks any recognized personality in Slovakia. It is quite likely that one particular event preceding the election contributed to the party's success.

The Federal Assembly debated on 30 March a Slovak motion to approve the return of the hyphen to the official spelling of Czechoslovakia. The refusal on the part of the majority of Czech deputies and some Slovak deputies provoked a mass demonstration in the streets of Bratislava the next day, where once again the chant of an independent Slovakia was heard. After some acrimonious discussions, two compromises were reached: It was agreed that the hyphen could be used in Slovakia, although in the Czech Lands and abroad the unhyphenated spelling would apply. Then on 20 April, Parliament voted the name Czech and Slovak Federative Republic (CSFR, and in Slovakia C-SFR). This incident was the first to show how very different were the Czech and Slovak conceptions of their common state and brought into the open the need to reexamine the state of Czech-Slovak relations. The evolving political discourse took place at three levels: at the parliamentary level, that is to say in the Federal Assembly, the Czech National Council (CNC), and the SNC; at the public level, namely in public demonstrations; and in the media, in particular the press, which also covered the two other levels.

The task of forming a government was given to Meciar, leader of the VPN in the SNC. He formed a coalition government since the forty-eight seats the VPN had in an SNC of 150 seats were insufficient to form it alone. The second group, the KDH, had thirty-one seats. Its leader, Carnogursky, who had given up his post of deputy prime minister of Czechoslovakia before the elections, became vice-premier. The SNS received twenty-two seats as did the CPS while the DS had seven seats, the Green Party six seats and the Hungarian parties fourteen. The Slovak government was formed of representatives of the VPN, KDH and DS. In opposition were the SNS and the CPS along with the Greens and the Hungarian parties. Miklosko of the VPN became chairman of the SNC while Ivan Carnogursky of the KDH became vice-chairman. This coalition government had the task of governing Slovakia until the next elections, set for June 1992.

The government represented one of two centers of power in Slovakia; the other was the presidium of the SNC. It was composed of fifteen deputies chosen on the basis of electoral results and its chairman was the president of the SNC. It set the agenda for parliamentary debate, appointed legislative commissions, and ratified the election of the premier and the appointment of all government

ministers. It is in the SNC and its presidium that many acrimonious debates took place, often on the same issue, for example the proposal to vote the sovereignty of Slovakia, which was proposed four times between 1990 and 1992. Of all the issues that were debated in the SNC, the constitutional question was the one that produced many proposals and approaches, and a great deal of political maneuvering with Czech and federal representatives, and between the parties in the SNC. At the federal level, the reappointment of the Slovak Marian Calfa as prime minister of Czechoslovakia, a former Communist who had held that position before the regime fell, strengthened the federal presence in the debate in Slovakia.

CONSTITUTIONAL DISCUSSIONS

Two projects dominated the political agenda after the elections: Constitutional reform and the introduction of a market economy. Both were intimately related but produced a different approach in Slovakia as a result of a historical evolution whose main traits became clearer as the consequences of the economic transformation started to be felt and the constitutional debate was engaged. The need for a new constitution was dictated above all by the unsuitability of the Communist one. While this was a self-evident proposition after the fall of the old regime, for the Slovaks its replacement was also dictated by the fact that the Communist constitution had particularly deleterious consequences for their nation: "The pseudo-federation of the last twenty years, after fulfilling the personal power ambitions of Gustav Husak, tied into [Antonin] Novotny's program of pursuing an assimilatory policy toward the Slovaks. The latter was based on the methods and aims of the Memorandum on Slovakia"[6]. Not surprisingly, Slovak political leaders became, in the words of Czechoslovak President Havel, "the motor of the discussions"[7].

The Slovak government approached the question of constitutional reform on two levels; within the SNC where a group of specialists and lawyers worked under the leadership of Ivan Carnogursky—in the end it produced very little—and through the presidium of the SNC which engaged in discussions with representatives of the presidium of the CNC and the federal government. Four main series of meetings on constitutional reform took place which involved representatives of the CNC, the SNC and the federal government: In Trencianske Teplice in August 1990; in Lany on 10 May 1991; in Budmerice on 31 May 1991; and in Kromeriz on 17 June 1991. Before the Lany conference, there were meetings in Vykary with Havel on 4 and 12 February and 4 March 1991. The Trencianske Teplice conference tackled the question

of the respective powers of the federal government, the CNC, and the SNC. The agreement that was signed also stipulated that the Czech and Slovak Republics would seek to be incorporated in European institutions as separate entities. On 24 November, the CNC and the SNC ratified the 13 November agreement resulting from the Trencianske Teplice meeting and the Federal Assembly passed Law 556/90. It amended Law 143/68 which had transformed Czechoslovakia into a federation in 1968. As of 1 January 1991, each republic became responsible for its own economy. Slovakia was also given the right to establish a ministry of international relations. Political power, which under the Communists had been concentrated at the federal level, had now shifted to the republics.

In Lany, the discussion centered on the federal constitution. The Slovaks accepted the proposal that an agreement would be signed by the CNC and SNC on the principles of the new constitutional arrangement instead of a state treaty. In Budmerice, there was discussion on the different types of constitutional arrangement but no agreement; in addition, Havel expressed the wish that the constitution should be ready before the elections whereas some politicians suggested that the elections be postponed. In Kromeriz, it was agreed that a federal commission would draft a legal treaty between the two republics that could be revised but also would be approved by the CNC and the SNC and then passed back to the federal parliament for approval. The treaty would formulate the broad division of powers and the basis for a new constitution. The constitution would be prepared for ratification by the national councils. Finally, a Federal Council would be created to oversee all federal laws. It was agreed to bring the constitutional process to a successful completion before the end of 1991.

These conferences and agreements met with varying degrees of approval in Slovakia. They set the stage, in fact, not only for a debate on the future of Slovakia, but also for other political activities, in particular public demonstrations, all meant to have some influence on the constitutional process. It is somewhat ironic that the Communist regime, which had so favored organized public demonstrations of self-proclaimed successes and proletarian solidarity, had been itself brought down by street demonstrations. The message was not lost on the Slovak people, especially those who began to have doubts about the way the Slovak government was handling the question of the nation's future. In addition, certain specific questions also brought the people out on the street, a phenomenon that became known as *mitingova demokracia* (meeting democracy).

Among the most important demonstrations were those held on 1 April 1990 in Bratislava on the spelling of the name of Czechoslovakia; on 5 May in

Bradlo to commemorate the death of Milan R. Stefanik; on 26 August in Ruzomberok in honor of Andrej Hlinka, where calls for the independence of Slovakia were made; on 29 August in Banska Bystrica to commemorate the 1944 uprising; on 5 October in Bratislava, organized by Matica slovenska, to make Slovak the official language throughout the Slovak Republic; on 11 March 1991 in Bratislava, also organized by Matica slovenska, to proclaim the sovereignty of the Slovak Republic; on 23 April in Bratislava when the Meciar government fell; on 8 June in [Turciansky Sväty] Martin, when Matica slovenska made public the new Memorandum of the Slovak Nation (in commemoration of the Memorandum of the Slovak Nation of 1861); on 19 September in Bratislava, again by Matica slovenska to ask the SNC once more to proclaim the sovereignty of the Slovak Republic; and on 22 September in Bratislava for a common state. There were also public hunger strikes in the fall of 1990 when the SNC refused to pass a law making Slovak the official language in all of Slovakia.

These demonstrations were in addition to the mass rallies before the June 1990 elections. Representatives of the federal government as well as the Slovak government appeared at the demonstration in Bradlo, Banska Bystrica, and Bratislava on 22 September 1991. The last two were counterdemonstrations to the Ruzomberok and 19 September Bratislava ones, which were deemed to have been very nationalistic, even separatist. There were also of a couple of specific demonstrations: the protest of metalworkers from all of Slovakia in Bratislava on 18 March 1991 against certain economic decisions of the Czechoslovak government and the ecological protest against the Gabcikovo dam on 1 August.

In addition to demonstrations, one political incident brought Slovaks onto the streets of Bratislava—the change of government on 23 April 1991. The coalition government that Meciar had formed after the elections experienced difficulties in governing Slovakia because of tensions between the coalition partners. In the fall of 1990, the language law issue provoked a crisis within the coalition. Two versions were proposed in the SNC, a moderate one by the government and a more radical one, prepared by Matica slovenska and supported by the SNS and some members of the KDH. The difference between the two proposals concerned the treatment minority languages. Meciar strongly defended the government bill and refused to bow to the public demonstrations that followed its passage in the SNC. There was also a famous incident on Slovak television where Meciar publicly berated Jozef Markus, president of Matica slovenska, for his nationalist stance.

There were also tensions within the main parties. The non-parliamentary leadership of the VPN under Gal gravitated toward Prague while the parliamentarians, led by Meciar and Knazko, concentrated on Slovakia and its

problems. As for the KDH, the division within its ranks revolved around the national question which the moderates under Jan Carnogursky preferred not to raise. The crisis that led to Meciar's ouster began when the tensions between the Gal and Meciar groups of the VPN came out into the open in March 1991. Other factors also played a role in this crisis: Meciar's popularity; his decision to form his own faction in the VPN; fears among some of his colleagues that he was too confrontational with his Czech counterparts in the constitutional process; the Andras affair;[8] and an economic report that outlined the consequences of the link of the Slovak economy with the reforms of Vaclav Klaus, federal minister of finance, which Meciar opposed. Under the still-existing rules of the Communist constitution, after Meciar lost a vote of confidence in the presidium of the SNC on 23 April, he was replaced by Jan Carnogursky, leader of the KDH. Meciar then formed his own party, the Movement for a Democratic Slovakia (*Hnutie za demokraticke Slovensko,* HZDS), and took some VPN deputies with him. This event was not without consequence on Slovak national life: "When he [Meciar] was forced into opposition, only one path was left for him to fight successfully a return to power, the national one."[9] He became an ardent defender of Slovak interests and the continued attacks against him merely increased his popularity in Slovakia.

Some of the public demonstrations, especially during 1991, as well as the government crisis, fed into and were fed by the extraordinary constitutional debate that was taking place in Slovak political and public life. The Slovak press faithfully reported not only the pronouncements of Slovak as well Czech politicians, especially Havel, but also made itself available to multiple analyses from observers, specialists, and academics. The theme of renewal of Slovak national life focused primarily on this question: How has the Czech-Slovak relationship been beneficial to the Slovaks? A Czech writer, Ludvik Vaculik, launched the debate. In an at-times bitter tone, he railed at the fact that the Slovaks, to whom he referred as little brothers, refused to share the common bed with the Czechs. He did not think, furthermore, that they were ready to sleep in their own. In his refusal to accept a Slovak approach and in his steadfast conviction of the importance of Czechoslovak statehood, he stated: "To develop our own Czech state—it is after all a step backwards. Not long ago I went to Bratislava and all my friends said to me why are you getting so agitated because those nationalist noises come from careerists, idiots or else intrigue-makers. I heard this with pleasure."[10]

Vaculik did not have to wait long for a reply; the Slovak writer Vladimir Minac took him head on. Rejecting the notion of a "little brother" and examining generally the meaning of Czechoslovakism, Minac retorted: "Vaculik writes that 'it is an honest duty to be a Czechoslovak.' However, what

you find behind a Czechoslovak is a badly covered pure Czech who in some peculiar way has made the land of the Slovaks his own; and if he has not done so, then he wants to do so. But a Slovak does not want to be a Czechoslovak, he does not want to be shoved behind a foreign facade, he wants to be himself, independent and equal. Is that so difficult to understand?"[11] At the root of this exchange and generally in most writings on the question of the Czech-Slovak relationship was the question of Slovak self-determination: "After the fall of the totalitarian regime, no one put in doubt the right of self-determination of the Czech nation. What is the situation with regards to the right of self-determination of the Slovaks? If we do not want to quibble with half-truths, we have to conclude that the right of self-determination of the Slovaks is yet to be achieved."[12]

Not surprisingly, many writers looked at the history of the relations of the two nations in the common state to seek to understand the reasons for such a development. According to a historian: "With the creation of Czecho-Slovakia [it would seem] as if the Czech nation lost its Czech national identity and took on a Czechoslovak one . . . . Historically, the entire Czech nation was prepared to accept the theory of Czechoslovakism. The Slovak nation [on the other hand] rejected this theory even if there were Slovak Czechoslovaks."[13] If the result was paradoxically "discipline and obedience" on the Slovak part, as another commentator pointed out, he also added that: "In the last seventy years, the history of our 'coexistence' has shown us that Czech politicians always honored Slovak compliance with an increase of their hegemonic pressure on Slovakia and by pushing aside disobedient and uncomfortable Slovak politicians."[14]

This historical record as well as the acknowledgment of the Slovaks's right to enjoy the right of self-determination brought many commentators to ponder how this record affected the current state of Czech-Slovak relations. At the heart of the problem was a double standard: "When a Czech identifies with his nation, he is considered to be a great patriot. But if a Slovak so much as identifies himself in a national way, the Czech political machinery labels him a nationalist, chauvinist, clero-fascist and destroyer of the state."[15] In a similar vein, when Prague recognized the sovereignty and independence of the Baltic nations, a writer commented: "When the Slovaks want to do something similar, Prague immediately 'spews fire and brimstone.'"[16] The Czech perception of the Slovaks explains why the signature campaign launched by a close adviser of Havel in the autumn of 1991, in a project called *Za spolecny stat* (For a common state) which gathered some two million signatures, mostly in the Czech Lands, "was understood in Slovakia as a further example of the attempts to maintain Czech hegemony in the Czechoslovak federation, as well as the continuation of efforts to rule Slovakia from Prague."[17]

The debate in Slovakia also looked at the economic dimension in the Czech-Slovak relationship. There were mutual accusations and misunderstandings. What caught the attention of some observers was a contradiction in the Czech press: "Instead of a realistic approach to the current [economic] situation in Czecho-Slovakia, there is in the pages of some Prague dailies a campaign which hardly contributes to . . . [Czech-Slovak] relations. On the one hand, they seek to convince Czech readers how badly the Slovaks would suffer if they separated from the Czechs, yet on the other, they claim that the Czech Republic is subsidizing Slovakia."[18] The economic reality in Slovakia since the abandonment of the command economy and the introduction of the market principle as well as new directions in foreign policy, away from arms sales, resulted in a proportionately greater unemployment rate than in the Czech Lands. In April 1991 around 100,000 persons, representing in total numbers more than twice that of the Czech Republic, were unemployed. By January 1992, a peak unemployment rate of 319,000 persons or 11.8 percent of Slovakia's work force was recorded.[19] Slovakia had 70 percent of the state's arms manufacturing industry; in 1988, its budget was 18.8 billion crowns; by 1991, it had fallen to 2.1 billion.

These developments raised the possibility of creating an alternative independent Slovak economy. However, a report from the Economics Section of the Czechoslovak Academy of Sciences in Prague indicated that separation would bring about an unemployment level of 300,000 in each republic, which meant that there would be twice as many unemployed in Slovakia as in the Czech Lands. The report also estimated that there would be a 50 percent loss of finished goods in each market and that Slovakia would experience more problems as it received 27 percent of its finished goods from the Czech Lands but sent in only 11 percent. The assumption was that the Slovak economy could not make up the difference internally.[20]

But a Slovak economist argued that the current economic problems, which were likely to get worse, were the result of Slovakia's historical and current relationship to the general economic situation in Czechoslovakia. He pointed out that Slovakia's contribution in 1990 to state offices was 19 billion crowns of which only 17 billion were for such offices in Slovakia. From taxes raised, the Slovak economy received from Prague in 1989–1990 115 billion crowns and in 1991, 146 billion crowns; he argued that if Slovakia were independent, it would collect 200 billion crowns. Finally, to illustrate the difficulties Slovakia faced in getting what it needed from the federal economy, he cited the decision to finance 250 kilometers of highway construction in 1991; only 18 kilometers was allotted to Slovakia on the strength of the argument that the most vital highways had to be the ones that could favor exports to Western European countries, in other words, those in the Czech Republic.[21]

Using a similar line of argument, a group called the Independent Union of Economists from Slovakia took a critical look at the economic course and concluded that it hit Slovakia particularly hard, favoring above all the Czech economy. The group proposed that the SNC declare the economic sovereignty of Slovakia and noted: "One need not worry about the capability of the Slovak economy to thrive in the extreme conditions of full independence, if it had to come to that."[22] Apart from economic arguments against it, the centrally run economic reform program was unacceptable because its consequences on the status and the future of Slovakia. One commentator explained:

> Our historical experience proves that the reverse approach to the delega-
> tion of powers—not from independent, sovereign states to the center but
> the opposite—hides a great danger. Access in Slovakia to economic reform
> determined by the center confirms this possibility and does not give us a
> guarantee against a fall into deformation which will lead us in the end to
> a unitary state and in this way to the factual denial of the sovereignty of
> Slovakia.[23]

Much of the debate in Slovakia, including the historical and economic discussion, concerned specifically the constitutional question, particularly during the time when negotiations between the two levels of governments were taking place. At the center of the constitutional debate in Slovakia was one basic question: What constitutional arrangement will best correspond to the needs and aspirations of the Slovak nation? Three corollaries also required an answer: First, how can this arrangement be linked to the sovereignty of the Slovak nation? Second, what is to be the relationship with the Czech nation? And finally, how does one change the current constitutional system?

Many of the participants in the debate reflected on the nature of the federal system. One commentator remarked:

> I cannot escape the feeling that on the territory of the C-SFR there are
> three nations: Czech, Slovak and federal. In the republic, the Czech and
> Slovak nations are more or less tolerated, but the creator, owner and ruler
> is the federal nation. In numbers, the federal nation is not very big, lives
> just about entirely in Prague but owns 70 percent of the state's property,
> has all the executive powers and has all the laws on its side. It is a nation
> with only one layer but it is a layer of rulers. It is in fashion to speak of
> Slovak nationalism and separatism. In fact, it has nothing to do with
> fashion, it is a seventy year old evergreen. If there is any sort of nationalism
> which is truly capable of breaking up the republic it is federal nationalism.

It is a nationalism which claims that Czechs and Slovaks are unable to
agree mutually, that they are like children who are not legally independent
[and] whom a careful tutor with a long whip has to force into the common
home.[24]

It is not just the history of less than seventy years of "Pragocentrism," as
centralized federal power was often referred to, that was troublesome for many
Slovaks, but the fact that federal officials continued to preach the necessity of
maintaining such power. Havel, in his first major speech to the Federal
Assembly in September 1990 on the need for a new constitution, wanted not
only the retention of a federal state, arguing that there existed a "federal people,"
although accepting the need to rebuilt federal organs, but he also cited American
federalism as an example to emulate.[25] Jozef Prokes, the new leader of the SNS,
in a letter to Havel, responded: "Your reference to the American Constitution
has left the strong impression that you wish to continue with the ideology of
Czechoslovakism, that is to say one nation in this state which, it seems, your
statement about a federal people confirms. Until now this has not brought
anything good in the relations between Czechs and Slovaks."[26] At the root of
the suspicions about the federal proposal was the historical record: "Czech
internal politics, especially the politics of the Castle since 1918, in fact to this
day, do not look for an ally in Slovakia for the idea and stability of a common
statehood for Czechs and Slovaks, but only an ally for the idea of unitary
Czechoslovakism."[27]

The constitutional debate in Slovakia left no doubt that the federal
solution proposed by federal officials was unacceptable. The main reason was
that it did not recognize the sovereignty of the Slovak nation. This is a basic
point that cut across the spectrum of all the Slovak solutions proposed and was
the object of heated debate in the SNC. However, it was not always clear what
was meant by sovereignty. The Slovak language has two words for sovereignty:
zvrchovanost and *suverenita.* In any Slovak dictionary they have the same
meaning; yet during the debate on Slovakia's constitutional future they acquired
different meanings. The first term, *zvrchovanost,* referred to the sovereignty of
the nation, that is to say its right to pursue its own national life. The second,
suverenita, meant state sovereignty as understood in international law.[28] The
three public demonstrations of March, June, and September 1991 on sovereignty addressed the sovereignty of the nation. The SNC refused, however, to
heed the public call to declare it, in part because Havel condemned such a
declaration on 12 March as an attempt to achieve independence by unconsti-
tutional means. There was also the split in the KDH; the nationalist group was
in favor whereas Jan Carnogursky's moderate wing was opposed to such a

declaration. There were three attempts by the nationalist group in the KDH to have the SNC declare the sovereignty of Slovakia, on 8 November 1991, 1 April and 7 May 1992. None succeeded.

While a centralized federation was rejected, a decentralized federation was acceptable to some, because it recognized implicitly—without stating it—the sovereignty of the nation. Dubcek, the respected leader of the 1968 Prague Spring and a supporter of a decentralized federation, stated: "I see a federal arrangement as an alliance of republics with equality of the nations, rights and citizens which will allow the development of the identity of nations, develop the statehood of the republics and create the conditions so that the CSFR and its republics are prepared for a dignified entry into an integrated Europe."[29] Dubcek's terminology was anything but clear and he did not use the term sovereignty. However, had he put the accent on the republics, he could have been speaking of a confederation. Dubcek was not the only one guilty of confusion. Jozef Moravcik, who later became the last foreign minister of Czechoslovakia, noted that "the present discussions and presentations of views of the political representatives of both republics assure us that each side understands the federation to mean something different."[30] Among the main political parties in Slovakia, the VPN supported this type of federal solution.

An alternative, which was articulated with some variations, was that of a confederal arrangement. Meciar, when he was prime minister and leader of the VPN, supported the federal solution, but opted for this alternative when he created the HZDS. Markus, president of Matica slovenska, also favored it, but with a slightly different variation.[31] Paramount in this proposal was the sovereignty of the constituent republics: "Compared to a federation which as a federal state is one state, a confederation is an association of states which in the international sphere maintain their sovereignty and are themselves objects of international law."[32] The two definitions of sovereignty were fused into one, giving this option a particular appeal: "in Western understanding, a nation is a state. If we reverse this proposition, the regrouping of a people, of a 'nation' which does not have its own state, is not a nation. According to Western understanding, the Slovenes are becoming a nation, the Slovaks were not a nation in the last forty-five years and if they stay in the federation, they will not become one either."[33] When Meciar spoke of this option, he underlined that between the republics "a common market would be kept, the human relations that were created would be maintained and respected and common organs would be created which would have powers in common dimensions."[34] Those who opposed it, as did Dubcek, argued that a confederation would lead "to the destruction of the common Czecho-Slovak statehood."[35] Another staunch opponent of the confederal solution was another Slovak, Calfa, the Czechoslo-

vak prime minister, who spoke openly against it in public interviews and on television.

These two solutions represented the two ends of what was an acceptable spectrum for many Slovaks. Close to the confederal solution was the approach taken by Jan Carnogursky and his wing of the KDH. His concern was centered on two preoccupations: First, the negative reactions in Europe and in the world that would result from the breakup of the common state of the Czechs and Slovaks, and second, the way that the Slovaks could join a united Europe as an "independent subject," an idea he first made public when he was still deputy prime minister of Czechoslovakia. Later he suggested that Slovakia could join Europe in the year 2000. In an interview to the influential weekly *Literarny tyzdennik,* he combined both preoccupations:

> The simplest way to get Slovakia onto the conscience of Europe is to create a reliable legislative system, starting with the protection of foreign investment and ending with a legal democratic order, including that of parliament. Slovakia must also enter the society of European nations as a legal subject, on whom everyone can rely. My vision is that we achieve an equivalent status. I say equivalent because Slovakia has already achieved a position of equal rights. Equivalent is also a matter of protocol, so that we can be a subject of international relations. Slovakia should achieve this kind of status not by breaking up Czecho-Slovakia, but by entering a broader European society as equal in rights and equivalent in status.[36]

Carnogursky, although a lawyer, remained vague when asked to define constitutional arrangements, an approach probably dictated by tactical and strategic necessity. He often stressed the need not to frighten the Czechs, whom he called the Slovaks' "natural allies."[37] His vagueness was meant not to offend or confuse. As in the case of Dubcek's defence of the federal solution, Carnogursky knew that it was politically expedient to avoid specific terminology. As Meciar remarked: "After analyzing the program of many parties in Slovakia, we have come to the conclusion that they are giving a confederal content to the common existence but are afraid to call it a confederation because right now they do not know how the public would react to it."[38]

Independence was the final option, although no one really knew how viable an option it was and whether it truly enjoyed popular support. The electoral success of the SNS was not an accurate indication: "Not all the voters for the SNS were for the absolute separation of the Czech Lands and Slovakia. Many saw the SNS, including their radical pronouncements, as a useful counterweight against centralizing tendencies. It was at best the only party

which had the courage to criticize openly the Castle. And this many voters found attractive."[39] Nevertheless, independence was on the program of the SNS since its creation. Under Prokes, the party put the emphasis on the need to be a good parliamentary citizen. Yet the aim to achieve independence remained and was dictated by the current economic situation and the integration process in Europe. According to Prokes:

> We believe that we should use the enthusiasm of the population to create something new before we fall into a political depression as a result of economic factors. . . . [Also] we should understand an integrated Europe as a cooperative Europe, not a Europe of one state. An integrated Europe will be stable only then, when all nations which live in it will have equal rights and duties. If there were so much as one unhappy nation, it would be an instrument of tension, for while it is possible to suppress the national factor or a national movement, it is not possible to eliminate it.[40]

While the debate on these options was taking place, the results of a public opinion poll taken in August 1991 on the constitutional future of Czechoslovakia were published. The poll produced some interesting results. Respondents were asked to chose between five outcomes: A unitary state; a federal state; a union of associated republics; confederation; and independence. In the Czech Republic, 70 percent of respondents opted for the first two outcomes (42 percent for a unitary state; 28 for a federal state) whereas in Slovakia, only 45 percent chose these outcomes (11 percent for a unitary state; 34 percent for a federal state). As far as the three other options are concerned, 17 percent of Czech respondents chose a union of associated republics; 8 percent independence and only 3 percent a confederation. In Slovakia, the confederation scored 23 percent; independence 16; and a union of associated republics 9 percent. Those who refused to answer totalled 2 percent in the Czech Republic and 7 percent in Slovakia.[41] A number of conclusions can be drawn from these results: The most evident one is the clear rejection in Slovakia of the status quo and its more centralized equivalent. In the Czech Republic, it is its acceptability that was overwhelmingly endorsed. The poll also showed that Slovak opinion was divided on the alternative solutions to the status quo, with a confederation as a leading favorite. We can also infer the strong support for the sovereignty of Slovakia from this poll. Among those in Slovakia who opted for a federal state it is likely that many did so without necessarily rejecting the sovereignty of the nation which all the other options (except a unitary state) accepted and reflected. Last but not least, the poll indicated that the constitutional debate not only involved politicians and specialists but also evoked interest in the general public.

It lasted until the June elections of 1992, without any indication of which option could achieve an absolute majority. In fact, the debate on this issue was so confused that it had prompted one newspaper to publish a series of articles explaining the different concepts and solutions being proposed.[42] The choice was in the hands of the elected representatives; at the end of December 1991, the government of the Slovak Republic submitted its constitutional proposals. The government of the Czech Republic did not.

The constitutional discussions and public debate in Slovakia were closely followed in the Czech Lands, as the poll showed, and in particular by President Havel. He visited Slovakia on a number of occasions where the reception was not always cordial and he also intervened in the debate. In March 1991 he proposed a referendum to determine what the Slovaks wanted. The reaction was one of skepticism and suspicion: "They threaten us with a referendum. Do they know ex ante that the Slovaks will decide in a certain way and in no other?"[43] In order to hasten the process and also to influence the outcome, Havel declared on 24 September 1991 in a speech to the Federal Assembly:

> We have only two alternatives: our first alternative is to build rapidly a democratic common state based on the federal principle. This would mean a state which exists out of the sovereign will of the republics which create it together and for themselves and which delegate it certain powers. . . . The second alternative is to break up in a legal and civilized way into two independent states which will then seek forms for future political and economic cooperation. As far as I am concerned, there is no third alternative.[44]

Havel's speech did not produce the results he expected. The meeting on 12 November between representatives of the SNC and the CNC in Papiernicky ended in failure. To counter this, Havel went on television on 17 November and "asked the people in a most dramatic speech to support him against their elected representatives."[45] Again he proposed holding a referendum on the future of the country. Once more his suggestion was ignored. On the Slovak side, work continued on a Slovak constitution; it was ready on time and was published on 27 and 28 December 1991. Despite the June Kromeriz agreement, the CNC had no constitutional proposals to offer by year's end.

The Slovak constitutional proposals offered the Slovak public four options: (1) the present federal system; (2) a common state with the Czech Republic on the basis of a treaty that recognizes the sovereignty of Slovakia with its own legislative assembly whose presidium acts as a collective head of state; (3) a common state in which Slovakia would have its own president and where powers would be divided

on the basis of a treaty with the Czech Republic; and (4) a confederation or any other form of union with other European states, including the Czech Republic.

While the Slovaks were considering their political options, Havel proposed and failed on 21 January to get the Federal Assembly to approve a law that would have given him the right to call a referendum before the June 1992 elections. His own constitutional proposals were rejected by the same body on 28 January. On 4 February, in Milovy, negotiations between representatives of the CNC and the SNC took place to hammer out constitutional proposals, and eight days later a text was agreed upon. However, on 25 February, after a particularly acrimonious debate where some members of the KDH voted with the HZDS, the SNC rejected the Milovy proposals.

THE 1992 ELECTIONS AND INDEPENDENCE

There were no further constitutional talks after the SNC's rejection of the Milovy proposals. The attention shifted to the forthcoming election, although the campaign was not devoid of discussion on the constitutional question, especially in Slovakia. The constitutional program of the mainline parties did not depart significantly from the one they developed during the constitutional talks. The electoral debate centered above all on the economic future of Slovakia. At issue was the challenge posed by the transformation of the former command economy into a market one; in contrast to the Czech Lands, such a perspective was problematic for the Slovak economy which would experience serious difficulties in privatizing major state industries such as mining, smeltering, and arms production. Most parties, in particular Meciar's HZDS, argued for a mixed approach in order to avoid major unemployment and other social problems, but also to allow the Slovak economy to modernize and become competitive. The HZDS also linked its social and economic policies with the need to find a constitutional solution and proposed the transformation of Czechoslovakia into a confederation of two national republics. The Communists, renamed Party of the Democratic Left (*Strana demokratickej lavice,* or SDL), had a left-wing platform with a strong nationalist content. As for the KDH, its program remained essentially Christian Democratic. Moreover, it split eight weeks before the elections with the nationalist group forming the Slovak Christian Democratic Movement (*Slovenske krestianske demokraticke hnutie,* or SKDH) under the leadership of Jan Klepac. The SNS continued to articulate the independence option.

Meciar's message was accepted by the Slovak electorate which gave the HZDS seventy-four seats out of 150 in the SNC. The SDL obtained twenty-

nine seats while the KDH won eighteen and the SNS fifteen. There were two independents, and Hungarian parties elected twelve deputies. The SKDH failed to get anyone elected. In the Czech Lands, Klaus, who had formed his own party, the Civic Democratic Party (*Obcanska demokraticka strana,* or ODS) was a proponent of a swift transformation to a market economy, the privatization of all state-owned industries, and the retention of the federal system. He won a majority of seats in the CNC. In the Federal Assembly, both parties also had the most seats, though not absolute majorities: In the Chamber of the People where deputies from the Czech Republic were allotted ninety-nine seats, the ODS had forty-eight deputies; from an allotment of fifty-one seat for Slovakia, the HZDS had twenty-four; the SDL ten; the KDH and SNS, six each; and there were also five Hungarian representatives. In 150 seat the Chamber of Nations with seventy-five seats each for Slovakia and the Czech Lands, there were thirty-seven ODS and thirty-three HZDS deputies; in addition, thirteen deputies were elected for the SDL; nine for the SNS; eight for the KDH; seven Hungarian representatives; and five Slovak Social Democrats. The decision about the future of Czecho-Slovakia was in the hands of these two political leaders. The outcome was determined not only by the success or failure of hard bargaining, but also by a certain events in Bratislava and Prague.

The first meeting between the representatives of Meciar and Klaus took place on 8 June in Brno where each premier laid out clearly its position. Three days later, on 11 June, there was another meeting in Prague of representatives of the ODS and the HZDS; there was no change in their positions, except that the Slovaks were insisting on international representation in a common state. When party representatives met in Prague on 17 June, the ODS went as far as it could to meet Slovak demands, but would not accept a confederation. The result was that "the Rubicon was crossed at this third negotiating round."[46] At the next meeting in Bratislava on 19 June, the constitutional options were significantly narrowed to a decentralized federal state or, what was seen as more likely, the breakup of Czechoslovakia. The month of September was also set as the deadline to conclude the constitutional negotiations. However, following this meeting, a series of events happened that hastened the process in the direction of Czechoslovakia's breakup.

The first event was the refusal by Slovak deputies to the Federal Assembly to vote Havel's reelection as president of the republic on 3 July 1992. Two weeks later, on 17 July, the SNC voted to proclaim the sovereignty (*zvrchovanost*) of Slovakia. That same day, shortly after the Slovak declaration, Havel announced his resignation from the presidency, which took effect three days later. It was by far the clearest signal from a Czech politician that the common state could not accommodate a sovereign Slovak nation. Klaus and

Meciar met on 22 and 23 July, and both once more reiterated their positions; Klaus insisted on the retention of the existing federal system, as it allowed the necessary centralization to effect the transformation of the economy. Czech politics had come full circle, back to its initial approach to the Slovaks whom the Czechs expected to accept and integrate into their own agenda. Meciar, on the other hand, stressed not only the need for a less rapid economic transformation program, but above all constitutional reform that would convert Czechoslovakia into a confederation. His approach represented not just the culmination of the history of Czech-Slovak relations since 1918, but also the only option the Slovaks were ready to envisage in a common state. It is at this meeting in the Slovak capital that the modalities of the breakup and how to get parliament to approve it were discussed.

If Klaus had thought that if push came to shove the Slovaks would buckle under, Meciar proved to be a determined defender of the nation. Representatives from both parties agreed in Brno on 26 August to bring about the dissolution of Czechoslovakia on 1 January 1993. Until the separation was effected, both sides negotiated the division of federal property. The SNC adopted a new constitution and a new flag on 1 September. On the same day, the Slovak nation learned of Dubcek's car accident that would eventually take his life on 7 November. On 25 November, the last necessary step to legitimize the breakup took place when the Czechoslovak Parliament, after an emotionally-laden debate, voted to dissolve Czechoslovakia. On 1 January 1993, another Slovak Republic was born. Meciar became its first prime minister and the National Council of the Slovak Republic, composed of the deputies of the old SNC, voted Michal Kovac to the presidency on 15 February 1993.

The dissolution of Czechoslovakia, according to a group of Czech and Slovak commentators who favored the continued existence of the common state, resulted from the interplay of a series of factors: The inability of the Czechoslovak state to solve certain social and constitutional problems since 1918; the legacy of the Communist regime; the adaptation crisis resulting from the passage from a single-party state to democratic pluralism; the lack of experience of the leaders of the Velvet Revolution; the absence of Czechoslovak parties in the post-Communist era; and the provision in the 1968 constitutional law that allowed Slovak deputies to block federal legislation that was not deemed to be in Slovakia's interest, the clause known as "*majorizacia*," that is to say, preventing the outvoting of the Slovaks by the numerical Czech majority. In their view, the dissolution was not the result "of the national emancipation efforts of the Slovak people."[47] However, not all agreed on this latter point.[48]

In terms of the Slovak struggle for survival, such factors point to the failure of one of the two options the Slovaks had since 1918, the roots of which go far

back in Slovak history: The pursuit of their national development in cooperation with the Czechs. The constitutional debate in the period preceding the declaration of Slovak independence clearly indicated that a majority of the population, in terms of the support they gave to the main political parties, was willing to entertain a continuation of this cooperation, but under new conditions. However, no agreement was arrived at. The inability to reach one was the ultimate historical failure of the Czechoslovak state to provide an acceptable framework for Slovak national development. It can also be seen as "the consequence of an inadequately strong consciousness of a 'Czechoslovak WE'"[49] with which the Slovaks could identify. Czechoslovakia had emerged out of the Czech agenda, had maintained it, and meant to carry on with it. However, even with all the advantages it gave them and the progress it brought, the common state put the Slovaks in a position of having to continue their struggle for survival. In the post-Communist era, they reached a point where they did not wish any longer to continue this struggle. The Slovak nation had undergone an evolution since 1918 that gave them all the means to take their future in their own hands. The other option, that of independence, was available. Their elected representatives simply took it.

If the Slovak struggle for survival in Czechoslovakia was over, another one was about to begin. A struggle no different from the one other nations in Central Europe are experiencing: to survive, through cooperation and development of democratic societies, in a world directed by global economic forces and standardized cultural values, subjected to major population movements, and last but not least, forced to search for new ecological standards.

Epilogue

WHAT'S PAST IS PROLOGUE[1]

It is relatively easy to be optimistic about the future of independent Slovakia. The factors in its favor are almost exceptional. Its population, which exceeds 5 million, does not by any means overpopulate its territory. There is a good balance between the urban and rural sectors, and most cities, towns, and villages are able to take care of their inhabitants. There is no major regional imbalance. As a nation, the Slovaks are sufficiently homogeneous and educated to organize and run an efficient economy, to manage the environment, and to ensure the social development that one expects of a modern society and economy. There are excellent universities and research establishments throughout the country, the arts and culture are on a par with the rest of Europe, and many Slovak artists, musicians, and athletes have achieved world renown.

Slovakia's agriculture is developed and is able not only to feed the population, but has also foodstuffs for export. Its industrialization offers many opportunities, if it is redirected and modernized, but it is Slovakia's natural resources, if properly managed, that can be the basis for modern industrial development as well as a recreational industry second to none in Central Europe. Its geographical location places it at the crossroads of Central Europe with a modern road, rail, and water navigational system that gives direct access to neighbors and the major markets of Wester, Eastern, as well as Central Europe.

What tempers optimism about Slovakia's future to some extent is the fact that Central Europe's newest state has appeared on the map with certain historical as well as contemporary political liabilities. The resolution of these

liabilities will determine whether future Slovak generations will finally escape what has been for over a century a cycle of hope and repression, and avoid emigration to other parts of the world as so many have done before them. Not all of these liabilities are of Slovakia's own making; nevertheless, they have exerted an influence on Slovak society and especially Slovak politics in this century and cast a shadow on Slovakia's future.

The greatest and perhaps most difficult problem with which the Slovak people have had to deal until recently, and which has had a major influence on Slovak politics, is the reticence of the international community to accept the Slovaks' right to self-determination. Even though this right was denied in the Kingdom of Hungary, it is with the creation of Czechoslovakia that this reticence appeared and became a factor in European politics. Self-determination as an organizing principle for the political map of Central Europe was put into effect at the end of the Great War when the American president, Woodrow Wilson, made it one of his Fourteen Points. As the map was being redrawn, the principle of self-determination did not necessarily prevail; rather, security requirements, especially those of France, and regional geopolitical considerations, as we saw in Chapter 8, argued for a common state of two small Slavic nations, the Czechs and Slovaks, rather than two small and weak national states.

A second factor that played a major role in strengthening this international reticence was the Czech definition of the common state. When the Allies accepted Czech arguments about the Slovaks and gave legitimacy to a state of the "Czechoslovak nation," any Slovak challenge to it, however legitimate the reason, became an attack on the status quo as well as the vested interests of the Great Powers, and had to be rejected. There was no international institution where the Slovaks could make their claim to self-determination since the "Slovak question" was deemed to be a matter concerning internal Czechoslovak politics.

It would take almost three-quarters of a century before the challenge could be made and be accepted by the international community. Among the factors that made this challenge possible were the changes in the security requirements of Great Powers as well as new geopolitical considerations in Europe. In addition, the failure of the Communists to resolve "the national question," which they proclaimed as a merely theoretical and historical problem, made the international community understand that the selective application of the principle of self-determination that had taken place in 1918 was not a satisfactory way to reorganize Central Europe. It is no coincidence that the second independence of Slovakia happened at a time when a similar demand from the Baltic and some Yugoslav nations had been made and accepted.

These two factors, the Czech definition and control of the common state and its international recognition, severely tested the strength and resolve of the Slovak nation in the last seven decades. Its leaders faced an almost impossible task when they sought to have their nation recognized by the international community. The difficulties they faced split Slovak opinion. For most of the century, international recognition of a nation came only with statehood; when the Slovaks achieved it in the first Slovak Republic, it was under exceptional circumstances and at a time when Europe was on the brink of another war. Thus, except for a few months in 1939 prior to World War II, the Slovaks did not have statehood in peacetime until 1993. They were considered either as a branch of the "Czechoslovak" nation or else as a minority nation that was neither the object nor the subject of international law. As a result of the postwar political situation in Central Europe, from the end of the war until the fall of communism in 1989, only Slovak emigre organizations, particularly in the United States and Canada, without any support from Slovakia, fought to regain their nation's international recognition.

With the overthrow of communism, the debate that took place from 1990 to 1993 on the future of Slovakia indicated that many Slovaks were not necessarily uncomfortable with international recognition through the Czechoslovak Republic; in addition, they would have been satisfied with the recognition of the sovereignty of the nation within a renewed Czecho-Slovakia. Others, on the other hand, wanted full state sovereignty and international recognition as defined in international law. As a result of the elections of June 1992, Slovakia achieved both definitions of sovereignty and the Slovaks took their place among the family of nations. For some Slovaks independence was a psychological leap that they have not found easy to make.

The absence of international recognition also brought about a subjective factor that marked both Slovak society and Slovak politics. Many Slovaks came to accept the Czech agenda in the common state and to serve it. The difficulties that the Slovak nation had experienced in affirming itself since the middle of the last century had convinced these Slovaks, especially if they studied in Prague, that their nation had no future except in a union with the Czechs. Some prominent Slovaks were held as examples of Slovak acceptance of the Czech agenda. As a result, neither in democratic (1918–1938, 1945–1948 and 1989–1993) nor in Communist (1948–1989) Czechoslovakia, could a Slovak political agenda be developed and pursued, except in reaction to the one set by Prague. And those who sought to set one found against them not only their colleagues in Prague, but above all the Prague government itself. Consensus politics did not define the "Slovak question" in Czechoslovakia. The result was not only constant confusion in Slovak political life, but in particular a situation where

others determined the legitimacy of Slovak political demands. During the worst of times, Slovak politics was in a state of virtual paralysis and was replaced by politics in Slovakia.

Slovakia's political future will be compromised if the political legacy of Czechoslovak politics, in particular that of the Communist period, is not put in the past. All Slovaks must understand that, having achieved international recognition, their fate is now in their own hands. The Slovak political agenda must henceforth be defined by the needs and future of the nation. A serious effort must be made to achieve consensual politics. The political scene in Slovakia must avoid radical polarization, political responsibility must be accepted by all citizens as well as the politicians, and full political accountability must be anchored in the system. The press and the media, without limiting any freedoms, also must be made accountable as well as responsible. The presence of many former Communists in positions of responsibility give some cause for concern. They worked in and sustained a system whose values were not democratic. The enactment of an effective lustration law for all positions of responsibility in all walks of life and not just in politics and state adminis-tration would be a signal to Slovak society as well as the international community that the democratic process is alive and well in Slovakia. In addition, the pluralist aspects of Slovak political culture would be greatly strengthened by a significant decentralization of political power to the local level, be it the city, town, or district (okres). Such a devolution would give citizens greater participation and responsibility in the political process. Many of the problems of ecological clean up and control, industrial restructuring, housing, and employment can best be handled at the local level. After eighteen months of independence, it is clear that some problems still await resolution. The government crisis that saw Meciar replaced by Jozef Moravcik and the formation of a coalition government in March 1994, and the holding of early elections in September suggest that Slovak political life is in ferment, a good sign on the health of the democratic process, but also an indication of the absence of consensual politics.

Another major liability that must be overcome quickly is the ignorance that Slovaks have about their history; in this case, this ignorance is of their own making. A major effort will have to be made to educate them about their past. It is true that each epoch reinterprets somewhat a nation's history to suits its needs and objectives. However, the necessity for the Slovak people to know more about their past is more than a temporal political requirement. A nation unsure of its history is unsure of itself and thus cannot be an effective member of the family of nations.

In a reexamination of Slovak history, particular attention must to be paid to the theme of Czech-Slovak relations. As we pointed out in the introduction, Slovak history has been presented as a corollary of Czech history in much of Western historiography. In addition, until recently, Slovak historiography in Slovakia was submitted to specific political imperatives that were tied directly to the Czech-Slovak relationship. It is undeniable that the Slovaks have shared a common state with the Czechs for sixty-eight years and that this chapter has played an important role in modern Slovak history. But it is only a chapter in a history that is otherwise over a thousand years old, a history that has its own dynamics, its own issues, its own heroes and villains, and its own criteria. The Slovak nation will find it difficult to determine its future if it is unaware of the efforts of past Slovak political leaders to chart a Slovak course, if it does not understand previous objectives, if it does not appreciate the difficulties that were encountered and how the obstacles were overcome. The Slovak people have a right to be made aware of their past, to have it interpreted on its own merits and not as part of the history of another nation. There is much they can be proud of, and in comparison with other nations the Slovaks are not wanting under any circumstances. The world will accept such conclusions if the Slovak people identify with, research, and write about their own past. Slovakia's international recognition can be but enhanced if the writing of its history is not burdened by inaccurate or tendentious interpretations.

In the last three years many Slovak politicians have expressed the hope that their country eventually will become a member of the European Community. This is not likely to happen for some time because of the current state of Slovakia's economy. On the other hand, the second Slovak Republic is being given the opportunity to join the world market economy, provided it is willing to accept the principles of free enterprise and the laws of the market. Little in the experience of the last four decades has prepared the Slovak people for the challenges that this involves. How Slovakia's economy and Slovak society face these challenges will depend on the willingness of all political parties to find solutions, on the readiness of the population to accept sacrifices, and on the ability of policymakers to be flexible and to see and make use of opportunities. The social and political climate must be stable enough to attract foreign investment. Many industries will have to be closed down either because of obsolescence and their inability to compete on world markets or because of the cost of modernization and pollution controls. The tourist industry has enormous potential. It is an industry, however, that must be carefully planned and managed. There must be control of the natural environment of the mountains, valleys, and plains of Slovakia and the development of a highly sophisticated hotel and tourist industry. This means not only institutions specializing in

recreational and hotel management, but also the training of personnel in foreign languages to serve properly an international clientele.

There will no doubt be many years of trial and error, and mistakes will be made. Policymakers will often face the temptation of achieving short-term gains at the expense of long-term development; it must be resisted. Particular attention must be paid to social policies so as to avoid polarization between those who are making the transition quickly and successfully and those who experience difficulties of adaptation. It is important to understand that raising Slovakia to this new level is not an easy task, because economic and social policies in a period of restructuring have few constants. On the other hand, a state's foreign policy is usually based on a number of constants.

It is perhaps because of its history rather than despite it that Slovakia does not have historical enemies. It has not been involved in a major conflict with any neighbor; during World War II, it attacked Poland only to recover Slovak territories that Poland had been given by Prague two decades earlier and in the Vienna Award, and its participation in the war against the Soviet Union was more symbolic than real, not based on territorial conquest, but on a desire to defend the Slovak nation against Soviet ideology. Slovakia's frontiers are internationally recognized and can be considered stable. Its foreign policy can thus be based on normal relations with all of its neighbors. Sharing a common frontier with five states (Austria, Hungary, Ukraine, Poland and the Czech Republic), Slovakia also has opportunities for participating in a regional arrangement.

With the exception of Hungary, Slovakia's neighbors have no claims and can be said to view relations with it in equally positive terms. All but Austria find themselves in a similar period of transition and restructuring; a willingness to work together is clear in the creation of the Vysegrad Group composed of the Czech Republic, Hungary, Poland, and Slovakia. But it is only one aspect of European security which is in a process of redefinition; it will take some time before a new regional security system emerges that incorporates the states of post-Communist Central Europe. Membership in the North Atlantic Treaty Organization may not be immediately forthcoming. On the other hand, Slovakia's membership in the Council of Europe, in the United Nations Organization and in the Conference on Security and Cooperation in Europe offers opportunities in foreign affairs, yet it would be wiser if Slovakia concentrated for the moment on her domestic problems and on maintaining good relations with neighbors.

The presence of the Hungarian minority along the border with Hungary can be cause for concern. As with any minority in a state, the Slovak leadership has to show sensitivity to Hungarian demands; its handling of the issue of

Hungarian-language road signs in Hungarian areas and the use of Hungarian first and last names has not been felicitous and had international repercussions. Council of Europe experts came to Slovakia in January 1994 after receiving a letter from leaders of the Hungarian minority in August 1993 complaining about unkept promises about minority rights by the Slovak government. However, the group reported, in the words of its spokesman, that "there are no disagreements between the experts of the Council of Europe and the Slovak Republic." It is clear that the road sign and language issue was being used for domestic political purposes by some politicians. The treatment of the Hungarian minority must not be seen as an unimportant issue and it also must avoid becoming an international problem. The direct involvement of the Hungarian minority in the Slovak political process, the respect of the rights that the Slovak Constitution gives them, a constant dialogue with the Slovak minority in Hungary, and open and direct links with Budapest at all levels will prevent the minority question from becoming the problem that it was in Central Europe in the interwar period.

The Slovak nation faces many challenges. Perhaps the greatest is to have faith in itself. If the Slovaks can acquire this faith, the liabilities will recede and the future will look good. The past seven decades will merely have been a prologue.

NOTES

Introduction

1. Bibliographies of works on Slovak history in Western languages as well as those in Slovak published in the West appeared in *Slovak Studies,* 7 (1967); and 17 (1977). An update to be published in *Slovak Studies* is in preparation under the editorship of Jozef M. Rydlo.
2. Joseph A. Mikus, *Slovakia, A Misunderstood History* (Hamilton, Ont.: The Battlefield Press Ltd., 1979).
3. Ibid., p. 6.
4. Ibid., p. 16.
5. Ibid., pp. 6-16.
6. Ibid., p. 15.
7. Among the first to ask this question was Hans Lemberg in "Gibt es eine tschechoslowakische Geschichte? Versuche einer nationalen Geschichtsintegration," in Hans Lemberg, Peter Nitsche and Erwin Oberlander (Hrsg.), *Osteuropa in Geschichte und Gegewart. Festschrift für Günter Stökl zum 60. Geburtstag* (Köln-Wien: Böhlau Verlag, 1977), pp. 376-91.
8. Alexandru Zub, "Themes in Southeast European Historiography," in Stanislav J. Kirschbaum, ed., *East European History* (Columbus, OH: Slavica Publishers, 1988), p. 12. Although Zub refers to Southeastern Europe in this passage, it is applicable to all of Central and Eastern Europe.
9. Thomas Capek, *The Slovaks of Hungary* (New York: Knickerbocker Press, 1906).
10. Julius Botto, *Slovaci. Vyvin ich narodneho povedomia. Dejepisny nakres,* 2 vols. (Turciansky Sväty Martin: KUS, 1923).
11. Scotus Viator (Robert W. Seton-Watson), *Racial Problems in Hungary* (London: Archibald Constable, 1908).
12. Ernest Denis, *La question d'Autriche—Les Slovaques* (Paris: Delagrave, 1917). Some years before, a doctoral dissertation on a specific Slovak subject had been published by Hélène Tourtzer, *Louis Stur et l'idée de l'indépendance slovaque*

(Paris: Cahors et Alençon, 1913). Denis may be considered the father of the Czechoslovak approach to Slovak history in the West, as his interpretation was based on Czech theses and political aims.

13. A. J. P. Taylor, *The Habsburg Monarchy 1809-1918* (Harmondsworth: Penguin Books, 1967), p. 258.

14. Daniel Rapant, *Slovenske povstanie roku 1848-1849,* 5 vols. (Turciansky Sv. Martin: Matica slovenska, 1937-1972). Rapant worked on this subject for three and half decades and included the years when the Communist regime put major constraints on his research and publications activity.

15. Frantisek Hrusovsky, *Slovenske dejiny* (Turciansky Sv. Martin: Matica slovenska, 1939). It was published in German four years later: *Geschichte der Slowakei* (Bratislava: Slowakische Rundschau, 1943).

16. Frantisek Bokes, *Dejiny Slovenska a Slovakov od najstarsich cias az po pritomnost* (Bratislava: Slovenska Akademia vied a umeni, 1946).

17. Richard Marsina writes that "In the years 1945-1948, Slovak historiography was a young historiography.... With the exception of short syntheses of Slovak history of a pedagogical character, defined by the period of their publication, there was no basic synthetic view of Slovak history." See Richard Marsina, "Slovenska historiografia 1945-1990", *Historicky casopis* 39, no. 4-5 (1991): 370-71.

18. Jozef Skultety. *Sketches from Slovak History,* trans. O.D. Koreff (Cleveland, OH: First Catholic Slovak Union, 1930).

19. The problems experienced and the constraints under which Slovak historians worked in the period from 1948 to 1990 are outlined in Marsina, pp. 371-79.

20. The imposition of political criteria introduced many "deformations" in Slovak historiography. For example, as Marsina writes: "An even greater deformation was the 'loss' of Slovak history as an independent discipline in the 1950s at the University and its inclusion in a discipline called Czechoslovak history." Ibid., p. 376.

21. Selected articles were translated regularly in various Western languages and published in the review *Studia Historica Slovaca,* which first appeared in 1963.

22. See Joseph M. Kirschbaum, ed., *Slovakia in the 19th and 20th Centuries* (Toronto: Slovak World Congress, 1973, 2nd ed., 1978) and Joseph M. Kirschbaum, ed., *Slovak Culture Through the Centuries* (Toronto: Slovak World Congress, 1978).

23. Joseph M. Kirschbaum, *Slovakia. Nation at the Crossroads of Central Europe* (New York: Robert S. Speller & Sons, 1960) and Joseph A. Mikus, *Slovakia. A Political History 1918-1950* (Milwaukee: Marquette University Press, 1963).

24. A list of Kirschbaum's scholarly publications can be found in the *Festschrift* published in his honor by Stanislav J. Kirschbaum, ed., *Slovak Politics. Essays*

on Slovak History in Honour of Joseph M. Kirschbaum (Cleveland, OH: Slovak Institute, 1983), pp. 373-76. A list of Mikus's writings can be found in the *Festschrift* published in his honor by Joseph Stasko, ed., *The Shaping of Modern Slovakia/Tvorcovia noveho Slovenska* (Cambridge, Ont.: Friends of Good Books, 1982), pp. 245-52.

25. Milan S. Durica, *La Slovacchia e le sue relazioni politiche con la Germania 1938-1945* (Padova: Marsilio Editori, 1964).

26. Frantisek Vnuk, *Kapitoly z dejin Komunistickej strany Slovenska* (Middletown, PA: Slovak v Amerike, 1968), and *Sedemnast neurodnych rokov (Nacrt dejin slovenskej literatury v rokoch 1945-1962)* (Middletown, PA: Slovak v Amerike, 1965).

27. Gilbert L. Oddo, *Slovakia and Its People* (New York: Robert S. Speller and Sons, 1960).

28. Kurt Glaser, *Czecho-Slovakia: A Critical History* (Caldwell, ID: The Caxton Printers, 1961).

29. Jörg K. Hoensch, *Die Slowakei und Hitlers Ostpolitik* (Köln: Böhlau Verlag, 1965).

30. Lisa Guarda Nardini, *Tiso: una terza proposta* (Padova: Ceseo-Liviana editrice, 1977).

31. Ludwig von Gogolak, *Beiträge zur Geschichte des slowakischen Volkes*, 3 vols. (München: Verlag R. Oldenbourg, 1963-67).

32. Stanislav J. Kirschbaum and Anne C. R. Roman, eds., *Reflections on Slovak History* (Toronto: Slovak World Congress, 1987).

33. Four works from younger scholars stand out by the access their authors had either to archival material or to Slovak historians: Dorothea H. El Mallakh, *The Slovak Autonomy Movement 1935-1939* (Boulder, CO: East European Monographs, 1979); Yeshayahu A. Jelinek, *The Lust for Power; Nationalism, Slovakia and the Communists 1918-1948* (Boulder, CO: East European Monographs, 1983); Owen V. Johnson, *Slovakia 1918-1938. Education and the Making of a Nation* (New York: Columbia University Press, 1985); and Wolfgang Venor, *Aufstand in der Tatra: der Kampf um die Slowakei 1939-1944* (Königstein: Athenäum, 1979). In 1983, Matica slovenska, while seeking to establish scholarly relations with Slovak scholars abroad, also named those with whom it would not have any contacts. See "?Slovak Studies Association?," *Slovensko* 8 (1983): 3.

34. Stanley Z. Pech, "New Avenues in East European History" *Canadian Slavonic Papers* 10, no. 1 (1968): 14-15.

35. Jaroslav Prokes, *Histoire tchécoslovaque* (Prague: Orbis, 1927). After World War II, another Czechoslovak history was published in English by an American historian. See S. Harrison Thomson, *Czechoslovakia in European History* (Princeton, NJ: Princeton University Press, 1953).

36. Robert W. Seton-Watson, *A History of Czechs and Slovaks* (1943; reprint, Hamden, CT: Archon Books, 1965). The title indicates that he was not entirely comfortable with the notion of a "Czechoslovak" nation; on the other hand, he dedicated the book "to the Czech people loyal and steadfast."

37. A recent bibliographic guide well illustrates the Czechoslovak bias in Western scholarship, first in the selection of works mentioned and second in the comments that accompany each selection. See David Short, *Czechoslovakia* (Oxford: Clio, 1986). This bibliography is organized according to subject matter, and is in this respect useful especially for aspects other than the history of the Czechs, the Slovaks, and Czechoslovakia. For works dealing with modern history, see pp. 47-67; for those dealing specifically with Slovak history, see pp. 71-77.

38. It is worth noting what Marsina writes in this respect: "No serious historian or sociologist can assume that the Slovaks, who since the 10th century lived in the Magyar sphere of interest and later in a state ruled by the Magyars, could have had a common ethnic consciousness with the Czechs, a Czechoslovak one." Marsina, "Slovenska historiografia," p. 376.

39. A good example are some of the survey histories of the Czechoslovak Republic; see, for example, Victor S. Mamatey and Radomir Luza, eds., *A History of the Czechoslovak Republic, 1918-1949* (Princeton, NJ: Princeton University Press, 1973) and Jörg K. Hoensch, *Geschichte der Tschechoslowakischen Republik 1918 bis 1965* (Stuttgart: W. Kohlhammer Verlag, 1966).

40. Two authors, one Czech and one Slovak, write that Slovak separatism is "an aberration of the past, excusable perhaps under the circumstances of the day, but otherwise the sooner forgotten, the better." See John Gellner and John Smerek, *The Czechs and Slovaks in Canada* (Toronto: University of Toronto Press, 1968), p. viii.

41. Josef Korbel, *Twentieth-Century Czechoslovakia. The Meaning of Its History* (New York: Columbia University Press, 1977), p. 160.

42. This is the case of Jozef Lettrich, *History of Modern Slovakia* (New York: Praeger, 1955) and Yeshayahu A. Jelinek, *The Parish Republic* (Boulder, CO: East European Monographs, 1976).

43. Stanislav J. Kirschbaum, "An Act of Faith and Integrity: Bishop Korec's Letter to Czechoslovak Television," *Slovakia* 34, nos. 62-63 (1989-1990): 80. For more on the comments of Bishop Jan Ch. Korec and especially about the impact Marxist interpretations have had on Slovak history and for an English translation and an analysis of the Korec letter, see ibid., pp. 61-126. The Slovak original is "List biskupa J. Ch. Korca c.-s. televizii k relacii 'Kriz v osidlach moci,'" published in *Kanadsky Slovak* (Toronto), 8, 15, 22 July, 12, 19, 25 August, and 2, 9 September 1989.

44. Two works stand out: that by Samo Faltan, *Slovenska otazka v Ceskoslovensku* (Bratislava: Vydavatelstvo politickej literatury, 1968) and by Lubomir Liptak, *Slovensko v 20. storoci* (Bratislava: Vydavatelstvo politickej literatury, 1968).

45. *Dejiny Slovenska I-VI* (Bratislava: Veda, Vydavatelstvo Slovenskej akademie vied, 1986-1992). Volume III was the last volume, and although published after the fall of the Communist regime, it had been in preparation for some years before that.

46. Marsina writes: "As far as Slovak historiography is concerned, in addition to what we may call Marxist pressure, there was also Czech, if not Czechoslovak pressure which obliged aspects of Slovak history to be judged and evaluated from a Czechoslovak, in fact from a Czech viewpoint." Marsina, "Slovenska historigrafia," p. 376.

47. See, for example, David W. Paul, *The Cultural Limits of Revolutionary Politics: Change and Continuity in Socialist Czechoslovakia* (Boulder, CO: East European Monographs, 1979).

48. The most recent is by Stanislav J. Kirschbaum, *Slovaques et Tchèques. Essai sur un nouvel aperçu de leur histoire politique* (Lausanne: L'Age d'Homme, 1987).

49. For other areas that beg examination, see Josef Anderle et al., "Uncharted Areas for Research on the History of Slovakia and the Slovaks," *East Central Europe/L'Europe du Centre-Est* 7, no. 1 (1980): 49-88. Since 1989, some of these topics have been the object of conferences in Slovakia with the participation of Western scholars; see *Slovensko v politickom systeme Ceskoslovenska* (Bratislava: Slovenska narodna rada, Historicky ustav SAV, 1991); *Andrej Hlinka a jeho miesto v slovenskych dejinach. Zbornik prednasok z vedeckeho sympozia* (Bratislava: Vydavatelstvo DaVel, 1991); *Slovensko v rokoch druhej svetovej vojny* (Bratislava: Slovenska narodna rada, Historicky ustav SAV, 1991); *Pokus o politicky a osobny profil Jozefa Tisu* (Bratislava: Slovak Academic Press, 1992); and *The Tragedy of Slovak Jews* (Banska Bystrica: Datei, 1992).

50. Carol Skalnik Leff, *National Conflict in Czechoslovakia. The Making and Remaking of a State, 1918-1987* (Princeton: Princeton University Press, 1988).

51. An initial analysis can be found in Stanislav J. Kirschbaum, "Czechoslovakia: the Creation, Federalization and Dissolution of a Nation-State," *Regional Politics & Policy* 3, no.1 (1993): 69-95; also published in John Coakley, ed., *The Territorial Management of Ethnic Conflict* (London: Frank Cass, 1993), pp. 69-95.

52. Matus Kucera and Bohumir Kosticky, *Historia. Slovensko v obrazoch* (Martin: Vydavatelstvo Osveta, 1990); this survey ends with the creation of the First Czechoslovak Republic; Anton Spiesz, *Dejiny Slovenska: na ceste k sebauvedomeniu* (Bratislava: Vydavatelstvo Perfekt, 1992); and R. Marsina, et al., *Slovenske dejiny* (Martin: Matica slovenska, 1993).

53. Spiesz, unfortunately, died in 1992 while doing research in Germany. He was a prolific historian, specializing on the Slovak economic and social history of the late Middle Ages.

54. Renée Perréal and Joseph A. Mikus. *La Slovaquie. Une nation au coeur de l'Europe* (Lausanne: L'Age d'Homme, 1992).

55. Josef Spetko, *Die Slowakei. Heimat der Völker* (Wien: Amalthea Verlag, 1991).

56. These statistics are taken from Jozef Busik, et al., *The Slovak Republic. Country Report* (Vienna: Bank Austria AG, May 1993), pp. 7-9.

57. Even today, the existence of the Slovaks still seems to puzzle certain people; commenting on how close the Slovak language is to Czech and Polish, Eva Hoffman writes: "It must have taken a special pertinacity to maintain a distinct Slovak identity"; see Eva Hoffman, *Exit into History. A Journey Through the New Eastern Europe* (New York: Viking, 1993), p. 182.

58. "Archbishop Giovanni Cappa, Vatican Ambassador to Slovakia, Expresses Ambassador's Sentiments Accredited to Bratislava," *Jednota*, 3 January 1993.

Chapter 1

1. These statistics are taken from Busik et al., pp. 9 and 11.

2. The Slavic nations of Europe are divided into three groups: the Western Slavs composed of the Czechs, the Poles, the Ruthenians, the Slovaks and the Sorabs; the Southern Slavs namely the Bulgarians, the Croats, the Macedonians, the Serbs, and the Slovenes; and the Eastern Slavs who are the Bielorussians, the Russians, and the Ukrainians. For more on the Slavs, especially the states in which they have lived and are found today, see Paul Robert Magosci, *Historical Atlas of East Central Europe* (Toronto: University of Toronto Press, 1993).

3. According to Francis Dvornik, the original homeland of the Slavs is in the Pripet Marshes. See Francis Dvornik, *The Slavs. Their Early History and Civilization* (Boston: American Academy of Arts and Science, 1956), pp. 3–13. However, for Samuel Hazzard Cross, "The habitat of the primitive Slavs before their dispersion was . . . an irregular oblong area northeast of the Carpathians, extending eastward from the basin of the middle Vistula to the course of the Dnieper north and south of Kiev, bounded on the north by the rivers Narev and Pripet, and along its southern edge touching the headwaters of the Prut, the Dniester, and the Bug, which are all rivers flowing into the Black Sea." Samuel Hazzard Cross, *Slavic Civilization Through the Ages* (New York: Russel & Russel, Inc., 1963), pp. 7–8.

4. "To be sure, the Slavs do not begin their historical career under this name, but under another which is etymologically related to the English term 'Wends' or the German 'Wenden,' frequently applied to the Slavs in our own day. . . . The name 'Slav' first appears in a Greek text written about 550, and from that period becomes more and more frequent." Ibid., pp. 5 and 9.

5. John Wymer, *The Palaeolithic Age* (New York: St. Martin's Press, 1982), p. 268.

6. Marsina et al., p. 13.

7. Wymer writes: "Only when a community became *more* dependent for their food supply on cultivated crops and domestic animals than on the food obtained by hunting and gathering can it be said to have achieved a true Neolithic economy. When a community became totally dependent on cultivated crops and domesticated animals, it can be said to have had a full Neolithic economy." Wymer, p. 268. (Italics in the original.)

8. Alasdair Whittle, *Neolitic Europe: A Survey* (Cambridge: Cambridge University Press, 1985), p. 307.

9. Kucera and Kosticky, p. 11.

10. Bokes, p. 16.

11. Marsina et al., pp. 14–15.

12. T. G. E. Powell, *The Celts,* rev. ed. (London: Thames and Hudson, 1959), p. 40.

13. Pavol Valachovic, "Die vorslawischen städtischen Siedlungen in der Slowakei." In Richard Marsina, ed., *Städte im Donauraum* (Bratislava: Slovenska historicka spolocnost, 1993), p. 22.

14. Spiesz, p. 8.

15. Marsina et al., p. 18.

16. Ibid., p. 10.

17. Joseph G. Cincik, "Relations Between Roman and Slovak Civilizations." In Joseph M. Kirschbaum, ed., *Slovak Culture Through the Centuries,* p. 124.

18. Kucera and Kosticky, p. 15.

19. Dvornik, *The Slavs. Their Early History and Civilization,* p. 33.

20. *Dejiny Slovenska I,* p. 61.

21. Ibid., p. 65.

22. Spiesz, p. 13.

23. Frantisek Kalesny, "Über den Weinbau und den Weinverkauf in Preßburg bis Ende des 15. Jahrhunderts," in Marsina, *Städte im Donauraum,* p. 187.

24. For the debate around the question of a single or multiple authorship of the Chronicle, see *Fredegarii Chronicorum Liber Quartus cum Continuationibus/The Fourth Book of the Chronicle of Fredegar with its Continuations,* Translated from the Latin with introduction and notes by J.M. Wallace-Hadrill (London: Thomas Nelson and Sons Ltd., 1960), pp. xiv–xxviii.

25. The problems Samo had with Dagobert are described in chapters 68 and 75 of *Fredegarii Chronicorum,* pp. 56–58 and 63.

26. Ibid., pp. 39–40. The Slovak translation found in *Dejiny Slovenska I* is somewhat different: "There was a man by the name of Samo, a Frank by birth, who took with him a number of merchants and proceeded to establish commercial relations with the Slavs. Samo immediately went to the side of the insurgents [against Avar power]. His military talents provoked admiration and the Slavs began to be victorious. Within a short period of time, the Slavic tribes were not only victorious over their conquerors, but also lords in their own lands. Familiar with Samo's courage and usefulness, they elected him king. He ruled happily for 35 years. He had 12 Slavic wives and his family produced 20 sons and 15 daughters. During his reign, the Slavs successfully defended themselves many times against attacks by the Avars who were trying to reestablish their rule"; p. 66. For another Slovak translation of the chronicle which respects the Latin, see Peter Ratkos, ed., *Pramene k dejinam Velkej Moravy,* 2nd ed. (Bratislava: Veda, Vydavatelstvo Slovenskej akademie vied, 1968), pp. 55–59.

27. *Dejiny Slovenska I,* p. 68.

28. Marsina et al., p. 9.

29. Dvornik, *The Slavs. Their Early History and Civilization,* p. 42.

30. F. Tiso, "The Empire of Samo," *Slovak Studies* 1 (1961), p. 21.

Chapter 2

1. The question of the name of Great Moravia and the people is examined by Arved Grebert, "Die Slowaken und das Großmärische Reich (Beitrag zum ethnischen Charakter Großmährens)," *Slovak Studies* 3 (1963): 126–34.

2. Jan Dekan, *Zaciatky slovenskych dejin a Risa velkomoravska* (Bratislava: Slovenska akademia vied a umeni, 1951), p. 43.

3. Christianity had already penetrated the territory of Slovakia before this period, but had not left permanent traces; see Joseph Papin, "Christian Inroads into the Territory of Present Slovakia prior to the Cyrillo-Methodian Era," *Slovak Studies* 3 (1963): 9–19.

4. Dvornik, *The Slavs. Their Early History and Civilization,* p. 75.

5. Francis Hrusovsky, "The Relations of the Rulers of Great Moravia with Rome," *Slovak Studies* 3 (1963): 22.

6. There is some dispute as to the date; Bokes, p. 33, gives the date as 833, whereas Marsina et al., p. 23, consider this consecration to have taken place in 828.

7. The main document that informs us of Pribina and Nitra is the *Conversio Bagoariorum et Carantanorum* of A.D. 870.

8. Marsina et al., p. 23.

9. Ibid., p. 9.

10. According to Dvornik, Rome did not answer Rastislav's letters for the simple reason that the Holy See was in agreement with the religious and political objectives of Louis the German vis à vis the Slavs. See Francis Dvornik, *Les légendes de Constantin et Méthode vues de Byzance* (Prague: Orbis, 1933), p. 232.

11. Ibid., p. 229.

12. Dvornik, *The Slavs. Their Early History and Civilization*, p. 87.

13. Hrusovsky, "The Relations of the Rulers of Great Moravia with Rome," p. 50.

14. Ibid., p. 51.

15. Marsina et al., p. 30.

16. *A liturgia sclavinica ad provinciam slovacam. Ad initia cultus Cristiani in Slovacia* (Bratislava: Bibliotheca universitatis, 1992), pp. 15–16. This book contains the original Latin text as well as Slovak and English translations.

17. Richard Marsina, "Conclusion" in ibid., p. 37.

18. Marsina et al., p. 31.

19. Ibid., p. 31.

20. Hrusovsky, "The Relations of the Rulers of Great Moravia with Rome," p. 68. Much of the text that follows is taken from ibid., pp. 21–77. His account of the activities of Cyril and Methodius and especially their relations with Rome is very well documented and quite detailed.

21. In the matter of the creation of a new alphabet for the Slavs, Michael Lacko writes: "We know that there exist two Slavonic scripts, Cyrilica and Glagolica. It might be assumed at first that Cyril devised the Cyrilica. And indeed such was the general belief for many centuries. Even [Josef] Dobrovsky in the last century was of the opinion that the Glagolica dates back only to the 13th century. But after the discovery of additional Old-Slavonic records inscribed in Glagolitic letters, especially of the *Kiev Manuscripts* the opinion is now generally held by Slavists that St. Cyril devised the Glagolica and that the Cyrilica arose in the 10th century in Bulgaria." Michael Lacko, "The Cyrilomethodian Mission and Slovakia," *Slovak Studies* 1 (1961): 43.

22. Cross, p. 57.

23. The original document was not preserved. References to it go as far as back as the eleventh century; the most extensive reference is found in the sixteenth century chronicle by Aventinus, *Annales Boiorum* (1552), translated in German in 1566 as *Bayerische Chronik.*

24. Hrusovsky, "The Relations of the Rulers of Great Moravia with Rome," p. 50.

25. Ibid., p. 64.

26. Ibid., p. 68.

27. Ibid., p. 72.

28. Lacko, p. 42.

29. According to Dvornik, ". . . the Life of S. Cyril was well known to the southern Slavs. . . a number of works known to have been written in [Great] Moravia in S. Methodius' lifetime are now found in Bulgarian manuscripts. Curiously enough, the Life of Methodius has survived to our days only thanks to copes made of it in Russia." Francis Dvornik, *The Making of Central and Eastern Europe* (Gulf Breeze, FL: Academic International Press, 1974), pp. 241–242.

30. Joseph M. Kirschbaum, "La littérature de la période cyrillo-méthodienne et la Slovaquie," *Slovak Studies* 3 (1963): 96.

31. George Vernadsky, "The Beginnings of the Czech State," *Byzantion*, 17 (1944–1945): 315–28.

32. Marsina et al., p. 33.

33. An affirmative answer is given by Tomas J. Veteska, *Velkoslovenska risa* (Hamilton: MSA–ZMS, 1987), p. 9.

34. For more recent research on these questions, see Michal Lacko, "Great Moravia in the Light of Recent Research, 1945–1975," in Joseph M. Kirschbaum, *Slovak Culture Through the Centuries*, pp. 70–96.

35. Marsina et al., p. 33.

36. This was the official view, among others, also of Slovak Communist historiography: "it is an indisputable fact that the period of Great Moravia belongs to the history of the Slovak and Czech nation." Peter Ratkos, "Postavenie slovenskej narodnosti v stredovekom Uhorsku," in Julius Mesaros, ed., *Slovaci a ich narodny vyvin* (Bratislava: Veda, Vydavatelstvo Slovenskej akademie vied, 1966), p. 9.

37. Dekan, p. 77.

38. *Dejiny Slovenska I*, p. 149.

39. Jaroslav Pelikan, Jr., "The Significance of Christianity for Slovak National History," in Joseph M. Kirschbaum, *Slovak Culture Through the Centuries*, p. 63.

40. For an outline of this tradition, see Joseph M. Kirschbaum, "The Role of the Cyrilo-Methodian Tradition in Slovak National and Political Life," *Slovak Studies* 3 (1963): 153–72.

41. Skultety, p. 30.

42. Kucera and Kosticky, p. 59. For these two authors, "national liberation" means 1918. This tradition extends beyond 1918 and is likely also to play an role in the political life of the second Slovak Republic.

Chapter 3

1. According to a Magyar historian, this took place sooner, namely in 902. See Laszlo Makkai, "The Hungarians' Prehistory, their Conquest of Hungary and their Raids to the West to 955," in Sugar et al., p. 12.

2. C. A. Macartney, *Hungary. A Short History* (Edinburgh: At the University Press, 1962), p. 8.

3. Laszlo Makkai, "Hungary before the Hungarian Conquest," in Sugar et al., p. 7. According to Lucien Musset: "In 889, the Magyars of Ukraine came under attack by the Pechenegs and broke up into groups. The principal group elected Arpad king and soon headed toward Pannonia where they entered in 895 through the Carpathian mountains, in all likelihood simultaneously through the northeast and southeast passes." See Lucien Musset, *Les invasions. Le second assaut contre l'Europe chrétienne (VIIe - XIe siècle)* (Paris: Presses universitaires de France, 1965), p. 60.

4. Macartney, p. 10.

5. Erwin Pamlenyi et al., *A History of Hungary,* trans. by Laszlo Boros et al. (London: Collet's, 1975), p. 24.

6. Ibid., p. 25.

7. Macartney, p. 9.

8. Rudolf Krajcovic writes: "In this period, the Slovak language developed independently with internal dialectical characteristics which manifested themselves in the fact that along with integrative phenomena (setting Slovak apart from neighbouring Slavic languages in their totality) there developed at the same time phenomena which differentiated its territory." See Rudolf Krajcovic, *Vyvin slovenskeho jazyka a dialektologia* (Bratislava: Slovenske pedagogicke nakladatelstvo, 1988), p. 16.

9. Eugen Pauliny, *Dejiny spisovnej slovenciny od zaciatkov po sucastnost* (Bratislava: Slovenske pedagogicke nakladatelstvo, 1983), p. 48.

10. Although the Slovaks are now in the Kingdom of Hungary, as this is a history of the Slovaks, the Slovak spelling of Magyar names, where applicable, will be used with the correct Magyar spelling in brackets. Where there is a universally accepted English name, such as Stephen, it will be used (rather than the Slovak Stefan).

11. Jan Lukacka, "Uloha slachty slovanskeho povodu pri stabilizacii uhorskeho vcasnofeudalneho statu," in *Typologia rane feudalnich slovanskych statu* (Praha: Ustav ceskoslovenskych a svetovych dejin CSAV, 1987), p. 198.

12. According to Musset: "Perhaps worried about the too exclusive influence of the German clergy, he welcomed Italian missionaries—among others those

whom the famous ascete from Ravenna, St. Romuald, was instructing for Central Europe—and made contact with the Papacy." See Musset, p. 70.

13. Dvornik, *The Making of Central and Eastern Europe*, p. 8.

14. There is some indication that parts of Slovakia were occupied by the Czech Premyslide kings toward the end of Gejza's reign. See *Dejiny Slovenska I*, p. 168.

15. Marsina et al, p. 36. According to Spiesz, an agreement was concluded between Boleslav and Stephen in 1018 to give Slovakia back to Hungary. See Spiesz, pp. 20–21.

16. Dvornik, *The Making of Central and Eastern Europe*, p. 215.

17. According to Slovak historians: "The actual archdiocese of Ostrihom, other than a bit of territory around Ostrihom itself, extended to about three quarters of the territory of Slovakia, from Moravia and the White Carpathians to Roznava and Spis. It is quite likely that it was the same territory of the original Nitra diocese, established in June 880. Eastern Slovakia (later the counties Abov–Turiec, Saris and Zemplin) belonged to the bishopric (diocese) of Jager." Marsina et al, p. 42.

18. Balint Homan, *Geschichte des ungarischen Mittelalters*, vol. 1 (Berlin: Verlag Walter de Gruyter & Co., 1940), p. 158.

19. Erik Fügedi, *Castles and Society in Medieval Hungary (1000–1437)* (Budapest: Akademiai Kiado, 1986), p. 18.

20. Macartney, p. 23.

21. Ibid., p. 33.

22. Pamlenyi et al., p. 62.

23. Macartney, p. 34.

24. Bokes, p. 76.

25. Engel Pal, "The Age of the Angevines, 1301–1382" in Sugar et al., p. 37.

26. See for example Bokes, p. 75; *Dejiny Slovenska I*, p. 315; Francis Dvornik, *The Slavs in European History and Civilization* (New Brunswick, NJ: Rutgers University Press, 1962), p. 135; and Spiesz, p. 36, who furthermore argues that "Matthew Cak was not a Slovak patriot as was claimed in the nineteenth century. His goals were those of an oligarch of his period. He did not create a territory with definite frontiers and a political administration which the Slovaks could claim."

27. *Dejiny Slovenska I*, p. 315.

28. Kucera and Kosticky, p. 75.

29. Ernest Denis, *Huss et les guerres des hussites* (Paris: E. Leroux, 1930), p. 8.

30. According to a Czech historian: "Hussitism is the movement of a young nation, full of energy, which, after having steeped itself in the ancient Western civilization seeks to create a new Christian way of life on the old bases. This

Czech religious movement is less preoccupied with speculative research of a theological nature than with practical experience; it struggles not for the theoretical interpretation of the Holy Scripture, but for the application of the principles of the Gospel to daily life." See Jaroslav Prokes, *Histoire tchécoslovaque* (Paris: Orbis, 1927), p. xiii.

31. According to an American historian: "Taken in its totality this larger movement can fairly be regarded as the embodiment of the Czech spirit and a determinant of Czech history." See S. Harrison Thomson, *Czechoslovakia in European History* (Princeton, NJ: Princeton University Press, 1953), p. 69.

32. Branislav Varsik, *Husitske revolucne hnutie a Slovensko* (Bratislava: Veda, Vydavatelstvo Slovenskej akademie vied, 1965), p. 11. According to another Slovak historian, they had appeared already in 1423; Bokes, p. 84.

33. Kucera and Kosticky, p. 104.

34. Bokes, p. 88.

35. Varsik, pp. 288–289.

36. Marsina et al., p. 35.

37. Arved Grebert, "Slovakia within the Framework of Hungary," in Joseph M. Kirschbaum, *Slovak Culture Through the Centuries,* p. 204.

38. Marsina et al., p. 42.

39. Belo Polla, *Kosice Krasna. K stredovekym dejinam Krasnej nad Hornadom* (Kosice: Vychodoslovenske vydavatelstvo, 1986), p. 303.

40. Joseph Tomko, "The Development of Church Organization in Slovakia," in Joseph M. Kirschbaum, *Slovak Culture Through the Centuries,* pp. 151–52.

41. The first recorded grant of such privileges dates back to 1238 to the town of Trnava.

42. Stefan Kazimir, *Pestovania vinica a produkcia vina na Slovensku v minulosti* (Bratislava: Veda, Vydavatelstvo Slovenskej akademie vied, 1986), p. 121.

43. Spiesz, p. 25.

44. Of these counties, ten were in Slovakia proper (Liptov, Orava, Nitra, Bratislava, Spis, Saris, Tekov, Trencin, Turiec and Zvolen) while in the remaining nine, Slovak territory represented only a part of the original Hungarian counties (Gemer, Hont, Abov, Zemplin, Novohrad, Turna, Uz, Komarno and Ostrihom).

45. Juraj Zudel, *Stolice na Slovensku* (Bratislava: Obzor, 1984), p. 14.

46. Pamlenyi et al., p. 109.

47. Macartney, p. 27.

48. Pamlenyi et al., p. 51.

49. Janos Bak, "The Late Medieval Period, 1382–1526" in Sugar et al., p. 65.

50. Ibid.

51. Ibid., p. 66.

52. Laszlo Makkai, "Transformation into a Western-Type State, 1196–1301," in Sugar et al., p. 33.

53. Macartney writes: "Louis standardized the obligations of the peasant to his lord at one-ninth of his produce—neither more or less. As he also had to pay the tithe to the church and the *porta* to the state, the peasant's obligations were thus not inconsiderable, but do not appear to have been crushing in this age of prosperity; his right of free migration was specifically re-affirmed." Macartney, pp. 45–46. The *porta* was a house tax levied on a peasant household.

54. According to Makkai, "vineyards were the origin of such important cities as . . . Pozsony [Bratislava]." Makkai, "Transformation into a Western-Type State, 1196–1301," in Sugar et al., p. 29.

55. Ibid.

56. Richard Marsina, "Preßburg im Wandel der Geschichte," in Marsina, *Städte im Donauraum*, p. 11.

57. Spiesz, p. 32.

58. Ibid., p. 34.

59. Macartney, pp. 54–55.

60. Some Slovak historians prefer to refer to it as a university. See Peter Ratkos, "Vztah Jana zo Sredny a Juraja Schönberga k univerzite Istropolitana," in Ludovit Holotik and Anton Vantuch, *Humanizmus a renesancia na Slovensku v 15.–16. storoci* (Bratislava: Veda, Vydavatelstvo Slovenskej akademie vied, 1967), p. 66 and Marsina et al, pp. 68–69.

61. According to Theodoric J. Zubek: "In most European countries, including old Hungary, the period of Humanism and the Renaissance has been thoroughly studied and evaluated. The same cannot be said, however, about Humanism and the Renaissance in Slovakia." See Theodoric J. Zubek, "Humanism and the Renaissance in Recent Slovak Studies," in Joseph M. Kirschbaum, *Slovak Culture Through the Centuries*, p. 239. Zubek does, however, recognize that the Holotik and Vantuch volume goes a long way to redress this situation.

62. Jaromir Homolka, *Levoca, Hlavny oltar v kostole Sv. Jakuba* (Bratislava: Slovenske Vydavatelstvo Krasnej Literatury), 1965, p. 11.

63. Ibid., p. 9.

64. Spiesz, p. 29.

65. Emericus Szentpetery, *Scriptores rerum Hungaricum,* vol. 2 (Budapest: Academia litter. Hungarica, 1938), p. 625. This motto is taken from Stephen's admonition *(Institutiones morum)* to his son Imre and reads as follows: "Guests and newcomers bring so much profit [to the kingdom] that they may justly be ranked sixth in the order of royal dignities. For at the beginning, the Roman Empire became so exalted and the Roman Emperors became so glorious because many noble and

wise men streamed to them from all manner of different regions. Rome would certainly still be enslaved today had not Aeneas set it free. For as guests come from diverse regions and provinces, they bring with them diverse languages and customs, diverse examples and weapons, and all of this embellishes the country, increases the splendor of the court, and reduces the arrogance of foreigners. For a country which has only one language and the same customs is both weak and likely to perish. My son, I command you therefore, to hold newcomers in high regard and to assist them with good will so that they might wish to remain in your domains rather than settle elsewhere"; Ferenc Glatz, ed., *Magyarok a Kárpát-medencében* (Budapest: Historia Könyvek, 1989), p. 32. I am indebted to Professor Thomas Barcsay of Ryerson Polytechnic University in Toronto, Canada for this translation from the Hungarian.

66. Spiesz, p. 33.

Chapter 4

1. Macartney, p. 65.
2. Ibid., p. 70.
3. Vojtech Kopcan, *Turecke nebezpecenstvo a Slovensko* (Bratislava: Veda, Vydavatelstvo Slovenskej akademie vied, 1986), p. 184.
4. Ibid., p. 67.
5. Macartney, p. 65.
6. Kopcan, p. 35. According to Kucera and Kosticky (p. 121): "After a week of devastation, the Turks took a great deal of cattle from the burned out land, but above all, many tens of thousands of prisoners who represented rich merchandise for the Eastern slave markets."
7. David Turnock, *Eastern Europe. A Historical Geography 1815–1945* (London: Routledge, 1989), p. 324.
8. David Turnock, *The Making of Eastern Europe From the Earliest Times to 1815* (London: Routledge, 1988), pp. 210.
9. Kopcan, p. 174.
10. Ibid., p. 122.
11. Ludwig von Gogolak, *Beiträge zur Geschichte des slowakischen Volkes,* vol. 1 (München: Verlag R. Oldenbourg, 1963), p. 16.
12. Ibid., p. 27.
13. Spiesz, p. 50.
14. Vojtech Kopcan, "Der osmanische Krieg gegen die Habsburger 1663–64 (Im Hinblick auf die Slowakei)," *Asian and African Studies* 2, no. 2 (1993): 169.

15. Macartney, pp. 87–88.

16. According to Ferenc Szakaly: "the ethnic composition changed everywhere in favor of other nationalities: Slovaks in the north, Romanians in the east, Serbs in the south"; Ferenc Szakaly, "The Early Ottoman Period, Including Royal Hungary, 1526–1606," in Sugar et al., p. 99.

17. Kopcan, p. 8.

18. Szakaly, "The Early Ottoman Period, Including Royal Hungary, 1526–1606," in Sugar et al., p. 93. According to Macartney (pp. 76–77): "The Reformation was in itself an event of the first importance for Hungary. It breathed new vitality into a spiritual life which had become in many respects worldly, torpid and degenerate, lending fresh inspiration, and one which proved peculiarly well adapted to the national genius."

19. Marsina et al., p. 95.

20. Spiesz, p. 50.

21. David P. Daniel, "The Protesant Reformation and Slovak Ethnic Consciousness," *Slovakia* 28, nos. 51–52 (1978–1979): p. 52.

22. Language had been a factor. Calvinism had spread among the Magyars as a result of the translation into Latin of the works of Jean Calvin; translations had not been needed in the case of the works of Luther and other German Protestants whose teachings reached directly the German colonists in Slovakia.

23. David P. Daniel, "The Reformation and Eastern Slovakia," *Human Affairs* 1, no. 2 (1991): p. 182.

24. Szakaly, "The Early Ottoman Period, Including Royal Hungary, 1526–1606," in Sugar et al., p. 95.

25. Marsina et al, p. 108.

26. It should be noted that already during the lifetime of Ignatius Loyola, founder of the Society of Jesus, Trnava was being considered as a seat for a college in Hungary. See Emil Krapka and Vojtech Mikula, eds., *Dejiny Spolocnosti Jezisovej na Slovensku* (Cambridge, Ont.: Dobra Kniha, 1990), pp. 25–27.

27. Ibid., p. 55. The three priests were beatified by the Catholic Church in 1905.

28. Ibid., p. 79. A publishing house in Levoca published some 900 titles during the seventeenth century. There were publishing houses also in Kosice, Bardejov, and Bratislava. Another source indicates only 600 titles; see Marsina et al., p. 112.

29. David P. Daniel, "The Impact of the Protestant Reformation on Education in Slovakia," *Slovakia* 34, nos. 62–63 (1989–1990): p. 10. As far as Catholic education is concerned, Eva Kowalska writes: "A quality classical education and the possibility of university study with the Jesuits or an education oriented towards the practical with an emphasis on the exact sciences and the native language with the Piarists—these became the two kinds of Catholic schools

in Slovakia until the time of school reform at the end of the eighteenth century." Eva Kowalska, "Learning and Education in Slovakia During the Late 17th and 18th Centuries," *Slovakia* 34, nos. 62–63 (1989–1990): pp. 33–34.

30. Jan Tibensky, *Dejiny vedy a techniky na Slovensku* (Bratislava: Osveta, 1979), p. 84.

31. Marsina et al., p. 111.

32. Marsina et al., p. 113.

33. Ibid., p. 107.

34. Katalin Peter, "The Later Ottoman Period and Royal Hungary, 1606–1711," in Sugar et al., pp. 111–12.

35. Engel, "The Age of the Angevines, 1301–1382," in Sugar et al., p. 46.

36. Macartney, p. 61.

37. Peter, "The Later Ottoman Period and Royal Hungary," in Sugar et al., p. 108.

38. Macartney, p. 83.

39. Ernest Denis, *Fin de l'indépendance bohème,* 2 vols, (Paris: Armand Colin, 1890).

40. Marsina et al., p. 100.

41. Macartney, p. 86.

42. Ibid., p. 87.

43. Ibid., p. 92.

44. Gogolak, vol. 1, p. 129.

45. It is interesting to note how Marxist scholarship describes Janosik and his activities: "In his time, brigandage was one of the class warfare means used in the anti-feudal opposition of the oppressed population decimated by the frequent wars and epidemics; it had a profound influence on the consciousness of the popular masses. In the popular imagination and legends, brigand leaders symbolized warriors for right and social justice. For centuries, he was the symbol of the opposition of the working people against exploitation and national oppression, the hero of numerous Slovak, Czech and Polish popular fairy tales, stories, songs and dances." See "Janosik, Juraj" in *Slovensky biograficky slovnik,* II. sväzok (E-J), (Martin: Matica slovenska, 1987), p. 528.

46. Gerald Sabo, "'Jesuit Slovak' in Writings of Franciscans," Paper read at the 1993 Annual Convention of the American Association for the Advancement of Slavic Studies, Honolulu, HA, 22 November, 1993, p. 1.

47. Spiesz, p. 62.

48. Szakali, "The Early Ottoman Period, Including Royal Hungary, 1526–1606," in Sugar et al., p. 99.

49. Macartney, p. 93.

50. Ibid., p. 94.

51. Ibid., p. 100.

52. Horst Haselsteiner, "Cooperation and Confrontation Between Rulers and the Noble Estates, 1711–1790," in Sugar et al., p. 156.

53. Ernest Denis, *La Bohème depuis la Montagne Blanche,* vol. 1 (Paris: Ernest Leroux, 1903), p. 573. According to Macartney (p. 124): "The reign of Joseph II was perhaps the most dynamic in Hungarian history. No single aspect of the national life, political, social, economic, cultural or national in the modern sense of the term, was the same after it as before it."

54. Macartney, p. 110.

55. Ibid., p. 112.

56. Macartney adds: "It was especially unfortunate that the most treasured among them, the exemption of their land from taxation, entailed them in a direct conflict of interests with the peasants, so that their defence of it did breed among them a great class egotism. . . . The gulf had never been wider in the national history, or at least not since the old days of slavery, between the *populus* and the *misera contribuens plebs,* whose function in the state was still simply to work for his betters." Macartney, p. 113.

57. *Dejiny Slovenska II,* 1987, p. 416.

58. The demographic consequences of their occupation of the Hungarian plain were dramatic. At the time of King Mathias "Corvinus," some 250 years before, Hungary's population had totaled about four million inhabitants; in 1720, it was around 3.5 million, with more than two thirds living in the western and northern counties (Slovakia). See Haselsteiner, "Cooperation and Confrontation Between Rulers and the Noble Estates, 1711–1790," in Sugar et al., p. 142.

59. Ibid., p. 117.

60. Slovak historians indicate that "According to the census taken during the reign of Joseph II in 1785, the population of Hungary had a varied national structure. Out of 11,379 communities in Hungary, 3,668 were inhabited by Magyars, 2,762 by Slovaks, 1,849 by Croatians, 1,029 by Romanians, 890 by Germans, 702 by Ruthenes, 452 by Illyro-Dalmatians, and 18 by Serbs." See Marsina et al., p. 124.

61. Macartney, p. 99.

62. Kucera and Kosticky, p. 168. According to Tibensky: "It was a modern mining text that was used for nearly a century not only at the Academy in Banska Stiavnica, but elsewhere." Tibensky, p. 122.

63. Kucera and Kosticky write: "A great deal of freedom was given to the primary school system in the use of national languages, which at that time was a very democratic step. The entire school reform also received its normative direction, published in document form and known in our education history as 'Ratio educationis.' " Ibid., p. 169.

64. Eva Kowalska, *Statne ludove skolstvo na Slovensku na prelome 18. a 19. stor.* (Bratislava: Veda, Vydavatelstvo Slovenskej akademie vied, 1987), p. 21.

65. Gogolak, vol. 1, p. 189.

66. Marsina et al., p. 130.

67. Izidor Kotulic, "Vyznam trnavskej univerzity pre rozvoj kulturnej slovenciny," in Viliam Cicaj, ed., *Trnavaska univerzita v slovenskych dejinach* (Bratislava: Veda, Vydavatelstvo Slovenskej akademie vied, 1987), p. 73.

68. Ibid., p. 75.

69. Lubomir Durovic, "Slovak," in Alexander M. Schenker and Edward Stankiewicz, eds., *The Slavic Literary Languages: Formation and Development* (New Haven: Yale Concilium on International and Area Studies, 1980), p. 212.

70. Gogolak, vol. 1, p. 18.

71. Gerald J. Sabo, "Commentary," in Hugolin Gavlovic, *Valaska Skola,* edited and with commentary by Gerald J. Sabo, (Columbus, OH: Slavica Publishers, 1987), p. 620.

72. Ibid., p. 624.

73. Ada Böhmerova, "The Camaldolese Dictionary," paper read at the 1993 National Convention of the American Association for the Advancement of Slavic Studies, Honolulu, HA, 22 November 1993, p. 5. The dictionary was discovered in 1929 and the translation of the Bible two decades later. For more on the dictionary and the Camaldolese monks, see Michal Lacko, "Camaldulese Hermits in Slovakia" *Slovak Studies,* 5 (1965): 99–167; and Michal Lacko, "Camaldulese Red Monastery—Cerveny Klastor. According to its 'Liber Actuum Capitularium'" *Slovak Studies,* 9 (1969): 113–231.

74. According to Peter Brock, Bajza might well be considered the one to have launched the use of literary Slovak, were it not for the fact that he "lacked training in philology and his impetuous disposition was disinclined to acquire a sound knowledge of the subject." See Peter Brock, *The Slovak National Awakening* (Toronto: University of Toronto Press, 1976), p. 8.

75. Joseph M. Kirschbaum, *Slovak Language and Literature,* Readings in Slavic Literatures 12 (Winnipeg: University of Manitoba, 1975), p. 102.

76. Gogolak, vol. 1, p. 26.

77. R. W. Seton-Watson, *A History of the Czechs and Slovaks* (Hamden, CT: Archon Books, 1965), p. 258. Seton-Watson uses the word *race* in the same way as we use the word *ethnicity* or *nationality* today. We favor the latter.

Chapter 5

1. A. J. P. Taylor, *The Habsburg Monarchy 1809—1918* (Harmondsworth: Penguin Books Ltd., 1967), p. 24.

2. The literature on nationalism is voluminous. Suffice it to indicate two works. Hugh Seton-Watson proposes a classification of nationalism in *Nations and States. An Enquiry into the Origins of Nations and the Politics of Nationalism* (London: Methuen, 1977) and Anthony Smith explains its contemporary validity in "The Ties that Bind," *LSE Magazine,* Spring 1993, pp. 8–11.

3. Macartney, p. 125.

4. R. W. Seton-Watson, *History of Czechs and Slovaks,* p. 258.

5. According to Seton-Watson, the Magyars "had immense advantages in their central position, their control not only of the central, but still more of the local, administration, the strength of their social position and resources." Ibid.

6. Brock, p. 10.

7. Milan Pisut et al., *Dejiny slovenskej literatury* (Bratislava: Obzor, 1984), p. 184.

8. Ibid., p. 183.

9. Ibid., pp. 186–187.

10. Ibid., p. 224.

11. Ibid., pp. 220–221.

12. Joseph M. Kirschbaum, *Slovak Language and Literature,* p. 114.

13. Ernest Denis, *La question d'Autriche—Les Slovaques* (Paris: Librairie Delagrave, 1917), p. 158. In the second edition, published in 1832, Kollar added two more cantos, bringing the number of sonnets to 615, "more a result of his erudition and ambition to create a great work, than a document of his poetic talent or artistic maturation." Joseph M. Kirschbaum, *Slovak Language and Literature,* p. 136.

14. Brock writes: "Kollar was pained by the thought that it [Bernolak's codification] divided his people into two conflicting camps and shut them off from the invigorating influence of Czech culture." Brock, p. 26.

15. According to a Slovak literary historian: "He lived in an imaginary Slavic motherland which was in conflict with reality and the needs of the people. He considered literature the affair of educated people and for this reason he stuck with Czech even though those revolutionary times demanded that he turn to his people and their language." Pisut et al., p. 219.

16. Joseph M. Kirschbaum, *Slovak Language and Literature,* p. 145.

17. Pisut et al., p. 214.

18. Joseph M. Kirschbaum, *Slovak Language and Literature,* p. 164.

19. Quoted in Brock, p. 24.

20. Andrej Mraz, *Dejiny slovenskej literatury* (Bratislava: Slovenska akademia vied a umeni, 1948), pp. 126–127.

21. Brock, p. 36.

22. It is worth noting that an attempt at a compromise orthography, encouraged by Kollar, was unsuccessfully made by Michal Godra, a young Slovak pastor,

and was published by Hamuljak in *Zora*. This attempt in fact showed a willingness on both sides to move in each other's direction, which is what happened in the end. For more on Godra, see Brock, p. 28.

23. Pisut et al., p. 244.
24. Brock, p. 50.
25. Pauliny, p. 177.
26. Joseph M. Kirschbaum, *Slovak Language and Literature*, pp. 185–186.
27. Peter Petro, "The Challenge of Slovak Literature," in Stanislav J. Kirschbaum and Anne C.R. Roman, eds., *Reflections on Slovak History* (Toronto: Slovak World Congress, 1987), p. 145.
28. Pisut et al., p. 249.
29. Ibid., p. 260.
30. Ibid., p. 262.

Chapter 6

1. Peter F. Sugar writes: "It was inevitable, once nationalism began to germinate in eastern Europe, that the thinking of patriots took a historical bend. Not only did the various institutions, traditions, values and beliefs to which they adjusted the new impulses reaching them from the West make sense only in an historical context, but it was history alone that could uphold their claims and hopes, which a dismal present did not justify. . . . History, particularly selective history, was full of lessons, examples, and badly needed encouragement." Peter F. Sugar, "Roots of Eastern European Nationalism," in Peter F. Sugar and Ivo J. Lederer, eds., *Nationalism in Eastern Europe* (Seattle: University of Washington Press, 1969), p. 39. See also Leonard W. Doob, *Patriotism and Nationalism. Their Psychological Foundations* (New Haven, CT: Yale University Press, 1964), pp. 47–49.
2. Gogolak, vol. 1, p. vii.
3. Ibid., p. 2.
4. Kucera and Kosticky, p. 188.
5. Macartney, p. 125.
6. Sugar, "Roots of Eastern European Nationalism," in Sugar and Lederer, eds., pp. 46 and 48–49.
7. Macartney, p. 131.
8. George Barany, "The Age of Royal Absolutism, 1790–1848," in Sugar et al., p. 180.
9. Jozef Simoncic, *Ohlasy francuzskej revolucie na Slovensku* (Kosice: Vychodoslovenske vydavatelstvo, 1982), p. 45.

10. *Dejiny Slovenska II,* p. 481.

11. Barany, "The Age of Royal Absolutism, 1790–1848," in Sugar et al., p. 178.

12. Macartney, p. 128.

13. Ibid., p. 134.

14. Barany, "The Age of Royal Absolutism, 1790–1848," in Sugar et al., p. 193.

15. Ibid., p. 200.

16. Daniel Rapant, *Slovenske povstanie roku 1848–49,* vol. 1 (Turciansky Sv. Martin, Matica slovenska, 1937), p. 85.

17. Gogolak, vol. 2, p. 1.

18. Ibid., p. 3.

19. Ibid., p. v.

20. Kucera and Kosticky, p. 188.

21. Rapant, vol. 1, pp. 145–146.

22. Ibid., p. 88.

23. *Dejiny Slovenska III,* p. 32.

24. Stanley Z. Pech, *The Czech Revolution of 1948* (Chapel Hill: The University of North Carolina Press, 1969), p. 268.

25. Ibid., p. 273.

26. Macartney, p. 159.

27. C. A. Macartney, *The Habsburg Empire 1790–1918* (London: Weidenfeld and Nicolson, 1969), p. 376.

28. *Dejiny Slovenska III,* p. 49.

29. Spiesz, p. 83.

30. Macartney, *The Habsburg Empire,* p. 413.

31. It is interesting to note what R. W. Seton-Watson writes about the Kromeriz constitution: "Though it never took effect, it will always remain one of the most remarkable political documents of the century, proving, as it does, that with adequate good will and in a congenial atmosphere rival nationalities, with very divergent and strongly-held views, are yet capable of reaching a compromise on fundamentals." *A History of the Czechs and Slovaks,* p. 192.

32. *Dejiny Slovenska III,* p. 76.

33. Ibid., p. 100.

34. Taylor, p. 81.

35. Gogolak, vol. 2, p. 5.

36. Ibid., p. 280.

Chapter 7

1. Macartney, *Hungary*, p. 164.
2. About these uniforms Macartney writes: "The reference was to an elaborate pseudo-Magyar uniform, complete with flowing cloak, high boots and spurs, which Bach designed for them and made them wear. These uniforms, adorning the persons of honest Czech or Slovene postmasters' or small tradesmen's sons, were a constant subject for mockery by the Hungarians and incidentally, no less antipathetic to their unfortunate wearers, who found them extraordinarily difficult to put on and off, and to wear with dignity, besides eating up a substantial proportion of their salaries." Macartney, *The Habsburg Empire,* p. 479, note 2.
3. Macartney, *Hungary*, p. 166.
4. Taylor, p. 123.
5. Macartney, *The Habsburg Empire,* p. 546.
6. Macartney, *Hungary*, p. 182.
7. Bokes, p. 156.
8. Spiesz, p. 92.
9. Gogolak, vol. 3, p. 35.
10. Vladimir Matula, "The Conception and the Development of Slovak National Culture in the Period of National Revival," *Studia Historica Slovaca* 17 (1990): p. 177.
11. R. W. Seton-Watson, *A History of the Czechs and Slovaks,* p. 162.
12. Ibid., p. 283.
13. See Thomas G. Masaryk, *La résurrection d'un Etat. Souvenirs et réflexions 1914–1918,* trans. by Fuscien Dominois (Paris: Plon, 1930).
14. Owen V. Johnson, *Slovakia, 1918–1938. Education and the Making of a Nation* (Boulder, CO: East European Monographs, 1985), p. 39.
15. Scotus Viator, *Racial Problems in Hungary,* p. 166.
16. Edita Bosak, "Intellectual Currents Among the Slovak Intelligentsia During the Nineteenth Century," paper read at the Fourth World Congress for Soviet and East European Studies, Harrogate, England, 21–26 July 1990, p. 16.
17. Scotus Viator, *Racial Problems in Hungary,* p. 333.
18. Oskar Cepan, "Ideove a lieterarne suvislosti Martina," in Vojtech Sarluska, ed., *Martin v slovenskych dejinach,* (Martin: Matica slovenska, 1986), p. 243.
19. Johnson, p. 25.
20. Milan Hodza, *Ceskoslovensky rozkol* (Turciansky Sv Martin: Nakl. vlastnym, 1920), pp. 176–177.

21. Ivan Kusy, "Martin v slovenskej literature v rokoch 1848–1918," in Sarluska, ed., p. 252.

22. Stefan Haviar and Ivan Kucma, *V pamäti naroda* (Martin: Matica Slovenska, 1988), p. 10.

23. Macartney, *The Habsburg Empire*, p. 527.

24. Marsina et al., p. 173.

25. Macartney, *The Habsburg Empire*, p. 528.

26. R. W. Seton-Watson, *History of the Czechs and Slovaks*, p. 266.

27. Gogolak, vol. 3, p. 66.

28. Bokes, p. 238.

29. Michal Elias, "Martin v slovenskych dejinach," in Sarluska, ed., p. 23.

30. Scotus Viator, *Racial Problems in Hungary*, pp. 130–31.

31. Haviar and Kucma, p. 12.

32. Macartney, *Hungary*, pp. 183–184.

33. Bokes, p. 273.

34. "[Turciansky Sväty] Martin had become strong enough by the mid 1870s as a social centre to survive such a heavy blow as the closing down of Matica slovenska and the Slovak gymnasium." Alexander Simkovic, "Slovenske literarne casopisy v Martine do roku 1918," in Sarluska, ed., p. 260.

35. Scotus Viator, *Racial Problems in Hungary*, p. 356.

36. Elias, "Martin v slovenskych dejinach," in Sarluska, ed., p. 24.

37. Bokes, p. 281.

38. Ibid., p. 282.

39. Skultety, p. 186.

40. Quoted in ibid., p. 188.

41. See Jozef Hvisc, "Poliaci a Martin" in Sarluska, ed., pp. 283–290.

42. Haviar and Kucma, p. 13.

43. Marsina et al., p. 177.

44. Johnson, p. 39. About other publications, Johnson writes that they "eventually wound up in Budapest, where 68 different Slovak periodicals were published before 1918, more than double the number in [Turciansky Sväty] Martin." Johnson, p. 40. According to a Slovak scholar, what is important to stress is the fact that the newspapers published in Skalica, Budapest, and also Ruzomberok remained essentially local and locally oriented publications whereas those in Turciansky Sväty Martin had a national vocation and readership. See Simkovic, "Slovenske literarne casopisy v Martine do roku 1918," in Sarluska, ed., p. 257.

45. Spiesz, p. 108.

46. Gogolak, vol. 3, p. 88.

47. Sugar, "Roots of East European Nationalism," in Sugar and Lederer, eds., p. 20.

48. "If we understand that the western ideas underwent numerous changes during their eastward migration, that in the East they were not only understood in a sense that differed from the original, but also that in eastern Europe they were fused with local concepts, we see how they became the main causes of a historic transformation that was *sui generis* to a large extent. . . . As a result of this approach to nationalism, xenophobia, historicism and a forced feeling of superiority emerged as decisive forces in Eastern Europe." Ibid., pp. 20 and 34.

49. Macartney, *The Habsburg Empire*, p. 733.

50. Gogolak, vol. 3, p. 52.

51. Petro, p. 145.

52. Pisut et al., p. 346.

53. Ibid., p. 349.

54. Ibid., p. 323.

55. Edita Bosak, "Czech-Slovak Relations and the Student Organization Detvan, 1882–1914," in Stanislav J. Kirschbaum, *Slovak Politics*, p. 34.

56. Edita Bosak, "Czech-Slovak Relations from the 1840s to 1914," *Slovakia* 35, nos. 64–65 (1991–1992): 66.

57. Jaroslav Solc, *Slovensko v ceskej politike* (Banska Bystrica: M.O. Enterprise, 1993), p. 8.

58. Ibid., pp. 10–11.

59. Ibid., p. 26.

60. Bosak, "Czech-Slovak Relations from the 1840s to 1914," pp. 76–77.

61. Solc, p. 31.

62. Brock, p. 53.

63. Gogolak, vol. 3, p. 54.

64. Scotus viator, *Racial Problems in Hungary*, p. 342.

65. Karol Sidor, *Andrej Hlinka (1864–1926)* (Bratislava: Tlacou knihtlaciarne Sv. Andreja, 1934), p. 307.

66. Quoted in Karol A. Medvedsky, *Slovensky prevrat*, vol. 3 (Trnava: Vydal Spolok Sv. Vojtecha, 1931), p. 346.

67. Sidor, p. 314.

68. Susan Mikula, "Milan Hodza and the Politics of Power, 1907–1914," in Stanislav J. Kirschbaum, *Slovak Politics*, p. 43.

69. Solc, p. 36.

70. Quoted in R. W. Seton-Watson, *Masaryk in England* (Cambridge: Cambridge University Press, 1943), p. 125.

71. Bosak, "Czech-Slovak Relations From the 1840s to 1914," p. 77.

72. Solc, p. 43.

73. Marsina et al., p. 202.

74. *Dejiny Slovenska IV*, 1986, p. 467.

75. The details concerning the change of name are found in Stefan Osusky, "How Czecho-Slovakia Was Born," in Joseph M. Kirschbaum, *Slovakia in the 19th and 20th Centuries*, pp. 86–87.

76. *Dejiny Slovenska IV*, p. 486.

77. Spiesz, p. 124.

78. Macartney, *Hungary*, p. 187.

79. Gogolak, vol. 3, p. 56.

80. Ibid., vol. 2, p. 7.

Chapter 8

1. The counties that were on purely Slovak territory remained as they had been since the fourteenth century while those in the south had their territory redrawn according to the frontiers of the new state. Two small counties, Ostrihom and Komarno, were merged into one, Komarno, while Turna county joined Abov to become the Abov-Turna county. See Jozef Klimo, *Vyvoj uzemia Slovenska a utvaranie jeho hranic* (Bratislava: Obzor, 1980), p. 51.

2. Gogolak, vol. 2, p. 5.

3. Taylor, p. 258.

4. Denis, *La question d'Autriche—Les Slovaques.*

5. These statistics, with the exception of the Czechs and Slovaks, are taken from Vaclav L. Benes, "Czechoslovak Democracy and its Problems 1918–1920," in Mamatey and Luza, eds., p. 40. The statistics on the Slovaks are taken from Johnson, p. 79. Benes, using official Czechoslovak statistics that enumerated "Czechoslovaks" but not Czechs and Slovaks, does not give therefore figures on either the Czechs or the Slovaks. The figures on the Czechs are obtained by subtracting the figure on the Slovaks from that on the "Czechoslovaks" found in Benes.

6. The text submitted by Benes is found in Documentation internationale, *La Paix de Versailles,* vol. 10 (Paris: Les éditions internationales, 1929), pp. 53–54.

7. Over the years, two spellings have been used when quoting the passage in the Martin Declaration that deals with the question of the new nation: Czecho-Slovak and Czechoslovak. It is unlikely that at the time the declaration was being drafted, the question of spelling was thought to have any sort of significance. These later usages merely reflect different approaches to the common state.

8. Thomas G. Masaryk, *The Making of a State. Memories and Observations 1914–1918,* an English version, arranged and prepared with an introduction by Henry Wickham Steed (New York: Frederick A. Stokes Co., 1927), p. 220.

9. Vavro Srobar, *Osvobodene Slovensko* (Praha: Cin, 1928), p. 336.

10. Ferdinand Peroutka, *Budovani statu,* vol. 1 (Praha: F. Borovy, 1934–1936), pp. 446-447.

11. Srobar, *Osvobodene Slovensko,* p. 365.

12. Peroutka, vol. 2, book 2, p. 1227.

13. Ibid., vol 1, pp. 452–454; also C. A. Macartney, *Hungary and Her Successors* (London: Oxford University Press, 1937), p. 116.

14. This is what Srobar wrote in his memoirs; see Vavro Srobar, *Z mojho zivota* (Praha: F. Borovy, 1946), p. 474.

15. Peroutka also suggests that "Slovak Protestants did not need any encouragement from Prague to try to put down the Catholics; this answered their dearest, and probably their most hoped-for desires"; Peroutka, vol. 2, book 2, p. 1226.

16. Karol Sidor, *Slovenska politika na pode prazskeho snemu,* vol. 1 (Bratislava: Andreja, 1943), p. 71.

17. Peroutka, vol. 1, p. 406.

18. Ibid., vol. 2, book 2, p. 1226.

19. Milan Hodza, *Federation in Central Europe* (London: Jarrolds Publishers Ltd., 1942), p. 89.

20. Sidor, *Andrej Hlinka,* p. 331.

21. Peroutka, vol. 1, p. 448.

22. Victor S. Mamatey, "The Development of Czechoslovak Democracy 1920–1938," in Mamatey and Lua, eds., p. 102.

23. Sidor, *Slovenska politika,* vol. , p. 142.

24. Mamatey, "The Development of Czechoslovak Democracy 1920–1938," in Mamatey and Lua, eds., p. 108.

25. Manfred Alexander, "Slovakia in the Files of the German Foreign Office, 1918–1921," in Stanislav J. Kirschbaum, *Slovak Politics,* pp. 84–87.

26. Mamatey, "The Development of Czechoslovak Democracy 1920–1938," in Mamatey and Lua, eds., p. 109. Peroutka writes: "The decision to put Dr. Benes at the head of the government was a surprise for everyone except for the members of the Petka who played a special role and for whom all of the circumstances remained confidential." Peroutka, vol. 4, p. 2374.

27. Ibid., p. 2373.

28. Ibid., p. 2445.

29. Ibid., p. 2370.

30. Taken from H. W. V. Temperley, ed., *A History of the Peace Conference of Paris,* vol. 5 (London: Henry Frowde and Hodder & Stoughton, 1921), p. 470.

31. Czech personnel in Slovakia, whether in the state administration or in education, invariably used Czech as the language of work and communication. An effort was also made to Czechize the Slovak language.

32. Manfred Alexander, "Leistungen, Belastungen und Gefährdungen der Demokratie in der Ersten Tschechoslowakischen Republik," *Bohemia* 27, no. 1 (1986): p. 85. (Italics in the original.)

33. Edouard Bénès, "Discours aux Slovaques sur le présent et l'avenir de notre nation," *Le monde slave,* février 1934, p. 45. (Italics in the original.)

34. Peroutka, vol. 1, p. 213.

35. R. W. Seton-Watson, *The New Slovakia* (Prague: Fr. Borovy, 1924), p. 109.

36. Macartney, *Hungary and Her Successors 1919–1937,* pp. 123–131.

37. Peroutka, vol. 4, p. 2449.

38. Ivan Derer, *The Unity of the Czechs and Slovaks* (Prague: Orbis, 1938), p. 7.

39. Quoted in Sidor, *Slovenska politika,* vol. 1, p. 219.

40. In the first issue of 1928, Tuka argued that there had been a secret clause in the 30 October 1918 Slovak declaration of political union with the Czechs that gave the right to the Slovaks, after ten years in their common state with the Czechs, to review their status in that state. If dissatisfied, they had the option either of renegotiating their participation or of opting out. Until such a decision was taken, there existed a *vacuum juris* as far as the Slovaks were concerned. The secret clause was never found and Tuka was brought to trial and sentenced to fifteen years imprisonment after evidence was produced that he had been receiving funds from Hungary.

41. Marsina et al., p. 230.

42. Susan Mikula, "Relations Between Slovaks and Czechs in the First CSR," *Slovakia* 35, nos. 64–65 (1991–1992): p. 83.

43. Marsina et al., p. 228.

44. Ibid., p. 226.

45. Macartney, *Hungary and Her Successors 1919–1937,* p. 127.

46. Mikus, *Slovakia. A Political History: 1918–1950,* p. 47.

47. Dorothea H. El Mallakh, *The Slovak Autonomy Movement, 1935–1939: A Study in Unrelenting Nationalism* (Boulder, CO: East European Quarterly, 1979), p. 48.

48. Marsina et al., p. 234.

49. Sidor, *Slovenska politika,* vol. 1, p. 309. Edvard Benes was much more cynical about the meaning and effectiveness of this assembly (and the corresponding ones for Bohemia, Moravia-Silesia, and Ruthenia), characterizing them as "powerless provincial assemblies that were supposed to create the impression that the administration was being decentralized when in fact it was being further centralized" and describing the law as a "step backward." Edvard Benes, *Mnichovske dny; Pameti* (Praha: Svoboda, 1968), p. 10.

50. Leff, p. 276.

51. Marsina et al., p. 237.

52. Ibid., p. 239.

53. Ladislav Deak, *Hra o Slovensko* (Bratislava: Veda, Vydavatelstvo Slovenskej akademie vied, 1991).
54. Solc, p. 78.

Chapter 9

1. Unfortunately the archives do not cover the entire period of the existence of the Slovak Republic. Shortly after the outbreak of World War II, both consuls were recalled and official diplomatic representation in Bratislava ceased, as did the recognition of Slovakia. The files of the ministries, however, were not closed automatically. Interest in Slovakia remained, but the type of reporting changed, reflecting the changed situation in both countries.
2. Public Record Office (PRO, London), FO 371/24290, Doc. C612/58/12, 6 January 1940.
3. Ministère des Affaires étrangères, Europe, 1918–1940, Tchécoslovaquie, vol. 131, pp. 100–3 (hereafter MAE, and volume number).
4. FO 471/39, Doc. C3973/19/18, 20 March 1939; This document, like a few others, was published in the collection *Documents on British Foreign Policy,* Third Series, vol. 4 (London: H.M.S.O., 1951), pp. 406–408. (Hereafter *D.G.F.P.,* and volume number.)
5. MAE, 132, pp. 13–15.
6. FO 417/39, Doc. C5201/7/12, 11 April 1939; *D.B.F.P.,* 5, pp. 84–91.
7. Ibid.
8. FO 371/22903, Doc. C8828/2392/12, 20 June 1939.
9. MAE, 132, pp. 55–58.
10. FO 417/40, Doc. C.10876/7/12, 31 July 1939.
11. FO 371/22899, Doc. C16390/7/12, 12 October 1939.
12. FO 371/24290, Doc. C3310/58/12, 27 January 1940.
13. Edward Taborsky, *President Edvard Benes, Between East and West 1938–1948* (Stanford: Hoover Institution Press, 1981), p. 38.
14. Ibid., p. 39.
15. Ibid., p. 261, note 37.
16. Spiesz, p. 154.
17. Ladislav Lipscher, *Zidia v slovenskom state 1939–1945* (Banska Bystrica: Print-Servis, 1992), p. 30.
18. Katarina Zavacka, "The Anti-Jewish Legislation of the Slovak State," in Dezider Toth, et al., *The Tragedy of Slovak Jews* (Banska Bystrica: DATEI, 1992), p. 71.

19. Marsina et al., p. 248.
20. Ivan Kamenec, "The Deportation of Jewish Citizens from Slovakia in 1942," in Toth et al., p. 84.
21. Ibid., p. 89.
22. Ibid., p. 97.
23. Gila Fatran, "The Struggle for Jewish Survival during the Holocaust," in Toth et al., p. 111.
24. Quoted in Milan S. Durica, *The Slovak Involvement in the Tragedy of the European Jews* (Abano Terme: Piovan Editore, 1989), p. 13.
25. Gabriel Hoffmann and Ladislav Hoffman, *Katolicka cirkev a tragedia zidov v dokumentoch* (Pratizanske: Vydavatelstvo G-print, 1994), p. 17.
26. According to Gabriel Hoffman: "His abdication was rejected by the presidium of the Hlinka Slovak People's Party." Ibid.
27. Tiso testified at his trial: "As you heard from the testimony of many witnesses, the Jews themselves sent word and beseeched me to stay on because they felt they were more or less safe as long as I was there. That was the obligation which urged and sustained me . . . to go on." *Dr. Jozef Tiso o sebe* (Passaic, NJ: Slovensky Katolicky Sokol, 1952), p.24.
28. Kamenec, "The Deportation of Jewish Citizens from Slovakia in 1942," in Toth et al., p. 88.
29. Reitlinger writes: "On June 26th [1942] when the deportations were slowing down Hans Elard Ludin, the German Minister in Bratislava, telegraphed Weizsäcker that Dr. Tuka was asking for diplomatic pressure to enable the remaining 35,000 Slovak Jews to be deported 'in the face of the unpopularity of these measures among wider circles of the population and the growth of English propaganda.'" Gerald Reitlinger, *The Final Solution; The Attempt to Exterminate the Jews of Europe 1939–1945,* 2nd rev. and augmented edition (London: Vallentine, Mitchell, 1968), p. 420.
30. Durica, *The Slovak Involvement in the Tragedy of the European Jews,* p. 12.
31. Reitlinger considers Tiso's response to Georges Dunand of the International Committee of the Red Cross that "Slovak Jews had been spared previous to the rebellion" to be a "downright lie." Reitlinger, p. 394. On the other hand, in the view of Gabriel Hoffmann, "Tiso . . . did everything that was possible in the given conditions of power to save the Jews persecuted by Nazism." Hoffmann and Hoffmann, p. 218.
32. Reitlinger, p. 385.
33. Marsina et al., p. 247.
34. Gustav Husak, "O vyvoji a situacii na Slovensku," *Svedectvi* 15, no. 58 (1979): p. 377.
35. Ibid., p. 369.

36. FO 371/34337, Doc. C9206/372/12, 9 August 1943.
37. FO 371/34446, Doc. C1056/150/18, 22 January 1943.
38. FO 371/34446, Doc. C5526/150/18.
39. Husak, pp. 376–77.

Chapter 10

1. Correspondence concerning this issue is found in Joseph M. Kirschbaum, *Slovakia. Nation at the Crossroads of Central Europe* (New York: Robert Speller & Sons, Publishers, Inc., 1960), pp. 318–321.
2. Lubomir Liptak, "Politicky rezim na Slovensku v rokoch 1939–1945," in *Slovenske narodne povstanie roku 1944* (Bratislava: Vydavatelstvo politickej literatury, 1965), p. 26.
3. Marsina et al., p. 253.
4. Edvard Benes, *Sest let exilu a druhe svetove valky* (Praha: Cin, 1947), p. 197.
5. Ibid., p. 198.
6. Ibid., p. 202.
7. Edvard Benes, "Czechoslovak Policy for Victory and Peace," in *Czechoslovak Documents and Sources,* No. 10 (London: Czechoslovak Ministry of Foreign Affairs, Information Service, 1944), pp. 40–41.
8. Benes, *Šest let exilu a druhe svetove valky,* p. 243.
9. Ibid., p. 197.
10. Ibid., p. 199.
11. BBC Written Archives Centre, P400 Press Cuttings, 1943–1944, *Free Europe,* 15 January 1943. See also FO 371/34336, Doc. C521/372/12, 13 January 1943.
12. Benes, "Czechoslovak Policy for Victory and Peace," p. 46. Italics in the original.
13. Vladimir Clementis, *Odkazy z Londyna* (Bratislava: Nakladatelstvo Obroda, 1947), pp. 113.
14. BBC Written Archives Centre, External and Overseas Service, Czech Section, Program Planning and Broadcast 1943, Accession No. 65587.
15. Bundesarchiv, Koblenz, Handakten Ritter, Slowakei, Telegram from Ludin, 24. August 1944.
16. *Slovenske narodne povstanie: Dokumenty,* (Bratislava: Vydavatelstvo politickej literatury, 1965), p. 186.
17. Husak, p. 378.
18. Ibid.
19. Ibid., p. 379.

20. Benes, "Czechoslovak Policy for Victory and Peace," p. 40.
21. BBC Written Archives Centre, P400, Press Cuttings, 1943–44, Free Europe, 17 November 1944.
22. FO 371/38941, Doc. C10763/1343/12, 16 August 1944.
23. Ibid.
24. Bundesarchiv, R30/50, Bericht über die Lage in der Slowakei, Gauleitung Wien an Frank, 26. August 1944.
25. BBC Written Archives Centre, Summary of World Broadcasts No. 1871, 31 August 1944.
26. Tido J. Gaspar, "Z Pamäti," *Slovenske pohlady* 84, no. 12 (1968): p. 79.
27. Bundesarchiv, R30/52, Gauleitung Sudetenland, Gauamtsleiter Rudolf Staffen an Frank, 16. September 1944.
28. Quoted in Jozef Jablonicky, "Slovenska otazka v obdobi narodnej a demokratickej revolucie," in Mesaros, Julius, ed., *Slovaci a ich narodny vyvin* (Bratislava: Veda Vydavatelstvo Slovenskej akademie vied, 1966), p. 276.
29. Quoted in Ferdinand Beer, et al., *Dejinna krizovatka* (Bratislava: Vydavatelstvo politickej literatury, 1964), p. 491.
30. Quoted in ibid., p. 483.
31. Gustav Husak, *Svedectvo o Slovenskom narodnom povstani* (Bratislava: Vydavatelstvo politickej literatury, 1964), p. 584.
32. Ibid.
33. Lubomir Liptak, "Jozef Tiso—problem slovenskej politiky a slovenskej historiografie," in *Pokus o politicky a osobny profil Jozefa Tisu* (Bratislava: Slovak Academic Press, 1992), p. 14.
34. Solc, p. 204.

Chapter 11

1. Robert Letz, *Slovensko v rokoch 1945–1948. Na ceste ku komunistickej totalite* (Bratislava: Ustredie slovenskej krestanskej inteligencie, 1994).
2. Solc, p. 229.
3. Husak writes that this division in the CPS was primarily the result of personal factors, namely jealousy from those Slovak Communists who had not participated in the 1944 revolt. See Husak, *Nove slovo,* 25 July 1968. There is no doubt validity in this explanation; Husak, however, fails to mention the more important educational and national divisions in the ranks of the Slovak Communists. The group that formed the centralist wing of the CPS was composed primarily of workers, many of whom were not even of Slovak origin

and whom the CPCS had sent to Slovakia during the 1920s and 1930s. By their social origin and through their activities in Slovakia, despite their national origin, they felt they had a justified claim to the leadership of the CPS. In this they were opposed by a younger generation of Slovak-born and Slovak-educated Communists such as Clementis and Husak, both of whom had a university education (each had obtained the doctorate of law), who felt and probably claimed that they understood better the needs of the Slovak people.

4. Solc, p. 247.

5. Hubert Ripka, *Czechoslovakia Enslaved. The Story of the Communist Coup d'État* (London: Victor Gollanz Ltd., 1950), p. 109.

6. The full text of the memorandum was published for the first time in *Pravda* (Bratislava) on 29 March 1968.

7. Quoted in Frantisek Vnuk, "Retribucne sudnictvo a proces s Jozefom Tisom," in *Pokus o politicky a osobny profil Jozefa Tisu* (Bratislava: Slovak Academic Press, 1992), p. 387.

8. Marsina et al., p. 271.

9. Lubomir Liptak, *Slovensko v 20. storoci* (Bratislava: Vydavatelstvo politickej literatury, 1968), p. 296.

10. Hans Renner and Ivo Samson, *Dejiny Cesko-Slovenska po roku 1945* (Bratislava: Slovak Academic Press, 1993), p. 131.

11. Anton Hlinka, *Sila slabych a slabost silnych* (Zagreb: LOGOS, 1989), p. 76.

12. Frantisek Miklosko, *Nebudete ich moct rozvratit. Z osudov katolickej cirkvi na Slovensku v rokoch 1943–89* (Bratislava: Vydavatelstvo Archa, 1991), p. 66.

13. Ladislav Feierabend, *Agricultural Cooperatives in Czechoslovakia* (New York: Mid-European Studies Center, 1952), p. 72.

14. Ondrej Balaz, "Vyvoj polnohospodarstva na Slovensku v rokoch 1949–1960", *Historicky casopis* 9, no. 1 (1960): p. 9.

15. Jozef Markus, *Zaujem o planovanie a zaujmy v planovani* (Bratislava: Nakladatelstvo Pravda, 1988), p. 123.

16. Marsina et al., p. 277.

17. The term is Eugen Löbl's who was one of the fourteen accused in the Slansky trial; Eugen Löbl and Leopold Grünwald, *Die intellektuelle Revolution. Hintergründe und Auswirkung des "Prager Frühlings"* (Düsseldorf: Econ Verlag, 1969). See also Peter Hruby, *Fools and Heroes. The Changing Role of Communist Intellectuals in Czechoslovakia* (Oxford: Pergamon Press, 1980); and Vladimir Kusin, *The Intellectual Origins of the Prague Spring* (Cambridge: Cambridge University Press, 1971).

18. Jiri Pelikan, ed. *The Czechoslovak Political Trials 1950–1954. The Suppressed Report of the Dubcek Government's Commission of Inquiry, 1968* (London: Macdonald & Co. Ltd, 1971), p. 148.

19. Ibid., p. 215.

20. Ibid., p. 241.

21. Ibid.

22. Dubcek personally intervened to get Gustav Husak to work in the Slovak Academy of Sciences as well as a grant to write his book on the 1944 revolt. Ludwig Vesely, *Dubcek. Biographie* (München: Kindler Verlag, 1970), p. 244.

23. Robert W. Dean, *Nationalism and Political Change in Eastern Europe: the Slovak Question and the Czechoslovak Reform Movement* (Denver: East European Monographs, 1973), p. 13.

24. William Shawcross, *Dubcek* (London: Weidenfeld and Nicolson, 1970), p. 124.

25. Hviezdon Koctuch, "Ideologia a ekonomika po roku 1945," *Slovenske pohlady*, 82, no. 3 (1966): pp. 90–92.

26. Anton Dzuban et al., "Narodny dochodok Slovenska," *Ekonomicky casopis* 14, no. 8 (1966): pp. 721–40.

27. Quoted in Shawcross, p. 124. Dubcek did not, nor could he, make reference to a federal solution. Instead he spoke of returning to the principles of the Kosice program.

28. Galia Golan, *The Czechoslovak Reform Movement Communism in Crisis 1962–1968* (Cambridge: Cambridge University Press, 1971), p. 259.

29. The occasion was the centenary of the founding of Matica slovenska. Novotny suggested that the papers of Matica slsovenska be transferred to Prague rather than modernize the building: "A greater snub could hardly be imagined; Novotny was virtually saying that the Slovaks' beloved Matica should shut up shop. Vasil Bilak, standing nearby, was furious and asked Novotny, perhaps a little loudly, how he dared to be so offensive. The President summoned his car and his wife and left at once." Shawcross, p. 127.

30. At that meeting, Novotny had substituted certain documents that the Presidium had accepted and tabled for discussion by the plenum. When Dubcek asked Novotny why the substitution had taken place, the latter accused him of acting as a "Slovak bourgeois nationalist." See Pavel Tigrid, *Le printemps de Prague* (Paris: Seuil, 1968), pp. 184–5.

31. Jaroslaw Piekalkiewicz, *Public Opinion in Czechoslovakia, 1968–69. Results and Analysis of Surveys Conducted During the Dubcek Era* (New York: Praeger Publishers, 1972), p. 82.

32. It is interesting to note how Dean explains the differences between Slovakia and the Czech Lands: "As a common reference point of Slovak reformist activity the national question (in its manifold aspects) served to differentiate the Slovak body politic from the Czech in two ways, both before Novotny's fall and during Dubcek's rule. The first was with regard to objectives; generally

speaking, in Slovakia the predominant political activity centered around the struggle for increased national autonomy, while in the Czech Lands political activity was more clearly directed toward defining and achieving 'democratization,' understood as the institutional pluralization of society and the securing of individual civil liberties. The contrasting salience of these issues in either part of the state accounted in part for a second important difference namely that political cohesion—popular and elite—was greater in Slovakia. The drive for home rule generally did not raise as many of the fundamental differences, as did the political issue of social reorganization which, by its very nature, tended to sharpen political conflict at all levels. . . . The political coordinates of the majority of the Slovak elite differed from those of the Czech reformers inasmuch as they regarded the solution of the national problem as a precondition for democratic reforms in Society." Dean, p. 3.

33. Leff, p. 127.
34. Vladimir Minac, *Navraty k prevratu* (Bratislava: NVK International, 1993), p. 21.
35. Viliam Plevza, *Socialisticke premeny Ceskoslovenska* (Bratislava: Pravda, 1983), p. 420.
36. Eduard Sarmir, "Ekonomicke vyrovnavanie SSR a CSR v procese vystavby socialistickeho Ceskoslovenska," *Ekonomicky casopis* 13, no. 7 (1974): p. 587.
37. Jan Fischer, *Kulturny rozvoj Slovenska v piatej patrocnici (1971–1975)* (Bratislava: Obzor, 1978), p. 219.
38. Peter Prusak, "Niektore vysledky vyskumu religiozity na Slovensku," *Sociologia* 1 (1970): pp. 65–82.
39. *Pravda,* 14 April 1970.
40. Miklosko, p. 124.
41. Hlinka, p. 186.
42. Leff, p. 268.
43. Alexander Dubcek, *Hope Dies Last. The Autobiography of Alexander Dubcek,* ed. and trans. by Jiri Hochman (New York: Kodanska International, 1993), p. 264. On Slovak participation in Charter 77, Dubcek writes: "Out of some 2,000 signatories of the charter, there were only three Slovaks, two of whom lived in Prague." Ibid.
44. Minac, p. 29.
45. Ibid., pp. 32–33.
46. An English translation and an analysis of the letter is found in Stanislav J. Kirschbaum, "An Act of Faith and Integrity: Bishop Korec's Letter to Czechoslovak Television," pp. 61–126.
47. Minac, p. 61.

Chapter 12

1. According to Zdenek Jicinsky, the Communist policy of normalization after the 1968 invasion explains the absence of an organized dissidence that articulated alternative policies distinguishing Czechoslovakia from other Communist states like Poland and Hungary: "Even after the introduction of the so–called Soviet perestroika, there was no development of opposition forces, political parties, newspapers and so forth, and dissident activity, as far as its representatives were concerned, was limited, as was its social influence." Zdenek Jicinsky, "Ke ztroskotani ceskoslovenskeho federalismu," in Rudiger Kipke and Karel Vodicka, eds., Rozlouceni s Ceskoslovenskem (Praha: Cesky spisovatel, 1993), p. 68.

2. Jan Mlynarik, "Historia cesko–slovenskych vztahov," in Kipke and Vodicka, eds., p. 31.

3. Vladimir Repka, "Co ma tesi, trapi, zlosti," Novy Slovak, 5 September 1991.

4. According to Jan Mlynarik, "The Czechs became definitely opposed to communism, especially after 1968, while the Slovaks came to identify with its material growth. Slovakia was transformed from a wooden to a modern residence only under communism (in the Czech Lands this process took place in the first half of the twentieth century). The Slovaks became accustomed to communism, even though, in contrast to the Czechs, they had rejected it in 1946." Jan Mlynarik, "Historia cesko–slovenskych vztahov," in Kipke and Vodicka, eds., p. 31.

5. Miroslav Janek, "Pestre politicke spektrum na Slovensku," Slovensko 15, nos. 9–10 (1991): 2.

6. Bohuslav Findo, "Ako to vidim ja," Slovensky narod 1, (1990). The "Memorandum on Slovakia," as we pointed out in Chapter 11, was a document that Czechoslovak National Socialist Party, the party of President Edvard Benes, prepared in 1946 for the assimilation of the Slovaks.

7. Vaclav Havel, "Zaklad identity spolocneho statu," Narodna obroda, 18 September 1990. This is the text of a speech to the Federal Parliament of Czecho–Slovakia.

8. Anton Andras, minister of Justice and a KDH deputy was asked to resign his ministry in November 1990 by Meciar on grounds of incompetence. At first Andras refused but in the end did resign. The incident worsened the already tense relations between the KDH and the VPN.

9. Jicinsky, "Ke ztroskotani ceskoslovenskeho federalismu," in Kipke and Vodicka, eds., p. 75.

10. Ludvik Vaculik, "Nase slovenska otazka," *Literarni noviny*, 3 May 1990, reprinted in *Nove slovo*, 24 May 1990.

11. Vladimir Minac, "Nasa cesko–slovenska otazka," *Nove slovo*, 24 May 1990.

12. Findo, "Ako to vidim ja."

13. Dusan Kovac, "Korene neporozumenia," *Nove slovo*, 31 January 1991.

14. Jaroslav Hontan, "Slovenska poslusnost a ceska odplata," *Slovensky narod*, 9 July 1991.

15. M. Bohus, "Rozvod?," *Slovensky narod*, 14 August 1991.

16. Milan Ferko, "Maturita nasej zrelosti," *Pravda*, 2 April 1991.

17. Jicinsky, "Ke ztroskotani ceskoslovenskeho federalismu," in Kipke and Vodicka, eds., p. 77.

18. Igor Cibula, "Benesov duch stale strasi," *Narodna obroda*, 13 September 1991.

19. Busik et al., p. 14.

20. "Rozvod zbytocny aj nakladny," *Narodna obroda*, 16 September 1991.

21. Frantisek Kosorin, "Kto na koho doplaca," *Kanadsky Slovak*, 17 August 1991. According to another source: "At present 40% of federal tax revenue goes to the Czech budget, 25% to the Slovak one, and 35% to the federal budget. The latter is then redistributed again, with 66% going to the Czechs and 33% to the Slovaks. In the first five months of 1991 the Czech republic generated tax revenue of Kcs 89.2 billion, and received after redistribution Kcs 78.8 billion; the Slovak republic generated Kcs 35.2 billion, but received Kcs 45.6 billion. In other words the Czechs subsidized the Slovaks by Kcs 10.4 billion—a rate of about Kcs 25 billion a year." *Eastern Europe Newsletter* 5, no. 20, 7 October 1991, p. 6.

22. "Tvrdo postihuje Slovensku ekonomiku," *Narodna obroda*, 4 March 1991.

23. Jaroslav Toma, "Zvlastny pripad—Slovensko," *Nove slovo*, 28 March 1991.

24. Emil Komarik, "Federalne tahanice," *Slovensky dennik* 180/1990 quoted in *Slovensky narod*, 1 December 1990.

25. Vaclav Havel, "Zaklad identity spolecneho statu," *Narodna obroda*, 18 September 1990.

26. Jozef Prokes, "Otvoreny list prezidentovi CSFR," *Slovensky narod*, 24 October 1990.

27. Imrich Minar, "Nevyhnutnost spoluzitia a spoluprace," *Literarny tyzdennik* 22 (1991).

28. Jozef Markus. "Interview," *Slovensky narod*, 18 July 1991.

29. Alexander Dubcek, "Na konfederaciu treba partnera," *Narodna obroda*, 10 June 1991.

30. Jozef Moravcik, "Nevyrieseny problem," *Narodna obroda*, 20 June 1991. Moravcik himself caused some of the confusion. In another article he writes: "If a federation is to be the form of solving the relations between national formations,

then the only possible solid basis of federal statehood is a treaty. It is often suggested that a treaty as a basis for the creation of a common state formation is characteristic only of a confederation. You have to indicate here that nations which resolve their constitutional relations are not tied by some generalized schemes, but above all by their own interests and needs." See Moravcik, "Narodne ustavy a federalna ustava," *Narodna obroda*, 11 October 1990.

31. Markus stated: "The creation of inimical, oppositional, economically and culturally disjointed states, the Czech Republic and the Slovak Republic, I consider personally as an extreme solution. The creation of two independent but closely cooperating states whose mutual borders of the 'future,' that is to say borders with no passport and customs controls I do not consider at all extreme, rather as a rational possibility for a future constitutional order. Technically speaking, there would be a customs and monetary union and a common market between an independent Czech Republic and an independent Slovak Republic. This is no utopia, for such a model of relations exists for some time between Belgium and Luxembourg and there are similar relations between the North European states." See Markus, "Interview."

32. Viktor Knapp, "Nedorozumenia okolo suverenity," *Narodna obroda*, 18 May 1991.

33. Igor Uhrik, "Nasa suverenita," *Slovensky narod*, 13 October 1990.

34. Vladimir Meciar, "Kto nositelom suverenity?," *Narodna obroda*, 10 July 1991.

35. Dubcek, "Na konfederaciu treba partnera."

36. Jan Carnogursky, "Rovnopravni sme, rovnocenni nie," *Literarny tyzdennik*, 12 March 1991.

37. Ibid.

38. Vladimir Meciar, "Mame podporu obyvatelstva," *Narodna obroda*, 6 June 1991.

39. Svetozar Krno, " . . . a problemy ujdu bohom," *Nove slovo*, 5 July 1990.

40. Jozef Prokes, "Hranice nemusia byt barierou," *Nove slovo*, 15 August 1991.

41. "Hojda sa stat, hojda . . . ," *Smena*, 28 August 1991.

42. "Vysvetlujeme niektore zakladne statopravne pojmy," *Praca*, nos. 218, 219, 220, 222, 223, 226, from 17 September to 26 September 1991.

43. Hvezdon Koctuch, "Kto chce partnerske spoluzitie," *Narodna obroda*, 13 September 1991.

44. Vaclav Havel, "Odporucam demokraticku federaciu," *Narodna obroda*, 25 September 1991.

45. Karl–Peter Schwarz, *Tschechen und Slowaken: der lange Weg zur friedlichen Trennung* (Wien: Europaverlag, 1993), p. 222.

46. Karel Vodicka, "Koalicni ujednani: Rozdelime stat! Volby '92 a jejich dusledky pro ceskoslovenskou statnost," in Kipke and Vodicka, eds., p. 94.

47. Rudiger Kipke and Karel Vodicka, "Predmluva," in Rudiger Kipke and Karel Vodicka, p. 11. Bernard Michel also writes that "the current independence of Slovakia does not have anything to do with a classical movement of national emancipation. Independence did not have seek to modernise and liberate Slovak society and the Slovak economy but, on the contrary, to block the process of reform." Bernard Michel, "Les racines historiques de l'indépendance slovaque," *Revue d'Europe centrale* 1, no. 2 (1993): p. 131.

48. One of the contributors to the discussion, and a former leader of the VPN, offers a more subtle interpretation: "The breakup of Czechoslovakia was not the inevitable result of the emancipation process in Slovakia, but rather an unforeseen consequence of the actions of the political elites. As such, it 'authorizes' the breakup of Czechoslovakia." Fedor Gal, "Rozpad Ceskoslovenska v politickej perpektive," in Kipke and Vodicka, eds., p. 162. These factors make an interesting autopsy report on the former common state of the Czechs and Slovaks.

49. Martin Butora and Zora Butorova, "Nesnesitelna lahkost rozchodu," in ibid., p. 126. According to Schwarz: "It [Czechoslovakia] broke up because the state idea which it had upheld had lost its meaning." Schwarz, p. 226.

Epilogue

1. This is a revised English version of an article entitled "Buducnost Slovenska" (The Future of Slovakia) that appeared in *Slovenske pohlady 93* 5, (1993): 10-19.

SELECTED BIBLIOGRAPHY

Books

A liturgia sclavinica ad provinciam slovacam. Ad initia cultus Cristiani in Slovacia. Bratislava: Bibliotheca universitatis, 1992.

Andrej Hlinka a jeho miesto v slovenskych dejinach. Zbornik prednasok z vedeckeho sympozia. Bratislava: Vydavatelstvo DaVel, 1991.

Balawyder, Aloysius, ed. *Cooperative Movements in Eastern Europe.* Montclair, NJ: Allanheld, Osmun & Co., Publishers, 1980.

Barto, Jaroslav. *Riesenie vztahu Cechov a Slovakov.* Bratislava: Nakladatelstvo Epocha, 1968.

Beer, Ferdinand, et al. *Dejinna krizovatka.* Bratislava: Vydavatelstvo politickej literatury, 1964.

Benes, Edvard. *Mnichovske dny; Pameti.* Praha: Svoboda, 1968.

Benes, Edvard. *Sest let exilu a druhe svetove valky.* Praha: Orbis, 1946.

Bogdan, Henry. *From Warsaw to Sophia. A History of Eastern Europe.* Santa Fe, NM: Pro Libertate Publishing, 1989.

Bokes, Frantisek. *Dejiny Slovenska a Slovakov od najstarsich cias po oslobodenie.* Bratislava: Slovenska akademia vied a umeni, 1946.

Bosl, Karl, Hrsg. *Gleichgewicht-Revision-Restauration. Die Außenpolitik der Ersten Tschechoslowakischen Republik im Europasystem der Pariser Vororteverträge.* München: R. Oldenbourg Verlag, 1977.

Bosl, Karl, Hrsg. *Die Slowakei als mitteleuropäische Problem in Geschichte und Gegenwart.* München: Verlag Robert Lerche, 1965.

Botto, Julius. *Slovaci. Vyvin ich narodneho povedomia. Dejepisny nakres,* 2 vols. Turciansky Sv. Martin: KUS, 1923.

Brock, Peter. *The Slovak National Awakening.* Toronto: University of Toronto Press, 1976.

Brunner, Georg, and Lemberg, Hans, Hrsg. *Volksgruppen in Ostmittel- und Südosteuropa.* Baden-Baden: Nomos Verlagsgesellschaft, 1994.

Busik, Jozef, et al. *The Slovak Republic. Country Report.* Vienna: Bank Austria AG, May 1993.

Butvin, Jozef, *Slovenske narodno-zjednocovacie hnutie (1780–1848)*. Bratislava: Veda, Vydavatelstvo Slovenskej akademie vied, 1965.

Capek, Thomas. *The Slovaks of Hungary*. New York: Knickerbocker Press, 1906.

Carnogursky, Pavol. *14. marec 1939*. Bratislava: Veda, Vydavatelstvo Slovenskej akademie vied, 1992.

Cicaj, Viliam, ed. *Trnavska univerzita v slovenskych dejinach*. Bratislava: Veda, Vydavatelstvo Slovenskej akademie vied, 1987.

Clementis, Vladimir. *Odkazy z Londyna*. Bratislava: Nakladatelstvo Obroda, 1947.

Coakley, John, ed. *The Territorial Management of Ethnic Conflict*. London: Frank Cass, 1993.

Conte, Francis. *Les Slaves. Aux origines des civilisations d'Europe centrale et orientale*. Paris: Albin Michel, 1986.

Cross, Samuel Hazzard. *Slavic Civilization Through the Ages*. New York: Russel & Russel, 1963.

Culen, Konstantin. *Po Svätoplukovi druha nasa hlava*, 2 vols. Cleveland, OH: Prva katolicka slovenska jednota, 1947.

Deak, Istvan. *The Lawful Revolution. Louis Kossuth and the Hungarians 1848–1848*. New York: Columbia University Press, 1979.

Deak, Ladislav. *Hra o Slovensko*. Bratislava: Veda, Vydavatelstvo Slovenskej akademie vied, 1991.

Deak, Ladislav. *Slovensko v politike Madarska v rokoch 1938–1939*. Bratislava: Veda, Vydavatelstvo Slovenskej akademie vied, 1990.

Dean, Robert W. *Nationalism and Political Change in Eastern Europe: The Slovak Question and the Czechoslovak Reform Movement*. Denver, CO: The University of Denver Monograph Series in World Affairs, 1973.

Dejiny Slovenska I–VI. Bratislava: Veda, Vydavatelstvo Slovenskej akademie vied, 1986–1992.

Dekan, Jan. *Zaciatky slovenskych dejin a Risa velkomoravska*. Bratislava: Slovenska akademia vied a umeni, 1951.

Denis, Ernest. *La Bohème depuis la Montagne Blanche*, 2 vols. Paris: Ernest Leroux, 1903.

Denis, Ernest. *Fin de l'indépendance bohème*, 2 vols. Paris: Armand Colin, 1890.

Denis, Ernest. *Huss et les guerres des hussites*. Paris: E. Leroux, 1930.

Denis, Ernest. *La question d'Autriche—Les Slovaques*. Paris: Delagrave, 1917.

Derer, Ivan. *The Unity of the Czechs and Slovaks*. Prague: Orbis, 1938.

Documents on British Foreign Policy. 3d series, vol. 4. London: H.M.S.O., 1951.

Dokumenty z historie ceskoslovenske politiky 1939–1945, (Acta occupationis Bohaemicae et Moraviae), 2 vols. Praha: Academia, 1966.

Doob, Leonard W. *Patriotism and Nationalism. Their Psychological Foundations*. New Haven, CT: Yale University Press, 1964.

Dubcek, Alexander. *Hope Dies Last. The Autobiography of Alexander Dubcek.* New York: Kodanska International, 1993.

Durica, Milan S. *La Slovacchia e le sue relazioni politiche con la Germania 1938–1945.* Padova: Marsilio Editori, 1964.

Durica, Milan S. *The Slovak Involvement in the Tragedy of the European Jews.* Abano Terme: Piovan Editore, 1989.

Dvornik, Francis. *Les légendes de Constantin et Méthode vues de Byzance.* Prague: Orbis, 1933.

Dvornik, Francis. *The Making of Central and Eastern Europe.* Gulf Breeze, FL: Academic International Press, 1974.

Dvornik, Francis. *The Slavs in European History and Civilization.* New Brunswick, NJ: Rutgers University Press, 1962.

Dvornik, Francis. *The Slavs. Their Early History and Civilization.* Boston: American Academy of Arts and Science, 1956.

El Mallakh, Dorothea H., *The Slovak Autonomy Movement 1935–1939.* Boulder, CO: East European Monographs, 1979.

Elias, Michal, and Sarluska, Vojtech, eds. *Narodna svetlica. Vyber dokumentov k dejinam Matice slovenkej.* Martin: Matica slovenska, 1988.

Faltan, Samo. *Slovenska otazka v Ceskoslovensku.* Bratislava: Vydavatelstvo politickej literatury, 1968.

Faltan, Samo, *O slovenskom narodnom povstani.* Bratislava: Vydavatelstvo Osveta, 1968.

Feierabend, Ladislav. *Agricultural Cooperatives in Czechoslovakia.* New York: Mid-European Studies Center, 1952.

Fischer, Jan. *Kulturny rozvoj Slovenska v piatej pätrocnici (1971–1975).* Bratislava: Obzor, 1978.

Fredegarii Chronicorum Liber Quartus cum Continuationibus/The Fourth Book of the Chronicle of Fredegar with its Continuations, trans. from the Latin with introduction and notes by J. M. Wallace-Hadrill. London: Thomas Nelson and Sons Ltd., 1960.

Fügedi, Erik. *Castles and Society in Medieval Hungary (1000–1437).* Budapest: Akademiai Kiado, 1986.

Fügedi, Erik. *Kings, Bishops, Nobles and Burghers in Medieval Hungary.* London: Variorum Reprints, 1986.

Gavlovic, Hugolin. *Valaska Skola,* edited and with commentary by Gerald J. Sabo. Columbus, OH: Slavica Publishers, 1987.

Gellner, John, and Smerek, John. *The Czechs and Slovaks in Canada.* Toronto: University of Toronto Press, 1968.

Glaser, Kurt. *Czecho-Slovakia: a Critical History.* Caldwell, ID: The Caxton Printers, 1961.

Glettler, Monika. *Pittsburg—Wien—Budapest. Programm und Praxis der Nationalitätenpolitik bei der Auswanderung der ungarischen Slowaken nach Amerika um 1900.* Wien: Verlag der Oesterreichischen Akademie der Wissenschaften, 1980.

Gogolak, Ludwig von. *Beiträge zur Geschichte des slowakischen Volkes,* 3 vols. München: Verlag R. Oldenbourg, 1963–67.

Golan, Galia. *The Czechoslovak Reform Movement. Communism in Crisis 1962–1968.* Cambridge: Cambridge University Press, 1971.

Golan, Galia. *Reform Rule in Czechoslovakia. The Dubcek Era 1968–1969.* Cambridge: Cambridge University Press, 1973.

Haviar, Stefan, and Kucma, Ivan. *V pamäti naroda.* Martin: Matica slovenska, 1988.

Hlinka, Anton. *Sila slabych a slabost silnych.* Zagreb: LOGOS, 1989.

Hodza, Milan. *Ceskoslovensky rozkol.* Turciansky Sv. Martin: Nakl. vlastnym, 1920.

Hodza, Milan. *Federation in Central Europe.* London: Jarrolds Publishers Ltd., 1942.

Hoensch, Jörg K. *Die Slowakei und Hitlers Ostpolitik.* Köln: Böhlau Verlag, 1965.

Hoensch, Jörg K. *Geschichte der Tschechoslowakischen Republik 1918 bis 1965.* Stuttgart: W. Kohlhammer Verlag, 1966.

Hoensch, Jörg K., Hrsg. *Dokumente zur Autonomiepolitik des Slowakischen Volkspartei Hlinkas.* München: R. Oldenbourg Verlag, 1984.

Hoffman, Gabriel, and Hoffman, Ladislav. *Katolicka cirkev a tragedia slovenskych zidov v dokumentoch.* Partizanske: Vydavatelstvo G-print, 1994.

Hoffman, Eva. *Exit into History. A Journey Through the New Eastern Europe.* New York: Viking, 1993.

Holotik, Ludovit, and Vantuch, Anton. *Humanizmus a renesancia na Slovensku v 15.–16. storoci.* Bratislava: Veda, Vydavatelstvo Slovenskej akademie vied, 1967.

Homan, Balint. *Geschichte des ungarischen Mittelalters,* 2 vols. Berlin: Verlag Walter de Gruyter & Co., 1949–1943.

Homan, Balint. *King Stephen the Saint.* Budapest: Études sur l'Europe Centre—Orientale, no. 11, 1938. First published in *Archivum Europae Centro-Orientalis 4,* nos. 1–3 (1938).

Homolka, Jaromir. *Levoca, Hlavny oltar v kostole Sv. Jakuba.* Bratislava: Slovenske Vydavatelstvo Krasnej Literatury, 1965.

Hruby, Peter. *Fools and Heroes. The Changing Role of Communist Intellectuals in Czechoslovakia.* Oxford: Pergamon Press, 1980.

Hrusovsky, Frantisek. *Slovenske dejiny.* Turciansky Sv. Martin: Matica slovenska, 1939.

Hrusovsky, Frantisek. *Slovenski vladari.* Scranton, PA: Obrana Press, 1948.

Husak, Gustav. *Svedectvo o Slovenskom narodnom povstani.* Bratislava: Vydavatelstvo politickej literatury, 1964

Husak, Gustav. *Zapas o zajtrajsok.* Bratislava: Nakladatelstvo Obroda, 1948.

Jablonicky, Jozef. *Povstanie bez legiend.* Bratislava: Vydavatelstvo Obzor, 1990.

Jablonicky, Jozef. *Slovensko na prelome. Pociatky narodnej a demokratickej revolucie.* Bratislava: Vydavatelstvo politickej literatury, 1965.

Jablonicky, Jozef. *Z ilegality do povstania.* Bratislava: Nakladatelstvo Epocha, 1969.

Janics, Kalman. *Czechoslovak Policy and the Hungarian Minority, 1945–1948,* English version adapted from the Hungarian by Stephen Borsody. New York: Columbia University Press, 1982

Jansak, Stefan. *Slovensko v dobe uhorskeho feudalizmu. Hospodarske pomery od r. 1514 do r. 1848.* Bratislava: Nakladom kuratoria cs. zemedel. muzea, 1932.

Jelinek, Yeshayahu A. *The Lust for Power: Nationalism, Slovakia and the Communists 1918–1948.* Boulder, CO: East European Monographs, 1983.

Jelinek, Yeshayahu A. *The Parish Republic. Hlinka's Slovak People's Party 1939–1945.* Boulder, CO: East European Monographs, 1976.

Johnson, Owen V. *Slovakia 1918–1938. Education and the Making of a Nation.* New York: Columbia University Press, 1985.

Kalvoda, Josef. *The Genesis of Czechoslovakia.* Boulder, CO: East European Monographs, 1986.

Kamenec, Ivan. *Slovensky stat.* Praha: Anomal, 1992.

Kann, Hans. *The Multinational Empire,* 2 vols. New York: Columbia University Press, 1950.

Kazimir, Stefan. *Pestovanie vinica a produkcia vina na Slovensku v minulosti.* Bratislava: Veda, Vydavatelstvo Slovenskej akademie vied, 1986.

Kipke, Rüdiger, and Vodicka, Karel, eds. *Rozluceni s Ceskoslovenskem.* Praha: Cesky spisovatel, 1993.

Kirschbaum, Joseph M. *Slovakia. Nation at the Crossroads of Central Europe.* New York: Robert S. Speller & Sons, Publishers, Inc., 1960.

Kirschbaum, Joseph M. *Slovak Language and Literature.* Readings in Slavic Literatures 12. Winnipeg: University of Manitoba, 1975.

Kirschbaum, Joseph M., ed. *Slovak Culture Through the Centuries.* Toronto: The Slovak World Congress, 1978.

Kirschbaum, Joseph M., ed. *Slovakia in the 19th and 20th Centuries,* 2nd ed. Toronto: Slovak World Congress, 1978.

Kirschbaum, Jozef. *Nas boj o samostatnost Slovenska.* Cleveland, OH: Slovensky ustav, 1958.

Kirschbaum, Jozef M., and Fuga, Frantisek, eds. *Andrej Hlinka v slove a obraze.* Toronto/Ruzomberok: Zahranicna Matica slovenska, 1991.

Kirschbaum, Stanislav J. *Slovaques et Tchèques. Essai sur un nouvel aperçu de leur histoire politique.* Lausanne: L'Age d'Homme, 1987.

Kirschbaum, Stanislav J., ed. *East European History.* Columbus, OH: Slavica Publishers, 1988.

Kirschbaum, Stanislav J., ed. *Slovak Politics. Essays on Slovak History in Honour of Joseph M. Kirschbaum.* Cleveland, OH: Slovak Institute, 1983.

Kirschbaum, Stanislav J., and Roman, Anne C. R., eds. *Reflections on Slovak History.* Toronto: Slovak World Congress, 1987.

Klimko, Jozef. *Vyvoj uzemia Slovenska a utvaranie jeho hranic.* Bratislava: Obzor, 1980.

Kohn, Hans. *Le panslavisme, son histoire et son idéologie.* Paris: Payot, 1963.

Kopcan, Vojtech. *Turecke nebezpecenstvo a Slovensko.* Bratislava: Veda, Vydavatelstvo Slovenskej akademie vied, 1986.

Kopcan, Vojtech, and Krajcovicova, Klara. *Slovensko v tieni polmesiaca.* Bratislava: Osveta, 1983.

Korbel, Josef. *Twentieth-Century Czechoslovakia. The Meaning of Its History.* New York: Columbia University Press, 1977.

Kowalska, Eva. *Statne ludove skolstvo na Slovensku na prelome 18. a 19. stor.* Bratislava: Veda, Vydavatelstvo Slovenskej akademie vied, 1987.

Krajcovic, Rudolf. *Vyvin slovenskeho jazyka a dialektologia.* Bratislava: Slovenske pedagogicke nakladatelstvo, 1988.

Krapka, Emil, and Mikula, Vojtech, eds. *Dejiny Spolocnosti Jezisovej na Slovensku.* Cambridge, Ont.: Dobra Kniha, 1990.

Krejci, Jaroslav. *Ethnic and Political Nations in Europe.* New York: St. Martin's Press, 1981.

Kruzliak, Imrich, and Okal, Jan, eds. *Svedectvo jednej generacie.* Cambridge, Ont.: Dobra kniha, 1990.

Kucera, Matus. *Slovensko po pade Velkej Moravy. Studie o hospodarskom a socialnom vyvine v 9–13. storoci.* Bratislava: Veda, Vydavatelstvo Slovenskej akademie vied, 1974.

Kucera, Matus, and Kosticky, Bohumir. *Historia. Slovensko v obrazoch.* Martin: Vydavatelstvo Osveta, 1990.

Kusin, Vladimir. *The Intellectual Origins of the Prague Spring.* Cambridge: Cambridge University Press, 1971.

La Paix de Versailles. Volume 10. Paris: Les éditions internationales, 1929.

Leff, Carol Skalnik. *National Conflict in Czechoslovakia. The Making and Remaking of a State, 1918–1987.* Princeton, NJ: Princeton University Press, 1988.

Lemberg, Hans, Nitsche, Peter, and Erwin Oberlander, Hrsg. *Osteuropa in Geschichte und Gegewart. Festschrift für Günter Stökl zum 60. Geburtstag.* Köln-Wien: Böhlau Verlag, 1977.

Lettrich, Jozef. *History of Modern Slovakia.* New York: Praeger, 1955.

Letz, Robert. *Slovensko v rokoch 1945–1948. Na ceste ku komunistickej totalite.* Bratislava: Ustredie slovenskej krestanskej inteligencie, 1994.

Liebich, André, and Reszler, André, eds. *L'Europe centrale et ses minorités: vers une solution européenne?*. Paris: Presses universitaires de France, 1993.

Lipscher, Ladislav. *Zidia v slovenskom state 1939–1945*. Banska Bystrica: Print-Servis, 1992.

Liptak, Lubomir, ed. *Politicke stany na Slovensku 1860–1989*. Bratislava, Vydavatelstvo Archa, 1992.

Liptak, Lubomir. *Slovensko v 20. storoci*. Bratislava: Vydavatelstvo politickej literatury, 1968.

Löbl, Eugen. *Svedectvo o procese s vedenim protistatneho sprisahaneckeho centra na cele s Rudolfom Slanskym*. Bratislava: Vydavatelstvo politickej literatury. 1968.

Löbl, Eugen, and Grünwald, Leopold. *Die intellektuelle Revolution. Hintergründe und Auswirkung des "Prager Frühlings."* Düsseldorf: Econ Verlag, 1969.

Loebl, Eugen. *My Mind on Trial*. New York: Harcourt Brace Jovanovich, 1976.

Macartney, C. A. *The Habsburg Empire 1790–1918*. London: Weidenfeld and Nicolson, 1969.

Macartney, C. A. *Hungary. A Short History*. Edinburgh: At the University Press, 1962.

Macartney, C. A. *Hungary and Her Successors*. London: Oxford University Press, 1937.

Macartney, C. A. *Maria Theresa and The House of Austria*. London: The English Universities Press Limited, 1969.

Magosci, Paul Robert. *Historical Atlas of East Central Europe*. Toronto: University of Toronto Press, 1993.

Mamatey, Victor S., and Luza, Radomir, eds. *A History of the Czechoslovak Republic, 1918–1949*. Princeton, NJ: Princeton University Press, 1973.

Markus, Jozef. *Zaujem o planovanie a zaujmy v planovani*. Bratislava: Nakladatelstvo Pravda, 1988.

Marshall, Sherrin, ed. *Women in Reformation and Counter-Reformation Europe*. Bloomington, IN: Indiana University Press, 1989.

Marsina R., et al. *Slovenske dejiny*. Martin: Matica slovenska, 1993.

Marsina Richard, ed. *Städte im Donauraum*. Bratislava: Slovenska historicka spolocnost, 1993.

Masaryk, Thomas G. *The Making of a State. Memories and Observations 1914–1918*, An English version, arranged and prepared with an introduction by Henry Wickham Steed. New York: Frederick A. Stokes Co., 1927.

Masaryk, Thomas G. *La résurrection d'un État. Souvenirs et réflexions 1914–1918*, trans. by Fuscien Dominois. Paris: Plon, 1930.

Medvedsky, Karol A. *Slovensky prevrat*, 3 vols. Trnava, Vydal Spolok Sv. Vojtecha, 1931.

Mesaros, Julius, ed. *Slovaci a ich narodny vyvin*. Bratislava: Veda, Vydavatelstvo Slovenskej akademie vied, 1966.

Miklosko, Frantisek. *Nebudete ich moct rozvratit. Z osudov katolickej cirkvi na Slovensku v rokoch 1943–89.* Bratislava: Vydavatelstvo Archa, 1991.

Mikus, Joseph A. *Slovakia, A Misunderstood History.* Hamilton, Ont.: The Battlefield Press Ltd., 1979.

Mikus, Joseph A. *Slovakia. A Political History 1918–1950.* Milwaukee, WI: Marquette University Press, 1963.

Mikus, Joseph A. *Slovakia and the Slovaks.* Washington, DC: Three Continents Press, 1977.

Mikus, Joseph A. *La Slovaquie dans le drame de l'Europe.* Paris: Les Iles d'Or, 1955.

Minac, Vladimir. *Navraty k prevratu.* Bratislava: NVK International, 1993.

Mraz, Andrej. *Dejiny slovenskej literatury.* Bratislava: Slovenska akademia vied a umeni, 1948.

Murin, Karol. *Spomienky a svedectvo,* Hamilton, Ont.: Zahranicna Matica slovenska, 1987.

Musset, Lucien. *Les invasions. Le second assaut contre l'Europe chrétienne (VIIe—XIe siècle).* Paris: Presses universitaires de France, 1965.

Nardini, Lisa Guarda. *Tiso: una terza proposta.* Padova: Ceseo-Liviana editrice, 1977.

Nolte, Ernst. *Les mouvements fascistes. L'Europe de 1919 à 1945,* trans. by Paul Stéphano. 3 vols. Paris: Calmann-Lévy, 1969.

Oddo, Gilbert L. *Slovakia and Its People.* New York: Robert Speller and Sons, 1960.

La Paix de Versailles, vol. 10. Paris: Les éditions internationales, 1929.

Pamlenyi, Erwin, et al. *A History of Hungary,* trans. by Laszlo Boros, Istvan Frakas, Gyula Gulyas, and Eva Rona. London: Collet's, 1975.

Paul, David W. *The Cultural Limits of Revolutionary Politics: Change and Continuity in Socialist Czechoslovakia.* Boulder, CO: East European Monographs, 1979.

Pauliny, Eugen. *Dejiny spisovnej slovenciny od zaciatkov po sucastnost.* Bratislava: Slovenske pedagogicke nakladatelstvo, 1983.

Pauliny, Eugen. *Slovesnost a kulturny jazyk velkej Moravy.* Bratislava: Slovenske vydavatelstvo krasnej literatury, 1964.

Pauliny, Eugen. *Zivot a dielo Metoda, prvoucitela naroda slovienskeho.* Bratislava: Tatran, 1985.

Pech, Stanley Z. *The Czech Revolution of 1948.* Chapel Hill, NC: The University of North Carolina Press, 1969.

Pelaez, Manuel J., ed. *Public Law and Comparative Politics. Trabajos en homenaje a Ferran Valls i Taberner,* vol. 17. Barcelona: Promociones y Publicaciones Universitarias, S.A., 1991.

Pelikan, Jiri, ed. *The Czechoslovak Political Trials 1950–1954. The Suppressed Report of the Dubcek Government's Commission of Inquiry, 1968.* London: Macdonald & Co. (Publishers) Ltd, 1971.

Peroutka, Ferdinand. *Budovani statu,* 4 vols. Praha: F. Borovy, 1934–1936.

Perréal, Renée, and Mikus, Joseph A. *La Slovaquie: une nation au coeur de l'Europe.* Lausanne: L'Age d'Homme, 1992.

Piekalkiewicz, Jaroslaw. *Public Opinion in Czechoslovakia, 1968–69. Results and Analysis of Surveys Conducted During the Dubcek Era.* New York: Praeger Publishers, 1972.

Pisut, Milan, et al. *Dejiny slovenskej literatury.* Bratislava: Obzor, 1984.

Plevza, Viliam. *Ceskoslovenska statnost a slovenska otazka v politike KSC.* Bratislava: Praca, 1971.

Plevza, Viliam. *Socialisticke premeny Ceskoslovenska.* Bratislava: Pravda, 1983.

Pokus o politicky a osobny profil Jozefa Tisu. Bratislava: Slovak Academic Press, 1992.

Polla, Belo. *Hrady a kastiele na vychodnom Slovensku.* Kosice: Vychodoslovenske vydavatelstvo, 1980.

Polla, Belo. *Kosice Krasna. K stredovekym dejinam Krasnej nad Hornadom.* Kosice: Vychodoslovenske vydavatelstvo, 1986.

Powell, T.G.E. *The Celts,* rev. ed. London: Thames and Hudson, 1959.

Prokes, Jaroslav. *Histoire tchécoslovaque.* Prague: Orbis, 1927.

Rapant, Daniel. *Slovenske povstanie roku 1848–1849.* 5 vols. Turciansky Sv. Martin: Matica slovenska, 1937–1972.

Ratkos, Peter. *Slovensko v dobe velkomoravskej.* Kosice: Vychodoslovenske vydavatelstvo, 1988.

Ratkos, Peter, ed. *Pramene k dejinam Velkej Moravy,* 2nd ed. Bratislava: Veda, Vydavatelstvo Slovenskej akademie vied, 1968.

Ratkos, Peter, ed. *Velkomoravske legendy a povesti.* Bratislava: Tatran, 1990.

Reitlinger, Gerald. *The Final Solution; The Attempt to Exterminate the Jews of Europe 1939–1945,* 2nd rev. and augmented ed. London: Vallentine, Mitchell, 1968.

Reitzner, Almar. *Alexander Dubcek. Männer and Mächte in der Tschechoslowakei.* München: Verlag "Die Brücke", 1968.

Renner, Hans, and Samso, Ivo. *Dejiny Cesko-Slovenska po roku 1945.* Bratislava: Slovak Academic Press, 1993.

Ripka, Hubert. *Czechoslovakia Enslaved. The Story of the Communist Coup d'État.* London: Victor Gollanz Ltd., 1950.

Rudinsky, Jozef F. *Ceskoslovensky stat a Slovenska republika.* München: Akademischer Verlag Peter Belej, 1969.

Rupnik, Jacques. *Histoire du Parti communiste tchécoslovaque.* Paris: Presses de la Fondation Nationale des Sciences Politiques, 1981.

Rydlo, Jozef M., ed. *Slovensko v retrospektive dejin.* Lausanne: Liber, 1976.

Sarluska, Vojtech, ed. *Martin v slovenskych dejinach.* Martin: Matica slovenska, 1986.

Schenker, Alexander M., and Stankiewicz, Edward, eds. *The Slavic Literary Languages: Formation and Development.* New Haven, CT: Yale Concilium on International and Area Studies, 1980.

Schmid, Karin. *Die Slowakische Republik 1939–1945. Eine staats- und völkerrechtliche* Betrachtung, 2 vols. Berlin: Berlin-Verlag, 1982.

Scotus Viator (Robert W. Seton-Watson). *Racial Problems in Hungary.* London: Archibald Constable, 1908.

Seton-Watson, Hugh. *Nations and States. An Enquiry into the Origins of Nations and the Politics of Nationalism.* London: Methuen, 1977.

Seton-Watson, Robert W. *A History of Czechs and Slovaks.* Hamden, CT: Archon Books, 1965.

Seton-Watson, Robert W. *Masaryk in England.* Cambridge: Cambridge University Press, 1943.

Seton-Watson, Robert W. *The New Slovakia.* Prague: Fr. Borovy, 1924.

Seton-Watson, Robert W. *Slovakia Then and Now.* London: G. Allen and Unwin, 1931.

Shawcross, William. *Dubcek.* London: Weidenfeld and Nicolson, 1970.

Short, David. *Czechoslovakia.* Oxford: Clio, 1986.

Sidor, Karol. *Andrej Hlinka (1864–1926).* Bratislava: Tlacou knihtlaciarne Sv. Andreja, 1934.

Sidor, Karol. *Slovenska politika na pode prazskeho snemu.* 2 vols. Bratislava: Andreja, 1943.

Simmonds, George, ed. *Nationalism in the U.S.S.R. and Eastern Europe in the Era of Brezhnev and Kosygin.* Detroit: University of Detroit Press, 1977.

Simoncic, Jozef. *Ohlasy francuzskej revolucie na Slovensku.* Kosice: Vychodoslovenske vyvdavatelstvo, 1982.

Skilling, H. Gordon. *Charter 77 and Human Rights in Czechoslovakia.* London: George Allen & Unwin, 1981.

Skilling, H. Gordon. *Czechoslovakia's Interrupted Revolution.* Princeton, NJ: Princeton University Press, 1976.

Skilling, H. Gordon, ed. *Czechoslovakia, 1918–1988.* London: Macmillan, 1991.

Skultety, Jozef. *Sketches from Slovak History,* trans. from the Slovak by O. D. Koreff. Middletown, PA: First Catholic Slovak Union, 1930.

Slovakia and the Slovaks: A Concise Encyclopedia, compiled and edited by Milan Strhan, and David P. Daniel. Bratislava: Encyclopedical Institute, SAV, 1994.

Slovenske narodne povstanie: Dokumenty. Bratislava: Vydavatelstvo politickej literatury, 1965.

Slovenske narodne povstanie roku 1944. Bratislava: Veda, Vydavatelstvo Slovenskej akademie vied, 1965.

Slovensko v politickom systeme Ceskoslovenska. Bratislava: Slovenska narodna rada, Historicky ustav SAV, 1991.

Slovensko v rokoch druhej svetovej vojny. Bratislava: Slovenska narodna rada, Historicky ustav SAV, 1991.

Slovensky biograficky slovnik, 6 vols. Martin: Matica slovenska, 1986–1993.

Solc, Jaroslav. *Slovensko v ceskej politike.* Banska Bystrica: M.O. Enterprise, 1993.

Spetko, Josef. *Die Slowakei. Heimat der Völker.* Wien: Amalthea, 1991.

Spiesz, Anton. *Dejiny Slovenska. Na ceste k sebauvedomeniu.* Bratislava: Vydavatelstvo Respekt, 1992.

Srobar, Vavro. *Osvobodene Slovensko.* Praha: Cin, 1928.

Srobar, Vavro. *Z mojho zivota.* Praha: F. Borovy, 1946.

Stasko, Joseph, ed. *The Shaping of Modern Slovakia/Tvorcovia noveho Slovenska.* Cambridge, Ont.: Friends of Good Books, 1982.

Steiner, Eugen. *The Slovak Dilemma.* Cambridge: At the University Press, 1973.

Storia religiosa dei Cechi e degli Slovachi. Milano: Cooperativa editoriale La Casa de Matriona, 1987.

Suda, Zdenek. *Zealots and Rebels. A History of the Ruling Communist Party of Czechoslovakia.* Stanford, CA: Hoover Institution Press, 1980.

Sugar, Peter F., et al. *A History of Hungary.* Bloomington, IN: Indiana University Press, 1990.

Sugar, Peter F., and Lederer, Ivo J., eds. *Nationalism in Eastern Europe.* Seattle: University of Washington Press, 1969.

Sutherland, Anthony X. *Dr. Jozef Tiso and Modern Slovakia.* Cleveland, OH: First Catholic Slovak Union, 1978.

Szentpetery, Emericus. *Scriptores rerum Hungaricum,* vol. 2. Budapest: Academia litter. Hungarica, 1938.

Taborsky, Edward. *President Edvard Benes, Between East and West 1938–1948.* Stanford, CA: Hoover Institution Press, 1981.

Taylor, A. J. P. *The Habsburg Monarchy 1809–1918.* Harmondsworth: Penguin Books, 1967.

Temperley, H. W. V., ed. *A History of the Peace Conference of Paris,* vol. 5. London: Henry Frowde and Hodder & Stoughton, 1921.

Thomson, S. Harrison. *Czechoslovakia in European History.* Princeton, NJ: Princeton University Press, 1953.

Tibensky, Jan. *Dejiny vedy a techniky na Slovensku.* Bratislava: Osveta, 1979.

Tigrid, Pavel. *Le printemps de Prague.* Paris: Seuil, 1968.

Tigrid, Pavel. *La chute irrestible d'Alexander Dubcek.* Paris: Calmann-Lévy, 1969.

Tiso, Jozef. *Dr. Jozef Tiso o sebe.* Passaic, NJ: Slovensky Katolicky Sokol, 1952.

Toth, Dezider, et al. *The Tragedy of Slovak Jews.* Banska Bystrica: DATEI, 1992.

Tourtzer, Hélène. *Louis Stur et l'idée de l'indépendance slovaque.* Paris: Cahors et Alençon, 1913.

Turnock, David. *Eastern Europe. A Historical Geography 1815– 1945.* London: Routledge, 1989.

Turnock, David. *The Making of Eastern Europe From the Earliest Times to 1815.* London: Routledge, 1988.

Varsik, Branislav. *Husitske revolucne hnutie a Slovensko.* Bratislava: Veda, Vydavatelstvo Slovenskej akademie vied, 1965.

Vatikan a Slovenska republika (1949–1945) Dokumenty. Bratislava: Slovak Academic Press, 1992.

Venor, Wolfgang. *Aufstand in der Tatra: der Kampf um die Slowakei 1939–1944.* Königstein: Athenäum, 1979.

Vesely, Ludwig. *Dubcek. Biographie.* München: Kindler Verlag, 1970.

Veteska, Tomas J. *Velkoslovenska risa.* Hamilton, Ont.: MSA-ZMS, 1987.

Vnuk, Frantisek. *Dedicstvo otcov. Eseje na historicke temy.* Toronto—Bratislava: Kruh priatelov boja za samostatnost Slovenska, 1991.

Vnuk, Frantisek. *Kapitoly z dejin Komunistickej strany Slovenska.* Middletown, PA: Slovak v Amerike, 1968.

Vnuk, Frantisek. *Mat svoj stat znamena zivot. . . Politicka biografia Alexandra Macha.* Cleveland, OH: Slovensky ustav, 1987.

Vnuk, Frantisek. *Neuveritelne sprisahanie.* Middletown, PA: Literarny almanach Slovaka v Amerike, 1964.

Vnuk, Frantisek. *Sedemnast neurodnych rokov (Nacrt dejin slovenskej literatury v rokoch 1945–1962).* Middletown, PA: Slovak v Amerike, 1965.

Whittle, Alasdair. *Neolitic Europe: A Survey.* Cambridge: Cambridge University Press, 1985.

Wymer, John. *The Palaeolithic Age.* New York: St. Martin's Press, 1982.

Zbornik o Slovenskom narodnom povstani, 2 vols. Toronto: Nase snahy, 1976–80.

Zudel, Juraj. *Stolice na Slovensku.* Bratislava: Obzor, 1984.

Articles

Alexander, Manfred. "Leistungen, Belastungen und Gefährdungen der Demokratie in der Ersten Tschechoslowakischen Republik." *Bohemia* 27, no. 1 (1986): 72–87.

Anderle, Josef, et al. "Uncharted Areas for Research on the History of Slovakia and the Slovaks." *East Central Europe/L'Europe du Centre-Est,* 7, no. 1 (1980): 49–88.

Balaz, Ondrej. "Vyvoj polnohospodarstva na Slovensku v rokoch 1949–1960." *Historicky casopis,* 9, no. 1 (1961): 3–28.

Benes, Edvard. "Czechoslovak Policy for Victory and Peace." In *Czechoslovak Documents and Sources,* No. 10, London: Czechoslovak Ministry of Foreign Affairs, Information Service, 1944.

Bénès, Edouard. "Discours aux Slovaques sur le présent et l'avenir de notre nation." *Le monde slave,* February 1934: 1–72.

Böhmerova, Ada. "The Camaldolese Dictionary." Paper read at the 1993 National Convention of the American Association for the Advancement of Slavic Studies, Honolulu, HA, 22 November 1993.

Bosak, Edita. "Czech-Slovak Relations from the 1840s to 1914." *Slovakia* 35, nos. 64–65 (1991–1992): 63–77.

Bosak, Edita. "Intellectual Currents Among the Slovak Intelligentsia During the Nineteenth Century." Paper read at the IV World Congress for Soviet and East European Studies, Harrogate, England, 21–26 July 1990.

Bubrin, Vladimir. "Prince Pribina and the Pre-Cyrillomethodian Political and Missionary Activities in Great Moravia and Pannonia." *Slovak Studies* 12 (1972): 135–47.

Carnogursky, Jan. "Politicke procesy." *Pohlady* 6 (1988): 62–122.

Daniel, David P. "Hungary." In Pettegree, Andrew, ed. *The Early Reformation in Europe.* Cambridge: Cambridge University Press, 1992: 49–69.

Daniel, David P. "The Impact of the Protestant Reformation on Education in Slovakia." *Slovakia* 34, nos. 62–63 (1989–1990): 9–27.

Daniel, David P. "No Mere Impact: Features of the Reformation in the Lands of the Austrian Habsburgs." *Archiv für Reformationsgeschichte,* Sonderband (1993).

Daniel, David P. "The Protestation Reformation and Slovak Ethnic Consciousness." *Slovakia* 28, nos. 52–53 (1978–1979): 49–65.

Daniel, David P. "The Reformation and Eastern Slovakia." *Human Affairs* 1, no. 2 (1991): 172–86.

Durica, Milan S. "Der slowakische Anteil an der Tragödie der europäischen Juden." *Slowakei,* 27 (1984): 109–48.

Dzuban, Anton, et al. "Narodny dochodok Slovenska." *Ekonomicky casopis* 14, no. 8 (1966): 721–40.

Gaspar, Tido J. "Z Pamäti." *Slovenske pohlady* 84, nos. 6–12 (1968).

Grebert, Arved. "Die Slowaken und das Großmärische Reich (Beitrag zum ethnischen Charakter Großmährens)." *Slovak Studies* 3 (1963): 126–34.

Hrusovsky, Francis. "The Relations of the Rulers of Great Moravia with Rome." *Slovak Studies* 3 (1963): 21–77.

Husak, Gustav. "O vyvoji a situacii na Slovensku." *Svedectvi* 15, no. 58 (1979): 367–82.

Kamenec, Ivan. "Snem Slovenskej republiky a jeho postoj k problemu zidovskeho obyvatelstva na Slovensku v rokoch 1939–1945." *Historicky casopis* 17, no, 3 (1969): 329–62

Keller, Hans. "Auf Aussenposten in Bratislava." *Revue suisse d'histoire* 30, no. 2 (1980): 246–57.

Kirschbaum, Joseph M. "La littérature de la période cyrillo-méthodienne et la Slovaquie." *Slovak Studies* 3 (1963): 89–104.

Kirschbaum, Joseph M. "The Role of the Cyrilo-Methodian Tradition in Slovak National and Political Life." *Slovak Studies* 3 (1963): 153–72.

Kirschbaum, Joseph M. "Slovakia in the de-Stalinization and Federalization Process of Czechoslovakia." *Canadian Slavonic Papers/Revue canadienne des slavistes* 10, no. 4 (1968): 522–56.

Kirschbaum, Stanislav J. "An Act of Faith and Integrity. Bishop Korec's Letter to Czechoslovak Television." *Slovakia* 34, nos. 62–63 (1989–90): 61–126.

Kirschbaum, Stanislav J. "Andrej Hlinka ako politik v prvej CSR." *Historicky casopis* 40 no. 6 (1992): 694–706.

Kirschbaum, Stanislav J. "Czechoslovakia: The Creation, Federalization and Dissolution of a Nation-State." *Regional Politics & Policy* 3, no. 1 (1993): 69–95.

Kirschbaum, Stanislav J. "The Czech Question in Slovakia in the Post-War Years." *Slovakia* 35, nos. 64–65 (1991–1992): 97–108.

Kirschbaum, Stanislav J. "Die Entwicklung des Föderalismus in der Tschechoslowakei." *Zeitschrift für Ostforschung* 24, no. 2 (1975): 272–87.

Kirschbaum, Stanislav J. "Federalism in Slovak Communist Politics." *Canadian Slavonic Papers* 19, no. 4 (1977): 444–67.

Kirschbaum, Stanislav J. "La fin des mythes? Les Slovaques et la Tchécoslovaquie." *Revue d'Èurope centrale* 1 no. 2 (1993): 147–56.

Kirschbaum, Stanislav J. "National Opposition under Communism: The Slovaks in Czechoslovakia." *Slovak Studies* 19 (1979): 5–19.

Kirschbaum, Stanislav J. "Nationalism in Eastern Europe: Disease and Cure." *Slovak Studies* 26–27 (1986–1987): 125–36.

Kirschbaum, Stanislav J. "L'opposition en régime communiste: le cas des intellectuels slovaques." *Canadian Slavonic Papers/Revue canadienne des slavistes* 17, no. 1 (1975): 1–43.

Kirschbaum, Stanislav J. "Slovak Nationalism in the First Czechoslovak Republic 1918–1938." *Canadian Review of Studies in Nationalism* 16 nos. 1–2 (1989): 169–87.

Kirschbaum, Stanislav J. "Slovak Nationalism in Socialist Czechoslovakia." *Canadian Slavonic Papers/Revue canadienne des slavistes* 22, no. 2 (1980): 220–46.

Kirschbaum, Stanislav J. "The Slovak Republic and the Slovaks." *Slovakia* 29 nos. 53–54 (1980–1981): 11–38.

Kirschbaum, Stanislav J. "The Slovak Republic, Britain, France and the Principle of Self-determination." *Slovak Studies* 23 (1983): 149–70.

Kirschbaum, Stanislav J. "Turciansky Sväty Martin and the Formation of the Slovak Nation." *Slovak Review* 2, no. 1 (1993): 113–23.

Koctuch, Hviezdon. "Ideologia a ekonomika po roku 1945." *Slovenske pohlady* 82, no. 3 (1966): 90–92.

Kopcan, Vojtech. "Der osmanische Krieg gegen die Habsburger 1663–64 (Im Hinblick auf die Slowakei)." *Asian and African Studies* 2, no. 2 (1993): 169–89

Kopcan, Vojtech. "Türkische Briefe und Urkunden zur Geschichte des Eyalet Nové Zamky. V," *Asian and African Studies* 1, no. 2 (1992); 154–69.

Kowalska, Eva. "Historicke koncepcie slovenskych obrodencov P. J. Safarika, J. Holleho a J. Kollara." *Slovansky prehled* 3 (1989): 249–57.

Kowalska, Eva. "Kontroverzna tolerancia: Protestanti a skolske reformy osvietenskeho obdobia." *Historicke studie* 34 (1993): 55–76.

Kowalska, Eva. "Learning and Education in SLovakia during the late 17th and 18th Centuries." *Slovakia* 34, nos. 63–63 (1989–1990): 28–49.

Kraus, Michael. "The Kremlin and the Slovak National Uprising August—October, 1944." *Slovakia* 34, nos. 62–63 (1989–1990): 50–60.

Lacko, Michal. "Camaldulese Hermits in Slovakia." *Slovak Studies* 5 (1965): 99–167.

Lacko, Michal. "Camaldulese Red Monastery—Cerveny Klastor. According to its 'Liber Actuum Capitularium.'" *Slovak Studies* 9 (1969): 113–231.

Lacko, Michal. "The Cyrilomethodian Mission and Slovakia." *Slovak Studies* 1 (1961): 23–49.

Lacko, Michal. "The Union of Uzhorod." *Slovak Studies* 6 (1966): 7–190.

Liptak, Lubomir. "Priprava a priebeh salzburskych rokovani roku 1940 medzi predstavitelmi Nemecka a Slovenskeho statu." *Historicky casopis* 13, no. 3 (1965): 329–65.

Liptak, Lubomir. "Slovensky stat a protifasisticke hnutie v rokoch 1939–1943." *Historicky casopis* 14, no. 2 (1966): 161–218.

Lukacka, Jan. "Majetky a postavenie Ludanickovcov na Slovensku do zaciatku 14. storocia." *Historicky casopis* 38, no. 1 (1990): 3–14.

Lukacka, Jan. "Uloha slachty slovanskeho povodu pri stabilizacii uhorskeho vcasnofeudalneho statu." In *Typologia rane feudalnich slovanskych statu.* Praha: Ustav ceskoslovenskych a svetovych dejin CSAV, 1987: 191–200.

Marsina, Richard. "Slovenska historiografia 1945–1990." *Historicky casopis* 39, nos. 4–5 (1991): 370–79.

Matula, Vladimir. "The Conception and the Development of Slovak National Culture in the Period of National Revival." *Studia Historica Slovaca* 17 (1990): 150–189.

Michel, Bernard. "Les racines historiques de l'indépendance slovaque." *Revue d'Europe centrale* 1, no. 2 (1993): 121–31.

Mikula, Susan. "Ludovit Stur and the Panlsavic Movement." *Slovakia* 14 no. 39 (1966): 104–15.

Mikula, Susan. "Relations Between Slovaks and Czechs in the First CSR." *Slovakia.* 35, nos. 64–65 (1991–1992): 78–96.

Mikus, Joseph A. "Slovakia. A Political and Constitutional History." *Slovak Studies* 24 (1984): 7–193.

Papin, Joseph. "Christian Inroads into the Territory of Present Slovakia prior to the Cyrillo-Methodian Era." *Slovak Studies* 3 (1963): 9–20.

Pech, Stanley Z. "New Avenues in East European History." *Canadian Slavonic Papers* 10, no. 1 (1968): 3–18.

Prusak, Peter. "Niektore vysledky vyskumu religiozity na Slovensku." *Sociologia* no. 1 (1970): 65–82.

Ratkos, Peter. "La conquête de la Slovaquie par les Magyars." *Studia Historica Slovaca.* 3 (1965): 7–57.

Reszler, André. "Identité nationale et héritage culturel: le cas de la Slovaquie." *Revue d'Europe centrale* 1, no. 2 (1993): 157–63.

Rydlo, Jozef M. "Slowaken in Westeuropa." *Slowakei* 21 (1983): 82–141.

Sabo, Gerald. "'Jesuit Slovak' in Writings of Franciscans." Paper read at the 1993 Annual Convention of the American Association for the Advancement of Slavic Studies, Honolulu, HA, 22 November, 1993.

Sarmir, Eduard. "Ekonomicke vyrovnavanie SSR a CSR v procese vystavby socialistickeho Ceskoslovenska." *Ekonomicky casopis* 13, no. 7 (1974): 582–93.

Smith, Anthony. "The Ties that Bind." *LSE Magazine* (Spring 1993): 8–11.

Stolarik, Marian Mark. "The Role of American Slovaks in the Creation of Czecho-Slovakia." *Slovak Studies* 8 (1968): 7–82.

Sutherland, Anthony X. "The Fathers of the Slovak Nation: From Juraj Tranovsky to Karol Salva or From the Reformation to the Rise of the Populists (1500s–1890s)." *Slovak Studies* 21 (1981): 5–187.

Tiso, F. "The Empire of Samo." Slovak Studies 1 (1961): 1–22.

Vernadsky, George. "The Beginnings of the Czech State." *Byzantion* 17 (XVII, 1944–1945): 315–28.

Vnuk, Frantisek. "Slovakia's Six Eventful Months (October 1938—March 1939)." *Slovak Studies* 4 (1964): 7–164.

INDEX